A Wedding in Cornwall

Books 1-6

This is a work of fiction. Names, characters, and events are a product of the author's imagination. Any resemblance between characters and persons either living or dead is purely coincidental.

A Wedding in Cornwall Books 1-6

ISBN-13: 978-1973750178

ISBN-10: 1973750171

Cover Image: "Cornish Cottage." Original art, "House in the garden" by Elena Mikhaylova. Used with permission. http://www.dreamstime.com

Dear Reader,

I'm so glad you've chosen to pick up an anthology of my best-selling romance series, A Wedding in Cornwall. But before you dive into its pages with a cozy cup of tea (or maybe a glass of lemonade) there's something that you should know: the fictional village you're about to enter is just that – fictional. A magical, romantic place that's truly different from real Cornish villages and Cornish life, from geography to language. And if you're a reader for whom geographic and regional accuracy – and real-life drama – are important, this book may not be for you. And you deserve to know that in order to save yourself a possibly disappointing read.

But I hope that you, like many other readers, will still find yourself "transported" by this fictitious village, and the fun and excitement of staging glamorous events at a gorgeous manor house. Even though I've never had the good fortune to visit Cornwall, I love the idea of an American finding herself transported to one of England's most unique counties, living as a 'fish out of water' far from home – and never dreaming how many changes await her in a new place.

Writing about the adventures of a wedding planner, however – and the sometimes-chaos that leads up to the big day – is very familiar territory for me. In a lot of ways, *A Wedding in Cornwall* and its sequels are a tribute to my most popular wedding romances. Six years ago (I can't believe it's been that long!), I penned *The Wedding Caper*, where meek bridal assistant Gwen mistakenly finds herself suddenly in charge of a socialite wedding. It became a hit with US readers, their enthusiasm turning it into my first bestseller and inspiring three more stories about Gwen's adventures in love and wedding planning.

My road trip romantic comedy *Late to the Wedding* found equal success with romance fans in the UK, whose enthusiastic reviews inspired more readers to take a chance on it than I ever hoped for. So, in honor of those readers—both from the UK and the US—I decided to launch a new wedding-themed series with an American heroine who takes a trip 'across the pond' to a new life, a new job, and— of course—a new romance.

Happy reading!

Table of Contents

A Wedding in Cornwall

By

Laura Briggs

I took a deep breath. And reminded myself to let it out again and take another, before I could pass out from sheer lack of oxygen. Because life-changing moments like these could send even the most rational person into a dead faint.

But this was going to be perfect, I told myself. This was exactly what every event planner dreams of: being at the top of her professional game someplace where every celebration seems like magic. And it happened by pure chance, all because the senior planner at Design a Dream, the firm where I worked, had to miss her interview due to a few red spots breaking out on her face. Spots which turned out to be a full-blown case of the chicken pox at the age of thirty-seven. What are the odds of that happening? Seriously, WHAT are the odds?

I didn't know, and I didn't care. I was too busy ransacking my closet, looking for the right combination of shoes, clothes, and, accessories for the interview of my life. The interview my fellow planner had skipped in order to wallow in anti-itch cream at home. I would have gone to that interview sporting a face full of pockmarks and calamine lotion if I had to, but that's just me. Anything to become the new event planner for a country estate in breathtaking Cornwall, England.

See what I mean by 'magical'? This was the grown-up equivalent to a kid's Disneyland fantasy. I was definitely enchanted by photos I viewed of Cornwall online, and the Travel Channel's episode I watched on England's southern counties made me even more desperate to land the position before a lucky rival could snatch it up.

And it worked.

Seventy-two hours later, they hired me. *Me,* Julianne Morgen, your average American girl was about to venture 'across the pond', as they say, for a new life. Pulling up roots and packing half my belongings into storage until I could find a permanent residence in the Cornish village whose name I still couldn't pronounce after locating it on a map. It was hard to believe, and yet it was really happening, my friends and family throwing me a farewell party the night before I left. Their words of encouragement and advice were still ringing in my head as I nervously boarded the plane that would take me to a new life in England.

Now, taking my first deep breath of English sea air, I was just a few train rides away from the elegant country house in South Cornwall. A place called Cliffs House, an old family estate that was among the rare and beautiful country houses of Cornwall, now turned into a bed and breakfast that hosted events from weddings to charity galas.

Everything I owned that was worth bringing was stuffed into the bags I carried with me: clothes for every occasion; the collection of high-heeled shoes that fed my ever-growing addiction to footwear, and books on everything from flowers to French baking, all part of my old job in the States.

I had never really belonged at Design a Dream. Truthfully, my creation of lemon poppy seed petits fours with lavender-infused frosting for an English tea-themed reception had been the only time my employer ever paid me a compliment. I was always overlooked, the best opportunities for creativity being handed to others, the firm's favorite event planners — including Francine, who was offered the job as a Cornish event planner before the chicken pox struck. Our boss, Nancy, had never found my designs to be 'to her taste' as she put it.

"It's too niche," she complained, quirking her eyebrow one time as she studied my sketches for an engagement dinner's flower arrangements. "It's all sleek lines and symmetry. Where are the vases overflowing with beauty? Where's the stuffed-to-burst elegance that we pride ourselves on, Julianne?"

"I was under the impression," I began, trying to sound confident under this interrogation, "that sleek was what our client wanted. She chose a venue with modern nineteen-twenties' architecture, inspired by Frank Lloyd Wright. Her colors were black and white. Simple and elegant." I did my best not to study the toes of my shoes as I made this point — a pair of red Jimmy Choos that had cost me four months of 'everyday luxuries,'—and that was for getting them at a bargain price, mind you.

"It's not what our florists want," said Nancy. "They want us to order show stopping arrangements, don't they? If we don't keep our friends happy, how will we keep our clients happy?"

By doing what they want? I wanted to reply.

"Triple the number of flowers in those vases, Julianne," said Nancy, dismissing me. When I was halfway out of her office, she added, "And as a gentle suggestion — find some more 'sensible' shoes for the office tomorrow. All right?"

Meaning ones that didn't come from a famous designer, I supposed. Senior planners at Design a Dream didn't care for junior lackeys showing off any luxury fashion labels they happened to own.

I hoped whoever managed Cliffs House estate didn't mind. Especially since the first wedding I was supposed to coordinate happened to be for clients worlds above any Design a Dream catered to, supposedly.

You, Julianne, are going to be helping someone famous make their dream day come true. Cakes, dinner menus, flowers, invitations — your color palettes and sketches will be going places they've never gone before. Just like I, Julianne Morgen, would be walking along rugged pathways to the shores of the English Channel on my days off. Letting the wind whip through my dark chestnut hair, closing my eyes before the spectacular view, and imagining that a fairytale English prince would come riding up on his horse —

I opened my eyes. Enough of that. The only eligible prince left in England was moving to America, according to the tabloids I had glimpsed in the airport newsstand while buying a postcard for my best friend Aimee back in Seattle — and all the other unmarried royal males were in 'nappies and nursery schools.' With a grin, I turned away from the restless channel waters along the shores outside the Newquay tea shop and made my way towards its cobblestone walkway to meet the cab that would take me to the railway station.

It got me there with several minutes to spare, so I parked myself on a bench beneath the fabric canopies. My luggage surrounded my Valentino-clad feet as I waited for the train to Par. Next would come Truro, where someone from Cliffs House would be waiting to drive me the remaining distance to the estate. Just thinking about it sent my nerves tingling again. With my WiFi connection fairly sporadic, I found myself resorting to people watching as a means of distraction.

There were some obvious tourists among the crowd, their dazed but happy expressions similar to what I had seen in the mirror that morning. Some of them carried guidebooks; others brandished their cameras like a weapon, as if they were members of the paparazzi, preparing to ambush a celebrity off the next train. There were some other, more casual-looking travelers too: a group of twentysomethings chatting and laughing among themselves on a bench, and a couple of bored-looking teenage girls who shared the ear buds to a music player. A tall, dark-haired man stepped from the doorway to the nearby café.

Hmmm. Not bad looking, I thought. Even from this distance, I could tell he was attractive. There was something rugged about his appearance, further enhanced by his natural tan and careless dark hair. Strands of it brushed against his nicely sculpted cheekbones as he adjusted the leather portfolio under his arm. Was he a businessman, perhaps? He didn't look quite polished enough for that, but he didn't strike me as part of the surfer crowd either. *Maybe he's a student or a teacher somewhere.* Definitely not a prince—though a galloping white horse might have suited him rather nicely.

I realized I was making up fantasies for a total stranger, and watching him as if he was the last attractive man on earth. *Don't be stupid, Julianne.* I must be jet lagged, or maybe just sleep deprived to scrutinize someone this way. He couldn't be all *that* handsome, could he?

His dark orbs flicked in my direction, and I quickly turned away, blushing hard. Had he noticed me studying him? My face blazed hot at the idea — with mortification that made me want to melt into the ground. He might very well be used to women staring at him and think nothing of it. *Or else, he's vain about it.* That was more likely, I knew. Deciding to ignore the weird uptick in my pulse for those dark eyes meeting mine from across the station, if only for a second.

After studying the pointy toes of my pumps for awhile, I dared to glance back in his direction. But the stranger was gone.

I glanced around, checking all directions. Now that he was gone, I regretted looking away, at least without gauging whether he was nice or rude, interested or insulted — made brave by his absence, of course. But no tall, mysterious men were anywhere in sight. He must have gone back inside the café, or else made his way from the railway station to one of the nearby shops.

Oh, well. His destination, no doubt, was somewhere miles away from my own. A peek at my watch showed I would be on the move again soon anyway. The next-to-last stop in my journey to the magnificent Cliffs House. This realization was enough to put the stranger's good-looks out of my head as I prepared to board the next train.

***

"Miss Morgen, I trust?"

The man holding the sign at the railway station in Truro didn't look the part of an English chauffeur, which I had rather stupidly been picturing after falling asleep on the plane from Seattle while reading an old Du Maurier gothic romance that Aimee had given me as a goodbye present.

"That's me," I answered, with a bright smile. I tried to hide the lump of nervousness I was sure was visible in my throat by swallowing. Was this my new boss? A fellow employee at the estate?

"My name is Weatherby," he said. "Geoff, as you may call me, if you like. I'm the estate manager for Lord William, the heir of Cliffs House." He was wearing a damp canvas mackintosh over a tweed coat and wool trousers, a tie perfectly knotted above the neckline of his wool pullover.

Lord William. I hadn't realized the house's owner was titled. "Um, is Lord William living at Cliffs House?" I asked. "Or at a town house in London now?" Vague notions of 'society' and 'the Season' popped into my head from old Regency-era novels from high school.

Mr. Weatherby, or Geoff, laughed. Gently, as if he read my mind and didn’t want to embarrass me too much. "He lives at Cliffs House," he answered. "And he manages it as much or more than I do. If you're imagining something from one of Jane Austen's novels, I hate to disappoint you. Lord William and Lady Amanda are the picture of the modern English country house's heir. Preservers of history, overseers of proper land management, business owners, and promoters of local tourism and trade." He lifted my heaviest bag and produced an umbrella from underneath his arm. “Lord William himself is quite handy at repairing walls and planting trees — and no stranger to the use of a chainsaw."

A chainsaw? I would have to amend the picture in my head of someone in Mr. Darcy's velvet frock coat, sawing through fallen trees amidst an electric *buzz* and a cloud of petrol smoke.

"A little rain today," he commented. "I hope you're not from the deserts of America, or this place may come as a bit of a shock. Cornwall may have sunnier days than many parts of England, but she has her share of rain, and heavy ones, too."

"I'm from Seattle," I said. "It's sort of like ... America's version of England's drizzly day." I clutched the strap of my second bag, one that held assorted books on event planning and design, and probably several pairs of stiletto heels and sleek sandals. "Pretty much every Seattle resident owns a good umbrella. That is…a brolly," I added. Thankful I had brushed up on some English slang and hadn't called it a bumbershoot, say, in an effort to sound quaint, like some character in an old movie.

"Perhaps you're well on your way to understanding Cornwall's weather," Geoff answered, with a smile, one which quickly became a look of concern. "I hope you brought a coat as well," he added. "Cornwall is a warmer part of England in general, but not in the summer, necessarily. You won't encounter the sort of temperatures you're accustomed to in America. It might seem a bit cool to you at times."

"I'm sure I have a coat or two warm enough to fix that," I answered him, thinking of the ones I had packed after reading a quick online guide to Cornwall's weather.

North Cornwall's cool morning had made me wish I'd worn a thicker pullover like the ones I saw tourists buying in a nearby shop as I had my first real cup of English tea. But I got a taste of the kind of cool, rainy day that Geoff had described a moment later, when I felt the wet breeze against my face. I gasped and gulped in the air, almost believing I could taste the salt of the sea even though the Channel wasn't exactly running alongside the station like a stream.

The estate's car that drove me to my new home wasn't a pristine Bentley or Jaguar, but clearly Mr. Weatherby's everyday vehicle, an economy Asian model. But it didn't matter, because the view from the windows was worth it. I had my second glimpse of Cornwall's beauty since my train ride from Newquay to the city. I had been amazed by the quick transition from the metropolitan-esque scenes of Newquay to the surrounding countryside, and here it was no different. As the city of Truro, with its mix of impressive Georgian architecture and sleek, modern businesses, slipped away, I saw the rugged fields and open countryside of rural Cornwall unfold around me.

"How far is the estate?" I asked. "Is it in a town nearby?"

"Ceffylgwyn. A mere dote on the map between here and Falmouth," he answered. "Falmouth's the next village of size in Cornwall, as you no doubt know by now. Although it's quite popular with tourists now, it's still a quiet place compared to England's more metropolitan counties. But, as the natives will tell you, that's its charm, and they're perfectly right."

"You're not from here?" I asked. I had a feeling that his accent wasn't Cornish vernacular. It sounded too much like broadcasts of the BBC I'd seen at night in my hotel room.

"No. I'm from London," he answered. "I moved here to manage Lord William's estate after his father died — that was six years ago, when he was still at university. The previous land manager retired, and Lord William needed someone who had a more modern view on a 'working' estate, as you might call it."

"Do you like Ceffylgwyn?" I asked, my tongue having a little trouble with the name. "Is Cliffs House a good place to work?"

"I love the charm of Cornwall," he answered. "I used to come here when I was a lad, which was a long time ago," he added, with a chuckle. "They call South Cornwall the 'Cornish Riviera' because of the tourism and the cultural highlights, but to me it's very much about the rugged countryside outside of Truro and Falmouth. And, of course, Mevagissey, which is a lovely place. It's the moors and the cliffs, the snug inlets along the Channel. There's a lovely walk to the cliffs that oversee the shore not far from Cliffs House — that's where it gets its name. In English and in Cornish."

"And the village name?" I asked. I wondered if there was a simpler name to call it than the one that Geoff mentioned.

"It means 'white horse,' in Cornish," he answered. "A little anglicized over the years, but still with the Cornish heart in its name."

As he spoke, he turned the car's wheel and we were swept along a curve that revealed the Channel's water. I caught a glimpse once again of a Cornish beach, and of stone walls cupping a part of the water, where the waves seemed strangely calm as they swept between the stone cracks I imagined lay there. Perhaps this was the kind of view Geoff was talking about on the path somewhere between Cliffs House and the sea.

I definitely knew how I'd be spending my first day off from planning events at the country house. It was like a dream come true, the world I could see on the other side of the windscreen.

I cleared my throat, trying to rid myself of a little of the nervousness still clinging to me. "So, what can you tell me about my job at Cliffs House?" I asked. "Any hints before I meet my boss?" I tried to sound lighthearted as I asked.

"Very little," he answered. "My job is second to Lord William's in managing the grounds and the practical purposes of the land, you see. Conservation, agriculture, and grounds management, that's my task, with Lord William overseeing it, and managing the financial side of the estate. He's also currently the chair of the local business and tourism union in Ceffylgwyn."

"What about the tourism side of Cliffs House?"

"That's Lady Amanda's field," answered Geoff. "She manages the estate's event planning and books guests and clients. She also designs all promotional and public literature for the estate and many of the business union's members. It was her idea to hire a full-time event planner at Cliffs House — there's no local event planners available for the task, you see."

"How much do you know about the wedding that's taking place there?" I asked. I had already reviewed some of the details, of course, but in my excitement over the move they had become slightly muddled. If they were truly celebrities, surely even a tiny village like Ceffylgwyn was abuzz with the latest gossip about it.

"Donald Price-Parker and Petal Borroway," he answered. "He's an English football player, quite successful and quite popular; she's a model of sorts, I've been told, working on the runway recently in the States. It should be quite the fashionable affair."

I'd never heard of either of them — then again, I didn't watch British football or any of those 'how to become a model' shows, much less read *Vogue* and *Vanity Fair* outside the dentist's office. "Wow," I said. "That's a big assignment for my first day at work. I hope I don't disappoint." I tried to sound like I was kidding, but I wasn't. I was impressed and nervous, feeling a shiver travel from my spine to the soles of my feet.

"Have you much experience in planning celebrity weddings?"

"None," I answered. Too openly, I realized too late. And was glad I didn't mention anything more, like the fact that I'd never planned a wedding completely on my own. Something that Lady Amanda must surely know, but apparently didn't care about since I was here.

Geoff Weatherby didn't say anything else about my work experience, I noticed. We were both fairly quiet until after we passed a road sign for Falmouth, and one for the turn to Ceffylgwyn and Cliffs House. The car traveled a stately driveway, bordered by neatly-trimmed hedges that still managed to affect a certain freedom and carelessness in their greenery that gave them character and life as they moved in the breezy rain. I glimpsed a large willow tree, and beautiful garden paths bordered by wild and colorful blossoms, untamed and rugged, with stones peeking out in between overgrown blooms and branches. I turned away, and before me was Cliffs House.

Tall and stately. Not imposing, but reserved and dignified with its elegant stone exterior, a color between ivory and yellow, with little adornment except for the carved bowers above its arched windows, and the impressive stone carvings above its vast formal entrance, a set of double doors facing the cobblestone drive of olden days. A soft grey-tiled roof above, and multiple chimneys which signaled any number of gorgeous fireplaces somewhere inside. I fell in love at once, and my friends will tell you that doesn't happen easily — except for a pair of truly exceptional designer stilettos, perhaps.

But this was something grand and hallowed. The closest I had ever seen to this impressive building was my first and only trip to the Guggenheim in New York, which impressed itself on my eight year-old mind and replaced Seattle's Space Needle as the world's most incredible building. I couldn't stop staring, even as I climbed out of Geoff's car and collected my bag from the back seat.

"Welcome to Cliffs House, Miss Morgen," he said.

***

"I'm so glad you're here," said Lady Amanda, with a little gasp of relief. "I thought I was going to be buried under fabric swatches and flower books for the rest of my life!"

Lady Amanda definitely wasn't a dignified lady with a stiff upper lip and strings of pearls. She was ginger-haired, tall, and curvy, wearing a rather worn but beautifully-knit Guernsey style sweater and designer jeans. She greeted me like a long-lost school chum mere minutes after our formal introduction as employer and event planner, ushering me into a little sitting room on Cliffs House's main floor that had been converted into her office, where she managed Cliffs House's image as a public attraction.

"I've been planning events on my own these past two years. Me and the kitchen staff," she continued, flopping down on an antique sofa. "It's exhausting how much I've handled, between that and the public relations work, which is every bit as important. But with the size and scale of these events growing every year — and tourism's on the rise again, thanks to television audiences — I can't possibly handle it on my own. So enter you, Julianne Morgen — chief event planner and coordinator to Cliffs House's growing number of guests."

"I'm flattered," I answered. "I can't tell you how much so, actually." It felt surreal, sitting in this room that felt both historic and modern, surrounded by antiques and the soft colors and clean lines of modern decor. From the overstuffed pink armchair and gleaming, carved walnut desk to the silver floor lamps and Warhol prints, it was comfortable, cozy, and unbelievably elegant after the sterile flowers-in-a-frame-and-sentimental-smiling-brides decor of Design a Dream's workspace.

"You must be planning a lot of events to hire someone full-time," I said. Even though I could see plenty of evidence that Lady Amanda was swamped with work — there were piles of half-printed brochures everywhere, and sketches for a printed tour guide to Cliffs House pinned to her design board, a cloth one covered with a soft print of architectural blueprints.

"I want someone to take my place in the process," she answered. "If you haven't guessed already, event planning wasn't my chosen career."

"Interior design?" I guessed, one eyebrow lifting. I had cast my eye over the books in her shelf while I was admiring her office. Several were on fabric, and on furniture history. "Or architecture?" I had seen the books on London city design and Venice's construction, and the well-marked one on historic Cornwallian building methods.

"Clever girl," said Lady Amanda, sounding impressed. "It was interior design at first, but I had a turn for marketing that persuaded me to change my goals. Hence, my role in promoting tourism both for Cliffs House, and then for Ceffylgwyn itself."

She poured a cup of tea from the silver service on the neighboring table, and passed it to me as she lifted her own. "William's as involved as he can be, given how little time he has between managing the estate's adjacent lands and the financial side of running a modern-day estate," she continued. "So it left us with no choice but to find someone to hire on permanently. Someone who could handle all the details big and small — from food to flowers, to emergencies. Everything but the kitchen sink, you might say."

"Everything?" I echoed. "You mean that you — you don't want a hand in the process?"

"Coaxing clients to choose the garden for a reception, or spending days on the telephone with the vicar of the nice little chapel in the neighboring village, trying to coax him into conducting a wedding service for strangers?" said Lady Amanda. "No, thank you. I am content booking events and greeting the clients as the lovely lady of Cliffs House — I have absolutely no interest in knowing what pattern of china they want for their wedding breakfast, or what Vera Wang designer gown they insist on having shipped here for their engagement party. I'm happy to let *you* worry about all of those things, and hear the juicy details later from the girls downstairs."

My head was floating above my shoulders now. I wasn't sure if I was scared or elated — after all, I was now in charge of every event planned at Cliffs House. I was the person whom brides of any background or nationality would look to for answers. I took a firm grip on my teacup's saucer and steeled myself for it. I knew what I was doing. I'd spent years studying it, practicing it on a smaller scale at Design a Dream, so what could possibly go wrong that I couldn't deal with?

"Why did you hire me?" I asked. "An American? Surely somebody English would make more sense."

"You'd be surprised how many international guests we host now," said Lady Amanda. "I didn't necessarily need local knowledge or the 'stiff upper lip' image, as you would put it. So many of our visitors are American these days, too — that's television's doing, again." She took another sip of tea. "I interviewed several candidates from Exeter, Oxford, even London. But when your name popped up on a list of employees from a U.S. business that planned a wedding of a friend of mine...well, something about it just seemed right."

Maybe it was kismet, I thought, remembering my grandmother's old-fashioned term for destined good luck. Maybe it was karma, as my spirituality-seeking friend Nate back home in Seattle would say. Or maybe it was destiny, as Lady Amanda suggested. Me finding a place of my own after years of languishing at the bottom of Design a Dream's career ladder.

"There's a list of local resources, businesses that cater, florists, musicians, and so on," said Lady Amanda. "As well as ones available from everywhere from Devon to London — anyone you might need to hire, from chamber orchestras to couture designers — although you look like a bright young woman who knows how to use the internet and a mobile to learn things." Here, Lady Amanda's impish smile returned.

"The staff here is capable of handling quite a bit," she continued. "Dinah is our chef, a graduate of a French cooking academy, and Gemma and Pippa assist her in catering any number of events. We have a hothouse and gardening staff, with quite a selection of flowers, with no small thanks to a brilliant horticulturist currently residing in Cornwall."

"It sounds so elegant," I said. "Like a four-star hotel." I pictured escargot and French pastries alongside a perfectly-carved rib roast, and vases brimming with English roses. Cliffs House was not the size of a manor like Pemberley or a castle from Arthurian legend, but it was such a beautiful, romantic spot. Who wouldn't want to have their wedding near the rugged English moors, overlooking a ribbon of water curving along those ancient cliffs?

"I'll see to it that you're settled properly in the office closest to mine. A former morning parlor, in case you're interested — just shove aside whatever antique andirons and stuffed birds are cluttering up the place."

"I'm sure I'll be very comfortable," I answered, with a grin. "Even if I have to rearrange whatever empty suits of armor are taking up my desk's spot." Lady Amanda hid her smile behind her teacup, but her eyes were still twinkling.

"So let's get to it," said Lady Amanda, after she set aside her tea. "The only event of importance in the diary right now is the Price-Parker -

Borroway union, of course. The groom-to-be booked us six months ago after announcing his engagement, and now the bride-to-be will be here to finish planning the reception for the next couple of weeks or so. Starting today, actually." She checked her watch, then sprang up from her chair. "I'll introduce you to the staff, then take you to meet them after I change into something a bit more suitable."

I was amazed. Fifteen minutes of chat, and I was already on my way to meet the celebrity couple. Quickly, I set aside my teacup and rose to my feet, smoothing my charcoal pencil skirt, hoping my hair's loosely-pinned style was sensible enough for whatever standards Cliffs House had for its newest representative. Lady Amanda had forgotten to clue me in on how I should dress, speak, and behave when talking to clients, especially since I was from 'across the pond.'

Her glance fell to my feet as I walked with her to the office door. "Lovely shoes," she said. "Are those Valentino?"

"They are," I admitted.

"Divine," she answered. "That's really my only reason to venture into the boutiques of Truro these days — shoe shopping. I always find that slipping on a perfect pair makes me feel as if I could conquer the world. But how did you ever find a pair in such an exquisite color?"

I had a feeling that Lady Amanda's standards, whatever they were, would suit me just fine.

***

Bride-to-be Petal Borroway was originally from Southampton, but had spent the last decade modeling in Milan, New York, and a dozen other places, where she was most famous for appearing in an advertisement for chip-resistant nail varnish — and for getting engaged to Donald Price-Parker, who was something of a heartthrob in Great Britain.

Petal exuded glam — I would have declared her a model, or a wannabe model if I hadn't known already. Flawless skin, perfect makeup, delicate bone structure that seemed almost sculpted. Her clothes were casual, yet screamed expensive. As did those of Donald, whose body was a trifle over-muscular beneath his tight t-shirt and summer jacket, his blond hair cut short against his head. He had the powerful brooding-and-sullen stare that makes many women go weak in the knees, but for me it was a little too much. Tarzan in designer clothes, exerting his animal prowess over women.

They were side by side on the velvet sofa in Cliffs House's main drawing room. Petal's hand rested constantly on some part of Donald's body — hand, shoulder, arm, thigh, shifting gradually and possessively every time he moved — and showing off the spectacular diamond on her finger.

"So why choose Cornwall?" I asked, in my best professional voice. "What makes this part of England so special to both of you?"

At Design a Dream, standard operating procedure had been to ask the bride and groom why they chose their wedding location. It helped determine how central to the wedding's theme the marriage or reception site would be — and how much of it would be brushed over or disguised to avoid clashing with said image. Since my job would primarily be coordinating their reception, I needed to know as much about their choice as I could.

"Weekends and what not," said Donald. He had a rather lazy drawl that surprised me. It made him sound as if he wanted to fall asleep. "I've had a place in Cornwall on and off for the past few years. Surfing in Newquay and so on. Weddings in London feel rather hack these days." He looked away from his mobile for the first time since Lady Amanda had introduced us, finally paying some attention now that the topic of his wedding was at hand.

"But you chose Ceffylgwyn," I said. "It must be special to one of you."

"Donald races in St Austell," answered Petal. "A hobby of sorts, now that he's not surfing in Newquay anymore. He was a big fan of the Trelawny Tigers. That's why we're taking a place along the coast in Truro instead of our old one."

Maybe it was my imagination, but I was picking up on signals that Petal wasn't exactly thrilled by this move. Maybe it was just the tiniest arch of her eyebrows as she said it, or the fact that she inspected her nails for a brief second when mentioning Truro — her presumably chip-resistant nail varnish. Nevertheless, she snuggled closer to Donald's body.

"Anyway — here we are," said Donald. "Doing the whole 'Cornish thing' for the big day and so on."

"A traditional Cornish wedding?" I ventured.

I hadn't been anticipating something like this, not so quickly, and I felt a quick patter of panic in my chest. This couple had no idea, of course, that I had only been in Cornwall for a day. I wondered what sort of traditions a Cornish wedding entailed — especially for two people who weren't natives, as they just explained.

"Just a few touches, here and there," said Petal. "We want something to make us feel at home in Cornwall, since we'll be splitting our time between here and London. At least for awhile." She smiled at Donald with a lingering, lovey-dovey glance passing between them, then looked at me with a smile. "And some of my friends will be coming from America, so we want them to have a taste of Cornwall. It's such a chic place right now. Who wouldn't want to show it off a little?"

At first impression, I didn't like her. Maybe it was the bored look in her eyes when her fiancé talked for more than a few sentences, or the way she looked annoyed during Lady Amanda's guided tour of Cliffs House's large music and dining rooms reserved for the wedding, curling a lock of her long hair around one finger at times, and sighing quietly. But her smile for me, inclusive and almost friendly, made me soften a little bit.

"Let's talk about what you want to show off most, then," I said, switching subjects. "You want touches of Cornwall, so that will obviously be part of your wedding theme. A country wedding — or city sophistication, with touches of the country?"

"A city wedding," said Petal at the same time as Donald said, "Country." They exchanged glances. For a moment, I thought Petal looked tense — or upset — but it cleared from her eyes when Donald spoke.

"Whatever. I'll be off at St Austell most of the time. Not as if I care." He shrugged. "Just something that'll look good in the papers. Champagne, expense. So on."

"I think we can manage that," said Petal, looking at me as she spoke. "Donald just wants something elegant...but simple. My dress is couture fashion, the cake is from an exclusive bakery in Newquay — I'll send you the details on them. The ceremony and reception should be just as exclusive ... if a touch dressed down, of course."

"Simple but expensive," clarified Donald, in case I hadn't understood this.

"Besides, I was thinking it *would* be nice to return to our roots," said Petal. "I've been away from England for several years, and Donald's been traveling the continent. I suppose it makes sense to have a little nod to tradition for this wedding, don't you agree?"

"Absolutely," I said. Country sophistication, a dash of Cornish culture — surely I could do that, with a little help from Cliffs House's knowledgeable, local staff. "I'm sure we can plan an English wedding you both will be proud of."

"But with a few American touches," piped up Petal. "I don't want to *completely* forget where I've been the last few years. And Donald loves cultural fusion, don't you, darling?" She was sidling close to him, draped effortlessly against his shoulder. The two of them certainly seemed fused together as he rested his cheek against her hair with a soft grunt of agreement — except his eyes hadn't left the digital screen of his phone.

"Cultural fusion," I repeated. "All right. Let's talk details."

The bridal party, including the chief bridesmaid and best man, was due to arrive in Cornwall in less than a week. The engagement celebration would be in Truro, but there would be a champagne lunch at Cliffs House, open to the press, on Saturday two weeks before the big day. The wedding ceremony would take place in Cliffs House's most beautiful formal garden, and the reception would take place in the largest music and drawing rooms, which opened to each other through a series of sliding double doors.

They were elegant rooms, done in pale pink, seafoam green, and antique gilding, the drawing room mostly cream and gold. The bride and groom had brief romantic bickering — followed by a rather long kiss — over which room would host the reception, with the drawing room's muted elegance winning. The wedding colors were cream and black with touches of burgundy and rose, with a hired classical quintet providing music at the ceremony, and a semi-famous pop artist playing for the reception.

Flowers, food, a few ceremony details — these were places where Cornwall's culture was supposed to shine. It would be my job to find a way to include it as I pulled together all the pieces they had chosen, and the ones yet to come. Trying not to sound ignorant, I pressed them both for details about what they loved most about Cornwall. Anything would help.

"Pasties," answered Donald. Who was still interested in texting someone else.

"The sea," said Petal. "I simply love the shore."

She hadn't mentioned any florists or flower arrangements being chosen yet, I noticed. "What about local flowers?" I asked. "Trees or special places?" I thought with a name like 'Petal,' surely she had someone or something in her past that was tied to the English landscape. It might be something I could weave into the wedding plans.

"I have no interest in flowers," she answered. "Anything will do, so long as it doesn't clash with the room." She wrinkled her nose, then laughed. But it wasn't a good-humored laugh — and Petal's smile was a trifle different — or maybe I was mistaken. Not that it mattered. I made a note *no favorite flowers* in my digital planner's app.

Moving on. "What about the cake?" I asked.

***

Dear Aimee,

Remember how you thought Cliffs House would be like the Grantham's home on Downton Abbey? Well, let me tell you, the bedroom I'm staying in would <u>NOT</u> disappoint you. It's so beautiful I don't even know where to start. An antique four poster bed, wallpaper with a delicate floral design, an antique wardrobe made out of oak, my very own fireplace and mantle—it's like waking up on the set of a BBC period drama miniseries! Even the drapes are so beautiful, I'm tempted to pull a Scarlett O'Hara and fashion them into a chic gown for my first big event here. Of course, I would be jailed for the destruction of valuable property but wouldn't it be worth it to make that grand entrance on the staircase?

My ridiculous postcard message to Aimee was interrupted by the sound of my mobile phone's alarm going off. After just two days in my new surroundings, I didn't trust my internal clock for any appointments, so I was relying on alarms to prompt me. Setting down my pen, I turned off the phone alarm and prepared to go downstairs.

My workspace was almost as nice as the bedroom I was so kindly being allowed to use until I could secure a place in the village. Despite Lady Amanda's laughing advice, there were no stuffed birds or antique andirons cluttering it up. Just a beautiful white mantelpiece and an antique globe that stood beneath my wall chart — I had copied the wedding's timeline from Lady Amanda's file, so I could see step by step each day between now and the ceremony. I had already marked deadlines — flowers chosen by this date, cake arriving by that one — and programmed reminders into my mobile so I wouldn't miss even one.

Just breathe. I inhaled slowly, reminding myself I had planned events before. Not ones like this, true, but they were still real celebrations with real people. I had everything under control. Repeating this one last time, I slipped on my tan sandals, grabbed the sketches from my desk, and went downstairs to talk with Dinah the chef.

Dinah's kitchen was an old-fashioned one transformed into a modern cook's paradise of efficiency. No utensils without hooks, no pots without a place within easy reach of her stove and range. Dinah, Lady Amanda had explained, cooked everything from simple meals for the house's family and staff to French cuisine for visiting dignitaries and businessmen at Cliffs House's galas and conferences.

"This is how I envision the cakes for the Saturday luncheon," I said, showing her a few sketches I had made, as well as some pictures I had copied from my books on formal receptions. "Light saffron and orange flavors sandwiched together with marmalade — Cornish and English flavors," I said. "Covered in fondant stenciled with a Cornish tartan design, and served with chocolate truffles and ginger and orange spiced biscuits."

I was proud of myself. I had spent two days reading up on Cornish cuisine and consulting the menus of several Cornish bakeries. I wanted this first step in the wedding planning to include the Cliffs House staff before I turned to any bakeries, local or not.

"Well, it's not an impossibility," said Dinah, studying the pictures. "And I rather like the idea of saffron and citrus, maybe even with a hint of cinnamon. But with the citrus being the primary one, of course."

"Those are pretty," commented Gemma, who was one of the local girls who assisted Dinah. "Who're they for?"

"For the wedding party," said Dinah.

Her accent, while not as strong as Gemma or Pippa's, was stronger than Geoff Weatherby's, with lots of rich 'r's' — I was guessing that Dinah was native to Cornwall.

"For Donald Price-Parker's wedding?" asked Pippa, sounding awed.

"That's the one," I answered.

Gemma sighed. "Isn't he lovely?" she asked. "I had a poster of him on my wall when I was fifteen. 'My 'ansum' as my mum used to call it — I'd blush roses every time, but his looks was rich enough that I didn't take it down."

Pippa groaned. "I can't *imagine* ending up with the likes of him. I've seen the model he's marrying, and there was no hope for me." She laughed. "Still, I had dreams of it until he went off to America and met that girl from the nail varnish advertisements."

"Do you think she looks like that other model — the one who's dad isn't a man anymore?" asked Gemma, confidently. She was briskly stirring a pan of melted chocolate as Dinah measured out flour — my mouth was watering, imagining a chocolate cake at the end of this process.

"*I* think she's not pretty enough for him, since he could've had that actress instead," said Pippa, who was peeling potatoes for tonight's soup. "What do you think?" she asked, glancing at me.

"He's definitely handsome," I answered, since this was the safest choice of words, rather than admitting that he wasn't my type. "In a ... beefcake sort of way."

Do they use 'beefcake' to describe a man's physique in Cornwall? I wondered how much of what I said was basically a foreign language to them, and if I could ever learn enough about their culture to pass muster with the locals.

"*I* think it's the other way round between the two of them," said Dinah, cracking an egg against her bowl. "But who am I to know anything? Especially compared to you two, who read every celebrity mag there is and gossip over it with your besties until the wee hours, no doubt, until not a boy in the county could compare with him in your eyes."

The two girls exchanged glances. "No boys in the county look that good in a football jersey," answered Pippa.

"Except for Ross," supplied Gemma, with a saucy grin.

"Ross is no boy," scoffed Dinah. "He's got nearly a decade on you both."

"Besides, he doesn't play football — he's too busy with the dirt and the like," said Pippa. They left me wondering who Ross was, and why it was important that he played — or didn't play — football. English football, I imagined, and found I had a hard time remembering what the uniforms looked like.

Pippa studied the mini cake pictures I had shown Dinah. "That's a proper treat for a to-do," she said. "Did you think it up yourself?"

"I did," I confessed. "That's actually what my old job mostly entailed — me coming up with wedding favors, or bridal shower treats. Nothing big, just something attractive for the serving table."

Pippa blinked. "You mean you didn't plan weddings before now?" She raised her eyebrow.

"No." I realized that making this confession was probably a mistake. Both of the girls exchanged glances, this time with a mixture of surprise and skepticism. That's what I read in the slight uplift of Pippa's eyebrow, and the bemused smile on Gemma's face, which quickly vanished as she busied herself with pouring the chocolate into Dinah's dry ingredients.

"There's a first time for everything," said Dinah. She lifted my sketches and slipped on her eyeglasses. "Hmmm...spice biscuits...truffles in milk chocolate?"

"The bride wants a little touch of the U.S.," I answered. Suddenly, I felt a tiny little doubt spring up inside me, one I tried to quickly crush. *Had* I taken a leap too big for my abilities? "So both dark and milk chocolate truffles would be served at the luncheon."

I still had sketches to make of possible flower arrangements and a consultation with Lady Amanda about how to rearrange the drawing room for the champagne luncheon, but I thought I would get a breath of air and steady my confidence first. A walk was what I needed. A chance to breathe in some Cornish sea air and refocus my thoughts, reminding myself how long I had waited and prepared for this.

"I'm going out for a walk," I said. "I thought I would take the path to the Channel overlook that Mr. Weatherby suggested. Which way is it?"

"To the right — just past the hedge opening that leads to the formal garden," said Dinah. "It's a view not to be missed. If you've been here two days already and not seen it, that's two days too long."

"Out walking?" said Gemma, looking up from the soup. "In those shoes?" Another funny smile crossed her lips. I glanced down at my tan sandals, and envisioned a steep, rocky path to the cliff and me stumbling down it after breaking a heel on the rocks.

"In these shoes," I said, with a confident smile. I thought I caught a cool, impressed glance in the girl's eyes as I turned to leave, hoping I wasn't heading to my doom along the garden path.

"... maybe she's got 'moxie' as they say in the States," I heard Pippa say before the door closed behind me.

One of Cornwall's milder breezes swept across me as I found my way past the formal hedgerows to the winding little path to the sea. I buttoned my green pea coat as I climbed down, gradually moving from the craggy slate walkway carefully built like a natural stair to the soft, wild grass growing alongside it. I angled my way towards the view of the water below, hearing it surge and crash against the cliff's walls.

The wind rose and batted my hair across my face. I could see the Channel below, washing its way between the shores. I could see the beach, the stones and sand lost along the shallow edge whenever water rushed up from the sea. I sucked in my breath, imagining the power of the waves if I were below, walking along the strip of white foam instead of the soft grass and delicate purplish flowers around me.

That's when I noticed I wasn't alone. A man was kneeling near the edge of the cliff a few yards away at the foot of the stone path, watching the water also. Wind swept his dark, unruly hair back from his brow, and fanned the edges of his worn brown canvas jacket. Between his fingers was a sprig of something dark green, a plant or a leaf of some kind.

Sensing my gaze, he turned towards me. I felt my breath catch. He was attractive. But more than that, he was… familiar.

The handsome stranger from the railway station, his dark good looks even more impressive against the stunning backdrop of the cliffs and water below. A day's worth of stubble made his well-formed features even more pleasing: features that were accented by eyes that I imagined as dark as coffee beneath those perfect lashes and sculpted brow. For a moment, we stared at each other. Then he spoke.

"Do you mind getting off the heath?" A gruff, commanding voice that was filled with disgust — even though he was practically shouting over the ripple of wind and tide, I could detect that much.

I gaped at him. "What?" I asked. His manners weren't as pretty as his looks, apparently. I felt a surge of annoyance along with my confusion for the accusation in his voice. Why was he talking this way to a perfect stranger? Who did he think he was anyway? Besides a good-looking…but no. That wasn't enough to justify the rudeness etched in his perfect face, or the scowl he offered my shoes.

"You're standing on it," he said. "The heath. What are you doing off the footpath? Can't you see you're trampling it with those spiky shoes of yours?"

I looked down and saw that I was standing in the middle of a bright patch of soft, green needles and the purplish flowers I had been admiring before. Quickly, I stepped aside, seeing that my heels had indeed left indentation in the soft earth around the plant.

So? I thought. I was pretty sure I recognized it from a website as a native wild plant here in Cornwall. "Sorry," I said, although my tone was a little annoyed with this apology. "But it's just heath, isn't it? It's not as if I killed it by walking on it."

"That's still no reason for you to crush it, is it?" he retorted. "It's a protected plant, by the way."

"Don't you think you're being a little rude?" I asked. Fed up with this insensitive behavior. He might be gorgeous enough to rival the view of the Channel below, but that didn't mean he could treat me like a criminal.

"I think I provided a pathway for people to walk on so they wouldn't walk on my plants," he answered, his voice still loud because of the distance between us. "Didn't you see the sign?"

I hadn't, actually. I had walked down the pathway without noticing any posted warnings or requests. "It's a wildflower that will bounce back in no time, I'm sure," I snapped. "There are dozens of patches of it between here and the house —"

"All of which deserve a chance to grow and propagate," he countered.

I had retreated to the stone path now, not sure why he was so angry.

What right did he have to order a stranger around over a little plant? "Who are *you* — the wildflower rescuer of Cornwall?" I asked, sarcastically.

"No," he answered, in the same tone. "I'm the gardener of Cliffs House."

Oh. Well, then. Question answered.

Way to go, Julianne. Putting your foot in it—literally.

I was aware that my cheeks were turning several shades of color equal to the heath along the pathway. "I see," I answered. I sounded lofty, even though my voice had a thousand cracks in it. "Well, that's hardly a great way to greet the guests of Cliffs House, is it?"

With that, I turned and walked quickly back up the path. I thought I heard his voice behind me, and I glanced back. I could see him scrambling to collect something — a tool belt of some sort, I thought — so I turned away and walked as fast as I could towards the house.

I retreated inside before he could catch up with me. I imagined that a pair of legs as long as the ones I'd glimpsed, clad in worn, corduroy trousers could walk fast, too. Safely inside with the door closed, I peered out from behind the lace curtains. I could see a man's shape on the path near the formal garden. He had stopped, gazing all around. Probably trying to spot the tourist woman in the green coat somewhere among the ornamental gardens. The one who went around trampling Cornish beauty beneath her expensive heels.

My cheeks blushed several shades of fire again. The gardener. Would I have to see him often? Or could I never see him again, if I played my cards right while living here at Cliffs House? Maybe I could avoid ever needing table arrangements from his garden. Imagine what he would think when he found out that it was the estate's new event planner who had been out crushing his life's work. I felt terrible, even though the whole thing was a silly misunderstanding involving a hardy and resilient Cornish weed. At least, according to the website I'd been reading on Cornish facts ... which, come to think of it, might have said something about it being a rare species after all.

"Is that you, Ms. Morgen?" Dinah was in the hall, appearing from the direction of the kitchen with a tea tray.

"Yes. It's me." I forced a smile to my lips.

"Tea's in the main parlor, if you're hungry."

"Sounds great." I hoped that the gardener was not invited to join us. Not until I had time to humble myself to an apology, or think of a better retort than 'don't be rude to tourists.' That made me sound crass and entitled, and definitely wasn't the start I wanted as a newcomer to Cornwall. And for all I knew, Lord William might have a passionate fixation on his valuable heath plants that explained why the gardener hated my intrusion on the open ground.

***

For the champagne luncheon, I couldn't avoid flowers, even if I wanted to do it. I had planned simple and elegant centerpieces featuring hothouse lilies. I had been at a loss when choosing local flowers, so I decided to stick with what I knew. I needed more time and research to choose native blossoms on my own, ones that would complement the lightly-Cornish theme Petal wanted.

Dinah had assigned Gemma and Pippa to round up and polish four elegant crystal vases for the table, but I was arranging the flowers myself. This was a task — sometimes monotonous — that Design a Dream's senior planners had delegated to me many times, whenever clients wanted simple and inexpensive arrangements. Since Petal didn't want to be bothered with choosing florists or flowers, it was up to me to decide.

"There's no local florist who would make you a centerpiece as nice as we can arrange from the hothouse flowers," said Lord William. "Marian Jones in the village makes a fine one, but she'd be busy already with local weddings for such short notice."

"Are you sure?" I said. "I don't want to offend the likes of your celebrity guests on my first try." I was half-hoping Lord William would mention another local florist, someone who could send four vases of red roses, even.

"Our flowers are among the finest in this part of Cornwall," he said. "What could they possibly object to?" His smile was equally as disarming as Lady Amanda's, with an absolute lack of pomp and circumstance in his general appearance, one of work-worn denim and a frayed sweater. There were wood chips clinging to his sleeve — I imagined him cutting up broken trees for firewood somewhere on the estate, as Geoff Weatherby had described.

"Nothing at all," I said, shaking my head. I admitted defeat at this point, and asked Pippa to let the gardening staff know that I wanted as many white lilies as the hothouse had available.

"Don't you want to see them yourself?" asked Pippa. "Take a geek at the place and pick them out for your own?"

"She means 'look it over,'" supplied Gemma, who was polishing one of the vases. "But she'll be glad to do it for you if Ross is there."

Pippa didn't argue with her, glancing back at me. "Well, don't you?" she asked me, trying to banish the traces of a saucy grin which Gemma's words had inspired.

"No need," I answered. "Just white lilies."

I knew that the gardeners would know who wanted them and why, so there was no need to explain. Thankfully, whoever the gardener was who had ordered me off the heath the other day, I hadn't introduced myself as part of the staff. He would imagine me safely gone as a rude tourist.

When the lilies arrived the day before their scheduled arrangement, something else arrived with them, in a white florist's box unlike the lilies' basket. Pippa read the note taped to the top, then handed it to me.

"For you," she announced. "Looks like you've got an admirer already."

"Who?" I asked, with total shock. I opened the box and found a sheet of pale green tissue paper folded around blossoms — roses in a shade of deep, violet-pink.

"Oh, they're gorgeous," said Gemma. "Who're they from?"

I pulled out a card tucked near the blossoms. *I apologize for being rude to you. You were correct before — no visitor to Cornwall deserves a welcome less than warm. With my sincere wishes for your success here, Matthew Rose.*

I read the words aloud despite the faint blush on my cheeks for the episode in my memory. A little gasp of shock came from Gemma. "Ross sent you flowers?"

"Heavens, did he really?" Even Dinah was listening now, even though she was busy poring over a recipe for petits fours, a row of spices lined up before her like soldiers.

"What — here four days and you've hooked him already?" said Pippa, with amazement. "Ross never pays any attention to anyone — how on earth did you manage it?"

"Hold on," I said. "Who is 'Ross'? The card says it's from someone named Matthew Rose."

Gemma's jaw dropped. "What, you don't see the resemblance?" she asked. "Everybody sees it when they look at him."

"Sees what?"

"You know, the television programme. *Poldark?* Ross, the main character?"

"I've never seen it," I answered.

"Never? Not even once?"

"I don't watch PBS?" I said, meekly. Both of the girls exchanged glances once more — this time, of pity for my ignorance.

"Does he really look like this — Ross guy, I take it?"

"Dead ringer," said Pippa. "Why do you think all the women about go a bit soft in the knees whenever he comes by?"

He was handsome. No denying that. And in a way that Donald Price-Parker was not, which was precisely the reason I had found myself staring at him a few days ago in the railway station.

"Why was he apologizing to you?" Gemma asked.

"Oh, that." My blush was back, for reasons besides Matthew Rose — or the mysterious Ross's — good looks. "I, um, sort of ... stepped on his plants the other day."

From her place by the stove, Dinah let out a peal of laughter. "Dear me, I would have loved to have seen that," she said.

"Why?" I asked. "He was completely rude about it. And it wasn't intentional, what I did. Obviously."

"Ross is that way. Part of his charming manners." Pippa flashed me a grin.

"He's not rude," retorted Gemma. "He's nice. Funny and smart, if you know him well enough, I've heard. Trouble is, he's hard to get to know. He's a slave to the dirt, he likes to say, and that's no lie. Hardly ever goes out from that cottage he rents, except to the village to buy groceries."

"Leave him alone," scolded Dinah. "He's a grown man. He knows well enough what he's doing. At least he's not acting silly with his head in the clouds, or mooning about over some personal troubles the way so many others do." A look in her eyes made me curious to know exactly what she meant by this, but I hated to ask.

The grounds were proof of Matthew Rose's devotion to his work, anyway. I had seen both perfection and wild beauty in the tumbling foxglove and periwinkle, and carefully-tended roses, and marveled at whoever produced it. "Looks like his hermitage has paid off for Cliffs House," I remarked.

Maybe this was the sort of fantasy they were writing about in those gothic novels. A mysterious, brooding, dark-eyed gardener in the wilds of Cornwall, tending beauty while living in a tumbledown, ivy-covered cottage —

"I guess I owe Mr. Rose an apology, too," I said. "Maybe I missed the sign he mentioned. And it was my fault his plant got a little crushed. I just thought he could have been nicer about it."

"Sent you flowers, didn't he?" said Dinah. She gave me a look that made me feel self-conscious again — this time for the impossibility of myself paired with this mystery man of a gardener whom half the village was tracing.

I shrugged it off. "I didn't say he doesn't have good apology skills," I answered. My fingers stroked the soft petals of the roses. I hoped he hadn't taken them from one of the estate's rose plants, since I was pretty sure that would get him into trouble.

I put the lilies into a cool, dark closet so they could 'rest' for the hours before they were arranged. I put the roses in a vase on my desk. From my window, I could see Ross — or Matthew Rose — trimming the hedges in the garden. A blue shirt untucked beneath his wool pullover, a pair of faded jeans with hand shears tucked in his back pocket. It was sunny today, so he wasn't carrying the wool cap I had noticed the other day, when it had been slightly rainy in the morning.

A moment later, I crossed the lawn to where Matthew was working. For a moment, he pretended not to see me approaching — I could see it from the way his eyes twitched in my direction, then focused harder than ever on the hedge. But I stood there until he finally looked at me.

"Thanks," I said. "For the flowers."

He gazed at me for a long moment, studying me intently. His eyes were as dark as coffee — almost black, but with little glints of something lighter in them. My knees threatened to tremble ever so slightly, but I resisted by locking them firmly upright. It was silly of me to have that reaction to a stranger.

"You're welcome," he answered. He went back to trimming the hedge.

There was a touch of Cornish in his accent, I could hear that much, only it had softened over the years, and mixed with something else. A little of London, or maybe a little of something closer to home for me. Was it an American accent? New York, maybe?

I tilted my head. "Where are you from?" I asked.

"Here," he answered, snipping away more green branches.

"Yeah, but ... somewhere else, too. Are you from America?"

"Briefly," he answered. "I spent some time there, once."

I hesitated. "Is that why you sent me the roses?" I asked. "Because I'm a fish out of water? A foreigner from familiar shores?"

"No. I sent them to you because I felt you had a point," he said. "If you had been a visitor to Cliffs House, I would have given you a poor impression of its hospitality. If you *had* been a visitor," he clarified. "And not, let's say, the newest member of the staff. Who should have been able to read the sign by the path, for instance."

"In English or in Cornish?" I asked. This time, I wasn't irritated, but smiling. I wasn't flustered anymore, but bold enough to joke with him a little.

"Both," he answered. For a moment, I thought he wasn't going to smile. At last, however, that serious countenance broke a little with the faintest proof of a smile. "Regardless, I learned my lesson, thanks to you. I'll be nothing but politeness itself to the next rude tourist who wanders off the beaten path."

Victory. I tucked my hands in the pockets of my pea coat. "Well, as the newest member of your staff, I concede your point about the native flowers," I said. "And I hope your heath plant recovers."

"As someone wise pointed out — it is a resilient plant," he said. "Even if it is a protected one. It should be fine, given a day or two." He smiled, this time for real. It was worth the wait for that smile, I decided.

"So why are you cultivating it along the pathway?" I asked. "Doesn't it grow there naturally?"

"Not really. We're trying to introduce it to more regions in Cornwall by propagation, part of a botanical program at work locally. There was an errant cigarette fire along that part of the pathway not long ago and it cost me the first part of my work," he said. "I'm trying to hurry along the recovery process with a few transplants."

"Oh." Now I felt worse about stepping on his plants. "Um, sorry, then."

"Where are you from in America?" he asked. This complete change of subject bumped me from my thoughts back to the present.

"Seattle, Washington," I said. "Before that, Idaho. A very sleepy spot in it called Molehill." My hometown's name tended to garner snickers from anybody who heard it. It hosted a yearly festival that involved whacking moles in carnival games and a puppet that looked like a groundhog popping out of a paper-mache volcano painted green.

Matthew didn't crack a smile, oddly enough. He looked thoughtful. "Did you know there's a village close by called Mousehole?" he asked.

"Mousehole?" I echoed.

"Exactly so." He turned back to his hedge, although he glanced over his shoulder at me. "If you feel homesick, you can visit its road sign." He winked at me. No smile this time, but there was something almost flirtatious about that brief movement of his eyelid, and the expression in his dark eyes.

I felt a little shiver pass through me. "I'll keep that in mind," I said, as I turned back to the house. I couldn't help glancing over my shoulder one more time before I went inside. That glimpse of his good humor, the smile that brought warmth into those dark eyes. That must be the charming side that Gemma had mentioned, and I could see what she was talking about.

"Julianne," I said. "Morgen. That's my name, in case you didn't know it." Lame, since obviously someone on staff had told him about me and described me well enough that he knew I was the woman from the path.

"I know," he answered.

He was completely absorbed by his hedge trimming once again. Since he didn't look at me as he spoke, I went inside and went back to my own work.

***

No more thinking about Cliffs House's gorgeous gardener, I had resolved. I had work to do, and only a day before the big champagne luncheon for Donald and Petal's wedding. In a sudden switch, we transformed the main dining hall into a champagne buffet so we could throw open the glass doors to the terrace and garden just outside. Once, the room had been some sort of receiving hall or something like that, I had read in my *Guide to Cliffs House*, courtesy of Lady Amanda, but it had been transformed by Lord William's grandfather into a beautiful, modern room that still had the original stone archway and buttresses on display. The view was perfect, and so was the dining table, a long, elegant cherry one that I covered with a white linen cloth.

The press would arrive early, no doubt, on the day of the event; the family would be cloistered for privacy until the party begin, in one of the spare bedroom and dressing room suites upstairs: one that felt like a spacious apartment compared to my beloved two-room cracker box when I first graduated from college.

Today we were arranging the flowers while Dinah was putting the finishing touches on the petits fours, the last item made for the buffet. She had outdone herself — as Geoff Weatherby and Jackson, the apparent head gardener — had declared upon tasting the castoff pieces of sponge when she cut the perfect orange rectangles from it. Now they were lined upon baking sheets, waiting for their platters: ten dozen orange saffron cakes wrapped in Cornish tartan-printed fondant.

"They turned out lovely," she declared. "That was a clever thought you had," she told me, although she was shouting a little over the noise outside the window, where two repairmen had come to make building repairs to the outside wall. "Using the Cornish print to add a bit of local color — especially to saffron-flavored cakes."

"I just don't want my first big clients to be disappointed — in me or in Cliffs House," I answered. I felt a surge of pride for her compliment. Sure, it was only a design for bite-sized cakes, but it was the first step in a hopefully-successful, elegant wedding that I would coordinate into perfection. "Besides, you're the one who brought them into reality, so they're as much your creation as mine. And I didn't think of that creative geometric twist you put on some of them."

Dinah had altered the Cornish tartan pattern with a pattern of diamonds and stripes in the same colors as the tartan. It was a simpler, lighter design, and provided a visual contrast that made the tartan's lines stand out.

"Touch of a chef, that's all," answered Dinah, mildly, as she checked off the number of spicy ginger-orange snaps she had made, cooling on the platters before her. It was her way of accepting my compliment, I realized, smiling as I lifted the buckets of lilies from their cool storage space.

"So why did you leave Seattle to come to Cornwall?" Gemma asked me. She and Pippa were helping me arrange the flowers in the parlor. Beautiful white lilies peered over the buckets full of cool water and the special preservative secret I remembered from Design a Dream — a dash of carbonated lemon lime soda pop.

I sucked in a quick breath. "I don't know," I said. "There's no one reason. It was just such a great career move, being in charge of coordinating and planning events on my own. I couldn't believe I'd been given the chance, so I just snapped it up."

"And flew all the way across the pond to Ceffylgwyn?" said Pippa, sounding amazed. "Sorry, but I don't think I'd be tempted by a job that dropped me in the middle of some tiny American village with no proper spa or entertainment to speak of."

"Unless you like Troyls," piped up Gemma. They both giggled as Pippa stifled a snort in response. Her shears clipped off the excess greenery at the base of a lily's stem.

"What's 'Troyls'?" I asked. I had a feeling this was definitely a Cornish thing.

"It's a dance," said Gemma. "Old-fashioned. Not like going to a club in London, or the like."

"Folk dancing," added Pippa. "Some people 'round here get dressed up in the tartan or the black kilts to go. Fish wife's costume, even."

"That's more for festival than for Troyls' night," argued Gemma. "Anyway, not exactly rich entertainment unless you like that sort of music."

I imagined bagpipes, then realized this image must be all wrong.

"Ross used to go — I'll bet he wore a proper kilt and everything," said Gemma. "Just imagine," she said to me, and both girls had saucy grins as heat crept into my face.

"I think I'm better off *not* imagining any of my fellow employees in kilts," I answered, hoping to change the subject. I stepped away from the table, dropping my trimmed leaves and stems into the waste bin.

"Those shoes," gasped Pippa. "Where'd you get them?"

"These?" I glanced down. I was wearing a pair of red Jimmy Choos, the same ones I'd worn to Nancy's office when she lectured me on dressing the part of an underling. "I got them from a Seattle boutique — marked down, but they were still pricey."

"Gorgeous," she moaned. "I've wanted a pair like that ever since I saw that movie about the shoe designer — you know the one. Can I try them on?" she asked.

"Sure." I slipped off my heels, watching as the girl kicked off her clogs and slipped them on. She stood up, wobbling a little as she walked across the carpet in stiletto heels. "How do you wear these all the time?" she asked.

"I got used to it," I answered. "At Design a Dream, wearing silk and heels was all part of the image. Classy was encouraged — only you had to be careful not to dress better than the boss or her favorites."

"Around here, the only person wearing designer clothes for casual is the model whose flowers we're arranging," said Gemma. "I saw the dress she wore when she met with you yesterday. Sells for four hundred pounds in London. I read it online."

"It didn't look like it was worth it," said Pippa over her shoulder, who was walking with more confidence in the heels now.

I had to agree. The dress's impression, like that of Petal herself, fell flat after a moment or two. Without makeup and an artful hairstyle, she looked less glamorous and more like the cute-but-pouting sort. Her smile for everybody at Cliffs House felt like a practiced one, and unless she was surgically attached to her fiancé, she seemed more interested in talking about New York and London than any sort of Cornish traditions for her wedding. Without him, Cornwall apparently held no interest for her.

"What do you think?" Pippa asked, posing dramatically with one hand behind her head. "Do I have a future as stunning as Petal Borroway's in Milan?"

Before either of us could answer, the sound of a tremendous crash and a wail caught our attention — coming from the direction of the kitchen hall. Without a word, we took off running from the parlor, me barefoot and Pippa teetering in my heels.

We halted in the kitchen doorway. There, on the table, was a disaster beyond the proportion of any I could imagine. Shattered glass covered the floor, the table, and the newly-finished petits fours. What had survived of them, that is — because the ladder which had crashed through the window had landed in the middle of Dinah's creations, creating a pile of sponge and marzipan mush.

"Sorry," said the workman, meekly. Dinah moaned again.

***

"Okay," I said, forcing my reeling mind to work. "Okay, we can fix this."

"Ten dozen sponge petits fours?" Dinah whipped her head to look at me, incredulously.

"We have — what? Twelve hours?" I tried to calculate how soon the tea spread had to be on display — early enough for the press to photograph it, including some journalists from prominent society magazines. "It's not impossible. I can cook — I'll help you mix up new sponge, cut the cakes out —"

"It's the decorating, though," pointed out Gemma, her voice seconds away from a wail of her own. "It took hours to stencil on that Cornish tartan —"

"And that was *with* mistakes," finished Pippa. "And we've got to make new fondant, because we used the last of what was in the fridge."

I felt cold sweat beneath my cardigan. The sweat of panic, something I hadn't felt since the time one of Design a Dream's clients delightful pond locale for their reception had turned into a mosquito-infested bog the morning of, and I'd been delegated to deal with the bugs.

"All hands on deck, then," I said. Inspiration was striking, and I was seizing it. "Gemma, quick — go get anyone who can be spared. Gardeners, Lady Amanda's assistant, anybody — tell them to be ready to help assemble mini cakes as soon as the sponge cools."

"What?" Gemma said. "Are you quite serious?"

"Yes, I am," I said. "We need anybody who can help us out."

"What about the stenciling? There's no way any of that lot's artistic enough to pull it off."

"We'll just have to go simpler," I said. I tried to ignore my sinking heart at the thought of Dinah's beautiful tartan and geometric designs pushed to the side. "Saffron cakes are still Cornish-inspired. We'll do a simple flower on top or something." I pushed up the sleeves of my cardigan. "So where's the saffron and the flour?"

We worked as fast as we could, me and Dinah mixing batter, with Pippa and Gemma cutting the cakes as they cooled. By the time we were ready for decoration, we had extra help. Geoff spread marmalade between cake layers as Pippa and I carefully spread a buttercream frosting over them in place of the fondant. With each smooth glide of my heated knife, I hoped that the final presentation would be even half as elegant as Dinah's poor, smashed creations.

I looked up from my work and caught a pair of dark eyes watching me. Matthew the gardener was seated close by, helping layer the cakes. I hadn't realized that he was here, I'd been so busy with my own work. I couldn't help but notice that Gemma's cheeks were blazing fire red whenever he spoke to her or anybody else at the table. She and Pippa would look at each other and giggle ever so often.

"Less giggling and more working," ordered Dinah. Her stout-as-steel patience was beginning to waver a bit as she removed her latest batch of sponge. She was feeling the pressure every bit as badly as I was — as the chef of Cliffs House, her reputation was at stake if these cakes weren't scrumptious *and* beautiful by tomorrow morning.

"A pity about the last ones," said Matthew. "I glimpsed them through the window an hour before the disaster. You were doing a beautiful job." He was speaking to Dinah, but he glanced at me at the same time. Dinah merely shook her head.

"Disasters happen," I said, trying to sound confident that this would all work out for the best. "I'm only sorry that no one really had a chance to see that handiwork. But I'm sure these will be just as beautiful, as soon as we put something decorative on top."

"Whose idea was the design? Cornish tartan?" he asked. "Was it yours, Dinah? I liked them better than the ones I've seen in London bakeries."

"Hers," said Dinah, nodding at me. I tried not to blush.

"Really?" He studied me again. That long glance that made me feel like he could see inside me, maybe see what was in my head. I hoped not, because it was the vision inspired by the girls earlier — him in a kilt, a picture that randomly popped into my thoughts in order to embarrass me at this moment.

"I thought it would be a good way to pay tribute to local culture," I said. "A twist on Saffron cakes, draped in Cornish colors."

"You're taking to Cornwall quickly," he said. Another smile, one that made my heart skip a beat. "Or maybe you're simply clever enough to do a quick internet search." In a second, the smile had become a sly, teasing one that infuriated me the way Nate's sometimes did, a friend who was almost like a brother to me. Matthew didn't seem like the brotherly type, I felt. So what *was* I feeling?

"Maybe Cornwall's colors were already my favorites," I retorted. "And this was all a coincidence." I didn't stick my tongue out at him, but I was tempted to. I wondered what would happen if I did. Would he tease me some more? I was surprised to find that I wanted that to happen.

"What was it for? There's no festival this week. Troyl, maybe?" As he said this, I heard Gemma stifle another giggle. I managed to stuff the image of Matthew Rose in tartan somewhere else in my mind, and was now working hard not to think about those rather strong-looking hands across from my own.

"It's for the wedding," said Pippa. "You know, the smashing Donald Price-Parker who's marrying the model? Petal Borroway, from the nail varnish advertisements?"

"Ah." This sound was somewhere between a growl and a grunt from Matthew's throat. I guessed he wasn't a fan of celebrity gossip.

"You know, she emailed Lady Amanda about the colors for the champagne luncheon," said Pippa, confidentially. "What do you think — odds are she shows up in a matching frock?"

"Bet a quid," said Gemma.

Matthew pushed his chair back from the table. "I have to finish the project I was working on a bit ago," he said to Dinah. "I can't finish helping with these, I'm sorry." He glanced at me. "I wish I could help more, but —"

"Of course," I said. I was startled by how abruptly he was leaving. "Fine. We've got more than enough people to finish these, I'm sure."

"Best of luck," he said. He wasn't looking at any of us, but busy collecting his tool belt, one fitted with spades, rakes, and augers instead of hammer and nails. He lifted a potted plant from beside it, opened the kitchen door and left.

"Why is he going?" Gemma said. "It's just some plant."

"You know how he is," said Pippa. "Well — Julianne here does, anyway."

It was their first time to openly tease me, and even if it happened to be about a sensitive subject like Matthew Rose, I decided to put up with it. "Maybe he's way too busy to spend his whole afternoon assembling tiny cakes," I answered.

"Matthew doesn't have to do anything he doesn't want around here," said Dinah to Gemma. "He came as a favor to help. We're lucky to have him, and if he says there's something pressing in the garden, I'm sure Lord William would prefer he finish it than slice cakes in here."

She made Matthew sound privileged for a gardener. It struck me as odd, and I wondered what made his relationship with Cliffs House so unusual. Was Matthew a relative of Lord William? Had he been in some kind of accident and wasn't supposed to be working right now? Any number of weird and wild solutions popped into my head — including a romantic one in which he was the rightful heir to a neighboring estate, and working as a gardener until he could wrest his place from the grip of a scheming relation —

"Last one," announced Dinah. "Now all we need is a decoration for the top."

Nothing came to mind that seemed original or perfect, especially since the original Cornish colors were the only real solution, given the biscuits and chocolates. We mixed up marzipan dough, looked through the kitchen's collection of decorative molds and books on creative cake toppers, but nothing seemed right.

"I suppose we could just do orange roses," began Dinah, with a sigh.

A quick knock sounded on the kitchen door, and Gemma ran to answer it. She and Pippa had been splitting an Indian curry takeaway since they were both hours past their usual working shift at Cliffs House.

"These are for you," said Jackson the gardener, handing Dinah a basket. "He said you might find 'em helpful. G'night." He tipped his gardening hat at all of us, and went back out again.

"Who said it?" Dinah wondered aloud as she pulled back the damp cloth over the top. Inside were edible flowers — little delicate white and pink petals, and bright yellow and gold ones that I recognized from my grandmother's flower pots.

"Dearovim, it's lady's smock and marigolds," said Dinah, whose accent slid gently into strong Cornish with these words. "The one's common, though I've not seen any in the garden — and where'd he ever find so many of the lady's smock? So few of them go to seed around here."

"He grows stuff at his cottage, so maybe it's from his own garden," said Pippa. "I've seen it before when passing by — all sorts of stuff grows there."

Pink, white, and gold. It would change the colors slightly, but not enough to matter. And once these were dusted with rock sugar, they would be perfect atop the cakes, and would add the 'Cornish touch' that we were missing.

I had never been so grateful to anybody in my whole career. Not even the shop who sold me the ornamental citronella candles at half price for the bug-infested reception.

***

Guests seemed impressed by the Cliffs House champagne luncheon, judging from the 'oohs' and 'aahs' when Dinah's decorative spread was revealed. Antique china trays of cream-colored cakes decorated with sugared flowers in pale pink and bright gold-orange, milk and dark chocolates lightly sprinkled with candied orange, and spicy ginger and cinnamon biscuits with only a hint of citrus in each crisp bite.

Lord William played host briefly, popping the cork on the first bottle of champagne to pour a round for toasting the bride to be. Petal was blushing, but in a way that only enhanced the pink rouge dusted over her flawless cheekbones. As Gemma predicted, her dress was a pale orange-brown print featuring white butterflies, matched with a pair of shoes so expensive I couldn't imagine ever dreaming about them, much less owning them. An engagement present from Donald, she told the girl at her elbow, the American chief bridesmaid Trixie Nelson.

Until now, I hadn't been aware that anybody in the world was still named Trixie, much less anyone as young and supposedly chic as Petal's fellow model. Trixie dabbled in acting, apparently, which she informed a few members of the press as she brushed aside the strands of platinum blond hair swept across her face by the breeze.

"Looks like it's gone off smashingly," whispered Pippa as she passed me, circulating one of the trays of champagne. I smiled, feeling as proud of Cliffs House's success as she did. It was my first big event, and it was going smoothly by all accounts.

I circulated the room, making sure that the cakes remained ornamentally stacked and that the truffles weren't running low. I helped Gemma chill more champagne, then edged closer to a journalist who seemed to be taking a strong interest in Dinah's beautiful citrus saffron cakes.

Only the journalist was really interested in the conversation taking place between Petal and Donald. Who were arguing over something about the wedding.

"And I *hate* the thought of carrying them down the aisle!" hissed Petal. "It's hideous, and I won't do it, Donald. I want something from the shops in London. Anything. Even a bundle of half-dead roses."

Her beautiful features had twisted into a scowl. I realized, with chagrin, that she was talking about the sketches we had discussed yesterday, the ones for her flower bouquet. I had prided myself on coming up with a Cornish bouquet that would match her wedding colors — a mixture of blooms the color of heath in autumn, paired with orchids and colored daisies — and had mentioned that most of the flowers were available in the manor's hothouse. Apparently, Petal's polite smile for my suggestions had been extremely fake.

"Why? It's a bunch of dead leaves and flowers, love," said Donald, disgustedly. "Toss 'em in the dustbin after it's over."

"You *know* why I feel that way," she said. "It's uncomfortable, Donald. I simply prefer to bring something down from London the day before and be done with it. Besides, it would go better with the dress. It's a couture gown, Donald. Not some fish wife's costume." She muttered this last part.

Donald rolled his eyes. "This is the Cornish Riviera, love," he said. "Stop moaning because it's not the beach house at Newquay. We were both bored there, and half the crowd's in Truro now for the summer."

"Then why couldn't we get married there?" she said. "Why did you have to pick this shabby little spot in the middle of nowhere where I'm reminded of a past I loathe every time I'm here?"

The color drained from my face, and I burned with indignation on behalf of Cliffs House and the impossible-to-pronounce Ceffylgwyn described as 'shabby.' I wanted to snap at Petal that a place that breathed this much history and local pride was too good for *her*, but I bit back my words.

I remembered my role at this event, and that this was their party, and they were entitled to their privacy, even if it was privacy for the sake of trash-talking the venue. Even with their voices low, people around them could still hear their argument, and I didn't want that — for both Petal and Donald, and for the sake of Cliffs House's reputation. "Sorry," I said, nudging the listening-in journalist as I passed him. "Oh, did I do that?" I said, as his champagne sloshed over his wrist. "My apologies. Can I get you a towel?"

"Watch where you walk next time!" he snapped. Obviously he was annoyed that he had lost track of their conversation. Petal and Donald had noticed him standing nearby and moved to a more private part of the room. A moment later they were both laughing at the best man's stories, and feeding each other pieces of saffron cake.

I retreated through the open glass doors for a breathing moment. I wanted to slip off my heels and relax, but there were still hours to go. But since nothing disastrous was happening at the moment, I took off in the direction of the garden paths where some of the wedding party's guests were wandering.

On the other side of the hedge, I could hear a woman's laugh, a high falsetto one that sounded a little like a yapping dog. Curious, I stepped through the opening, and found Trixie the chief bridesmaid and Matthew Rose the gardener. There were two glasses of champagne present, one in Trixie's hand and one on the lawn beside Matthew.

He had been in the middle of tending the roses, but now Trixie was sitting on his wheelbarrow tilted on its side, her dress's ornamental wrap slipped low enough to bare her shoulders to him. Matthew was laughing, though not as heartily, at whatever had struck them both as funny a moment ago.

"Sorry," I said. I stepped backwards. "I didn't realize anyone was here." Not true, but I said it anyway.

"Oh ... the wedding planner, right?" said Trixie, squinting at me. "Yes, I do remember meeting you earlier." That was all the attention she was willing to give me, turning her attention to Matthew again. "Did you *really* meet David Bowie?" she said.

"Only once," he said. "And at a party of a friend, who merely wanted me to give him some advice on landscaping. Nothing very exciting, I'm afraid."

"I wanted to hear you tell that story — I've always been jealous when other people get to meet famous people that *I* wanted to meet." She leaned closer to him. "So how many *other* famous people have you met?"

Matthew blushed. Her face was much closer to his than before, her whole body sidling towards his. The look in his eyes was strangely conflicted — even confused — but it wasn't the look of someone utterly shocked or repulsed by this bold maneuver.

Two champagne glasses — obviously the two of them had been here for a little while, getting acquainted. I tried not to let my feelings show, those of disappointment and mortification, as I turned and left without bothering with any polite farewells. Obviously I wasn't wanted at this little gathering.

I made myself busy for the next hour or so back at the reception, although blood was thundering in my ears. What was wrong with me? It wasn't as if Matthew ever suggested he was attracted to me. I made it all up in my imagination, based on some silly roses and a couple of glances. He sent those edible flowers to save Dinah's reputation, not mine. And those roses — that was just his way of flirting with the newest female employee on the estate, or maybe his way of flirting with every woman he ever met.

I was pretty sure I wouldn't be fond of seeing roses around for awhile.

More people were strolling around the grounds, and the press was almost finished with 'exclusive interviews' or 'one on one' questions, and beginning to make small talk in the dining hall. I discreetly swept some crumbs off the table and removed an empty truffles platter.

Petal was on the stairs as I passed through the hall to the kitchen. Someone else was with her, and it only took a second before I recognized the platinum blond hair and gold party dress from before.

"... he was just so attractive," said Trixie, who was almost whining. "Don't be such a stick, Pet. There's nothing wrong with me hooking up with him for a few weeks, anyway. It's not as if he's private property, is he?"

"It's inappropriate," said Petal. "I don't want you doing it, Trix."

Automatically, I stepped back against the wall. It was my second time to eavesdrop today — this time intentionally — and I found I didn't want to be seen before this conversation ended.

"Why? Because I'm an American on vacation here?" her friend retorted. "Or is it because —"

There was a crash from the kitchen. "Dearie me, there goes a bucket of ice!" I heard Dinah say, the last threads of patience in her voice wearing out.

"Sorry," squeaked Pippa. "It just slipped." The sound of ice clattering as they swept it up.

Both Petal and Trixie had been listening, too. Trixie tossed her hair. "I don't care what you say," she said. "I want him and that's that." She trotted up the stairs quickly, ignoring Petal's pouting scowl and crossed arms.

I waited until they were both gone to finish walking to the kitchen. Even if Matthew was a flirt and probably deserved someone like her, I still didn't like the idea of her 'hooking' him for a few weeks time. I tried not to think too hard about why as I helped Dinah and Pippa finish cleaning up the spilled ice.

***

"We'll put the arbor for the ceremony here, I believe," said Lord William, waving his hand towards a neat square of green lawn in front of a flower bed. "The foxglove will still be in bloom, but I'm afraid those annuals will be spent by then. It'll look rather shabby, but this is by far the best spot."

"We could patch those spots with something else," suggested Geoff, studying it with a frown. "Bit of green, if nothing else."

"I think we should simply bring round some potted flowers from the garden behind the kitchen," Lady Amanda intervened. "There's lovely color in them, and it would fill the gaps nicely without having to plant anything more. Transplant is an art."

Lord William sighed. "Let's ask Matthew's opinion on it," he said. "We want this to be as striking as possible. Maybe he'll have a brilliant thought on what would be ideal."

I didn't offer an opinion as the three of us studied the wedding ceremony site in the garden. Absently, I plucked a few leaves from a vine in a heavy cast-iron urn, blossoms of vinca trailing along its sides. I was still peeved at Matthew — for no good reason, really — and didn't want to venture an opinion that might include his name.

Lady Amanda sighed. "This is the part of event planning that *always* lasts far too long," she said. "Making up one's mind to the details, be it ever so small." She checked her watch. "Fortunately for me, I have an appointment with the boat rental on the port that can't be missed."

"What — leaving now?" Lord William asked. "But we haven't made a decision."

"Their new website is nearly ready and we have to discuss online scheduling." She kissed his cheek, then tucked her handbag under her arm and strolled quickly towards the garden's exit. Over her shoulder, she gave me a conspiratorial smile — the smile of a woman finally escaping to her true calling, and leaving me to mine.

Both of the men present now looked at me. "Then I suppose it's your opinion that will be the final word, Julianne," said Lord William, with a smile. "That, and Matthew's, of course."

"Right," I answered.

Reluctantly, I set off in the direction of the hothouse, where Matthew was busy working, apparently. I picked my way around a pile of broken clay pots and fertilizer, opening the door to a long, glass room which might as well be a conservatory joined to the sunniest side of the house.

Inside, Matthew was busy testing soil in a row of potted plants — at least that's what I assumed he must be doing. He was examining smears between glass lenses, a pile that resembled chemical test strips from my old chem lab days lying on the table in front of him.

"Um, sorry to interrupt," I began, trying hard not to look at him. "But Lord William wants to know if you can do something special for the central bed in the formal garden." I studied the heavy green vines, vinca and flowering peas, which trailed past the windows from the blanket of green covering the glass roof. It was somewhere over Matthew's right shoulder, but far from the direct line to his dark eyes.

Not that he noticed. He was too busy reading whatever sample was in his hand, held up to the sunlight. "I see," he answered.

"If you could just say 'yes' or 'no,' that would be fine," I said.

"Can it wait?" he asked. "Or are you rushing off somewhere?" He looked directly at me now. I gave the little flowers on the vine considerably more study, giving him only a fraction of a glance. I didn't leave, so that seemed like an answer in itself.

He studied the sample a moment longer, then laid it aside. "Are you angry at me?" he asked.

The direct question took me by surprise. "What?" I said. I broke my own rule and looked at him for a moment. He looked amused, and vaguely puzzled. Time to study the flowers again, I reminded myself.

"No," I said. "I'm not angry. What makes you think that?"

"I'm fairly sure I can recognize anger at this point."

"That's a rather stupid question to ask someone," I said. "Whom you hardly know, anyway."

"I thought maybe we were back to the debacle of the heath plant," he said. "Or perhaps you had a problem with the edible flowers."

"No," I said, slightly softened by this mention of the flowers.

"Or perhaps you have a problem with me personally." He studied his project on the table now, but not with any real focus that I could detect. "With something I said or did. You didn't speak to me yesterday, I noticed."

"You were busy enjoying your champagne," I muttered, a little tersely. That was a mistake. I could see from Matthew's face that he figured it out.

"What — with the chief bridesmaid?" he said. "She brought me that glass, you know. I didn't ask her to — I didn't invite anyone into the garden to chat." A deep red blush crept over his face, and suddenly he looked very boyish and embarrassed. "I was polite, but I wasn't ... flirting."

I'd made him uncomfortable, which surprised me. It wasn't a crime for him to notice a woman as gorgeous as Trixie, since he was apparently unattached. And, like I had told myself before, there was nothing between us but my silly little fantasy now and then.

"If you were, there's no law against it," I reminded him, although it cost me a blush — just a little one. "Besides she was very pretty. And thoughtful."

"That's not the point," he muttered. But more to himself than to me. "Anyway, I was being polite in the garden to — to a guest of the house. But not quite as polite as all that." He seemed to have recovered now, offering me a smile. It seemed perfectly friendly, yet sad. I wasn't sure why it struck me this way, but it did.

"Well, as I said before, it's none of my business." My voice softened. "But when you get the chance, if you would give Lord William and Lady Amanda a few ideas on how to make the flower bed more impressive, they would appreciate it." I turned to go.

"Do you still want to make a better acquaintance with Cornish culture?" he asked.

I glanced back. "Sure," I said. I didn't think this was a trick question — although back home, with a friend like Nate or Aimee, this kind of proposal sometimes ended with the kind of mean joke friends play on each other, a cube of ice down the back of my shirt, or a spoonful of salt in my coffee. But me and Matthew weren't close enough for me to worry about that, were we?

"Then come with me to lunch," he said. "If you're not busy with other plans."

"No other plans." The voice that answered him had come from me, yet it was soft and entirely different from my usual one. That was good, because a sudden and quiet astonishment had swept over me when he suggested this.

Ceffylgwyn itself was a place I hadn't thoroughly explored until now — but by Matthew's side, I saw everything anew through the eyes of someone who lived here and clearly loved it. From the harbor port with its strong smell of fish and saltwater, the shacks and wood supports stained grey and black by the water, to the quaint whitewashed and slate structures that reminded you of Old England at every turn. The water was always there, making Cornwall feel like an enchanted island every time I glimpsed the curves of the Channel and the beaches. I peered through the windows of shops, some of them selling tourist souvenirs; others were proof of Cornwall's everyday population, with modern fish and chips and takeaway spots, and tobacco shops and grocery stores.

"How long have you lived here?" I asked Matthew, as we walked.

"Four years," he said. "I was a boy here, though, for most of my life. Long before university, I used to bike along the shore. I worked at a fish and chips shop — my first real job."

"You weren't a gardener then?" I asked.

Matthew laughed. "I'm not a gardener now," he said, sounding amused. "Not in the way you think."

I stopped walking. "What do you mean by that?" I turned to stone. Had Matthew — had everyone — been lying? Playing some elaborate joke? It made no sense — hadn't I met him digging on the grounds at Cliffs House? Defending its plants against clumsy visitors?

"I'm a horticulturist and botanist," he said. "I used to teach those subjects at a university when I was in America. I worked in crossbreeding and hybridization, disease control, preservation of historic plants — that last one was a position I held for some time at a historic garden in Massachusetts. When I came back to England, I did a little of the same, in London and then here in Cornwall. I studied landscaping on the side. Purely a hobby, you might say."

"What — what exactly are you doing at Cliffs House?" I demanded. I crossed my arms as I faced him. "If you're not a gardener just replacing singed heath and potting foxglove, or whatever."

"William is a friend of mine from university. We may have grown up in separate parts of Cornwall, but we both love it...and since I was between positions, he asked me if I would be kind enough to consult on the gardens at Cliffs House."

I considered this as I gazed at the shop across the street. "So you *are* a gardener," I said. "And you are gardening at Cliffs House."

"Technically, I'm restoring the gardens of Cliffs House to their previous glory," he said. "While solving a few bacterial and disease problems among the roses and some of the shrubbery."

"Hence all the test strips and soil smears this morning," I said. I shook my head. "Why didn't anyone mention what you did?"

"Why does it matter?" he asked. "Does it matter to you whether I'm an undergardener who trims shrubbery, or a former professor who treats its diseases?"

"I guess it doesn't," I admitted. "Still, I wish I had known. I should have been addressing you as *Doctor* Rose, for one thing." I smiled a little, seeing that I had embarrassed him slightly.

"It's not a title I use right now," he said. "Just Matthew Rose is fine. Matt is better, actually."

"Matt," I repeated. Shyly, to my surprise. Was I in danger of melting again under his good looks and boyish charm? Shaking off the possibility, I told him, "Okay. I'll remember that." I slipped my hands into my coat pockets. "So why did you give up teaching — or your job in Massachusetts, whichever came last?"

Matthew's face dimmed. "I needed a change of scenery," he said. "I needed to come home." A moment later, he smiled at me.

"I'll show you where I grew up, if you don't mind walking a little further," he said. "We'll find something to eat there as well. If you want to taste the best in Cornish pasties, then my childhood haunt is the proper place to go."

"By all means," I said. "Besides, I'm starving. Whether they're the best or not, I'll probably eat two."

When Matt said his childhood home was very different from Lord William's, I hadn't believed him at first. Not until I saw that it was a small house near a part of Cornwall that didn't make the mention in my 'visit Cornwall' research. This was the poorer part of town, reminding me a little of places near my first home in Seattle. There were fewer historic sites here, far fewer tourist havens or boutiques. I noticed a tobacco shop and a chemist's, a fish and chips shop with a neon sign.

"I didn't realize this was what you meant," I said, gazing at the now-empty house. A black iron fence spliced with chain link on the sides kept us from passing through the rickety, ornamental gate to the miniscule lawn on the other side. The old-fashioned shutters were closed upstairs; the whole place needed a new paint job, its white, weathered surface turning grey from years of neglect.

"My father died when I was young," he said. "My mother worked to raise me and my sister, alone. I was bright enough to earn a scholarship, which was how I ended up in public school, then at university."

He was being modest, I thought. When he said 'bright,' he was downplaying his accomplishments. During our walk, I had used my WiFi connection to sneak a few internet searches of his name and discovered words associated with it were a little more glowing. Like 'brilliant,' 'innovative,' 'genius,' paired with terms like 'a leading figure in plant disease research,' and 'the foremost expert in preserving antique plant breeds for the future.' He had been an Ivy League professor, a consultant and landscape architect at the oldest and most pristine rose garden in Massachusetts.

"Then my mother died, and I helped my sister finish school. She wanted to be a nurse and that's what she does now. Only in the military, which wasn't quite what I had in mind for her future." His smile was one of pride and worry.

No noble background, I perceived. Except for that of a hero to his family, and one of the most brilliant minds in modern day botany. And that was so much better than a prince on a white horse.

"Here we are," he said, opening the door to the modern fish and chips shop. "Lunch."

"G'day, m'love," said the woman behind the counter. "Haven't seen you 'round here for a week."

"Too many plants," he answered, with a lopsided smile. "Julianne, this is Charlotte Jones, my former employer and baker of the best Cornish oggies this side of Falmouth. Charlotte, this is Julianne Morgen, the new event planner at Cliffs House."

"Pleasure to meet you," said Charlotte, with a smile. "What'll it be?"

"Two oggies," he answered.

"What's an 'oggy'?" I asked, not exactly sure I wanted to eat it. I lowered my voice for Charlotte's sake as I asked.

"It's the local nickname for a pasty," he said. "Trust me, you'll love it."

I did. At first bite. Beneath the brown, crispy crust was the savory taste of beef, onions, and spices. I practically gobbled mine up in two bites, savoring its taste as I licked my fingers. Matt, who was savoring his, laughed aloud at me. It was the first time I heard him laugh, except for the muffled sounds through the garden shrubbery that fateful afternoon with Trixie. It had a warm, natural sound that made me feel as if I had a pleasant little fire lit deep inside me as I listened. Strangely enough, that made me shiver in response.

"These are delicious," I said to Charlotte. "The best thing I've eaten in the whole county."

She laughed heartily. "Go on now," she said. "Everyone 'round here eats them all the time. Like fish and chips or bangers and mash."

I knew the pasty was an iconic Cornish dish, and I had a few poor American imitations, but not even the meat pie served at my first English hotel stay was this good. Something this sweet and savory from a kitchen in Ceffylgwyn ... didn't it deserve to be served alongside an exclusive baker's cake from Newquay? At an event where some of the most influential English and American socialites might be present?

"Can you make these in a miniature version?" I asked.

Charlotte gave me a puzzled look in response, but after some pleading on my part, she promised to try it. A tray of the 'trial versions' would be sent to Cliffs House for everyone to sample—but with the caveat they wouldn't be 'proper oggies' in miniature size, given the hearty contents of a full-size one. But I was pretty sure they would still taste scrumptious, and with only a few days before the bride, groom, and their party arrived to stay, I needed every last impressive detail to be perfectly in place.

Since Petal had emailed me with a definite rejection of the Cornish flower bouquet I designed, I was left with no choice but to pay tribute to Cornwall through the centerpieces and the food. The days were ticking away, and I clutched at every possible solution I could find. Something like Charlotte's tasty 'oggies' was exactly what I needed.

"You're thinking of something else, aren't you?" Matt asked.

"Who, me? I'm just thinking how lucky it was that I left my good stilettos in the closet today," I answered. I was glad for once that I was wearing a pair of sensible boots, nothing too spiky or delicate. Not the way my legs ached after walking what felt like ten miles between here and Matt's car.

"I thought you were thinking of work," he said.

"This from an accused workaholic?"

Matt grimaced. "I am a little ... too devoted these days," he said. "I've thrown myself into projects these past few years. A good way to fill empty spaces in my life."

Loneliness wasn't something I imagined for him. I had assumed his self-induced exile in Cornwall was for the sake of working hard despite distractions — not the opposite reason. "Are there very many?" I asked him, softly.

"Oh, no more than anyone else has, I suppose," he answered, with a faint smile. "Maybe I was away from Cornwall too long to truly come home again. Or maybe I gave up on other possibilities in my life too soon." For a moment, I thought I heard him sigh after these words.

"For what it's worth, I've enjoyed my tour of Ceffylgwyn," I said. "My first full day of Cornish culture. I owe you for that." I glanced at him with a smile.

"You could do better than a walk through the village and a few pasties," he laughed. "The locals would be happy to take you into their fold. Quiz nights at the pub, euchre circle at the fish and chips shop on Tuesdays, a bout of Cornish wrestling now and then —"

"A night of Troyl?" I suggested. "Complete with Cornish tartan and kilt?" If I was saying any of this incorrectly, he didn't bother to correct me, I noticed. A lesson for another day, maybe.

"Exactly," he said.

We were both quiet again. "Do you ever get a day off?" he asked me.

"I just took two hours off," I answered, with a laugh. "Um...with all the work I have to finish before the big event, I'm not sure."

"If you do," he said, "there's somewhere I'd like to show you. The place I worked before now. Well, consulted, really," he added. "Sort of like for Lord William, only on a slightly bigger scale. It's a beautiful part of Cornwall, one no visitor to our county should go without seeing."

I imagined it must be quite a bit bigger, given Matt's tendency to depict things as less than they actually were. "I'd love to," I said.

"Let me know when you're free," he said.

"What about your time?" I asked him. "When do you have a day off?"

"Whenever I want one," he said. "Remember?"

Right. The whole 'consulting on his own time' thing. So Matt didn't *have* to be the 'slave to the dirt' that Pippa and Gemma imagined him to be. Well, if it encouraged him to give it up for a few hours to shuttle a newcomer around the county, I would happily oblige. It was the least I could do in return for the edible flowers, wasn't it?

"Do you speak Cornish?" I asked him.

"A little. Why?"

"What's the house's name in Cornish?" I asked. "Cliffs House?"

He thought about this for a minute. "Chei Klegrow," he said, with an impossible pronunciation I could never match. "That's as close as I can come off the top of my tongue, at any rate."

"I think I like it better in English," I said. "But I think the village's name is growing on me."

"That it does," he answered. Whether he was talking about the Cornish name or the village itself, I wasn't sure, but it didn't matter. I agreed with both of them wholeheartedly.

***

"So where are we going?" I asked.

I was trying to calm the little cloud of butterflies that took flight in my stomach now and then, ever since I climbed into Matt's car. We were just friends having a day out, I reminded myself. He was being nice, showing me the countryside around Ceffylgwyn. No need to make it into something more.

Nevertheless, I was wearing my cutest casual dress, a soft cotton knit printed with lacy white flowers, and a pair of semi-sensible tan sandals that were a decent imitation of a top designer. Trying to seem more casual, I pulled my hair back in a ponytail, using the excuse of the coastal wind and today's warmer temperatures. It had nothing to do with last-minute guilt making me want to dress down a little, in case Matthew got the wrong message. And not at all about feeling guilty over wishing he'd notice me a little.

"I told you," Matthew answered. "It's a place that every visitor to Cornwall should see."

"If it's Newquay, then I've already been there once. My first day in Cornwall," I added. Hesitating a moment, I told him, "You were there, too, actually. At the railway station. I saw you outside the café."

His brows lifted in a look of surprise. "You know, I was there recently," he said, after a moment. "But I would have noticed…that is, I think I would remember if I saw you before," he told me. The blush creeping over his face proved he meant this as a compliment. It surprised me a little, his reaction.

"Well, it was only for a moment," I said, trying not to read too much into this and reawaken the butterflies inside me. *A moment where he saw the back of your head, most likely,* I reminded myself. I was glad he hadn't noticed me staring at him, at any rate.

"So why were you there?" I asked him, eager for the subject to move forward again. "You don't seem like the surfing type exactly. Was it the nightclub scene that drew you there? Meeting up with friends for a pub crawl later that evening perhaps?"

He laughed at my teasing suggestions. "Nothing so scandalous, I assure you. I was waiting for a cab to take me to Newquay airport. A colleague of mine was giving a lecture in Edinburgh on behalf of the garden society he serves as chairman for. I was there for moral support and to glean some of his knowledge on plant preservation and propagation. His work is quite similar to what I'm doing for the estate, you see."

Mmm. So he didn't have a secret life in Newquay, with a girlfriend and a group of rowdy drinking buddies. Good to know, since I rather liked his image as the hermit of Ceffylgwyn, whose quiet but smoldering good looks were tragically wasted on plants.

"Well, then," I said. "Back to the subject of where you're taking me. Is it someplace urban? A burgeoning tourism district lined with shops that cater to your every whim?"

"It's like no other place you've been before," Matthew said.

He smiled at me. A smile that guaranteed that was the last of his hints.

That 'place' popped up on a road sign after we had driven several miles, talking mostly about the estate, and a little about colleges and universities, now and then brushing against a more personal subject, which made my butterflies a little worse. I saw the Cornish name printed below the English one first.

"'Lowarth Helygen,'" I said, doing my best to pronounce it. "Wow. It has a beautiful name in Cornish." A romantic phrase right out of Arthurian legend, I thought.

"The Lost Gardens of Heligan," he translated, smiling. "One of England's most beautiful historic gardens. I spent a lot of time here when I first returned to Cornwall."

"You mean you worked there," I corrected him with a knowing smile.

"Yes. Correct. I was a consultant," he said. "And it was a place worth every minute of my experience there."

The Lost Gardens had fallen into neglect after World War One, and had only been restored to their former glory in more recent decades. They were part of a family estate, like the gardens at Cliffs House. Only these gardens were a showcase of Victorian English gardening design. Lakes and fountains, antique shrubbery in summer bloom, flower and vegetable gardens carefully planted and tended. As I wandered the grounds beside Matt, I could imagine him loving this place. It was peaceful, alive, and filled with color at every turn.

He showed me the rhododendrons he had helped protect against a fungal infection: beautiful, tall plants whose weathered bark revealed their age. They were antiques, he explained with a smile, cared for and cultivated for decades. I gazed up at one, its shadow falling across me, as soft and cool as I imagined its glossy leaves would be if I touched them.

There was a 'jungle' of fern trees that made me feel like I was lost in the wilds of Borneo; and flower beds filled with European specimens that I had never seen pictures of, much less admired in person. Matt knew nearly everything about this place, so there was no need for a printed guide. He walked me from place to place, pointing out special plants that I would have otherwise missed, and telling me stories about the people he'd met here, and the experience of working in a garden this historic and famous.

We stopped and chatted with a few of the current gardeners, who were tending a less-crowded part of the estate, one of whom recognized Matt and, clearly, had enjoyed working with him. I couldn't help but feel proud, even though we were practically strangers. Something about seeing Matthew in his element was getting to me. Maybe that explained why I couldn't help the urge to move closer to Matt while exploring the jungle, where a sudden childhood fear of monkeys diving down from the trees came over me. Or maybe it was just because he seemed strong and protective.

Not every part of the garden enchanted me — when we reached the pineapple pit, I couldn't help my reaction to his explanation of it. "You mean it's full of manure?" I asked, repulsed.

"Fertilizer, yes. It produces heat, which is what protects the trees from cold, and encourages temperatures for fruit production," said Matthew. "It's just science, Julianne."

"It's manure," I corrected him. "Which, I'm sorry, is really gross where I come from." I tried not to imagine a squishy, smelly floor on the bottom of the pit, and look only at the lush, tropical leaves of the trees themselves.

"Gardeners are used to the idea," he said. "Fertilizer, compost — it's all part of a plant's life. Don't worry — I won't toss you in there to check the pH." A sudden, wicked smile played across his lips with this statement.

"Don't ever suggest something like that again," I said, in mock warning. Just to be safe, I retreated further away, where the garden path traveled elsewhere. "You feel free to stay here and enjoy the scent of compost," I called back over my shoulder.

It took him a moment to catch up with me. "Two more things you have to see," he said.

"Not more pineapple pits full of slimy sludge, I hope?"

"It's not," he promised. "I have to introduce you to the Giant and the Mud Maid."

They were definitely nothing like the science behind the pineapple pit. Heligan's Mud Maid was a living sculpture of plants, earth, and stone. She reclined on her side, almost smiling dreamily, I felt. Suddenly my playful fight with Matt was entirely forgiven, as I stood there admiring her.

"What do you think?" Matt glanced at me.

"I think she's gorgeous," I answered. "I think someone was incredibly talented and brilliant to think of creating this." I sneaked a glance at him now. "It wasn't you, right?"

He laughed — loudly, and more heartily than I'd ever heard him laugh. "Not at all," he said. "Believe me, I don't possess garden sculpting skills, and it was never my job to look after Heligan's living sculptures in any form, I'm afraid. I just enjoyed visiting them."

We stayed a little longer, visiting the Giant's Head also before we made our way back to the car. We stopped for a late lunch at a restaurant with the view from our table's windows of a little country cottage, where I had my first taste of fresh Cornish sea food.

I was feeling energized, not tired, even though the day had been a long one. I was a little disappointed when the road sign for Ceffylgwyn came into view through the windscreen. Maybe Matt sensed this, because he cleared his throat and looked at me.

"Would you like to see my home?" he asked. "Before I drive you back to the country house?"

"Of course I would," I answered. These past couple of weeks, I had been curious to know more about Matthew's 'reclusive hole' after listening to Gemma and Pippa's remarks. It could be anything from a shack in the woods to a crumbling gothic carriage house, I felt.

But it was none of these things. Matt turned onto a sleepy side street in the village, then parked outside a battered picket gate and fence surrounding a two story cottage covered in white lime wash aged grey in places from the wind, and a slate roof with grey-painted shutters bordering each of its windows. On the lower story, window boxes tumbled forth vinca and pea vines, covered in small summer flowers, while upstairs, I could see a chimney, oddly painted red, peeking from behind the house.

I was struck speechless for a moment, as I had been outside Cliffs House. This was a completely different world, this tiny cottage compared to Cliffs House's size and stateliness ... but there was something enchanting about it. Like something special was hidden in those walls, in the red chimney and the most crookedly-hung shutter on the second floor.

Of course, there were gardens — and maybe that was the source of the magic, Matthew's talent and dedication come to life. They wrapped around the whole cottage, tangled and wild, with plants almost as tall as me, and some so small and delicate they barely brushed against the toes of my shoes. Foxglove, hollyhocks, snapdragons, and delphiniums, mixed with asters and heaths, and tufts of the delicate lady's smock he had sent me, alongside tiny Cornish daisies.

I recognized a lot of these from a website on Cornish flowers I had visited, trying to learn more after accidentally trampling an endangered variety. Even without flowers, I could now spot familiar leaves among some of them, enough to guess what native and domestic flowers Matthew cultivated.

"There's a hothouse behind the cottage," he said, closing the rickety white gate behind us. "I had hoped for a place with a conservatory, but when I couldn't find one affordable, I simply built a greenhouse myself. There's a path along the side of the house — the right one, where the ivy is climbing up."

"The roses you sent me —" I began.

"I grew them," he said. "The roses are in the hothouse. A few antique climbers have the trellis back there ... but most of what you see around you does what it wants. I just helped it along a little."

Inside, the old parlor was furnished with mismatched things, both modern and antique, most of them looking as if they'd been rescued from junk shops or from abandonment on the curb as rubbish. Stuffing popped out of the arms of an old, comfortable club chair, while an antique dining one served as a makeshift side table next to one of Matt's many crowded bookshelves.

"This is my home," he said, pulling open a pair of worn plaid curtains covering the windows — Cornish tartan, I couldn't help but notice. "Where I spend what little time I'm not outdoors."

"You read a lot of books," I said, picking up one from the chair. A volume of poetry, one of English myths. "A folklore fan?" I held up the copy of *Cornish Tales and Legends* as I spoke.

"I'm a fan of local culture," he said. "And I don't do much reading, really. The books are deceptive." He smiled.

"Here's one in Cornish. You can read Cornish, too, can't you?" I said. "As well as you speak it?"

"If by that you mean 'not well,' then certainly," he said. He took the book from my hand and flipped through it, glancing at its pages as if trying to remember where he'd found it before. "I know a little, of course. The name of the house I could guess, for instance, based on a crude vocabulary of Cornish I've learned over time."

"The name of the gardens today?" I asked.

"Lowarth means 'garden,'" he said. "Heligan's from the Cornish word for 'willow tree.'"

"Willow Tree Gardens," I said. "I like it." I looked out the window, where the late afternoon sunshine played across the petals and leaves in the window boxes. "So what's the name of your garden?"

"It doesn't have a name," he said. "But the cottage is called Rosemoor."

Roses on the moor, I thought, automatically. And realized it probably meant something quite different in Cornish. Maybe I could study the language eventually. Learn enough that I could recognize the meaning of Cornish words on road signs here and there, at least. Leaning against his windowsill, my view to the back of Matthew's garden, I smiled at him. “Did you pick the cottage because you shared a name?” I asked. “Matthew Rose of Rosemoor Cottage?”

"It's a coincidence," he said. "I picked it because ... well, it's a romantic spot, I suppose. It was close to the estate, and it had room for a garden. What else could I want?"

What else indeed. I could think of something, but I knew better than to say it. When Matthew moved closer, I tried not to tremble, because I felt drawn to him more than ever. He laid the book I'd handed him on the chair once again, his hand resting on its cover. This close, I caught the scent of his skin, and could almost imagine the fabric of his sleeve brushing against my arm. It was mere inches from my skin now, as was the rest of his body.

For a moment, I thought he might kiss me. I thought I might kiss him. Slide my arms around his body, pull him close to find out if it felt as good as I was imagining it right now. When his dark eyes met mine, I felt my legs tremble in response. We were both looking deep into each other’s eyes ; his features softened, his expression growing tender. I could feel my own changing, and wondered what it was telling him. I was afraid it was revealing something even I didn't know, but I felt powerless to stop it. In a way, I didn't want to.

His glance broke from mine after a few seconds — a space of time which felt longer to me. I caught my breath sharply. I hoped he didn't notice.

"Tea?" he asked me. "Or anything else I have on hand?" He had moved a little further away now, snapping on a lamp beside the chair.

"A cup of tea would be nice," I answered. I was developing a taste for it, and I needed something to steady me after feeling that much electricity. It left me feeling alive but exhausted for a moment.

Matthew made tea as I curled up in the ratty club chair and watched the insects buzz around the flowers in his garden. As we drank it, we talked about nothing as dangerous as kissing, only about Ceffylgwyn and other places we'd each lived. Our conversation felt like it lasted only minutes, but it was actually an hour long by the time we finished; time had sped up crazily after those few seconds of looking into his eyes, which had halted the world spinning around us from my point of view.

He drove me back to the estate afterwards, and walked me inside. There was a visitor, I noticed, judging from the car parked near the camellia bed, a sporty, foreign red model. I walked through the main door which Matthew held open for me, waiting for him to follow me inside.

Lady Amanda was emerging from her office, and with her, the bride-to-be from the wedding that was now only days away.

"There you are, Julianne," Lady Amanda said. "Thank heavens, because we have a few last-minute issues that need discussing."

Petal had arrived early, it seemed, with a final list of requests for the big day. As always, she was flawlessly dressed, this time in a blouse that cost three figures, and designer jeans so tight and thin I imagined them permanently bonded to her skin. A pair of oversized designer sunglasses were propped on her head.

The door closed behind me. Matthew had entered, taking a few steps before he stopped short. Petal had seen him enter, and was staring at him as if she, too, were rooted in place.

The color drained from Matthew's face. He looked as if he had seen a ghost. On Petal's face, a mask of complete blankness — but there was something in her eyes that looked like she wanted to turn and walk away as quickly as she could.

"Matthew," she said.

Matthew's lips moved. "Petal," he said. A slight tremor in his voice. No other emotion.

"You look well." I thought these words had been squeezed from her chest, forced into the open.

"So do you." It took him a moment to say this aloud.

Petal was now paying extra attention to the set of keys in her hand. Lady Amanda was looking very uneasy. And as for Matt — he didn't look at me, or anyone else. For a moment, he seemed not to see anything, until he turned to me with the ghost of a smile.

"I'll say goodnight," he said. I had a feeling this was meant for the whole foyer. I thought maybe my eyes were burning, but the confusion I felt was making my head feel too empty to notice that detail.

"See you tomorrow," I said. My voice sounded normal, thankfully, although I could hear my confusion in it, too. Matthew didn't say anything. He was already gone.

A second of awkward silence ticked past, then Lady Amanda seized the situation. "Shall we have Geoff bring in your luggage?" she said to Petal. "And Julianne can show you what she had in mind for the circulating trays at the reception."

"Of course," said Petal. She seemed fully herself now. "I can't wait to hear about it."

***

I was trying hard to be in a good mood as I sat in the kitchen, helping Dinah put the finishing touches on the squares of Cornish fudge, each one topped with candied marzipan blossoms resembling a sprig of purplish-red heath, and one of sugared rosemary.

"When's the groom coming?" Gemma asked. She had volunteered to work extra hours in the kitchen today, all in hopes of catching a glimpse of the football heartthrob, I suspected, who was due to arrive with the best man today.

"Never mind Donald Price-Parker," said Dinah. "We've got six dozen more of these to decorate for the catering trays. Unless he's coming to the kitchen to help out, he's of no interest to the three of us."

"Not until after lunch," I answered her, as I placed another finished square of fudge aside. "Don't worry, you won't miss him. Lord William said he's driving here in a racecar, straight from the track at St Austell."

"Imagine," sighed Gemma. "Soon as I'm done with studies, I'm moving somewhere more exciting than Ceffylgwyn."

"Off to Land's End, are we?" quipped Dinah. "St. Ives, perhaps?"

"Sure," said Gemma. "Truro, if nowhere else'll do."

How about Mousehole? I might have suggested this jokingly, now that I knew enough Cornish village names to understand the difference between a port village and the kind of places Gemma wanted to see. But I wasn't in a joking mood, and the memory of Mousehole's name only brought me back to thoughts of Matthew.

I didn't need to be thinking about him. What did it matter if Matt and Petal clearly knew each other at some time or other? Or clearly had a connection that left them both tongue-tied? So what if Matt had clearly been avoiding me and the grounds immediately around Cliffs House for the past twenty-four hours or so since they'd seen each other?

Get your mind back on work, I scolded myself. Only one day was left between now and the big event I was in charge of pulling together. If my stomach wanted to tie itself in knots of confusion, it should be doing it for that reason, and no other.

The clatter of high-heeled shoes sounded in the hall — for once, they weren't mine — and the chief bridesmaid appeared. With a yawn, Trixie surveyed us, sleepily.

"I'm starving," she announced. "Is there anything to eat around here? Pet's being totally dull and didn't send anybody out for breakfast."

"I can make you some toast, if you like," said Dinah. I thought I detected a slight crack in her civil tones.

Trixie wrinkled her nose. "No, thanks," she said. "Got any more chocolate?" she asked. She lifted one of the pieces of fudge from its airtight container and popped it into her mouth.

"Oops — are these for the wedding?" she asked.

"They are," I answered.

"Sorry." But she didn't sound as if she was. "Guess I'll make do with the raw stuff." She lifted a bar of chocolate from the cook's table, one that Dinah had been coarsely chopping to decorate the whortleberry tarts that would be topped with clotted cream. Taking a generous bite out of it, she sat down at the work table where the three of us were decorating the fudge squares.

"Oooh, aren't they cute?" she said. "You're making little flowers to go on top. Isn't that sweet. It looks kind of like Play-doh covered in glitter, doesn't it?" She laughed. "Let me try one. I'm totally bored, with Petal spending hours chatting online with all our friends back in New York."

We exchanged glances. Gemma looked slightly amused, trying to stifle a laugh as she popped a finished piece of fudge into the storage case. Trixie was putting three marzipan heath sprigs on one piece of fudge, making it into an impossible mouthful.

"Just one is fine," I told her, trying to figure out the nicest way to get rid of her. "Guests are meant to notice that it's a sprig of heath and rosemary — two native Cornish plants."

"Oh, the Cornish thing," she said. "Right. Donald's so into that, and Petal's *so* not. But she'd do anything for him, so I guess that's why she's agreeing. He's got this 'let's be all English country as a couple' and she's all 'let's go back to civilization.' You can imagine." She popped another heath sprig — crookedly — on top of a square of fudge. I tried discreetly to fix it after she placed it in the box.

"Of course, she didn't want to come to Cornwall in the first place, but after she found out her ex was here, she was really mad," continued Trixie. "He's from Cornwall, see, and that's partly why she doesn't like it here. That, and they broke up because she knew she could do better — and now she's marrying a football player who wants to live in the country. Go figure, right?" She plopped two badly-decorated pieces of fudge into the box, and popped one of our perfect ones into her mouth. "He works here, actually, her ex," she continued. "At this place."

Gemma, who had been drinking it all in with a curious and incredulous smile, now looked as if she had swallowed a whole chunk of fudge herself. Her eyes were like saucers when they met mine — I wondered if she, too, knew it was Matt.

"I think Cornwall's a great place to live," I said. I was surprised how firm my tone was. "It's beautiful here. And everyone's so friendly. Who wouldn't love it?"

"Pet doesn't," said Trixie. "But she's hooked on Donald, so what can you do?" She shrugged her shoulders, dramatically.

"Donald's totally cute," said Gemma, speaking up at last, since the subject of the football player's looks was a safe one. Plus, I suspected she was dying for more details, the clues that Trixie had carelessly dropped about Petal's old love life. The same clues that were twisting me into knots, and making my fingers too shaky to apply the false heath sprigs properly.

"I thought her ex was hot," said Trixie. "I met him once or twice when they were still together, and she used to talk about him when we were both modeling in New York."

"So she left him ... for Donald Price-Parker?" Gemma hesitated before saying this aloud. From the troubled look in her eyes, I knew she was probably picturing Petal dumping Matt. It hurt too much to think about, so I was trying not to have the same picture pop into my head.

"No, she met Donald later. She just ... broke up with him. Broke his heart into a million pieces," said Trixie. "It was totally scandalous, I thought. She always said he was a bit of a nerd...but he was so totally into her, he'd do anything to make her happy. He even offered to move to New York for her. But it wasn't enough."

Trixie's conversation was pouring gossip into the room like syrup — we were all trapped in it, her words wrapping around us like a sticky mess of tentacles, making me learn about a side of Matt that had been hidden from me until now. Imagining him in America, madly in love, then brokenhearted and back in Cornwall, bitter and alone. Hadn't he said work was filling the empty space in his life? The one that had been Petal's, it would seem.

She leaned towards Gemma. "I'm totally into him. If he didn't spend so much time hiding from Pet, I would be asking him out for a weekend. Have the full English experience before I go home. A girl like me shouldn't let someone like him go to waste, right?"

She was talking about Matt like he was a tempting piece of candy she was planning to steal. My face burned hot. Her words made me angry, and I broke one of the candied stems without meaning to. Quickly, I hid the pieces under a dish towel.

"Maybe you should see if he's hiding on the grounds where Lord William's working, behind the estate," I suggested, sweetly. "There's a path leading towards the woods. It's a little rocky, and the field is probably extra hot today...and there are a few teensy little insects since it's summertime ... but that shouldn't stop you, right?"

Trixie looked at me, a pair of cold eyes boring straight through my innocent look. "I don't do the outdoors unless it's mowed," she said.

"Oops. My mistake," I said, with a shrug. "I guess you can keep helping us. Would you lift that super-heavy pot from the wall behind the stove? Someone has to start melting the chocolate to make another batch of these. We need a few thousand, at least."

"A few thousand?" Trixie froze, a piece of hard chocolate halfway to her lips. I could see Dinah was hiding a smile as she listened.

"Oh, yes," she chimed in. "It's a good thing you've turned up. You don't want your friend's wedding to be anything less than perfect, do you? And we've a long ways to go to finish it all."

"It should only take half the day," Gemma assured her. "Making the fudge itself, I mean. The decorating's just 'til late tonight probably."

"Midnight, at least, I should say," chimed in Dinah. Trixie now looked as if she'd eaten the whole tray of fudge before her.

"The man with the cake's here." Geoff popped his head through the open kitchen window. "We're bringing it in directly."

"Oh, mercy — have I cleaned out a spot in the fridge big enough?" Dinah's attention was momentarily transferred from the fudge to the arrival of the culinary masterpiece from Newquay. I noticed Trixie had completely disappeared by the time the cake's layers were carefully transported into cool storage.

I could see from the picture of the soon-to-be-completed creation that it was a simple ivory-colored tower that resembled a modern building, studded here and there with expensive-looking silver cake decorations. Clearly Petal's metropolitan tastes had trumped Donald's 'let's be English country' ideas this time.

Trixie might have made herself scarce, but her words were still lingering in my head. I found myself wandering in the garden after I finished decorating the marriage bower with its sprigs of greenery and dried heather, leaving room for the fresh flowers to be added early on the wedding morning.

I took the path to the cliff. Maybe with the idea I would find Matt there, even though it seemed unlikely he'd be around. He was probably off in some remote corner of the estate ... I was really being pathetic, wandering around in hopes he was in the gardens close to the house.

Halfway down the garden path to the cliff, I spotted Matt. He was gazing at the water, sitting on one of the rocks arranged close to the edge. I knew for sure that I had been hoping he would come here; that I had sensed that this was a place where he came to think. From the look on his face as he watched the Channel, he was doing a lot of it.

He waited until I came closer to speak. "I'm sorry I left so abruptly," he said. "After I brought you back. It seemed rude. I didn't realize it until later, I'm afraid."

I tucked my hands in the pockets of my green coat. "Why didn't you tell me?" I asked. "That you knew her? That you had broken up with her?" I sighed. "Did anyone know, or was it a secret from everybody?"

"Not a secret," he answered. "Some people knew. But I generally avoided talking about it with anyone."

"Is that why you haven't been around the last few days?" I asked, quietly. "You could have told me you needed some space. You didn't have to avoid me — the house, I mean." I changed this quickly, feeling awkward. Perhaps Matt hadn't really thought of me as someone worth avoiding — only that he'd been rude to a fellow employee of the estate, for instance.

I wasn't sure he heard me over the distant roar of the water, until he answered. "I wasn't avoiding you," he said. "Or anyone. I ... was giving some thought to things. Ones I haven't thought about for some time."

I didn't say anything in reply. I wanted to say that this was fine, and that I understood. And I did...except for the tiny part of me that was hurt by all this, of course.

"Petal and I met here," he said. Matt had finally broken the silence. "As a girl, she came here with her family on holiday. And I ..." He paused. "We met again when I was working in Boston, where she was trying to become a model and give up her job in retail. We reconnected. I fell...very hard. It lasted for three years until she changed her mind." He swallowed. "I was foolish. I made desperate promises I couldn't possibly keep, about myself and everything in our lives — none of it was enough. It couldn't be."

There was so much left unsaid in those words. His voice was calm, yet it was impossible not to see the brief flicker of pain that crossed Matt's face. I imagined him begging her to stay, even promising to go wherever she wanted, be whatever she wanted. My stomach felt sick in response.

"I didn't like her when I first met her," I said, with a forced laugh. "Now I have a good reason for it. She broke your heart. She's still breaking it, I guess."

"I don't love her."

"Doesn't mean she can't hurt you," I said. "I don't think you can pretend that part away, Matt." I swallowed hard, because a lump was forming in my throat. "It's understandable. You don't have to hide it. Not from me, certainly." Me, the understanding friend and almost-stranger, who didn't have anything to lose by listening to him.

That Matt and I had been growing closer in those hours before he and Petal had appeared face to face — that truth was burning a hole in my own heart right now. I had been a second away from kissing him before; it was crazy that I felt this way, but it was as if she had taken away something I hadn't fully realized I wanted.

I wanted a chance with Matt — to have him look at me the way he did that afternoon, only with more than just a little spark of attraction in his eyes. And, somehow, Petal had taken it away with one glance.

"The other day, Julianne," he said. "What might have passed between us..." He looked at me as he stopped speaking. But not the way I had been fantasizing about. "It isn't a rebound, or an attempt to lead you on. Nothing like that."

I didn't want to hear the rest of whatever he planned to say; I didn't want to see the hurt in Matt's eyes become that of someone guilty of hurting me. An apology in those dark eyes would be unbearable on top of everything else.

"Please," he said. "Don't think of it that way."

I didn't answer. I chose to do the only thing I could, which was turn to leave. After taking a few steps, I stopped for a moment and looked back.

"What made you notice me?" I asked him. "What made you ... be nice to me?"

I was fighting hard for control of myself with this question, because it seemed dangerous. The door between us, one side friendship and one side attraction, was swinging between the two. We hadn't defined it, and I didn't want to with my choice of words.

Matt looked at me. "When the sunlight shines through your hair, there are strands of red that shine like fire," he said, gently.

I hadn't been prepared for that answer, and my heart skipped a beat. "Really," I said. Feigning skepticism. Any other time this would be playful, but now it was only that way on the surface; underneath, I was losing control of myself, like his words were part of the tide below.

"It's true." He turned towards the cliffside view again. "But it's not the real reason. It was because I'd never met anyone so bold and brash and confident at first meeting — who could almost convince me I was in the wrong just by the sheer tone of her opinion."

He had been kidding me until now, at least a little; but the seriousness underneath this last answer was threatening to take my breath. It was only the glimpse of sadness in that tender smile that kept things together for me.

"Nice to know it wasn't just my looks," I answered, jokingly — but I was really past being able to joke at this moment, his words had rattled me so. I only hoped he couldn't see it from my smile before I turned around and walked back up the path.

The house came into view when I crested the top of the path, the sun shining against the face of Cliffs House. Any other time, this would make me happy, and put a little more speed in my step as I approached. After all, I was happy here — my dreams had begun to come true, and even though my work was hectic, it was satisfying.

I took a few steps more. Slow ones.

It didn't really matter what I thought right now. It didn't really matter what I felt. All that mattered was the job I was supposed to be doing, making sure Petal and Donald's fairytale wedding fell into place.

It shouldn't matter at all that Matt's heart was still too broken for me to have a place in it. We were practically strangers, barely friends for more than two weeks. It made perfect sense not to fall in love with him, and to accept that he cared about someone from his past.

He still loved her. Big deal. It only hurt to know he was hurting, right? But that wasn't the only reason I felt crushed, and that was the hardest part for me to accept.

Voices and laughter from the house's front drive. I could see a flashy race car painted in neon orange and black parked out front, Donald Price-Parker leaning against it, striking a casual pose as he talked with the best man — no doubt Gemma was watching from behind the house curtains, enjoying a glimpse of the football player's rippling muscles as he lifted the car's bonnet and pointed out something about the motor to his friend.

For the rest of the day, I worked frantically, keeping my mind elsewhere. I wrapped the stems of the flowers for decorating the rest of the ceremony's arch, the delicate white roses and sprigs of fresh heath blooms and rosemary. I checked on the cases of champagne and re-polished half the serving platters and waiters' trays until they gleamed like mirrors.

"Still working?" Pippa was in the doorway of the silver pantry, pulling off her cleaning apron. "You should be ready for a bit of a rest by now. I'm going home to put my feet up and have a curry."

"There's just a few more things to be done," I said, lightly. I made sure to avoid my reflection in the polished silver surface — there was a tiny chance that it showed my cheeks were colorless and my eyes were bloodshot from holding back a few tears whenever I thought too hard about this afternoon.

Pippa was staring at me. I knew it without looking up. "Look, whatever these incomers are saying about Ross," she began.

"Incomers?" I repeated.

"You know. Outsiders like them. Rich snobs what comes around and thinks they're better than everybody else." It was the first time Pippa had ever said anything less than complimentary about a celebrity, so for that reason I couldn't help but look up. "Anyway, Ross is worth twenty of them. I'll bet he's not still thinking about some petty little tart who spends her days on chat shows talking about chipless nail varnish and all."

I stifled a giggle. "She's definitely beneath him," I said. "But I think it's more complicated than that."

"So? I still say he's doesn't care a fig for her." She smiled at me, crookedly. "Or that Trixie person. Otherwise, half the girls in the village would get their hearts broke. Including the likes of us."

I hid my smile for this idea, and applied more vigor to polishing the silver platter as I tried to hold to Pippa's philosophy. But when she was gone, I turned my focus to the next item in need of attention, a champagne tray.

***

"Come with me," said Lady Amanda, who found me in the kitchen, wolfing down a quick piece of fried bread before throwing myself back into the fray of setting up the reception rooms.

"What is it?" I asked. I followed her quickly upstairs — not to one of the offices, but to the private suite assigned to the bridal party. Specifically, Petal Borroway.

The bride was on the phone. From the tense and angry look on her face, I sensed that something was wrong. When she hung up a moment later and faced me, however, she forced a tiny smile into place.

"It looks as if we have a teensy little problem," she said. "The flower delivery was late — when I called, it turns out that the London florist lost my order somehow. It seems they can't provide a suitable replacement, and no other florist in the city can send one on time ... so I'll need you to have that bouquet you designed ready by tomorrow morning."

My heart sprang high in my chest, then crashed down just as quickly. "The Cornish bouquet?" I said. *The one you hated?*

"Donald will love it. It's so traditional," she said. "Such a perfect complement to the wedding's theme, don't you think? Now that there's no possibility of the London florists sending the one I selected." There was a smile on Petal's face, but I was fairly sure the only thing holding its serenity in place was the thought of scoring a few points with Donald due to his recent Cornwall obsession.

"I do," I answered. But my voice didn't reflect the confidence I had felt when I first suggested this. The flowers I had chosen — the manor hothouse might not have enough of them left, to begin with. And at this short notice, where would I ever find enough orchids that resembled the heath-spotted ones along the coast? The only thing that would be easy to find would be actual heath — if I raided Matthew's beloved patches of it, that is.

Matthew. He was the only one who could find half of these things easily, much less pull together a bouquet filled with elegant blossoms and the colors of Cornwall's native flowers. How could I possibly ask him to do it now, given what I knew about him and Petal?

"I'll see what I can do," I said, with my brightest smile. "By tomorrow morning, I'll have a bouquet for you assembled from the best that Cliffs House's gardens can offer." That much of the promise I could keep, although I couldn't promise it would be what Petal envisioned for her wedding day.

As soon as the door closed behind us, I looked at Lady Amanda. "What am I going to do?" I asked her. "She waited until it's nearly impossible — how will I ever find what we need?" I ran a hand through my hair in frustration. "Do you have numbers for all the florists around Ceffylgwyn?"

"I do — and ones in Truro, too," answered Lady Amanda. "Let's hope they have the answer." We hurried off to her desk, where the 'master list' of South Cornwall businesses was stashed in a drawer beside her telephone book.

The garden could provide some flowers the color of heath's blooms, Lord William assured me — not protected flowers, but domestic varieties in a few shades of pink and purple. Maybe not the brightest or most colorful blossoms at this stage, but that was the least of my problems. Cliffs House's greenhouse had only a couple of orchids, only one of them in bloom — and it wasn't the same color as the wild orchid's purple and pink blush. All the other blossoms had been showcased this past week as centerpieces at an afternoon charity tea.

"Hi, Flowers by the Sea? I was wondering if you could provide me with a dozen purple and white orchids..." After I finished explaining all the details, I listened with disappointment as florist after florist told me they had too few blossoms, or the wrong type of orchid. Several of them were handling big orders for other weddings or special occasions, and couldn't meet a request this last minute, not for orchids or for daisies in pink, white, or magenta.

I sighed as I hung up. All I had were lilies, a few white roses, and maybe six orchids if the two florists I had spoken with truly had those in stock. I had no painted daisies to fill the bouquet — there were none planted at Cliffs House currently, I learned, not in any color, much less what I needed. Just a few cultivated wildflower blossoms whose shades might pass as Cornish native ones.

I was sunk — just like a boat ramming against a rock wall, my first big assignment had rammed against the fickle rock of Petal Borroway's wedding tastes. I would have to find a way around this crisis, and the only choice left was to assemble a bouquet from the hothouse's best flowers and give my apologies to Petal tomorrow.

***

The day of the wedding dawned with a morning drizzle of rain. I watched it through the windows, holding my breath as I waited for it to stop. The arbor in the main garden needed its protective tarp removed and its living decorations added before the photographers arrived, and the chairs hadn't been set up on the open spaces around the main flower bed.

So many details were left, and I felt slightly dizzy at the thought of it all. *Stay calm*, I told myself. I took a deep breath, trying to tell myself it would be all right. But I had yet to face Petal with her substitute bouquet and explain that the one she had requested at the last minute was simply impossible. Telling someone like Petal Borroway that what they wanted was out of reach — I had a feeling those moments were unpleasant ones for whoever confronted her with the truth.

I could hear Dinah's anxious voice coming from the drawing room, where the cake was being assembled in its modern, skyscraper form, and the sound of guests coming to and from the breakfast room, where a complimentary spread was laid out before the ceremony.

The press would begin taking pictures within an hour. The wedding photographers were scheduled to shoot photos two hours before the wedding, in the main garden. Hopefully, Petal would be over her anger and disappointment by the time she was posing for portraits with the rest of the wedding party.

I didn't have time to listen in when press photographers covering the wedding paid compliments to its simple beauty. A few last-minute questions and issues, a few quick adjustments, and it was time for the bridal party to descend from the suite.

"...and I need to fetch my bouquet," Petal was saying. "Trixie, will you fix my veil, *please*? It's catching on my dress." Petal was descending the stairs, flanked by her chief bridesmaid, her mother, and a handful of friends.

Her dress was a beautiful, fitted white silk, studded with delicate seed pearls and tiny, glimmering stones, a thin, gauzy veil descending from the tiara crowning her hair. A pair of white and silver sandals studded with semi-precious stones were matched with her wedding dress, shoes I heard whispered were original Prada creations.

No wonder Petal was so eager to have a bouquet as original as her outfit. I sucked in a quick breath, thinking of the simple design of white lilies and garden-variety heath sprigs that I had managed to assemble. It was tucked in the basket beside the door, along with Trixie's smaller bouquet of white roses and sprigs of wild rosemary.

I was steadying myself for this moment, one which had been delayed as long as possible due to all the little tasks I had been hurrying to finish. As Petal approached, I made myself smile, calmly. The bride looked at me expectantly.

"Do you have my flowers?" Petal asked.

"She does." It wasn't my voice speaking, but Matthew's. He had approached behind me, and stood in the open front doors to Cliffs House. No dirt stains, only a neat, clean shirt tucked into his trousers, a corduroy jacket and clean boots. In his hands was a white floral box, tied with a single cord.

"This is yours, I believe." He was speaking to Petal, but looking at me as he placed it in my hands. He smiled at me.

I opened the lid. Inside was the bouquet I had designed — or a creation every bit its equal and better. Large white orchids flecked with pinkish purple and lavender, with bright pink and purplish-hued daisies that resembled the summer blooms and fall foliage of heath and heather. A small, delicate pink daisy interspersed among them, along with baby's breath and soft silvery-white sprigs of the rosemary herb. All bound with a simple pinkish-white ribbon that trailed from the base of its blossoms.

It was stunning. My eyes flew from the blossoms nestled in tissue paper to Matthew's face. He glanced from me to Petal, then back again.

"Best of luck," he said. With that, he left.

I looked at Petal. Her face had turned pale, then her cheeks flushed bright red. She looked as if she was on the verge of saying something — but whatever it was had died on her lips, apparently.

I lifted the bouquet from the box, and held it out to her. "Best of luck," I repeated. With a smile, I handed Trixie her smaller one, and stepped aside for the wedding party to make its way outside for the photographers.

As the wedding party assembled in the garden, I couldn't help glancing around me, seeing the members of Cliffs House staff who were watching discreetly as they finished up the last minute touches before the ceremony. I glimpsed the gardening staff taking away the hand carts that had been used to wheel in stacks of chairs — and among them stood Matt.

I could see his face clearly enough from here. He didn't look angry or hurt as he watched Petal and her husband-to-be pose for the camera. He stood there calmly, turning aside after a moment to answer someone who spoke to him. A second later, he was gone again.

Who had told him about the bouquet? Was it Lady Amanda? Or did one of the girls let it slip that I was struggling to find the flowers for the very bouquet Petal had rejected? One thing I felt very certain of, however, was that he hadn't done it for her. He hadn't raided his greenhouse and clipped blossoms from his carefully-tended plants for the woman who had crushed his heart to pieces years ago.

Maybe that's why two bright spots of pink invaded my own cheeks momentarily. I turned my thoughts somewhere else, to the immediate task of adjusting the front edge of the carpet rolled across the pathway for the bride's aisle.

I stood up and gazed at the carpeted walkway sprinkled with petals, and the beautiful arbor decorated with dried flowers and fresh blooms, reflecting the colors of wild Cornish blossoms. Everything was perfect. Cliffs House could be proud of itself at this moment, and that was what mattered to me.

Thank you, Matt, I whispered inside. I owed him more than I could say for this moment of satisfaction.

***

The reception's party was in full swing an hour after the ceremony was over. The string quartet had been replaced by the pop singer and a band, and the modern skyscraper of a cake had been dissected for the hundred or so guests of the bride and groom.

Petal and Donald looked happy as the best man toasted them with champagne, and as they posed with friends and family for private photos snapped by mobile phones. Petal seemed especially pleased by how much attention her dress and shoes were garnering from the handful of exclusive feature journalists and photographers who were allowed to stay for the event. As I checked on the progress of the catering staff, I caught a glimpse of her serene smile as she lifted the hem of her long wedding dress to let a photographer take a close up of the glittering designer shoes. For once, it made me glad that I was wearing a pair of plain, unadorned heels.

"Isn't it exciting?" Gemma asked me, under her breath. I could see her cheeks were flushed with excitement, in contrast to her dignified black and white service uniform. In her hands, a nearly-empty tray that had once held Dinah's mini whortleberry pies topped with clotted cream and dark chocolate shavings.

"I think we've pulled it off," I said, forgetting momentarily whether this had the same meaning in English vernacular or not. "That is, it's a success. For all of us. It couldn't have been a better day if we had designed every part of it."

"It's a good thing Dinah made a little extra fudge," Gemma added, in a whisper. "The kitchen's almost out of tarts *and* pasties."

Charlotte had decorated her mini meat pies beautifully, with elegant crimped edges and a decorative swirl of pastry on each one. I knew she would be proud of how many famous people had declared them the best they'd ever eaten. Even if they *weren't* the hearty full-size 'oggies' she was famous for in the village.

"Is there still enough champagne?" I asked.

"A crateful," she answered, then slipped back to circulating among the crowd.

I felt Lady Amanda squeeze my arm, briefly. "A smashing success, isn't it?" she said, echoing part of my words from before. She was wearing an elegant dress — her best frock from a London designer, she informed me, which she generally wore to formal events at Cliffs House.

"Are you pleased with today?" I asked, feigning curiosity with this question. "Did I meet your standards for a proper event planner? Because now's your chance to fire me, if not."

"Silly of you," said Lady Amanda, with a no-nonsense look. "Of course we're pleased. And don't think you're going anywhere anytime soon. We have a charity ball for the Tsunami Recovery Foundation *and* a wedding booked with an American couple in the diary for next month."

"So soon?"

"Not feeling quite up to the job of chief event planner?" Lady Amanda's eyes twinkled.

"I've never felt better about it, actually," I answered. "Now, if you'll pardon me — boss — I think I'll grab a quick bite to eat and make sure Dinah doesn't need an extra hand finishing those caviar canapés." I gave her a smile as I slipped from the room.

A few couples were dancing in the main hall to the strains of music from the reception. A cluster of guests were giggling loudly as they viewed something on the screen of a mobile phone — I was guessing that a few extra rounds of champagne influenced their good spirits. Shrugging my black wrap more securely around my satin party dress, I crossed the room, not to the kitchen but the open main doors of Cliffs House.

Outside, the garden was peaceful, the light soft as the sun moved behind a cloud for a moment. It was my first moment to myself since the wedding began, and I spent it thinking of Matthew. I couldn't help it, partly because the unused bouquet of flowers I had made — the vastly inferior one — was now sitting in a vase on the table close by.

A smile tugged my lips again. This one, a softer, more wistful one than before. I rested my head against the door's frame for a moment, remembering the look in his eyes when he handed me the box of flowers. Had I been imagining it — or was that look —

"Quite all right, Ms. Morgen?" Geoff was behind me.

"Fine," I answered. "Just getting a quick breath of air."

"If you say so." He smiled as he continued on to the kitchen. "And, by the way — congratulations on your first assignment."

"Thanks," I answered. My first congratulations, I thought, in my first moment as a full-fledged event planner. One who knows that everyone who helps you with the smallest of tasks is the real reason you didn't fail.

There was still a couple or two dancing in the main hall by the time the event was over. Donald and Petal Price-Parker had driven away in a sporty foreign car, destined for a private plane and a honeymoon in Rio de Janeiro. Trixie, who had not caught the bouquet, had pouted until the best man and a group of 'fresh young things' from the couple's circle of friends swept her off in a red convertible to some party spot in Truro. The last of the empty trays and glasses had been carted away by the serving staff, the last of the food and drink stored away once more.

I stepped out the hall's main doors, into the cool evening air. The sun was setting, the last of the sunset disappearing on the horizon, transforming the garden into shapes and shadows, even where a couple of guests had requested — and lit — lawn torches along the pathway from the front courtyard to the gardens. I walked in that direction, hugging my wrap around myself, and ignoring my pinched toes from too many hours on my feet in high heels. In my arms, the bouquet of lilies from the vase in the main hall, their water-soaked stems and damp paper carefully wrapped in floral plastic.

I was halfway to the cliff's path when I saw him standing by the shrub-lined walkway outside the main garden. Matthew, only wearing a suit instead of his clean, casual clothes from earlier. He looked handsome, dashing, and as if he was waiting for someone. Seeing him there caught me by surprise.

"Hi," I said, at last.

"Hello," he answered.

I was flustered. The words I should be saying had gotten lost, probably because I hadn't expected to say anything. "I, um, was going to leave these for you," I said. "Along your seat by the cliffs. A way to say 'thank you' for the ones you brought this morning to save me from an apology."

I paused, then kept talking, because Matthew hadn't said anything. "Actually, I owed you an apology anyway," I continued. "Not just for being rude in the beginning, but for not being as understanding as I should be. I was hurt. I had no right to be hurt that you hadn't told me, but I was, and it made me less of a friend ...."

I was babbling now. What was I saying? Matthew was still looking at me, but I imagined he was looking at an insane, flustered woman. I was sure I was blushing, and I was afraid even the growing darkness wouldn't hide it.

I took a deep breath. "So here," I said, holding the flowers out to him. "It's a little weird, I know, but it was the only thing I could think of right now."

"I accept it," he said. "The gift and the apology." He smiled at me. "But I didn't come here for that."

"Oh. Of course not." I was recovering a little now — since I had managed to avoid any physical contact with Matt, I could hide my confusion better the longer I talked. "I'm sure you have plans. I just wanted to leave those for you. There's a card tucked in there, by the way. Just a quick note — but it says things better than I'm saying them now."

"You said them perfectly fine," he answered.

If he didn't stop looking at me, I was going to start crumbling apart again. The heat in my face was spreading everywhere. I had run out of words to say, so we were both going to stand here silently unless Matt had something to add.

"I want you to believe me when I say I'm not in love with Petal anymore," he said. "I won't deny that it hurt to see her. But it was more about my pride than my heart after all these years. I had been avoiding facing her, and when I finally did, I knew for sure that while I might change many things about my past ... I wouldn't change the part where she and I parted ways."

I had stopped breathing as I listened. As I looked into those dark eyes, in what little daylight was left to us. "I believe you," I answered, softly.

"Do you?" he said.

"Of course," I said. "You have a very honest face. I can tell you're not lying to me." I managed to remain serious and not crack a smile with this reply. But I could see Matthew's tugging at the corners of his mouth.

"I'm glad," he said. "I assume that you're not going anywhere — that you're not packing up and leaving Cornwall now that the wedding is over?"

"According to Lady Amanda, I'm indispensable," I answered, with a shrug. "She already has two more events she wants me to plan. So, no, I'm not going anywhere."

"Good," he said. And smiled again.

I stepped closer to him. "I'm sorry," I said. "It's just ... there's something I have to do. Because a bouquet really isn't enough to say thank you —"

I ended this statement short by pressing my lips against Matt's, gently. It was a quick, soft kiss, but enough to tell me that a longer one would be just as good. My hand brushed against his sleeve, the distance between us as close as it was before in the parlor at Rosemoor Cottage.

I drew back, giving myself a moment to catch my breath. "Anyway, that's my thanks," I said. "For everything." I glanced up at his eyes quickly, then looked away. My skin tingled with the electricity of this decision, my brain swept away by the sudden boldness of actually doing this.

Matt stood very still afterwards. The look on his face — the tender one I remembered from the cliffs — gave me hope that this hadn't been something very stupid on my part.

"Why are you here?" I asked. My voice was soft.

"To ask you if you were free this evening," he answered, just as softly. "And if you would like to go for a walk. With me."

"I would love to," I answered.

He held out his hand to me. I took hold of it, feeling my arm tucked protectively beneath his own a moment later as we entered the avenues of the hedge-lined gardens. I glanced back at the lights of Cliffs House before they disappeared from sight, then turned back to the path, and the view of Matt walking beside me.

It was amazing the difference a few words and a single kiss could make. Even with only his arm through mine, I could feel the electricity from crossing the line between friendship and something more.

"Is there a garden on the grounds worth seeing by moonlight?" I asked. Partly joking as dusk enveloped us, deepening the shadows of the rhododendrons around us.

I felt Matthew's laugh even before it escaped his lips. "Funny you should ask," he said.

Even without seeing them, I could imagine the look in his dark eyes. I found it was everything I thought it would be and more. I had my chance, and wouldn't trade it for anything — not a prince in shining armor or a hero brooding in a gothic manor.

And definitely not for a football player with a flashy sports car.

A Christmas in Cornwall

By

Laura Briggs

"Goodness, I feel exhausted!" Lady Amanda pushed aside a stack of glossy tourist pamphlets and stretched out dramatically in her armchair. "Are there any more details we need to discuss? Or at long last, are we at an end?"

"Just one more thing for today," I answered. "The Christmas tree in the main hall — red and white?"

"Lovely. Throw in a bit of blue and we've got the Union flag and the American one," quipped Lady Amanda. "I'll be serious now, promise. Red and white would be perfect with the rest of the event's motif, so I'm sure those colors will do."

I made a note in my planner. "And the staff Christmas party —?"

"Oh, I'd completely forgotten." She smacked her forehead. "Do ask Lord William if he's arranged for a couple of geese yet. I suppose turkey is more traditional, but goose is making a bit of a comeback, isn't it? And even though Dinah usually has powers of persuasion over the local butcher, William was hoping to surprise her with a fine pair to stuff for the party."

"I'll talk to him," I promised. "We'll make certain it's a great event for everyone." I pictured the fun of the event — a real Cornish Christmas, something which Geoff and Dinah had hinted was a festive occasion.

It wasn't anything like Tiny Tim's Christmas dinner in Dickens' novel, I was sure, but I couldn't imagine what a real English village Christmas was like. And since this would be my first one, I intended to make the most of it — and not just for the sake of sending a quaint postcard to my friend Aimee back home, either.

I hurried away to get started for the day on the never-ending tasks of Cliffs House's event planner. Muffled voices greeted my ears from somewhere in the hall, and turning the corner, I encountered Gemma and Pippa hanging a festive wreath in the main hall. Glass balls of gold and red shone cheerily beneath the lights as both girls giggled, trying to balance the heavy creation until it was secured in place on the wall.

"Don't let go yet!" shrieked Pippa, as Gemma released her half of the wreath.

"Sorry!" squeaked Gemma. "Is that better?" She shifted it more to the left.

"You two be careful," scolded Dinah. "Someone's going to end up on their backside if not." She had bustled forth from the kitchen passage, a tray of cookies in her hands — three different kinds, all of them tempting beneath decorative piping or colorful sprinkles.

"What do you think?" she asked me. "I've tried six different recipes, but these are the best. Ginger first, then the butter biscuits, then a nice cinnamon lace."

I took a bite of the ginger biscuit. It melted in my mouth after one crisp bite. "Heavenly," I declared. "I don't think any guests will be able to resist."

"These aren't for the charity ball," said Dinah with a laugh. "These are for the Christmas party. Proper to save the best for our own celebration, isn't it?" She winked at me.

"Julianne, coming to the pub tonight?" Gemma asked, looking over her shoulder. "There's a quiz tonight — all American television programs. My bloke Andy says you could beat anybody there." Andy was Gemma's latest boyfriend — one who bore more than a passing resemblance to one of the rugby player posters she adored, albeit a thinner, more awkward version.

"Not tonight," I answered. "I'm having dinner out." My voice shrank a little for these words, trying to go unnoticed — but my cheeks both had a very bright pink spot in the middle of each.

"Ooh...with Ross, I'll bet," teased Pippa. She and Gemma exchanged glances — I had been on the receiving end of more than one good-natured joke recently regarding things between me and Matthew. "Is he taking you someplace nice?"

"I'll bet he looks the part of a proper gentleman, all dressed up," mused Gemma, dreamily. "Imagine him in a tuxedo, like James Bond."

"It's just dinner at a restaurant he visits sometimes," I answered. Trying to sound casual about it. "He says it's one of the best examples of South Cornwall's seafood."

All things said, I was getting used to the constant teasing over Matt and me. Matthew Rose, former professor and brilliant horticulturist, now a consultant gardener at Cliffs House — but the two young girls employed at the country house had nicknamed him after the handsome hero from *Poldark* due to his looks.

I had only seen pictures of the actor from the series, but the biggest proof of Matthew's looks was in the reaction of women to him. Women in Ceffylgwyn teased Matthew every bit as badly as Pippa and Gemma when it came to his looks. Even at a quiet restaurant just outside the village, I detected a couple of admiring glances cast in his direction by female patrons. And I could see the blush on Matt's face whenever he detected one, too.

He pretended not to notice as he sat down across from me at our table. "What will you have?" he asked, as I glanced over the menu. "Would you like a recommendation from me? A favorite dish?"

"No, I want to select it completely on my own," I answered. "I think I'm even going to point randomly to an item and eat whatever it is."

"You're risking ordinary fish and chips with vinegar," he said. "Or even boiled calamari." I could tell he wasn't being entirely serious, due to the glint of humor in his eyes.

"I'll take the risk," I said, smiling. "Besides, I need a risk. I have to be prepared for the upcoming charity ball. Surprises keep event planners on their toes, you see."

I found the idea of a ball on Christmas Eve a little surprising at first, I had to admit. Until I learned the primary sponsor for it was a business based out of Tokyo, Japan, where Christmas isn't quite the phenomenon it is in other parts of the world. And since the proceeds were going to an international program dedicated to bringing clean water sources to impoverished nations, it seemed rather a lovely way to spend the eve of the most charitable holiday on the calendar.

"Your life sounds exciting compared to mine," Matt answered. "All I've done is coddle a few grafted roses through their first frost."

"Lord William appreciates it," I said. "The rose garden is definitely short on varieties since the previous gardener had an all-consuming passion for herbs and annuals, I've been told."

"On the other hand, I might have an opportunity for a tiny bit of excitement myself," he said. "The university has invited me to give a lecture in the spring. A review of my work in breeding disease-resistant antique roses during the Massachusetts project."

"Really?" I said. "That is exciting, Matthew! You must be so pleased."

"I am," he admitted. "Until their invitation arrived, I hadn't realized how much I missed the academic world. Yes, it's less hands on than what I've been doing these past few years ... but there's something about exchanging ideas in a classroom that can't be dismissed."

I detected a little note of eagerness, and maybe yearning, deep in

Matthew's voice. I hadn't thought about him regretting his decision to leave his Ivy League post after his broken heart. He had said more than once that he didn't regret Petal's decision to leave him, and all that happened as a result of it; but I knew that leaving his life behind, even for the place he loved most, had probably been hard.

"Spring, huh?" I said. I took a sip of my wine. "I guess it seems kind of far away right now, doesn't it?"

"It gives me plenty of time to prepare," he said. "I've been in touch with the president of the university. We've been emailing quite often. Maybe this will open the door to more lectures in the future, at some of the other colleges as well."

"I'll bet they miss you," I said. "Miss having you teach and lecture full time. Definitely miss your input in landscape architecture and plant propagation on their historic grounds." I swirled the wine in my glass, imagining the liquid's whirlpool was a tight spiral of rose petals — almost the same color as the blossoms Matthew had given me for an apology after our first meeting/argument.

"You think they're trying to lure me back?" Matt teased. He took a sip from his own glass. "Coax me back into their fold permanently, so I'll give lectures in the mornings and treat diseased begonias and wayward rose canes in the afternoon?"

"They wouldn't be so scheming," I replied, with a pretend scowl of indignation. "Besides, all they would have to do is ask. I'm sure that no one has to bribe you to use your gifts."

Matthew flushed, briefly. I wondered if a tiny part of him almost wished our made-up scenario was true — if it would seem like a rescue, now that he had no real gardening challenges to pursue in South Cornwall. In fact, he had little to do right now, between consulting jobs, short of completing a few odd jobs on Lord William's behalf.

"Perhaps if I apply my gift correctly, I can force that carefully-coaxed rose into blooming in time for Christmas," said Matt, setting aside his glass, and changing the subject at the same time. "The first time in many years."

"The one you brought back from the brink of death?" I echoed.

"That's the one," he said. "It's developed a flower bud or two already. It's a matter of keeping it healthy, warm, and well-watered so it can bring them into fruition."

The rose was a rare antique variety that had been left neglected in the greenhouse for years. Lord William had discovered it languishing there when he and Geoff Weatherby took over managing the grounds — a pitiful brown and green stick with only a few leaves, he had claimed. But in Matthew's hands, it had begun to slowly recover its life, sprouting new green canes, and unfurling reddish-green leaves.

"Lord William says his mother was probably the last person to see it bloom," I said. "Decades ago. How long do roses live, anyway?"

I had the bare minimum's knowledge of botany, horticulture, or plant taxonomy despite my attempts to memorize plant names and gardening terminology since arriving in Cornwall. Matt had done his best to teach me a little more, loaning me books from his shelves, but I was still a hopeless beginner.

"Roses can live long, rich lives, just like human beings," he said. "Providing they have the right care. But it depends on the variety. Some live less than twenty — some live a veritable century."

"So Lord William's rose might outlive me?" I asked, jokingly.

"Probably not." Matt's smile was one of amusement. "It already has a good thirty years' advantage. And it's rather amazing it lived so long, given its condition."

I wanted him to tell me the variety's name again, so I could commit it to memory, along with other things he'd taught me lately, but the waiter appeared with our food just then. So I settled for praising the dish set before me, grilled fish in a chef's sauce, steamed asparagus beside it.

I glanced at Matthew as he ate, half-expecting him to tease me about my luck in randomly selecting my dinner. Lately, he teased me more often when we were talking. A lot of barriers had come down between us since that night I kissed him impulsively in the garden.

What were we, exactly? Tonight felt like a date, as had the other times we'd been out together — less than a dozen over the past few months, from casual evenings at the pub to a couple of restaurants like this one, with both of us in 'posh' clothes and on our best behavior.

We were comfortable together, even though there were still little awkward moments, where separate cultures or personalities collided; and there were moments of attraction, where I thought that I could lose myself in those dark eyes as we gazed into each other's. And there had been more kisses...but not the words that would mean no going back for either of us, emotionally-speaking. Even with all the butterflies and sparks of electricity that Matt's touch produced in me, not being quite sure where we were — or what we both wanted this to be — was definitely a problem we couldn't escape.

No one called us 'boyfriend and girlfriend' yet, I noticed — and we didn't even call ourselves that. It was as if something was standing between us, some final barrier that kept us both from planning a future together. Pieces of our different pasts were still in the way, somehow.

In a way, I was hoping tonight would change that, but it didn't. Matt was handsome in his suit, charming as always, and deep inside, I knew I was falling in love with him — desperately and helplessly so. But the words that would make everything between us fall into place — well, those feelings couldn't seem to become words in my brain. And they didn't seem to be coming from Matt's lips, in between the jokes and stories, no matter the tenderness and longing in his eyes. Lock glances, deep stares of emotional desire and unspoken feeling, look away — could this be an actual routine in our romance? And leading to what?

At least I knew it wasn't Matthew's formerly-broken heart that stood in the way. And I was pretty sure it wasn't my own romantic mishaps, either. So maybe it was something as simple as our unsettled goals: my life of less than six months in Cornwall, and Matt's tenuous career as a horticultural consultant.

Or maybe we were both just a little afraid what would happen if one of us admitted we were really, truly falling in love.

Matt poured a second glass for both of us. "What shall we drink to?" he asked. "It's been six months to the day since you arrived in Cornwall, you know."

I felt as if he'd read my mind. "Really?" I said. I hadn't kept up with the exact date — the anniversary of my arrival at Cliffs House last summer.

"I'm certain of it," he said. "Even if I did have to ask Geoff Weatherby to be certain." There was a twinkle in his eyes as he lifted his glass. "Well, Miss Morgen?"

I thought about it. Nope, no toasting to a future as Matt's one and only love, I decided, even jokingly. "To a bright and happy future, I guess," I answered. "And to a happy Christmas in Cornwall."

"To your happy future, then," he said. "Now and always." His glass clinked against mine, and we both took a sip. Our eyes met, and I looked deep into his own, seeing the gentleness and the passion that had taken my breath more than once in our time together.

There was something so clear, so alive in that gaze. I wanted it to become words, so I could tell him I loved him. If it wasn't true yet, it wouldn't be long before it was; the more time I spent with him, and the better I knew him, the harder it was to resist that feeling. The real him — the passionate gardener, the chivalrous gentleman, the kindhearted friend, and the veritable genius, among his many sides — was breaking down every defense of friendship that still held me in place.

Dusk had given way to darkness when we walked to Matt's car outside the restaurant. I could hear the restless water in the dark, and see the movement of the waves by moonlight. Moonlight transformed the coast into something both beautiful and menacing — the jagged edges of an island of dark rocks rising from the waters, a sheen of pale light on the waters rising and falling with the tide. A flash of navigation light was visible from the point where we stood in the harbor, from a fisherman's vessel at sea.

"What are you thinking about?" Matt asked me. His hand rested on my back, the passenger door of his car opened for me as I gazed towards the sea.

"I'm just imagining a lighthouse somewhere near that outcropping. The one that looks like a little peninsula," I said. "It seems like the perfect spot."

He laughed. "But not very practical," he said. "This isn't the shore for deep-sea fishing vessels or commercial ones, either. I'm afraid the romantic lighthouse you're picturing is the Lizard's lighthouse. It's a bit further south."

"The Lizard," I said. "That name always sounds so weird to me. I'm picturing a big desert lizard, the kind with all the little spiky horns on its back."

"It has its share of spiky rocks," said Matt. "And it is covered in a type of rock known as 'serpentine.' But most historians agree its name is really derived from the Cornish language. 'Lys Ardh' means 'high court' in Cornish. It's a beautiful place, full of rare plants and natural wonders…but its waters can be treacherous for vessels to navigate sometimes."

His voice grew softer with these last words, his cheek almost against mine. I could feel the heat from his skin mere inches from mine as he stood close behind me, gazing out at the moonlit sea. It would feel natural to lean back against him right now, and feels his arms encircle me in return — but I resisted the urge to do it, even with the fantasy tugging at my mind.

After a moment, Matt stirred. “Sorry,” he said. “I was lost in thought for a moment.”

“So was I.” I glanced at him over my shoulder, with a smile that I hoped didn’t betray my blushing cheeks. Had we been thinking the same thing until now? Or had Matt’s mind been somewhere else — exploring the Lizard to document rare specimens for instance?

We talked about the pub's quiz nights and the awful programs on television as we drove back to Ceffylgwyn later that night. Matt paused at the road sign for a moment.

"Would you like to come back to Rosemoor Cottage for an hour or so?" he asked. "It's not late, and I had a cutting in a pot that I wanted to give you. Nothing valuable, but it's tough, hardy, and blooms beautifully with minimal care — a good choice for your first plant, I thought."

"A plant? For me?" I answered, dramatically. "Are you sure you trust me with such a treasure, Mr. Rose?"

"I think you're ready," he answered, trying to look serious as he said this. "After all, you've only damaged one or two protected Cornish heath plants, and un-potted a Japanese peace lily by accident. A relatively mild record of attempted plant homicide, really."

"The heath was an accident," I reminded him. "And that peace lily was in the way when we were trying to wrestle the furniture aside for the harpist due at the Cancer Awareness Foundation's tea. It was a victim of circumstance."

"You'll find the plant I'm giving you much harder to kill," he answered. "So, shall we stop by?"

"Love to," I said. "Except I have to finish organizing my list of possible caterers for the ball. I didn't have time this afternoon after Lady Amanda and I finished double-checking the holiday decor. Another time?"

"Of course," he said. "Tuesday. After the pub's quiz night."

"Sounds perfect," I said.

I loved Matt's cottage, with its too-full bookshelves and its garden running amok with every kind of English wildflower known to mankind. Even in the midst of winter, there were still touches of green and splashes of color. It was a place I could never picture as grey or gloomy, even on the rainiest days.

"What would you like to do for our next outing?" Matt asked me.

I gave this a moment's thought. "How about a picnic for the two of us in a cozy garden spot?" I asked.

Matt laughed. "Cornwall winters may be milder, but that doesn't mean it might not be a bit cool for sitting on a blanket on the grounds," he pointed out.

"Then how about I cook dinner for us?" I suggested. "At your cottage. I'll buy the ingredients and bring everything I need."

"You can cook?" Matt didn't quite raise an eyebrow, but I thought he was tempted. I put on my best indignant expression.

"Of course I can," I answered. "It's just a myth that American women burn everything they bake. I can assure you that I'm handy with a saucepan and a casserole dish — besides, Dinah has been giving me some pointers, and says I'm coming along nicely, thank you."

"I trust her judgment," said Matthew, solemnly. I swatted him on the shoulder.

"Take me home," I said, crossing my arms. "If we keep talking, I might end up hitting you again." Even in the car's darkness, I could spot his grin as he shifted the car into gear.

I kissed him goodnight after he circled and parked in Cliffs House's courtyard. A kiss on the cheek, lingering for just a second to notice his aftershave, and the heat of his skin. Our lips brushed, but we both hesitated before the kiss began; we both knew what happened afterwards, the electricity making it hard to stop with just one.

"Goodnight," I said, softly. I waved goodbye as I watched Matt drive away. With a sigh, I imagined a different ending — one in which I had whispered the truth in Matthew's ear, then waited to hear him whisper back the same words.

Or heard silence in response. Even though I felt sure of his feelings, there was no guarantee, after all. Maybe deep inside, Matt still had doubts about us. Surely he didn't think I had them. Not after what these months had meant to me.

I turned and walked towards the house's main door, which was standing open even though the family wasn't expecting guests and all public visitors had gone home hours ago. Someone had arrived, however, and not someone local, since they hadn't used the informal entrance.

A man in a business suit and overcoat had been chatting with someone in the main hall, exiting the house as I approached, the door closing behind him. As I crossed his path, he glanced at me, and stopped. The visitor had blond, curly hair, a carefully-trimmed beard of light, short stubble that didn't hide his attractive, youthful features. But that wasn't why I was staring at him. And he wasn't staring at me because I looked irresistible in my red dress and wrap, either.

"Julianne?" he said.

My heart had fallen to the bottom of my chest. "Dwight?"

***

I hadn't laid eyes on Dwight Bradshaw since the day we broke off our casual but somewhat promising relationship outside a coffee house in Seattle. That was almost a year ago, back when I still worked for Design a Dream, and Dwight was the financial advisor for one of the biggest digital security firms in the city. He hadn't changed a bit from what I could see in the dim light of the manor's courtyard. Still handsome, still polished and perfectly dressed for the role of a successful businessman. Only with a startled look on his face as he gazed at me from mere feet away.

"It *is* you," he said after a moment, features breaking into a grin of disbelief. "I thought I might be imagining things for a second there."

"Me too," I said. Feeling another jolt of surprise as he gave me a quick hug, the stubble from his beard brushing lightly against my cheek. Me and Dwight's breakup, while not the stuff of soap operas, hadn't exactly been cheerful, so this warm gesture wasn't exactly what I expected upon first meeting. Maybe a few awkward, forced polite lines instead.

"You look fantastic," he said, stepping back to assess my appearance with a glance. "Red always was your color, Julianne. Fiery and full of life—just like the girl who's wearing it," he added, with a teasing note in his voice.

I felt grateful for the dim lighting, since red had began to infuse my cheeks with the compliment. Dwight had a certain charm with words that I had forgotten about since our breakup. Not so much the words themselves, but the way he made them sound—warm, playful, and completely sincere. It was a talent I imagined came in handy for his job, as well as his dating life — whatever his dating life was, these days.

"Thanks," I told him, summoning a smile in response. *Be polite, Julianne.*

He smiled back, tucking his hands in the pockets of his wool trousers. Executive wear was practically Dwight's everyday attire, I remembered. The closest thing to casual I had seen him wear were designer khakis and pullovers, and that was usually just for the time spent on his yacht. A sailing enthusiast, Dwight belonged to a Seattle yacht club, where he participated in several races—and frequently placed first— throughout the year.

"Are you here on vacation?" I wondered, thinking it wasn't likely. Dwight had always preferred a metropolitan atmosphere, except for when he was out on the water, of course. Maybe he came here for the sailing then. But December was hardly the best time of year for that sort of activity in Cornwall, was it? And Dwight seemed more like the Newquay type than someone interested in sleepy little Ceffylgwyn.

Dwight shook his head. "I'm here on business. The firm is helping to sponsor the big Christmas Eve gala they're hosting at this place. I'm crunching the numbers for them, as usual, so I thought I would nip over here and have a word with the host and hostess on some budget expectations."

"Nip over to Cornwall from Seattle?" I raised an eyebrow. "That's kind of extreme isn't it?" Dwight chuckled at the words.

"It's not as far as you think. I've actually transferred to one of the company's international offices. You're looking at the newest chief financial advisor for the London branch of Spencer's Digital Security."

"Really?" I hugged my wrap closer to my arms, conscious of goosebumps breaking over my skin. From the cold, of course, not Dwight's unexpected words. Still…it was quite a coincidence. A stunning coincidence, even — me running into my ex just as things were finally comfortable, and my chances of starting anew were brighter than ever. My face was pale now instead of red, my head not quite sure how I felt about this.

"What about you?" Dwight asked. "Design a Dream must be treating you well, if you can afford a Christmas vacation in a setting this idyllic." With a nod towards the manor before us, its stone exterior and elegant carvings stretching far overhead, with bowers and chimneys that were faintly etched amid the glow of moonlight.

"I'm not working for Design a Dream anymore. In fact," I told him, pausing for a breath, "I'm working here now. As the new event planner for Cliffs House."

Surprise flooded his cobalt eyes. "So we're both expatriates, I guess."

The words held a conspiratorial edge beneath the humor, making it seem as if this were some kind of bond we shared. Leave it to Dwight to make it seem as if we never lost touch with each other. As if we hadn't fought about all the little differences that added up to the bigger reasons we couldn't work as a couple. Or maybe he'd forgotten that last, awkward exchange outside the coffee house that ended with me taking the bus back home instead of accompanying him to our friend's anniversary party. Curled up on my couch, I had devoured a carton of caramel salted ice cream for some post-breakup comfort, if memory served correct.

But that should be water under the bridge, shouldn't it? After all, I had that episode to thank for helping me cut ties with Seattle without a second thought to come to Cliffs House...and find Matt's tender gaze waiting to meet mine.

"Expatriate seems a little strong for me," I told him. "But Cornwall is an amazing place to live. The staff here is fantastic, and I've never been happier than I am working for Lord William and Lady Amanda. It's definitely beginning to feel like home."

That was the truth. Although I'd only been here a few short months, Ceffylgwyn and Cliffs House felt as familiar — as comfortable — as my own hometown. And this without me being able to speak a word of Cornish, understand half the speeches of anybody using strong dialect, or explain to Aimee what exactly a 'Troyl' involves, even after more than one email on the subject.

"You? You were such a Seattle girl," said Dwight, sounding amazed. "And I thought by now you'd be in a serious relationship there — I mean after what happened. After all, I knew I didn't break your heart for good."

Although he spoke these words lightly, I could tell he sneaked a glance to see what effect they had on me.

It wasn't that Dwight hadn't touched my heart in some way, of course. It had taken more than one cry to get over the way things ended—but I *had* got over it. And look or no look, I was sure that Dwight had too, given the ease with which he referred to our mutual past. Anything else would be pure imagination on my part.

"My cab to the train station is arriving any moment now," Dwight said, checking his watch. "I have a meeting in Westminster bright and early in the morning."

"Exciting," I replied. Secretly, I was relieved he would be leaving Ceffylgwyn in a matter of minutes. No matter how innocent our re-meeting was, I didn't relish the thought of reliving any part of it. And I didn't want to explain to Matt that yet another one of us had an ex hanging around the manor for a short time.

How would Matt feel if he knew I was chatting with an old flame? Jealous? Trusting? Confident that I was in love with him, though I hadn't said it? Or perhaps he'd feel exactly the way I felt when I learned his ex-fiancée, Petal, was the bride-to-be in the first wedding I supervised at Cliffs House. Which meant he'd be a little bit hurt that I didn't mention this recent attachment in my past. Threatened even, although I didn't think Matt seemed like the insecure kind.

All this speculation was going nowhere, since I didn't plan to bring it up with Matt, even to know what he was thinking. For now, I'd prefer that part of our relationship to remain a mystery. Besides, he needn't feel threatened or jealous, since things with Dwight had ended the way they should, and I didn't regret it for a second. Even if seeing him again had proved to be weird and unsettling in some way I couldn't quite explain.

England's a big place, I reminded myself. *No reason you can't share it with Dwight—and no reason this has to be awkward or a big deal in any way at all.*

And it wasn't. At least, not for the few minutes we stood there waiting for his cab to arrive. Catching up on news about friends back home, most of whom Dwight had seen more recently than I had. Being overseas made it hard to keep up with even my closest friends, aside from the occasional phone call or video chat with Aimee and Nate.

When his cab pulled up, Dwight gave my hand a parting squeeze. "It was great seeing you, Julianne. A familiar face on foreign shores is nice. And who knows? Maybe we'll bump into each other in London. Have a cup of tea and catch up." He grinned as he climbed into the cab and shut the door.

I waved goodbye to him from the other side of the glass. Certain I would never see Dwight Bradshaw again, least of all for a cup of tea and a 'catch up' as he put it, not if I had my way. And those are not the words of a bitter ex, in case you're wondering.

But we can't really know the future, can we? This time, my instincts turned out to be quite wrong.

***

"I haven't done this since kindergarten. Honestly, that's why it looks so bad," I explained, folding a strip of green paper into a loop that looked more like an oval than a circle. It promptly squashed itself flat beneath my thumb.

Gemma giggled. "You didn't have to tell us that, Julianne. I think we both reckoned paper arts weren't your strong point." From the chair near the hearth, Pippa let out a quiet groan as her own scissors cut a crooked path through a sheet of red.

The three of us were assembling paper chains in festive colors for decorating the tree in the Cornish estate's library. Its theme was a throwback to an old-fashioned holiday, the only tree in the house that wasn't bedazzled with colored or clear lights and ornaments of a more elaborate nature for tourists and the upcoming charity gala. Instead, simple berries and paper chains would decorate its branches, along with some antique lace ornaments from the manor's bygone days. Only my paper crafting skills were all but nonexistent after twenty-something years of not bothering with them.

Luckily for me, Pippa was in the same boat, struggling to paste her crookedly-cut paper strips together as the glue stuck to her fingers and hair. Watching us fumble around, Gemma let out a snort of derision. "Look at you two! I mean really, any nursery group could do this with their eyes closed."

"They've had more practice," Pippa pleaded. "I was hopeless at paper crafts in school, anyway — must be the maths behind it."

"Rubbish!" said Gemma. "I remember you in primary, making paper stars as good as mine."

"They were crooked, I solemnly swear. You've just forgotten after so many years."

Meanwhile, I was busy trying not to glue my paper to my hair again. I lifted my eyes and laughed as I caught sight of Dinah watching us in the doorway. She shook her head, a hopeless smile on her face.

"I was about to ask if you were having tea this afternoon, but I think it's best you carry on here," she said, eyeing the drop cloths we had placed on the floor to cover the rug from possible spills and gummy glue bits. "At this rate, the lot of you will still be folding little strips of paper when dinner's laid out tonight."

"No I won't," I argued. "This is just me getting warmed up. Once I find a natural rhythm, the work will fly by. You'll see." As I mangled another strip of paper, tearing it nearly in half as I tried to loop it onto the chain.

Without further comment, Dinah turned and disappeared back down the hall. Pippa and Gemma had glimpsed my latest monstrosity, and the three of us burst into giggles again. I let my scissors fall to the floor as I gave up all pretence of salvaging that part of the chain.

"So," I told them, retrieving my scissors after I controlled my giggles again, "tell me about some Christmas traditions at the estate. Just a hint or two at least."

All my co-workers were being coy about what Christmas at Cliffs House would be like, despite the fact I had prodded them for examples multiple times the past few weeks. All I knew was the menu consisted of goose with all the trimmings, and that presents would be exchanged at some point, with possibly a bowl of punch on hand to toast the holiday. It conjured up images from the 'Wassail' carol, but that wasn't nearly enough information in my opinion.

"Well," Gemma began, "don't tell her that I told you, *but*—" and she lowered her voice, glancing round as if to be sure we weren't being eavesdropped on, "— Dinah's making her special plum pudding recipe for dessert this year."

"Plum pudding?" I was lost, envisioning something like the cups of store bought pudding my mother used to pack in my school lunches, my nose scrunching automatically in response. Or was it more like the blackened bowling ball that Tiny Tim cheers for in the movie *A Christmas Carol*?

Pippa quickly cleared up my confusion. “No, not like the nasty sort you lot probably eat — all processed fruit like gumdrops and the like."

"It’s suet with raisins," said Gemma. "Cinnamon, nutmeg, and ginger add a bit of spice to it, and black treacle makes it rich and moist.” She sighed, a hint of longing in the noise, as if anticipating the taste of said pudding.

My mouth was already watering from the description, aware that Dinah’s skills in the kitchen would be at their best for such a special event at the Cornish manor. As of yet, I'd only sampled a handful of Cornwall's famous dishes, becoming a virtual 'oggy' addict at this point, thanks to Charlotte's pasties in the village.

“My Auntie Ruth used to hide a treasure inside the pudding at Christmas,” Pippa said, folding another strip of paper into a loop. “A coin or a button with a fancy design. ‘Course, me cousin Freddie always made sure to get at it first. Right spoiled little brat he was back then—and still is, come to think of it.”

“We always make Christmas Cake instead of pudding at my house,” Gemma said. “Then everybody watches the Queen’s Speech as we tuck into the chocolate again. Oh, the sweet pleasures of a proper holiday chocolate. Mmmm.”

I grinned. “Sounds a lot like my family. Too many sweets, so we’re snoozing by early afternoon.”

It would be the same as always this December at my family’s home back in the States, only without me, of course. Not for the first time, I felt a wave of homesickness, one of many I had experienced since moving overseas. At least I would get to see them open presents via the laptop video chat we were planning. And at least all this distance was for the sake of an amazing experience — which I hoped would include a liking for goose at the holiday dinner. I had yet to admit to several people that I'd never tasted any bird besides chicken and a good ol' holiday turkey.

“How about snow?” I asked. “Any chance for a white Christmas in Ceffylgwyn?”

The girls looked at each other, as if debating how much hope to give me. “Not much of one,” Pippa admitted, adding another link to her gold and red chain. “We’re more likely to see storms than snow.”

"Just think," said Gemma. "We could go storm watching on Christmas."

Storm watching—an activity popular with tourists in Cornwall's wintertime—was a pastime I had yet to develop a taste for. I knew plenty of Americans loved chasing storms in the Midwest in hopes of seeing a tornado — and plenty of English tourists had done the same in Kansas, too.

Then again, I had only tried storm watching once so far, so I wasn't being fair. Matt and I had walked down to the sand, keeping a safe distance from the waves. Waves that seemed to rise as much as twenty or thirty feet high before they crashed against the tall, majestic cliffs along the shore. Beautiful yet terrifying at the same time. I had buried my face in Matthew's coat at one point and blocked out thoughts of giant tidal waves sweeping us away, breathing in the familiar scent of his aftershave as he held me in his strong, secure arms.

Well, maybe storm watching wasn't *all* bad.

Too late, I realized the others had noticed my dreamy little smile for this memory, their expressions revealing how transparent I was. Those secretive smirks — were they picturing me and Matt raging with the same tempest as the sea? They probably were. After all, they were all dying to know how serious Matt and I were.

I blushed fire red. "Well!" I said, brightly, trying to dispel any of these thoughts by showing off my latest handicrafts attempt. "Look at this—over half way done now. And definitely better than some of the paper crafts I sent my grandmother when I was in grade school." I held up the chain in my lap, showing its gradual improvement from my mangled paper wads.

Pippa's was looking much better than mine, but Gemma's was nearly perfect by comparison to both of us. Hmmm. It would take some creative arranging, but I was sure we could disguise the varying degrees of quality when we finally wound these around the fir tree.

Paper chains finished, it was time for decorating the mantel. Carefully, Gemma and I wove a garland from evergreen clippings, holly berries, and wintersweet, a fragrant flower with yellow-golden blossoms that Matt had sent over that very morning from the garden. Pippa located some scented candles from the pantry, their metal antique holders flanking each end of the plain white mantle. The final result was simple but elegant, and even the tree had a quaint, pleasing feel with its homemade decorations. It would feel like home, and that was exactly the point.

Gemma and Pippa were needed back in the kitchen by the time we were done, so I retreated to my office, intending to go over some of the unfinished details for the charity ball. As I sat behind the desk, my work mobile rang. The number on the screen was unfamiliar. The voice that greeted me when I answered, however, was not.

"Dwight," I said, feeling my breath hitch, cautiously, with this word. "What a surprise." It was, and I wasn't sure it was entirely pleasant. I didn't have a longing to hear from my ex-boyfriend again, really. While I was curious why he called, I was still a little annoyed, although not as much as I thought I would be.

"Is it bad timing?" he asked. "I can phone back—"

"No, no. It's fine." What could this be about? Surely he didn't mean what he said about having tea together, at least not this soon. It must be something for the charity ball, I thought.

"I had a favor to ask of you," Dwight continued. "Well, more like a favor for some friends of mine, actually. They're planning a Christmas wedding, but their planner has just dropped them last minute due to scheduling conflicts. Some big London agency, I think. They're devastated, of course."

"That's terrible," I said. "They need help finding another agency, I presume? I can recommend some places—"

"They've tried that, Julianne. It's too close of a deadline and the best planners are already booked through spring anyway. I thought…well — *hoped* — you could help them somehow. You know, give them some advice, help them to fill in the missing pieces, that sort of thing."

"Um, well…"

My hands were basically full with the details for the Christmas Eve ball, and I couldn't let anything interfere with my duties at Cliffs House. If I were to somehow disappoint Lord William and Lady Amanda at the biggest event of the season…well, I just couldn't think of it even.

"You were the best at Design a Dream," he continued. "They should've promoted you if they had any sense. Anyway, I thought someone with your talent, and with your heart, was exactly the person who could help a friend with a problem like this."

"I'm sorry, Dwight, but I'm fairly swamped here," I began. "The charity gala is coming up, as you know, and that's something I have full responsibility for. I wish I could help, I just don't think I have the time to commit to a wedding on top of my current duties."

Harsh and formal and cold. That's how I sounded, no doubt, even though that wasn't how I meant it. I was being overly-careful to keep Dwight at arm's length, that's all. But I was being honest about having more on my schedule than I could handle.

Dwight sighed faintly over the phone. "Of course," he said. "What was I thinking? Except that it's Christmas and I could appeal to your sense of charity. I know that you wouldn't give an answer like that if it wasn't true." His joke was a halfhearted one at best, with this flat and sober ending tacked on. I felt a pang of conscience.

"I really am sorry Dwight. If I only had the time— maybe I could help with a few little —"

"It wouldn't be a huge time commitment." Dwight had leaped on my words, eagerly. "Most of the details were taken care of already, so you would just be double checking those. You know, making some phone calls to the appropriate business contacts, finishing up a few little perfect touches. You probably have an address book filled with the best of the best in London's bridal industry by now," he added, with a chuckle.

I did, actually. My role as chief event planner at Cliffs House might be relatively new, but I had covered a lot of ground since my first assignment. I was now a familiar face to several of the reputable bakeries, florists, and caterers from Cornwall and Devon to the heart of London and could probably arrange something for Dwight's unfortunate friends, even with a big event monopolizing my time. With a sigh, I gave in.

"I could probably manage a couple of trips to London before the holiday," I answered. "I'll see what I can do. That's all I can promise for now, I'm afraid."

"You're an angel," Dwight replied. "Thanks a million, Juli. They'll really appreciate having you rescue them, I promise."

An angel, hmm? That didn't explain why I felt vaguely like a traitor as I penciled a meeting time with Dwight and his friends into the diary on my work desk. Was it my work schedule at Cliffs House I was afraid of betraying, or my relationship with Matt? The little seed of conflict over which one was the bigger problem was sprouting more quickly than I wanted to admit.

***

A hearty fire was blazing in the hearth of the Fisherman's Rest as Matt and I walked through the door on Tuesday night, its rosy glow illuminating the pub's small interior. Stone hearth, high wooden beams, and a bar of rich cherry wood. It was the quintessential English pub, the way I had always pictured one would look. Strands of clear Christmas lights trailing from the beams only added to its cozy charm tonight, as Matt and I shrugged out of our coats and scarves inside the doorway.

We had agreed that skipping quiz night twice in a row would be an unkindness to our teammates, since we were two of only seven members in our regular group. And, since tonight's trivia theme was American cinema, a variation on last week's television trivia, I stood a fair chance of helping us win for a change. Though I couldn't help wishing we were back at Rosemoor cottage instead, sharing that romantic dinner I had planned to make for Matt as soon as Dinah's cooking lessons assured me it was time for such a gutsy move. Something involving pheasant, maybe, but definitely not the ox heart from Dinah's *The Best of English Cooking Through the Centuries.*

The pub was packed inside, anywhere from eighty to a hundred locals showing up for pub nights on average. Matt kept his hand on my back as we searched the crowd, a warm and protective touch that I was loathe to lose as our friends spotted us from across the room.

"Julianne, Ross, over here!" Gemma waved to us from a table in the corner near the hearth. Her boyfriend Andy was beside her, his athletic, yet lanky build unmistakable. Across from them was the rest of our team: Rosie, the administrator for the local cat shelter; Susan, a hair stylist from Falmouth; and Susan's husband, Clive, who used to work as an undergardener at Cliffs House before retiring to his own garden work at a cottage by the sea.

"How's it going, mate?" Andy greeted Matt with a handshake, as the two of us took our places at the table. My seat was directly across from Matt's, next to Susan, who turned to greet me with a smile.

"Don't you look smart tonight?" she observed, glancing over the tartan skirt and boots that I had paired with a blouse and fleece jacket. "That hairstyle isn't bad either," she added, with a glance at my reddish brown layers that I had pinned back with a clip, rather than do battle to tame it with my straightening brush and curling iron at the last minute. "Suits you better than your usual look, I think. Not that I'm saying it couldn't do with just a *bit* more of something...off the sides, maybe."

I hid my grin for this compliment, since Susan was forever nagging me to get my hair cut at her salon in Falmouth. She was obsessed with persuading me to change my look, claiming my features were crying out for something short and daring, a touch of Emma Watson's pixie cut from the celebrity magazines on her salon's waiting room table. Given her dedication to adding me to her pool of customers, it was quite a concession for her to admit any look I sported 'wasn't bad.'

"Thank you, Susan," I said, with a smile of victory. "I rather like it myself."

It hadn't taken long before I had begun to feel a part of these weekly gatherings at the Fisherman's Rest. I never had my own hangout back in Seattle, so to speak, but I much preferred the idea of a pub to a bar anyway. And Ceffylgwyn had a way of pulling people into its fold, if they were really interested in being part of it — just like the small towns and villages from television and novels.

Of course, they teased me endlessly about my accent. And my wretched attempts at using Cornish and English slang. Try as I might, I couldn't remember the right time for saying I was 'chuffed' about something or that something was 'daft'. Or saying I would do something 'dreckly'—a Cornish phrase similar to 'directly' but meaning the speaker might accomplish their task anytime between now and next year, from what I had gathered. Their good-natured ribbing reminded of a Washington college classmate I had teased occasionally over his Alabama accent. If this was comeuppance for that particular episode, I was getting off easy in punishment.

Matt was chatting with Clive about gardening, while Andy and Gemma shared some private confidence that involved her giggling quite a bit. From the seat on my left, Rosie 'the cat keeper' as she was known in the village, studied me with an arched brow before leaning closer. "No sea food cravings for the two of you tonight, I take it?" she asked.

So news of our little dinner date had made the rounds in the village gossip. I merely smiled and shrugged, determined not to give in. Everyone who asked was simply fishing around to determine how serious the two of us were — and they probably thought my polite or vague answers were merely being coy.

I wish they wouldn't ask — at least until we're both on the same page for sure, I thought. I felt a twinge of longing as I pictured myself finally being open about my feelings for Matt. With him, at least. That would be a start.

Tell him, a voice seemed to urge. What's the worst that could happen? But I knew what, feeling a shiver at the thought of driving him away with a sudden declaration of love. Well, not *that* sudden, but everyone has different timing. What if Matt felt I was rushing him after a handful of dates and kisses? What if I panicked as soon as I told him and wished I had waited? I didn't want to blow this, with everything going so well between us.

Such anxious thoughts were forced aside for the usual small talk. Rosie was telling someone who stopped by our table about the basket of tuxedo kittens someone had left on the shelter doorstep that week, and Susan was pondering whether a kitten was an appropriate gift for her niece. Matt was chatting with Clive about how to winterize Cornish Palms, and Andy and Gemma were arguing over which of them would get more answers correct for tonight's quiz.

"It won't be all Marvel movies," said Gemma. "There's bound to be a few chick flicks in the lot."

"When's the last big box office smash been a *chick* film?" retorted Andy. But I was only half-listening to them, because I was busy watching Matt, and trying to untangle the quandary that surrounded us as a couple.

Around seven o'clock, the quizmaster took the floor, and Matt gave me a subtle wink across the table, which I just as subtly returned. It was down to business, with a series of musical-themed questions that put us safely in the lead, thanks to my Saturday afternoons with Aimee. I always knew that watching *Singin' in the Rain* over a hundred times would come in handy someday. But it was Andy's fondness for time travel movies that proved a lifesaver in the second round.

The end of round two found us hanging onto that first place, just barely, and round three found us beaten by a group of senior-age women, who raised their mugs in a triumphant toast for the final score tally. The prize, appropriately enough, was a set of cinema discount coupons.

"You almost got us those, Julianne," said Andy, with a mournful shake of the head.

"I guess my knowledge of John Hughes' comedies wasn't as strong as I thought," I quipped, since the last few questions on the director had left us stumped. "Still," I said, "Rosie knew almost as many answers as me. Maybe a few more really," I said, glancing at the animal lover, whose smile was one of quiet satisfaction.

"Yeah, Rosie," said Andy, tipping his bottle in her direction, "how'd you get to be such an expert on American cinema then?"

Rosie merely shrugged. "Dated an American bloke once, I suppose."

This set off a chorus of 'ooohs' from the other women at the table, so apparently this was not common knowledge in Ceffylgwyn. "What?" Rosie asked, glancing round at us. "Don't be acting so surprised now. I wasn't a crazy cat lady me whole life, you know. I had quite the adventurous side back in my university days."

"I think it's lovely," said Gemma, a dreamy look in her eye. "The stranger from foreign shores that sweeps in to steal your heart." Beside her, Andy looked decidedly less charmed by this idea.

"I don't know about that," said Rosie, laughing. "He was a looker, though. Tall and athletic with a pair of cheek bones you could cut your steak with. And he was me last great chance at romance, before I moved to this hole-in-the-wall village," she said, with a grin that was only half-joking. So maybe being a middle-age cat lady was a second choice for Rosie.

"You've a point there." Susan shook her head. "I had to go all the way to Falmouth to find my own happiness. It's not a home to many eligible bachelors, our Ceffylgwyn. Especially when Julianne here has already hooked the most desirable catch in the pond."

"A nice bit of angling that was, Julianne," agreed Rosie, with a wink in my direction.

Matt was talking to someone at the next table, having taken a moment to stretch his legs, and hadn't heard this comment. I was sure discomfort was etched on my face in the form of a fiery blush. Fishing metaphors were not a good choice for my relationship with Matt and seemed particularly ill-timed, given the thoughts I'd been having this evening. The image of me trapping him like a fish with a hook…not good. And it made me tread carefully when answering.

My weak laugh didn't fix things. "That's hardly true is it?' I said. "I mean, Matt and I — we're just spending some time together. We're really still friends, mostly. We're seeing where things go."

But friends didn't exchange the kind of kisses Matt and I had recently, did they? Deep inside, I knew this was true.

"Friends," Rosie scoffed. "That's a lot of rubbish now, isn't it? Don't think you have to keep it a secret from us, or that we'll hold it against you, sweeping in and stealing that handsome bloke from us." She glanced at Gemma. "Tell her it's no use to argue the truth."

I looked at Gemma, hoping she would let this subject go. "Really, there's nothing to say," I insisted. "Trust me, I'm not trying to romance Matt into a corner or anything like that."

That was when I realized Matt was looking right at me as I said these words. His dark eyes held a look I couldn't quite identify, but my mind instantly leaped to guilt and hurt without reason. No one bothered to reply to me, because they were all talking about something else now. Luckily for me, Andy chose that moment to start telling a story about a Cornish wrestling match he'd attended last year.

"I think I'll have a pint," said Matt. He offered a polite smile to our group as he excused himself — I felt as if he barely glanced at me — before he turned and headed towards the crowd at the bar.

Great. Just perfect. He probably thought I had disowned our relationship in front of our friends, that I was just toying with him all these months. What had I been thinking, brushing off the idea of a romance between Matt and I? As if he would suspect me of making mountains out of molehills by confessing that I felt something for him, after those passionate kisses? *You weren't thinking, you were panicking. And now Matt thinks...oh, who knows what Matt thinks.*

But I had to find out, and the sooner the better. Resisting the urge to follow him immediately, I waited for a discreet moment to pass before I left our table. Matt was near the end of the bar, where his pint was only now being filled and set before him. A dark amber liquid that took on a hazy glow in the light from the Christmas bulbs overhead.

"Not thirsty?" I asked, moving next to him. My smile feeling a tad meek as I waited for him to say something in response.

"Merely giving myself a moment for thought," he answered.

“Get you something, Julianne?” The bartender, Pete, had noticed me there, his smile one of expectation.

“A hot chocolate,” I said quickly, wishing I had a more private place for this discussion. But I couldn’t suggest we leave just yet, so this would have to do. Pushing aside the steaming mug that Pete delivered a moment later, I steeled myself for explanation.

“Matt,” I began, quietly, “I’m sorry about what I said at the table a minute ago. I was just feeling a bit cornered and I …well, sort of panicked, I guess. It wasn’t what I meant to say at all. I didn't mean it."

He looked at me. "Didn't mean what?" He looked puzzled.

Oh. Rats. He hadn't heard a word I said at the table. I felt my face grow hot. "Um, I — I thought you — I thought you got the wrong impression."

"Wrong impression of what?"

I was in this conversation now, whether I wanted to be or not. *Might as well take your chance, Julianne,* I thought, desperately. *Looks like this is your moment after all.*

"What I said back there, about not wanting to force things between us, was true ... but it didn't mean I didn't want a romance with you. I do. Really. I only wanted them to see that I wasn't rushing it.”

He looked at me again. A definite, pointed look that made me shiver, despite the pub’s warm and toasty atmosphere. “Are you sure, Julianne?” he asked. Not skeptically, but earnestly. "There's no reason you would want to think about ... us ... a little longer?" Quietly, his eyes searching my face for the answer.

My stomach seemed to twist, the noise around us fading to a dull hum. *Was he uncertain? Was he thinking that I'm not the one for him?* "What doubts would you think I had?"

Matt was hesitating. "We haven’t known each other very long. Not by some people’s standards," he said. "I wouldn't be angry if you thought that weeks aren't enough to build a true flame. Disappointed — for reasons I think are fairly obvious, given what's happened between us. But not angry.”

Something about the way he said it made me think that 'disappointed' was Matt's substitute for a stronger emotion. It was the look in his eyes when he said the word, before he looked away.

I cringed at the word ‘doubts,' imagining he believed that's why I might hold back. Doubts that we could be more than what we were at the moment.

Doubtful I was not, and no matter what came of it, I wanted him to understand how I felt. *Here goes nothing*, I thought, without need of a pint to brace my nerves.

"No," I said, the word carrying a firm edge. "No doubts. Not about you." His brows went up, and I immediately lowered my voice. "Not about how much I enjoy being with you," I continued, softly. "How close we've grown lately and how I'm—"

I almost said it. Almost said, 'I'm falling in love with you' right there in the middle of the village pub. But the noise of our fellow patrons, the loud guffaws that echoed suddenly from a group of rowdy construction crew members two tables away, caused me to hesitate a fraction of a second about the here-and-now stance I was taking to declare my love for Matthew — right in the middle of someone else's crude punch line about a Cornish farmer and a fish wife.

I could see that Matt was waiting for my next words, but any chance of my finishing them was put on hold by another patron joining our end of the bar. The elderly gentleman known as Old Ned among the locals, his status as a fixture at the Fisherman's Rest all but legendary in the village. He was there nearly every evening, and from what I observed in previous visits, spent a great deal of his time in hopes of getting one of his neighbors to buy him a round at the bar.

Sitting down on the vacant stool beside us, he offered Matt and me a doleful greeting. "We'll be havin' a harsh winter, then," he said, with an air that indicated this was the opening of a much longer observation on the climate and weather patterns of Ceffylgwyn.

"How's that then, Ned?" Matt tore his glance away from mine and was indulging Ned's comment. A moment later, I could see a wry smile growing at the corner of Matt's mouth as his eyes met mine in mutual surrender. With despair, I could feel my chances to fix this conversation slipping away, as Ned continued.

"The holly berries, lad. Up above us on the mirror there," he said, with a nod to the garland surrounding the antique looking glass that hung above the shelves of bottles. "Bright and red as can be, aren't they? That means a bitter cold is on its way this winter. Ice and maybe even some snow, though snow's a rare sight indeed."

“Snow for Christmas might be nice,” I said, still looking at Matt as I spoke, my lips moving automatically, with words that had nothing to do with what was in my head. In my eyes, I hoped he could read an apology for our unfinished conversation. If only I could be sure he understood what I had been planning to say.

From his seat at the bar, Old Ned gave a melancholy sigh.

“Now the February of my sixteenth year *that* was as harsh a winter as any I’ve ever seen," he began. "Snowed something fierce and broke through the roof of the old school house. Brought down many a good tree on me dad’s old farm, too. We’ll not be seein the likes of that winter again soon.”

"Maybe so," said Matt. "I fancy there's some around here who wouldn't mind a touch of white at Christmas. Reminds them of home." He was still looking at me, and neither of us was making the slightest move to look away. I felt him take my hand, and felt relief that if nothing else, Matt understood that I hadn't been trying to get rid of him.

Ned sighed again. “What’s that in your glass there, lad?" he asked Matt. "A bit o’ rum perhaps? I could do with a touch of something strong to warm me up on a night like this….”

***

I was still kicking myself for not finishing that sentence at the pub. The rest of the evening had flown by, and our group of friends broke apart shortly after Matt and I extracted ourselves from Old Ned at the bar—Matt’s pocket missing a few coins more as a result. The drive home was all too short, our conversation consisting mostly of the floral arrangements for the charity ball. Matt had agreed we should meet at the hothouse to go over possible selections. None of it had been about what either of us were feeling, and whether we were taking our relationship to a more serious step. Such as me calling Matt my 'boyfriend' in public, and not just secretly in my head whenever I watched him trimming hedges at Cliffs House.

First, though, I had a meeting in London with Dwight and his friends, who sounded really anxious to escape their dilemma. Of course, I hadn’t told Matt about it yet, or about an old flame of mine moving to London. Now seemed like a bad time for bringing it up.

Dwight had arranged for us to meet in one of the conference rooms at the firm where he worked in Westminster. I had been to this part of London several times now, taking in the landmarks from Big Ben to the Royal Opera House. It had a palpable feel of excitement, this constant motion and hum of thousands of people in one place. A different world from Ceffylgwyn, to be sure, but not so different from Seattle.

Normally, I would be happy to lose myself in the shops, but today was about work, not pleasure. I was doing a favor for someone and needed to be amicable, polite, and on time to prove there were no hard feelings between me and Dwight now.

The bride and groom were younger than I expected: the bride was still at university, and the groom was an intern at the company Dwight worked for. Dwight introduced us in the conference room, where posh chairs and an armless sofa stood against a glass wall that overlooked the busy street below.

"Coffee, Julianne?" he asked, reaching for a phone on the nearby table. "Water or tea, if you prefer."

"Nothing, thanks." I still didn't feel quite right about this somehow, even though I wasn't exactly shirking any of my duties at Cliffs House to be here. Things with Matt must have me on edge, perhaps, making me feel more restless than usual.

"We're just so relieved you could fit us in," said the bride, whose name was Daphne. She was petite and slender, with dark locks that were cut in a fashionable pixie style that made me wonder if Susan didn't have a point about my hair after all. Her clothes were equally chic, with designer jeans, a spotless white cardigan, and a pair of diamond stud earrings that could only be genuine.

She seemed a little bit nervous, constantly fiddling with the pair of designer sunglasses she held in her lap. I warmed to her instantly, as well as the groom, a shy sort named Benjamin, whose face was freckled beneath a shock of auburn hair.

"We've been so worried," he explained, taking his fiancée's hand as they sat on the sofa across from my chair. "Christmas is a busy time for our families as it is, you see. Having this mix-up with the wedding agency has been rather stressful for all of us."

"Let's see if we can't sort it out," I said, putting on a reassuring smile. "I'm sure I can take care of a few things left on your list."

As Dwight had promised, much of the work had already been done for the ceremony. Leafing through the wedding portfolio, I was relieved to see the bridal couple had very definite ideas of what they wanted: a ceremony in the colors of silver and blue for a modern but tasteful Christmas theme, with orchids for the bouquet and blue roses and white lilies for the table centerpieces at the reception. The bride's dress had already been commissioned from a designer in Paris. Two of the biggest obstacles were already handled, albeit pricey ones. I wondered how an intern and a student could afford this extravagant wedding — short of paying off charge cards for the next twenty years, of course.

"This is very impressive," I told them, refraining from comment on its extravagance. "And it shouldn't be hard for me to follow this plan at all. It looks like your previous planner just hadn't confirmed some of your reservations...or helped you choose a caterer."

They both relaxed in response. Having been dumped by their previous wedding planner, they were probably apprehensive about trusting someone else — even someone whose services were being volunteered for free. "Very chic and elegant," I continued, closing the book on my lap. "So let's talk about the caterer first."

"We've had some trouble agreeing on that choice," admitted the bride. "I wanted something rather simpler, but Benjamin—" with a glance at her soon-to-be-husband "—thinks it should be a formal dinner rather than champagne and hors d'oeuvres. But a dinner seems a bit much this late in the season. I mean, it's already practically Christmas, isn't it?"

"I think either choice works," said Dwight. "I'll bet Julianne has some good ideas on this issue. Maybe some contacts in the city who could offer you a great deal, too."

Thinking practically when it came to their budget, I noticed. I sensed this was an area of contention between the couple, maybe: of practicality versus pride. Maybe Benjamin was the one in favor of having a showy wedding with lots of flowers and a towering cake, no matter the expense.

"Why don't we go over the types of foods each of you have in mind?" I suggested, pulling a sketch pad and pencil from my shoulder bag. "I think we can find a compromise on paper."

By the time our meeting was over, we had covered several possibilities for the reception food, including a platter of beef tenderloin sliced thin, rolled into finger-size pieces with a mustard sauce garnish that would surely resemble a meal despite appetizer servings; and finger foods ranging from asparagus tips in hollandaise to chocolate truffles frosted to resemble mercury glass Christmas balls in the wedding's colors of silver and blue.

That last idea was mine, and the happy couple had deemed it perfect, especially as a wedding favor for their guests in lieu of the old-fashioned "cake slice." I arranged to email them a list of suggestions for caterers who were skilled enough to provide this menu — and known to discount large packages — then to contact the top three for price negotiations once they had narrowed it down. I promised to negotiate the best price possible from their choice. After all, the groom was only an intern, the bride a student — wanting to impress their family with beef tenderloin in *any* size slice wouldn't be cheap, I knew.

“You were brilliant back there,” Dwight told me, as we walked through the lobby afterwards. “Really, Julianne, Design a Dream didn't appreciate what they had."

I blushed and rolled my eyes. "Thanks," I said. "Maybe I should drop my old boss a taunting letter, listing all my accomplishments. She'll beg me to come back."

"You should think about doing this freelance,” said Dwight. “You could charge thousands for that kind of insight. I'm a consultant. I could help you set it up, make it possible. And all at the discount I reserve for friends when I consult.”

Friends. That word to describe us felt slightly weird, I decided. Maybe I wasn't quite ready to forget all of our relationship's bitter moments after all.

“No, thanks," I answered, smiling. "Freelance doesn't suit me as well as being part of Cliffs House full time. Even the promise of thousands wouldn't lure me away.”

“I can see that.” He smiled. At the lobby doors, he stopped me with a hand on my arm. “Let me buy you an early lunch,” he said. “In thanks for salvaging my friends' wedding.”

“Oh…” I glanced at the time on my phone. “There's no need for you to do that, really,” I answered. “I know you must be busy and I should really be getting back to Ceffylgwyn.”

“Even busy people have to eat,” he remarked, with a persuasive grin. “Why not, Julianne? For old times' sake. A quick bite is all I'm suggesting. There's a charming fish and chips shop about a block from here. What do you say?"

"All right," I said. After all, fish and chips was a quick meal, as he said, and there was nothing remotely romantic about splitting it with an old-flame-turned-ex, except to maybe the wildest imaginations in Ceffylgwyn's gossip circle. There would still be plenty of time for me to catch a train back to Cornwall, especially since the train would probably be late. This I had learned the hard way from using public transportation regularly.

"Are you living at Cliffs House, then?" Dwight asked. He was seated across from me at a table by the window. The shop was crowded with hungry customers, but Dwight and I had been fortunate enough to nab a table shortly after we walked through the door.

"I'm living there for now," I explained, pulling a piece of fish from the basket between us. "It's difficult to find a place for rent near Ceffylgwyn—at least for reasonable rates. Lord William and Lady Amanda have been incredibly gracious, though, letting me stay until a good accommodation becomes available."

"They sound like perfect employers," he mused.

"They are. It's the best position I've ever had." My cheeks colored slightly, thinking of one particular reason I was so happy at Cliffs House. One I didn't feel like discussing with my ex. "So," I began, clearing my throat, "how does London suit you?"

"It's great," he said, reaching for his cup of coffee. "In fact, better than Seattle at times. It's hip, it's modern, but there's a kind of dignity about it. Not the sleepy, quiet atmosphere one pictures so much of the time when hearing about England," he added, sipping his coffee with a smile.

Meaning a village like Ceffylgwyn, presumably.

When Dwight and I had been together in Seattle, his love of the city had been obvious. Of the two of us, he was the virtual addict to convenience — takeout delivery, valet parking, ATMs — while I was the one who was always out of patience with public transportation, long lines, and 'out of order' signs on elevators and escalators.

Then again, I was the only one of us who had to make my way everywhere by bus or by foot, since Dwight owned a car. Until after we broke up, I never thought about the fact he never offered to go a little out of his way to give me a lift to work, or to run errands on my day off, as if

I liked the harassment of foot traffic and broken crosswalk signals.

He seemed to guess my thoughts. “Clearly village life agrees with you, Julianne. Convenient locale, a slower pace of life. You used to hate Seattle sometimes, remember? All those times you complained about the smog, and the rain, and how every coffee shop had about a billion customers?"

"Sure," I answered. "Not that I didn't like Seattle. Just not the inconveniences, sometimes."

"You look as fantastic now as you did in that red gown the other night," said Dwight. "Coming here has obviously been amazing for you. I've never seen you look so content. Like there's this glow about you or something."

There was the old smile that I remembered well from our time together, and it made it easier to remember why I had once been attracted to him. The rainy day movies we shared, the waffle lunches at my place on Saturday afternoons...those were better memories of our time together than ones of Dwight's underlying insensitivity towards others.

“What about the yacht club?” I asked. “You must have hated to leave it for your job transfer.” This was a good, safe subject, even thought it was tied to several disagreements that Dwight and I had over Saturdays spent on his boat, painting or cleaning it, or taking it out for a practice sail on a blazing hot afternoon before an upcoming match.

“Oh, I can sail over here just as easily,” he replied, breaking a chip in half. “You probably see a lot of that activity in …Kettlegwyn was it?”

“Ceffylgwyn,” I answered. “And yes. Lots of boats on the water.”

I hadn't been out to sea yet in Cornwall, not even with the most seasoned of sailors among the village population. I shivered, imagining a cold, choppy sail in the Channel, me huddled in a parka against salt sprays and a cutting wind; then shuddered, thinking of being on the water for the winter storm Matt and I had witnessed.

“Made a lot of friends there yet?” he asked.

“A few,” I answered, shrugging my shoulders. “They’ve adopted me into euchre circle and quiz nights, that is.”

He laughed at this, but not in a bad way, I hoped. I knew quiz nights and card games wouldn't be Dwight’s idea of a burgeoning social life; no doubt he was picturing me surrounded by a lot of little old ladies, hopeless spinsters, and middle-age couples desperate for a night away from the kids. He hadn't even liked our weekly Bunko-and-wine tasting with his two closest friends.

"Speaking of friends," I said, "Daphne and Benjamin seemed a little different from your usual choice." They were much younger than Dwight, for starters, and I couldn't imagine him choosing an intern as his closest pal in an office full of mid-level executives with sailboats and golf games. "Have you known them for long?"

"No, but they're good kids," he said. "Benjamin has a lot of promise at the company, so we'll be working together in the future, I'm sure. I just wanted to step in and help, since their big day was at stake. Not to mention their Christmas. "

"That's nice of you," I said. Aware that my eyes had softened with the words, in response to the sparkle in his own. Maybe the move to London had been good for Dwight after all. Maybe it changed his priorities and his attitudes in a way that our relationship — and breakup — would never have done.

"Rats, I'm going to be late!" I said, sneaking a peek at my phone's clock. "I have a meeting with someone later today about flower arrangements for the ball." I wished I was making this up, but I wasn't, since the next train probably wouldn't get me back to Ceffylgwyn before my appointment.

It wasn't just 'someone' I was late in meeting, but Matt. And that was enough to hurry me to the station in a London cab traveling faster than my usual comfort speed.

***

"A wedding in London? Isn't that a bit much to handle, given your work on the charity ball?" asked Matt.

Matt was in the greenhouse working when I arrived for our meeting late that afternoon. A long, glass structure with rows of potted plants, trees, rose bushes, and bulbs, it was heavily infused with the smell of potting soil and wet earth. I found it to be overwhelming at times, but Matt was clearly at home there, from the dirt under his nails to the stains on the knees of his corduroy trousers. At the moment, he was overwintering some flower bulbs that had been deemed too delicate to stay in the ground, moving them into a crate where he layered them with vermiculite.

"It's not a big deal," I answered, thinking of the ease of the meeting that morning, and of making a few simple persuasive phone calls on behalf of Daphne and Benjamin. "Just a few catering issues and some last-minute touches. Nothing your average event planner couldn't handle in their sleep."

"I see." Matt dusted off his clothes, bits of vermiculite clinging to the sleeves of his pullover. "I'm sure you know what you're comfortable handling — and I'm sure you don't want to let your friend down, either."

There was a pause on my part. Now was the time for complete honesty. "Dwight wasn't exactly a friend," I said. "That is, we sort of dated for a while back in Seattle. Not for very long though — and it's been over a year ago since I spoke to him even. So you could say ... technically ... he's sort of like my ex-boyfriend."

My ex-boyfriend, whom I don't really like. Will never, ever like again. That's the important part about this, Matt, in case you're wondering, I thought.

Matt listened without speaking. He looked thoughtful, but not cheerful — I wondered if it had been a big mistake, calling Dwight a 'friend' in the first place, even if we were much more amicable here in Cornwall than in Seattle.

"You can imagine how surprised I was to see him at Cliffs House," I continued. "Of course, there's absolutely no spark between us now. We're not bitter about breaking up or anything — just, you know, being polite acquaintances."

Matt's hands rested on the crate of flower bulbs. "It must have been an amicable breakup for you to be helping him in this way," he said.

"It was," I said. It hadn't exactly been a pleasant goodbye between us, but how many actually were? "We were both ready to move on," I continued. "It wasn't a long relationship. We weren't ever even friends, really. Friendship makes the difference."

This was how I had chosen over time to interpret that experience, although it wasn't based on anything Dwight and I had said in our split outside a Seattle coffee house.

"Friendship does make the difference," agreed Matt. In his voice, the familiar spark of playfulness, matching the twinkle in his eye when he looked at me. I felt the pleasant reaction of butterflies released inside me.

“About the other night, Matt," I said, softly. "I didn’t mean to —”

“Julianne, don’t feel you have to explain,” he said. “I know that Rosie can be a little too inquisitive. I’m sure that you had good reason for whatever you said, so let’s just forget it, shall we?”

“I just wish it had gone differently,” I told him. I was not, repeat, *not* ready to forget about it, not without breaking the final boundary down. “It seemed like it ruined the whole evening for us.”

“There will be other evenings,” he promised. Smiling as he moved the crate of flower bulbs aside temporarily.

"For what? Quizzes on *American Bandstand* and the Presidents?" I asked. "No, that's not what I mean, Matt —"

"I meant for the two of us to talk about something more important," he answered. "For instance, how we both feel ... and what we both want. If neither of us has doubts about the other, it means something. And it's time we should decide exactly what."

"Oh." His words had left me speechless. "Oh ... well, that's exactly what I meant."

We could talk about it here and now, despite the earthy, leaf-mold smell of the hothouse, and the presence of dirt-covered tulip bulbs all over Matt's work table. I took a step towards him, then heard the trill of my phone.

"Hello?"

It was Lady Amanda. "Have you talked to Matt about the centerpieces?" she asked. "I've had this lovely idea about little Japanese paper flowers folded in Christmas print —"

When this conversation was finished, I was fairly sure the moment between me and Matt had passed. At least, Matt's cheerful whistling and genuine interest in inspecting the bulbs' condition didn't leave me with much room for steering the subject back to serious romance.

"That was Lady Amanda," I said. "Worried about the flowers for the ball."

“We should discuss those flower selections now, before time slips away and Dinah wonders why your place is empty at the dinner table,” Matt said, setting aside his last box of bulbs.

“Right,” I said, switching my brain back to work mode. Which was not an easy task with Matt before me, looking handsome in his faded pullover and trousers, his dark, unruly mane falling across his face as he bent over a sketch, in a way that made me want to brush it back again.

Normally, we tried to keep things professional at work; but the close quarters of the greenhouse made it difficult, with every accidental touch reminding us of all the purposeful ones we had started to allow in our moments alone together. He caught my eye, and I felt my cheeks burn scarlet. My hand brushed his when I retrieved my sketch, and felt the slightest tremble from his fingers in response.

But, as always, we kept on with our work. Much to my disappointment.

I cleared my throat. "I know we agreed on poinsettias alternated with amaryllis, and I still think it's a perfect combination, *but—*" and I could see his wry smile appear as he waited for this caveat, "—I'm starting to wonder if we should mix in some white lilies or roses even. Something simple but elegant to provide a nice foil to the bolder shades of red."

"It might be possible," said Matt. "Let me take an inventory on the lilies again, see if there's enough promising blossoms to make it work. Roses, I'm afraid, are out of the question. As you can see, most of them have already bloomed once this December, and those that haven't are just now starting their first buds." He gestured towards the hothouse's collection, all enjoying their warm environment. "I wouldn't trust myself to coax enough of them into healthy blossoms in time for your big event. You'd need a florist's help for that."

I could see the various roses potted along the wall behind him, both climbers and beautiful tea roses. Green, healthy canes were a lovely sight, even without colorful blossoms to adorn them.

"Which one is your special patient?" I asked. "The one Lord William discovered languishing on its own?"

"Ah, that one," said Matt. With a fond smile, he pointed out the rose we'd been speaking of at dinner a few nights ago.

My attention zoned in on the rare antique one Matt had rescued from neglect and certain death. It was smaller than the others, and its bare canes were struggling to put on new growth.

"Look how beautiful it is now." I bent down to study the delicate buds that were forming in shades of pinkish red. Leaf buds, I noticed — but maybe one or two were actual roses. "Will it be scarlet when it blooms? Or is it a shade of pink when its buds finally open?"

"It will have to be a surprise," he replied, crouching beside me to admire the plant in its newfound health. "I'm not entirely sure what breed we're dealing with — I can only hazard a guess. And one this delicate —" he touched one of the limbs, lightly, near what I felt sure was an actual flower bud, " — it needs all the help it can get if we want to see its colors."

I glanced at his face as he spoke, seeing the pride and satisfaction for the fruit of his labors. The rose that hadn't bloomed for decades was going to make its comeback in time for Christmas, maybe even with blooms. A tiny miracle of gardening that Matt had somehow orchestrated, thanks to his brilliant skills in botany and horticulture.

"You should document its progress for your lecture in the spring," I teased, rising to my feet. "Give a lecture on rescuing stray roses to the Ivy League students." We were back at Matthew's work table, its surface crowded with bags of potting soil and empty plant containers.

A funny look crossed Matt's face, and my smile dimmed in response. "What is it, Matt?" I asked. "Did something happen with the lecture?"

"Not exactly," Matt answered. He looked slightly hesitant, picking up a spool of garden twine from the table, winding the loose cord around it. "Truthfully, I heard from the university again this week. It seems you're a bit psychic, Julianne. They've had a last-minute opening in their botany department, and they've offered me a teaching position for the spring term."

A teaching job in Massachusetts. I shouldn't be surprised, but I was — as if the conversation we had at dinner a few nights ago had summoned this into being. I wasn't sure what to say.

"That's wise of them," I said. "They definitely have excellent judgment when it comes to choosing faculty. They must regret letting you slip away before."

So maybe Matt's conversation about our future would be different than I pictured it. The hazards of long-distance relationships loomed before us, suddenly, and I wasn't sure I was prepared for it. If I thought about it very long, I felt as if the breath would be sucked from my lungs.

He shook his head. "They were simply surprised I hadn't been employed by another university somewhere in England," he said. "And, no, they hadn't been thrilled when I left before, of course. It was sudden, to say the least. And in their eyes — and mine, until Petal's departure — it had been going extremely well."

“What did you tell them?” I asked. My heart was hammering in my ears as I waited for his answer to emerge. I watched Matt standing across from me in the glass house of plants, while the late afternoon sunlight filtered through the panes above us. Suddenly I was imagining I might not see him like this again for a long time. Maybe not ever again.

Stop being silly. He hasn't said 'yes' yet. And even if he does, that won't mean the end of everything, will it?

“I told them I would have to think about it,” he said. He glanced at me, as if trying to gauge what I was thinking.

"You should," I said. "Of course. It's a great opportunity. And I'll bet you were great at it before." I knew he was probably a brilliant professor. I imagined his students probably loved him — and probably half the girls in his classes had crushes on him.

“Of course, it’s not as if I could actually accept it, not with such last-minute notice. But I could hardly tell them ‘no’ right away either, without giving it thorough consideration. It’s a matter of courtesy, I guess.”

His laugh was slight for this explanation. I sensed he was uncomfortable, sharing this truth. He didn't have to tell me that a part of him wanted to do it, at least a little.

If that's what he wanted, I wanted it for him. But the thought of losing him stung deeply. Distance made relationships hard. An ocean would separate the two of us, who had never even said the three magic words that would keep us together. And what made it worse was the fact that I was actually *in* love with him now, whether he knew it or not.

But I couldn’t live with myself if he made his choice for any reason other than his happiness. Even for mine.

“Don't dismiss this so quickly,” I said. “Take your time. Because if you want to go back, you don't want to regret missing your chance.” I bit my lip, but managed to force my expression into a smile a second later. *Please don’t regret saying that, Julianne.*

I touched his hand as I spoke, stroking the skin browned by the summer's sun. I felt his fingers cover mine for a moment, squeezing them tightly. The strength of it surprised me, given how mild our conversation was about his leaving and me staying behind.

He released my hand, and set aside the roll of twine inside a box of gardening tools. “Perhaps so," he said "But it would be difficult for me to go now, you realize. Leaving Cornwall behind with all her beauty.

Leaving everything behind that has come to mean so much. Other sources of beauty." His smile flickered to life again, his glance meeting mine for a moment. I knew he wasn't thinking of the Heligan Garden's Mud Maiden with these words.

"You've done it before," I said. "And you've come back. Everything was fine."

"That's true," he answered. "That I have done it before. But that was before I knew you, Julianne Morgen."

The warmth in his voice and his eyes was almost too much for me. I could kiss him right now, I decided — if only I felt it wasn't so horribly out of place while we were talking about being apart for months. Maybe a year, even.

Everything will be fine. Just keep telling yourself that, Julianne. He might not leave. Any worries or doubts might be for nothing a few short days from now.

"You don't want me to leave, do you?" he asked, quietly.

"No." My voice was slightly above a whisper, forcing me to make it stronger. "Of course not. But I want you to be happy ... and I don't want you to languish with only one antique rose's fate to keep you busy." This part was a little more joking than I really felt, but we needed to cut the tension of this moment. At least while Matthew's decision was just that — a decision.

"So you're willing to shove me off to Massachusetts now this bloke from your past has shown up?" Matt asked. He, too, was trying to joke; but I thought I detected a shred of snark in the question.

Was he a little jealous of Dwight? I felt a little pleased by this, even though I didn't want anything to come between Matt and myself. As if there was anything to fear from the presence of an ex who had the indecency to call me two weeks after breaking up to see if I'd return his rental DVDs for him, while I was still in my alone-and-pouting phase of recovery.

"No, of course not," I retorted. "If I wanted to be rid of you, I could find much more creative ways than that. Shove you off the cliffs ... or flirt with Ned at the pub one too many times."

"Would you now?"

"Not ever," I answered, shaking my head and laughing. "But promise me you'll think about what you want." My voice grew serious again. "I mean that. It's important for you to be happy." *Even if it means I'm not quite so happy as I have been these last few months.*

"I will," he said. "And you'll be the first to know my decision. I promise."

"Good," I said. But I could feel unhappiness welling up inside my chest. And when Matt laid his hand over mine again, I found myself leaning against him for a moment, my eyes closed. I felt his arms around me in a gentle hug. His arms tightened around me as I returned his embrace, and we stayed like that several minutes before he released me.

"Now then, what else can I do for you?" asked Matt, softly. "More last-minute flower requests for elaborate manor house events?"

"Nothing like that," I said. "Though you do owe me a plant. The one you promised to give me over a week ago? Something hearty and hard to kill, as you'll recall."

"Ah, yes," he said. "Come by Rosemoor and claim it any time you like. Let yourself in with the spare key if I'm not there — keys under the front pot, the plant's on the table near the door."

"Okay." I would infinitely prefer he was there, even though I felt almost at home any time in Matt's little cottage, with its tumbling gardens and crooked fence. I knew I had better savor every one of those moments while I still could — just in case, as impossible at it seemed, Matt really did choose Boston over Cornwall's shores.

***

"The ladies luncheon will be on the seventeenth and then, of course, we have a tour group in the diary for the twenty-first. A man will be in to clean the chimneys before then, and I believe the greenery for the ballroom will arrive on the twenty-third." Lady Amanda sighed. "Heavens, how will we do it all in time?"

This statement ended this list of impending activities from the diary on her office desk; my own planner was filled with notations of a similar nature. The smaller festivities leading up to Christmas Eve — then came the charity ball and the New Year's Day open house on its heels. I felt as if my head couldn't possibly hold any more details as I calculated the number of necessary tea sandwiches and truffles.

"The ladies luncheon will mean yet another tree, I'm afraid," Lady

Amanda said, "this one for the little sitting room near the ballroom. I've asked Geoff to bring it 'round later today. Don't worry, though — I won't ask you to make a paper chain this time," she added, her smile taking on an impish quality with the remark. "All modern ornaments in very sleek silver, to match the theme of 'Silver Years Holiday Goals.'"

"My chain *was* wretched," I admitted. "I had to redo it almost three times to make it presentable. Even then, I'm not sure a group of school age children couldn't have done it more justice."

"William didn't think so," Lady Amanda replied. "He told me it puts him in rather a nostalgic frame of mind. It makes him think of stories his grandmother told about Christmastime during the war, when a lot of people couldn't afford decorations from the shops, so almost everything was made by hand, even the presents. Quite a different Christmas from the one we're celebrating at the manor today."

Her voice was gentle for the remark, perhaps remembering a story from her own family history of those difficult times that rocked the world so many years ago. I knew that Britain's taste of World War II had been much harsher than that of my own grandparents in the United States.

"Very different," I said. "But it's good to remember the past."

"How are you managing with the holiday rush, by the way?" Lady Amanda studied me over her coffee mug with a keen eye. "Christmas at Cliffs House can be a chaotic time, as well as great fun. Believe me, this time last year, I was wishing for an event planner to help me cope with it all," she said, with a laugh. "Not knowing you yet, of course."

"I'm holding up great," I said. My voice lacked the enthusiasm I meant for it to have, however. It wasn't because of the work—everything was going right on schedule. It was more about Matt, and how unsettled everything felt between us. The little nagging voice in my head urged me to tell him, as if my love would sway his decision. And as if I'd be selfish enough to plead with him to stay — Matt, who would never dream of asking *me* to drop my career and Cornish experience to follow him back to the USA.

"Well, don't hesitate to come to me if you start to feel overwhelmed," Lady Amanda said. "I think you've already earned the right to a nice holiday somewhere next year. If we can find a way to do without you for a week or so," she quipped, setting her mug down on the nearby desk.

What would I do with a holiday? See more of Cornwall, perhaps.

Maybe visit The Lizard Peninsula, with all its rare and wonderful plants and insects. Or go spend a week in Mousehole, the village whose name had become a sort of inside joke for Matt and me after he learned the name of my birth town in Idaho was Molehill.

Mousehole would be fine with me, if Matt could be my guide there. But the chances that would happen suddenly seemed very slim compared to only a week ago in that candlelit restaurant.

Downstairs in the kitchen, Gemma was slicing strawberries as Dinah added the final dollop of whipped cream to the squares of sponge cake by the oven. From something Dinah had said earlier, it was meant to be a variation on a popular Japanese Christmas Cake. We had decided the hors d'oeuvres at the ball would pay tribute to its chief sponsor's cultural home. That meant platters of sushi and filled daikon radish curry boxes, sticky rice and shrimp balls, and squid and cucumber bites for the hors d'oeuvres, and a sake cocktail alongside the more traditional champagne.

"Shall we sample these for you Dinah?" Gemma asked, hopefully, as she eyed the latest batch of trial sponge cake desserts. They looked every bit as chic and metropolitan as the finger foods on Dinah's sampler platter. I had to admit the sight of them made my own stomach growl despite the sandwich and crisps I had for lunch.

"Go ahead then," said Dinah, untying her apron and giving a sigh of surrender. "Taste away and tell me what you think. And no lies out of politeness or heaven help our unsuspecting guests."

Gemma had washed her hands and was tugging her apron off already, her task of slicing strawberries at an end. "Try one, Julianne," she said, handing a square of sponge cake across the table as she pulled out the seat catty corner to mine.

"Mmmm, delicious looking." I popped the dessert appetizer in my mouth without a second's hesitation. Its texture was light and airy, the cream and strawberry blending perfectly for a just right sweetness that lingered in my mouth.

"These are scrumptious, Dinah," I declared, eating it down to the last crumb. "The guests will be snatching them up." I resisted the temptation to lick my fingers, too.

"They're not bad," she conceded, trying one from the platter on the counter. "Perhaps a bit overbaked, but that's easily remedied. A touch more sweetness wouldn't go amiss, though." A thoughtful frown on her face with these words.

Like most chefs, Dinah was harder on her work than it deserved. Gemma and I exchanged sly grins behind her back, both of us accustomed to hearing that some masterpiece of baking wasn't quite up to her standards. I would have gladly devoured half the platter, but I settled for just one more before I returned to my notes for the ballroom decorations set to arrive next week.

Pippa stuck her head through the doorway. "Geoff 's brought another fir tree for you, Julianne. A tall skinny one with branches out to there," she said, extending an arm to indicate the length.

"That'll be for the sitting room," I said, remembering Lady Amanda's instructions for the ladies luncheon. I kept forgetting it since Lady Amanda handled most of its details, preferring a hands-on approach to events involving our neighbors in Ceffylgwyn.

"He said he'd bring it 'round to the back entrance," Pippa informed me, still leaning in the doorway. "Ross came along to help," she added, giving me a knowing look.

My pulse quickened a little. Matt was in my thoughts way too often these days, but I couldn't seem to get rid of him there. He popped up every other second, as if Cliffs House and Cornwall were one big reminder of my secret feelings.

Geoff Weatherby was the estate manager for Lord William, a man of middle age and quiet charm from London. He was looking slightly overburdened by the long tree, even with Matt's help in maneuvering Cliffs House's hall.

"Bring it through to the sitting room, please," I said, leading the way to a lovely space down the hall near the ballroom, where double glass doors overlooked the terrace and garden beyond. Most of the plants were dormant at this point, but I could see a few blossoms from the winter varieties, and the scarlet red of the holly berries Old Ned had claimed were a sign of potential snow.

We positioned the tree in front of the glass doors, selecting an ornamental pot for it among the ones available on the terrace. Stepping back to admire the effect, I couldn't help saying, "This will be my third Christmas tree to help decorate this month."

"So many?" chuckled Geoff.

"I'm not tired of it, believe it or not," I assured him, as I carted the boxes of silver ornaments into the sitting room. "Actually, it's kind of relaxing." *When you don't have to construct a paper chain for it, that is.*

"As long as you enjoy it," said Geoff. "As for me, I have a little ornamental ceramic one that merely plugs into the wall. No decorations needed, I fear."

"I haven't bothered putting up a Christmas tree in years," Matthew said, adjusting the tree's upright angle. "Not since my sister's university years. She was rather the one who decorated it."

With his mother gone and his sister far away, I realized that Matt had fewer reasons than some people for observing the traditional festivities of the season. I felt sad, suddenly, at the thought of Matt spending Christmases alone while his sister was overseas, and no real holiday cheer at home.

"Did you hear that?" I glanced at Geoff with a smile. "How can a man this devoted to the world of fauna and flora *not* have a Christmas tree? It seems unfair that no one's given him one, doesn't it?"

"It's not that I don't want one," said Matt. "I just never had the time to put one up."

Beside him, Geoff chuckled mildly. "I'm afraid it's a lost cause sometimes, Miss Morgen," he said. "I say that as an equally-busy bachelor."

I crossed my arms. "That is just so incredibly sad. I had no idea men were this helpless on their own when it came to celebrating the season." In my mind, I was calculating how easy it would be to sneak a fir into Matt's cottage while he was busy in the hothouse. Or leave it on his porch like a Christmas tree foundling. How could he not be moved to take it inside and decorate it afterwards?

"One finds their consolation elsewhere," said Geoff. "In my case, the staff Christmas party at Cliffs House, for instance. Where Dinah's plum pudding is a treat that's fit to serve the Queen. A treat not to be missed, I assure you."

"Mmm," I said, politely, although I was still trying to balance the mouth-watering description of Gemma and Pippa versus the blazing bowling ball in Christmas movies. Was it really to die for? Or was it actually like a giant, scorched breadball with bits of fruit in it?

"Is there anything else we can do for you, Miss Morgen?" Matthew asked, affecting a serious air as he bowed. This was the first bit of silliness between us in awhile — almost like the beginning of our love-or-friendship's uncharted waters.

"Nothing at the moment, Mr. Rose," I answered, feigning equal loftiness. "You're dismissed."

Maybe I could ask Geoff if there was a spare tree or two on the estate that needed a good home this Christmas.

***

Dwight's friends had narrowed down my list of potential caterers to their top three, all of whom were located in Westminster. It would take a considerable part of the day to visit them all, so I decided to use my day off for my next expedition to London. I boarded the train early that morning with a finished reception seating chart that had taken me most of the night to complete, but I was sure would make both of them happy.

To my surprise, Dwight insisted on accompanying me to the caterers. "I'm afraid my conscience wouldn't let me rest, with you doing all the work," he said, as we descended to the Underground that would take us to the first caterer on the list. "I'm sure you have things you would rather do with your time than chase around London for the friends of a friend, after all."

"It's my day off," I explained, tucking my portfolio in my lap on the train. "You don't have to feel guilty about eating into my work time. And as you said before, they're two young people in need of help."

"So you're giving up your leisure time. That's still a sacrifice," he said. "Tell me, what would you be doing in Ceffylgwyn with a day like this? Are there lots of festive events for the holiday? You know, Christmas markets filled with cheap souvenirs and so on."

"Not really," I said. "There's Troyls' night, but that's a sort of cultural dance. I haven't been to one yet, but maybe I'll go if they have one for Christmas."

Gemma and Pippa had tried to educate me on this, where some of the villagers embraced tradition by dressing up in traditional tartan and kilts. Matt, they claimed, had done so in the past, although I wondered if this was more wishful thinking on their part than anything. I hadn't dared ask him yet, though I couldn't help being a little curious if it was true. Matt in a linen shirt and kilt made a very appealing picture.

No thinking about *that* right now, I scolded myself, wondering what kind of expression Dwight had seen on my face.

"Most of the time, things are very laid back in Ceffylgwyn," I continued, quickly. "The main attraction is quiz night at the pub. More than a hundred locals turn out to compete sometimes. My team almost won — a nice package on movie tickets was ours for the taking, if only we had brushed up on our comedies."

"Is there a movie house in this village of yours? I sort of pictured it being the library and Ye Old Medieval Museum type, with relics of the past and bored teenagers on every corner."

"Well, we would have to go to Truro to see one," I admitted reluctantly. "But it isn't that far, all things considered."

"How far is far?" he laughed. "In Seattle, you complained if the bus took more than fifteen minutes to reach your stop across town."

"That was different," I said. "It was hectic in Seattle, and I was nearly always running late — but here, people take their time. And it's only a short drive when me and M—when we go catch a new film." I finished this part without Matt's name. Chatting romance with an ex was never a great idea, I felt.

Dwight had caught my slip of the tongue, however. "Who is 'we'?" he said. "This mysterious 'M' you speak of. Someone special?"

I blushed, wishing I had been more careful. Still, now that I was caught, I decided to be honest about it. "Maybe someone a little more special than the others," I admitted. "He's a really great guy. Brilliant, kind, funny ... but we're still not quite a couple." At least, Matt hadn't said he loved me. Or that he was falling in love with me, even. I only knew that he cared about me, and that he found me attractive.

"Hmm," said Dwight, thoughtfully. "I'm surprised that it's not something more by now. A girl as perfect as you in a village that size. I thought there would be no end of dashing, rugby playing or cricket-loving 'chaps' who would ask you out."

I didn't like his tone for this remark. And I resented being metaphorically presented as a piece of meat in a hungry kennel of animals, as if Ceffylgwyn's female population was mostly eliminated from the menu by wrinkles, warts, and toothless mouths. I wrinkled my nose, and changed the subject.

"What about you? I heard you were serious about someone in

Spokane. Aimee said you were a good match." I pulled this piece of gossip from the recesses of my memory. Aimee had kept tabs on my ex long after I had stopped, mostly in hopes of delivering awful stories about Dwight, I knew — a gesture which never worked out, much to her disappointment.

"Not that good of a match, I'm afraid. We broke up after a couple months or so. After that, I didn't really have time for seeing anyone new. I think my last truly serious relationship was with you. Which shows how out of practice I must be," he admitted. "I guess there's probably a reason for that."

I could have pointed out plenty of reasons in the past, but now I was past that need, and wasn't certain all of it was true anymore. After all, time changes people. Maybe Dwight was as different now as I was. It hadn't completely been his fault we had broken up, anyway, as I had eventually admitted to myself.

I tried to conjure the pieces of me and Dwight's past together, mentally pasting them into a timeline. The first meeting at a mutual friend's birthday party; the weekends of rented movies, fast food pizza, and nights out with our group of friends. It had been brief, and some of it had been fun, but there had always been something missing between us. It had never felt completely right. Spending time with him was never as satisfying or fulfilling as I had wanted it to be.

It was different with Matt. With him, it felt the way it was supposed to be. With butterflies and secret glances, and a touch that had become its own language — everything I had dreamed about before. Everything I was about to lose, perhaps.

At our meeting, Dwight was more concerned with the catering negotiations than I was, insisting on all the special details Daphne and Benjamin loved most. He was devoted to making sure the price range fit the wedding budget, sticking to that point even when the caterer grew stubborn over the bottom price for his sliced tenderloin on toasted baguette bites. *He's practically their event planner at this moment, not me,* I thought. *He must really like them.*

By the time it was over, and we exited the shop, my feet were sore from my tall, Valentino pumps, and the tight pencil skirt I was wearing felt constricting each time I boarded the Underground. Dwight checked his watch as we stepped from the last shop to the sidewalk.

"What do you say to a real English afternoon tea?" he asked. "You know, the British thing. Take a break before calling Daphne and Benjamin to confirm their choice."

"I don't know," I said, hesitantly. "Isn't it sort of early for afternoon tea?" A peek at his watch had told me it was still nowhere near the traditional tea time—although I had heard that some London restaurants served these refreshments closer to lunchtime to accommodate tourists. This was hardly a tourist outing, though, and I was impatient to be back on the train home. It would give me some time to myself to rest. And maybe to come up with the perfect Christmas gift for Matt, which had been eluding me for days now.

"Come on, Juli," Dwight persisted. "I know the perfect place, not far from here. I don't know about you, but I'm starving."

"I'm sorry, Dwight," I said. "I had no idea it would take this long." Of course, he had volunteered to come, but I felt that I should have found a way to end the debate over prices more quickly, so we could have both salvaged this day for other things.

"Never mind," said Dwight. "The cakes and sandwiches should more than make up for it. What do you say?"

I was about to tell him that tea was probably not the best idea for me, when I saw something—or rather *someone*—that caused me to lose all train of thought.

Matt was here.

Dressed in a suit and overcoat, his silk tie a deep shade of crimson. His dark hair was tamed against the winter breeze, revealing the finely chiseled features beneath it. Matt was here in London, emerging from the Underground entrance and standing not ten away from us on the crowded sidewalk.

He saw me at the same moment, surprise lighting his dark eyes as they looked into mine.

"Hi," I said, somewhat breathless with amazement. "You didn't say you were coming to London today." I would have to explain Dwight in a moment, I realized — and that was something that didn't thrill me, given the status of Matt and I.

"There was a garden show at the university," Matt explained. "A lecture on propagating orchids, given by an old professor of mine. A few friends from university were there, so we had lunch together."

"That sounds great." I could feel Dwight watching us, no doubt observing the profound effect Matt's appearance had on me — changing my voice, my expression, making me flush whenever I looked into his eyes too long. It would be pretty obvious to anybody that this was the 'someone special' I had mentioned before.

I glanced to my right. "Matt, this is Dwight Bradshaw from Seattle," I said, gesturing to him. "He's an old friend of mine. The one whose friends are having trouble planning their wedding."

"A ghost from Julianne's past," Dwight told him, holding out his hand with a smile. "I think she's mentioned you a time or two."

"It was strange to see another face from Seattle across from me on Cornish soil," I supplied. To Dwight, I said, "Matt is a horticulturist and botanist and a friend of Lord Williams' from university. Right now, he's working at Cliffs House as a landscaping consultant."

"So the two of you are co-workers, then," Dwight said.

"Matt has been my saving grace since I moved overseas," I said. "He lived in the States for awhile, so he's good at putting up with my American quirks. And he's been the perfect guide, introducing me to the local customs and culture in Ceffylgwyn." I smiled at Matt.

"And all I had was an *A-Z London* guide for getting around my first few weeks," said Dwight.

Matt smiled at this joke. I could tell he was unsure what to think of Dwight, which was making me nervous somehow. As if Dwight might turn into an obnoxious American suddenly, who poked fun at Matt's accent and told stories about the cutesy things we used to do while dating.

Tucking my hands in my coat pockets, I searched my brain for something brilliant to say so I could escape any stories from the past. Instead, it was Dwight who spoke again.

"Julianne and I were just about to go to tea. I booked a table at The Golden Swan, a hotel not far from here. It's not exactly the Ritz, but it's a favorite with most of our clients. You're more than welcome to join us."

He had booked a table? Now it would be harder for me to turn him down. Nevertheless, I intended to, when, to my surprise, Matt turned to me and said, "Why not? I have the rest of the day free. If you're certain it won't interfere with your work—"

"Not at all," I said, quickly. There was no way I was going to tea alone with an old boyfriend while Matt went back to Cornwall on the next train.

"Let's split a cab then, shall we?" suggested Dwight.

The Golden Swan was every bit as beautiful as its name suggested. Marble columns flanked the entrance to a dining hall with gorgeous golden-yellow walls and glittering chandeliers. Exotic palm trees had been placed throughout the room in decorative pots, and a harpist provided musical ambiance in the form of lilting classical tunes.

My chair was across from Dwight's, with Matthew seated at my right. The table before us had been spread with a silver tea service and delicate gold-rimmed chinaware. A selection of sandwiches, scones, and biscuits were arranged on the tiered cake stand in the center of the table.

"This is amazing," I said, unable to help the gushing remark as I sampled the scrumptious treat from my plate. A golden baked scone with raspberry preserve and clotted cream that melted in my mouth. Pure heaven.

Matt looked slightly amused. "Better than Dinah's?" he asked, teasingly.

"Sorry," I murmured. "But I'm not being disloyal, I promise." I noticed cream was all over my fingers too. But I resisted the urge to lick them.

"Julianne makes your village sound nice and cozy," said Dwight, turning to Matthew. "She was telling me all about trivia night at the local pub. It sounds rather ... casual ... I have to admit."

"It is," said Matt. "The village doesn't have a lot of excitement, as I'm sure you must have guessed. It's a quiet place, but that's its charm."

"I got the idea," said Dwight, chuckling slightly. "Mind you, all I saw of it was a glimpse from the cab window. Though, it's starting to sound as if a glimpse is all it would take to see the highlights," he joked. "Maybe Julianne will show me around sometime."

"Dwight's more of a city dweller," I explained, feeling myself wince inwardly at his critique of the village. "He really loved Seattle." I remembered Dwight repressing a shudder whenever his hometown — one with a respectable population of a hundred thousand or so — was mentioned in his presence, as if it conjured horrible memories for him.

"You must prefer being in London, then," said Matt.

"London's fantastic," Dwight agreed, taking a scone from the tiered cake stand. "Though, I have to admit that I did find Cliffs House a promising little spot for a conference, perhaps. I'm going to recommend it to my boss for the next company retreat. A little R-and-R in the Cornish wilderness, and a stroll through those primitive gardens." He glanced at me. "Does its garden have those big mud sculptures that are so famous around here? I think I saw them once on *National Geographic* or something?"

"I'm afraid not at Cliffs House," said Matt. Whose tone was decidedly polite and cool.

When the conversation shifted to sailing, I was almost relieved. At least Dwight sounded friendly when he asked Matt for some recommendations on local sailing spots.

"Helford River in Falmouth is a popular choice," Matt said. "So is Fal River. If you're more experienced on the water, The Isles of Scilly have anchorages well worth visiting."

"Is that the place I've heard referred to as the English Caribbean?" I asked. Picturing glistening golden sand and crystal clear waters surrounding an atmosphere akin to the Bahamas.

Matt nodded. "It is. A very different side of England from what you've seen, but quite beautiful in its own way."

"You've sailed it before?" Dwight asked him.

"I've followed the route to Tresco once. It can be a fair bit more challenging than the rivers in Falmouth, though."

I pictured Matt on a boat. The breeze playing through his hair as he hoisted the sail, and steered the rudder through choppy waters. Maybe in an open shirt ruffled by the wind, a little manly afternoon stubble on his face, and a smile on his lips when he looked at me. Well, maybe it wouldn't be so bad to be sailing out on the Channel, even in winter. Myself snuggled in my parka, feeling a refreshing sea breeze against my face...and just like with the kilt scenario, I caught myself wandering into this fantasy and stopped it in time.

"Julianne here can vouch for my skills with a sail boat," said Dwight, calling me back to reality. "She helped me celebrate at least one of my victories with the SYC. Seattle Yacht Club, in case you've never heard of it. Remember that night?" he asked, turning to me again. "Champagne and a catered gourmet dinner beneath the stars on Teddy's long liner. There's nothing like eating on the water, I always say. Especially after a big victory."

"Sounds charming," said Matt. Blandly.

I was very glad when tea was over.

***

It hadn't been a disaster, but it could have gone better. That was how I thought of our tea, the three of us making conversation that seemed awkward and disconnected. Afterward, Matt had taken a train back to Truro while Dwight and I called on Daphne to review the winnowed to-do list before the ceremony.

"I'm sure I can handle the rest of this by phone," I said, glancing over my itinerary one more time. "After the caterers and the harpist, that just leaves the horse-drawn carriage. Are you sure about that one?" I asked Daphne. I felt worried about the pricey cost of that escort. I imagined the headache of bills for a young student-age couple when this was over and wished that they would rethink it before I booked anything. Already the harpist had demanded an extravagant rate, and the flower bill was tremendous.

"Oh, yes," said Daphne. "It's essential. I've always dreamed of one and Benjamin promised me. I really couldn't imagine my special day without it."

"All right," I said. "I'll call and arrange one." After all, it wasn't my business to argue, was it? Not after I'd made my professional point regarding their budget.

"See what I mean? She's brilliant, isn't she?" said Dwight to Daphne. "You're in the best hands possible for this wedding." Despite myself, I blushed as the two of them beamed at me.

Dwight's compliments kept coming as the two of us left Daphne's flat.

"You really are something, Julianne," he said, shaking his head. "No wonder Cliffs House stole you away."

I gave a modest shrug. "I was only too happy to be stolen, in that case." Anyone who had seen my resume before my role at the Cornish manor house would marvel at my ability to handle this level of responsibility. But I was doing it, and somehow, it was working. I just hadn't flexed those muscles at Design a Dream.

"You've been to London but didn't visit the shops?"

Pippa was scandalized I had returned without any kind of shopping bags from the boutiques. I was tempted to tell her it was work, not pleasure that took me there, but I hadn't really made the others privy to my favor for Dwight — mostly because it would mean explaining who Dwight was.

"I always have a peek inside Topshop at least," she continued, polishing the platter Dinah had laid out for serving the chocolate mousse on at dinner. "You must've done *your* holiday shopping already."

"I've done most of it," I said.

"Any hints at what might be under the tree for a certain girl who works here?"

"No way," I answered. "You'll have to wait until Christmas morning, like everyone else."

I had packages of gifts ready to mail to family members, and I had the staff's gifts wrapped and waiting for the big Christmas Day party. All except for Matthew. I had found nothing special, nothing personal enough for someone who mattered to me as much as he did.

But what would do? A rare plant? I would never know what one to choose. A gardening tool? I had no idea what kind of tools he might find useful in his gardening work. It needed to be something special, and I had yet to decide.

It came to me when I turned the corner in the main hall the next morning, lugging a box of brochures on having an 'Active Senior Christmas' to the sitting room for the ladies' luncheon. The Christmas tree with ornaments of red and white caught my eye. It was one of several green firs that Lord William had either felled or dug up this season for decorating Cliffs House and other parts of the community.

Matt's tree. That was the answer. Not only would I take it to his cottage, I would decorate it completely. I would make it as beautiful and personal as I could, so it would remind him of the family Christmases he'd been forced to do without for so long.

I felt my enthusiasm for the idea began to grow, my steps turning in the direction of the kitchen, the heavy box of brochures left behind in the hall.

"Do you know if Geoff is here yet?" I asked Dinah. "I might need his help picking up another fir tree."

"Good heavens, another one?" Dinah sounded incredulous.

“Wherever will you put it? We’ll be drowning in fir needles soon if you keep on."

“This one isn’t for Cliffs House,” I promised her. “It’s a gift for a friend.”

***

"Merry Christmas!" My voice was muffled behind the bushy branches of the tree in my arms.

"Merry — what? Julianne, what are you doing?"

"Giving you a Christmas present," I answered, shoving it forward, and emerging from behind the branches. "My gift to you. One Christmas tree, delivered and decorated by yours truly, as proof of my undying affection. For you and for Christmas."

Matt gazed at me in pure astonishment as I stood on his doorstep bearing a small, scrubby fir tree, its roots wrapped in burlap. “Did you uproot it yourself?” he asked, a moment later, ushering me inside with a laugh. He took the weight of it from my arms, his laugh becoming a grunt of exclamation. "Julianne, you could have hurt yourself, carrying something this heavy!"

“Geoff helped me bring it through the gate, actually. He drove me over," I said. "And I thought you might appreciate the kind with its roots still intact. This way, it’ll go back to being part of the tree line for the estate once its stint as a Christmas tree is over. Or in your garden, if you want.”

Matt paused, the tree now upright before the windows. He was gazing at me with a look that could mean any number of things, but the warmth I detected in his dark eyes was all that mattered to me right now. "You're quite amazing," he said, softly.

"Thank you," I said. I shrugged the heavy bag on my shoulder to the floor. "Ornaments in here, by the way."

He dragged a heavy ceramic planter from the garden into the corner of the room, and the two of us managed to maneuver the tree's burlap-wrapped root ball into it, and watered it thoroughly. I could see the smile on Matt's lips as he watched me decorate it, using a series of ornaments I purchased at a shop, brightly-colored balls, and silvery tinsel, and a few old-fashioned paper ornaments that had taken me all of yesterday afternoon to fold properly.

"You have a decorator's eye," he teased me, as I switched two ornaments' positions after studying the effect on the tree.

"Call me a perfectionist. Even as a kid, I was a meticulous tree decorator. It took me hours to hang mine, while the rest of the family was already settling in with cocoa, cookies, and *Rudolph the Red-Nosed Reindeer*," I answered.

"'Your' ornaments?" said Matt.

"In my family, everybody had their own," I said. "Special ones, favorite ones, handmade ones, ones that people gave you as gifts." I hung a silver star on a branch, then a red pinecone close by. "My favorite was this little snowman snow globe my grandmother bought me at a souvenir shop in Toronto. I used to hang it on the tree and dream about foreign travel." I glanced over my shoulder. "Not that I ever imagined being lucky enough to be in England for Christmas."

"Mine was a reindeer," said Matt.

I glanced at him again. "It was?" I said. "What did it look like? Besides, obviously, a reindeer."

"It was nothing special. It was only plastic with brown felt glued over it, some painted white spots and very large blue eyes. Glitter on its little horns, which were made out of some kind of pipe cleaner."

I smiled. "It sounds adorable," I answered.

"It sounds very old, and like a very poor depiction of a reindeer," said Matt, who was smiling, too, despite these words. "My mother got it secondhand from a resale shop. I wore a little patch of its fur off from petting it." He looked slightly sheepish with this admission.

"Awww, that part is even more adorable." I melted a little in response to this story. "How old were you?"

"Oh, I don't remember, really. Three, four — possibly even seven. Maybe closer to seven, since I don't remember my father being around."

Matt's father had died when he was only a boy. I imagined his Christmases as a child, his mother working long hours to support herself and two children, and a little boy playing under a Christmas tree with a velvety toy deer. Maybe petting it because he was alone except for his little sister and the neighbor who would watch them until his mother's shift ended late in the evening.

I bit my lip and turned towards the tree again, so Matt wouldn't see that his story had made me a little sad, too.

"Can I make you some tea?" Matt asked. "Hot chocolate would be more appropriate, I know, but I doubt there's any in the cupboard."

"Tea sounds great," I replied. The little catch in my voice disappeared as I mastered my emotions again.

Maybe Matt hadn't experienced the cozy Christmases of my childhood, but things would be different this year. I was determined to make sure of it. I hadn't told him yet, but I was planning to bring him to the Christmas charity ball as my guest. I had already reserved a tuxedo for him, and couldn't wait to surprise him.

The two of us dancing beneath Christmas lights twinkling like stars, me in my emerald satin gown pressed close to Matt looking splendidly handsome in a tuxedo. Toasting Christmas Eve's midnight bells with glasses of champagne. It couldn't possibly be more perfect, could it?

I smiled to myself as I hung a paper star on a branch near Matt's bookshelves, brushing against his collection of hardbacks on the shelves. The fire was smoldering in the hearth of the chimney, the one curiously painted red atop the cottage's slate roof. I realized how much I loved Matt's cottage, the ramshackle feel of the sardine box size rooms and the wild beauty of the plants in the flower beds and window boxes. And I loved him, which was the real explanation for the previous statement.

It was so true. As I watched him in the kitchen, a red ornament dangling between my fingers, I let this feeling steal completely over me. It was the first time I had let it happen, myself feeling how completely I cared about him, and I didn't know if it was because I was afraid he was leaving, or just because I was ready to tell him.

"Do you have any ornaments from your childhood?" I asked. "Anything special we should hang on the tree?"

Matt was putting the kettle on, the wallpaper behind him a faded buttery gold that still seemed cheerful in the small surroundings. The cabinets were a distressed white, with glass window panes that showed off the dishes stacked inside. I knew the chipped-edged plates well, and the blue ceramic bowl beside them that I planned to use for serving pasta when I finally cooked dinner for him.

"Me?" he said.

"You. I know the reindeer might not still be around, but you must have something left from your childhood," I said. "Macaroni and cardboard picture frames — pipe cleaner santas —"

"Ah, those." He smiled faintly as he thought it over for a moment, fingers drumming against the counter. "They're in a box in the closet in the hall, it seems. There's not much to choose from, I'm afraid. We had a shoestring budget for Christmas most of the time. But I saved a few, mostly for Michelle." Michelle was Matt's sister, now an Army nurse.

Matt had shown me his childhood home when I first came to Ceffylgwyn. A weathered old house in a poorer section of the village where Matt's family struggled to get by for several years afterward. They had leaned on Matt to survive, eventually, with him looking out for his sister after their mother died.

"I think it would make your sister happy to know you have a tree right now," I told him, sensing his thoughts had drifted that direction as he searched the little cupboard in the parlor. "We'll take a picture and send it to her, so she knows you haven't forgotten about Christmas."

He laughed, a sound both deep and warm. "Perfect," he said. "She's good at getting her way, my sister. Like some other people that I know."

The look he gave me was unmistakable; I stuck out my tongue at him.

"You're extremely stubborn, Julianne Morgen."

"Another compliment — you're spoiling me, Matthew Rose," I replied.

We took the box from its hiding place in the closet in the hall, a teapot and two cups on the table behind us, the brown china ones from the cupboard. Matt was right. It didn't contain much in the way of ornaments. Some snowflakes made out of paper and a few that were made out of lace. A few brass bells, and tin stars, and a set of Christmas balls worn and scuffed from use.

"Ohh, you *did* keep him." I couldn't help melting again as I lifted a worn reindeer whose felt was mostly gone from one side, its tiny antlers now holding only the barest fibers of gold tinsel. "Look at him. He's so cute. Oh, but he only has one eye — what happened to the other one? It's been rubbed off."

"Licked it off, I suspect," said Matt. In response to my wrinkled nose, he added, "In my defense, I was seven, remember?"

"True," I conceded. After all, I had once spent an afternoon as a three year-old licking a pink plastic Popsicle. The things children do. "We'll just paint it back on sometime." I retied the little loop coming from the reindeer's brow, so he could hang on the tree.

Below it, there were holiday images cut from magazines or greeting cards and pasted onto some kind of stiff backing. At the very bottom of the box was a tiny felt doll with a mop of golden yarn for hair. She wore a plain muslin robe, and had badly-quilted wings sewn from felt and batting. Around her brow was a crooked loop of gold pipe cleaner.

"The angel for the top," Matt explained. "Michelle made it. She was around eight, I believe, and quite proud of her craftsmanship." He grinned as he turned it over in his hands. Remembering things connected to it, I imagined, and the sister he missed so much.

I thought it was lovely, these pieces from his past. They might seem poor in comparison to the ornaments I'd been decorating with for days now, but they were rich with a different kind of history. Gently, I picked up a star and hung it on one of the branches. Matt looped a bauble onto the branch above it, the red and gold paint still pretty despite being rather flecked in places.

"You have to hang the reindeer," I reminded him.

"It's only right I suppose." He smiled. He tucked it between two glitzier ornaments of blue and silver. "There you are, Bobo. Safe and sound."

"Bobo?"

"A children's book," he said. "I wasn't a creative child. That was Michelle. Her penguin ornament was named 'Louis Valois the Fourth,' as I recall."

The stuffed penguin was missing his eyes — was it an epidemic in the ornament box? I wondered, jokingly — but both his little felt wings were intact. We hung him close to a cutout of a Currier and Ives sleigh ride, and a glittery card of a bass drum-beating teddy bear leading a toy parade.

A comfortable silence descended over us as we finished decorating the tree, the contents of the box slowly vanishing as the branches on the tree grew crowded. Matt found a pathetic string of lights in the back of the closet and wound them around it despite the ornaments. Then he poured a cup of tea for me, placing a mint biscuit on the saucer beside it.

"It's not The Golden Swan, but it will do, I hope," he said, handing it to me.

"It will do perfectly," I assured him. "I'm not spoiled by London, I promise." I studied him over the rim of my cup, but his face was giving nothing away. Had the snark in his voice been for my enthusiasm for the restaurant's biscuits, or for the way Dwight had rubbed his posh tastes in Matt's face? I had been a little embarrassed by that, having forgotten Dwight's tendency to show off.

"How was the garden show?" I asked. "We didn't really get a chance to talk about it the other day."

"Very enjoyable," he replied. "It was a nice change from being in the hothouse all day. A few of my former students were there, even. From my job at the London university, of course," he added.

"Right," I said. "Although, some of your students from Boston are probably working overseas now. It's a very popular thing to do, isn't it?"

It was stupid of me to hint around like this, trying to gauge his reaction to the idea. But the subject of his job offer, though largely unspoken, still hung between us like an invisible curtain. Dividing us in ways that I didn't notice until conversations like this, when my skin tingled with a combination of nerves and curiosity. Matt merely shrugged.

"I suppose it's possible. I haven't kept up with very many of them, I'm afraid. A few emails and the like. Perhaps we'll meet again in person someday." A half-hearted smile and shrug for this, as if it wasn't important right now.

"If you were working there again, for instance," I suggested. I studied his reaction again, looking for clues.

His gaze met mine, holding it in place as he said, "If I was, yes. But it's not a decision I'm taking lightly. And I don't know if I'll go at all."

I sipped my tea, outwardly calm. Inside, however, I wished desperately for an answer. Matt hadn't made a decision about the job yet. That meant he wasn't automatically rejecting it. Which should be a good thing, since it affected his future and the dreams he had of returning to the academic world.

But I couldn't shake the growing certainty that more than Matt's career options were at stake here, since our friendship, and the 'something more' we had been dancing around these past few weeks were coming to a crossroads. If Matt and I were in separate places in a week or two, I might never find myself in Rosemoor cottage like this again. I might be the friend who is forgotten due to time and distance —

and what if Matt decided to stay in America for good?

No, not Matt. Not given how much he loved this place.

Shutting this last possibility out, I finished my tea. But it was hard not to think of it again as we hung the last few decorations, and strung some of the tinsel on the tree.

Matt handed me the angel. “Will you do me — and Michelle — the honor of topping the tree, Julianne?”

“I would be honored,” I answered. Placing the doll carefully over the very top branch, I tucked her into a leaning-and-holding position around its top, her benevolent smile now overlooking the worn yet dignified ornaments hung below. Matt took my hand to steady me, and I felt the warm reassurance of his fingers holding tight to mine. Just like the day in the greenhouse when he talked about leaving. The little ache inside me coiled tighter in response.

“There’s something I have to give you, as well,” said Matt, afterwards. Reaching under the table, he retrieved a clay pot with a small but healthy-looking green plant inside. “The hardy and hard to kill variety. I’ve chosen it especially with you in mind.”

“How touching,” I quipped, making a face. Nevertheless, I took hold of the pot, the stems inside it bearing a vaguely cactus-like appearance. “What is this variety’s official name?” I teased him, grinning at this inside joke about my bad luck with plants. "And is it stiletto-proof? That's important around me."

“It’s a type of succulent known as a Kalanchoes,” he replied. “It’s a hybrid that blooms flowers in a vibrant shade of pink. You should see the first blossoms sometime in early spring. And so long as it's nowhere near your feet, it should be safe.”

“It’s lovely,” I told him. “Thank you.”

I leaned up and kissed his cheek, wishing this moment wouldn't end. Wishing that the happiness inside me on this perfect afternoon would never fade, as I cradled Matt's gift between my hands.

***

“Julianne, be careful!”

Gemma squealed nervously as the ladder wobbled beneath me. I shifted my weight, feeling slightly nervous myself. I had never climbed this high before, a twelve-foot ladder needed for changing the drapes in the manor house ballroom. Lady Amanda and I had agreed that red and gold, while very fetching, was not the best choice for the upcoming charity ball. A classic ivory would be a much better backdrop for the bright red of the poinsettias and amaryllis I planned for the display.

A few more tugs, some minor readjustments, and the new curtains were finally in place. A Christmas tree as tall as my ladder would be placed in front of the large glass windows later this week and decorated with clear white lights, and ornaments in the shape of stars and snowflakes. Simple, elegant, but eye-catching—that was my vision for the upcoming gala.

"I'll take these off to the laundry room then," said Gemma, piling the red and gold fabric onto a nearby trolley. "Need help getting down?" she asked, teasing me as I clung to the top of the ladder. I don't have a fear of heights per se, but this had been a little much for me even. The sooner I got back on the ground, the better.

"Thanks Gemma, but I think I'll be okay," I said, grinning down at her. "If I take it slowly, there shouldn't be any spills. Or broken bones or sprains."

"Let's hope not, with the ball right around the corner," she answered, laughing. She watched me safely descend a few of the steps before pushing her trolley towards the door. I reached the bottom step without so much as a wobble. Grinning, I tucked my feet back inside the pair of three-inch heels I had slipped off for this exercise. No way was I teetering on *those* twelve foot up. They were impractical enough already, given the amount of dashing around my job often called for.

Pippa stuck her head through the doorway. "Julianne, there's a bloke here to see you. A Mr. Bradshaw, he said. I've left him to wait for you in the parlor." She tossed me a curious look as she imparted this information. No doubt wondering why a cute American guy was waiting to speak to me.

I was curious, too, since Dwight and I hadn't spoken since I finished Daphne and Benjamin's catering menu. Surely nothing had gone wrong with the wedding plans. I had delivered the final payment to the caterers, and the reception's seating charts and harpist's song list were finished, although it had cost me all my free time to bring it all together so last-minute. If something was wrong, wouldn't he have just phoned my work mobile, rather than make the long trip to Cornwall?

Puzzled, I pushed open the door to the parlor, where Dwight was standing by the mantel, a bouquet of red roses in his arms.

“For you,” he said, holding them out with a smile. “One last thank-you gift for stepping in and saving the day. My friends couldn’t be happier with the wedding arrangements, and that makes me very happy.”

“They’re lovely,” I said, feeling puzzled, still. “But Dwight, you’ve already thanked me enough. It’s not necessary, really. Gifts especially.”

“You deserve it,” he insisted. I tried not to wince as I felt a stray thorn from one of the bouquet's flowers. Obviously the florist wasn't meticulous, whoever they were.

“This is nice,” he said, looking around. “In an over-the-top, old-fashioned way, that is. You know me—a minimalist at heart. All this stuff is kind of ... I don't know ... stuffy.” Dwight’s apartment in Seattle had been all-white walls and chrome fixtures, although, to be fair, he lived in a neutral-tones building that forbid tenants from painting. “Is the rest of the house this swanky?”

“Definitely,” I answered. Hesitating before I added, “I hope you didn't come all the way to London to give me these. A phone call to say 'thanks' would have been just as good. And I'm sure you're as busy as I am." I was eager to wrap this meeting up, especially before anyone stumbled upon the two of us chatting alone in here.

“Actually, I was hoping maybe you could give me a tour,” he said. “I showed my boss the website for this place, and he thinks it could be a great site for our spring conference. Of course, he needs a little more information to be sure. He has several options to consider. And I need to be sure I can make it worth his while before he'll consider this one.”

“I can’t, Dwight,” I said. “Today I've got a lot to do. There are public tours this afternoon — they're given by appointment only, but I'm sure they'll let you come —”

“Come on. I’m sure your employers wouldn’t mind if you showed a friend and prospective client around. Not if they’re as understanding as you say.”

“Even if they didn’t mind, I have too much work do," I protested. "But I know for sure there's a tour booked for Monday at two. Why don’t I just put you in the diary for that?"

"Are those roses satisfactory?" he asked suddenly, changing the subject as he frowned at the bouquet I was holding. "I was thinking maybe I should get you violets. Weren't violets your favorite? This is meant to be a thank you, after all. I mean, you've done *so* much already, and I'm truly grateful."

"Um, actually, it was —"

"You know, all I need to know is, if you could possibly —" He touched my shoulder with these words, but that was as far as he got before another voice spoke up.

“I’m sorry to interrupt. Lady Amanda wondered if I could restock the wood box for her. Apparently, she's hosting a tourism board meeting in here shortly."

Matt was standing there, a bundle of firewood in his arms. At the sight of him, I automatically put space between myself and Dwight, and dropped the roses low in one hand, the petals brushing against my skirt.

“You’re not interrupting,” I said, hastily. “Dwight was just asking about a possible tour. His company is interested in booking Cliffs House for a conference this spring.”

“If they can get a better deal on it than a castle in Scotland,” Dwight joked. "You know how corporate budgets are — and how tight English prices are."

Matt nodded, his expression hard to read. I suspected he didn't like that joke about Cliffs House's rates all that much. I could see he’d been working in the garden that morning, his trousers and canvas jacket spattered with mud in contrast with Dwight’s business suit and immaculate shoes. I detected a slight sneer in Dwight's gaze for Matt's untidy appearance.

“You know, I’ve always assumed that houses like this just paid people to do all the menial tasks," said Dwight. "I thought you were a botanist — but you're bringing in the firewood?"

“That's how it works around here,” I said. Bristling a little on Matt's behalf. “Even a great scientist isn't above helping out with the chores. And Lord William actually cuts the firewood himself. He works on the grounds almost as much as the gardeners and the estate manager. Right, Matt?”

“He does, yes.” Matt was keeping his answers short apparently. He pulled another log from the bundle, his glance falling once on the bouquet I was holding.

My face had turned a similar shade of crimson. "A thank you present," I said. “For my work on the wedding. Totally unnecessary, of course, but thoughtful — and something I should probably find a vase for and put in the front hall for guests to admire. Be back in just a moment,” I told them.

It took me longer than I planned to locate a proper vase. There were more flower arrangements in the house than usual due to the holiday season, and I finally had to resort to using a crystal pitcher from the kitchen pantry, one whose handle had parted ways from it years ago. By the time I had the roses on display and made it back to the parlor, a good ten minutes had passed. Dwight was ensconced in the armchair near the fire, busy texting someone. He didn't look up as I entered.

“Where did Matt go?” I asked. Glancing round as if he might be tucked away in a corner somewhere. Dwight gave a shrug.

“He said something about a project in the greenhouse. Guess he had to hurry back to his plants." He gave me a quick smile.

“I have you in the book for a tour on Monday,” I told him, having made a note in the house's diary. “Two o’clock. If you think your boss is interested, feel free to come and take some photos to show him.”

“Right,” he told me. “I’ll see you then, I guess.”

With Dwight gone, I made my way towards the greenhouse. Matt was inside, but I couldn’t see any evidence of the project he mentioned to Dwight. He seemed to be lost in thought, crouched in front of the rose that hadn’t bloomed for thirty years or more. I stopped a few feet away, knowing the gravel crunching beneath my shoes had given away my arrival. “Will it bloom in time for Christmas?” I asked him.

“It may.” He didn’t turn around, I noticed, but was busy concentrating. Not on the plant, but on the phone in his hand, the screen of his mobile.

"Is something wrong?" I hinted.

"No," he said. "Nothing's wrong." He looked up at me at last and gave me a quick smile — but the distraction in his voice was something he'd done a poor job of hiding.

Was it a text from someone? Or was it because of Dwight? I didn't want to ask if he was jealous. After my assumption about him and Trixie the friendly bridesmaid last summer, I thought we might both be a *little* more careful about romantic misinterpretations, if that was the case.

"If you have time, I thought we could take a final look at those flower selections for the ball," I told him. "Lady Amanda agreed that adding lilies to the mix could be a brilliant combination."

Climbing to his feet, Matt said, "It will have to wait, I'm afraid, Julianne. I have an errand to run this afternoon."

"Of course," I said. "There's still plenty of time. Even if there wasn't, event planners thrive off the time crunch of a last-minute decision."

He didn't smile for this joke, I noticed. There was definitely something on his mind. "We'll talk later," he said. He touched my arm, gently. "I promise."

"Of course. See you then," I said. But I felt worried.

I didn't have a clue how to find out what was on Matt's mind, but I had a feeling it was probably his offer from the university. And if he was making up his mind — well, if I pressed him for answers, it might make him think I was trying to influence his decision, and that was the last thing I was trying to do.

Although maybe not the last thing I *wanted* to do. But that's another story.

***

"Time for a coffee, Julianne? You look as if you could you use the boost."

Pippa shot me a questioning look as she sat across from me at the kitchen table. Her coffee smelled like hazel and nutmeg, tempting me despite the fact I wasn't all that hungry lately. I probably looked as if I needed that 'boost' she talked about.

"Thanks, but I'm holding up without it so far," I answered, bravely. "Just a few more days and we'll be celebrating what a big success the ball was." I had almost checked every box on my giant to-do list, from polishing serving trays to meeting with the orchestra.

"Right before we host the entire village for the New Year's open house," Pippa pointed out with a wicked grin.

I let out a moan. "One worry at a time, Pippa. Please."

"Never mind. Christmas will make it all better, I promise," said Pippa. "Wait 'til you taste Dinah's menu."

"I'm sure it's heavenly," I answered, although my mind was far away from the visions of sugar plums and roasted geese I had begun to associate with a Cornish Christmas. Instead, it was much closer to the quandary of becoming Matt's girlfriend or staying Matt's friend.

Over the past two days, we had been so busy that we had scarcely seen each other. I'd called him, but each time I missed his return call. He might be ensconced in the greenhouse, of course, coaxing the lilies to open in time for my modified flower display for the ball. Or he might be working on some project for Lord William I knew nothing about, since my knowledge of the grounds management was limited to what concerned my work in the house. Either way, we hadn't crossed paths, and it was beginning to worry me. Time was ticking away, and Matt's decision hadn't been made. And even though I wanted to believe I was prepared for him to leave, deep inside I knew I wasn't.

Rather than suffer through a third day in suspense, I plucked up my courage and returned to the greenhouse early that morning, determined to face the truth, whatever it was. I walked the pathways lined with frost-rimmed grass. Mist hung like a grey-white blanket over the estate's distant fields, drifting like smoke around the hothouse's walls, its windows fogged by the warmth inside.

Rapping on the door, I opened it and stuck my head inside. "Matt?" I called out.

No response. I stepped inside, shutting the door behind me. It was balmy in here, compared to the temperatures outside, with every day seeming colder than the one before it lately, the breeze from the Channel extra brisk. Perhaps Old Ned was on to something with his theory about holly berries. Having seen a touch of glittering frost on the holly hedges which bordered the estate's northern fields, I could almost believe that snow had dusted them instead.

I glanced around, seeing nothing but the rows of plants that Matt had spent the winter nurturing into states of perfection. The hothouse was silent, the smell of earth and peat moss strong enough to make me crinkle my nose a little.

Matt wasn't here. A pair of pruning shears lying on a bench near the roses was the only sign that he had been at work here this morning. I noticed the buds on the rescued antique rose seemed even firmer and fuller than the last time I saw it, although I couldn't tell if they were ready to open. A few had been removed, so I wondered if Matt had pruned them to help the rose conserve its strength.

They were so beautiful, I had to remind myself not to touch them. Instead, I only marveled at the transformation this plant had undergone under Matt's expert care.

I hung around awhile, hoping that Matt would show up and we could finally talk. He didn't, however; so I trudged back up the pathway to the house with a feeling of defeat.

Outside my office, Matt was waiting. He'd been doing the same thing I was doing, and, he, too, was on the verge of leaving.

A laugh escaped my lips, even though I felt nervous. "We were at cross purposes," I told him. "I've just been to the greenhouse, looking for you."

"I haven't been there today," he said. "I had to catch a train...then I had to find you."

I noticed he wasn't wearing his work clothes today, but rather a nice button down shirt and trousers. He must not be working on the grounds today either then, which puzzled me even more.

"Come inside," I said. "If this is about flowers, then please tell me you have good news about my lilies and my poinsettias." I cleared off the chair opposite my desk, as I perched on its corner.

"Julianne," he said.

His brown eyes told me the rest of what he was going to say. I knew that Matt was going to America.

I took a deep breath. "It's great, Matthew," I said. "I'm glad for you."

His features relaxed. "I hoped you would be," he said. "I — I didn't know what you'd think. The university told me I had to decide by today. I thought about what you said from before. About my needing a challenge and a change of pace. And I knew you were right. I walked away from my career before because of blind emotion, and I want to give it a second chance."

"Of course you do," I said. "That's great, Matt. Really great."

I mentally kicked myself for that past observation, even knowing it was the right one. It didn't make this hurt any less, however, to know that I was responsible for Matt's decision to go back to America. And Matt — my Matt, whom I was falling madly in love with — had no idea how I really felt.

"William admits the grounds are well in hand now, practically restored to their best. It would be nothing for an experienced landscape artist to take over for me. Truthfully, the only obstacle I face is purely personal." His eyes met mine.

Personal. As in me? As in us? I felt a flutter of hope deep inside me.

"I want to thank you, Julianne," he said. "For all that you've done...for all that you mean to me. These aren't the right words, really...perhaps there are none...." In his gaze, I saw something that made my heart skip beats and sink into despair at the same time. He trailed off as if it was suddenly hard to speak; I felt a lump rise in my throat.

Gentle, warm, kind words from Matt. Just not the ones I had wanted to hear.

"You deserve a chance for something like this after all you've done for Cliffs House," I answered. "The life you gave up when you were hurting. It wasn't fair that you lost it, and now you've got a chance to have back the job you loved. You did the right thing."

“Is that really what you think?" he asked, softly. "You can tell me the truth, Julianne. Please."

He had sounded almost worried as he asked this question. I wondered if my disappointment was starting to show despite my best attempts to keep it hidden. I felt his hand on my shoulder, its warm pressure. I wanted to touch his fingers, but I didn't, not until I was sure I really meant those words. So he wouldn't feel my fingers trembling or clinging to him desperately.

This was about Matt, after all. Not me, or whatever expectations I might have for our relationship. If I couldn’t be proud of him for embracing this opportunity, then I didn’t deserve him anyway.

I rose to face him. “Of course I think so," I continued. "You’ll be in your element, back in the classroom, Matt. I really am glad for you. Really." I took both his hands in mine, squeezing them, gently. *And can’t help wishing that you weren’t doing this, at the same time.*

His hands felt perfectly still in my hold. I heard Matt's voice murmur something close to my ear, but I didn't catch the words. We stood without speaking for a moment, avoiding each other’s gaze. It felt as if we had suddenly reverted to our former, awkward selves, back when we first had a disagreement and didn’t know how to behave around each other.

Matt was the first to speak again. “I should talk with William now," he said, gently. "I'll tell you everything later."

"Of course," I said.

I waited until he was out the door and out of sight before I sank into the chair and buried my face in my hands, even though I was determined not to cry a single tear.

***

There was no time to fall apart.

That's what I told myself as the countdown to the charity ball kicked into gear, my presence required in six different places at once it seemed. I was barely sleeping anyway, my mind a commotion of event planning details and Matthew's news running constantly through my brain like a tickertape announcement that our chance to be a couple had expired. It kept popping into my head as I moved from the kitchen to the ballroom and Lady Amanda's office in between.

The look on his face as he said the words; the hurt I had glimpsed in his dark eyes before they looked away. Each memory was weighing me down a little more every time I thought of it.

Stop being stupid and tell him you love him. No matter what, tell him you love him.

I had forgotten to tell him I was taking him to the charity ball. Forgotten about the tuxedo reservation until I found the receipt on my dresser this morning. All those visions of me and Matt dancing to the orchestra, cheek to cheek — had that been changed by Matt's announcement?

"Are you quite sure you don't need some caffeine, Julianne?"

Dinah was keeping fresh-brewed coffee on hand for the staff as we ran ourselves ragged each day, and a pot of hot water ready for a 'cuppa' whenever the staff was in desperate need of rejuvenation. I could only think it would make me more on edge, though.

"I think I'll manage without it," I said, doing my best impression of a perky smile. "Who needs coffee when they have a to-do list to keep them on their feet?"

Neither Gemma nor Pippa was fooled by it, judging by the glances they exchanged at the kitchen table, where they were polishing champagne flutes; and neither was Dinah, whose sharp eye detected it was more than just my work that was preying on my mind when we discussed last-minute changes to the hors d'oeuvres.

She reached over and patted my hand. “Feeling a bit homesick, are we?” Dinah asked, giving me a sympathetic look.

“A little," I said. "But I'll be fine." I couldn't be honest with her about everything in my head, either.

Geoff pushed open the kitchen door, a smile on his face. “They’re ready to bring the flowers in from the hothouse, Miss Morgen,” he said. “If you have a place for them, that is.”

“Yes,” I told him. “Bring them over. We’ll put them in a dark closet so they can rest awhile before I do the arrangements.”

Matt didn’t appear with the delivery from the hothouse, as I had hoped. Instead, a couple of undergardners brought in the buckets of lilies, poinsettias, and amaryllis I would be arranging before the splendor of the Christmas Eve event. It was hard to say if I was more relieved or disappointed that I didn’t have time to face him right now. My feelings seemed to fluctuate by the minute, and I was so wrapped up in them I all but jumped out of my skin when my mobile phone started to ring.

“Miss Morgen?” said a voice posh but friendly sounding. “It’s Daphne Freemont.”

I almost said ‘who?’ before I remembered: Dwight’s friend, the would-be-bride in London. “Miss Freemont,” I replied, trying to sound cheerful. “How lovely to hear from you. Everything is going well I trust?” As I silently prayed there wasn’t some dilemma requiring my presence in London, with so little time left before the ball.

“Oh, brilliantly,” she said. “Well, except for the carriage.”

“Carriage…?” I tapped my fingers against the phone's case, trying to remember what she was talking about. Wait. The transportation to the church, the one I had tried to veto over its expense....

“The horse drawn carriage?” Daphne supplied, helpfully.

“Yes, of course. I booked that place in Westminster. There isn’t a problem, I hope?” *Please, please, nothing I can’t fix with a simple phone call.*

“It’s just a tiny thing,” said Daphne. “They’ve put us with a gold carriage and chestnut horses, but I feel that to keep with the wedding colors, we really *ought* to have a blue carriage and white horses. Do you think you can talk them into it? I’ve tried phoning them, but the line is always busy, and Mr. Bradshaw said you wouldn’t mind.”

Mr. Bradshaw? Of course ... she meant Dwight. That was awfully formal for a friend, I thought.

"I can take care of it for you," I said. After all, it was only a phone call, wasn't it?

"That's brilliant," she answered. "Really, I don't know how we could have managed this dream wedding without you. Or Mr. Bradshaw for that matter. He's been an absolute dear to help us this way."

"Well, I'm sure Dwight was happy to do it," I said. "Being friends with your fiancé and all."

"Oh, but he isn't," she chirped.

I hesitated. "He isn't?" I repeated. Cleary, I had misheard her.

"Benjamin met him once, I think, at a meeting at the firm. Or maybe it was lunch at his uncle's office. Yes, that was it. Benjamin's uncle is the chief executive for the firm, you know. "

"I...didn't know that."

A sudden wave of fury had crept over me with the revelation. So Dwight's 'friend' just happened to be the nephew of his boss? It wasn't a coincidence, obviously. Dwight had seen a chance to impress the chief executive at his firm by 'rescuing' the nephew's wedding debacle, or something like that.

So I had been a pawn in Dwight's corporate ladder games. I felt disgusted by this idea. Dwight wasn't being friendly to let 'bygones be bygones' between us, but because he needed my skills to be offered for free.

From the other end of the phone, Daphne was thanking me in advance for arranging the carriage swap.

"No, Miss Freemont, *thank you*. I'm very glad you decided to get in touch." I hoped my voice wasn't as frosty as I felt as I hung up the phone.

***

My anger was still palpable the morning of Dwight's tour. I deftly avoided the group he was with by sequestering myself in the main dining hall, where the Christmas decorations from the ladies luncheon were being replaced with a simple table runner and bouquet of winter flowers. I thought I might run him through with a fireplace poker if he came near me. How *dare* he use me like that? And after the callus way he treated me after our breakup before.

The tour was drawing to a close, and to my chagrin, Dwight spotted me through the doors that Gemma had left open for a moment. He walked in with a smile, obviously expecting a friendly greeting in return.

“There you are,” he said. "This place is really great. I think I'm definitely recommending it to my boss. So ... expect a very posh reservation to come your boss's way."

“Enjoyed your tour, did you?” I gave him a fake smile as I trimmed the stems on some flowers for the table’s centerpiece. I gave them an extra-hard snip with the shears.

“Sure,” he said. “Although I was hoping to see the place with you instead. You know, so we could talk privately about the booking." He paused, noticing the flowers whose stems I was fiercely trimming. “Those look nice,” he commented. “Did your friend grow them? Somehow I pictured him as more of a 'potatoes and carrots' kind of gardener.”

“Matthew oversees the flower gardens, yes," I answered, coldly.

“I’m sure they look more impressive in the spring,” said Dwight. “Not so dead and dull. At least, I hope so, since the conference takes place in March.”

“It was beautiful when I got here in the summer, so I’m sure it’s even better in the spring."

“Not that the gardens matter. We're talking corporate, so it's some trust exercises, some teambuilding, some slide shows. So... maybe you and I could work through the details? Maybe over dinner some evening? If you're free, that is.”

“In London or Cornwall?” I asked, forcing myself to play along. He gave a warm laugh.

“London probably has more, shall we say, ‘suitable’ dining options,” he suggested. Meaning expensive, chic, restaurants, I presumed. I wondered if his company would pick up the tab, or if he was planning to fund that part of the assignment himself. And probably take it out of a travel allowance later. "If you're not busy on Tuesday — I'm not, either."

“Maybe it’s because you just haven't thought of another way to give your career a boost on that day,” I said. Tucking the final blossom in place as I offered Dwight a meaningful smile. "Not since Benjamin and Daphne's wedding gave you brownie points with your boss, I mean."

He made a scoffing sound. “What gave you that idea? I’m here to see you, Julianne. We're friends. That’s the real reason I’m trying to sell this place on my boss,” he said, lowering his voice, as if it were a secret. “I thought it would be a boost for you. After all, we could let bygones be bygones, couldn't we?" He moved a little closer. "Good business for me, good business for your boss. Event planners need events, right?"

“No,” I snapped. “I *don't* need your event, Dwight. You’re trying to ‘sell’’ this place to your boss, as you put it, because you think I’ll give you some kind of special discount. Why didn't you tell me in the first place that your 'friend' in trouble was really the nephew of your boss?"

“Who lied? Benjamin is a great guy with a lot of promise. I’ll be working with him in the future and helping him out was the nice thing to do. So what it if happened to benefit my standing at the company if I save him a little pocket money? That was just a bonus, really. Besides, it'll look great on your resume, Julianne. Planning the wedding of a future CEO.”

He was trying so hard to sound sincere, and all the while his selfishness was leaking through. I remembered all the little incidents in the past where Dwight had made a decision solely for himself, and tried to twist it into something for me, or for one of his friends. That was then, however — and I didn't have to listen to it anymore.

So I slapped him. Hard.

“That's for reminding me of all the reasons we broke up," I hissed. "Mostly because you were a self-serving, arrogant, know-it-all. I can't believe I trusted that you wanted to be friends again."

He glared at me, an angry red spot appearing where my slap had landed. “This from somebody who stranded herself in this dinky little village where card games pass for the local entertainment — and whose only crush is the gardener.”

I didn't bother to lower myself to reply to him. I simply walked out of the room.

In the hall outside the crystal closet I found Gemma standing with a vase in either arm, her eyes wide. "Julianne — did you just smack that bloke?"

I let out a sigh, pushing my hair back with a frustrated motion. “Gemma, I think I could use that coffee now,” I answered.

***

It would take more than coffee, or even a cuppa, to get me through the next twenty-four hours. That was my fear as the day of the ball dawned, a cold and blustery wind appearing now and then to rattle the panes in the windows. If it ended up storming, I would find it an ominous sign for the ball, and not just because the weather would be imperfect.

Now that everybody knew Matt was going back to the States, I had to hear mention of it every single second. There was surprise for him leaving, but not really; most everyone had imagined that Matt wouldn't stay in Cornwall forever. Everyone except me, it seemed — well, and the two kitchen staffers Pippa and Gemma.

“What’s he leaving for?” Pippa whined, slicing strawberries for the final batch of Dinah’s variation on Japanese Christmas Cake. “It’s not as if he was happier in the States. Some girl broke his heart there. He should stay here — there's not a model to be seen in Ceffylgwyn, that's for certain.”

“It won't be the same without him," said Gemma. She sighed. "What will we do when there's only Jackson trimming the hedges? He looks awful in that ratty old coat — sixty if he's a day."

“Mind your work, both of you,” Dinah scolded them, taking a batch of sponge cake from the oven and working quickly to cool it. "We've got our hands full today without moaning about your opinions on people's looks." I knew without turning around as I whipped the cream in a chilled bowl that both of the maids were rolling their eyes.

I hadn’t cried in front of anyone yet, but my eyes were puffy in the morning from a quick cry in the utility closet when I couldn't stand the strain any longer. When Matt and I exchanged glances and smiles for one of the last times in the presence of the staff at the morning meeting, I had been afraid that tears would begin to well up without warning, and I would humiliate myself in front of everyone.

Even though no one had asked me how I felt about Matt leaving, it must have been fairly obvious that things between us hadn't worked out. After all, if he was in love, he might not have chosen to leave, right? Everyone knows that long-distance relationships are risky — not something you choose lightly, as opposed to amicable goodbyes.

He was packing up his cottage this week. Lord William had sent over some empty crates and boxes to help. The thought of Rosemoor devoid of Matt's belongings—or worse, populated by someone else's—was something I didn't want to think about. The tree stripped of its lights, planted in the garden; the ornaments back in their box, from Michelle's angel to the faded fuzzy reindeer.

Who would take care of the garden? It was such a part of him, I couldn't fathom how it would survive under another's care. And in the weeks that were left, what would we do together? Would we talk about a future when he came back? Would we be friends and promise to write and call each other? I had no idea at this point.

The orchestra arrived and begin to set up in the ballroom by four. Mr. Tanaka, the head of the Tokyo based company had gotten there earlier in the day and was meeting with Lady Amanda and Lord William in one of the private suites upstairs. Soon, the caterers would be here, bearing the chilled champagne and platters of hors d'oeuvres that would serve in addition to Dinah's creations. I would have to swap my apron for the gown and wrap in emerald green I had specially purchased in London. I would circulate in the ballroom, making small talk with various guests, checking the number of champagne bottles being chilled, the supplies for the sake cocktails, and whether enough finger foods were circulating.

Of course, originally I had planned in between to dance with Matt. How had that gone wrong? And if I found the courage to tell him how I felt — if I told him that all I wanted —

"Where are you going at this hour? Hadn't you better get changed?" Dinah cast a worried eye at me, standing frozen in the hallway and seemingly staring at the big Christmas tree waiting to greet our guests.

"I have something to do," I said. I had come back to myself now. And with those words, I collected my scarf and coat and put them on. My determined expression must have puzzled Dinah even more, judging from the way she was staring at me.

"I'm just going out to stretch my legs. And clear my head," I explained, winding the scarf around my neck. "I'll be ten, fifteen minutes tops."

"Well, mind you stay clear of the cliffside," she answered. "That winds picking up something fierce." As she cast an eye towards the gloomy Cornish sky outside the glass pane.

I fully intended to follow her advice, carefully picking my way through the pathway that led to the greenhouses. But I paused as I caught a glimpse of the rocks overlooking the Channel, and something happened inside me. A deep longing connected to memories of this place filled me, ones connected with Matt, and our first, heated exchange when I accidentally trampled his heath plant.

Other times we had walked there since, making this place more special than any words could explain. A smile, half-sad, half-hopeful tugged my lips as I stood before it, on the verge of following the path to the overlook. Closing my eyes, I tilted my face towards the breeze for just a moment, absorbing its smells, hearing the distant roar of the water rolling against the rocks. The sound of the weather changing, of a storm rolling towards us on the back of the wind.

Somehow, I couldn't imagine its summer self at this moment, the breeze's balmier in their restlessness, the sunlight beating down on my hair.

"Julianne."

I turned around at the sound of his voice. With timing as perfect as in the movies, Matt was standing behind me on the path. Maybe there was a psychic connection between us after all — a joking thought that I didn't find funny at this moment, with my head and heart so full of serious reflections.

"There's something I need to say to you," he said.

He walked towards me, the distance narrowed between us with each of our strides. "I can't leave without telling you," he began. He took a breath, but I was the one who spoke next.

"I'm in love with you," I said. "I love you, Matt. I have almost since the start, but I've known it for certain for weeks now. Maybe longer."

The words came out on their own, without any hesitation or wobbling tones. They had been waiting for me to say them, and no matter what, I couldn't wait any longer.

Surprise flooded his dark eyes. "Truly?" he asked.

"Matt, how could you think I would feel otherwise, after all these months of spending time with you? There's no one but you. I only wish I had told you sooner, instead of waiting until you were leaving."

I stopped speaking, waiting for him to reply. Waiting for anything.

The look in his dark eyes was serious, almost somber. "My mistake," he answered, "was not telling you first that I've loved you since that day on the cliffs. That determined girl who was so willing to scold a stranger and hold her ground."

He moved closer, his hands cradling my face. I wrapped my arms around him and held him tightly for our kiss. When he released me, he rested his forehead against mine, the two of standing there as if we were frozen by the chill of the wind.

"What will we do now?" I asked. Gazing up to see the same question reflected in Matt's eyes. "If you're in Massachusetts and I'm here." Not sure how to finish that sentence, I let it stand with just those words. Even knowing how we felt about each other didn't change the fact that Matt was leaving, I realized.

"It will be difficult," Matt said. "But not impossible. Not for us."

"Not for us," I repeated.

His fingers stroked my hair, their touch warming my face. I could tell he was thinking, searching for the assurance that neither of us had. Not yet, anyway.

"Can you come with me?" he asked, softly. "Come to the cottage? There's some things I want to talk to you about — and we're short of time —"

"I wish I could," I answered, honestly. "But there's so much for me to do. Tonight's the ball, you know, and we're swamped with preparations at the last minute."

"Of course. You're working," he said. "You know, for a moment I forgot everything but you." A wistful smile crossed his lips as he stroked my hair.

I put my hand on his arm. "Come with me tonight," I said. "As my guest. I was planning to bring you, I've been planning it for weeks." I thought of the tuxedo receipt on my dresser and was glad now that I hadn't tossed it in the garbage. "We'll dance and we'll sip champagne, and have one last moment together in Cornwall."

The wind was picking up, sending chills from head to toe. Matt started to say something else, when he noticed I was shivering. "We best get you back inside," he told me. "Come on."

He kept his arm around me as we made our way back up the path. Nestled this close, I could breathe in the familiar scent of his jacket: the smell of fresh earth and dried flower blossoms; the vague aroma of Matt's aftershave; all comfortingly familiar. My head rested against his shoulder as we crested the top of the hill.

In the courtyard to the house, a vehicle was parked that I recognized instantly as the caterers. It brought with it a sense of reality, the fact that the ball would be in full swing mere hours from now. And even Matt's arm around me couldn't change that.

"You're coming, right?" I said. "I already rented you a tuxedo, so don't worry. I'll have Geoff bring the ticket by. All you have to do is find me in the ballroom." I squeezed his hand before releasing it and taking a step towards the house. I glanced back and saw a look on Matt's face that seemed odd.

"I can't," he said, softly. "I wish I could, but I can't. My flight for Christmas night was rescheduled — it's been moved up because of the coming storm. And I had already told the university I would arrive as early as I could to discuss the syllabus."

I felt crushed. Matt was leaving tonight? I had no idea. No wonder he had come to find me — no wonder he wouldn't be holding me tonight on the ballroom floor as the midnight bells rang. I wouldn't even be able to go with him to Heathrow.

Tears stung my eyes, and not just from the cold. "I see," said. "I guess you can't help that, can you? No control over the weather." I tried not to sound too hurt by this news.

"I wish I could," said Matt, with an ache in his voice. "I wish you all the best tonight, Julianne. As always. And knowing you, tonight will be perfect."

Before I could say anything, he stepped forward and pressed another kiss to my mouth. Shorter, but no less tender, before he turned and walked away. Despite the cold wind, I waited and watched until he was out of sight before I hurried inside.

***

The ball did go perfectly, or nearly so. With the orchestra playing a medley of Christmas favorites, the guests mingled in black tie dress, exchanging conversation, dancing, and enjoying the sumptuous hors d'oeuvres made by Dinah and the caterers. The sponge cake appetizers were a hit with everyone, including the Japanese business men and women whose holiday dessert was the model for her creation.

I made a few new acquaintances and had a few requests for my business card. I sampled a few appetizers, and dealt with a few small crises, but the evening ran smoothly. And as I stood watching others dance, without a partner for myself, I missed Matt more than ever. The dreams of the two of us sharing tonight had dissolved with Matt's plane ticket's altered date.

But I had told Matt I loved him. There was no going back from it, and I had never felt freer. It was as if I was a different person from the one who left the house for a walk that afternoon. Right now, that was all that mattered.

Geoff joined me for a moment, a champagne glass in hand. "I have something for you," he said to me. "An early Christmas present, it would seem."

"For me?" I said. I felt surprised, and a little guilty, since I had intended to give the staff their gifts tomorrow at the staff Christmas party. Geoff placed a small package in my hand.

"It's not from me," he said. And with a knowing smile, he moved on, leaving me to open it.

I untied the ribbon and opened the lid. Inside, atop a folded note, was a tiny, perfect rose blossom, with petals of a shade somewhere between pink sunset and rosy dawn.

Lifting it carefully, I caught a whiff of the sweet perfume. A scent like honeysuckle, only subtler, with a hint of spice. A perfume that had been lost for thirty years, until Matthew brought it to life again. With the same hand, I unfolded the sheet of stationary with Matt's handwriting on it.

Julianne,

This first blossom from the restored rose is my Christmas present to you. I truly wish I could give it to you in person. To have seen the look on your face when you opened it, and to see your smile ... I wanted to be there for it.

I came to the cliffs today to tell you I was leaving early. But all I could think to say was that I loved you, and that leaving you hurt me deeply. I didn't plan for you to say it back. The fact that you did has been the best Christmas gift of all. And it made me regret that something is taking me away, even though I was looking forward to this opportunity.

There were reasons I had to go. You knew what most of those reasons were before I did. You understand me in a way no one else ever has, or ever will. And though this choice takes me far from my home in Cornwall, I hope the same is not true for your heart. For you have never been very far from mine since the time we met, Julianne Morgen.

It wouldn't be impossible, we said. Difficult, but not impossible. I believe that's true, or else I could never board the plane tonight. Always remember that.

All my love,
Matthew

Tears spilled over my cheeks as I finished reading his note. Not because I was sad, exactly, although I was. It was just that seeing Matt's love in words made it all the more real to me. As if I was holding a piece of it in my hands.

And there was the rose. The beautiful, perfect rose that Matthew had known would be the just right Christmas present. I held it close, smelling the sweet aroma once more. Its memory was something I could treasure long after the petals would start to fade and curl, turning slowly to rose-colored dust.

***

"The storm is what woke me up," Gemma insisted, pulling back the curtain to look out at the scene in the courtyard again. "Started right before dawn, it did. I heard it pelting the windows something fierce. First the rain and then the sleet—"

"And then the snow," I finished. Gazing past her at the light dusting of glittery white that covered the cobblestones and ground. And everything in between, its presence a rare and welcome sight in Ceffylgwyn, or Cornwall, for that matter.

"Never have I seen such a sight on Christmas before," Dinah exclaimed, bustling into the parlor, her tray laden down with another round of truffles for the hungry manor staff. We tucked into breakfast, to be followed by gift opening and party games.

Pippa held out a Christmas Cracker, instructing me, "Give it a twist and a tug on the count of three, Julianne. There's a bit of holiday cheer inside for the winner — small prizes, but loads of fun."

"The best part's the hat," said Geoff, chuckling. "That was my opinion when I was a lad."

We gave it a firm tug, the shiny wrapper splitting apart to reveal its treasures. Paper party hats, hard candies, and some very bad jokes—but we all laughed at them anyway.

It was destined to be a glorious afternoon of board games and loads of chocolates, and, of course, the dinner. Dinah's splendid Cornish feast, making the dinner table groan beneath its buffet.

"Dinah, you've outdone yourself," Lord William declared, cutting into another slice of goose. "The Queen herself couldn't ask for a better Christmas dinner."

"A toast to the chef," said Lady Amanda. "My own mum couldn't have done it better, and she was forever slaving over a hot stove for the holidays."

"To mothers everywhere," said Geoff. "And excellent cooks, as well."

Any moment now, the pudding would be served — promised to be more sumptuous than I could imagine, everyone said — but I slipped away from the table for a moment to gaze at the snowy world outside. Cornwall in the snow was a rare treat, I realized. Even a dusting on the green of the holly hedges and the privets, and a little blanket in the flower beds, made this Christmas a little more special than usual.

Amid the laughter and cheerful conversation, I was having a little moment of sadness, truthfully. Not just for home, but for missing Matt, who was supposed to be here for today. He would spend Christmas adjusting to his life in Massachusetts, unpacking his things and planning his syllabus. I pictured him organizing his office, then meeting with students and fellow faculty members. Finding a place to live that wasn't at all like Rosemoor, with its red chimney and faded white wash exterior, but someplace where Matt's books and gardening tools could still feel at home.

I wanted him to be happy there, and I wanted to find a way to be part of his life there, somehow. That nice holiday Lady Amanda said I had earned—who said it couldn't be spent in Massachusetts? Maybe Matt could be my guide in Boston, the same as he was in Ceffylgwyn those first few weeks. My smile grew as I pictured this scenario, until my reflection was almost beaming in the window's glass.

It was a good match for the view outside, where the fine dusting of snow glistened like crystal against the dark green hedge leaves and the branches bared for winter, and tucked itself like sugar into the crevices of the ornamental garden urns. I would have to rejoin the others at the table soon, but, just for a moment, I wanted to savor this image of a perfect Cornish Christmas morning. Perfect, except for the fact that Matt wasn't here to share it with me, of course.

When I spotted a figure crossing the courtyard a moment later, I thought it wasn't real. A mirage, perhaps—one of Matt carrying gift wrapped packages and wearing a tuxedo beneath his overcoat, no less.

I was out the door and down the steps to meet him in mere seconds. His brown eyes met mine, his breath forming clouds in the air as he reached me.

"I don't think any storm has ever had better timing then this one," he said. "When my flight was delayed last night, it seemed like fate. And when they rescheduled it…well, I decided that one could be delayed, too. For me, anyway."

"But I thought you had to leave." I thought I was going to cry, even though I was smiling. "You had promised the university..."

"I think they can wait one more day," said Matt, smiling. "Christmas is best spent with those you love. Especially when it's your first one together. And I couldn't possibly let a hired dinner jacket go to waste, could I?"

He set his packages in the snow and took hold of both of my hands. His fingers were cold, but I didn't care. I leaned against him, burying my face against his wool scarf for a moment as we stood together.

He picked me over his work? How very dashing and romantic. I wanted to throw my arms around him in a bear hug, instead of fighting not to be utterly overwhelmed by happiness at this moment.

"What do you think, Julianne Morgen?" he asked. "Are you free to spend this day with me?"

I settled for a teasing smile as I drew back from his hold.

"I'd be very flattered," I said. "Lucky for you, you're just in time for plum pudding. Dinah's special recipe, so you know it's perfection."

"Then let's have some of it, shall we?" Matt gathered his Christmas gifts from the snow, his free hand taking mine as we walked side by side to the house.

A Cottage in Cornwall

By

Laura Briggs

"He's going to prison? Nooo!" moaned Pippa. "No, it's not fair!"

"Hush up, will you?" said Gemma. "I can't hear the telly!" She pressed the volume button and pumped the sound several decibels louder as the characters onscreen murmured their way through a British drama. No less than the famous *Poldark*, the show the two of them had talked about constantly during their kitchen work. "Just imagine him in some dank, dirty little cell —"

"— probably shirtless," completed Pippa, as they both stifled a giggle. "And sweaty."

Between them, barefoot with the bowl of popcorn balanced on my lap, I popped several kernels in my mouth as I watched the screen in silence, where the handsome, smoldering Ross Poldark suffered persecution and overwhelming odds.

Pippa and Gemma, part of the staff at Cliffs House, where I was the event planner, had hounded me for months to watch this series when I first came to Ceffylgwyn, a village in Cornwall. Finally, I had joined them on the sofa to watch episodes — in part out of curiosity, and in part because they were right about Ross Poldark and Matthew Rose bearing a strong resemblance to each other.

Matthew Rose. My Matthew, as I thought of him, persistently. And with all this distance between us, physically and emotionally, my heart found a strange comfort in seeing someone who reminded me of him standing on a Cornish cliffside, wind whipping aside his dark hair. It made me think of the first time I met Matt on Cliffs House's walkway to the sea. Of course, he was yelling at me at the time for stepping on his plants, but that's an understandable reflex for a serious gardener. And his roses and his charming note of apology to the newest 'visitor to Cornish shores' more than made up for it.

My only problem is, he's not my Matthew. Not now. And I, Julianne Morgen, know that full well even as I watch the gorgeous figure onscreen suffer his latest conflict since returning home to Cornwall from foreign shores. While somewhere across the pond, Matthew's only conflict while teaching in Boston was our weeks-old heated argument.

"Oooh, here comes a possible duel!" squealed Gemma. "You know, Francis is fairly dreamy himself, when you think about it —"

"Not so loud — I can't hear what they're saying," said Pippa, grabbing the remote and turning the sound still louder.

Matt — I mean, Ross — was gone from the screen temporarily. And silly as it was, I missed him, even though he had nothing to do with the real-life man I knew.

****

"Breakfast?" Dinah asked, when I walked into the manor's kitchen. "There's marmalade and fried bread on the platter. It was Constance's breakfast, but she's too busy to touch it, apparently."

"She must be really deep into her masterpiece," I said, taking a bite from the unwanted toast, slathered in Dinah's spicy, sweet-and-tart marmalade from her own special recipe.

"Ah, Lady Amanda tells me she can spend days on one little part of a canvas. Painting away at the same tree or flower until it's near to life as she can make it. Won't have so much as a cup of tea until it's right, apparently." Dinah dusted flour from her hands and covered her bread's proofing bowl.

"I love the painting she gave Lady Amanda," I said. "The one of the driftwood on the shore." It was so bright and soft, exactly like a clear morning along the coast. I had spent a lot of mornings walking along there, the cool, wet sea air against my coat and scarf, wet sand beneath my sensible boots — boots Matthew coaxed me into buying so I could explore places in natural Cornwall where three-inch designer stilettos just won't do. So, in a way, it was like a part of him came along for every walk through Cornwall's rugged coast or breathtaking groves.

Cut those thoughts out right now, Julianne Morgen, I scolded myself. It was time to quit thinking about Matt every other minute of my life. Eight weeks of not talking to a person was a sign of deep trouble, even if my heart didn't want to fully admit it.

"That was one of her first paintings, from when Constance was only a girl," said Dinah, who continued our conversation, unaware of the thoughts in my head. "Her gift to Lady Amanda for her eighteenth birthday. Worth a decent sum now, not that she'd ever part with it."

"Not in a million years," I said, smiling over the rim of my teacup before I took a sip. Constance Strong was practically Lady Amanda's godmother — at times a fairy godmother, from the description of the holidays they had shared traveling in England, and in France, where

Constance used to live when her career was in its prime. Now, nearly sixty, she had left France behind for England; and though her canvases were fewer and far between, each one was a meticulous masterpiece that commanded thousands in galleries. Constance Strong was now one of the foremost botanical watercolor painters in all of Europe, maybe in all the world.

This summer, she was painting the indigenous flora of Cornwall, so she had accepted an invitation from Lady Amanda to spend a month or two here at Cliffs House. It was common around the estate's grounds and Ceffylgwyn's natural spots to find Constance cross-legged on the sand or ground, a small easel propped in front of her, her fingers making a rough sketch of a purplish sprig of Cornish heath, or one of the tenacious plants clinging to recesses in the cliffs' rocks. A strong, weathered figure with a calm face and spiky grey-white hair beneath a simple straw gardening hat, her sensible denim or tweed trousers, and her buttoned linen shirt and boots always a little stained by grass or mud from close contact with nature.

Today, she was painting in Cliffs House's 'natural garden,' where Matt had planted an extremely fine specimen of Cornish Moneywort last year, thanks to the Cornish Natural Preservation Society's propagation arrangement. The wind whipped the scarf around her hat's crown, while her brush deftly sketched a leaf's angle with soft, painted lines. She had glanced up at me as I passed her on my way inside, revealing a pair of blue eyes, deep facial creases, and a Mediterranean tan. She raised her hand in a friendly wave.

"Morning," I said.

"Good morning," she called. Her voice a bit cracked and hoarse, but still full of energy, even for two little words. "Lovely day with a bracing wind, isn't it?"

"It is," I agreed. A sunny day in Cornwall was perfection, even in its imperfect details. Like a strong wind off the coast, the one that was tearing at my coat and scarf and ruffling the leaves of the plant Constance was painting. "But it's a little strong for my tastes," I continued.

"Puts the energy into one, though," said Constance. "Must be the breath of spring rolling off the coast. I feel twenty-five again — and me with rheumy fingers, as you know." She waved her hand again, revealing the knobby, crooked fingers — like ballet dancers have twisted toes, I suppose artists are supposed to have roughened hands.

"Must be spring in the air, like you said," I echoed cheerfully, although I found the wind mostly played havoc with my carefully-tamed dark auburn tresses when I most wanted them to be smooth. But Constance's unruly hairstyle looked carefree and at home in the breeze. I envied it as she turned back to her painting, reaching for the glass of water and the open paints on her little folding table.

Polishing off Dinah's toast, I made my way to Lady Amanda's office, which was close to my own. My space as Cliffs House's event planner in residence commanded a beautiful view of the estate, and an impressive display of antiques in between more modern furnishings and conveniences. Just like my room, in fact — which was a guest room I had promised myself months ago to vacate for more permanent housing.

Lady Amanda had wanted to see me first thing this morning, and I arrived just as she was finishing her phone conference with a local inn whose brochures she was designing. Lady Amanda wasn't just the wife of Lord William, lady of the regal manor like in old-fashioned British dramas — like most modern-day ladies of title, as I had learned, she was actively involved not only in Cliffs House's role as a tourist site and event host, but had devoted herself to her career of promoting local business, tourism, and Cornish cultural preservation in Ceffylgwyn. Which was exactly why she needed me, an event planner transported from the U.S. by a lucky resume submission, to run the day-to -day process of hosting events at the manor.

She moved aside the heap of glossy printer paper on her desk and blew a few stray bangs away from her eyes. "Well, that's a morning's work done," she said. "Julianne, I'm glad to see you. There's something we need to discuss before I leave for my sculpting class."

Lady Amanda had taken back up a hobby from her university years recently, partly because of Constance's presence in England. Lady Amanda's friend had been quick to ask if she'd kept up with her talent — a talent that Lady Amanda decried as pathetic in comparison to her quick digital skills for whipping up tourist brochures, or designing programs for recitals and theatrical events.

She checked her watch. "I'll have to make it quick. Close the door if you will."

Close the door? That was new. I felt a jolt of worry. For the first time,

I wondered if I was being scolded; if I had made some horrible error recently with regards to an assignment.

"If this is about the Brown-Phelps wedding —" I began, wondering if the angry mother-of-the-groom had complained about my unwillingness to decorate the reception's petits fours with her favorite berries — a beautiful but somewhat poisonous variety which guests were just 'supposed to pick off' before eating, as she explained, but would look *so* much better than edible ones...

"No, no," said Lady Amanda. "It's something quite secret, actually." She moved from behind her desk to the armchair in her office's sitting area. I sat down on the sofa.

"No one knows but me — although everybody will find out soon enough — but the fact is, my friend Constance told me last night that she's in love. In truth, that she's going to be married very soon."

I knew my surprise showed in my face — but not for someone falling in love with the senior-age artist. "Really?" I said. "That's wonderful." I felt relief that this discussion was about good news, and not some problem with one of Cliffs House's paying guests.

"Isn't it?" said Lady Amanda. "It's just such a surprise to me. All these years, she's lived alone, had a boyfriend here or there, but no one serious. But last night she says, 'I've met the love of my life at last, Amanda. Me, at my age, in love like a schoolgirl.'"

On Lady Amanda's face a fond smile appeared, one that was proof that her thoughts were drifting into the past, no doubt for exploring hiking paths and forgotten gardens in her own school days with the artist.

"Who is he?" I asked.

"I've never met him — but he's coming here shortly so they can be married. He's a friend of the gallery owner who's hosting Constance's exhibition this month. A former vineyard owner named Joseph, whose farm was only a hundred miles from the village where Constance always stayed in Italy. She's driven past it dozens of times, it would seem, when traveling there."

"Wow," I said. "Think if she'd only stopped for a quick tour."

"I know. All those years, they never crossed paths, but now —" Lady Amanda spread her hands, dramatically. "It was love at first sight, apparently."

It was an incredibly romantic story. I was thrilled for Constance, even with my own heart still recently sore and heartbroken — but I didn't see why Lady Amanda needed a secret conference with me to reveal it, unless there was more to this story.

"When's the wedding?" I asked. "Are we planning it?" That would make sense.

"Two weeks," said Lady Amanda. "Right after the gallery show closes." She poured a cup of tea from a pot on her sitting-room table, then poured one for me. "But here's the problem, Julianne. Constance keeps saying 'it's just a small affair, just a little ceremony.' A mere piece of paper between them after some vows before a magistrate, and then they're off to Switzerland for a week so she can paint the plants emerging with the spring thaw. It's practically nothing — all she wants me to do is ring up and enquire about the license and putting an announcement in the London paper afterwards."

I was pretty sure I understood now where this would lead. "And you want something special," I said.

"Of course I do," said Lady Amanda, emphatically. "Constance is my oldest, wisest, and best friend in all the world — more so than half the close chums I still have from my school days, believe it or not. I can't possibly let her be married to the love of her life in her old hiking togs, with nothing but some ginger biscuits and tea before she takes off again. It wouldn't be right."

I pictured this slapdash ceremony taking place — with stained trouser knees that reminded me painfully of Matt's gardening clothes — and couldn't agree more with Lady Amanda taking issue with her friend's arrangement.

"I'm persuading her to be married here, at least — and I want the two of us to add a few special little touches to make it a celebration worth remembering." Lady Amanda set aside her teacup. "Something worthy of Constance, whether she believes it or not. And I need your help to pull it off."

"You've got it," I promised.

***

Constance's wedding would be just the distraction I needed. Something to take my mind off the silly fight I'd had with Matthew, the one that had brought our long-distance romance crashing down around us.

I tried to tell myself it was inevitable: couples separated by an ocean have the odds against them. Long phone calls and webcam chats, and love letter emails eventually become too little; every little disagreement becomes bigger just because you can't reach for someone's hand to say it's really all right.

And it had been such a stupid, petty argument — all about whether Matt should take time off to visit some remote South American region where a new virus had appeared among a rare rain forest species of flower. It sounded dangerous, I pointed out. And didn't he have a big test coming up for his students?

"I do, but a teacher's aide will give it to my class, and take over my syllabus while I'm away," said Matt. "It's only for a few weeks, and it's the best chance we have of saving this species. They want a team representing all fields of plant sciences."

"It's an honor to be asked, I'm sure," I answered. "But you get why I'm concerned, don't you? It's a jungle, Matt. Literally. People get eaten there. By big snakes, and crocodiles, and — and bugs and fish, even." I dredged for further memories of South American nature specials, and came up short.

"I'll be very careful," he promised. And laughed, which actually made me a little angry. "It's a few weeks, Juli. Just long enough to observe, collect samples, and see if an antiviral program can be developed." He sounded more serious now. "If it wasn't so important, I wouldn't consider it. You know that."

I knew. I also knew that I was jealous of South America, and a dying plant. It had been weeks since we'd seen each other for my vacation around Valentine's Day, which we'd spent hand in hand in Boston. I was tired after a long day's work and bitter over a whiny wine tasting host's insufferable demands for his upcoming event in the garden. That's partly why I had reacted poorly to words like 'virus,' 'jungle,' and 'weeks in a remote place,' where Matt would be without cell phone coverage or internet for nearly a month. But truthfully, I was lonely for him, and the one smidge of vacation he would have for spring break was being spent even further away from me than usual.

So we argued. And, eventually, fought with harsher words about whether this was a practical choice, whether Matt could get hurt, or at least stuck in a foreign country and miss his students' final exam; and, underneath all those words, whether we were both too lonely and too tired to keep our relationship from crumbling under the strain.

Even then, I could hear how much it was hurting him to have me even hint that his feelings weren't as strong as before. This, after he had bought my ticket to Boston, and barely let me out of his arms at the airport in time for me to board my flight. It hurt me to admit that I sometimes regretted his choice after I had tried so hard to be supportive and happy for his return to the university.

He would never ask me to leave my job in Cornwall to come back to the U.S.; I would never ask him to give up his work as a scientist and a professor to make me happy. But somewhere in between those truths was a lot of wistfulness and heartache, and it had finally emerged in the form of a major disagreement. We hung up without resolving our differences, both too peeved to talk about what was really bothering us the most.

A few days later, I received a short email from Matt before he left for his trip, one that felt a little more distant in its words than I wished it to be, even with 'all my love' at the bottom. I was still too sore to write back. And that was the last time I heard from him, even though it had been weeks ago, and by now, Matt would be back in Boston, probably administering the final to his class.

It was my stupid pride's fault, I thought. I hadn't emailed him until it was too late, and even then those emails had gone unanswered. After all those weeks, our relationship had cooled to the point that Matt apparently didn't need to write me again, as if those distant words from his emailed goodbye had been the last ones. So Matt's pride was at fault, too. And now I was lonely, sad, and missing him like crazy. I almost wished I'd gotten on a plane to South America ... well, maybe not. Not with man-eating snakes and piranhas there. But if I hadn't been so bitter that last time he wrote me ... if Matt wasn't *so* stubborn sometimes ....

See? Constance's wedding had come at the perfect time. Time for me to face facts that Matt and I had reached an impasse — that maybe that perfect love we had celebrated at Christmas wasn't so perfect after all. My heartache would have to find a way to fix things between us — or find a way to heal itself, so I could stop thinking of how much I missed him.

And the way to that healing seemed, ironically, to be through plants.

After all, Constance Strong was a botanical artist, Amanda pointed out, so the wedding obviously needed a strong natural theme. I had suggested she find a way to pay tribute to her friend's artwork as part of the wedding — maybe finding a rare cultivated species of flower to give to Constance and Joseph as a gift, maybe similar to one which Constance had painted in the past. The idea of paying tribute to Constance's art thrilled Amanda, who was already eagerly researching possible choices.

Since it was spring, we could host the ceremony out of doors. Amanda had chosen the 'tea garden,' as I called it. Right now, it was in need of a trim, however, and some of the plants had been burned by a winter frost. Not exactly a magical site for a wedding, but I knew that a gardener's touch would make the difference.

Unfortunately, that also meant I would have to talk to Billy.

Cliff House's longtime gardener Jackson had retired this winter, and until a full-time replacement could be hired, Lord William had arranged for a neighboring estate to 'loan' him an experienced caretaker for Jackson's job — a longtime Cornish native who was a little past his prime, they explained, but had spent decades caring for their public botanical gardens. He arrived two days later, a hunched, sour-looking figure who glared at the gardens as if he was facing off a mortal enemy. He wielded pruning shears like he was cutting his way through the wilderness, and the only time I saw him smile was when he was savaging a stray hedgeling with his machete.

While Jackson and I had been friendly coworkers, Billy and I ... well, we hadn't exactly hit it off. In simple words, I was fairly sure he detested me.

Determined, I walked towards the hedges that Billy was busily trimming. "Billy," I said. "I need to talk to you about maintenance for the little garden on the house's east side."

He squinted at me. "What'bout'em?" he asked.

His words were unfathomable to me most of the time — maybe his remarks were occasionally in Cornish, maybe not, but either way, I couldn't understand him. "Lady Amanda wants the garden to be in pristine show condition two weeks from now," I said. "It's for a wedding for a friend of hers."

"Garden'sa'right now," he said. He gave me a mean, calculating look, as if I'd accused him of neglecting it. My brain tried to translate his last sentence in the meantime.

"She wants it to be special," I repeated. "I was thinking maybe some nice spring bulbs — some daffodils and paperwhites, and some early crocuses in the big urns."

Billy spat — viciously — into the bushes. "Wales'r'dils," he said. "Nowannaput t' likes of 'em round 'ere." From the look he gave me, I gathered I had insulted him deeply with this suggestion.

I opened my mouth to reply, trying to fathom the meaning of his words. "Do you have some flowers in mind?" I asked. "Again, it's in two weeks, and it's important to Lady Amanda —"

"Donwanna foolin' around w' that spot for 'nother fortnight or so," he mumbled — grumbling — under his breath as he began scissoring away hedge branches again. "Tisn'twhat've amind fer it ... not fer 'nother few weeks. N'of it."

Was that an outright refusal? I couldn't be sure, but I couldn't let it go at that, if it was. "Listen," I said, firmly. "What Lady Amanda wants, we do. Is that clear? She wants spring flowers in bloom in the east patio garden in two weeks." I held up two fingers, in case this number wasn't clear.

"G'onw'ye!" he snarled. "I'vegiv'n ye answer, and it be. Meddlin'wench," he muttered under his breath after this, as the vicious pruners snapped their way through more limbs. There was a *squeak* from the mechanism with every clip of the blades, like a squeak of protest from the poor hedge.

"We're not done with this issue," I said, firmly. "And I would suggest that you start cleaning out the urns and trimming back the frost-bitten plants so we can get started on putting in the new ones."

As I walked away, I heard more muttering and snarling behind me, none of which was intelligible, except for maybe the word 'Yank' thrown in a time or two. I knew my face was flushed with anger, and that my Valentino heels were clipping an angry pace along the walkway.

I passed Pippa who was tugging on a pair of wellies for visiting the kitchen garden, her dark, spiky hair hidden beneath her wool cap. "What's with you?" she said, looking at me with a puzzled expression. I folded my arms and scowled.

"I was attempting to have a discussion with Billy the gardener, but I obviously need a lesson or two in Cornish," I said.

"He doesn't speak Cornish," said Pippa. "Well, except when he swears," she added. "He's a tough old stick, Billy, isn't he? Not very friendly with the lot of us, but that's his choice. Got a chip on his shoulder, it seems. He's not exactly taken a shine to you anyways, I've heard."

"Is it because I'm an American?" I asked. "Is that why he dislikes me?"

"Probably. He's got a bone against foreigners of any kind, seems. French, Italian, Spanish, Welsh..."

"Welsh visitors aren't exactly foreigners, are they?" I asked.

"Neither's Devon's folk, but he's got a real bone against *that* lot," said Pippa. "Anybody that's not proper Cornish. Not even me — me dad's from Cheshire."

Weren't daffodils the official flower of Wales? I thought. Maybe that's what he took issue with in my suggestions.

"Well, if he won't listen to me, he'll have to listen to Lord William," I said.

Lord William, the titled master of Cliffs House, was in the manor's spacious, stone-built garden shed, the former carriage house from the Victorian era. I found him greasing a chain saw at his work bench, oil spattered on his old pullover and a worn pair of denim jeans. Far from the picture I'd first had of him, before I knew that modern-day estate owners were often as handy with tools, agricultural planning, and gift shop cash registers as they were with financial portfolios and business plans.

He listened sympathetically to my problem. "Billy is rather stubborn, unfortunately," said Lord William. "I've had a difficult time myself getting him to understand how things are done at Cliffs House. It seems he's set in his ways — he has a particular way of doing things at his usual post, and wants to stick to it. I suppose thirty years of the same routine rather does that to a person."

Any other time, I could sympathize with a senior-age gardener needing his routine, but not now. "Will you speak to him?" I said. "It's very important to Lady Amanda that he do something about the garden before Constance's big day. If it's just a few sad-looking plants and tufted grass in those flower urns and beds, I'll never forgive myself." *I'll get on my hands and knees and plant cheap bulbs myself first*, I thought.

"Not to worry," said Lord William. "I'll see to it. I'll have a word with him and I'm sure he'll change his mind." He laid aside his oily rag, giving me a cheerful smile that made me feel much better about the prospects of getting Billy to plant a few of the much-despised daffodils.

On my way back to the house, I heard my cell phone ringing in my coat pocket. I pulled it out, a part of me hoping against hope that it was Matthew's number on the screen — and, instead, saw one that had become familiar only these past few weeks: the number to a local estate agent, one of Lady Amanda's friends.

I answered it. "Hello, Denise," I said. "Do you have good news for me?"

I crossed my fingers as I spoke, since Denise had been combing all of Ceffylgwyn and the outlying villages for an affordable rental house or flat for me. A few possibilities had come up, but I had found myself reluctant to take any of them. Not because of the shabbiness of a couple of choices, but because they were outside the village. After months of living here, of quiz nights and quiet strolls along Cliffs House's walkways, I found I didn't want to live in another village, even one that would be just as charming. Not sleepy, quiet Ceffylgwyn, where all my American friends no doubt pictured me spending dull evenings knitting scarves and longing for the metropolitan atmosphere, coffee shops, and movie theaters of my old life in Seattle.

Finding something in Ceffylgwyn itself would be challenging, Denise had warned me. But I was willing to take even the crumbliest of one-room flats in the village itself to stay.

"I found you something at last," said Denise. "It's just come back on the market — the owner has been holding it for someone else, but hasn't had word that they're interested, so they're making it available."

"Where is it?" I asked. "It's here, right?"

"Right in the heart of Ceffylgwyn. It has —"

"One room, I know, I know," I said. "A cold water flat with a view of some shacks and the fish and chips shop's neon window sign, but I don't care."

"It's better than that," laughed Denise. "It's a proper house, with a kitchen and bath, and all the modern conveniences we all expect, and they'll be yours alone. And at a decent rate, although still a little pricier than you'd probably wish. But I think you'll be able to afford it. There's even a little wiggle room outside, should you want to take up gardening."

Gardening. That little wistful longing in me for a certain someone stirred itself at this word. "Um, I'll take it," I said. "I'll meet you there, and get the keys, and I'll bring the deposit." It would take me a day or two to move everything — that with the help of Geoff, the kindly estate manager and fellow Cornwall transplant who shuttled me around in his car whenever I needed a lift.

"It'll be tomorrow afternoon at the very soonest," said Denise. "I'll come and pick you up, and bring the rental agreement with me. You should see it before you sign, of course."

"As if I'd pass on a place that sounds this great," I answered.

I hadn't seen it yet, of course. But when Denise pulled up outside its gate and parked, I felt my heart give a great *thump* before it seemed to plunge all the way to the bottom of my chest.

It was beautiful. It was charming, small, and exactly how everybody pictures a Cornish cottage. I loved it already, because I had always loved it — ever since Matthew had first invited me inside.

"Isn't it a beauty?" said Denise, as she climbed out of the car. "The owner was quite shocked the previous tenant didn't renew his lease. They're a bit hesitant about renting to just anybody, you see. But I persuaded them that *you* would be a model tenant."

I crossed the threshold, feeling like I was entering a ghost house. None of Matthew's things were here — his books weren't on the shelves, his pictures gone from the walls. The furniture was still there, everything positioned exactly as it was the last time I was here. Decorating a Christmas tree with Matt, trying to bring back a little of the childhood happiness he had lost all too soon to adversity.

"The place has a name," said Denise, checking the listing on her mobile. "Ah, yes. Rose-"

"-moor Cottage," I finished, at the same time as Denise. "I know."

The room sounded empty and hollow, my footsteps echoing a little as I crossed the wooden floor in my stilettos. I bent down and lifted a silvery piece of tinsel which had fallen behind the shabby old armchair. It was dusty, marring the shiny, silver surface.

"Needs a bit of cleaning, of course," said Denise, referring to the cottage's neglected rooms. "But I'm sure you'll love it once you've made it a bit more personal."

"Why didn't the previous tenant come back?" I asked, softly.

"Haven't the faintest idea, really." Denise dusted her hands after pulling open the worn tartan curtains across the front windows. "She simply said he hadn't renewed. Something about him being overseas — maybe he's staying a bit longer than planned. Either way, the place is available, and it won't be that way for long. It's yours to take or leave, Julianne." She paused. "Shall I bring the papers?"

I gazed at the garden outside. The first spring blossoms had appeared, although the grasses and long-leafed, wild stalks seemed tangled and forlorn. A lump rose in my throat.

"I'll take it," I said.

I didn't want to, yet I did. I wanted to be here, and not have a stranger pulling up the plants and putting the old armchair out by the curb — as if that would actually happen, given the owner's feelings on tenants. Even though the last thing I needed was to be surrounded by memories of Matthew, I felt at home here. The coziness of this room, of this view, meant too much to me to let it go yet.

After the papers were signed, Denise drove away and I was alone in the cottage. It felt strange, with only my presence in these rooms. I'd never been here before without Matthew. I walked through each one, finding dust and empty shelves and the wrought-iron bed frame I hadn't realized was in the bedroom. I opened a narrow door which led to a closet, and saw a flannel shirt lying crumpled on the floor. One of Matt's, which he had obviously forgotten.

In my mind, I still pictured his books and his glossy brown tea pot on the table. But the teapot wasn't in the kitchen's glass-door cupboards when I opened them, one by one in my exploration. Only the chipped plates I remembered fondly from having a takeaway lunch here with Matt a time or two, when we were still in the 'will we?/won't we?' stage of our relationship.

Out the kitchen door, to the little hothouse Matt had loved. I stepped inside, standing beneath its glass ceilings choked with overgrown sweat peas, climbing roses, and other flowering vines that had crept up the frame and filtered the sunlight. The glass panes around me were grimy with pollen and dirt, making it hard to see the little green leaves budding out on the vines; the space around me was vacant, except for a few empty clay pots. Matt had found someone to care for all his plants before he left.

I took a deep breath. It smelled like him, earthy and green — but also like leaf mold and manure, which made me sneeze, then wrinkle my nose after a second breath. I moved aside, and felt a broken piece of ceramic beneath my shoe. I caught sight of a hole near the corner, where Matt had dug up an impressive climbing pink rose that had always seemed to be in bloom.

Oh, Matt. I wish you were here. I sighed. It would be a very long time before I didn't wish that, I was certain. I wondered if he was in Boston, missing me and wishing things between us were different. I wondered if I should try one more time to write him an email, to be the first one to break my pride and offer an olive branch.

Maybe it wasn't too late. But I thought of the black hole into which my last three letters had vanished as I stepped outside the greenhouse and closed the door.

***

"To Geoff Weatherby — the finest Londoner ever to come to our fair village," said Lord William. "May he have many a happy birthday among us." He lifted his glass as the rest of us did the same.

"Here, here," echoed Gemma. "Three cheers for Geoff!"

For the estate manager's birthday, Lord William had arranged a luncheon at Ceffylgwyn's finest restaurant — a quaint, semi-casual seafood bistro that served the freshest catch and had an outdoor seating area that overlooked the ever-moving waters of the Channel. We were toasting our beloved estate employee, who looked rather modest and somewhat embarrassed over being the center of attention — Geoff was typically the quiet and stoic type, who remained placid, whether Cliffs House experienced a crisis of garden blight, hoodlums trampling a newly-planted timber grove, or storm damage to the east side of the manor right before a major public event.

"Make a birthday wish, Geoff," said Gemma. "Just like in the movies. Maybe it'll come true." She lit the candle on a tempting-looking cake — a scrumptious recipe from Dinah's kitchen which Lady Amanda had arranged to have brought to the table after lunch.

"Bet he wishes for a raise," said Pippa, with a wink in the direction of our employers.

"Bet he wishes for a million pounds," said Gemma.

"*I* think he'll wish that the lot of nosy young things at the manor would hold their tongues," snorted Dinah, as Geoff leaned over and gently blew out the flame.

"Tell us, Geoff," said Pippa.

"If you tell it won't come true," I protested. "Don't listen to them, Geoff."

"Oh, that's a superstition," said Lady Amanda. "Do tell so we'll know if it's going to come true."

"I think I will hold to superstition, Lady Amanda," he answered. "I'm afraid I'm rather too old to believe that one million pounds will arrive by magic into my possession, since I never play the lotto." Despite his usual calm, grave tone, I detected a hint of humor in Geoff's voice as he glanced at me, accepting a slice of Dinah's cake.

Afterwards, we trickled away from the restaurant towards the cars parked along the street. I was arm in arm with Pippa, our best luncheon dresses — my semi-casual pink and white flowered chiffon and her electric-blue polka dot minidress — clashing a little as we picked our way in high heels past the pavement cracks in need of repair.

Even being careful, I felt the jolt of a stiletto trapped between a pavement gap. "Stuck," I announced, as I pulled free of Pippa's arm. She had practically pulled me off my feet before I spoke, not even aware that I had stopped.

"What?" she asked, glancing back a second later. "Something wrong?" I shook my head, motioning for her to go on. Remembering plenty of times when I was every bit as lost in my own daydreams as she was on an afternoon this beautiful.

"Ah, the young," said Dinah, who was passing by now. "Do you want a hand?"

"I'm fine," I said. I wiggled the shoe a bit, being careful not to scrape the leather. I winced, thinking of the scrape that would undoubtedly show once it was free — shoe polish doesn't cover everything. While this was a knockoff pair, I was fond of them anyway.

I stood up, feeling the breeze on my face, carrying the heavy smell of sea air that has a distinctive flavor, an acquired taste that you get only from living on and loving the coast. The buildings looked white in the bright sunlight, except for the striped awnings, the green buds peeking from window boxes, and the black and white cross of a Saint Piran's flag.

I heard the security *honk* of a horn as Gemma bumped against Geoff's car before he had unlocked its door. I smelled the scent of pasties cooking in a nearby shop, and I saw a man emerging from the chemist's, a backpack slung on his shoulder, dark hair contrasting with his blue shirt.

Matthew.

The figure had turned the other way, walking the opposite direction from me. I know I shouted his name, because I felt my lips move and heard the words in my ear. I knew that everybody was looking at me — Dinah and Geoff and the girls, Lord William and Lady Amanda who were catching up behind me — but I didn't even notice their expressions. I had taken off in that direction, pausing only to pull off my heels and carry them in one hand as I ran like a crazy person down the streets of Ceffylgwyn.

I knew it was him. I knew it. The unmistakable profile, the color of his hair, the expression on his face — all unmistakable. Matthew Rose was here in Cornwall.

"Matthew, wait!"

I shouted again, trying in vain to close the distance. The figure never turned to acknowledge me. *Was it a mistake?* Was I chasing a stranger? I hurried past a boy walking a dog, a girl busy watering a tub full of spring daffodils. Ahead of me, the figure turned the corner and disappeared.

When I reached the next street, he was nowhere in sight. Frustrated, I stopped running, biting my lip as I gazed at my surroundings. The usual shops and houses, only without a soul in sight. A motorbike beeped at me as it passed by, but the driver was a stranger. There was no sign of anybody I knew. Not even a glimpse of a stranger who looked remotely like Matthew.

Disappointed, I turned around. The woman rearranging the window display to my left was staring at me, undoubtedly wondering who I'd been chasing. I turned the corner onto the street where Geoff and Lord William were parked, and ran directly into a man in a blue shirt as he exited the side door of a shop, his cologne so familiar that I lost my breath at the scent of it.

I looked up into Matthew's eyes. He was looking at me as if he'd seen a ghost. I was looking at him as if he was a mirage. At last, his lips moved.

"Julianne," he said.

"Hi," I answered. I wanted to bite my tongue. *Hi?* How about, 'what are you doing here?'

We both stared at each other. "I ... I didn't know you were back," I said. Because nothing else came to mind at this moment. "I mean — I thought you were in Boston."

"I was." His voice sounded hoarse, almost far away. "That is ... I've only been back for a day or two. Since the end of the semester."

"Right. The semester." My lips tried to smile, but couldn't. It didn't feel right...not like meeting an old friend on the street. This was awkward, painful, and hurt in the pit of my heart.

"I didn't think I would see you this soon —" he began. "That is —"

"Are you here for long?" I made my tone extremely polite and casual, only I wished my voice wasn't trembling, because it ruined the effect.

"I don't know," he said. "Not if ... I may have to go to London for awhile." He glanced away, studying the flag rippling in the wind above a pot of half-open daffodils.

"Oh." I paused. "Well ... I suppose I'll see you around," I replied. "You can tell me about your class." I didn't mention South America, or the poor plant Matt had been trying to save.

"Yes," said Matt. But it was as if the word had been dragged out of him. He didn't want to look me in the eye, I could see. That sudden sheepishness — avoidance — on his part made me feel angry.

The politeness would kill me if I stood here much longer.

"I...um, I'm renting the cottage," I continued. *Your cottage*, I almost said, before I sternly corrected myself. "There are some things there that you forgot."

"I'll pick them up," he said. "Thank you."

"You're welcome," I said.

"It's good to see you," he said. But he didn't look as if it was good. He looked as if he was miserable — as miserable as I felt standing here. "I'm sorry it's been so long." He looked at me for a moment, his dark eyes flickering to my own.

"Me, too." If it hadn't been for how mortified I felt, that gaze might have melted me. But Matt's pain was accompanied by body language that said clearly that he wanted distance, more than simply an arm's length apart.

He hesitated. "I should — I should go," he began.

"Of course." Right now, I didn't care if that was reluctance or desperation in his voice. "I have to as well. Goodbye." I touched his arm, briefly, then moved past him, walking towards the rest of the manor staff. Trying to seem as calm and normal as if my chasing down someone while barefoot was a perfectly ordinary experience, as if nothing in meeting Matt and finding that he'd dreaded this moment could actually hurt me like a red-hot poker shoved into my chest.

I wanted to feel as over it as he seemed. I wasn't going to cry, I wasn't going to let it show that our breakup hurt. I was going to cling to my dignity, and be perfectly adult about the fact that relationships end.

I was not going to picture myself in Matthew's arms, no matter how badly I ached to be there.

***

"So why didn't you tell us he was coming home?" demanded Pippa. She was tying ribbons on the little complementary gifts for the wine tasting tomorrow, while Gemma and I were working on cutting cheese cubes for the appetizer platters. "I can't believe he hasn't come to see us at all!"

"You know, I had a dream about Ross just a few nights ago," said Gemma. "Now, I think maybe that was a sign." She blushed a little a second later, since, after all, I was supposed to be Matt's girlfriend.

"Well, he's not sure he's staying long," I said. "He might be going to London." I repeated this part of Matt's answer, hoping they wouldn't press me for details.

"You must've been surprised," said Gemma. "Did he mean to surprise you? Was he planning to show up at your place without warning — let me guess, you spoiled it by chasing him down?"

"I was surprised, yes," I said. It wasn't a blush of pleasure that was suffusing my cheeks with these words, whatever they might think. "He definitely intended something else." *Like sneaking into Cornwall and avoiding seeing me as long as possible.*

"How romantic," sighed Pippa. "I wish a bloke would try to surprise *me* with something special. Last thing Gregory did for me? Brought me a bunch of half-dead flowers picked out of his mum's window boxes. And some poor excuse for missing my birthday for a wrestling match."

"Wrestling? Ick! And I thought he was the rugby type." Gemma tsked with sympathy after this. "Know what Andy did to *me* this past week?"

"No! What sort of cad has *he* been?"

I was glad for this change of subject. No one knew yet about my falling out with Matt — or that I hadn't the slightest idea what he'd been doing for almost two months now. I wanted to gradually slide into the truth, which would be easier when Matt was in London. And even easier when I finally wasn't still in love with him.

As for the possibility that Matt would be sticking around...I couldn't think about that yet.

I had to face facts and talk to him soon, to get it over with. First, to berate him for not having the decency to email me back those last few times. Then I intended to point out that he could have simply called me when he got back from South America and told me it was over, rather than leave me hanging on for — what? Two weeks now? Three? How long had he been back from the wilderness, and avoiding communication with me?

Yes, that was definitely what I was going to do. Then, when I had time to lick my own wounded pride after wounding his, maybe I would stop being in love with Matthew Rose.

Today, I had an appointment at Willows Floral, where I had recently explained Lady Amanda's wish to purchase a rare, domesticated version of the Alabama canebrake pitcher plant. Constance had painted a grove of the endangered plant back in the 1950's, only ten years after its discovery in a handful of U.S. counties. Lady Amanda had shown me the postcards of the unusual plant, with its tulip-like maroonish-brown blossoms, and the late season 'pitchers' of yellow, threaded with spidery orange veins here and there, rising like trumpets from the plant's base.

I had shown those same postcards to Harvey Willow, along with a complete printout on the *Sarracenia alabamensis* and its limited availability as a preservation-oriented propagated species. Now I hoped that he had word on how soon the plant would arrive from the U.S.

"Ah, well...let me see." Harvey scratched his head, almost dislodging his glasses. "A — a what did you say? An Alabama lily?"

"A pitcher plant," I explained, patiently. "Remember — I showed you a printed picture?"

"Mm-hmm. I have a stack of those around here — pictures for orders,

I mean." He shuffled through some papers next to a computer. An outdated, boxy monitor that was shut off and covered by a cloth, I noticed. "What did you say your name was?"

"Julianne Morgen," I said. "You've met me before, remember? I work at the estate." I tried not to feel exasperated, although this was the second time I'd explained to him who I was.

"Yes, of course — Miss Morgen. The one Lord William hired from America," said Harvey, snapping his fingers. "I certainly hope you've taken a liking to Cornwall, Miss Morgen."

"Yes," I said, weakly. "It's lovely. But if you could just check on the status of the plant I ordered for Lady Amanda, that would be really great."

"Ah. The plant. Yes. What was that again?"

"The Alabama canebrake pitcher plant," I said. "That's it in that pile of papers — no, not that pile, the other one — no, to your left, Mr. Willow. The other left —"

"This one? No. Well ... good heavens, this one's a month old." He frowned with puzzlement as he stared at the latest sheet of paper from his stack. "Hmm...I wonder if Lorene still needs it..."

"About the pitcher plant?" I suggested again.

"Hmm? Oh, yes. Terrible mess around here," said Harvey Willow. "My boy's doing, I'm afraid. I'm supposed to be retired, you know. Just helping with the arrangements and the hothouses and what not. He's running things now — had to go and break his leg up at St Austell a few weeks ago. Hasn't mastered crutches at all yet."

So Harvey's son David must be entirely in charge of the business side of Willow Florists, something I hadn't realized until now. But with him gone, there was nothing else I could do, unless I wanted to deal with a London florist, who might be twice as busy — the only other florist local to Ceffylgwyn was on vacation in Spain for a month.

"Knew it would be trouble the moment that rich footballer bought the racetrack up there last year," Harvey muttered. "What's-his-name, married the model 'round here, didn't he?" Inwardly, I winced over this reference to Donald Price-Parker and Petal, Matt's ex. "Thought we got rid of that sort when the Trelawny Tigers folded, what had David moping about for weeks. Hoped it would stay closed after sane folk crushed St Eval's bid over noise, but money speaks to everyone sooner or later these days. Even so, it did put a stop to the boy's running off every weekend to race with that club in Launceston —"

"Are you sure we couldn't call David?" I interrupted, eagerly. "Maybe he could talk you through the computer program's steps?" Surely the information was trapped inside that hard drive, more so than Harvey's precariously-positioned stacks of paper.

"No need, no need. Now, what was the Latin name of this plant?" He lifted the sheet from the pile, squinting at it. "I can't make it out — must've left my glasses in my other pocket."

"*Sarracenia alabamensis*," I said, reading it for him. "Um, your glasses —"

"When the boy gets back, this will all be easier. He knows computers like a proper genius. Took a class in school." Harvey searched carefully for the monitor's 'on' switch, the screen sputtering from blue lines to an old command prompt that one only saw in nineties-era movies now.

One finger picked its way across the keys. "I've got two weddings this month, you know. Plus the regular order for the manor house that they can't fill on their own. Heard they lost their gardener. And that chap who used to look after the hothouse, one of Lord William's school chums."

I tried hard not to blush at this inadvertent reference to Matthew once again. "Um, Mr. Willow," I tried again, tapping the top of my head.

"Blasted little keys are so hard to see," the florist mumbled, not noticing my gesture. "Ah. Well. It seems there's not an order for Lady Amanda, miss," he said.

No order? But I had brought this printout in days ago. "Is something wrong?" I asked. "Is it out of stock — is there a ban on it in Customs?"

"Not if I've got the proper import forms, likely ... and the nursery's certified and inspected...I just haven't put in for it yet, it seems."

"You mean you forgot?"

"Exactly, Miss Morgen. Exactly." He shook his head. "It flew out of my mind, it seems."

My heart sank. "How long...exactly ... will it take for one to arrive?"

"Oh, with the Customs forms...the inspection ... a bit of wheedling here and there with the Ministry of Agriculture's special permits and so on ... a couple of weeks or so."

"If you send it today?" I said.

He looked away from the screen. "What? Oh, of course, Miss Morgen.

I'll see to it directly." He laid the piece of paper atop the keyboard, and searched his pockets with both hands. "Now, if I could just find my —"

"Your glasses, Mr. Willow." I pointed to the top of my head. His eyes traveled up to his own, which were propped there.

"Ah. Well, I actually meant a pen. For the forms."

Ah. So those, too, had gone astray since the last time I was here. With a sigh, I accepted a pen and the sheets of paper and began filling in the blanks once more.

***

I reheated a pasty in Rosemoor Cottage's tiny oven, and popped it quickly in my mouth in four bite-size pieces. I slung my jacket across the worn kitchen chair and pictured kicking my high heels off for a pair of sequined mules as I settled in with the sketches for Constance's bouquet.

A simple little one of ivory and lavender blooms, we decided. Lady Amanda had already coaxed Constance into at least purchasing a new dress for the wedding, and the two of them were off to London for the first half of this week. I suspected if Constance hadn't needed to meet with a gallery owner there to transfer some paintings for the exhibit that Lady Amanda never would have convinced her to agree.

I heard a knock on the front door. "Coming!" I shouted, swallowing the last of my tea before I hurried to answer it. There, on the doorstep, was Matt.

I was so shocked at the sight of him that I lost my words for a moment — and *why* must my heart give that crazy flutter at the same time? "Oh. Hello," I said. Still polite. And still using my polite-but-reserved smile. "It's you."

"I'm sorry to bother you," he said. "I wanted to get my things out of your way." He looked as if he planned to stay on the doorstep, as if I would simply close the door and leave him there while I fetched them. Well, if he thought I was going to be petty about this, he was completely wrong. Justifiably angry, but not petty.

"Come in," I said. I opened the door fully. He crossed the threshold, looking around at the room. Where, shamefully, I'd done very little personal decorating, except for hanging a few pictures of friends, and sticking some Cornish souvenirs on shelves. I even had the same old tartan curtains over the windows. For a moment, I thought I saw a little wistfulness in his face.

I softened, just a little. "It looks a little empty, doesn't it?" I said. I could be polite a little longer. No need to scold him for being an insensitive coward straightaway.

"It looks fine," he said. He smiled. "I remember seeing that picture in your office at Cliffs House. The one of you and Aimee."

His smile was only a weak, half-hearted attempt at one, really, but it still did strange things to my heart and head, unwilling as I was. "I'll just ... grab the box."

I made my escape, trying to contain the heat inside me the longer I was in Matt's company — part longing and part anger. The cardboard box with Matt's stray possessions was in my closet. Nothing valuable, just some 'bits and bobs' that I had discovered while cleaning. Since I shouldn't be keeping any reminders of Matt, probably, it would be better to give them back to their rightful owner.

I handed it to Matt. "It's just a few things," I said. "A shirt, a coffee mug ... a paperweight I found in the back of a shelf."

He lifted a paper star from its contents, studying it with a faint smile. I tried not to blush, remembering folding it myself back in December. The two of us decorating the tree in this room, on the verge of being so much more than friends....

"I, um, was so surprised you didn't rent this place," I continued. Was my tone actually cold at this moment? "Even if you're only staying a few weeks." *Before you rush off to London, which is the only way I have a chance of forgetting about you.*

"Like you said, it was only for a few weeks." His voice sounded distant, too. "I missed Mathilda's emails about the lease ... by the time I read it, I thought it wouldn't be fair to beg a few weeks' permission from her. I thought I'd stay someplace further from the village's center." He didn't say where.

"So are you working in London?" I asked. "Or is it just the precursor to somewhere else — Oxford, maybe? Cambridge? Eton? Another class of bright young minds destined for botanical greatness?" I knew I should ask about his South American trip, in order to clear the air. Then the subject of our breakup would deal with nothing but our personal failures.

"None of them," he said. "I'm not working in London. I'm ..." he hesitated. "I'm not sure what I'll be doing." He sounded evasive — and unhappy — and not in a way that made me think he was uncomfortable chatting with his former girlfriend.

"Before you go, you owe me an explanation, at least." I crossed my arms, planting my feet squarely apart in my heels, which gave me enough height to be level with Matt's gaze. "For why you never answered my letter after I apologized to you. And why you didn't have the decency to break up with me using something other than silence, Matt."

A cornered look crossed Matt's face. He looked more uncomfortable than ever, avoiding my eyes.

"Because I didn't —" he began. "I never —" He stopped speaking, running one hand through his hair in frustration. "I have no idea where to start." He let out a bitter laugh at this point. "I hadn't wanted to say anything. That was the whole point of being out of the way and not seeing anyone here. Not seeing you especially." His eyes wouldn't meet mine, but I could see frustration in them.

"Never what?" I said. "Don't you think I deserve the truth?" At this moment, something about Matt's words made me feel a tiny bit of dread, because we were no longer talking about our silly argument over piranhas.

Carefully, Matt set the box he was holding on the nearby chair.

"Before I left for South America, I had a physical," he said. "Routine blood work and vaccinations. I wrote to you the day I left, then I was out of touch for six weeks ... when I came back, there was a phone message waiting for me from the medical clinic. Several messages. They'd been trying to get in touch with me for weeks, because there was an abnormality in my white cell count."

I drew a sharp breath. *Cancer*.

"They wanted to do some tests as soon as possible. And they — they thought they might have found something." He lifted his gaze to mine. Oh so briefly, but in it, I read oh so much.

"When I got the news, I didn't know what to do," he said. "It was a shock. Crushing. They scheduled a biopsy. And they told me if the results are positive, then it's likely an advanced stage."

And a poor prognosis. He didn't have to say it, because I knew that already from his voice, which was trying so hard to be calm and careful, but couldn't hold everything back.

"I read your messages. But by then I already knew, and I couldn't ... I couldn't ask you to deal with this. I couldn't ask that of anyone." He swallowed. "I had one week of classes left, and I decided to leave for London for the test, and come home to wait ... and if it turned out that it was negative, I would come to you and explain, and everything would be fine again ...."

It wasn't only misery in his voice and face, I noticed. His cheeks were hollow, his body gaunt from worry. He had spent the past two weeks worrying that he had only months left to live, and was planning to hide from everyone in the place he loved most until he knew the truth. He hadn't left my messages unanswered because he was scared of breaking up with me, but of breaking my heart by making me watch him die.

"And if it was positive?" I asked. Quietly.

Matt didn't answer for a moment. "It would be better for me to let you go," he said. His voice broke slightly. "I would have said goodbye to you."

"How could you?" I realized that tears were gathering in my eyes, and I worked hard to blink them back. "How could you keep this a secret?"

"Julianne, we're talking about weeks. Months at most. I couldn't ask you to wait — even if I took treatments in London, they might not work. I couldn't hurt you by making you go through it, too. I don't want to hurt the people I love more than I have to with this. And this isn't what you deserve in life. "

That was it. I was really angry now. I took my hands off my hips and took two quick steps across the floorboards, my arms closing around Matt. Holding him as tight as I could, possibly squeezing the breath out of his chest, but I didn't care.

"Don't you ever, *ever* again suggest I could care so little about you that I would walk away now." My cheek rested against his, my lips close to his ear. "Do you understand, Matthew Rose? If you ever so much as think about breaking up with me again over a little thing like a medical diagnosis, I'll honestly kill you myself."

I felt a tremor in his frame. Laughter, I realized. "Julianne," he began.

"No, honestly," I said. I drew back from my hold on him. "I thought you were holding my stupid jealousy over a sick plant against me. If I had even dreamed that you needed me, I would have been on a plane to Boston in ten seconds, holding your hand."

"Missing out on your life," he answered, softly. I laid my hand against his cheek.

"This is part of my life," I said. "I'm not saying it doesn't hurt that this is what we're facing ... but I'd rather face it with you than have you shut me out to be protective. That's my choice, Matt. And if you try to banish me again, you'll see what I'm like when I'm *really* angry. Not just peeved over some unanswered emails and — and piranhas, or whatever."

When he chuckled, the unhappy lines in his face relaxed, at least a little. The burden of keeping it secret from everyone had been too much for him, a lonely exile that was exhausting him. I cupped his face as I kissed his cheek, then his lips. It was the first time in weeks, and it felt good.

He kissed me back, tenderly, then eagerly. His arms tightened around me, and I felt the hunger from our last moments together in Boston, and also felt the tension melting away from Matt's frame.

When he released me, I drew free from his embrace and lifted my jacket from the sofa. "I need to pack," I said. "And you need to put that box back in the closet so it isn't cluttering up this place. That's the only decent chair for company."

"What? Why put it back?" Matt sounded mystified. "And where are you going?"

"Someplace else," I said. "Because you're staying here from now on, where you belong."

A look of resistance crossed his face. "Julianne, no," he said. "This is your place now. I'm not taking it from you. And I'm not having you sleep in an inn because of a sentimental idea."

"I have a place to stay," I answered. I reached into his jacket pocket and drew out his keys. "We'll get things swapped around later, but for now, I'll just keep my stuff here until yours is shipped back."

"I can't let you do this," Matt protested. He was being stubborn — he obviously hadn't realized I'd seen the wistfulness in his eyes when he looked around at his former home.

"Too late," I said. "Garden's a mess, by the way. Know somebody who can deal with that?" I kissed his cheek again, and gave him a saucy look as I went to pack a few things for tomorrow before scrounging up a suitable dinner and tea for two.

***

Matthew's temporary residence in Cornwall was a 'rent by the week' flat in a house on the edge of Ceffylgwyn: one room and mini kitchen close to the 'water closet.' Its best asset was a beautiful view of one of the Channel's inlets, even more forlorn and haunting than Cliffs House's coastal view. I savored it as I folded one of Matt's shirts that had been draped over the rumpled single bed.

Unsatisfactorily, not much of Matthew was present, but there were a few books on the nightstand, on tropical plant diseases and taxonomy of Brazilian flora. Reading way too dry for me when I paged through them, compared to the Cornish folk tales and nature guides I'd borrowed from Matthew. But I made myself read a little, to make up for my unfair remarks about South America, before I restacked them, neatly.

Sketches of a dissected plant on the wall, of an unusual little white-and-purple blossom cluster with droopy, sleepy-looking leaves. These reminded me of Constance's artwork, the sketches in her portfolio, although I knew Matt was probably thinking about the scientific application as much as their beauty when he drew them. They were the only decorating Matt had done for his week of exile.

I admit it — my tidying up Matt's place was really an excuse to snoop a little. I smiled when I found his printed photos from South America and his trip journal tucked beneath today's paper. Wistfully, I paged through his meticulous notes on culture smears, microscope slides, and climate temperatures, and the glossy images of Matt and other members of his team at their base camp, or smiling as they posed before a breathtaking waterfall.

I wished that things had been different, and that we had never fought. I wished there had never been a message in his voicemail from a worried medical staffer, and that he had called me first thing when he landed, with us chatting over a webcam connection as he shared his photos and adventures.

That couldn't be changed now, of course. But we would make sure that things were different from now on. No matter what the answers to Matt's biopsy revealed to us.

Unfortunately, the one thing I had forgotten to do while camping out at Matt's for the night was to set my alarm. I woke up groggy and late at eight-thirty in the morning, my face buried against a pillow that smelled vaguely of Matt's brand of shampoo and soap, then raced to put on the cashmere cardigan and wool skirt I had brought. Shoving my Prada heels on my feet and grabbing my clutch and mobile, I hurried out the door.

Lady Amanda would be back at any moment, if she wasn't home already, and I was supposed to meet her and Constance this morning. And I still needed to talk to Billy about the tea garden's makeover — thus far, he didn't seem to have touched it, despite Lord William's promise.

I marched up the pathway to the main English garden, the path flanked by perfectly-trimmed hedges that fenced it in like a maze's walls. In the heart of it, Billy was aerating the rose bushes, a cigarette between his lips flicking ash on the compost as he stabbed through the ground savagely with a long-handled fork.

"Good morning, Billy," I said.

"Nonuvit," he grunted.

"I kind of noticed that you haven't started on the east garden, like we discussed before," I said, taking a polite tact for opening the discussion. "Didn't Lord William tell you that it was a priority right now? As in 'must be done immediately?'"

Billy looked up from his work, eyes fixed on me in a glare of revulsion. "Dnwhat ye blabberin' on," he said.

I thought I understood that remark, strangely enough. "Lord William and Lady Amanda want the east garden readied for spring," I said, firmly. "Now. If you didn't get that impression from his remarks, then you're quite mistaken about whatever impression you *did* get." I planted my hands on my hips, bracing in battle stance for his reply. Obviously, Billy hadn't taken Lord William's arguments to heart.

His lip curled. "T'eastgard nowhat be done fer a fortnight. Daftwomn, didyeno hear t'first time?"

An insult. That much I made out. "Billy," I said, firmly. "I want flowers in the east garden. Please. I don't care about schedules or routines right now. It's an order from Lady Amanda, and I don't care if it has to be daffodils by the dozen or paperwhites, but it *will* be in bloom before two weeks. Is that understood? Now do this or else!"

I turned on my heel, the stiletto sinking into the earth a little bit, which ruined my exit somewhat. And poked a hole in the lawn, which might explain the final burst of vitriolic speech from Billy, aimed at my departing self. None of which sounded English to me as he shouted it over the hedges, but a great deal like the words some of the old fishermen down at the pub used whenever they spilled a pint.

I could hear Lord William's heavy-duty truck cart rumbling along the wide path to the field, so I cut through the 'shortcut' in the hedges and followed the decorative walkways leading to the mansion's rear gardens. Geoff was with him, spotting me waiting near the kitchen gardens, the vehicle slowing down as I approached.

"Lord William, I don't know what you said to Billy, but he simply doesn't believe he has to improve the east garden," I said. "I spoke to him this morning, and he was definitely not receptive to the idea."

Lord William groaned. "Of course," he said. "Julianne, I'm so sorry. I'm afraid that I completely forgot to have a word with him."

"Could you talk to him now?" I asked. "Just give him a firm hint?"

"I would, but I'm afraid we've got a crisis on the reforested acres," said Lord William, apologetically. "We have to dash off just now. But tell him that I've said it must be done. I'm sure that if anyone can persuade a gardener to finish a project, it's you." He gave me a quick smile, shifting the vehicle into gear again as he and Geoff drove away to whatever agriculture emergency awaited.

I could feel my expression fall with disappointment. "As if Billy will ever listen to me," I muttered. Clearly Lord William's confidence was misplaced when it came to my powers of persuasion over his substitute gardener.

I entered the house through the kitchen, where Dinah was busy lifting fresh-baked biscuits onto cooling racks. "Morning, lass," she said. I sneaked a broken cookie from her pile of imperfect ones.

"Dinah," I said. "Do you speak Cornish?"

"Oh, a bit here and there," she said. "Why do you ask?"

"I just wondered what something meant," I said. Hesitantly, I repeated a few of the words Billy had fired after me earlier. In response, I saw Dinah's eyebrow lift sharply.

"Where on earth did you hear *those* words?" she demanded.

"Oh, just ... somewhere," I said.

"I've never in all my born days used such language. They ought to be tarred and feathered, whoever said it in your company," she answered, as she slid the last cookie on the rack.

Lady Amanda was back from London and in her office, having a morning cup of tea with the artist. She had left her door open on purpose, so I would catch sight of her before I disappeared into my own. When I rapped on the door frame and peered inside, I saw a series of London shopping bags taking up the chairs and desk, and Constance buttering a muffin while settling into Lady Amanda's armchair.

"How was London?" I asked, as Lady Amanda motioned me inside.

"Diverting, as always," said Lady Amanda, assuming a snooty accent for this answer. "It was lovely, of course," she added, in her own voice. "The best part *being* that I talked someone into purchasing a very beautiful gown."

"Pish-posh," said Constance. "A waste of money, that dress. Where will I ever wear it after the wedding? While riding 'round in an open jeep in Italy? Hiking the Alps for a glimpse of spring snowdrops?"

"You'll wear it to parties, of course," said Amanda. "Maybe the opera in Milan, or to the Proms sometime. The point is, you'll look lovely for your wedding day."

"Let me see it," I said.

Constance rose and lifted a garment bag from the sofa. "Behold, the sensible, elegant choice for a bride-to-be of sixty," she said, and I suppressed a laugh, knowing she was probably quoting the London salesperson who presented it. "A work of splendor in fashionable ivory."

She unzipped the garment bag's folds. Inside was a beautiful, soft gown of champagne-colored satin with a wide halter strap, a modest v-neck, and no embroidery or seed pearl studding anywhere, only some light ruching on its bodice. A matching wrap of champagne was draped over a second hanger inside.

It was modern, elegant, and classy — while nothing about it was necessarily 'fashionably taboo' for a woman of Constance's age, it was a bold choice, given how many older women opt for long sleeves and a shorter hemline than the almost train-length one on Constance's gown. But I thought the young-at-heart artist would pull it off beautifully.

"Isn't it gorgeous?" said Lady Amanda. "The moment the salesperson brought it out, I knew it was Constance's. She looked smashing in it."

"As if I'll have need of it for a quick minute in front of the local magistrate," said Constance, with a smile. She zipped the garment bag closed and laid it aside, taking up her teacup and muffin again.

"At least you should have some flowers at the ceremony," I coaxed. "I could whip up a beautiful bouquet to match your dress. Something small but very elegant." In fact, I already had in the form of a sketch, and I was pleased to see it would go really well with Constance's choice of gown.

"A few flowers would be nice. As a botanical enthusiast, I'll never say 'no' to one, even though I prefer them in the ground rather than in the vase," said Constance. "But no fuss, mind you. Neither of us expect any fuss. Joseph is bringing a bottle of his best vintage for us all to drink a toast, and then we'll be off in no time on our sketching holiday."

"A little fuss never hurts," said Lady Amanda. "*You* told me that, remember? When I was fifteen, and I didn't want a posh frock for Lydia Chansom's wedding? All pimples and adolescent angles back then," she explained to me. "I was mortified at the thought of drawing attention to myself in grown-up heels and that short little blue dress. But when I look back at the photos, I was actually quite lovely — at least when someone managed to coax a smile out of me for the picture. Constance was right. I don't regret that fuss in the least."

"So why not let us plan something special for you?" I asked Constance. "This is your special day, after all. You're marrying the love of your life."

Constance smiled. "The love of my life," she repeated. "True enough. Until now, the love of my life was painting. And nature in all its splendors." She polished off her marmalade muffin. "Of course, half my friends are saying it's come too late. 'What a pity, what a shame. If you'd only stopped in for a glass of wine, you would have met him.' 'If you'd only met some nice bloke on that sketching holiday in the Lake country when you were really in your prime.' Not Amanda, of course," she said, waving her hand towards Lady Amanda, who was busy snipping a price tag from a newly-purchased scarf, but looked up and smiled at hearing her name.

"I don't agree with them," I said. "I think it's romantic. I think romance can happen any time, right? It's the sort of thing everyone dreams about — that loneliness can turn into love at any moment."

Constance laughed. "Like in novels," she said. But her smile told me there was something more to this statement. She took another sip of tea.

"My special day has already happened, you see." She set aside her teacup. "I was on a sketching holiday in the Ardennes last month. Took a train down from France for the weekend, and Joseph came with me. I thought he'd wander around some of the shops, look for a bottle for his collection, perhaps...but instead, he came with me to the place where I was painting.

"It was this beautiful little place in the middle of the woods. Just where the trees part, and a shaft of sunlight comes down. It landed on this cluster of wildflowers, sleepy little crocus-kin bulbs, just at the base of an old black log covered in white mushrooms marching across it just like little fan-shaped soldiers. It was like something out of a fairytale, I said to Joseph. The sort of thing one pictures in enchanted forests, where all the mushrooms circle fairy rings.

"He said, 'Maybe it is one. Maybe it's a part of a story here and now, and we're in a fairytale ourselves.' I thought he was being silly, of course — he does rather like to be silly sometimes, when it's the two of us going off on a lark, or having a time painting up impossible stories about what people are doing, or where they're going.

"But he reached into his pocket, and took something out. And he took my hand. And then I knew...and for a moment, I honestly thought I would cry. Me being silly enough to do it, there in a spot of sunlight, before those little white flowers. And Joseph with his serious smile and a diamond between his fingers."

I thought I detected the glint of tears in Constance's eyes now — but the artist blinked them back, shaking her head with a smile. "A diamond for me — it's not as if I needed one, is it? But that's Joseph, you see, always being sentimental about things."

The ring on Constance's finger wasn't a mere diamond chip — it was a row of three diamonds in a beautiful antique setting, with a filigree band. I imagined Joseph scouring antique shops or Old World jewelers for it, knowing that a modern cut and a glitzy, faceted stone wouldn't be the right choice.

"I would have said 'yes' for the ring alone," I joked.

Constance laughed heartily. "He does have good taste — although I suppose most people find it pityingly old-fashioned that it's not something custom made. But I never liked everything to be glitzy and new, even when I was young. I like the present when it's *alive* — breathing, and growing, like a plant or a bulb pushing earth aside to come out, not merely all of us rushing about like ants on the march or glued to the telly at night. And I like to remember the past and keep it alive in bits and bobs. Old brushes and old postcards and the like."

"Oh, *do* go on about 'bits and bobs,'" said Lady Amanda, sarcastically. "Your flat in France was as cluttered as a packrat's nest. Hardly room to swing a brush for all your souvenirs and things — when you were teaching me a few years ago, I must have painted half a dozen wine bottles, shadow boxes, and heaven knows what else by proxy. I can only imagine the one in England must be every bit as bad by now."

"Your problem was your talent didn't lie with a brush," said Constance, with a snort. "You were obviously a sculptor, and anyone could see it by your hands. It was for the best that you gave up on my lessons."

"Never mind that. I only know that you're every bit as sentimental as Joseph is, apparently. Otherwise, your move from France to England wouldn't have required toting quite so many boxes."

Yup. I was right. Joseph's choice had been perfect.

***

Lord William believed that I could convince Billy to start on the east garden on my own, but I decided I needed backup for this campaign. When I explained to Matt what the issue was, he immediately volunteered to discuss things with the gardener himself the next morning.

Hand in hand, we walked up the main path to Cliffs House, the first time Matt had been back to it since his semester in America. I glanced at him, giving his fingers a quick squeeze.

"Does anybody else know?" I asked him, softly. "Besides me?" I didn't have to say about what.

He shook his head. "Not even Michelle knows," he answered. "And I don't want anyone to know, if I can help it. Not until the results are in."

I nodded. If this was what Matt needed, then I would respect it. I would keep his secret until he was ready for everyone to know.

Billy was in the shed, cleaning dirt from the hand tools as Matt and I approached. I stepped back a little, letting Matt be the one who addressed Billy first. The gardener squinted at me hanging around the rhododendron bushes, then looked at him, a look of suspicion in his eyes for a stranger.

"What'b'ye doin' here?" he asked.

Matt, who had been studying the shed with an air of aloof interest, now nodded towards the row of pots on the table, where some twigs were poked above the dirt, a little leaf on each one. "Your cuttings have a good size," he said. "You've got a good skill with rooting them."

Billy grunted. "V'been at i' long nuff," he said.

"Mark of a gardener's best service is his palm," said Matt. "Let's see yours." He held out his hand, his own palm still weathered and callused from his work in the university's greenhouses. Billy surveyed it with reserve, then clapped his own work-worn hand in Matt's.

They shook hands solemnly, then began talking about something with words that sounded to me like gibberish — Matt's speech had slipped into Cornish dialect, something I'd scarcely heard him use before more than a word at a time. Billy's squinting glare hadn't disappeared, but he was nodding occasionally. They both gestured at times in the direction of the east garden, making me hopeful that this was progress.

A few minutes later, Matt strolled out of the shed and joined me. "It was simple enough," he said to me. "A reasonable chap. You should have told me that before." But there was a twinkle in his eye that proved he was teasing me. "I wonder why you didn't settle this sooner."

I rolled my eyes. "Maybe because I don't know the secret Cornish gardeners' handshake," I answered.

"Pshaw," said Matt. And I enjoyed hearing him tease me again, because a little of the worry had lifted from Matt's face with it. He seemed more like himself, and I would happily endure any ribbing over Billy's malevolent grunts to see it return.

With a truce between Billy and the east garden apparently in place, I left Matt in one of the gardens and went to the manor kitchen to take advantage of Dinah's morning 'cuppa,' and to discuss Constance's wedding buffet. I had a few ideas — more elaborate than the 'bottle of wine and quick bite of crumpets' suggestion that Constance had offered Lady Amanda on the subject, and wanted to see how possible they were.

"A log cake?" Dinah lifted an eyebrow. "But not a Yule log, you say?"

"It's the same, really — a Swiss roll with chocolate ganache and cherry compote spread inside it," I said. "It's for the groom's cake. Lady Amanda says Constance mentioned Joseph is fond of chocolate gateau, and I thought fashioning a cake to look like a log would be perfect." I thought of Constance's story about the Ardennes forest, and thought it was a stroke of luck that I'd already sketched out this cake.

"What's the bark made of?" She peered more closely at my supply list, pushing her eyeglasses further up the bridge of her nose.

"Flakes of chocolate, gilded along their edges," I said. "Layered like bits of bark over a mirror ganache, see? And with little meringue mushrooms spotted with chocolate, and some sugared rosemary to look like fir needles on a forest floor."

The wedding table's theme was meant to suggest a forest floor — lots of meringue mushrooms, and sugared marzipan crocus blossoms and buds on teacakes. Savory biscuits topped with a creamy spread, rosemary needles, and edible kale and spinach stems crowned with mini roasted garlic-and-shallot blossoms; and delicate little wild lilies made from candied citrus peel atop Dinah's famous iced orange saffron sweet biscuits.

"It's quite elaborate," said Dinah, studying my menu and my quick little drawings. "It wouldn't be terribly hard to pull it off for such a small affair, providing Pippa and Gemma have quick enough fingers to keep from snapping all these little stems. But what about a wedding cake?"

"I'm glad you asked," I said. If she thought *these* were elaborate, she had yet to see the wedding cake that Lady Amanda had dreamed up. Two layers of cream-sandwiched vanilla sponge with edible flowers and miniature bunches of gold and red grapes glowing like gems in an arrangement atop the cake. A marriage between the respective passions of the bride and the groom, Lady Amanda had declared it.

"Goodness me! This with the teacakes and the gateau — isn't this supposed to be a small affair?"

"Well, Lady Amanda might have sort of ... expanded ... the guest list," I admitted. I knew full well that she had arranged not only for members of her own family to come, but also for several of Constance and Joseph's respective friends, and even some of Constance's colleagues. It totaled thirty guests now — plus a few local friends in Cornwall and Devon whom Constance herself had invited to witness the ceremony.

"Well, that's reasonable, I suppose," said Dinah, when I handed her the guest totals. "But you say Constance knows nothing about this?"

"Not a word," I said. "So don't tell her, because Lady Amanda will be crushed if Constance makes her cancel the reception. It's practically her gift to the couple."

Except her real gift hadn't arrived yet, the special rare plant on order. Since I hadn't heard the progress on its shipping status, I made a note to stop by and ask Harvey Willow how many more days until it arrived. Time was passing quickly, and I knew it would disappoint Lady Amanda to have it arrive too late to present it before the couple's Swiss vacation.

I hoped she wouldn't ask me questions about its delay — Harvey Willow clearly wasn't filling my inbox with information, since he could barely turn on the shop's old computer. Fortunately, Lady Amanda was much too distracted as she rushed through the door.

"Rats, is that the time?" she demanded of me, looking at the antique grandfather clock near the stairs. "I'm terribly late for my appointment — Wallace Darnley is going to be peeved at me, as *always.*" Wallace Darnley, a local sailor known for his short temper, was starting a coastal cruise business to take tourists on pleasure cruises highlighting the wonders of the Cornish coast, and had far too many opinions on Lady Amanda's brochure designs for him.

"Did you have a flat tire?" I asked, noticing her hair was slightly disheveled. She rolled her eyes.

"Heaven forbid," said Lady Amanda. "No, I was 'kept after school' by my instructor, who had rather an issue with the shape of my bowl."

Lady Amanda's sculpting instructor, I surmised. "What was wrong with it?" I asked. "A bowl's a bowl, right?"

"Apparently, not," she answered, with a scowl. "He said my edges were far too fluted, to begin with, and that one side being slightly higher wouldn't have the artistic affect I wanted...and that my choice of orange paint with metallic gold would clash after it was glazed...oh, a dozen little things in between. 'Too ambitious, aren't we, for only a third attempt?'" she said, mimicking what surely must be his voice. "Plus, he said I should cut my nails, because they're only impeding my artistic progress."

"At least it looks like a bowl," I supplied, helpfully. "That's a start, right?"

"At least I wasn't the only one. Neddy Cox and Vince Ho were both in the same murky waters as me," she said. "I wish I were a proper artistic genius like Maddie Smith — she's making a fluted vase that looks like a Calla lily. I can't imagine anything but a single Calla lily will fit in it, but it *does* look impressive."

"Would you like me to call and tell Wallace you'll be late?" Not that I wanted to listen to his complaints, but it would make Lady Amanda feel better, I thought.

"No, I think I'll reschedule," she said. "He'll be in a rotten mood either way. And I do need to get the clay out from underneath my nails." She studied the skin beneath her long, tapered red nails, as if bits of clay were lodged there now. She sighed. "He really has no respect for a decent manicure."

Despite the frustration in her voice, I sensed that this was good-natured complaining on Lady Amanda's part, mostly for the sake of today's class. I knew for a fact that she secretly loved the challenge of it, even staying after class on her own a time or two to practice, so it couldn't be all bad.

Pippa and Gemma were in the smallest sitting room, fitting little votives in short hollowed birch logs, artificial ones I had purchased as candleholders of varying sizes for the table's decoration. Lord William had obtained an impressive-sized driftwood log to use as an altar for the marriage ceremony, and I was planning to tuck some trailing strands of soft, white goat's beard moss in its crevices, along with little white flowers.

"These are so pretty," said Gemma. "Are they just for the table alone?"

"Mostly," I said. "In groupings of two or three with some pinecones, in between the platters."

"Menu sounds scrumptious," said Pippa. "Hope we can sample a tidbit or two. I *love* Dinah's savory paste."

"Is it all still a secret from Constance?" asked Gemma. "How will we keep her from noticing all this?"

"Easy. She's out painting most of the day," I said. "We'll just keep these things hidden in the pantry."

"Besides, she's so busy with her gallery show, she'll be gone several days," said Pippa, inserting another candle. "Running up to London to meet with the gallery owner and see how they're arranging her work. She's looking forward to it. Supposedly, it'll draw a big crowd of art lovers — not that I'd know anything about that lot."

The lack of metropolitan atmosphere in Cornwall was always a subject of regret for Pippa and Gemma. Whereas for me, the opposite problem existed, since I was woefully uneducated about village life, and about Cornwall especially. My ears still burned sometimes with the laughter I received the first time I pronounced the village name of 'Mousehole' for a Cornish native — with literal English phonetics, of course. One of Matt's more wicked teasing tricks on me in our earliest days of knowing each other.

Gemma carried the finished table decorations to the box near the mantel, but stopped halfway across the room. "Is that Ross?" she said, with amazement.

"What? Ross is here?" Pippa scrambled up from her seat. "It is him!"

The windows in this room, like the French doors of the main parlor, faced the tea garden. When I reached the view, I saw Matt in the midst of it, kneeling before one of the beds and planting bulbs from the large sacks beside him. Already he had trimmed away the frost-bitten ornamental grasses from the beds, and swept aside the weathered mulch using a narrow gardening rake.

"Why didn't you tell us that he was coming here to work today?" said Pippa.

"I didn't know he was doing this," I said. And I didn't. There was no sign of Billy, but there was Matt, with the same mud patches as before on the knees of his trousers, and on his boots.

"Come on, then! Let's go say hello!" said Gemma. The two of them hurried off to fetch their jackets and greet their real-life 'Ross' from all those *Poldark* fantasies, leaving me alone at the window. Matt turned around to fetch another handful of bulbs and saw me, giving me a smile and a wave.

I waved back, my smile one of surprise and gratitude. Matt gave me a subtle wink in response, then turned back to his work. A second later, Pippa and Gemma were racing up to him, both throwing their arms around him in a hug before eagerly bombarding him with their questions.

I knew they were asking him all about Boston, and why he hadn't come to see everyone sooner. I knew he was going to smile and tell them that he didn't know how long he would be here, and that everything had gone well in America.

And I knew that he had never asked Billy if he would kindly restore the east garden for me.

"Good heavens! Is that Matthew in our garden?" Lady Amanda had joined me, her eyebrows lifting with surprise. "Don't tell me he's popped in to manicure our gardens without even saying 'hello'?"

"He knows how much it means to you to have this garden at its best for the wedding," I said. "I don't think you could stop him even if you opened the window and yelled at him."

She sighed. "He really *is* the best, isn't he?" she said. "Utterly incredible. Julianne, you really must keep him here this time. Don't let him slip off to America again. We'll find something to keep him busy."

I felt a tiny bit of discomfort over Matt's real reason for coming home. "I'm sure he'll always spend as much time in Cornwall as he can," I said. "He loves this place more than any other."

"If nothing else, maybe we could ask him to consult again, until we find another gardener," mused Lady Amanda. "Then we could get rid of B—we could be sure the gardens were in good hands," she supplied quickly, covering her slip of the tongue. "Not that there's anything wrong with the way things are done now, of course. They're managed swimmingly, I'm sure. Just not quite as well as Matthew would do it."

I hid my smile over these remarks. We watched Matt auger holes in the center of an ornamental urn's soil and place tiny bulbs, covering them gently with soil. Such care and seriousness on his face as he worked, even when there was a hint of a smile on his lips.

He really was utterly incredible, I thought. I couldn't agree more with Lady Amanda's words.

Even though we still had a few decisions to make about arranging the tea garden's parlor for the big event, I decided to postpone them in favor of checking on Lady Amanda's wedding gift. I knew she was anxious to give her friend something special and personal to keep, not just finger food trays and a place to stand on the patio facing the sea. I only hoped that she wouldn't have to baby-sit it for two weeks until Constance and Joseph returned from the Alps.

When I opened the door to Harvey's shop, the entrance bell rang cheerily, but there was no one behind the counter to greet me. After waiting several minutes, I finally located the service bell under a pile of dirty gardening gloves, and gave it a couple of taps. Several minutes later, Harvey appeared from the back of the shop.

"Mr. Willow. Hi. It's me — Julianne Morgen?" I crossed my fingers that he would remember me this time. There was something doubtful in his gaze, however.

"What can I do for you, Miss Morgen?" he asked.

"You ordered a plant for me from overseas a few days ago," I said. "On behalf of Lady Amanda at Cliffs House. Remember?"

A thoughtful expression appeared on Harvey Willow's face. "Ah, yes. Well...let me see." With a sigh, he dug through some papers stuffed beneath an old ledger. I noticed the computer monitor was turned off again, and covered by the vinyl cloth.

"You *did* order it, didn't you?" I asked.

"Did I? Yes...I'm quite sure about that...let me think." He searched his pockets for his glasses, eventually locating them in the pouch of his gardening apron. He propped them on his nose, peered closely at the piece of paper in his hand, then shook his head.

"Not the right one. Where is it...let me see.... Oh, yes. Here 'tis." He pulled a stack of rather crumpled and woefully dingy forms from underneath a pile of tiny little bulbs.

"Ah. Oh. Hm. Meant to call you, it seems. Seems they returned the forms that afternoon. The nursery, that is. Application denied. Something about a customs embargo on that species — some red tape with the government."

Denied? My heart sank. "So this plant is *not* on its way here from America?" I clarified.

"Nope. Needs sorting out with the Ministry of Agriculture. Months of red tape. Dunno as I've ever had this trouble before. The boy knows all about those things, I'm sure, but he's still not stumpin' about on his cast yet," he said. "Anyways, here's the forms you filled out, all nice and stamped by the nursery. Bit sorry about the plant," he said.

A nice red stamp of doom on my order form. I felt utterly defeated. How could I ever find a replacement for Lady Amanda in time?

***

I was still feeling blue about the plant two days later, and had come up with nothing for Lady Amanda in its place. She was deeply disappointed, and I knew she was racking her brain for new possibilities. I'd seen her scouring art websites looking at reasonably-priced gallery canvases, and making lists of everything from plants to plant-inspired jewelry to art cases. Most of them were crossed out, however.

I tried to banish it from my mind the day of Constance's gallery opening. Matt and I went up to London by train that morning, walking hand in hand through the doors of an old London warehouse converted into a modern art gallery.

Matt was a tremendous admirer of Constance's artwork, I had learned; he had a book of her sketches from southern France, color prints that revealed the colored pencil strokes bringing to life a cluster of tiny moss flowers, or a twig engulfed by a broken chrysalis.

"How long have you been a fan?" I asked. I turned the pages of the book, one he'd bought at a gallery in New York, apparently, looking at the glossy copies of Constance's art.

"Five or six years," he answered. "I stumbled upon an article in a botany journal, about the sketches she made of a university class's plant dissections, trying to better hone her understanding of what she loved most. I was intrigued by that story ... so I looked up her artwork, and found myself developing a deeper respect for it with each new canvas."

"You should have said something before," I said. "Oh, this one is so beautiful," I added on impulse, touching the print of a budding willow tree. "I wish I had seen it before I designed the petits fours."

"So you wish I had told you so you could have access to my books, I gather?" Matt smiled.

"Of course not," I said. "Well ... maybe a little access. After all, this book would have been incredibly helpful, since websites just don't do justice to her work...and I didn't have time to track down any interviews about what inspired her, I just went with Lady Amanda's words on it. You were clearly holding out on me."

To prove I was teasing him, I pinched his shoulder. As Matt grinned, I closed the book, reluctantly shutting it on the beautiful view of a long-vanished palace's garden turned wilderness.

"What I meant was, that you could have met her at the estate," I continued. "You could have spent the last few days watching her paint in person." I imagined that as a true fan, Matt would have enjoyed the progress of Constance's brush even more than I had, as a few painted black lines quickly took shape as the stems and leaves, then gradually became a complete rendering of a new-budding plant in the heart of one of Cliffs House's gardens.

He took a deep breath. "Any other time, I would have liked that," he said. "But right now, I think I prefer working in Rosemoor's garden. As you said before, its neglected state needs attention, and looking at the pitiful state of dead stalks and overcrowded seedlings is too much for me."

I knew that was Matt's way of saying that he needed to be working right now, to take his mind off other matters. I suppose even watching a famous artist at work wouldn't be as distracting as having his hands deep in the earth, rooting out persistent weeds or aerating the soil around that vivid tangle of overgrown English wildflowers.

There was a sign outside the gallery with Constance Strong's name and the title of the show — *A Walk in an English Wood.* All of Constance's paintings and sketches from her return to England were on display, three years' of work traveling from county to county.

Watercolors of leafy forest floors, of graceful or crooked branches loaded with buds or naked beneath frost or ice. A flower washed up on the seashore; a hoary tree with a yellow-flowered plant springing from its hollow; a ring of orange-red toadstools, huddled together like a group of confidants converging in a circle. In black and white sketches clustered here and there between canvases, I glimpsed some Cornish cliffs, with resilient plants tucked in the recesses of those jagged stones.

Constance was surrounded by enthusiastic patrons in the middle of the gallery floor. I spotted her, my hand reaching again for Matthew's as he caught up with me just past the *Sea Strawberries after a Storm* canvas.

I glanced at him. "Will you let me introduce you while we're here?" I asked. "You really should meet her. She's a great person, and tells wonderful stories. You'd like her, I'm sure of it."

"I would be honored," he said. "She won't mind?"

"Constance? Not at all," I said. "Trust me." We made our way through the cluster of admirers. Constance spotted me among the attendees, and motioned me forward.

"This is the lovely girl who's making my bouquet for the ceremony," she said to her guests, introducing me to a few art students who had been eagerly peppering her with questions. "I'm very glad you've come," she added to me. "I thought you might only be humoring a friend of Lady Amanda when you said you enjoyed my work. One can never be sure these days whether they're on the receiving end of politeness or enthusiasm."

"I really should thank you again for these tickets," I said. "But there's someone I'd like you to meet first. Constance Strong, this is Matthew Rose." I laid my hand on his arm. "He's a scientist, gardener, and friend of Lord William's, who very much admires your artwork."

"Matthew Rose?" repeated Constance. "Why, I'm quite sure I've heard your name before — you treated the bacterial outbreak among the historical garden's spotted orchids, didn't you?"

"A few years ago," said Matt. "And it is a tremendous honor to meet you, Ms. Strong. It's my first time to see your canvases in person, except for the one you exhibited at the Met a few years ago."

"Ah, yes. My *Frozen Bittersweet*," said Constance. "I'm quite fond of that one. It's the last one I painted in England before moving to France."

"I remember reading that in the guide to your canvases," said Matt. "Do you ever lend *Lilies of Marseilles* for exhibit, or is it still in your friend's private collection? I've seen its photographs in art and science journals, and it's truly one of your most striking canvases."

Constance laughed. "Fancy you knowing about that arrangement," she said. "You must have a friend or two in the art world. Yes, I'm afraid Horace still has it under wraps. I'm going to twist his arm for the upcoming show at the Orsay, however. I hope you can attend. I'll send you tickets, if you can possibly visit France then."

"Thank you," said Matt, who seemed surprised by Constance's swift generosity to someone she'd scarcely met. "I'd be quite happy for them. As to whether I can make it will depend on other matters," he continued, a grave expression flickering in his dark eyes for a moment. "But I wouldn't miss it, if I can help it."

"Splendid!" said Constance. She glanced at me. "You didn't tell me you had such a famous chap attached to you," she said. "Never breathed a word about your young man."

"Sadly, it hadn't occurred to me that you would recognize his name," I confessed. "I hadn't thought about the fact that artists and scientists in botany would probably be studying the same plants in their work. Not until Matthew showed me the book he had of your sketches — and there was even one on the cover of a botany textbook he used in the class he taught."

"I think I'll invite you both to my wedding as guests," said Constance, thoughtfully. "It's a small affair, as you well know —" she glanced at me in particular with these words, so I almost thought she was suspicious that Lady Amanda was up to something, "—and we're only bothering a few friends to rouse themselves to a morning train to Cornwall for it. But I suppose since Amanda's wrestled me into that lovely dress that I should make a show of having people attend."

There was no suspicion in Constance's voice, at least. I thought of the growing guest list — the decorations and wedding buffet — and bit my lip to prevent an ironic smile from appearing. Matthew caught my eye as he listened, however, and nearly ruined my best efforts to resist it.

"It's just a little thing. Quick vows, a toast with a bottle of Joseph's ninety-four blush, and a bite to eat if I remember to ask the kitchen for some biscuits. But you're still welcome to come, especially to meet Joseph."

"That's so kind of you," I said. "If you don't mind, I'd love to help out with just a few little things that day, on Lady Amanda's behalf," I added, since I could hardly tell her what those things might be. "And I'm sure Matt would love to be there, if he doesn't have another engagement."

Constance smiled at him. "It's been quite an honor to meet the scientist who helped cure the spotted orchid's last crisis. Clever chap. Quite handsome and charming, too," she added, jokingly to me. "You've done almost as well as I have in that department. You haven't seen Joseph yet, but you'll agree come the wedding day."

"He's an extremely lucky fellow," said Matt. "Julianne has told me the story behind your romance. It's rather the stuff of novels, as they say,"

"I suppose it is, in some ways," said Constance. "But plenty only see it as an old woman desperately hitching myself to a semi-retired gent with a bottle shop in the Cotswolds."

"I think that's a terrible description of it," I said. "Did someone really say it to you?"

"Oh, they say things that mean the same thing. 'Why bother at your age?' 'How long until you lose each other?' they say — but they don't see that it doesn't matter. Time doesn't matter. What difference does it make if we live a year or fifty years together? What difference does it make when it comes to loving someone?"

"What other reason would you have besides love?" asked Matthew. "You're a successful artist who couldn't have been short of admirers in the past. And whose life has been quite adventurous, according to what

I've read about you in articles."

A dreamy look entered Constance's eyes, briefly. "Yes, exactly so," she answered. "I've lived a full life until now. And now, I'll live a full life with Joseph. I've been very fortunate. So how could I choose to be unhappy? It would be rather wrong of me. So long or short, I choose to be happy with what Joseph and I have."

Her words were beautiful — they filled me with happiness and sadness at the same time. I looked at Matthew, wondering if he was feeling the same way. And, for the first time all day, the thought that I could lose him for good hit me, and felt worse than ever before. Even Matthew going to Boston when I thought perhaps he wasn't yet in love with me — it didn't have the ability to produce the sudden ache welling up inside me.

I looked into Matthew's eyes for a moment. My hand felt for his again, my fingers closing around his tightly.

"No one could have put the truth any better than that," I said to Constance.

***

I showed Matt the plans for Constance's wedding and reception that night, when the two of us were curled together on the tiny love seat in Rosemoor's parlor. He couldn't help but chuckle over the vast difference between Constance's offhand, casual version of how events would unfold, and Lady Amanda's celebration, which expanded 'wine, biscuits, and maybe a crumpet or two' into the forest floor buffet and 'flowers and fruits' wedding cake.

"Constance will be very surprised," he said, after admiring my sketch of the chocolate log gateau. "Every little detail is perfect. Lady Amanda has outdone herself, and so have you. The chocolate mushrooms are an inspired touch; I think Constance will appreciate it greatly."

"I just hope it won't come off as an unpleasant surprise, somehow," I said. "Maybe her heart was set on a quick ceremony at Lady Amanda's, and an afternoon's walk or something."

Matt shook his head. "I don't think it will be," he said. "Having met her, I think she's simply a person who doesn't fuss over herself a great deal, only her work and other people. I think when she sees how deeply

Lady Amanda cares for her, she wouldn't have it switched back to the simple signing of the license and a toast afterwards."

"Let's hope you're right." I settled my head comfortably against his shoulder. "When you hear Constance talk about Joseph ... it seems right. They're in love with each other, and they don't try to make their reasons for being together anything other than that."

I released a small sigh as I thought of Constance's description of Joseph's proposal. Not a gushing, flowery story — but one that drew its romance from the look in her eyes when she told it. Its words were strong and straightforward, just like Constance herself, but full of deeper emotions.

"If Constance is going to love it, then there's only one problem left for me," I said. I lifted myself and set my portfolio on the tiny, square table piled with some of Matt's books he loaned me on flowering South American plants.

"And what would that be?"

"Lady Amanda's gift to the couple." Here, I repressed a second sigh. "The rare plant she wanted from one of Constance's sketching holidays isn't available. And Harvey Willow, who's in charge of the shop right now, apparently, forgot to tell me until it was too late to do anything about it."

"Find another plant," suggested Matthew. "I could do a little research and help you find another international nursery, if you like. I have plenty of contacts in that quarter."

I smiled. "I know you do," I answered. "And thanks for volunteering them. But Lady Amanda wanted it to arrive in time for the wedding, and I'm pretty sure I can't find something that would be special enough on this short notice without forcing her to spend a fortune. I'm afraid she'll have to settle for a more conventional gift."

"It seems to me that Lady Amanda's already spent tremendous effort and more than a little money on Constance's big day," said Matt. "No expensive wedding gift could ever compare with the ceremony and reception she's planned."

"I kind of suggested that already. But Lady Amanda really wants Constance to have something more permanent from her than just memories, and photographs of them eating truffles that look like mushrooms."

"Hmmm," said Matt, thoughtfully.

"I suppose I could always suggest a nice photo album. Or maybe a wedding portrait." But none of these sounded like the right choice, I knew. Too cliché. And they seemed more like additional wedding expenses than a thoughtful gift, anyway.

Matt stretched further back against the sofa's pillows. The arm which had been resting behind me, along the back of the sofa, now pulled me a little closer, something I didn't object to at all. I settled close against him, my hand resting on his chest, near his heart.

"You know, you haven't finished telling me about South America," I said, lifting my gaze to his.

"That's true. What do you want to hear about next? The crocodiles or the piranhas?"

"Stop it," I said, giving him a playful little smack. "I don't want to hear about made-up jungle encounters, thanks." Those dark eyes couldn't hide their spark of humor, not from me.

We hadn't talked about the elephant in the room, either. And it wasn't the piranhas or the man-eating snakes of the Amazonian jungles. We'd been carefully avoiding the subject of Matt's biopsy for days now, ever since he had revealed the truth to me. Instead, we talked about his research trip, and my busy life in Cornwall while we were apart.

In this calm and comfortable moment, the last thing I wanted to think about was that moment in the future. But I couldn't help but think about it, with my hand so close to Matt's beating heart.

"When will you know?" I asked, softly.

The humor faded from his gaze. "A week," he said. "Possibly sooner ... but there could be a delay, even, depending upon the number of tests the lab is processing."

A week. I pictured the biopsy mark beneath the bandage, and tried not to feel afraid.

"Let's not talk about it," he said, softly. His fingers stroked my shoulder, lightly. "Not yet."

"Not if you don't want to," I said. Talking about it would be painful, especially for Matthew. I desperately needed to do it, though, before he knew the answers about his health. "I only want you to know that whatever it is ... it doesn't change anything for me."

It changed everything else, of course. We both knew that. That's why

Matt's eyes grew still more tender, and why my own burned for a moment with tears gathering just beneath the surface. This moment felt fragile, like something we were holding in our hands, about to let it fall and shatter below.

Fiercely, I blinked those tears away. Matt was working hard to hide the worry lingering just beneath his surface. "I did see a big python in South America," he said, after a moment, in a lighter tone of voice. "Twelve meters long, and quite capable of eating someone."

"You didn't," I challenged, picking up on his cue.

"There's photographic proof," he said. "I'll have to show you the photos. There's a beautiful one of the plant we were observing, when its flowers were only beginning to open. I took it one morning just after sunrise."

"No chance you brought back a cutting, smuggled in your pocket for transplant?" I asked. "Lady Amanda would probably give you a hundred pounds for it."

"Not on your life," said Matt, smiling. "No self-respecting scientist would steal a rare native plant. Even for *two* hundred pounds."

Gazing at him, etching his face into my memory permanently, I felt how completely I was in love with him. The feelings I had for him were so strong and deep. I hadn't even known Matthew for a full year of my life yet, but I couldn't picture it without him. And what if I had to? Constance's words on love being all that mattered, no matter the length of one's life, came back to me now with the full force of its meaning for myself.

My eyes traced Matt's features, drank in the beauty of his dark coffee eyes that seemed almost black. And I realized that I wanted more than anything to spend our lives together, no matter how much time we had. I wanted to tell him that no matter what the test revealed, that's what I intended to do.

Me throwing my arms around Matthew Rose and proposing marriage — I imagined the reaction that would provoke in the calm, self-possessed gardener beside me. I imagined myself doing it in the middle of one of Cliffs House's flower gardens, telling him to marry me here and now despite his muddy trousers and boots, my impractical heels and skirt, and the lack of a vicar on the grounds.

I found myself almost laughing aloud at this point. I wondered what

Matt would say if he could read my thoughts now, and knew that despite that ludicrous picture, the feelings behind it were still real. I wanted to marry Matthew, for a year or a hundred of them, as Constance would say.

Matt's hand traced the skin just below my blouse's sleeve as he gazed at the candle burning on the mantel. "What are you thinking?" I asked him.

He glanced at me. "Nothing," he said, softly. "Lost in thought. But nothing that matters now."

So he wasn't thinking the same thing I was. It would have been too much of a coincidence, I supposed. It was impossible for Matt to read my mind every time I wanted it, right?

"Maybe Lady Amanda needs to think outside the box," said Matt, after we had both been silent for a little while. "Perhaps you could persuade her to think of something that wouldn't necessarily need to be purchased, but something that would be a connection between herself and Constance. A journal from when they traveled together, for instance ... or maybe just a letter telling her how much those experiences meant."

"Something with sentimental value only," I said.

"From the heart. Exactly," said Matt. "That's what Lady Amanda needs in a gift for her friend."

It made sense. And I tried hard to think of how to put that into words for my employer as I snuggled closer to Matt, feeling his free hand cover mine.

***

I knew Lady Amanda would be in her office in the morning, as soon as she returned from a meeting with a local businessman about his new website. She breezed in hurriedly around ten A.M., dropping her tote bag near her desk, and brushing aside the trailing ends of her scarf headband as it swung against her shoulder.

"Fancy seeing you here!" she said, as I sat up straighter in the cozy armchair across from her desk. "Did we have a meeting this morning? If so, it's completely flown out of my head, what with the website crashing — *again* — due to some sort of hacker's virus. Some arrogant schoolchild genius's idea of fun, I suppose."

"Don't worry, we didn't have anything scheduled," I said. "I just wanted to talk to you about a few things."

"Is it the wedding?" Lady Amanda asked. "I think everything's been handled splendidly, Julianne. Dinah assures me that the cakes will be perfectly easy to assemble, and she already has four dozen savory biscuits popped in the freezer for safekeeping. You know, Joseph is bringing the special vintage for toasting their nuptials — and I was thinking for the other guests, it would be nice to have a glass apiece from Joseph's old vineyard, so I persuaded William to let me order a dozen from the bottle shop. A very reasonably priced red wine, and we can serve the unopened ones later at table ...."

"It's nothing about the reception, really," I began, trying to decide where I was going with this speech, one that was likely to disappoint the woman before me. As Lady Amanda had been talking, she had also been emptying the contents of her tote bag, a pile of brochures and business plans forming on her desk, among them being what looked like a green ceramic blob. I noticed it in particular at this moment.

"Did a knickknack from your desk end up in your bag?" I asked, puzzled.

"Oh, this?" Amanda laughed. "No, it's my first sculpture from my class, actually. My instructor finally remembered to give it to me yesterday — he had left it next to the drying oven last time."

I lifted it. What I mistook for a green, glossy blob took on the definite form of a tree one held upright; one with curvy, droopy limbs and clusters of foliage, its jade green streaked with emerald.

"Rather silly, isn't it? It's supposed to be a bracelet tree for Mum," said Lady Amanda. "I made a paperweight for William with my second try, which was much better-looking than that. He uses it to hold down receipts from the gift shop."

I remembered seeing a modern-looking sculpture on William's desk, a marbled white and brown object shaped almost like a cliff, with little waves of grey rippling along its base.

"So what does your instructor think of your work?" I asked, placing the tree on her desk. A little vision of possibility had begun to take form in my head. "Constance said you had the hands of a sculptor."

"Oh, rubbish," said Lady Amanda. "He says I'm decent enough for a beginner, but I'll hardly be the next Michelangelo. I'm rather struggling with his latest lesson ... sometimes I wish I'd taken pottery instead," she joked, as she tidied the papers from her carryall. "I could be making very useful clay jars and vases right now if I had."

"Lady Amanda," I said. "I have an idea."

***

The morning of Constance's wedding dawned with perfect weather, which was a testament to its uniqueness as England's southernmost county. No rain drizzled from the sky, only clear sunlight breaking above the restless shore, bathing the cliffs and sand in white.

In the tea garden, the daffodils and paperwhites that Matt had planted were in full bloom, a rising sea of blossoms in every bed and container, the breeze fanning the ornamental grasses and the ground cover's carpet of miniscule white flowers in between. It was a picture worth beholding when I opened the drapes, and began putting in place the final details to make this wedding perfect.

At the end of the garden pathway, I arranged tiny little battery-operated votives in birch candleholders and simple white tulips at the base of the driftwood altar where the couple would take their vows. In the parlor, the furniture had moved to create plenty of standing room, and a bower of evergreen and white tulips decorated the mantel. I draped the serving table with a flawless white cloth, and decorated it with the birch candleholders and pinecones. Now it was only waiting for Dinah's serving trays to arrive. Displayed in the very center, the bride's small bouquet of narcissus and lavender, placed in a crystal vase.

By the time guests began arriving from the train station — a mix of painters, vineyard owners, gallery curators, and businesspeople from various points in the U.K., Ireland, France, and Italy — Constance definitely knew something was up. Lady Amanda insisted on keeping her sequestered upstairs on a pretense of fussing with Constance's hair and dress, but it was obvious that the bride knew her friend had made some changes to the wedding's guest list.

"Who are all those people?" she asked. "I hear several voices — that can't possibly be only Toni and Angelo down there."

"Hold still, dear." Lady Amanda was using a light mousse to tousle Constance's hair into a slightly more elegant version of itself. "I can hardly finish your hair if you keep trying to spring up from the chair."

"Well, I'm quite concerned, if you must know. What on earth is going on down there?" said Constance.

"Oh, nothing," I said.

I had just finished a few last-minute, primping touches to Constance's bouquet on the table, and the smaller version meant for Lady Amanda, who was standing as chief bridesmaid, and one of the marriage's witnesses. "Just a little furniture rearranging in one of the parlors, that's all," I explained. "There's an event coming up soon."

I exchanged glances with Lady Amanda above the bride-to-be's head. Constance caught part of it in the mirror, however, and cast a decidedly suspicious eye at both of us.

When Constance reached the stairs, looking elegant in her simple gown and Lady Amanda's pearl teardrop earrings, the secret plans her friend had made were fully obvious. For the doors to the parlor were wide open, along with the French ones leading to the garden just beyond it. The candles were aglow, with the guests waiting on either side of the newly-decorated room, gazing expectantly towards the stairs. And Joseph, his morning suit's top hat in hand, was standing at the foot of the steps, holding out his free one to his bride.

Constance stopped short at the top of the stairs. I couldn't help but smile at the expression on her face, part astonishment, part exasperation, and — most definitely — part pleasure.

She looked at Lady Amanda. "And what's all this?" she demanded.

"It's your wedding," said Lady Amanda, cheerily. "What do you think it is?"

"All this fuss," began Constance, two pink spots appearing on her cheeks. "I thought I said it wasn't necessary."

"Nonsense," said Lady Amanda. "Come on now. Everyone's waiting for the bride-to-be's grand entrance." Lady Amanda handed her the bouquet. "And the handsome gentleman below doesn't deserve to wait any longer."

True to Constance's word, about Joseph's looks, the groom was handsome: a tall, active-looking man whose white beard was carefully trimmed, and whose skin was the same sun-drenched shade of Constance's own from years of outdoor living in Italy. His eyes lit up the moment Constance appeared, and a smile broke across his lips, illuminating his whole face. I was sure that Constance blushed as she took his hand.

He led her towards the garden, where the vicar waited behind the driftwood altar, as Lady Amanda and I followed, dressed in our best. Guests squeezed into the garden wherever there was room, or stood in the doorway of the parlor where the reception would be held.

All during the ceremony, Lady Amanda stood beaming beside Lord William, among the cluster of good friends and relations who were gathered between the flower beds and urns. I stood near the back, beside Matthew, who had arrived a little later than the rest of the guests.

He was wearing the suit I remembered from the night he came to take me for a walk in the gardens, the night of my first big wedding at Cliffs House (or anywhere, for that matter). It was then that I had first told Matt I had feelings for him, after knowing him mere weeks.

It had been nearly a year ago — time had flown by, but it felt like yesterday that I saw him on the cliffs for the first time. That I kissed him for the first time, on impulse, mere moments after my first triumph as an event planner. Now here we were, side by side, celebrating the surprise and happiness that love creates. I took a deep breath, catching the faint scent of fresh earth and spring flowers, the salt of the sea breeze, and a hint of Matt's familiar aftershave. A perfect combination, I decided.

Afterwards, everyone sampled Dinah's scrumptious savories and desserts, with plenty of impressed compliments paid to the mushroom-shaped chocolate truffles and the clever roasted garlic and shallot snowdrops. Joseph was obviously touched by the special effort made with his favorite dessert as he sliced the chocolate gateau log, its delicate ruffles of white chocolate mushrooms looking almost exactly like the real thing. And it tasted heavenly, too — Matthew and I split a piece of each cake, both arguing heartily about which one was the best.

When the bottle of wine was opened, it was Joseph himself who proposed the toast. "To the woman who has given me every reason to live as long as I may. The blessing of my life — Constance."

He lifted his glass, hearty cheers echoing his last words. Gemma passed me a glass of wine and I lifted it to my lips, tasting something rich and red with a fragrant bouquet.

"Isn't it romantic?" sighed Pippa. She took a sip from her glass. "Still— I hope *I'm* not sixty before I find the love of my life!"

"I don't think you have to worry about that," I said. "Plenty of blokes are chasing you — Gregory, for instance."

"Don't mention that name to me, thank you," muttered Pippa darkly. I surmised that Gregory, with his half-dead bouquet and thin excuses — was now history.

Constance held out her hand as I approached midway through the reception. "I suppose I owe you thanks for this sumptuous event, as Amanda's co-conspirator," she said.

"Well, maybe a *little*," I said. "But the credit's really all hers. I just followed along with the plan."

Constance scrutinized me. "I suppose I'll believe you," she said, at last, with a hint of a smile. "And here is your handsome escort, too. No pressing engagements held you back, Doctor Rose, did they?"

"None at all," he answered, with a smile. I realized this was the first time I'd heard anyone in Cornwall address him by his title. I wondered if it seemed strange to him, since people in Boston probably called him by it every day. But Matthew had always preferred being plain Matthew Rose, he had told me.

"I want you both to meet the love of my life," Constance continued. "Joseph — come and meet that young woman I was telling you about, and the young man who's been wise enough to offer her his attentions."

"A pleasure," said Joseph, shaking hands with us. "Constance had spoken a great deal about her friends in Cornwall. I could scarcely wait to come and meet them all."

His kind voice made me like him instantly — but what made me like him even more was the way he kept Constance's hand in his own when they were together. He lifted it to his lips when he thought no one was watching, and squeezed it tenderly before they were parted by friends in conversation.

I felt Matthew's arm around my waist. I glanced at him and we exchanged knowing smiles.

It was at this point that Lady Amanda made her way through the guests, with a small package in her hands, one wrapped in light pink paper and tied with several curly ribbons. Her smile was a nervous one as she placed it between Constance's own.

"It isn't quite what I hoped it would be," she explained to Constance, with an apologetic smile. "I certainly hope in this case that it's the thought that counts."

"You've already done too much," protested Constance. "I can't imagine what it is - I do hope you haven't spent a fortune, my dear." She untied the beautiful loops of ribbon around the box.

I slipped from Matthew's embrace and stole closer, watching Lady Amanda take a deep breath, trying to hide her anxiousness. Constance opened the box, lifting an object wrapped in tissue paper.

Its layers parted to reveal a pale, milky-white base from which fluted, curving stems rose, tinted softly with green. From each one emerged a flower, its head nodding towards the ground as if the blossoms were all sleepy. The petals were iridescent ones made of mother of pearl — polished oyster shells from the Cornish beach, I imagined — and transparent crystals that glittered in the light.

Pearly buds, broad, miniature leaves, delicate grace. I knew without seeing Constance's sketches from the Belgian forest that this was the plant she had painted the day Joseph proposed.

For a moment, Constance was simply silent. Her hands held the sculpture perfectly still; in her eyes, I saw the first glint of tears.

"Why ..." she began, softly. "Why ... I always knew you had a sculptor's gift." Her voice was slightly thick for these words.

"So you like it?" Lady Amanda asked. She looked relieved now, her breath coming out in a long sigh. "It's not quite right — you can see the little marks on the leaves where I —"

"It's perfect," said Constance. She took Lady Amanda's hand in one of hers, squeezing it tightly. "Quite perfect as it is, I assure you." Her arms closed around Lady Amanda, hugging her close.

Over her shoulder, I saw Lady Amanda wink at me as she hugged her friend. I smiled back.

***

The winds from the sea were ruffling my silk dress, and the petals of the first spring flowers in Cliffs House's garden as walked along the garden paths, hearing it rustle through the leaves of the shrubbery that Billy's clippers had been mangling when I confronted him about the east garden's renovations. I was strolling alongside Matthew, my hand tucked in his strong, callused one once again.

We were retracing the first walk we had taken together along this same path the previous year — a night walk we shared after a very different wedding, of course, that of Matt's heartless ex. Here and there, Matt would pause to inspect plants he'd added last year, crouching down to crumble mulch between his fingers or study the underside of leaves.

He rose to his feet. "I spoke to William yesterday," he said. "He wants me to consult again for a few weeks. It's temporary, of course, and I think he's mostly offering it to be kind — but I thought I might take him up on it. At least while things are still unsettled...and there's no permanent gardener at Cliffs House." He dusted the rose's mulch from his hands.

"You mean it?" I said. Matt back at Cliffs House — it seemed too good to be true, even with the real reasons for it lingering in the back of my mind every minute.

"It seems like the sensible thing to do," he said. "Besides, I'm not entirely satisfied with the progress the roses are making, or the beds along the cliffs' walk, either. They need a bit more care than they've received."

"So you're saying —"

" — that Billy will be restored to his real job elsewhere, yes," he supplied. A grin crept across his face now. "Does that give you relief?"

"Absolutely," I answered, laughing. No more insults or Cornish curses, or silent glares directed my way by the incorrigible old gardener on loan — it was like a dream come true.

Matt took my hand again; I didn't mind the dirt on his as our fingers intertwined. I leaned against Matt's shoulder, taking a deep breath of sea air as we emerged from between the hedge walls, to the open path leading towards the cliffs' view.

"They make a lovely couple," said Matt. "Constance and Joseph."

"They do," I agreed. "The sort of couple everyone wants to be. I would want to be that happy with the love of my life at sixty...seventy...and eighty." Our eyes met for a moment as I spoke, and the humor in my voice died away ever so slightly beneath the tenderness of his gaze.

Matt looked away. "You know," he said, softly. "I had wanted things to be very different when I came back from my research trip."

"Different from this?" I asked. Feigning a lightheartedness I didn't entirely possess as I squeezed his hand. "As in you strolling along Boston's shore with some other girl?"

Matt scoffed. "Of course not," he said. "I meant ... I had hoped to forget about our silly argument before I left. Put it behind us and move on with the future."

"We are moving on," I said. "I don't know about you, but I haven't wasted any time thinking about it these past couple of weeks. I hope you realize that I didn't really mean any of those things. I was just missing you horribly and having a rotten day."

"I know. And you know that I never meant to make you think that I chose work over you," said Matt. "That wasn't my intention when I went to Boston, or when I agreed to be part of the research team. I never should have put you in a position where you would feel that way."

"See? We're past it," I said. "Over it. Next expedition to the wilds, I'll be waiting passionately for your return. Counting down the days until you tell me what miracle you worked against virus and bacteria." I slid my arm through his, hugging it close.

Matt didn't say anything. We paused at the head of the path, where the first glimpse of the Channel's restless waters could be seen beyond the banks of heather and the craggy stones emerging from the earth. "I often think about that week in Boston," he said, quietly. "When you came for Valentine's Day."

Matt as my guide along the Freedom Trail, and through Faneuil Hall. The two of us having dinner at a restaurant near the harbor, both eager to talk, both equally as desperate to hear the other one's voice. Everything had been so warm and comfortable between us, so perfectly natural.

"We went ice skating at that indoor rink," I reminisced. "Do you remember how I nearly broke my ankle when that kid brushed past me? My weird little stumble must've looked like a sit spin gone wrong." A smile tugged at my lips for it, remembering how the two of us were laughing too hard for Matt to help me to my feet for a minute or two.

"I remember holding your hand every day," he said. "Everywhere we walked, every time we were sitting or standing together. And feeling sorry that I ever let go of it at the airport."

I shivered a little in response; the same memory had been in my own thoughts just a few days ago.

"I had wanted to envision a future between us," he continued. "A long one. And now ..." He hesitated. "Constance's speech about time not mattering — I'm not sure if I can agree with that. I couldn't ask you to choose a fleeting happiness. One that would be marred by pain, and spent shuttling back and forth between hospitals and clinics."

"I think you don't realize how much you mean to me," I said. "If that's what you think."

"Before this, I thought of nothing else," he answered. His arms slid around me, drawing me close. "And I was sure enough of your feelings that I had hope of something more."

Pressed against him, I felt the corner of a square box tucked in his pocket. A jewelry box, I realized. I lifted my eyes to meet his, imagining full well what must be in it.

His lips moved. "Before this, it was all I wanted," he said. "And it's still all that I want."

I didn't say anything. I knew that my eyes were filling with tears, and I didn't want to hold them back. "Yes," I said. "That's my answer. Yes, Matthew."

His hand reached into his pocket and pulled out a small velvet box. He opened it. The ring was nestled between two ivory cushions, a braid of small diamonds and pearls. It looked utterly beautiful, and utterly timeless, as if it had belonged in romances of the past, just like Constance's.

He lifted it out, gently, and held it in his palm. He was hesitating, but I could see the yearning in his eyes. My fingers touched the band as it lay there, watching the little diamonds glint like stars in the light.

"Well?" I said, my voice barely above a whisper. "Aren't you going to say something?"

"I love you," he said.

I felt his fingers take mine, separating one on my left hand from the others. The ring slid into place, its smooth metal encircling my finger. He took my hand in his and lifted it to his lips, kissing it, gently. And with that kiss, the promise between us was sealed.

***

I was trying very hard not to check the calendar daily, but the days until Matt's results would be back were slipping away quickly, and my brain was counting them down without my permission. By the day of the deadline, no phone call from his doctor came; and though Matt didn't mention it, I knew it was preying on his mind.

Matt wasn't due to start work at Cliffs House until the next week, so he was still spending his days weeding the gardens at Rosemoor Cottage. I wanted to take a few days off and help him — and be there when the phone call finally came — but there were two catered events planned at Cliffs House for this weekend, and it was my job to see that everything was in place for them.

Today was also the day for Constance and Joseph's departure for Switzerland, and Lord William and Lady Amanda were hosting a send-off breakfast for the couple. I was there, along with most of the house's staff, and a couple of wedding guests staying locally, Italian friends of Joseph's who were on a walking tour of Cornwall.

"Are you sure you won't eat a second muffin?" said Lady Amanda, passing the platter at breakfast. "Train trips are very long, you know. And dining cars have nothing on Dinah's cooking, as you know."

"I couldn't eat another bite," said Joseph. "My compliments to the cook. I've never had marmalade quite that delicious."

I knew Dinah would be pleased to hear that, once again, her special recipe was unbeatable among the manor's guests. I myself had guiltily slathered a generous spoonful of it over a muffin earlier in the morning, and wolfed it down while alone in the kitchen.

Already the artist's latest canvases and sketches were packed for travel, along with her battered little painting case. Joseph carried the disassembled easel and their duffel bags out to the boot of Lord William's car as Lady Amanda gave her friend one last farewell hug.

Constance shook hands with me once more as I stood in the courtyard with Gemma and Pippa. "Take care of yourself," she advised me. "And take good care of that young fellow who's so smitten with you. I'm quite grateful for all the help you gave Amanda. The wedding was lovely ... it couldn't have been more so in any other hands."

"I'm glad you loved it," I answered. "And I hope your sketches of Switzerland turn out beautiful."

"I've a little something for you," she said, placing a small brown paper-wrapped package in my hands. "Hang it in your office as a reminder of how happy you helped make a cantankerous old artist. Or perhaps you know someone else who has a good use for it." There was a knowing twinkle in Constance's eye with these words.

"Ready when you are, Constance," called Lord William, who opened the passenger door of his car. Constance waved goodbye to Lady Amanda and the staff of Cliffs House as she climbed in, settling beside Joseph. A moment later, the car drove away, carrying the two of them to the train station.

"What'd she give you?" asked Gemma, curious.

"Bet it's an autograph," said Pippa. "Or a bit of something she drew on her scratch pad."

I removed the paper from the flat package. Beneath it was a sketch, mounted on a plain cardboard back. Delicate brush strokes had brought it to life as a watercolor. A view of the house's cliffs, the Channel's water on the horizon, and the outline of the path leading to the plunging view of the beach below. In the corner, the unintelligible, slanting signature of Constance Strong.

A small note was folded on top of it. *One should always know one's special place*, it read. And that was all.

How did she know? I lifted my eyes, and noticed Lady Amanda's secretive smile before she turned and went inside the house again.

"It's our cliffs, isn't it?" said Gemma, peering over my shoulder.

"Part of the Cornish series she painted for the show, I believe," said Geoff, who was also admiring it. "I saw it in the catalog Lady Amanda brought back."

"Fancy that," whistled Pippa. "It's worth a good bit of money, I'll bet."

"I wouldn't part with it," I said. "Except to one person." Which, I knew, was exactly what Constance had implied before.

Gemma was no longer noticing the sketch I held, but the ring on my left hand. Her eyes grew wide as saucers. "What's that?" she demanded. She seized my hand. Beside her, I heard Pippa suck in her breath, sharply.

"Oh my gosh! Ross *proposed*?!"

"I was going to tell everyone," I began. "It's just I thought I'd wait until Co—"

"Are those stones real?" said Pippa. "Not 'real,' I mean, but *real*?"

"Where's Geoff?" said Gemma. The estate manager had already wandered towards the gardens, it seemed. "And where's Lady Amanda?

How could you not *tell* us first thing?"

Once explanations — and enthusiastic congratulations — from the two staffers had finally come to an end, I took the painting upstairs for safekeeping before anyone else could waylay me and ask about the news. I found it a temporary place of honor by propping it on a mantel (I would have it framed before presenting it to Matthew, I decided). At the same time, I heard the trill of my cell phone in my pocket.

When I pulled it out, I saw the word *Matt* on the screen. I felt my heart begin to hammer. Matt wouldn't call me at work for just any reason. Especially not right now. Not unless —

The phone was still ringing when I shoved it into the pocket of my jacket again. I didn't answer it, I simply took off for the stairs leading to the front door.

"Julianne, where are you going?" Lady Amanda called over the banister. "What's this I hear about a *ring*?"

"I'll explain later when I come back!" I called over my shoulder. "I promise!"

Halfway out the door, I pulled off my high heels and began running. Geoff was in the courtyard alone, placing a stack of empty crates in the boot of his car.

"Geoff!" I said. "Please, if you're going into the village, I need a ride home." 'Home' would be Rosemoor Cottage, of course. Everyone at the estate still assumed I was staying there, not Matthew.

"Of course," he said. He gave me a puzzled look. "I trust everything's all right, Miss Morgen?"

"Fine," I said. "Just fine. I just need to do something there."

When the car pulled alongside the street outside the cottage, I climbed out and gave Geoff a quick wave of goodbye as he drove on — thankfully, he hadn't noticed my ring yet. I opened the gate and hurried towards the back garden, where Matt met me halfway between the hothouse and the untamed English garden that sprawled towards the neighboring house.

I didn't give him a chance to speak. My hands cupped his face, and I kissed him, hard. When I drew back from it, I saw an expression of surprise in his eyes — but not a trace of worry or sorrow.

"How did you know?" he asked. Astonishment in his voice. "I hadn't told anyone it was negative yet — not even Michelle." I felt him touch my cheek, the first truly carefree smile I had seen from Matt in weeks lighting up his face. "You couldn't have possibly known."

"I didn't," I said, softly. My own smile was taking over my lips now. "I didn't know until now."

I heard Matt laugh. The relief in that laugh was worth a million pounds — worth more than anything in the world. He rested his forehead against mine, our lips a kiss apart once more. I wrapped my arms around his neck, holding him tight.

I felt his hand reach to take mine a moment later, closing around the one wearing our engagement ring. He brought it to his lips, kissing my fingers once again. I opened my eyes, smiling as I looked into his own.

"Let's go give everyone the good news, shall we?" I said.

A Manor in Cornwall

By

Laura Briggs

Every wedding planner wants an event to fall on a perfect day. I've had my share of good luck when it comes to sunshine and clear skies — even as an event planner in England, known for its drizzly days — but here in Cornwall, whose rainy days are fewer than England's northern counties, I didn't think that fortune would smile on my own wedding.

But it did. We took a chance, having the ceremony on a Cornish beach, instead of one of Cliffs House manor's drawing rooms, we knew. Matthew and I, however, felt there was no place more appropriate, since it was the view of Cornwall's water that brought us together. Well, the view from the flower beds growing along the garden path, that is. But our beloved cliffs' point was far too small to accommodate all our guests without squashing Matt's hard work in those flower beds — and the shore below it was, needless to say, mostly a rocky ledge.

I, Julianne Morgen, known for my love of designer shoes, stood barefoot despite any beach-swept rocks or shells, risking whatever might be buried underneath the sand — hand in hand with Matthew as the sea's breeze whipped our hair around our faces, and rippled the train of my ivory gown along the sea-washed edge of the beach. The gown I had chosen wasn't a designer label with a fancy price tag, but merely a simple, beautiful strapless dress with a sheer overlay.

I didn't care if it encountered salt water or seaweed, just as I didn't care that my hairstyle was completely ruined by the wind: the only thing I cared about today was being with the people I loved most. Even Matthew wasn't in a morning suit, although his silk shirt and linen trousers were definitely a step up from his gardening togs. This aspect definitely felt like an American wedding to me — although one straight from California's sunny beaches and not the rainy streets of my old home city Seattle.

My parents were there to watch us, looking proud, happy, and maybe just a little overwhelmed by the whirlwind of days they'd spent exploring Cornwall up until this morning. Aimee, my closest friend from the U.S., was there, too, in her brightest pink formal and acting as my chief bridesmaid; Gemma and Pippa joined her in the wedding party, wearing the matching pink, knee-length gowns I had chosen for my two local bridesmaids (with lots of input from both of them), and for Michelle, Matt's beloved younger sister. Even a few of Matt's colleagues from Boston were there, although his best man was Lord William himself.

"You may now kiss the bride," said the minister, as he closed his book of vows.

The words I had been waiting for. I hadn't cried through my vows, at least — being deliriously happy means you can't stop smiling even long enough to cry — but I was dangerously close to it now that I was facing Matt as his wife, and he was leaning down to kiss me.

Both of my hands were now enfolded by Matthew's strong fingers; I felt his lips brush my own, the touch between us a tender one that lasted longer than even we intended...after all, we had said beforehand, there would be plenty more later, right?

One look in those eyes as he released me, and I felt my tears melt away. It was as if fireworks were ignited inside me, lighting me up within with color and fire in breathtaking display. Aimee threw her arms around me in a bear hug as she handed me my bouquet, while Matt was engulfed in a similar hug by Michelle. We were eagerly surrounded by our loved ones now, all smiling from ear to ear as they wished us happiness.

A few moments later, my hand was safely back in Matt's hold again as I tossed my bouquet of freesia over my shoulder. A wail like a siren from behind me made us all turn to see the source of the noise — it was Pippa the romantic, whose expression was that of an astonished lottery winner as she clutched the bouquet in both hands. Someone snapped a photo at that exact moment, one of Pippa's delight and everyone else's laughter and smiles.

Like I said, it was a perfect day.

***

That beautiful day on the shore was almost five months ago, and since then, I couldn't have been busier. Maybe there was something in the air this fall that compelled people to plan major, life-changing events in Cornwall. A wedding for a couple from St Austell coincided with a financial guru's retirement, then two weddings back to back near the end of the summer, sandwiched in between a charity tea social and Cliffs House's role in the village fete.

Now, two more events were scheduled back to back, albeit at separate ends of the financial scale. The first was a major Cornish performing artist's album debut, being hosted here at Cliffs House, and the second was Pippa's wedding.

"You'll help me with it, right?" said Pippa. "I don't know the first place to start — I want a proper dress and flowers and everything. Something classy and elegant, like the big ones we've done here."

Pippa's knight in shining armor wasn't a football star, actor, or London millionaire like the ones she and Gemma had spent hours dreaming about while working in the kitchen. He was an incredibly likeable local boy named Gavin, who had just landed a good job in Hampshire and saw his opportunity to finally propose to the secret love of his life. More than one person had taken bets when he first began dating Pippa that she would break his heart — so almost everyone was surprised when she showed up one morning wearing a beautiful little sapphire ring.

"His gran's," she explained, as she showed it off to a wide-eyed Gemma and Dinah. "Not exactly the Hope Diamond, but it's pretty enough, I suppose." She blushed with these words, and I felt sure that Pippa was in love at that moment. "Better than a diamond chip like Tandy Newcastle's wearing. Practically invisible unless you hold it under a water glass — and her Ted's spent four thousand quid on that beater of a classic motorbike what everybody says is too rusted for anything but spare parts."

"Engaged?" said Gemma, who was just now recovering her speech. "Since when? Why didn't you tell me it was serious? You held out on me, that's what you did."

"Heavens, half the village thought you were running his heart ragged, the way you talked about him, not planning to marry him," said Dinah, half surprised and half scolding at this point. "All those criticisms of his looks and his manners and the way he mooned about, trying to get your attention since he was a lad —"

"I think it's great," I said, before Dinah's concern carried her too far into probing poor Pippa's love life. "He seems really perfect, and he's definitely in love with you. The look in his eyes whenever the two of you walk into the pub for quiz night, for instance —"

"—like the way Ross looks at Demelza," sighed Gemma. Because no conversation between these two on staff at Cliffs House was complete without a reference to *Poldark*, I knew.

"He's not exactly Poldark, though," said Pippa, who looked slightly wistful. "But he's a decent lad, it's true. And the way he proposed was romantic. Took me to a little place in Truro, and got down on one knee and everything." A blush burned in her cheeks after this admission.

Gavin was a wise man, I surmised, who knew the way to Pippa's heart better than anyone had thought. And he was a much better choice for her than her usual boyfriend, who usually spent hours loafing around with fellow football fans, and didn't mind giving other girls a glance whenever the two of them were at the pub or Charlotte's pasty shop.

"Well, I'm astonished, that's all I'll say," said Dinah, who made herself busy rattling pans again. I'd never seen her at a sudden loss for words with either of her assistants, whose silly stories and gossip she tended to address with a quick tongue. Pippa's news, however, defied that tradition.

"So I want it to be a special day," Pippa confided in me. "Gavin wants me to pick a nice dress and flowers, no matter what my mum says about the cost — and I want a place with a bit of class for the reception. I've not much money myself, though —" here, her face fell slightly, "— and I know Gavin's saving as much as he can for renting a nice little place afterwards. So I thought maybe you'd know some ways to make it elegant without costing too much. I don't want a quick ceremony at the magistrate's and a rowdy afternoon at the pub afterwards with me dad's crowd." She made a face.

"It'll be beautiful," I promised. "There are plenty of things that we can do that will make it gorgeous, trust me."

"Like a fairytale," chimed in Pippa, hopefully. "When I think of some of the things I've seen here — even just one of Dinah's cakes would be something." Her face lit up.

I suspected the manor's cook was softhearted enough that one of those would be Pippa's, with or without the money for it. "I'll talk to the florists for you, and find a reception site," I promised. "Some place better than the pub." For all our love of the local watering hole near the shore, there were limits to its romantic appeal, from the rowdiest patrons and their arguments to Old Ned the former sailor's penchant for sidling up to guests and wheedling a free drink out of them.

I had made Pippa that promise and I intended to keep it. The two of us had already gone through Pippa's 'wedding scrapbook' one Saturday afternoon, poring over the dresses and flower arrangements she had torn out of magazines. She had excitedly described all sorts of celebrity weddings she admired. Now it was up to me to find a way to add a little of the celebrity elegance that Pippa had always craved for her special day.

I laid out the magazine clippings on my desk on Monday, on top of the wine lists, florists' catalogs, sketches, and other paperwork that was beginning to take over my workspace. Pretty soon the stack would tumble to the floor in dramatic fashion, I imagined, as I blew a few wisps of auburn hair out of my eyes and tried to rearrange a few things to make more room. *Note to Julianne — take this afternoon and put some stuff away*, I thought, as I searched for a critical bill among the stack.

"Julianne, have we heard from Kelly Forrester yet?" Lady Amanda hurried into my office, as fast as her semi-practical high-heeled boots allowed. Kelly was the local antique dealer, who was supposed to be loaning us a few elegant props for our next event — notably, a hand-painted spinet formerly belonging to a French palace.

"Not yet," I said. "She's been gone this week to a china auction in London."

Lady Amanda released an exasperated sigh. "Is it just me or is *everyone* on holiday this week?" she asked. "Just when we need answers on the dot, too." She was gathering up a few of the floor plans for the ballroom's rearrangement, which she and I had been working on yesterday, shoving them into the portfolio in her arms.

"Did you talk to the caterers in Truro yet?" I asked her.

"Heavens, no? Was I supposed to do that? I thought you were," she answered.

"I *was,* until I ended up having to spend all day on the phone with the sound equipment place," I said. "And you said —"

"Never mind what I said, since I clearly forgot," said Lady Amanda. "I'm afraid you'll have to call them, Julianne, since after this morning's meeting I have an appointment with the tourism council."

Another thing on my list. I jotted it down on a sticky note, where three other essential tasks were already scribbled. "You know," I said, "I think we're going to need a lot of reinforcements for this event."

"I know," groaned Lady Amanda. "An army couldn't possibly provide all the security, decorating, and heavy lifting we're facing."

"Maybe we need one, anyway," I said.

"If you can organize one, then I commend you," said Lady Amanda.

"I'll see what I can do." I posted the sticky note to my lamp, where I hoped I wouldn't miss it when I came back. Between Lady Amanda and me, more than one important thing was at risk of being forgotten these days.

"As you all know, we have less than a month until Wendy Alistair's gala evening, and we have a tremendous amount of work left to do," said Lord William. "I know we're feeling the pressure, but we need our very best to be on display for the event."

This morning's staff meeting was in his office, where we sat in a circle — me, Lady Amanda, Geoff the estate's manager, Dinah, and the new gardener Pollock. Lord William had evidently been busy on the estate's property shortly beforehand; little chips and shavings of wood were caught in the yarn of his pullover, and a pair of work gloves were sticking out of his pocket.

"It's not too soon to start mobilizing the event staff, is it?" I asked. As always, Cliffs House would hire several locals — usually young and eager for extra wages — to help out with catering, cleaning, and anything else that was overwhelming the manor's modest full-time staff.

"The more the merrier," answered Lord William. "Ms. Alistair's people have been kind enough to supply their completed vision of her performance, and some of the details might be slightly daunting."

Wendy Alistair's name was on everyone's lips in Ceffylgwyn lately, and probably all over the county, for that matter. It wasn't every day that a Cornish singer became the leading soprano in a major opera company in Milan — or became an overnight singing sensation after an inspired public performance for the royal family. Wendy Alistair, former mezzo-soprano in Milan, had now recorded a project that was already number one on the U.K. classical charts even before its release.

"I still can't believe she's coming here," said Dinah. "I mean, we've had celebrities before — but never one this famous. Her poster's everywhere when you go into the village."

"Isn't it exciting?" said Lady Amanda. She had preordered the artist's CD, the receipt for it lying on her desk for the past two weeks.

"It's quite a boon for us," said Lord William. "I found it hard to believe that she didn't wish to choose some place a bit more famous. Tintagel Castle, or even Minack Theatre simply for its atmosphere. Although I suppose the weather might be a bit against anything outdoors."

"According to her biography, she was a Truro girl at heart," said Geoff, speaking up for the first time. "Perhaps she wished for a location close to her former hometown."

"I didn't know you followed celebrity gossip, Geoff," I said. While Lady Amanda and Dinah had been almost starry-eyed a moment ago like the manor's youngest staff members, Geoff Weatherby generally doffed a rather vacant, polite expression whenever details about actors' love lives or singers' latest pop hits were the subject at hand.

"I read *The Opera Lover's Digest,* from time to time," he said. "Ms. Alistair's *Madame Butterfly* was the toast of Venice in the March issue."

Lady Amanda was glancing over the latest set design for Wendy Alistair's performance — not the one she and I had been working on, but one from Ms. Alistair's representatives. Her eyes grew wide. "Good heavens, they want this many people in the ballroom?" she said. "And how on earth can a giant projection screen possibly be made to look nice in there?"

"I suppose we'll simply have to create the illusion of more room," said Lord William. "Quite un-simply, of course." His smile was wry.

For the project's debut party, a guest list of three hundred had been invited from all parts of the British music industry to enjoy a private concert by the artist, then champagne and hors d'oeuvres in the foyer. Lavish black tie events like these meant everyone had to be on their best behavior, including those hired just to pass around trays of champagne or mind the doors to the closed-off parts of the house.

"Ms. Alistair appears to be very particular in her wishes," remarked Geoff. "Are we quite sure we'll have everything satisfactorily in place by the time she arrives?"

"Fortunately, her representatives are sending someone here beforehand," said Lord William. "An event promoter of some sort who will 'double tick' the boxes on her behalf. He'll arrive shortly, and, hopefully, give his blessing to our progress thus far."

I studied the list of demands from the artist, and the performance design as Lady Amanda handed them to me. I definitely agreed with Lord William — we had a lot of work to do.

***

"Put away your digital devices," coaxed Matt. "It's nearly six o' clock, and you haven't even touched your pasty. Or, for that matter, talked to your husband."

I looked up with a smile of apology. "Sorry," I said. "It's just been such a day at work. Tomorrow, we're removing all the drapes and the furniture from the ballroom...plus, did I mention that we have an engagement party this week?"

"You've mentioned nothing else," he answered, smiling back.

"Sorry," I said, again. With a sigh, I turned off my tablet and laid it on the table, then stretched beside Matthew on the sofa. "How was university?" I asked, softly, leaning against his shoulder.

Matt had been between assignments when he first returned to Cornwall, and served a brief stint once again as Cliffs House's main gardener, but he was now lecturing at Oxford three days a week. Where I had no doubt that the *Poldark*-esque looks that had so charmed Gemma and Pippa probably had the same effect on his botany students.

"Good," he said. "I spoke with my friend John from Heligan Gardens a few days ago. He has a friend who is in charge of the grounds at Pencarrow, and would like me to come see a part of the gardens they're considering expanding."

Pencarrow was a historic estate in the northern part of Cornwall, I knew. "Really?" I said. "Not two days a week, I hope?" I crossed my fingers that it wasn't the case.

"No," he laughed. "More like a few times a month, mostly weekends. I'd love for you to come with me, if you could. You've never seen it, and it's one of the most beautiful historic sites in the county."

Between his travel and my hectic schedule, we hadn't seen much of each other lately, so the thought of traveling north by car with Matthew seemed romantic and incredibly relaxing. Unfortunately, when would I find the time? My last weekend I had still been catching up on Friday's to-do list.

"More than anything, I wish I could," I said. "I've seen pictures of it, and it's everything you've described...and the real attraction there would be you, of course." I took his hand, interlacing my fingers with his own. Watching Matt garden did the same thing for me that watching Ross Poldark in the tin mines did for Gemma and Pippa.

"Then come with me." He buried his face against my hair.

"What would I do about my work?" I asked. "These days, there's always something extra to do on the weekends. Lady Amanda can't possibly handle it herself, since she's already running a business on top of booking the manor's events."

I snuggled closer to him, catching a whiff of his cologne, but only the faintest traces of the earthy, outdoorsy scent I associated with his passion for gardening. Too much time in the classroom, too little time in Rosemoor's flower beds and hothouse, I decided.

"Find someone else to do it," he said.

"What? You mean, replace myself?" I echoed, incredulously. "Thanks a lot. I land my dream job, and now you're trying to talk me out of it."

"No, I mean find someone who will pick up the odd jobs you don't have time for. At least until this busy season is past," he said. "It will give you more time to concentrate on the details that matter, and more time for yourself."

I considered this idea. Who would it be? Not Gemma, who already had double duty between the manor's cleaning schedule and Dinah's kitchen. Not Pippa, who was leaving in a few short weeks. I couldn't think of anyone who would do, yet Matt's suggestion made sense. Especially if I wanted to spend more time with a certain consulting gardener in the coming weeks.

I closed my eyes, imagining myself strolling through the gardens in the crisp fall air, my hand in Matt's ... and not a worry in my mind that I was neglecting the celebrated Wendy Alistair's big album debut.

It was definitely worth considering.

***

"Most of you have worked here in the past, so you know the rules already," I said. "Just in case, however, I've made a short printout of 'dos' and 'dont's' for those of you who will be chosen to work at the actual event...." I passed out the sheets to my listeners with these last words.

The foyer was crowded with eager would-be staffers from the village, some of whom were volunteering to work for free, believing it was their only shot at seeing Wendy Alistair in person. I spotted several of Gemma and Pippa's friends among them, since virtually every village girl from seventeen to twenty-five — as well as a few boys — seemed to be here this morning.

"Of course, most of you will only be helping renovate the manor house's ballroom for the next few weeks," I said. "There's a lot of cleaning and repair work to be done, and you'll be supervised by Geoff Weatherby here and by Gemma Lawson and myself. And some of you will stay on for the event itself —"

"Will we get to meet Wendy?" A hand shot up in the air before I was even done speaking.

"This isn't a big chance to meet a celebrity, I'm afraid," I said. "This is mostly about serving the event's guests, then helping clean up afterwards."

"But she'll be there. So we might meet her, right?"

I had seen the list of demands for the artist, which included a mandatory force field of space between her and fans or staff, so I found it fairly unlikely. "Probably not," I said. "So if you're not interested in simply working for the manor's average part-time wage and going home with a box of leftover truffles and caviar, this isn't the event for you."

There was some grumbling and whispering from a few little clusters of friends. Beside me, Gemma whispered, "Better go ahead and pass out assignments." She had helped me comb over the names on the sign-up sheet, explaining various skills and limitations. I had to take her word for most of it, since I hadn't lived in the village as long, and barely knew most of them on a first-name basis.

"Don't let Billy near the kitchen — he'll eat us out of house and home by snitching what's not tied down," whispered Pippa, who had just joined us. "Oh — and Lina's good at organizing things, so she'd be the proper one to fetch and carry for you." Both the girls knew I was hoping to find someone who could help me out directly for this event.

Lina, a long-haired blond busy texting someone on her phone, had delayed her university entrance because her grandmother had promised to take her to France for a month. Her skills were listed as 'public speaking,' and 'sharp dresser' (no, I'm not kidding on that one) on the sheet from Gemma: qualities Lina shared with a handful of others, a girl named Janet and one named Sandy, who were the two giggling near the front of the crowd. Only one girl wasn't giggling at this moment, in fact: a dark-haired girl near the back, the only one who didn't have on nail polish or makeup, or a stylish pair of jeans beneath her weathered, drab canvas jacket.

"You'll be split into three groups for today, and see Geoff and Gemma for your assignments," I said. Gemma puffed with pride at this announcement.

I read their names off according to their group, then followed the second group, the one with sharply-dressed Lina and the dark-haired girl. This group consisted mostly of girls that Gemma and Pippa had recommended as capable and responsible, so they were helping the two of us finish up some last-minute details for tomorrow's wedding.

Everyone else was helping Lady Amanda and Pippa strip the ballroom down for its makeover, but our group was in the pantry, the long table crowded with flowers and bud vases destined to become centerpieces for the reception's tables. I shoved aside my color wheels and the flower samples for Pippa's wedding to make room for us at the table.

"Each one of these vases gets a sprig of baby's breath, three daisies, and a sprig of the white bellflowers," I said, using Gemma's pet name for this last one. "We need to fill forty vases with water and floral powder, and then use the remaining ones to make corsages for the ushers."

Three of our helpers — Lina, Darla, and Ella — immediately put themselves in the spots closest to the materials, sorting the blossoms into vases. Two others helped them by trimming stems, the five of them forming a group that resembled a school clique, all whispers and secretive glances, and the inside language only they really knew. This left a girl named Florrie and the dark-haired girl named Kitty with the job of filling vases with water and the flower-preserving powder from the box on the table.

"I hope we'll get to meet her," said Lina, as she arranged her daisies neatly in each vase. "I saw her sing in Milan when me and grandmother were there, and I got her autograph. Now I want her to sign the poster on my bedroom wall."

"I can't believe you actually got to *meet* her," sighed Darla. "She's sooo beautiful. I've read one of the star players for Manchester United has a crush on her. Think he'll come to her concert?"

I glanced at Gemma, and we both smiled. Apparently, my honest remarks hadn't completely squashed the dreams of our temporary staff for celebrity sightings.

"Don't fill the vases so full, please, Kitty," said Lina, in a smooth, polite voice. "They'll spill everywhere when we move them."

"I know what I'm doing, thanks." Kitty's tone of voice was, well, *rude*. Lina and Darla exchanged glances, both rolling their eyes as Kitty filled each vase three-fourths full, then began adding the powder, carefully. Florrie had completely disappeared, I noticed — the first defection from the crew?

"Did you see where Florrie disappeared to?" I whispered to Gemma, who was cutting strips of floral tape.

"No," she said. "But she was always wandering off in school. Headmaster used to find her hiding in the loo. Sometimes with her mum's cigarettes."

Great. "Maybe I should go look for her." I was beginning to regret my request that we rally an army to help us — looking for defectors would make every task twice as long.

"Do these go in the vases, too?" Lina asked, lifting one of the samples from Pippa's wedding. I turned to see that she had begun pairing some of them off into little piles — pink ones, red ones, yellow, magenta — and had put two reds and two pinks in each vase.

"Not those," I said, quickly. "Those are — that's not important right now — just worry about the ones for the wedding tomorrow." Lina shrugged, then finished arranging the neat little matching stalks in their vases before walking away.

The missing Florrie wasn't in the washroom, or in the kitchen with Dinah, or even smoking a cigarette in the garden. I gave up looking for her ten minutes later, making a note to speak to her if she materialized and wanted a paycheck without anyone having seen her working.

Lina and her friends were now transporting the vases to safety, while Gemma was cleaning water and petals off the table. Near its end, Kitty was studying the stalks of flowers and the open color wheel I had left beside them.

The color wheel — in this case, strips of varying shades and hues of every color, laid out in the spectrum's order — was a possible test I had mused as a way to choose my helper for the next few weeks. In high school, one of my favorite teachers had been an interior designer, and had told me that a person's perception of color, using it and identifying it, was the best clue to someone's organization skills. I had thought it would be a quick way to eliminate which ones were clueless when it came to decorative tasks, at least.

"Now what can we do?" asked Lina, who was giving me a smile that looked like it was kept in a cool, dry place until needed. I imagined her following me around, doing her best to hide the gleam of excitement at the mention of Wendy Alistair's name, and felt a little dread.

On impulse, I lifted the color wheel and held it out to Lina, spreading its strips wide. "Pick two different colors," I said. "Pretend they're for your birthday cake — but they have to be two completely different colors."

"Why?" asked Ella. "Is this a game?"

"It's too hard to choose," pouted Darla. I could tell right away this test wouldn't work with her.

"This one ... and this one." Lina confidently pointed to two test strips. One was a creamy white, while the other was a festive pink. Perfect matches, but that's because they were also completely safe and conventional choices. I felt disappointed.

"So what are we doing now?" asked Ella. Who kept glancing around, as if picturing Wendy Alistair showing up any minute, and maybe popping her head in to see if we were doing the centerpieces for her champagne celebration. I recognized that hopeful expression on sight.

"Next, we'll be wrapping the corsages," I said. "Then we'll be making a last-minute garland of boughs for decorating the punch bowl's table." A slight mix-up in the details for the reception's layout had created this problem.

"Is any of this for Wendy?" asked one of the high school girls who had been trimming flowers.

"Nope," I answered. "Not a bit of it." Her face fell with disappointment.

I noticed the extra vases by Pippa's flowers had been rearranged. Two sprigs of magenta-colored blossoms, one yellow, one orange — it caught my eye because it looked attractive, even though the stems needed trimmed to give the arrangement a tapering height.

"Gemma, did you try that combination for Pippa's flowers?" I asked. I had left the color palette open to a spread of reddish, pinkish hues, I noticed.

Gemma looked up from correcting the corsages. "Who, me? No. Not a bit," she answered.

I glanced around. Kitty was sweeping up petals on the floor, and Florrie had returned from unknown parts, now busy reading the back of the plant food package. "Where have you been?" I asked her.

She looked at me with a blank, innocent expression. "I went to the lavatory," she said.

"Why didn't you say something? You've been gone for twenty minutes."

"I didn't think you needed me. You had lots of people here working."

I glanced at Gemma, who offered me a not-so-subtle look of skepticism. I sensed this would be one of many in the days to come.

I lifted the color palette and opened it randomly, studying the bright samples. I took a deep breath and laid it aside, then removed the box of plant food from Florrie's hand.

"Florrie," I said. "We need to have a word."

"What? Why?" she said.

"Just come with me," I said, leading her towards the door. When I glanced back at Gemma, I saw Kitty looking at the samples, her fingers laid on two separate colors: a blue shade of lavender and a smoky red.

***

"I was thinking of driving to Bodmin this Saturday," said Matt. "Pencarrow's putting Sir William's Molesworth's recently-discovered garden sketches on display with the original blueprints of Pencarrow itself. It's the anniversary of Robert Allanson's final architectural design, I think, or something like that." He glanced at me. "You'll come with me, won't you? Or do you think that designing a diva's stage will occupy your time?"

"I don't know," I said. "But I've been thinking about your words, and I decided you were right. I'm going to pick someone from Pippa and Gemma's pool of temporary staff to lighten my work load this round." While I was still blenching at the thought of picking oh-so perfect Lina, it hadn't destroyed my desire to free up my time.

"Before Saturday?" he asked, hinting.

"Maybe so," I said. "I *would* like to see Pencarrow. And there's no one I would rather see it with." I drew his arm more firmly around my shoulders, holding onto his hand. My head rested on his shoulder, and the deep, smoky smell of the outdoors in autumn reached my nostrils from the fabric of Matt's shirt. The smell of smoke from our chimney, and of earth and dried leaves, clinging to Matthew's skin and clothes. That was the right scent, I felt.

"Were you gardening today?" I asked.

"I was weeding the foxgloves and the hollyhocks," he said. "How did you know?"

"I can just tell," I answered, my fingers tracing those belonging to his hand, now separating the one that wore his wedding ring, a thick, gold band engraved on the outside with the Cornish words for 'love,' and 'forever.' "You know where I wish you were gardening?" I asked.

He smiled, amused. "I think Lord William finally ran out of reasons to hire me," he said. "Besides, Pollock's a good gardener. You've never said you dislike working with him."

"And I don't," I said, quickly. "I just wish I were working with you. Then we would see more of each other. I'd open the drapes in the drawing room and there you would be, planting autumn mums or trimming the rhododendrons..."

"Maybe if you ask someone to help you at work," he whispered, "we'll see more of each other here. In our cottage, and our garden. And I could spend Saturdays teaching you how to root cuttings."

"Sounds exciting," I whispered back. "Tell me more, oh master gardener."

"It's actually very dull to explain," he answered. "Unless you happen to be a student of botanical science."

"You'd be surprised," I said. "I could listen to you talk about plants all day." I slid closer to him, succeeding in pushing to the carpet below a book on possible plant fossils in Antarctica's ice and my sketches of Pippa's wedding flowers, now in magenta, orange, and yellow, with a sprig of white added.

"You must be very desperate for companionship," he teased me.

"Desperate. For you. Yes, that's definitely the word I'm looking for right now," I answered, kissing him on the lips.

The next morning, the winnowed pool of part-time manor workers waited for their assignments. I had a checklist with names divided into two groups, one for Geoff and Lady Amanda and one for Pippa.

"As I read off the names in the first group, you'll be joining Geoff for stage construction," I said. "The rest of you will assist Pippa with moving the furniture into storage." I checked the name sheet once more. "Kitty — you'll be helping me for this afternoon."

Several pairs of eyes latched onto the dark-haired girl when I said this last name. Several more people were whispering. After a short pause, the girl began moving in my direction.

"What are you thinking?" hissed Gemma. "That's Kitty Alderson, for heaven's sake!"

"What?" I asked.

"She's a troublemaker," whispered Pippa. "Don't you know she's —" But that was as far as she got before she hushed herself.

Kitty stopped in front of me. She was slightly shorter than I was, but that was because my high heels and her battered red sneakers placed us at different eye levels. Her dark hair was almost black and rather untamed, while freckles were visible on her fair skin, across the cheekbones just beneath her greenish-blue eyes.

"Follow me," I said. And I led the way to my office, aware that Pippa and Gemma were both watching with disapproval.

"Basically, this is a simple job," I said. "I want the piles of paperwork on my desk sorted into separate stacks of bills, sketches, and receipts. Any file folders go in the cabinet by the big antique globe, in alphabetical order. And if I need an errand run, you'll pop out and do it for me so I don't have to leave while they're working downstairs. Does that sound manageable?"

Kitty stood in the middle of the room, her hands stuck deep in the pockets of her old canvas coat. Underneath it, she wore a red hooded jacket and a pair of jeans cuffed at the bottom because they were too long. The only time she took her hands out was to lightly touch the globe, her fingers giving it a deft spin on its axis.

"All right," she answered. She shrugged her shoulders. There was a decided lack of interest or enthusiasm in her voice, and a decided coolness — it was the audible expression of a poker face, almost.

"You arranged the flowers in the vases yesterday, didn't you? The ones Lina had put there by mistake," I said.

"Yeah?" Kitty said. Cautiously. "So?" She pulled off her old coat and, for lack of a better place to leave it, folded it on the floor.

"Did you ever work with flowers before yesterday?"

"Me gran had a shop once," she said. "I used to do flowers there. I learned some stuff from her. A bit, anyways." This part was added as if to keep me from getting my hopes up.

Hmm. Well, this was only a temporary arrangement, and if Kitty's eye for colors was a clue to her inner self, she could handle the mess on my desk without a problem. So I left her to it as I caught up on phone calls to the exclusive London caterer serving the private concert.

"What do you think, Julianne? Is it too much?" Pippa had appeared now, holding up a picture on her smart phone for my approval. It was a pale white dress with a sheer neckline and sleeves — simple, but very sophisticated, and very expensive, I imagined.

"It's gorgeous," I said. "Where did you see it?"

"In a shop in Truro. Right next to this *posh* bridesmaid's dress in bright pink," said Pippa. "So do you think I can pull it off?"

"Julianne, tell her not to buy a bridesmaids' dress!" protested Gemma. "I'll wear my old one from your wedding. With the fortune she's spending on that gown, she'll need to save every bit she can." She folded her arms and gave Pippa a look. "She's practically blowing her whole budget on it."

"But it's so beautiful," said Pippa.

"Maybe we can find something similar for a little less," I suggested. "Let me look around when I'm in Truro — maybe I can persuade them to lower the price a little, if nothing else."

In the past, I had dealt with more than a few shops that sold wedding clothes secondhand. Probably not what Pippa had in mind, but sometimes beautiful dresses were available through them for only a fraction of the original cost. Surely I could find a similar deal somewhere in Cornwall, I thought, and score a dream dress that fit Pippa's budget.

"Oh, Julianne, thank you, thank you!" said Pippa. "Even just a few quid lower —"

"What about your flowers? What about your reception site?" said Gemma. "Those things cost money, too, Pip. You can't possibly afford half of what you want." She looked at me now. "Has she told you she wants the Silver Perch?"

The Silver Perch was a swanky tea house just outside the village, newly opened by the well-to-do Lily Hammond, whose chic figure was the only one in Ceffylgwyn that kept up with London fashions on a monthly basis. I imagined the private room that Pippa undoubtedly had her eye on would cost just as much to reserve as Cliffs House's parlor, maybe twice as much, given Lily's exclusive taste.

"It's just an idea," said Pippa, meekly. "I mean, I'm never getting married again, am I? Well, probably not ... at least not with a proper dress and everything. I just want it to be a bit special."

"Then ask Lady Amanda to give you a proper discount *here*," said Gemma.

"But I don't want to have it here," said Pippa. "I want somewhere new, somewhere exciting! A bit of boiled lobster dining in Land's End or maybe with burning torches and candles on some beach in Newquay —"

I heard a snort from the area of my desk. Evidently, Kitty was listening to our conversation. Pippa had heard it, too, and wrinkled her nose at the girl.

"You can keep your opinions to yourself," shot Pippa in her direction, loftily. "You weren't good enough for the likes of Land's End in the first place."

"I think I'd rather be married in a posh old parlor than in some cheap tourist seafood restaurant that stinks of seaweed and fish guts," retorted Kitty. "*I'm* not daft."

"Since the chances of you ever catching a man's fancy —" began Pippa, before I interrupted.

"Kitty, would you mind running downstairs to ask Geoff for those measurements on the stage?" I asked. "If he's not around, just wait for him to show up and tell him I've asked him to double check them."

It was an excuse to avoid whatever quarrel was between these two, and I suspected Kitty knew it. But she simply rose and went out of my office, leaving behind the beginnings of two very orderly stacks of papers on my desk. She cast a sullen glance in Pippa's direction, who turned up her nose in response.

"What's all that noise?" Lady Amanda called. "I can hear you all the way from my office, where I'm trying very hard *not* to concentrate on the tourism board's exploitation of this concert!"

"Lady Amanda —" began Gemma. Pippa hurried after her — no doubt to stop her from booking Cliffs House's small parlor on her behalf. I decided to follow along, too, since they would probably be shouting for me in a few minutes' time.

"It's only that Pippa wants her reception to be at some posh, expensive spot —" I heard Gemma continue.

"I only want someplace nice and different, where I haven't been every day of my life," protested Pippa. "Half my crowd goes to the Fisherman's Rest after they've said their vows."

"Well," began Lady Amanda, thoughtfully, tapping her chin, "I suppose we could always —"

Gemma, who had sat down on the window seat during this discussion, now released a slow whistle. "Who's that dishy stranger coming up the path?"

"What?" Pippa replied, joining her at the window. Her whistle echoed Gemma's. "He's not from around here, is he?" she said. "Juli, you have to see him —"

"Looks like a proper billionaire in those clothes, right out of the romance novels."

"Let *me* see," said Lady Amanda, eagerly — I tried not to laugh, imagining if Lord William was watching. "Dearie me, he *is* dishy, isn't he? Julianne, come here!"

"Hurry, before he disappears!" said Pippa, beckoning me frantically.

"All right, I'm coming," I answered. I slipped off my spiky Valentino shoes in order to make better time crossing the room, wedging in between the three of them kneeling on the window seat. Below, a stranger with sandy blond hair was pacing along the gravel paths, dressed to the nines in a fashionable dark suit and overcoat. In one hand, he held a smart phone, and was obviously deeply engaged in conversation as he walked.

I sucked in my breath. "I'm in perfect agreement," I said. "He's definitely one of the handsomest guys I've seen. So nobody here recognizes him at all?"

"Who do you think it is?" repeated Gemma. "Imagine if it were someone like Ewan McGregor — or Chris Hemsworth?" She giggled. "Down below in our gardens."

"The event promoter," guessed Lady Amanda. "That must be who he is. He's arriving today, I think. One of you will have to go down and greet him, I suppose. I'd go, but I'm expecting a very important call from the president of the tourism council."

"Not me," squeaked Pippa. "I'm engaged now, remember?" Probably she was more horrified by the fact that she was covered in plaster dust than for the thought of offending Gavin. "Send Gemma."

"I'm not going down in *these* old togs! Not to meet someone who looks as dishy as him!"

"I'll go," I said. I was sure Matt would forgive me for my briefly-admiring glance at a tall and handsome stranger, since I clearly preferred the dark and mysterious type. "But you'll have to come down eventually, Lady Amanda — I need reinforcements for rounding up the staff." Shoving my feet in my shoes again, I made my way to the front hall.

I wasn't the first person to greet the new event promoter, however. Because through the front door propped open for the furniture's removal, I saw him turn around in time to collide with a swift-moving figure in the courtyard, carrying a crate of board trimmings. The figure, a girl in a red hooded sweatshirt, didn't slow down, even though the man's mobile phone fell and landed on the paving stones.

"Hey, watch it," he said, in a very American accent. "You could hurt someone with that stuff." He pointed to the jagged ends of the boards sticking out of her crate.

"You should watch where you're going," she retorted, now glancing back at him. "You're so slow and chatty that I could've stolen your wallet off you in two seconds and you'd never have felt it."

His eyes widened. "What?"

"You heard me," said Kitty, amusedly — but not nicely. It was still the first real emotion from her lips other than scorn.

"Even it if was somehow my fault, don't you think you owe me an apology since you nearly broke my phone?"

"Emmet." This muttered word was Kitty's parting shot as she kept on walking, paired with an eye roll that the stranger didn't see, but I did.

"That's not my name, thank you very much!" he retorted.

Unlike him, I knew this was local slang for slow and oblivious tourists, and I winced at this insult. I hurried outside. "Hi," I said. "You're Wendy Alistair's representative, right? Julianne Rose." I stuck out my hand and smiled.

"Oh, an American," he said, looking relieved. "Hi. Nathan Menton." He shook hands with me. Up close, I could see that he was every bit as attractive as from the window's view. He was in his early or mid twenties, his smile a charming one as he looked me in the eye.

"So, shall I show you around the place?" I said.

"I don't know if you're aware of this, but that girl who just came out is really —"

"This way to the ballroom, where I'll introduce you to all the staff," I said, quickly, escorting him through the door, and trying hard to change the subject from that of surly estate employees. "I think you'll love what we're doing."

Gemma and Geoff helped me assemble the staff in the middle of the workspace where the temporary stage was being constructed. I spotted Lina among them, looking somewhat sullen herself, her platinum blonde hair covered in a fine dusting of sawdust and plaster.

It took a few minutes to round everyone up again. I stepped forwards once the ballroom was quiet.

"Everyone, I have an important announcement," I said. "This is Nathan Menton, Wendy Alistair's public relations representative. He'll be spending the next couple of weeks here, helping stage the event, and we'll be assisting him with whatever he needs."

Midway through my opening sentence, Kitty had made her way back inside, to the fringes of the gathering. I thought the rest of my announcement would probably have an effect on her, and I was right — the girl's glance, after latching onto Nathan, had dropped to the floor for the rest of the statement. Maybe she was sorry for what happened previously.

"Thanks, everyone," said Nathan. "I'm sure we'll all make a great team, and I look forward to working with you." A giggle or two followed from some of the girls, no doubt for his American accent — or his good looks. He gave the group a broad, friendly smile ... but something about it made me think it was his business-only one.

The group dispersed back to their activities, helping Geoff measure for the stage's underlying supports, except for the two unlucky volunteers who were helping Gemma clean the walls with long-handled dusters. Kitty was still standing there, as if uncertain what her job was now.

I took a deep breath. "Kitty, if you've already had a word with Geoff, you can go back to sorting papers, if you like."

That cool glance didn't change, but she stuck her hands in her pockets and made her way towards the ballroom doorway. She brushed past Nathan Menton, who was traveling the opposite way — he glanced at her with obvious recognition.

"You're the girl from before," he said. "Look, if I owe you an apology —"

"You don't owe me anything," she scoffed, giving him a look that suggested he was crazy for suggesting it. From the look on Mr. Menton's face, I gathered he was thinking the same thing about her as she walked away.

So maybe Kitty wasn't sorry after all.

He turned to me. "Is that girl part of the staff?" he asked, jerking his thumb in her direction.

"Sort of," I hesitated. Imagining what he would think if he caught a glimpse of Kitty working in my personal office, for instance. "She's part of the temporary help at the estate this week."

"Well, I hate to break it to you, but I think she's a little psycho. Maybe you should find somebody else," he said. "By the way, after I talk to —" he sneaked a glance at his phone, where I realized he had been keying in all the names from my staff sheet, "—Geoffrey Weatherby, is there a place we can all meet?"

"Sure," I said. "Upstairs."

The ballroom didn't satisfy Mr. Menton's expectations, it seems. He had bigger — grander — ideas in mind for this album release party.

"Indoors, we're too confined," he said. "It won't cut it. This event is expanding lightning fast — we've already got ITV interested —"

"ITV?" piped up Gemma, excitedly. She and Pippa were supposed to be silent bystanders — both pretending to clean Lady Amanda's office while the rest of us — me, Lady Amanda, and Geoff — joined Nathan in conference.

"Exactly," said Nathan. "A televised special. That's why this has to be dramatic, see? We're talking tourism growth — fans flocking to this place, wanting to see where Wendy Alistair sang the classical standards they love. Flocking here, to Cliffs House — think of the boost this will be for visitors and clients wanting to come to this place. The boost in commerce for local businesses, who probably can't imagine the number of people this will attract to their part of the world."

I saw a spark of excitement in Lady Amanda's eyes for the words 'tourism,' and 'local commerce' — after all, Lady Amanda was part of the council working hard to promote Ceffylgwyn and surrounding villages as

English landmarks everyone should see. Their group hadn't been blind to the prospects presented by Wendy Alistair's visit these past few weeks, either.

"We need the grand scope of Cornwall in the background," continued Nathan. "Big rocks, sweeping waves. You get the idea, don't you? That's what people are coming to see — Cornwall's natural beauty."

"Why does this place have to finally get interesting now that I'm leaving?" moaned Pippa.

The part about natural Cornwall restored Lady Amanda to reality, it seems. "There's no place on the estate with a view of the sea where we could possibly seat hundreds of people," she said.

"You've got the sea right out your front door, practically," said Nathan.

Lady Amanda and I exchanged glances of horror. I imagined Matt's beautiful flower beds uprooted for a makeshift stage — hundreds of people trampling the lawn and gravel walkways to ruins, with big black light cables snaking along the ornamental boulders —

"There's not enough room in the cliffs gardens," said Lady Amanda. "Not for so many chairs. Or for building a stage, as far as that goes. We couldn't possibly rearrange the rocks or the cliffs, you realize."

"What about the rest of the estate's property?" I asked.

Geoff released a slight cough. "Most of the seasonal crops have not been harvested," he pointed out. The immediate acreage was planted in a winter food supply for livestock, I remembered, a favor to a local sheep farmer. "The fields were planted this season. Even without this fact, they're rather unsuitable for what you have in mind."

"One part isn't," said Kitty.

She stood in the doorway, hands in her sweatshirt pockets. "Papers are sorted," she said to me, as if the previous statement hadn't been spoken at all.

"What part are you talking about?" Lady Amanda asked. "What part of the estate?"

"That little clearing on the other side of the grove," said Kitty. "You can see the water from it. Behind some timber, anyway." Everyone was looking at her, so she shrugged her shoulders. "I cut through there sometimes," she said, even though this spot clearly wasn't on the way to anywhere.

Geoff looked thoughtful. "She's right. There is a little dell of sorts, running behind a natural stand of timber Lord William preserved," he said. "Not terribly large, and a little overgrown, perhaps —"

"Could we get power to it?" said Nathan. "Can we put in seats for the concertgoers? A camera and sound crew? Because if we can, then that's the spot."

"We could construct a stage, of course," said Geoff. "And perhaps we can conceal your power sources behind some distant trees and rocks...."

"Let's make the stage look like a natural rock rise, okay?" said Nathan, who was keying something into his smart phone, fingers moving like lightning. "I want this to look very natural, very beautiful. We'll bring in some boulders from a local quarry if we have to."

I exchanged glances with Lady Amanda again, who quirked one eyebrow upwards in amusement.

"Here's what I'm thinking," said Nathan. "Half the numbers are inside that ballroom. Very classy, very Old World charm in an intimate atmosphere with 'music room' decor —"

I thought of the spinet on hold with Kelly Forrester, and crossed my fingers that she was hurrying back from London.

"— then the rest is in this natural setting, sunset, dusk, darkness. I'll get a lighting crew out here to assess the possibility. And when darkness falls at the close, we shoot off some fireworks. What do you think?"

"It sounds ... exciting," said Lady Amanda. Who looked dubious, but interested.

It sounded over the top, but that was the point, I realized. Nathan Menton's job was to be the mouthpiece for Wendy Alistair, and this was what her people wanted. Granted, it was a lot more than we imagined, even from their list of demands — and this was a long list of commands from someone whose typical job description meant printing up posters and arranging radio ads and billboards for concerts.

"Can I see this grove?" asked Nathan.

"Now?" said Lady Amanda. "Lord William's in London today, I'm afraid, and Geoff is rather busy, as you can see. Could it wait, possibly?"

"Anyone can take me there," he persisted. "Or just give me a map and point me in the right direction. That'll do."

I pictured him getting lost in the fields somewhere, and thought this was a terrible idea.

"Miss Alderson undoubtedly can show you the way," said Geoff. "If Julianne can spare her, that is."

"Let's go," said Nathan. Even so, he glanced at Kitty, and I could see from his eyes this wasn't ideal, as a spark of concern appeared in them. Kitty crossed her arms, the look on her face not a happier one.

"Not unless you've got a pair of wellies," said Kitty to Nathan. "It's all mud and muck, that place."

"What?"

"Boots," I supplied, eyeing his expensive leather business shoes. Ones that did not look appropriate for hiking across farmland.

"I don't care," he said. "These shoes will be fine, I'm sure." The look of determination was still fixed on his face.

"It's your loss," said Kitty. With a tiny smirk, she disappeared from the doorway, forcing the event planner to catch up.

***

"Honestly, how could you choose *her*?" demanded Pippa. "Lina's a bit of a toff, but she's got a proper smile and speech for the visitors. Not like Kitty, who always looks like she'll bite the heads off puppies."

"I know she seems an unlikely choice, but she has certain instincts that were better than Lina and the others," I said. "There's potential underneath that arms-length attitude. I can sense it."

Granted, potential that it wasn't my job to unearth — it was my job to pick someone responsible, reliable, and organized, so I could have more free time for myself. And I had apparently made the poorest choicest possible.

"You should have asked us," said Gemma. "Or anybody. Everyone knows about Kitty Alderson."

"Like what?"

"Like the fact that she *steals* things," said Gemma.

"What?"

"Everyone knows she stole Roddy Fisher's bike. And she was always taking candy and cigarettes from the tobacco shop."

"She has a record?" I said. "Why didn't you put that on the staff sheet?"

"No one ever *caught* her, exactly," said Gemma, dubiously. "But everyone knew it, mind you. And she was definitely caught stealing apples out of Ted Russert's tree, too."

"She ran with the wrong crowd at school," said Pippa. "Rotten punks, they were. Loafing about corners on evenings. Playing tricks on people. Bit of vandalism going on with them, too."

For all I knew, Kitty had already shoved poor Nathan Menton into a marsh for being a bothersome 'emmet' whose shoes kept getting sucked into the mud. I was feeling remorse dig a deep pit inside me as I listened to all this.

"Don't speak so ill of another person," scolded Dinah, who was cooling crumpets on wire racks. "Kitty Alderson's got her problems, same as other folks. On the outs with her mum most of the time — *she's* a rum'un, mind you — but the girl was well enough when her grandmother was still around."

"She's been a loner ever since she came back from Land's End," said Gemma. "Runnin' off, all stuck up like about leavin', as if we weren't good enough for her. And back she comes before the year's out. I heard it was just so she could save up enough quid to leave again — as if she'll ever earn enough peddling fish and chips 'round the village."

"She and her mum have screaming fights all the time, so says all the neighbors. Kitty's been teasy since she was a kid — and her mum's been in a funk ever since her divorce."

"I'll bet she's never even worn a proper dress," said Gemma. "Julianne, you simply have to pick someone else. Pick Darla. Or Nettie. She's got a proper head for decorating things — used to do everybody's notebooks at school with little glittery stickers and the like."

I pictured Kitty as the neighborhood hoodlum, spray-painting walls, and stealing bicycles: a far contrast from the glimpses of the girl thus far, the one who picked such intriguing colors on the wheel. Maybe it was just a fluke or a mistake, those colors she chose. Maybe those flower arrangements were just a memory of one from her gran's shop.

"Why are we all hiding in the kitchen?" Lady Amanda breezed in, her business portfolio tucked under one arm. "Are those crumpets cool enough to eat?" she added.

"Help yourself," said Dinah.

"I'm on my way to rally the council. This news will be tremendous," said Lady Amanda. "I can't imagine the excitement for it. After all, we've had a decent number of visitors — day trips from Truro and so on — but not enough to keep the boat cruises afloat, or employ half the people desperate for a job in the village."

"I don't know if we need more tourists," said Gemma, wrinkling her nose. "Lot of emmets, likely enough."

"Unless they look like the dishy new event planner, maybe," said Pippa. They both giggled.

"Go along with you both," said Dinah. "Pippa, I believe I asked you to go fetch some garlic from the kitchen garden ten minutes ago." With a sigh, Pippa rose from her seat at the table.

"Anyway, I wanted to tell you that Kelly Forrester's back," said Lady Amanda to me.

"Finally! Some good news," I said. "I'll run along and have the spinet delivered ASAP."

"Hmm. Bit of bad news on that front," said Lady Amanda, reluctantly. "Seems that she sold it."

"What?"

"A gentleman from London saw its photos on her mobile while at the auction. Absolutely adored it. Long story short, he had it picked up by a removal van and carted away to some posh flat in London."

"No," I wailed. "What am I going to do?" The ballroom needed a musical atmosphere — it needed something special to give its stage a visual appeal besides Wendy Alistair and a microphone. I had been banking on the spinet as that perfect detail. "There's not anything else like it close by."

Lady Amanda looked thoughtful. "It seems to me that Lady Warrington owned a harp," she said. "A beautiful old instrument made by a Cornish craftsman, but it had gone to ruin over the years. Still quite handsome and striking, as I recall."

"Who's Lady Warrington?" I asked.

"Oh — a relation of William's," said Lady Amanda. "Quite eccentric, I'm afraid. She lived here some time ago, in Gossan Cottage on the upper half of the estate. She lives in Edinburgh now because of her health. Loved to collect all manner of things, and had the old barn positively crammed full of them. A hoarder, I suppose you would say."

"And there's a harp in it?" I asked. "A Cornish harp?"

"Unless my memory has failed me," she said. "But how we would find it, I haven't the slightest idea. *Her* memory's almost completely gone, and as I said before, everything was just crammed into the nooks and crannies of her shed. Even the old caretaker probably wouldn't know, and he's got rather particular ideas about looking after the place as it is." She polished off her crumpet with a second bite.

"Would she lend it to us?" I asked.

"Heavens, yes! If she was only sane enough to do it," said Lady Amanda. "Pity, because someday it will all be William's, anyway — she's left the money to her daughter, but not her 'collection' at Gossan Cottage, it seems. William was rather fond of her as a child, so I suppose she remembered that when writing out her will." She tucked a second crumpet, wrapped in a napkin, into her coat pocket. "Well, off I go, everyone."

I wondered if the caretaker could be persuaded to look through the 'collection' and find the antique harp. Surely if I had an hour or two to spare, I could locate it. A piece as beautiful as Lady Amanda suggested would be just the thing for the ballroom.

Gemma plucked my sleeve. "Have you talked Pippa out of the Silver Perch yet?" she asked.

"I haven't had time," I said. "But I'll find another place for her reception. Somehow," I added. I was so busy, I couldn't imagine when I would find time to search for an affordable one.

"You know, when she was a kid, Pip used to play at the old stone barn at Ted Russert's," she said. "It's empty except for some old junk, but nothing like Lady Warrington's old shed, don't worry. But it's quite big, and Ted would probably let someone use it for practically nothing."

"I'll go and look at it," I promised. "Maybe we could make it work." I pictured a little dressing up for the simple atmosphere, something to convince Pippa it was a lovely choice — surely a celebrity somewhere in the world had hosted a party in a similar spot.

I added it to my to-do list for tomorrow. Along with deciding if I should give Kitty Alderson a second chance.

***

First stop in the morning was Ted Russert's farm, where I hoped I could get permission to visit his barn, and maybe use it as an event site. And although I gave it a lot of thought last night — between kisses bestowed on Matthew — I couldn't decide on another staffer to be my temporary right hand. So it was Kitty, in her battered red sneakers, grey sweatshirt jacket, and old military coat, who walked up the lane with me to Ted's place.

Given the rough driveway, I envied Kitty's shoes just a tiny bit, since my Prada heels weren't meant for this sort of hike. And with the silence between us, I had plenty of time for my own thoughts.

I glanced at her. "So, you used to live in Land's End?" I said, hoping this might be a good subject.

"Once, yeah."

"Did you like it?"

A shrug. "It was all right." Kitty tossed this reply out in offhanded fashion.

"I guess you must have missed Ceffylgwyn," I added.

A slight snort from Kitty. One of contempt, I imagined, and I bristled a little, out of my own love for the village. "It's a beautiful place," I said. "I love how quiet it is. Of course, a lot of people prefer a lot of noise, activity, excitement...."

"Nothing wrong with quiet," said Kitty.

So it wasn't the village's sleepiness that had driven Kitty out, apparently. This topic hadn't quite worked out, so I shifted the conversation elsewhere. "What do you do in the village now?" I asked. "I know your grandmother doesn't have a flower shop anymore." I had gathered that much from Dinah, who told me that Kitty's grandmother had moved to Truro because of ill health, then died a few years later.

"I work in the pasty shop," she said. "The one at the bottom of the hill."

I knew she was referring to the modern snack shop — a fish and chips place near Matthew's childhood home, owned by one of his friends. "You work for Charlotte?" I said. "I love her food, especially the 'oggies.' I go there all the time." I had never seen Kitty there, however.

"I deliver fish and chips," she said. "I work the fryer when the spare cook's poorly. Nothing grand." An odd, biting humor to this last remark that seemed, well ... different from usual. For a moment, I half believed that Kitty had a playful side — hard-bitten and dark, perhaps, but still playful.

"And your mum?"

"She gets a pension. Doesn't do much of anything." Kitty's voice held no emotional clues for this one.

As we came into view of Ted's house near the end of the lane, I saw Kitty's steps falter. For a moment, I thought her cheeks were slightly paler than before, but maybe it was just the cold wind. She drew her hood on and hunched her shoulders forward as she trudged on towards Ted's place. The farmer himself was in the yard, splitting firewood.

"Hello, Mr. Russert," I said. "It's Julianne Rose — from Cliffs House?" I still tended to reintroduce myself in light of being Lord William's employee than being Matthew Rose's wife, my recognition as the event planner for the estate tending to prompt people's memories better.

"Of course. Bit out of the way, aren't you?" he asked, genially.

"We were hoping to get permission from you to see the old barn near the road," I said. "I've heard you haven't used it for sheep in years, and I was hoping to let some friends use it for an event."

"That old spot? Well, I suppose," he said. "I guess it's well enough. Not much of anything in it — had some of it carted off as junk a few years back. Probably the place is empty by now. Give it a geek, if you want." I smiled at the Cornish slang for 'look over,' which had such a different meaning in America.

"We'd be very grateful," I answered. But Ted had noticed the 'we' of right now, Kitty hanging back in the distance.

"Is that Kat Alderson back there?" he asked.

I remembered the story about the apples now, and my face grew hot. "It is," I said. "She's with me."

"I remember that lass," he said. "Caught her shimmying up my apple trees one fine fall 'bout this time. Gave you a hidin' you haven't forgotten, I'll wager," he said to Kitty, with a hearty laugh.

Kitty's face was definitely paler, but her scowl was still in place. She didn't reply, I noticed. But her body language suggested she wanted to sink into the earth.

"If you want a few more, there's some late ones on the tree," said Ted, who was still laughing. "You've got more pockets this time for carryin' em — before, she had an armful when she come tumbling down," he informed me. "Like to broke her crown that day, but still quick enough to scramble up with a handful."

Kitty must have been small, I realized. Not exactly the hardened thief yet of bicycles and cigarettes. Since she was not enjoying Ted's laughter for this memory, I quickly wrapped things up with the farmer.

Kitty was silent at first as we left, her hands shoved deeper into her pockets than before. "He didn't have to bring it up," she muttered. "It's been sixteen years, for heaven's sake."

"What were the apples for?" I asked. "Just for fun?" Maybe a few curious questions would be better than awkward silence this time.

Hesitation on Kitty's part. Then, at last: "I wanted my mum to make a pie. Not that she would've." Kitty directed her gaze elsewhere. "It broke most of 'em when I fell, so he gave me a smack for nothing but a couple of pulpy ones that I tossed into the brook afterwards." She sighed.

It was time for our second stop for the day, one concerning the much-needed Cornish harp. The path to Lady Warrington's cottage lay through the fields where Lord William was currently restoring the estate's timber holdings. When I came to the rotting rail fence that divided the tiny pasture from the tree rows, I found a padlocked gate, one that was extremely difficult to climb over in heels. On the other side, through the close-growing wood ahead, I could make out a small building in the clearing, one that must undoubtedly belong to Gossan Cottage.

I glanced at Kitty. "Do you know the caretaker?" I asked. Half hoping the answer would be 'no,' since I didn't want to repeat Kitty's embarrassment with another local farmer.

"No," she said. "I didn't know anybody lived here, now that old Lady Darlene was gone."

"Lord William said that his aunt was a little eccentric," I said. "And I gather the man who looks after the cottage for her might be, too." I pictured a little old man in house slippers and overalls, probably shuffling through the barn, meticulously searching for signs of rats and mice among his employer's 'collection.'

Gossan Cottage was in rougher shape than I imagined, in need of a coat of whitewash and new shingles on its roof. A great tangle of dead roses clung to one side, and its yard was littered with fragments of firewood, empty aluminum cans, and chicken feathers, ones belonging to the large flock of birds who scattered with panic at our approach.

I could see the barn which evidently contained Lady Warrington's possessions. An old, weathered wooden one, almost grey with age. It was a short distance from the cottage, on the fringe of the woods in this clearing, with rusted paint cans and an old wooden ladder lying beside it.

"I suppose we should find —" That was as far as I got in my remarks to Kitty, because the door to the cottage swung open with a *bang* and a large, vicious-looking dog emerged, snarling and barking.

I took several steps back — bumping against Kitty, where I stopped short. From the cottage emerged a large figure in a knit vest, worn trousers with suspenders, knee-high wellies, and an old fisherman's canvas coat and knit hat. Resting on one arm was a large shotgun, currently cocked open to reveal two shells in its chamber.

He shouted at me — not in English, I was fairly certain. But over the dog's bark, I couldn't be sure.

Kitty stepped forwards and shouted something back in the same language. The man turned and snarled a word or two at his dog, who sat down, growling as it stared at us.

"Don't want no curious types 'round here," he grunted. "'Tis private property. Be on your way, both of you."

"Please, Mr. Trengrowse," I began. "I'm from Lord William's — he would like to borrow his aunt's —"

"Nobody touches her ladyship's stuff!" he roared. "Be off now! I've had enough trouble with fool young hoodlums like her about —" he motioned towards Kitty," — and I've no interest in foreigners, neither."

"But I'm not a foreigner," I said. "Not anymore." Technically, I was married to a British citizen now. "And besides, I'm from Lord William's —"

"Get off with ye now, or I'll set me dog on you!" he answered. The dog rose and began snarling again, as if sensing its cue.

"Who made you king o' this lot?" demanded Kitty. "His lordship'll have a word or two to say about *you* to her ladyship if you keep on, so you'd best be a bit nicer to his mates."

That was bold. I looked at Kitty, whose stance was as tough — and fierce — as her voice. She didn't seem afraid of the dog half as much as she was of Ted Russert's teasing. Kitty's scowl made you think you'd best not cross her, but it didn't seem to have much power over Trengrowse.

"I've no reason to take lip from you," he replied. "Or your Yank friend! Now be off, the both of you!" He marched back inside the cottage, the dog following on his heels in response to his whistle, although it glanced back at us suspiciously one last time.

I scowled, too. "We'll just see about that," I muttered. I began walking away, but glanced back to see if the curtains covering the windows moved. They didn't. I turned right, and made my way to the barn instead.

On the other side was a large door. An ancient-looking handle and keyhole were visible, both looking rusty. The door didn't budge when I grasped the handle.

"It's locked," I said, although I wasn't surprised. No doubt Trengrowse kept all of Lady Warrington's things under lock and key. I was only surprised there was no rusty padlock and double chain around the handle for good measure.

"Tell Lord William," said Kitty. "Maybe he can get the key."

"I don't have the time," I said. I sighed, frustrated. "I don't even know if it's in there, or if Lady Warrington had another shed of treasures tucked somewhere on the property." There had to be another way in. Then I spotted the window high above, on the barn's second story. It was wide open, one old shutter hanging dangerously from a hinge.

"Kitty," I said. "Help me lift that ladder."

"What?" she said. "Are you daft?"

"Help me," I repeated. I seized one end of it, and, with a grunt, began dragging it around to the hidden side of the barn. I hoped that Trengrowse wasn't watching from a window in the cottage — possibly armed with a pair of field glasses kept handy for spotting would-be thieves.

Kitty helped me lean it against the front of the barn. It bowed slightly, and was a little rotten, but it didn't disintegrate as we stood it on its legs. It was propped just below the window's sill, a spot which seemed really high from down here, but I did my best to swallow my fear. I put my foot on the rung, teetering slightly as I reached for the next one above me.

"Stop," said Kitty. "Let me do it."

I looked at her. "I'm not going to ask you to do something like this," I said. It was dangerous, and it was my job that was involved, not hers.

"Shoes," said Kitty. I glanced down at my high heels, which were having a hard time finding a grip on the wooden rungs. They would be impossible to climb in.

"Good thinking," I said. I stepped off the ladder to remove them, and

Kitty, without another word, swung herself into place and began climbing.

"Kitty, wait!" I lowered my voice again quickly, since I was afraid Trengrowse might have a window open at the cottage. Kitty was already halfway up the rickety ladder, climbing to the sill high above. The ladder creaked and groaned in protest as she seized the window's edge and hoisted herself inside, disappearing from sight.

I waited a few minutes. I heard the sound of another creaky ladder or steps, then a scuffling noise. "Kitty," I said, leaning close to the door. "Kitty, can you hear me? Do you see a harp anywhere?"

I heard a clicking noise on the other side of the door. A moment later, it opened from the inside, Kitty behind it. In her hand, I saw a hairpin, pulled from her sleek, black locks — that was Kitty's key.

"Don't just stand there," she said. "Come on before he figures where we've got to."

Lady Amanda hadn't been lying about Lady Warrington's collection. Bread boxes, butter churns, toasters, radios — anything and everything was piled head high in the barn, leaving only a few paths here and there. It was as if the unsold merchandise of Portobello Road had been cast off in here, with trinkets and clothes piled in boxes among the furniture.

"Look at all this," I said. "How would she ever find anything?"

"Doubt she ever looked," said Kitty.

She had a point. I tried to ignore the twinge of despair I felt glancing around at the towering piles of unsorted goods. How would anyone ever find anything in such a place? Without a lot of hunting in dusty corners and bumping into things, that is. I imagined one false move might send the stacks collapsing against each other, domino style. That hadn't crossed Kitty's mind, evidently, as she was already clearing away a dusty sheet draped over some of the pieces of furniture.

I edged aside a stack of boxes blocking another pile, sneezing as a cloud of dust rose in the air. "Where did you learn to speak Cornish?" I asked Kitty, looking for a way to distract myself from the task at hand. "That's what you were speaking to Trengrowse, wasn't it?"

"My gran." Kitty was moving aside a broken chair and a termite-ridden coat rack, disassembling one of the biggest piles of bits and bobs. "She spoke Cornish. Spoke a bit of Welsh, too, as it happens. Old Cornish and Old Welsh were a bit alike in words — same goes for

Breton, too. But not as much."

"Breton. Isn't that in France?" I asked. Cursing my lack of geographical knowledge.

A snort from Kitty was the only reply I received. I might have been annoyed, but I had just spotted what I was looking for. In the rear of the barn, beneath the rickety stairs to the hay loft, stood the frame of a magnificent harp. It was covered in dust, but I could see the former glory of the wood, the intricate carvings and faded gilding that would appear with just a little polishing.

"There it is," I breathed. I forced my way between an upended parlor table and a box filled with old telescope parts, picking my way through the piles until I reached it.

"What are we going to do with it?" Kitty lifted an eyebrow as she watched me.

I turned around. "Do you think we could carry it?" I said. "Just beyond the trees?"

"You're thinking of coming back for it," guessed Kitty.

"In the dead of night, if I have to," I answered. "But I was thinking probably later today, with Geoff Weatherby and the little field truck."

"You're the boss." Kitty began climbing over the piles, too.

The harp was heavier than I thought. I had the foresight to remove my high heels, at least, but even so, Kitty and I nearly had several accidents that would have sent the instrument crashing into piles of glass bottles and jars, or crushed one of us beneath its frame. When we reached the main open space in the barn, we both set it down and caught our breath.

"Look," I said, when I wasn't gasping for air again. "Isn't that cute?" I pointed to an old metal dollhouse wedged beneath an old oxen yoke and a crate of vintage milk bottles. A two-story pink one made of tin, now coated with dust and grime, and exhibiting a few dents and crayon marks, too.

Kitty nodded. "I've seen it before," she said. "That's the old one that used to be in the Russert barn. Kids would play with it when they sneaked up there. Not that he minded." She brushed some dirt from her jacket, and I knew Kitty's averted gaze was probably because of our close proximity to the story of the apple incident. "Guess Lady Warrington must've found it in the junk he threw out."

So Pippa had played with this, too, probably. Hadn't Gemma said that the Russert barn was one of her favorite spots as a child? I opened one of the little metal shutters on the house, surprised that it still worked. The original design had been intricate, from the painted gingerbread trim to the curly roof trim and tiny little balcony rails. Cleaned up, it would look impressive. Maybe even as a centerpiece at a certain event.

Looked like I needed Kitty's hand for a second theft, too.

With a lot of struggling and effort, we managed to hide the harp in the middle of the grove, then I carried the pink tin dollhouse there, too, reasoning that since it would someday be Lord William's, he wouldn't object to my borrowing it for Pippa.

I brushed my hair — and some cobwebs — away from my face. "I wonder how often Trengrowse checks this lock," I said, as I closed the barn door again. I imagined him combing the woods for would-be thieves. Stumbling upon my hidden cache and locking it up again, maybe even calling the local constable. I didn't want Lord William embroiled in a local complaint lodged by his own family, more or less.

"He won't know we've been," said Kitty. From her pocket, she took the hairpin from earlier, and slipped it in the lock. I heard some soft clicking sounds, then watched as she pulled the handle afterwards. The door didn't budge.

"See? Your secret's safe." She tucked the pin into her black hair and began strolling towards the lane again. I shoved my feet into my shoes, dusted myself off, and followed. I decided I had no desire to ask exactly how Kitty came by those magic hairpin skills, or for what purpose she usually used them.

We cut across the back lane through the fields, which put us in view of the new stage under construction in the dell close by the sea. Extra workers were leveling the ground for the temporary seating area, while Nathan Menton had arranged for several decorative slabs of rock to be delivered for covering the sides and top of the stage, to make it look as if Wendy Alistair was standing on a craggy, cliffside ledge as she sang.

I had heard offhand comments about, 'candles burning in rock grottos' and 'a children's choir in gossamer robes' for the star's grand entrance to the stage. There was even talk of a 'level site for the camera crane' being readied for the big fireworks moment. I wondered what they had in mind for the ballroom's songs, given how grand the outdoor event was growing.

"Looks like they're only making a lot of mud," said Kitty, making a face as we watched as a small backhoe leveled an unused part of the field. A truck carrying granite slabs and lumber was struggling not to sink as the driver positioned it for offloading. The event promoter Nathan, ever focused and determined— this time, in sensible boots — was in conference with two laborers, holding a set of blueprints and motioning towards the surrounding glen.

"They're talking about making the stage a permanent fixture," I said. "Maybe hosting some of the surviving Cornish 'Passion plays' from the Middle Ages, if the local theatrical group is interested." Already, the community's drama club was abuzz about the possibility of an outdoor playhouse in Ceffylgwyn.

"Have you ever seen one of that lot's plays?" Kitty asked. She glanced at me with this question, and I tried to fathom its meaning — whether she was curious, or poking sly fun, or had been snubbed by them at some point — and found it was hopeless.

"No," I said. "Have you?"

"A few times." This was uttered in that same offhand tone as half of Kitty's statements. But not generally the half about things she disliked, I had noticed.

I started to ask her another question, but another voice at my elbow interrupted. "Are you going to let them do this?" An older woman clutched my sleeve, a stranger in a garish jumper and very sensible hiking boots, who wore a pink knit cap with a bobbin on top. "Let them murder the little innocents for the crass profits of tourism?"

"What?" I said, startled. "Who?"

"These heartless developers, that's who," she declared, pointing towards the laborers with the trucks and backhoe.

"They're only building a platform in the clearing," I said.

"Think of the noise! Think of the impact on the hundreds of helpless creatures who will be driven out by construction! Not to mention the impact of the lights and the noise when they bring in those dreadful amps and what not."

"Are you —?"

"Noreen Prowse," she supplied. "Chairwoman of the Cornish Natural Habitat Preservation Society. And your profiteers are in violation of the agreement we have with Cliffs House to forever preserve the sanctity of the red-billed chough whose nests along the Cornish coast have been threatened by the intrusion of mankind."

She thrust a piece of paper into my hand. "We intend to take action to stop this," she said. "We'll be addressing our complaints to the village government. I suggest you be there, if you wish to defend your so-called 'boon to the community.'" She turned and hiked away across the fields, a pair of field glasses on a long strap bobbing alongside her like a purse made of metal.

"Do you know her?" I asked Kitty. I felt bewildered as I glanced down at the paper in my hands — a notice about the meeting, apparently, for a complaint filed against the estate.

"Sure," said Kitty. "Old bat." She muttered this last part under her breath.

I sensed this meant a great deal of trouble was in store for us.

***

"Everyone knows Noreen Prowse," said Matt, with a chuckle. "She means well, truly. She's done quite a bit of good when it comes to raising awareness for the endangered flora and fauna of Cornwall ... but she can be a bit dramatic in her tactics, sometimes. And carry her point a little too far on some occasions."

He brushed the dirt from his clothes before he came inside Rosemoor. "I suppose it's possible that she could cause trouble for Cliffs House," he said. "But I rather think her complaints are mostly inspired by the thought of outsiders being drawn here. Increased traffic inspired by this event."

"'Emmets' and 'incomers,'" I said, using the local slang for thoughtless tourists and outsiders from other parts of England. "People like me, eh?" I folded my legs comfortably on the sofa's cushions.

"Not like you." He kissed the top of my head. "I think Noreen Prowse envisions noisy tourists who toss rubbish alongside scenic views and frighten away her beloved wildlife with too much noise and too many photographs.

"Right," I said. "Well, apparently, she's afraid for some kind of gull, or something like that. A red-billed something," I added, not too sure about the rest of its name.

"The red-billed chough?" said Matt. "Their nests are quite rare in

Cornwall now. Cliff erosion, predators, mishaps between the human and animal world — any and all of those have led to the decline. Even without those things, it was always a delicate and fragile existence for the hatchlings."

"Well, she's afraid we're going to drive them into the sea with the vibrations from the amps and the thunderous applause for Wendy Alistair," I said. "She's planning to ask the village to ban the event from taking place."

"I suppose it's possible the red-billed chough could be close by," said Matt. "Not likely, of course, but possible. Has anyone spotted one?"

"How would we know?" I asked. I had never heard of this bird, not that I had any knowledge of the average Cornish species. With my limited reading time, even the presence of Matt's naturalist volumes had left me with little more than the names of a few local flowers and some butterflies.

"We could ask the members of the birdwatcher's society," said Matt. "And I suppose we'll have to find out from William exactly what sort of habitat he's protecting in the glen."

I nodded and hoped that speaking with Lord William would help clear up the matter. Noreen Prowse seemed like a force to be reckoned with, though—or at least the kind who didn't willingly listen to reason. "At least my day wasn't all bad," I told Matt, leaning back against the sofa. "I found the antique Cornish harp to replace the missing spinet. Long story," I added, seeing his confusion as he settled on the cushion beside me. "Let's just say that Cliffs House's ballroom needed a few extra antiques for its television debut. Oh, and something else turned up that might prove useful."

I told him about the doll house and its connection to Pippa's childhood days. If it could be restored to its former glory—and I thought it stood a fair chance despite the evident wear and tear the years had given it—then it might be just the right touch I needed for Pippa's big day.

"What do you think?" I asked, uncertain what to make of Matt's smile as he watched me wax eloquent on my lucky find. "I know it might seem a little unconventional for a centerpiece choice," I continued, "but I really think it could work with the proper arrangement—"

"Julianne." He shook his head, the warmth in his glance assuring me that he wasn't questioning this decision. "I think it's a perfect choice. Thoughtful and rather touching, even. I think Pippa will probably feel the same way."

"That's what I'm counting on," I said, smiling back at him. "I know she has a lot of expectations for this wedding. I just want it to seem as special as she hoped it would be." *Minus the small fortune it would take for pulling off some of her ideas*, I added silently to myself.

"It will be," Matt told me. "How could it be anything less, with the finest event planner in all of Cornwall on the job?"

"The finest?" I glanced around, as if expecting a third person in the room to clarify his words. "Is there another person involved in this wedding that I don't know about? Because that's definitely not me."

With a subtle wink, he added, "You really do have a gift for this sort of thing, you know. And I'm not merely saying it because we're married."

"Flatterer," I scoffed. "I'm only doing my job." But I was pleased and reassured by the words. Maybe he was right about my instincts being spot on, at least about this. I knew that I loved the ideas I had in mind for Pippa's wedding—I just needed Pippa to love them as much as I did. And maybe she would. Maybe all I had to worry about at this point were the many demands of the Wendy Alistair concert.

Oh, and Noreen Prowse, of course.

"I don't suppose you know of a way to pacify Mrs. Prowse?" I asked Matt, seeing his smile grow wry in response. "Maybe a few facts on whether concerts scare away endangered birds?"

"I'll look into it," Matthew promised. "Maybe find an answer or two." He kissed my cheek, then my lips, having forgotten his errand to make a cup of tea now that his gardening was done. And since I didn't intend to remind him of it, I cupped his cheek with one hand and kissed him back.

***

On the subject of Noreen Prowse and the Cornwall Natural Habitat Preservation Society, Lord William had slightly unfortunate news.

"I did agree to preserve a natural habitat for a local nature group," he said. "The timber along the field has been left alone specifically for that reason. It seemed like a perfectly natural request, and I'm as fond as anyone else of seeing wildlife protected — even if a few of them nibble at crops and seedling trees from time to time."

"Do you think that they have a case?" I asked. "She claims we're driving them all away with the construction — and that the concert will upset the delicate life balance of endangered birds along the shore."

"The size of the habitat is fairly substantial," said Lord William. "It's hardly a little cluster of trees. That particular grove around the dell is so small, I can't imagine a large population of wildlife lives there, not compared to the rest of the acreage. And squirrels and mice and the like aren't usually greatly upset by the presence of humans."

"So what can we do?"

"I'll write a declaration that the habitat itself is not being touched — only the open dell where already plenty of humans are present during the harvest season and the peak tourism season. Perhaps when they see that the majority of the habitat isn't being threatened, they'll dismiss Mrs. Prowse's complaint."

"And what of the fireworks?" I asked.

"I can't possibly see how they could cause any more concern than the noise on Guy Fawkes Day," said Lord William. "Not to mention the children with smuggled firecrackers who are particularly prone to set them off in the woods. On the other hand, I'm not quite sure how the village government will react to permitting a rather noisy fireworks display simply for a concert."

"What does the event promoter think they'll say?"

"He's rather an optimist. Or perhaps the better word is 'tenacious.' But I suppose that must have been the reason that Wendy Alistair's people hired him."

"Hmm." I imagined his disappointment if the village wasn't keen on the concert's plans. He struck me as someone who was used to arguing his way out of any difficulty, something he would find a little more challenging in a place as quiet and, well, *settled* as Ceffylgwyn.

More disappointments lay in store for me when I took Pippa to see the barn. Ted Russert had unlocked the door for me and given me a spare key, giving me a chance to sweep it up in advance with Kitty's help, and removed a little rubbish still cluttering the place, so it was a space filled only with potential. But Pippa seemed slightly unhappy as she stood in the middle of the room.

"What do you think?" I asked. It was a wide open, rectangular space, with high stone walls and high, old-fashioned windows that were oddly glassed, as if the barn had once been a prosperous house. Old wooden beams and rafters were above us, while the packed dirt floor had all the firmness of real boards. Its weathered doors were propped wide open, letting in a strong presence of sunlight.

"We can put carpets down on the floor," I suggested. "A long wooden table down the center of the room. Add some candles, some flowers ... it will be very romantic. And very elegant."

"I suppose," said Pippa, reluctantly. "It's just ... it isn't exactly sophisticated, is it? It's just an old barn. I used to play with my dolls here when I was a kid."

"I know," I said. "And that's what makes it special, Pippa. I'm sure that Gavin played here as a boy, too. Half the kids in the village did, I've been told." I thought of Kitty's words from before. "And it will be beautiful when we've finished cleaning it and decorating it. Use your imagination — it's a blank slate right now, but with so much potential with these stone walls and those windows."

"Maybe," said Pippa. She sighed. "I guess I'm just thinking of what my mum and dad'll say. All about how it serves me right, having a send-off in an old barn after passing on the dining room at the Fisherman's Rest."

The dining room was about as impervious to the noise of a rowdy pub crowd after a football match as if the walls were made of tissue paper — and its only decoration was a big, glossy fish on a plaque and two rusty-looking anchors on either side. A great place for a stag party or a yachting club's meeting, but with zero potential for a romantic atmosphere. I knew that Pippa, however, was imagining this place would be a dusty, musty room with flies buzzing around her wedding cake. She couldn't imagine how a few simple touches could magnify its charms.

"I need you to trust me, Pippa," I said. "It will be beautiful the day of your wedding. You won't regret this choice if you say 'yes.'"

Pippa gazed around her. The doubtful look was still on her face, even as sunlight streamed through the windows as if they were the high arched ones in an old stone chapel. "I s'pose," she said, after a moment.

"You won't regret it," I repeated.

To console Pippa, I walked with her to the village, where I bought her a pasty from Charlotte's shop and window browsed the selection of new shoes and stylish tops in the local boutique. Poster after poster for Wendy Alistair's upcoming album greeted us in the shops, revealing the newly-minted diva's flawless profile and chestnut hair, a sparkling diamond earring on display in her earlobe.

"She's so gorgeous," said Pippa. "Gavin said he'll take me to a concert if she goes on tour. I wish we could actually meet her — but that warning sheet from her manager doesn't make it sound very likely."

"No, it doesn't," I agreed. "But at least we'll probably see part of the concert before ITV's audience, right?"

"I can't wait," sighed Pippa. "It's so romantic. Lucky thing Gavin didn't propose to me last month, otherwise I'd be in Hampshire by now."

Plenty of new posters had been added since the last time I was in the village, and there was a splashy article in the local paper about the upcoming concert being recorded by ITV for broadcast. I suspected that was the work of Nathan Menton and not Lady Amanda. I made a mental note to ask her next time I saw her — which, unfortunately, would be the local municipal meeting over the habitat.

"Have we got time for a quick visit to the chemist's? Mrs. Evans promised she'd show me the pictures of the newest labels at Topshop," said Pippa. "I haven't been there in ages." She sounded more cheerful now. I was glad to hear it — and especially glad that she hadn't changed her mind and reserved that costly room at the Silver Perch.

"Let's go see them," I said. After all, I had a few hours to kill until I faced the indomitable Noreen Prowse in the battle over birds.

***

"This meeting will come to order. Mrs. Prowse, I believe you wished to address a matter of importance to the residents of Ceffylgwyn?"

The meeting hall was sparsely-populated on this evening. At the head of the room, a few bored-looking council members sat in wooden chairs, along with Lord William and a few other local landowners. A small group I ascertained must be the Cornwall Natural Habitat Preservation Society sat facing them, with Mrs. Prowse clearly representing them.

I was seated near the middle of the room, with Kitty beside me, her grimy red sneakers propped on the back of the chair in front of her.

Somehow, I hadn't brought myself to go through with the plan to let Lina or Nettie take her place — not after yesterday's grand heist, anyway.

"Citizens of Ceffylgwyn. It has come to my attention that one of our beloved endangered species is at risk, due to a careless and incautious money-driven scheme tragically involving our own Cliffs House," Mrs. Prowse began. "As you all know, the planned concert for Ms. Alistair has been moved out of doors, and now involves an intrusion into our wilderness, with man-made lights, sound equipment, and plans for hundreds to pack themselves into temporary seats for two hours that will surely terrify the delicate ecosystem ...."

I squirmed in my seat, trying to find a more comfortable position, since Mrs. Prowse was clearly winding up for a long speech. I studied the members of the preservation society, wondering how many of them were also bird watchers.

I nudged Kitty. "Do you know any of the people with Mrs. Prowse?" I whispered. "Are they all members of the society — you know, keen on Mrs. Prowse's line?"

"The one on the left's Harry Tallack. He's a member, but he oughtn't be — he hunts for sport up at Mevagissey, and he's a bit of a poacher — though no one's supposed to know. Next to him's Julie Coad. Keeps a cat that eats birds."

I stifled a giggle. Kitty's dark humor was growing on me. "What about the others?" I asked.

"Newcomers from over Falmouth way," she answered. "I don't know about them."

I glanced around, hoping to see Matthew walking in. Instead, I saw Nathan Menton enter the hall, taking a seat on the opposite side of the room. He removed his overcoat and sat with his arms folded, listening intently to Mrs. Prowse's speech with an expression that looked ready for battle.

".... not to mention the dangers already incited by Guy Fawkes Night, particularly with the illegal bonfires and small incendiaries involving the village youth...."

Lady Amanda had slipped into a seat near the back of the room. She gave me a sympathetic smile when she spotted me.

"Is there anyone else who has something they wish to say?" Clearly, the village's official representatives were growing tired of this meeting already. I stood up.

"Actually, I do," I said. "Most of you know that I'm the event planner at Cliffs House. As you also know, Lord William has promised the habitat will not be included in any way in the aforementioned development of the clearing. Since humans are already routinely present in that clearing —"

"But we're speaking of the cliffs," interrupted Mrs. Prowse. "Of the harm that explosives and loud noises will cause to the natural habitats along the craggy banks of the sea —"

Nathan rose. "I have the necessary permits already to build a platform on sight," he said. "I have the permits to host an open-air concert on the property in question. What rules are we violating? If the issue of the birds was such a big deal, may I ask why those permits were ever issued?"

An offensive tact, the wrong choice for this time and place. I tried to signal him to be quiet, but Nathan clearly didn't see me. In the chair beside me, Kitty leaned back her head and rolled her eyes.

"Ms. Alderson, would you please remove your shoes from that chair?" said one of the council members. "Thank you." She looked at Nathan. "Might we ask who you are?" she said.

Hush and sit down, I thought, willing him to obey. But Nathan appeared not to notice the annoyed glances and tired attitude of the council members at this emergency meeting.

"My name is Nathan Menton, I'm an event promoter currently working in tandem with Wendy Alistair's representatives to stage an extremely important, extremely prestigious event here in Ceffylgwyn...."

"I think we've already established that Ms. Alistair is coming to the village," said one of the council members, dryly. "Might we hear something more pertinent to the issue of nature versus the concert itself?"

Lady Amanda stood up. "If I might have a quick word," she said. "We're not in any way trying to do damage to Cornish wildlife. If there are concerns about the birds, might we not have time to ascertain whether there are any birds actually at risk?"

"A very sensible suggestion," answered the council member. "Mrs. Prowse?"

"I think the estate has had a great deal of time — weeks," she answered. "And I have a signed agreement from Lord William himself regarding the acreage surrounding the clearing —"

We were losing, I felt. I cast a panicked look at Lady Amanda, whose suggestion was being steamrollered right now. Nathan looked ready to open his mouth again, which I felt would be a mistake, given he was a stranger, a foreigner, and trying to argue this like a business deal in a London boardroom.

"We've already established Lord William's role in the habitat, I believe," said the councilwoman, wearily. "I'm as fond of birds as everyone else present, but I *would* like this meeting to come to a point sometime tonight."

"Might I address the matter?" asked Matthew.

I turned to see him in the aisle. He caught my eye and gave me a smile and a wink — reassuring ones that made me close my eyes with relief. Matthew had kept his promise to find an answer.

"Yes, Doctor Rose," said one of the council members, eagerly. "Please, if you have something to say, we will gladly hear it."

"On the subject of the birds' safe habitat, no one could be more sympathetic than I am," said Matt. "However, as to the actual occupation of the cliffs at this time, I believe Mrs. Prowse is mistaken regarding the number and delicacy of the species present."

He passed a series of papers into the hands of the meeting's chairperson. "As you can see from these recent photographs taken by a renowned birdwatcher from Falmouth — Doctor Davies, who yearly tracks the life cycle of the birds nesting in the cliffs — the autumn migration has left the nesting sites abandoned ...."

***

"Three cheers to Matthew Rose," said Lady Amanda, lifting a pint. "For saving us all from a *very* long evening of tedious debate."

"I second the motion," said Lord William. We clinked our glasses together at the bar of the Fisherman's Rest. After Matthew's proof that the birds nesting in the cliffs—none of which turned out to be of the red-billed chough variety—would be safely beyond the impact of fireworks and music, the council had decided that canceling any permits was too drastic of a response to Noreen Prowse's objections. They had suggested she make a list of concessions for protecting the habitat and have these presented at a meeting as an amendment to the society's agreement with the estate. While Noreen wasn't thrilled, she had eventually accepted this proposal.

"I'm sure I'll have to make no end of concessions," said Lord William. "We'll have to put a barrier of some sort between the habitat and the clearing, possibly even the estate's fields themselves. I suppose it'll be costly, and it will have to be attractive in appearance — but perhaps it will all be worth it in the end."

"If Mr. Menton is correct, then Cliffs House will be seeing an uptick in the number of visitors and events," I said. *Which means more work for me*, I thought, remembering with a pang that I was supposed to be finding ways to lighten my workload.

"Nathan, please," said the event promoter, who sampled his pint with a face that suggested he wasn't a fan of the local brew. "And this isn't just about making money for Cornwall. It's about helping people realize that it's a place worth seeing. For the birds that are nesting on the cliffs — the beautiful countryside — the magnificent coast. All things that tourists miss when they only stop in England long enough to see Big Ben and Buckingham Palace."

"Have *you* seen them?" I asked. "They're pretty impressive."

Nathan took another sip from his pint. "You have no idea how hard I worked to get Ms. Alistair's people to even consider Cornwall," he said. "They wanted a big concert at Royal Albert Hall. It's easy to get a camera crew setup in there, it's a place everybody knows and loves. But it didn't really celebrate what made her music special. What made her story so unique in the world of classical music."

"That's a pretty passionate declaration from someone who's only supposed to arrange some P-R and set up a stage," I said.

"Yeah, well, I take my job way too seriously," said Nathan. He managed to drain his glass, although it cost him some effort — I imagined how Gemma and Pippa would feel at seeing this hint of an unattractive grimace on his handsome face. Setting the glass aside, he continued, "Not that I'm the only one who's dedicated to their work around here."

"Who, me?" I said. "I'm not married to my work. I'm married to the very brilliant scientist who just saved the day." Beneath the bar, I linked my fingers with Matt's, feeling their tender pressure in response even as he chatted on with Lord William.

"I was thinking about your staff. They seem pretty hardworking when it comes to events like this," Nathan said. "The work you guys put into the ballroom, and into making the place look so elegant. They're a great group of people." He pushed aside his empty glass, waving off a refill with a trifle more energy than was necessary. "Although the one who works with you sometimes is a bit of a pill. How do you put up with that? She's got all the friendliness of Genghis Khan."

"Kitty's just different," I said. I glanced her direction, seeing the girl looking a little aloof at one of the nearby tables, an empty shot glass in front of her. I hadn't realized until now that she didn't join us at the bar.

"Well, better you than me," he answered. "I mean, she seems like a hard worker. And she's not completely unlikable — she was almost nice part of the time we were in the field. Almost," he emphasized. "Even though she did laugh at me when I got stuck in the mud. And didn't exactly help me out of it, either."

He sneaked a glance at Kitty at this point — just a quick one, I noticed, while making sure she didn't notice him back. Not that I blamed him for it. Despite the grungy clothes and attitude, there was something interesting, even a little magnetic about Kitty. Dangerous electricity, as my friend Aimee would put it. Maybe the event promoter sensed that part, too, since when he looked away, he ordered a second drink — but a smaller one this time.

I pictured Kitty's smirk and laughter when the mud sucked Nathan earthwards. It probably wasn't the most charming picture in the world; especially for someone like him, who probably never had girls laugh at him.

At her table, Kitty rose to leave. I glimpsed her backpack slung over her shoulder, her figure disappearing through the door of the Fisherman's Rest. I gave Matt's fingers a quick squeeze and whispered, "Be right back," in his ear before following her outside.

I felt bad. We hadn't made her feel welcome, had we? I hadn't even thought about the fact that Kitty's aloof personality seemed to exclude her from local groups — or that her past led them to exclude her, whichever it was. Either way, I wanted her to feel that I appreciated what she had done for me the past couple of days.

"Kitty, wait!" I called. The girl was halfway down the sidewalk, but she stopped when I spoke, and turned around. I caught up with her, laying my hand on her arm. I felt it stiffen a little in return.

"What?" she said. She gazed at me, expectantly. "I'm off duty now, aren't I?"

"Of course," I said, awkwardly. Kitty had made me feel weirdly intrusive all of a sudden. "I just hated to see you leave early. You didn't even have a chance to talk to any of us. I meant to introduce you to Matt, my husband."

"Oh," said Kitty. "What would we talk about?" She sounded puzzled.

"I don't know," I said. I shrugged my shoulders, my mind a blank. "Tell me about the time you stole the bicycle," I suggested.

"What?" Kitty looked confused, and a little offended. "What bicycle?"

"The one that somebody said you stole."

"You mean the motorbike," said Kitty.

"You stole a motorbike?"

"I didn't steal it," she scoffed. "I borrowed it. Roddy Fisher was being a right sod, rubbing it in that he wouldn't give me a ride." Her face darkened for a moment. "Anyways, I wanted to know what it was like, so I fiddled with the starter's wires when he wasn't around. Took it around the block, and had a bit of an accident."

"How did it end?" I asked. I was guessing that Kitty had never ridden a motorbike before that day, much less driven one. Somehow this decision didn't surprise me.

"Oh, just a scratch. I took it back before he knew what happened. He blamed me, of course, when he saw it, but he couldn't prove it. He wrecked it himself anyways," she said. "He didn't need my help to wrap it around a village wall, riding around like a maniac."

I tucked my hands in my pockets. "Was it fun?" I asked, lifting one eyebrow. "Your ride?"

"Smashing," said Kitty, in reply. "Wind in my hair. Until I met with the village post box, anyways."

I caught Kitty's eye and saw the hint of a smile. I laughed, and to my surprise, Kitty laughed, too. Reluctantly, as if she wanted not to, but it was still coming out all the same.

"Don't go," I said. "Come back inside for awhile. I'll buy you a drink, anything you like — local brew, soda pop, you name it. It's the least I can do to thank you for helping me with some ... covert ... operations in my work." I smiled with these words, conspiratorially.

Kitty shook her head. "I should go," she said. "I've got work in the morning. I've had to shift my hours at the pasty shop for the manor job, so I promised Charlotte I'd come in early."

"Fifteen minutes, then," I said. "And you can go early tomorrow. I won't keep you late." I was planning to stay late myself, given the tight deadlines we were facing, but I couldn't ask that of any of the manor's temporary staff — even the supposedly-devoted Lina.

"I don't belong," said Kitty. She looked me in the eye for this statement, a square and unflinching gaze. "Not with that lot. I don't even belong here half the time." Her gaze moved from the pub towards the village in general, including it in this statement. It wasn't anger in her voice, but almost sadness in a matter-of-fact form. "I never did, and I never will, likely enough. So it's nice of you to make the offer, but I don't need it. I'm all right."

She turned to go home. I crossed my arms as I watched her, partly in stubbornness, and partly against the cool wind. "So why are you still here?" I asked. "And not in Land's End, or some other place?"

Kitty glanced over her shoulder. "I never said I didn't like it around here," she answered. "That's got nothing to do with the rest, does it?" A saucy smile appeared on Kitty's lips briefly, then she turned away and was out of sight in the evening's dusk. "See you tomorrow," she called, just before she was lost in the shadows on the other side of the lamplight.

"See you then," I answered.

Despite myself, I laughed. I had seen the first evidence that Kitty Alderson had a smile that did her face more justice than its scowl.

***

The days leading to Wendy Alistair's big debut had become a blur of activity — unfortunately for me, that blur was coinciding with my big promise to Pippa that her wedding day would be special.

In between worrying about the flower arrangements for the ballroom, I worried about the flowers for Pippa's reception, and the altarpiece garland for the ceremony, which featured lots of white roses and sprigs of bright pink heath and yellow 'chain flowers,' as Gemma called them, in bloom, thanks to Matt's generous donation from his hothouse plants.

The colors would match the ones for her reception — the ones that

Kitty's impromptu rearrangement had inspired — which would be featured in several small vases placed at intervals along the reception table's center, and in a ring surrounding the cake's platter. As of yet, all of those things were merely sketches, with the last-minute crunch of arranging the flowers left entirely to me.

After applying lots of elbow grease to Lady Warrington's harp, I had managed to unearth much of the frame's original beauty. The polished wood gleamed, while the carving was inlaid not with gold, but with mother-of-pearl forming the petals of several delicate-looking white flowers — that had been the gleam that caught my eye in the barn.

"Isn't it stunning?" said Lady Amanda, catching her breath. "It will look splendid onstage. With lots of candles lit close to the string quartet's section —"

"— and the new cream and gold damask drapes contrasting the wall color, but matching the gold and white trim," I supplied. "That, with the stunning portraits and the gorgeous antique carpet spread out across the newly-finished floor, should 'do Cliffs House proud' as they say."

I felt perfectly satisfied as I surveyed the work. Geoff and his carpentry crew had constructed a beautiful temporary stage that had been finished as dark, gleaming cherrywood. The portrait drapes were drawn open, revealing the sweeping oil portraits that predated even Cliffs House's long history. The whole room smacked of history and elegance.

"... and she's letting her parade around and *talk* to people, like she's one of them." Lina was talking in a low voice on the other side of the ballroom, where she and Darla were supposed to be adjusting the frames on the walls.

"Did you hear what she said to some tourist the other day?" said Darla, struggling not to laugh. "About Cliffs House being 'a proper job in Cornish architecture?'"

"I thought I'd die laughing. Imagine what they must've thought, hearing that awful stony voice chattering away some facts from a tour pamphlet."

"I just can't believe they don't have someone watch her every minute. She's practically a *criminal.*"

"If you two are done straightening those portraits," I interrupted, "then why don't you go find Pollock and assist his crew in planting the walkway to the new outdoor theater."

"Of course," said Lina, with a perky smile. "We'd love to." She and Darla walked away, still whispering together as they left. I stared after them, feeling annoyed by the conversation I had overheard. I glanced towards Gemma, expecting to read sympathy in her eyes, but saw nothing that resembled it.

"Why do you let them talk about Kitty that way?" I asked. "What if she heard her fellow employees talking about her like she's a convicted felon who escaped from prison?"

Gemma shook her head. "You haven't known her as long as we have, Julianne," she said. "Kitty's always been trouble. Even grown up, she still has a knack for rubbing people the wrong way. Anyway, she doesn't fit in here because the likes of her can't do the 'smile and nod' bit with tourists and guests."

"What if she just needs a chance to prove she can?" I asked. "Maybe she's learning how."

"Give her a chance, and she'll screw up in front of someone important," said Gemma. "You have to see that, Julianne. Honest. It's not about whether we like Kitty ... it's just a fact."

I sighed. "I thought you would understand," I said. "Imagine how you would feel if you were trying to fit in someplace like — like New York, or London, where maybe everyone made you feel like an outsider."

Not that Kitty was an outsider. She was born and bred here, I assumed. So was she an outsider by choice, or just because she made mistakes?

"Do what you want," said Gemma. "I'm just warning you. But wait long enough and you'll see it's true for yourself." She went back to polishing the mantelpiece's andirons.

In the pantry, the vases I had borrowed for Pippa's wedding were in a straight line down the middle, with my sketches in a haphazard pile. I had come here to have a little breather on my own before unpacking the candles for the 'grotto display' and candle stands at the new outdoor theater, but the pantry wasn't empty. Kitty was there, sitting on a stool, busy polishing a small piece of tin. It was the broken hinge from the dollhouse shutter, I realized. When I looked at the corner table behind me, I saw the dollhouse had been completely cleaned, scrubbed from top to bottom.

No crayon marks, no grime, no rust. Kitty had even managed to coax the dents out of it, and had painted over the damaged pieces. Before me was a glowing pink and white Victorian gingerbread house like the ones I had seen in a toy museum in Boston. Tiny little false flowers formed a garland of maroon, white, and pink around its base, as if a miniature shrubbery had grown there. Small battery-operated tea lights were inside the rooms, flickering visibly through the open shutters.

"Kitty, it looks amazing," I said. "When did you do all this?"

"This morning." Carefully, she attached the tiny shutter in its old position, using half a sewing pin in place of the old missing hinge pin. "Just thought it could do with a spot of tidying."

"I'm speechless," I said. "It must have taken you hours." The tiny windows had been covered by transparent paper squares — white, pink, and yellow — like miniature stained glass. It was a work of art, the entire effort. A perfect display piece for the reception. I hadn't asked her to do it — I hadn't even mentioned the fact that I needed it done.

Kitty's shoulders nudged themselves upwards in a quick motion, as if shaking off my compliments. "I used to play with this when I was a kid," she said. "Sometimes I skipped school and took my doll there. No one else would be around. There used to be little bits of furniture inside it — a toy chair, a table, some sort of wind-up clock. Somebody stole that one out of it ages ago."

She folded back the mini shutter on its new pin, testing it. "My mum would've had a fit if she'd known where I was. But I liked it, you know? Being on my own. No one to get you into trouble there, or be jumping all over you because you've done something wrong."

Her hooded sweatshirt had been swapped for a clean-looking pullover. Two small barrettes pinned back her untidy black locks of hair. She was making an effort, I realized. Trying to fit in.

I touched a small plastic sofa, a dollhouse miniature lying on the table. "You're good at this, Kitty," I said. "At making things look nice. I've really appreciated your help these past couple of weeks."

A low grunt was the only reply at first. "Good, I guess," said Kitty.

"You have an eye for arranging things to look their best," I said. "Flowers, decorations ... an instinct for what looks good. You pay a lot of attention to detail, and that's an important skill in my kind of work."

"S'pose," said Kitty, in a word that was almost a sigh of admission.

"There are jobs that need that kind of skill," I said. "We need people who can do what you've just done for Pippa — who think on their feet, the way you thought of the sea view when Mr. Menton needed one. You could learn to do what I do, even."

"Me?" Kitty let out a mocking laugh. "That'd be the day."

"I'm serious," I said. "I'm not making fun of you, Kitty. I'm not saying it wouldn't be hard work, or that you wouldn't need to change some things. Your appearance, for instance."

Kitty's fingers had stopped playing with the dollhouse's shutters.

"You would need to dress differently, maybe do your hair a little more," I said. "And you would need to talk differently to some of the people here at the manor, of course."

"And change my voice, I suppose. And my personality, and my background. Be more 'Downton Abbey' for a start." Flint in this chirpy voice from Kitty's lips, one of mockery. "You know, just not be me anymore."

"Kitty, no," I protested. "That's not what I'm saying —"

"That *is* what you're saying," she retorted. "That's what everyone says to me. 'Kitty Alderson, what's every bit the loser the rest of her folks are'— that's what everybody says needs changing about me. If I was only a simpering, conniving little liar like Lina Trawley, I'd be likeable enough."

"I'm not talking about changing who you are!" I said. "I don't even *know* Lina Trawley —"

"*I* don't need to change," muttered Kitty, who shoved aside her dirty rags and all-purpose cleaner, its lid clattering to the floor. "And I already have a job." She grabbed her backpack and marched out.

"Kitty, where are you going?" I called after her. "I didn't mean to offend you!"

But this time Kitty didn't stop, so I was only talking to myself, in a room empty except for the dollhouse and the newly-polished vases.

"She just ... flew off the handle," I said, feeling too exasperated for words. I rested my forehead on my hand. "Honestly, I don't understand why. Unless she thought I was trying to force her into a makeover or something."

I felt Matt's arms around my shoulders, drawing me into an embrace. I didn't care if anybody else was watching us from over the garden wall between Rosemoor and the neighboring house, since they would have seen us kissing multiple times in the garden anyway.

"Don't blame yourself," said Matt. "You didn't say anything wrong. You simply offered to help her explore a different path in life — learn a little more about the talents she possesses. But perhaps that isn't what she really wants right now."

"Maybe," I said. "Or maybe you're just trying to make me feel better."

"That, too," he answered. "But there was nothing else you could do except apologize, Julianne. She can accept it, or go on believing that you think of her the way everybody else seems to."

"Do you know about Kitty?" I asked. "Know all those stories about her?"

He smiled. "It's a small village. There are stories about everyone. Even me."

"You?" I said. "I can't imagine stories about the famous Doctor Rose."

He grimaced. "Not that, please," he said. "But yes, there are. Did you know, for instance, that I picked all of my neighbor's flowers once to give to my mother as a present?"

"No," I said. "You? Really?"

"Yes. I was five, and they were very lovely. And it was my mum's birthday, but since she was working very late, I simply left them on her pillow. And the next day — I was in very hot water with the woman next door, whose prize petunias I had stolen."

"Oh, Matt." I leaned my cheek against his shoulder. "You must have been a very adorable thief. I'll bet she forgave you immediately. One look into those dark little eyes, all full of repentance...."

Matthew blushed. "Never mind that," he said, with a gentle grin. "Nothing of the sort happened, I'm afraid. She made me plant all-new flowers for her the next spring."

"Was that your gardening start?" I asked, lifting my head to look into his eyes. "Repentance for theft?"

"Not quite," he said. "I used to plant seedlings for my mother, in the front window boxes. A hodgepodge of wildflowers, usually — some of which were far too big for that tiny space."

I imagined Matt as a boy, his tiny fingers poking holes in the soil. That same expression of concentration on his face even back then. Once again I wished I had a picture of Matt as a child, but he didn't have any around, claiming all the family photos ended up with his sister. I would have to beg Michelle to email me one if she had any with her on the base in Afghanistan.

I crossed my legs, guru fashion, and drew away from Matt's embrace. "All right, professor," I said. "Enough about my problems. Teach me how to identify hollyhock seedlings."

"Are you sure that you're interested?" he said. "If you're not, they'll all look like tiny squash plants to you. Only a practiced eye can tell the difference."

"Stop making it sound so hard." I swatted him on the shoulder. "Now show me what we're doing."

"First we examine the leaves," said Matt. "See the beveled edges? That's the first sign that we've found the right plant...."

Gardening with Matt on a weekend afternoon was the only time I had been able to spend with him lately. Between his teaching schedule and the trips to Pencarrow, and my never-ending schedule at work, we had seen less of each other than ever. I still hadn't had the chance to visit the beautiful northern estate with Matt, and was already kicking myself for missing the opening weekend of the anniversary exhibit.

Maybe if you'd just picked Lina in the first place, you'd be spending tomorrow there, a little voice in my head suggested.

No — I shook my head for this idea. I couldn't see myself trusting Lina with those tasks. Something about her had been too perfect, in all the wrong ways. Not just the safe color choices or the flowers lined up like soldiers in the vase — something simply hadn't fit with what I had in mind.

Mere days until performance time — and with Pippa's wedding only twenty-four hours afterwards, we didn't have her help at the estate now. Gemma, Lady Amanda, and I were the ones who chose the staff for serving champagne at the post-concert reception, the assistants for the stage and film crew, and the assistants to security — that, is the people who would prevent entry to private quarters on the estate, and prevent anyone unauthorized from sneaking around on the estate's grounds.

Plenty of eager part-time helpers — and even a few volunteers — were still around, but I felt more shorthanded than ever. For the past two days, Kitty hadn't returned. She had quit, apparently; and I hadn't chosen anyone to take her place.

A part of me had been hoping she would change her mind and come back. I left a message for her at Charlotte's shop, where I dropped by several times, hoping to find her there. Each time, however, Charlotte shook her head when I asked.

I even went to Kitty's house — at least, the house where I presumed she lived with her mother. Although I knocked several times, nobody answered the door at first, although I could hear the sound of a television blaring. At last, a mousy-looking woman with hair dyed a very orange red came to the door. Kitty's mother, Bets Alderson, according to the labels on the untidy stack of magazines piled by the door. She seemed suspicious of me until I explained who I was, and that I was looking for Kitty.

"She's not here," she said. "Gone off who knows where with her mates. That girl." She sighed. "Never listens. She doesn't get it from *my* side of the family." A tone which might be equal parts sad and bitter. "You're sure you're not coming about here selling something?" she added, sounding suspicious again. "None of your like ever came around looking for Katherine before."

"No, I just really wanted Kitty — Katherine — to call me, at least," I said. "I'll leave my phone number for her."

"No use in that. I haven't heard from her in two days," said Bets. "None of my business where she is, is it?" With another sigh of annoyance, she concluded our conversation and shut the door.

Back at the manor, the television crew was already setting up in the ballroom to record the indoor segment of Wendy's concert. Rows of elegant chairs which Lord William had rented from a major hotel all the way in London had been carried inside in stacks swathed in bubble wrap and mover's cloths — the temporary staff was now unpacking them and placing them in uniform rows to form two seating aisles in the ballroom — Gemma watching them like a hawk the whole time, using Lady Amanda's floor plan as a reference point for snapping out orders.

"It would be terribly exciting, if it wasn't so stressful," said Lady Amanda. She had taken a quick breather from hours on the phone with Wendy Alistair's team of personal assistants, who were eager to know about her dressing room, her crystal carafe of sparkling mineral water, and her complimentary basket of miniature oranges and white lilies, which were all essential for the singer's comfort, it seemed.

"Have you seen what they've done in the clearing?" I asked. I knew that the temporary seating — rows of sleek, uniform black metal folding chairs with black leather padding — had been arriving on a second removal van today.

"William took photos and sent them to me from his mobile," said Lady Amanda. "Not quite the Minack Theater, of course, but terribly impressive nonetheless. *I* wish I was going to sit in one instead of scurry around with members of the press in between checking on the staff."

Lady Amanda was taking full advantage of the entertainment reporters at the private concert as the manor's official spokesperson, to guarantee that the village's name appeared in as many publications as possible. No doubt the local business council was cheering her on, especially the struggling merchants and unemployed villagers who had heard Nathan Menton's speech about boosting the economy.

But then came the 'emmets,' I supposed, and felt a twinge of regret for the possibility. Would Ceffylgwyn be the same if the sidewalks were crowded with sightseers who ignored the village's ways or made fun of locals' manners? If the shore was packed with tourists trying to photograph rare birds, or packing themselves into boats for a pleasure cruise along the cliffs?

I tried to imagine lines for oggies outside Charlotte's shop, even though it was in the poorest part of the village. I imagined the possibility of pickpockets and petty thefts, as less scrupulous people paid a visit to the village, too.

I was still pondering the good and bad possibilities of change, when I felt a tap on my shoulder. "Julianne, the florist has a little problem with the flowers for the champagne reception," said Gemma, who was holding the manor's telephone. "And did you order something for Pippa's reception?"

"I did," I said.

"Well, it's all coming here tomorrow," she said.

"What?" I took the phone from her.

The florist confirmed Gemma's words. "We're terribly sorry about this," said Marian Jones, the local florist. "I *do* wish that there was another way, but we've been shorthanded, and completely overwhelmed with orders ever since David Willow closed his shop temporarily after the fire."

"But I really do need them delivered the day *of*," I said. "I can't possibly finish all those arrangements on my own — we're in the same boat you are, frankly." Not to mention, I didn't have room for so many half-finished arrangements, plus the loose flowers for Pippa — the rest of which were still waiting in Matthew's care.

"If we could just pick them up ourselves," I began, envisioning me, Geoff, and Gemma stuffing large bouquets into Geoff's tiny car and rushing back to the manor with them.

"I wish it were possible — I would even entrust you with my spare key — except the whole place is being fumigated. I can't let even the slightest blossom stay here, and I've no more room at home. I'm afraid the Silver Perch and the Trawley-Pennans wedding are having to do the same as you."

"All right," I said. "Any time this afternoon is fine."

The whole pantry was now crammed with flowers — big white gladiolas and lilies for the post-concert reception, and the modest, brightly-colored loose blossoms for Pippa's wedding. Even with Gemma's help, I found myself working late to snip stems on the newly-rested hothouse flowers to finish the last couple of arrangements that Marian Jones had been forced to put aside.

By suppertime, the clear vases and showy white flowers looked beautiful on tables in the foyer. By eight o' clock that night, I was still working on putting Pippa's flowers in the darkened closet to 'rest,' my fingers crossed that they would be fine until her big day. But a big knot of worry was in my heart for this decision, too.

"You look exhausted," said Matthew. I could see concern in his eyes as he greeted me — two hours late for our meal — when I opened the door to the cottage.

"I am," I admitted. I kicked off my red Jimmy Choo high heels, not caring that one bounced against the leg of our worn-out armchair. "Have you cut the flowers for Pippa's wedding yet?"

"I delivered them to Cliffs House late today," he said. "Dinah took charge of them. I thought I might see you while I was there, but you had dashed off to the outdoor theater to help arrange the seating, I gathered. But I didn't want the blossoms to be exhausted before you had them — the sun's been rather bright these last few days in the hothouse."

"Trust Cornwall's weather to keep the rain at bay just when I need a cloudy day," I said, with a wry smile. I accepted the cup of tea Matthew handed me as I sat down at our kitchen table.

I felt his hand take mine. "Forget about flowers for a little while," he said. "That's usually my concern, not yours."

"I know," I answered. I sighed. "My head is just too full of all these issues. It's crunch time, you realize...I can't let Pippa down for her big day after all the times I've reassured her it will be perfect ... and I can't help worrying about Kitty."

Matt's fingers massaged mine, a pleasant, reassuring sensation traveling through my skin in response. "I'll come and help," he said. "As soon as I'm home from university, I'll rush to Cliffs House and help you finish some of these tasks."

"Thanks," I said, smiling. "But I don't think it's a good idea. The place will be crawling with security by tomorrow, since Wendy's due to arrive. Even Lord William's word that you belong there probably won't be enough — all of us will be wearing color-coded badges, courtesy of the event promoter, to ensure we won't be ordered off the grounds."

"I could sneak in," he said. "I'll steal one of those security tags off an unsuspecting staffer."

"No, you won't," I said, imprisoning his fingers in mine now. "You'll be busy enough tomorrow with all the students who can't wait to ask you questions about their assignments...especially the ones who spent their whole class period daydreaming about you instead of paying attention."

Matt blushed. "I highly doubt that," he said. But he had heard more than enough sly comments and dreamy sighs from girls like Gemma and Pippa to have any doubt about my words' meaning.

I kissed his cheek, laughing. "Well, I don't," I answered. I drew back, gazing into his dark eyes. "So what have you cooked for dinner?"

"More reheated pasties, I'm afraid. I didn't have time to simmer a stew, or get some takeaway."

"Sounds perfect," I said. "Dish me up one. I'm going to change into something that *doesn't* have a fitted pencil skirt." I gave him a smile as I pulled off my business jacket and made my way towards the closet where more comfortable garments — like my fleece pajamas — were waiting.

***

"No one gets by without a badge, thanks. You have one? Good. Go on in." Nathan waved them inside with a smile. But despite that smile's calm exterior, I was fairly sure that he was a tense mass of concentration inside.

"Badge?" he said to me. I smiled and flashed a pink plastic card from beneath my overcoat. "Perfect," he said, breathing a sigh. "Go right inside." He glanced over my shoulder. "Hey, you — stop right there! Jim, hold them at the side entrance, will you?" he said, speaking into a small hand radio. With that, he was off, a determined look on his face that didn't bode well for the non-badge wearing member of Cliffs House's staff.

Chaos had descended over the house on the eve of the big day, with lots of grim-faced strangers in security attire inspecting every last corner of Cliffs House and its gardens. Two were posted at the house's drive, one stood at every entrance, and several others were patrolling the garden and the newly-landscaped pathway to the outdoor stage.

I checked my schedule on my mobile phone. *Meet with Lady Amanda; make sure complimentary gift baskets are delivered to blue spare bedroom (dressing room); phone caterers about canapé delivery; help Dinah with savory biscuit trays.... Pippa's flowers!!* with a double exclamation point, was at the very end of it.

It was definitely another late night in store for me, and all because I hadn't stayed longer last night. I was hoping that the weariness and stress I was battling could be put aside by a cup of Dinah's coffee — made 'American style,' as she put it, for me and the new event promoter.

Already a little crowd had begun to form at the gated-off drive to the manor. I saw lots of hopeful-looking teenage girls in t-shirts with the album cover printed on the front, holding balloons and flowers. The local kids puffed slightly with pride at the sight — they were safely on the inside of the gates, wearing the official 'badges' that gave them hope they might glimpse the diva when she arrived.

Lady Amanda and I had our hands full for most of the afternoon — a number of temporary staffers and a few of the manor's usual ones had neglected to wear their security badges, and we were forced to vouch for them before the security team and Nathan in order to get them admitted. Gemma was swamped with last-minute cleaning and furniture rearrangement — and when word came that the diva herself might be shuttled to Ceffylgwyn early with her chauffeur and assistant, panic broke out among staff and security alike.

Exhausted, I pushed open the door to the flower pantry at five o' clock. Normally, I would be finishing up my emails and logging my receipts in preparation for a long evening spent in Matt's company, but tonight would be a long evening spent with Pippa's flowers.

Except the flowers were done.

At first, I panicked — the row of freshly-cleaned vases was gone from the center of the table. Had someone mistaken them for a decoration for the post-concert party? I opened the cupboards, frantically, then the door to the 'resting closet' and found them sitting on its shelves. The original buckets which had held Matt's cuttings and the floral flowers were now empty, for in each vase the sprigs of magenta, yellow, orange, and white were arranged identically, stems trimmed to the just-right height.

I stared. In the middle, a bigger glass vase held the remaining blossom sprays, arranged with several of Matt's heather sprigs and the lilies I had ordered. In clean buckets of fresh water and plant preservative, I found the newly-cut flowers for Pippa's bouquet and the ones for the altar garland.

It would have taken hours of work to do all of this, and it wasn't me in my sleep who had accomplished it. *Gemma*, I thought. But no, Gemma hadn't seen my sketches — and Pippa hadn't been at Cliffs House for two days now —

Kitty had been here. But why? After she had been so annoyed, I couldn't imagine why she would do this.

"Have you seen Kitty — the girl who was helping me a few days ago?" I asked Nathan, who was posted at the door again, his fingers flying over his smart phone's keypad in a text.

"Who?" he said. "Her? No. Nobody comes through unless they picked up a badge yesterday morning, like I told them." He pulled up a digital checklist of names. "What name did you say?"

"Kitty Alderson," I repeated.

"No. No Kitty...no Alderson. Why?" He glanced up. "Was someone here unauthorized?"

"Maybe?" I tried to imagine how Kitty had gotten past security. Had she slipped through the back door when Dinah was out of the kitchen? The door on the other side of the manor? But security had been in place since last night, meaning Kitty must have used her reputed 'shady' skills to get inside.

"I need a quick word with security on the south and east sides of the estate," said Nathan, speaking into the radio's mouthpiece. "We might have a possible breach on one of those sides."

Charlotte wasn't behind the counter of the fish and chips shop when I pushed the door open, hearing the door's friendly bell jingle above. Instead, Kitty was sweeping the floor, a flour-dusted red apron covering her old tartan-print flannel shirt and worn jeans. She glanced up, a wary expression crossing her face at the sight of me.

"I guess I missed you at Cliffs House this morning," I said. "What time were you there? Four a.m.? Five?"

Kitty shrugged. "Just early," she answered.

"They looked great, by the way. I couldn't have done it better myself."

"Great," said Kitty. She swept out a corner beneath the counter.

"I still can't imagine why you did it, though," I continued. "You seemed pretty angry the other day. I didn't think you'd come back. Especially not to finish Pippa's flowers." She and Pippa didn't like each other, that much was clear. Wasn't finishing the flower arrangements for one of your least-favorite people one of the last things girls like Kitty were supposed to do?

"The big arrangement's short some," said Kitty, offhandedly. "But you could always fill it out a bit with some tulips. There's some that's been forced already in the hothouse."

I waited a moment, but she didn't say anything else. "You know," I said, "I could still use a little help tomorrow night for the concert. And there's something special I'd like to do for Pippa's reception site, and I need an extra pair of hands there, too...it could be kind of challenging. Especially on my own."

Kitty stopped sweeping. She turned to me. "What'd you have in mind?" she asked.

She rested one hand on her hip, her eyes on the portfolio in my hand. It was the first time she actually sounded interested in our conversation since we'd begun — the tough shell had cracked a little with her curiosity.

"Stained glass," I said, opening the folder on the counter and showing her the transparent sheets of colored paper, and the design I had drawn.

"It's your idea, really. When I saw what you did to the dollhouse, it made me think of those big, high windows in the barn. I had compared them to church windows before...so why not turn them into the real thing?"

Kitty's face was completely different when she looked at my sketches. A quick, alert gaze took in my pencil strokes for the window and the color patterns, and the delicate, slightly crinkled texture of the colored sheets. She couldn't hide her interest, and I imagined that mentally she had already applied them to the windows herself.

"Anyway," I said, closing the folder. "If you have some time, and Charlotte can spare you, I'd love to have a hand." From my pocket, I took a rectangle of pink plastic and laid it on the counter: a spare security tag from the event promoter's stash.

Nathan didn't have to worry about me leaving it on the counter for a possible stranger to find. I felt sure that tag would be tucked in Kitty's pocket the moment I was gone.

***

Wendy Alistair breezed into town five hours before her concert, her chauffeur making his way through the security barricade at the gates, where a growing crowd of screaming fans waved their heart-covered, glittery signs frantically despite the car's tinted windows blocking any view of the singer.

Wendy Alistair herself breezed through the foyer quickly as well, wrapped in a white silk coat and cashmere scarf. She paused long enough to take off her oversized designer sunglasses, admire the flowers, and give a charming smile to a photographer before making her way upstairs.

As per her assistant's demands, the staff kept their distance, including the almost-swooning Lina and Darla. When the singer and her entourage had retreated safely to her dressing room, I heard Gemma let out a squeal of excitement. "Oh my gosh, we just saw *the* Wendy Alistair!"

"Go on with you," said Dinah, sarcastically — who, nonetheless, had found an excuse to be upstairs, near the dining room doorway, when the star made her grand entrance. "I'm sure it was the thrill of her day, seeing you, too."

The concert was scheduled to begin an hour before sunset — it was being filmed out of order, with the sunset view of the sea and the fireworks display coming before the songs being performed in the ballroom. Of course, this timing meant a long evening lay ahead before the inevitable champagne toasts for Wendy's upcoming album, complete with costume changes, lighting mishaps, and other delays.

For the concert, I wore my most sensible black party dress paired with my red heels and minimal jewelry — it was my job to look nice while directing champagne waiters and crew assistants, but look more professional than the guests who would be in black tie and posh frocks. As security escorted them to their seats — and evicted a few desperate fans who had climbed over the west hedgerows — I made my way through the final checklist of serving trays, spare decorative candles, and uniform inspection for the nervous servers standing by.

"That's the last of the trays, Dinah says," Kitty announced, returning from the direction of the kitchen. "There's only thirty more coming than she expected. Bit of a mix up, but not bad."

Kitty had already helped me shoo away unauthorized members of the press and lay out two more last-minute trays of caviar spread and savory biscuits. Truthfully, she had made herself useful all day, showing up first thing this morning with the pink security tag I had given her clipped in place.

Tonight, instead of her worn jeans and hooded jackets, she wore a somewhat faded charcoal cardigan and a short grey skirt. Her hair was slightly crimped from being pinned up untidily before, but she had pulled it back neatly with a decorative hair clip; and her red sneakers had been traded for a pair of slightly scuffed ballet flats that I was fairly sure were several years old and a size too small.

The fact that she dressed up for tonight surprised me beyond words — but I knew to be careful when calling attention to the fact before Kitty herself. "You look nice, Kitty," I said. "Grey suits you almost as much as red does."

"It's just some old stuff I had lying around," said Kitty, feigning indifference. "I'm not dressed posh, or anything. Like any of this lot would care."

"I don't know," I said. "I think you'd be surprised." I imagined the surprise of the likes of Lina when she saw Kitty in something besides her baggy old togs; then I thought of an example that would probably interest Kitty more. "Imagine what Nathan Menton would think if he saw you now," I suggested. "He actually paid you a compliment the other day, despite the incident in the courtyard." Well, almost a compliment, I decided. "Besides that, I think he noticed you're quite pretty," I added. Which was true enough, I felt.

Two quick spots of color flashed in Kitty's pale cheeks, a scornful look on her face. "As if I'd ever be with a toff like that —" she began, then paused. "That is ... I don't think the likes of me and Mr. Menton are very compatible, are we?" she corrected. Her posture straightened, her arms crossed as she tilted her chin with affected airs. "We have differences of opinion."

A posh tone meant to be humorous, but somehow it worked for her. It gave me a spark of a notion that this was the hidden facet of personality that would carry Kitty through the next task on my list.

I had spoken to the pyrotechnics expert earlier about keeping the display short, tasteful, and avoiding anything that would leave a lot of debris or create a fire hazard by bursting prematurely, but I planned to follow up one last time with his crew. That left only the job of greeting the guests who arrived at the manor for the second half of the performance.

"So what do we do now?" Kitty asked.

In the distance, the heavenly sound of Wendy Alistair's voice rose with the trill of a classical soprano. I checked the time — less than fifteen minutes to go.

"I have to speak to the FX crew one last time," I said. "So you should wait by the door for the guests when they arrive at the manor. Security will check their V.I.P. cards, but someone has to greet them officially on our behalf before they enter the ballroom.

The color disappeared from Kitty's face. "Me?" she repeated. I thought I detected a slight note of panic in her voice. "Greet the guests? Those posh — I mean, the people who are at the concert?"

"Why not?" I said. I planted my hands on my hips now, too. "Think you can't handle a nice smile and a few simple words?"

Kitty looked away. I could see the gears were turning inside her. Debating whether to take my challenge — while I was wondering if I was taking a risk by suggesting it.

She sighed. "I guess I'm off to the door," she said. "See you later." She flashed me a smile that I felt wouldn't be a bad one for greeting the event's attendees — if it wasn't slightly sarcastic, that is — then marched in the direction of the front door.

I crossed my fingers that this was not the mistake everyone else would claim it to be.

Now that Kitty was gone, I took the pathway towards the concert, one lit by several battery-operated candles clustered in attractive groups or held aloft inside carriage lanterns on posts. No guests were here, only members of the film and sound crew hurrying back and forth on errands. Nathan the event promoter was there, too, having apparently been in the thick of things until recently.

"Double-checking the fireworks," I said, when he caught sight of me.

"Good thinking," he said. "It's ten minutes until the big moment."

He had shed his overcoat and his business jacket despite the cool evening, his shirt sleeves rolled up, revealing muscular arms beneath them. I had no idea what all he had been doing until now, but I could see telltale signs of exhaustion on his face, and even a little smear of dirt on the bridge of his nose. He looked younger than ever — especially since he was still feigning energy and cheerfulness.

"You have a little something..." I began, as I rubbed my own nose. Nathan picked up on the signal and brushed the streak from his own.

"Thanks," he said. "I got a little grimy helping them position those candles in the big rocks by the dell's entryway. Something about the spacing for the camera...you know how it is."

"This event's been a lot of trouble for you, hasn't it?" I said. "I think you'll be glad to say goodbye to us afterwards."

"I don't know," said Nathan. "This isn't a bad place to be. It's pretty, and it's got charm." He glanced around. The twilight grove was nothing but shadows of trees, with the pinpoints of real candle flames flickering in the dark. "I've never been in the country before, so I didn't know what to expect."

"I still can't believe you did all this just for Cornwall," I said. "Maybe for your career, or for Wendy's — but not for a place you'd never even seen."

"Why not?" he asked. "I think every place deserves to be recognized. Why not give this place a chance to be seen by people who don't even know it's on the map? Maybe by somebody out there who has always dreamed of somewhere like this one."

I smiled. "I hope you're right," I answered. "See you later." I cut across to the temporary footpath that led to the fireworks team's van, which was parked within sight of the display's zone across the way — placed far enough from the concert that the noise wouldn't interfere with the music.

Despite Lady Amanda's wish, she and Lord William weren't among the guests seated in the clearing, but they had staked out a spot to hear the concert further up the little hill leading towards the timberline. Stealing a few minutes before it was time for the event at the manor itself.

They weren't alone, however. Even in the dark, I recognized Matthew seated beside them on the lawn blanket, his suit jacket laid next to him.

"Matthew?" I said.

"Finally," he answered. "I was afraid I was going to have to sneak below and find you."

"I just had a last-minute conference before the fireworks," I said. "I didn't know you were coming tonight. How did you get in?"

"I slipped in across the fields," he said. "And William was kind enough to give me a ride in the field truck."

"I'm afraid he's been stuck with us the whole time, waiting for the fireworks to begin," said Lord William. "I hope it outdoes firecrackers on Guy Fawkes Day. I want something a bit more dramatic, comparable to the Queen's Diamond Jubilee, perhaps," he joked.

"We'll only catch a few minutes of it, really," said Lady Amanda. "We'll have to hurry back to the manor. The concertgoers can't very well show themselves inside, can they?"

"Don't worry," I said. "I've got that covered, at least for a few minutes. You can afford to catch the whole show." I calculated that Kitty could probably handle the first few guests without a problem, anyway. "Besides, I'll be hurrying back myself as soon as it's over."

"Until then, come for a walk with me," said Matt, who rose and stretched out his hand for mine. I took his hand and we strolled a short distance away from Lady Amanda and Lord William. The shadows of the trees surrounded us as Wendy's last song carried itself on the breeze beyond the clearing.

"I hope they pinned her hair back against the sea breeze," I said, leaning against him. "It murders every hairstyle I try, that wind."

"I think it looks beautiful," he said. "I like seeing the breeze play with it. In the sun, it brings out the bits of red and gold." I felt his fingers stroke it, tucking a strand gently behind my ear.

"Are you cold?" he asked. I was rubbing one arm with my free hand.

"A little," I admitted. "This is the first time I haven't been rushing around all day." I hadn't worn a coat, my sheer black cap sleeves barely even protecting my shoulders.

"Here." He draped his coat around my shoulders. "That should be better." I buried my nose against its collar, catching his scent on the fabric.

Matt drew me against him, his cheek resting against mine. "This is nice," I murmured. "I listened to your suggestion. I found someone to help me, and now I finally have a moment to myself."

"And here you are, wasting it on me," said Matt.

"Shut up. How else do you think I would spend it?"

"I don't know," said Matt, laughing. "But I wish you had more of them so we could find out. You with spare time...me with no lecture to rush off to, or garden in need of a consultation."

"Maybe I could find a way," I murmured. "I want to go to Pencarrow with you this Saturday. I want to stroll beside you in the gardens, meet your friends. Maybe have a picnic lunch. I don't want to spend it worrying about stray receipts or last-minute phone calls."

"It might be slightly cool for a picnic," said Matt. "You're forgetting about fall in Cornwall."

"Let me guess. There's rain on Saturday, too," I said.

In the distance, the first crackle and thunder of the fireworks began.

"We could have a nice tea somewhere," Matt suggested. "Just the two of us with a few cucumber sandwiches, watching the rain patter against the windows."

"While talking about everything we never have a chance to talk about," I said. "You know. Us."

Matt sighed. "I wish it could last forever," he said. "Moments like this. Just the two of us, no responsibilities or errands to pester us every second."

"Well, I hope you're pleased," said a different voice — this one belonging to Noreen Prowse, who was emerging from the woods. "You've gotten your way on terrifying the defenseless avian species of the county. Just listen to that horrible noise." In one hand, she held a stout walking stick, an outdoor satchel swung over the opposite shoulder. Bits of twig and leaf clung to her tweed coat and hat.

"Good evening, Mrs. Prowse," I said. "Lovely weather, isn't it?"

She sniffed. "I have greater matters on my mind than the weather, I fear."

"Rest assured, Mrs. Prowse, the resident birds have already migrated from our cliffs until spring," said Matthew. "I wouldn't have presented that point at the meeting if I had felt any doubt, I assure you."

"You always have been loyal to the natural species of Cornwall," said Mrs. Prowse, although she still sounded doubtful. "So I suppose I'll have to take your word for it. Goodnight, all." At this moment, a loud scarlet firework boomed overhead. "Oh, the noise," she groaned, clutching her head as she hiked away along the wood line, a pocket flashlight in hand lighting the way.

When she was safely out of earshot, Matt clutched his own head. "The birds, the birds," he groaned.

I giggled, but I smacked him on the arm all the same. "That's not polite," I said. "Although I do feel like she'd be happy if they ate us all, like in Hitchcock's movie."

"Sorry. She does mean well," he said, settling his arms around me again. "And I do enjoy the bird watcher's society. I once helped them pass a motion locally to ban cliff climbing in places where the native birds are nesting. It discourages people from disturbing the sites — and from stealing the eggs for profit, too."

"You did?" I said. "You never told me that."

"I can't tell you everything I've ever done," he chuckled. "If we told each other everything, we'd have no surprises left, would we? And I rather enjoy being surprised by you."

Overhead, a golden burst of sparks filled the sky. One more, maybe two more, I thought, counting on making these precious seconds last before the evening began again.

***

The morning of Pippa's wedding, a light shower of rain fell, but it didn't dampen her happiness. I had managed to procure a gown nearly identical to the one Pippa had loved so much in the bridal shop window, and a matching pearl and crystal tiara trimmed with a small white veil. Gemma wore a new bridesmaid's gown of a rich shade of magenta that matched Pippa's color scheme — this was the result of a few strings I pulled at a shop that owed me a favor.

I was worried about her reaction to the reception sight until the moment Pippa finally stepped inside the barn. I had lined the pathway to it with sea shells and white stones, and the outside looked rustic and inviting, but not like the glitzy Italian-piazza style of the Silver Perch's exterior, I knew. I was afraid Pippa would be disappointed, even with all the work that Kitty and I had done.

As she crossed its threshold, Pippa's eyes lit up, widening to take in all her surroundings. "Oh, heavens — it looks like a fairytale," she said. She squeezed Gavin's hand, then looked at me with an expression of astonishment.

Sunlight had broken from behind the clouds, now streaming through the faux-stained glass that Kitty and I had created. Squares of bright color flooded the long rustic table covered in a white cloth, where tiny glass vases held Kitty's flower arrangement; small faux white votive candles of ivory wax flickered wherever the stone protruded to offer a convenient ledge, alongside sprigs of heather blossoms.

In the middle of the table stood Dinah's cake, a beautiful three layer vanilla citrus concoction trimmed with candied peel and pink rose petals. On the buffet, where a catered spread waited, stood Kitty's large centerpiece trimmed with heather blossoms, its flowers looking vivid in the sunlight.

"The colors — it's like a chapel. And look at the flowers! It looks like something out of a magazine," breathed Pippa. "Angelina Jolie could be married in a spot like this." Her voice was full of pride, almost trembling with excitement.

"I'm glad you like it," I said. Inside, I breathed a deep sigh of relief.

"Wow," breathed Gemma, who entered right behind the happy couple. "Look at this old place! It's a proper job, isn't it? And is that the old dollhouse?" she asked, pointing.

"Where'd you find it?" Pippa asked. She had swooped down on it, opening and closing the little shutters with amazement. "I haven't seen this thing in years. It never looked this smashing when I was a kid, though. Like a fairy house, almost." She towed Gavin behind her, who feigned enthusiasm for the fairy house for the sake of pleasing Pippa, I detected.

The dollhouse stood against the wall on a separate table, ringed by Kitty's wreath of artificial blossoms in Pippa's wedding colors, and a few extra candles. The main table was already set for a wedding feast worthy of an English country party— I had rented water goblets and champagne flutes from a nearby restaurant's banquet room for a modest fee, and had helped Pippa's mum find a suitable caterer to provide a ham and trimmings, and ordered four dozen of Charlotte's pasties in a smaller size to serve as appetizers.

A few of Pippa's musician friends provided entertainment for the reception — folk tunes, including those I recognized from Troyls. With an eye roll, Pippa explained that it was Gavin's idea, not hers — but it didn't stop her from dancing to them after the champagne toast, I noticed.

The music was lively, the food was delicious, and there was plenty of laughter throughout the reception — all in all, it was a fun, relaxed afternoon that was ten times better than some of the stiff, formal events I had planned recently. Pippa and her friends and family — including the new additions of Gavin and his mother and cousins — had a wonderful time.

When she threw the bouquet, it wasn't Gemma who caught it, but a teenage girl I only half-recognized from the village. Her little sister laid claim to the bouquet afterwards, toddling around with it proudly, her tiny face buried in its blossoms.

Pippa seemed deliriously happy, right up to the end of the afternoon. When I embraced her at the close, I realized that she was sniffling against my shoulder.

"I don't know what I'm going to do, leaving here," she said, with a catch in her voice. "I've never gone off from the village before. And I'll be all the way in Hampshire — what am I going to do?"

"You'll have a great time," I said. "You'll live in a place all your own with a charming, dashing young man. How could it get any better than that?"

My hug wasn't as carefree as my words, however. In a few minutes, Pippa would be gone — not just from Ted Russert's transformed barn, but from Cliffs House and the village. No more *Poldark* viewing parties, no more celebrity gossip tidbits between her and Gemma in the manor house's kitchen.

"I don't know," said Pippa, with a choking sound suspiciously like a sob. "I mean, it's a pretty place, I s'pose. And there's always Highclere Castle," she added, with slightly more cheer. "But it's not the same as home. I always wanted to leave ... but it's not the same."

I wondered if that was how Kitty Alderson had felt. If leaving for Land's End, even to get away from a village that labeled her a troublemaker, hadn't been everything she had dreamed. Or was it only a matter of being a few quid short of the rent?

I drew back, giving Pippa a smile. "You're going to love it there," I said. "And you'll come back to visit all the time. It'll be like you never left, almost."

"Maybe," said Pippa, sniffling. "But I'm going to miss it, awfully, and I never thought I'd say that. And I'll miss Ross — I mean, Matt — too." She threw her arms around Matthew now, who put an arm around her gently, a smile of amusement on his face as he looked at me.

"I'll miss you, too," he answered her. "Things won't be quite the same at Cliffs House without you."

Pippa brushed a tear from her eye as she released him, and gave me a smile that was real, even if it was quivering a little. "Thanks again for everything, Julianne," she said. "It wouldn't have been half so lovely today if you hadn't done all this."

"I had a little help," I said. "Kitty did half the work for me. The flower arrangement was her idea — and the big centerpiece was, too."

Pippa looked taken aback by my words, and a little surprised. "I suppose you should say 'thanks' for me, then," she mumbled, at last. "They did look a proper job, I guess." Begrudgingly, but acceptingly.

I managed to hide my smile as I agreed with her.

Pippa took a deep breath, gazing around her at the happy guests, and the flowers wreathing the open barn door. "I can't believe all this is happening to *me*," she said. "It's like magic, in a way."

"Just think — it's the romantic adventure you always wanted," I said. "Now it's finally happened — and you're *not* sixty, as you feared you would be at Constance's wedding."

She giggled. "At least that's true."

One last hug from Gemma, one last photo snapped by her family, and Pippa was gone. She rolled the passenger window of Gavin's car down and waved goodbye to us one more time, her cheerful grin lost from sight as the car turned onto the main road. But the rest of us kept waving until the car disappeared from view.

"So," said Matt, putting his arm around me, as we lingered among the wedding guests outside the barn. "Are you free on Saturday, now that your latest happily-ever-after is in motion?"

"Maybe," I said. "Are you thinking about a certain picnic in northern Cornwall?"

"Rain, my bird," he answered, his lips close to my ear.

"What did you say?" I said, lifting one eyebrow as I gave him a look. I knew enough about British slang now to know the gist of this phrase, at least.

He chuckled. "It doesn't mean the same thing in Cornwall," he said, evidently aware what I was thinking. "It's a term of endearment here, for a woman you care for deeply."

"Oh. Then, by all means, go on," I said, snuggling against him again.

"I was saying the day will be ours, for doing whatever we like. Unless, of course, you have another pressing engagement," he teased.

"Me?" I said. "Nothing at all. Just a Saturday with my husband, that's all. Picnicking, sightseeing, whatever we want."

I wrapped my arms around his embrace, holding it in place. Smiling, we watched as the lucky recipient of Pippa's bouquet posed with it proudly for a selfie, no doubt dreaming of her future, too.

***

"I'm glad you stopped, Kitty," I said. "Charlotte said it was your day off, so I thought maybe you'd come by."

I had asked Kitty to show up on Saturday morning, on the pretense of returning the plastic security badge from the concert. Since I didn't have to leave for my day out with Matthew for at least a half hour, I was using the excuse of catching up on a last-minute catering menu to be in my office when she arrived.

"Here's the badge." Kitty shoved her hands into the pockets of her hoodie. "Anything else?"

"I was wondering," I said. "Have you worked for Charlotte since you came back to the village?"

"Yeah. Why?"

"Do you like working at the fish and chips shop?" I asked. "You sounded kind of attached to it before, but I wasn't sure if that was true."

"It's a job." She shrugged her shoulders. "I pop pasties into boxes and shovel chips. Nothing grand, really. Her sister-in-law bought my gran's shop...so I guess when I came back, she felt she'd offer me something, since there wasn't a place for me there."

I rose from my desk and moved to lean against its front edge. "I guess I was wondering if there's any chance you've ever thought about a different job. Maybe a job as an event planner's assistant?"

A brief silence. I saw a flash of surprise in Kitty's eyes as one eyebrow arched. "With you?" she surmised.

"That's right," I said. "I could use someone to help me. Cliffs House is already busy a lot of the time, and if things truly get busier, then I'll need all the help I can get. The estate would need an extra hand, and I think I'd like it to be you. Lady Amanda has already agreed to hire you, if you're interested."

"What makes you think I'd be good at it?" she asked, sounding puzzled. "I'm not what you imagine a proper assistant to be, am I? Everyone around here would tell you that I'm not posh enough to chat with the toffs who come to tea at a place like this."

"Do you think you could learn to be?" I asked. I raised one eyebrow, waiting.

Kitty met my gaze. "I could," she said, with a touch of defiance. "I know how to mind my 'p's and 'q's when it's necessary. But I suppose for a job like this one, I'd have to put in a bit more effort. Dress the part, and put on some airs and graces."

She made a face for this idea. But I was shrewd enough now to be fairly sure it was a fake effort.

"You definitely would," I answered. "So do you want to try it?"

Kitty pondered this, her expression a conflicted one. At last, she let out a deep breath. "All right," she said. "I'll give it a go."

I smiled. "I was hoping you'd say that," I said. Reaching over, I lifted a box from my desk, one wrapped like a present. "That's why I got you this."

"What is it?" said Kitty, suspiciously — but I saw the two pink spots on her freckled, porcelain cheeks as she asked. She untied the loops of ribbon and opened the lid. Inside was a pair of high-heeled shoes. Black leather ones from a designer knock-off label, with straps across the instep and fashionable heels that weren't quite a stiletto in width or height. They were the same size as the grimy red sneakers Kitty was wearing now, but infinitely more elegant.

Kitty made a face. "What am I supposed to do with these?" she asked, lifting one by the strap between her thumb and forefinger.

"Trust me," I said. "They'll come in handy. Whether you realize it now or not."

A Bake Off in Cornwall

By

Laura Briggs

"Which color would you prefer?" asked the sales clerk in the chic London baby boutique. "Blue is traditional for boys, of course, and pink for girls. But many people choose to switch them today — or prefer something neutral."

I studied the choices of tiny footed sleepwear in soft colors and miniature jumpers printed with bunnies or kittens, and bit my lip. Boy or girl — I had no clue at this point, and wouldn't for some time, but time was of the essence for this occasion. *Make a selection, Julianne*, I ordered myself. I felt a little bit nervous about it, however, since I needed it to be perfect. I wouldn't take anything less.

"Do you know the child's gender yet?" the clerk asked.

"Um, no," I said. "It's going to be a surprise."

"How about a nice duckling print? Ducklings are *always* in fashion, and perfectly neutral," said the sales clerk. "It comes with a free toy bath duck, too."

Would ducklings be the right choice? It was pretty adorable, the sleeper printed with baby ducks and soap bubbles, the one the clerk had pulled from the display rack. It was a soft, pale fleece that begged to be touched like a fuzzy stuffed toy. I envisioned it swaddled in tissue paper, the layers parting, the look of surprise as it was opened ....yup, it would definitely produce the effect I wanted.

"Perfect," I said. "Can you wrap it for me?"

"Of course."

Afterwards, I hailed a cab and hurried to the train station. The train to Ceffylgwyn — the village I now called home a year after leaving my old city of Seattle for English shores — was on time for once, leaving me scarcely enough leeway to board it.

Once again, I watched the countryside fly past my window as I thought about how much had changed for me, and how much everything was still changing. First, taking a leap of faith from my old event planning firm in America to become the chief event planner for the Cornish manor Cliffs House. Then my falling in love with professor-turned-gardener (and apparent Poldark look-alike) Matthew Rose, and becoming his wife nearly a year ago — months that had magically flown by despite the challenges my job sometimes provided. Now, things were changing yet again — me training Kitty as a fledgling event planner ...

Ceffylgwyn chosen to host one of the biggest summer events in all England ... and that was only the beginning of this year's new happenings, if the tiny gift sack beside me was any proof.

I had hours to reflect on my past, but my mind was firmly back in the present by the time I arrived home again in the evening. There were no cabs in Ceffylgwyn, but I caught a ride with the florist Marian Jones, who was close by, delivering some last-minute floral arrangements to the local church. I checked my watch — if I wasn't careful with my timing, I would miss my chance for today, and I didn't want to wait to see my gift recipient's face when they opened it.

Clutching the handles of the shiny sack decorated with pastel balloons, I hurried inside, a tiny smile twitching around my lips. Even so, I found my nerves were knotting themselves a little in my stomach — was it a mistake, a little too soon to do this? Would it be a welcome surprise?

Too late now, I thought, as I crossed the room's threshold.

"Sorry I'm late," I said. I paused with the gift in my hands. "This is for you." I held out the sack. The gift tissue rustled inside, the shiny paper sack crinkling as it was opened.

"Why ... how perfectly adorable," breathed Lady Amanda. "What charming little ducklings — and a little bath time duckling, too! Oh, Julianne, you really needn't have."

"I know you haven't told very many people yet ... so I hope it's not presumptuous to go ahead and give you a gift," I said, feeling relieved that she loved it. "When I saw the London boutique, I couldn't resist."

"It was a lovely thought," she said. "I love it. Come, let's go show William our first official baby gift." With one hand resting on the slight bump beneath her frilly pastel blouse, she led the way to Lord William's office, where the lord of the manor was busy with his agricultural schedules.

"What do you think?" she asked him, smiling as she pressed the little pajama sleeper against her stomach. "Isn't it a perfect fit?"

***

"Are you sure you love it?" Matthew asked.

"Of course I do," I said, indignantly, as I opened the thin, leather-bound book propped on my knees. "It's beautiful. And so thoughtful of you." I brushed aside the tissue paper from the sofa, letting it fall into the gift box on the floor, where the birthday wrapping paper was wadded, too.

"I know you said you were thinking about keeping a journal, but that seemed rather like a resolution made in haste on New Year's than an honest endeavour," he said, his handsome forehead creasing a little with these words, to match his rueful smile. "The necklace I knew you would love, of course. But if you've changed your mind about this gift, you needn't lie and say you love it, too. I won't be upset if you return it."

"To say anything else than what I already have would be a lie," I answered, drawing him close to kiss him. "I intend to follow through this time and seriously keep a diary."

"You *already* keep a diary," Matt pointed out, teasingly. Having learned long ago that 'diary' in England equals 'appointment book' in America, I replied with a playful whack on his shoulder.

"You know what I meant," I said. "My life here has been wonderful. It's been an adventure. And I've always wished I could put it into words. This place, the events I've planned...and you, of course."

"I'm flattered," he answered. "But I think I'll make a very boring subject on paper. You've seen what plant science becomes in written form — very dry reading for the average audience." Evidently, he had changed his mind about pouring a second glass of wine from the bottle beside my unwrapped birthday presents, choosing instead to ease himself closer to me, his arm encircling my waist.

Until recently, Matt had been working as a horticultural consultant at the northern Cornish gardens of Pencarrow; his two-week holiday had meant lots of time for the two of us, something that was about to come to an end ... but right now, with his arms around me, I was half-glad that Matt's season as a consultant was almost over.

"I beg to differ," I answered, half-whispering. "But I'm not going to show it to anyone in any case. It's just for me." *Well, and maybe for a few pairs of understanding eyes, like Aimee's*, I added mentally, thinking of my best friend back in the States, who had been a sympathetic ear to all my relationship ups and downs, in Seattle and Cornwall — and knew all but the juiciest, private details of my romance with Matt. "I want to make sure I don't forget anything about this experience."

"Would this be because you expect things to change?" Matt asked, softly.

"Of course not," I whispered back, firmly — well, as firm as I could sound with a quiet tone of voice, anyway.

His fingers brushed away the strands of hair resting against my forehead. "You're happy with everything the way it is?" he asked. "I sometimes feel you've grown to love this life as much as I do. But if it's ever not the case, we need to talk about it. Change isn't necessarily bad, Julianne."

"I know. But I don't want to change anything right now," I answered. "The life we have together, here, is the one I want most." I took a deep breath. "The only thing that worries me is you. You could be a professor on his way to tenure in an Ivy League school, for instance, instead of taking consulting jobs here and there."

He laughed. "You needn't worry about me," he answered. "I'll look after myself. I'm quite used to change, my love, and quite content with it. You know that as well as I." His face rested close to mine, against the cushions of our sofa, his eyes looking into my own. My heart skipped a beat for a second, proof that sparks of my initial attraction to Matthew were alive and well months after saying 'I do.' That was something I was sure would never change.

"Is there anything else you need?" he asked. "Besides my assurance that I'm content?"

"Well...maybe one thing," I said. "I would need your help to do it...it's a two person job, so to speak." I drew myself against him. "I'd look forward to maybe having you teach me a few things in the process, too."

"And what would this be?" he asked.

I moved my lips closer to his ear as I whispered the words, hearing a short laugh of surprise from Matthew in reply.

We had weathered a lot together. Like the time Matt was almost diagnosed with cancer, for instance; or, before that, when his Ivy League past summoned him to a classroom across the ocean. This period of happiness was hard earned in my estimation, since our chances almost slipped away more than once in the past.

So I let myself become intertwined with Matthew as we whispered to each other, and forgot all about putting my thoughts on paper for that evening.

***

There was plenty to keep my mind busy these days, besides Lord William and Lady Amanda's big news, and my own dilemma. As promised after the major concert hosted here by Wendy Alistair, Ceffylgwyn had experienced a steady uptick in tourism figures — and Cliffs House had been more popular than ever when it came to event bookings. It had definitely kept both me and Kitty busier than ever.

Kitty Alderson, my assistant — the 'event planner in training' at Cliffs House manor ever since the month of Wendy Alistair's performance. Although I never thought I would say it, she had become almost indispensable to me now. Kitty's penchant for surprising ideas continued to impress me — it had been she who came up with the design for the mini fruits-and-flowers centerpieces for the summer orchard wedding, and booked a first-class Cornish folk band for the contradance that gave one of the ale-tasting events a fresh look in place of the polka theme the corporation executives initially suggested.

Of course, there were still a few sharp corners that poked against the formal side of Cliffs House now and then. But she looked as at home in my office as I did while helping me come up with a suitable layout for the work tables in the special pavilion constructed on the green behind Cliffs House's rear gardens.

"Should we face the trees — or the manor?" I pondered, tapping my stylus against my cheek as I looked at the digital plan. "But they'll rearrange it when the camera crew sets up, I suppose."

"Or maybe face the hill and the woods," said Kitty. "That's better — you can see a bit of the stone wall dividing the fields that way. They'll want a bit of the country life in the picture."

I made a note about it — and about following up with the rental place providing the tables and appliances. "Have you spoken to the delivery service about the grocery shipments arriving early?"

"Twice." Kitty held up two fingers. But she didn't give me the 'look' anymore that I used to get for asking obvious questions. Kitty's self-restraint this past month or so had been pretty impressive.

Besides the two international corporations' ale-tasting weekends, we had hosted two private classical concerts and several weddings, along with the usual local charitable fetes. But that was nothing compared to the event that Cliffs House — and Ceffylgwyn — was about to welcome into its arms for one whole week.

My jaw had dropped when I first heard the announcement at the summer's beginning. "We've been chosen?" I said. "Us — for The Grand Baking Extravaganza?"

"So you've heard of it?" Nathan asked. "Lady Amanda said I might have to explain it to you."

I was tempted to swat him on the arm. "Hilarious," I said. As the estate's event planner, I had helped Nathan draft the proposal for the program when he first presented it to Ceffylgwyn and to Cliffs House.

I might have been behind the times when it came to *Poldark*, but my days of missing British telly trends was all in the past, thanks to Gemma's persistence.

"You'd have to live under a rock in Cornwall not to have heard of it," said Kitty, without looking up from the invoices laid out on her desk. "Everyone's been holding their breath to hear the big announcement, ever since the last broadcast."

That big announcement was which county and village would be chosen as the site for the competition, of course. Every section of England had its turn already — and some choices of villages for filming were obvious, like Cromer in Norfolk, or Thirsk in North Yorkshire. Locations across England's two southernmost counties had vied to host the week-long event, featuring the best local bakers and two tough professional judges.

For Cornwall — and Ceffylgwyn — to be the one chosen was, in a word, magical.

Rumor had it the baking auditions had been filmed weeks ago at a secret location in Dartmoor, disclosed only to applicants lucky enough to be among the final pool of would-be contestants from both Devon and Cornwall. That was how the show worked, the try-outs being filmed in one competing county, while the contest events were staged in the other.

“Didn’t I tell you that big things would happen for this place?” Nathan said. “The producers loved our pitch for the village. And wait for the best part — they especially loved this place.”

“Cliffs House?” I said. "You're serious?"

"Over Pencarrow, or Lowarth Heligan, or even a modern ‘hot spot’ like Newquay," said Nathan. "I'm telling the honest truth."

Ceffylgwyn — where the only ‘fast food’ was the fish and chips and pasty shop in one, and it only took a half hour for news to spread from one side of the village to the other? Where there was only officially one street of shops, and the village’s most exciting event was quiz night championship at the pub? It made Newquay, a haven for 'stag nights' and surfing enthusiasts seem like bustling city life by comparison.

“Anyway, I wanted Cliffs House to know first, because this is big," continued Nathan. "And you guys will have a lot to do to be ready for this.” He sounded pleased with himself; his ‘cheeky’ American confidence tended to linger just beneath his business persona. I remembered it well from this spring, when he’d orchestrated Wendy Alistair’s publicity campaign.

Nathan Menton was an American event promoter, who, like me, was a transplant on foreign shores. He first visited Ceffylgwyn while working for the promotional wing of Wendy Alistair's televised concert in Cornwall. Instead of continuing on with the singer's international tour, however, he had decided to stay in Cornwall and promote its attractions to tourists — Ceffylgwyn especially. He had been the leading voice in crafting the village's proposal for the producers of The Grand Baking Extravaganza, including Cliffs House's part.

My head might still be caught up in surprise, but my event planner self was kicking into high gear nonetheless. “Kitty, we need to contact the council about any site permits or construction permits ... and we’ll need to provide locations that won’t damage the gardens or the existing pathways.”

Kitty reached for her open assistant’s calendar, and, for the first time since his return visit to Cliffs House, Nathan seemed to truly notice my assistant: specifically, that the sleek figure in a dark business suit and patent heels had the same freckled, porcelain face as the girl who had insulted him when he first arrived.

Surprise flickered in his eyes. “If it isn’t Little Red Riding Hood,” he said, in reference to the red sweatshirt Kitty had worn back in the day she was my ‘unofficial’ assistant — and the person who made his first welcome to Cliffs House a cold one, also.

There was no flash of anger from Kitty in reply, except maybe a slightly scornful paling of her cheeks. Nevertheless, her expression never changed as she jotted a note on her memo pad.

“Do you want me to call Linda Green — or wait ‘til you’ve talked with Lord William first?” she asked me, as if Nathan wasn’t here. “You know — get an early start?”

“Wait,” I said. Time was of the essence, but there was such a thing as too early. “There will be plenty of phone calls to make after this is official. Let’s see if Lady Amanda wants to talk about the plan this afternoon.”

“You’re the boss.” Kitty rose from her chair and exited the room, still not deigning to look at the event promoter. I couldn’t help but notice that Nathan sneaked a puzzled glance at Kitty's departing figure, as if he still wasn’t quite sure it was really her.

“She’s your full-time assistant now?” he asked, looking at me. I had definitely been right about the shock in Nathan's reaction.

“She’s the best one I’ve ever had,” I answered. *And the only one*, I might add, but didn’t.

“Hm.” He stared towards the doorway a moment longer, then seemed to recover himself and offered me his usual business-y smile. “So, some news about the contest, huh?” he said.

“I’ll say,” I answered. "You seem as excited as the village itself will be."

"I'm feeling a little better after this win," he said. "Truthfully, I was a little nervous about deciding to go freelance after the concert. Trying to make a difference in a smaller market is tough. I'm more like the ... unofficial ... event promoter for Cornwall. Plus, working out of Truro feels a little weird after London. But since a train ride from London is pretty rough on the average working day, it was the only thing to do."

"You think you're staying on in Cornwall full time?" I asked.

"Sure. Why not? This proves my instincts weren't wrong. Event promoters basically just work to make attractions bigger, even if the firms and companies here aren't the biggest ones on this side of the Pond. Maybe I needed a change from an international machine like Wendy Alistair's," he said, with a rueful smile that made him seem much more relaxed and human. "Like convincing a popular British program to pick this place as a filming location."

"I told you this place has irresistible charms," I said.

***

Dear Diary,

Isn't it weird, writing a greeting to a book? But I guess that's how you traditionally start one of these, so I'll give it a chance. I want to show Matt that this is a serious endeavor on my part, and not just a passing thought. Because it was really considerate of Matt. Really. And I'm not just saying it because I loved the amethyst pendant he gave me, either. Regardless of this fact, I love the journal, and I love Matt...and always want to remember everything I can about Cornwall, so I can carry it with me wherever I go in the future.

Nobody knows I'm actually doing this, and I'll probably give up before page two. So keep it a secret for me, okay? — Julianne

***

Kitty:

"Katherine, is that you?" From the sound of her voice, my mum turned down the telly in the living room to ask this question. "Nigel, it's not you, is it? Not shiftin' about through my pocketbook for a quid, are you?"

"It's only me, Mum," I called back. I'd been hoping to sneak in and out without getting caught, but even full decibel sound from *Big Brother* can't hide the sound of a squeaky kitchen door from my mum.

I dropped my bag on the floor of my room and slipped off the pair of black heels that Julianne — my sort-of boss — gave me a few months ago when they took me on at Cliffs House. Time to put them back where they belonged after hours: in the closet, with my red sneakers in their rightful place on my feet. I had given the black skirt and coat a quick drape across a hanger, next to a charcoal-colored cardigan and a couple of proper dresses from a shop. The only ones I could afford for this job, but decent enough by my reckoning.

Posh togs compared to my old one at the pasties shop, anyway. No more cycling around with newspaper bundles in my basket, and the smell of fried fish and potatoes clinging to my clothes. Sadly, however, it wasn't the end of me having to crash at my mum's place. The ratty black and red sweater and denim leggings I pulled on weren't the only old clothes of mine lying about this room, which was now more a storage space for my gran's old sewing supplies than a place for me. Old fabric squares and loads of bits and bobs for her dilapidated sewing machine — a treadle one, believe it or not — that hadn't been touched since she died. Mum was always swearing she'd take up learning it after Christmas was over, or some such time.

"There's shepherd's pie in the oven, but don't touch it — it's for Nigel when he drops in," my mum continued shouting. "And give your cousin Saul a ring...he's been calling your mobile for hours."

Saul. He was only calling me because he wanted money, most likely. I snorted. All my Uncle Phil's lot was always desperate for cash for some scheme or other. And I wasn't the least bit surprised that Mum didn't want me to stay to dinner. The rare boyfriend of the moment usually had her attention, destined to be the recipient of more than one of her awful dishes, since when there was none around we subsisted off frozen pasties and beans on toast. Nigel, a retired salesman and widower, was one of the few men desperate enough not to be driven off by Mum's moods or her cooking.

"I'm going out, Mum," I shouted, as I pushed open the front door, my canvas and shoulder bag the only things I was carrying, besides the helmet for riding my motorbike.

"Already? Where are you going?" The telly's sound was still low, but Mum was still reclining on the sofa, I could tell. "If you've got an extra quid on you —"

"Gotta go, Mum." I closed the door behind me.

At my mate Talisha's birthday party at the pub, I found a quiet corner under some white twinkle lights and curled up with a book and a half pint, after the initial greeting. Talisha and I weren't close mates, so turning up was mostly an excuse to go out for an evening — and the book was nothing special, just an old book on psychology I found on a shelf. But the pint was good St Austell brew, so I was fine.

The place was crowded with loads of people, and was its usual noisy self as I turned pages on Freudian concepts and Jungian stuff that I imagined would help me understand the sort of crowd that was due at Cliffs House in another week for a mental health conference. One would have to be mental to read much of this, I was certain...but when I lifted my eyes, I wished I'd left them stuck to its pages.

The last crowd of patrons had brought a stranger into the Fisherman's Rest. Sandy hair spiked with a bit of product, leather jacket, a pair of jeans that had the decency to fit and not look too tailored. I didn't look twice: not because he wasn't dishy, but because I'd recognized that odious Yank Nathan Menton without his usual suit.

He'd ordered a drink and was chatting with some uppity types I recognized from school — a few girls who thought Truro was the high life after living in Ceffylgwyn. I turned the page of my book, and pretended not to see that Nathan Menton had noticed me.

Blast. He was drifting this direction. Wishing I was mistaken, and that he'd spotted some chum in the far corner wouldn't change it, anyway. I tried not to mutter an oath under my breath as I hoped he would walk right by.

He paused. One hand tucked in his back pocket, the other holding a half pint of a pale brew that was no doubt as watery as American beer.

"Kat," he said.

"Kitty." I corrected him without looking up.

"Right," he said. "I meant —"

"If you're going to do the Little Red Riding Hood bit again, you can leave now," I interrupted. I gave him a look — not a nice one — to prove I meant it.

I thought he actually turned red with embarrassment, but it was so quick it was probably just the heat of the room. "Sorry, I didn't mean it to offend you," he said.

"It offends me more to be called the wrong name," I answered. Kat was ... well, a name that belonged to a different period of my life. Off limits these days, by my rules.

He glanced around, awkwardly. If he wanted to leave, it was fine. I didn't know why he was sticking around at this moment, when his sort-of mates were across the room. "Are you a friend of Talisha's?" I asked. It would feel a bit odd to go on reading with him standing here like this.

"Um, more of a hanger-on," he said. "You know how it is. New person in town, you take any invitation you get. Some acquaintances invited me to tag along ... I kind of think it's more about my being single than about actually wanting my company."

A smile tugged the corner of my lips. "That might be true," I answered, archly.

"Well, I knew if anybody would agree, it would be you," he said. "The welcoming committee for my first day in the village."

My turn to feel a bit awkward. "Er, sorry," I said. Mumbling a bit, but still, the words made it out of my mouth.

"It's okay," he said. He sat down on a nearby chair, which, unfortunately, someone had left close by, and, with elbows resting on his knees, cupped his glass between both hands. A bit close for my taste — we were on eye level now, since I was curled up in the old armchair.

"I apologize for treating you like everybody's best friend's little sister," he said. "It's kind of a reflex, teasing someone I'm uncomfortable around. Not that you make me uncomfortable," he hastened to add, " — in a bad way."

"Nice to know." I tried not to smirk, but it was a challenge.

"You know, I think I'll stop here." Nathan took a long drink from his half-pint. "So there. I apologized."

"Apology accepted." I turned the page in my book. Not a clue what words were printed on the next one, but it gave me an air of indifference, you might say.

"Are you here alone?" he asked. "I'm not implying anything by saying that, before you take offense. Just putting that out there." He held up a hand, defensively.

"I'm friends with some of this lot," I said, glancing towards the crowd. "They're all right. I just felt like being on my own for a bit." I looked the part of a loner, I figured, sitting off in the shadows like this in a noisy pub. I could be playing darts with Charlie and Fez if I wanted, or listen to Talisha's latest moanings about posh customers at the salon, but my closest mates were part of a different crowd. Not that anybody believed I had close mates — even my own mum. And with me, 'close' still had its limits.

"You can hang out with my friends, if you want some company," he said. "We're over there." He pointed towards a group near the bar.

"With Melinda and her lot? No thanks." I shook my head.

"You don't like Melinda?" he asked. "What's wrong with her?"

"I didn't say anything was wrong with her."

"Let's just say it's implied."

"She's not my cup of tea," I answered. Why break tradition with a long reply?

"Can I ask why?" He shrugged his shoulders, as if implying he didn't care if I answered. "You tend to be very succinct in your explanations. Did anyone ever tell you that?"

"You can ask if you want. Doesn't mean I'll tell you," I said. "Melinda's a toff. If you like that sort, then it's fine."

Even from here, I could smell Melinda's rich perfume and the polish from her flawless, twice-weekly manicure. It wasn't being part of the Truro-loving crowd that bothered me — it was the keen recollection that Melinda had mocked me plenty of times at school, and probably still did when she was with that crowd.

"Toff. Right. Well, I guess since I'm one of those, I'm with the right group," said Nathan. "According to your definition of me from before."

I think he was waiting for me to say something else, but I wasn't going to contradict him. Not without proof, anyway. "One should always know one's place," I answered, in a fake snooty voice I used sometimes to make Julianne laugh.

Nathan laughed. It surprised me — and him, too, weirdly enough. "Thanks for the advice, Lady Violet," he said.

That must be a *Downton Abbey* thing. I hadn't a clue. But I hated to tell him I never watched anything on our telly except *Britain's Got Talent*, which had been the only program Mum and I could mutually endure.

"I guess I —" Nathan began, but now somebody from his group was saying something to him, and I was diving into the pages of some sort of ego versus superego case studies. I pretended I didn't notice him leave, trying hard not to. So what if he looked dishy enough out of his Hugo Boss togs?

I played a quick round of darts with Charlie and drank a shot toast with Talisha at the height of the party — everybody was joining in around the room, but I didn't see the American event promoter among them. I didn't see him again until I had left the pub, where I recognized the back of his jacket as he struggled with the driver's door of a small black car.

He wasn't drunk, I realized. His voice and the steadiness of the palm that smacked his window with frustration made that clear. He glanced at me, his face red with frustration, too.

"My keys are inside," he said. "I was such a moron to forget them — now I'm locked out."

"You could walk."

"To Truro?" He ran a hand through his hair, giving it a frustrated raking.

"Probably not," I answered. I stepped closer, seeing the keys lying on his driver's seat. He hadn't left a window cracked — shame, because that's always easier to manage that way.

"Is there a lock service in this town?" he asked.

"Nope." I reached into the twist of hair at the back of my head, pulling out the two pins that kept the braided part held back from my face. "Hold on a moment."

"What? Why?" he said. I bent the first pin and inserted it in the lock of his car. His ride was a newer model, but too economy to have an alarm system. It took a few seconds for it to pop.

"Did you just — pick my lock?" he asked. Astonished, he lifted the door handle, opening the driver's side.

"Best not leave anything you value lying on the seats when you're in Truro," I said.

"Thanks," he said. "I think." He was still looking at me with surprise. "Um — what do I owe you?"

"Nothing." I shrugged. "It was two seconds." I lifted my helmet from the seat of my bike.

"Is that yours?" he said, noticing my battered motorbike — one that had been a classic with black and chrome before my cousin did a horrible bit of painting on it in streaky seafoam green. Despite this, I thought maybe he gave it an admiring glance.

"Beats a cheap foreign car," I answered, tucking my loose hair out of the helmet strap's way. I started the bike's motor.

"I still owe you," he said. He jingled the keys in his hand, newly rescued from his car's seat.

"Yeah. Two hairpins." With a snort of derision, I pulled away from the pavement before he could do something stupid, like offer me a quid. If that was the sort of daft thought in his head, that is.

***

Julianne:

Ceffylgwyn is a small village — there's only one street of shops in the village, and only the florists and fish and chips besides. So when word spread that the baking contest would be hosted here, it spread fast and furiously. This was bigger than a televised concert special. This was *baking.*

"I've heard that Jenny Bryce over Falmouth way's been chosen," said Gemma, as she sampled a ginger-poppyseed biscuit. "Her bloke's been bragging about it at all the pubs — bought her a special whisk that's supposed to guarantee an airy scone."

"No whisk would ever make a difference in mixing a scone's ingredients," said Dinah, as she stirred her batter. "That's a lot of nonsense." Her batter sloshed onto the table, an unusual mess on the cook's part.

"Doesn't this recipe take baking soda?" I asked. I hesitated to point this out — after all, my own baking skills were pretty rusty, even after Dinah's coaching. Matt probably discreetly buried my scones when I wasn't around.

Dinah looked at me. "What?" she said. "Oh. Of course. Silly me. I'll go and leave off my own head next." She reached for the jar of bicarbonate of soda, nestled in a pile of flour beside the sugar canister.

"Everybody knew Leeman Lawson would be chosen from Devon — he used to have a bake shop near the border," said Gemma to me.

"Moved away five or six years ago, but couldn't resist coming back to show off. His apple tarts were always the talk of the village fete. People fought each other to be first in line for a dozen."

"The last winner had a mean tea cake, as I recall," I answered. "A really good one," I clarified. Sometimes I still forgot myself when it came to Americanisms — more than once I'd accidentally spoken the equivalent of gibberish to the rest of the staff.

"Even my mum's getting into it. Talking about making a proper pudding in grandmother's old tin, just to celebrate when the show's broadcast on telly. And she never cooks anything but bangers and mash."

A dish I was mostly good at burning — but I preferred the charming thought of tarts, pies, and cherry puddings more, anyway. If I were a local baking connoisseur, I would be molding little marzipan cherries covered in sugar, or learning the secret behind a good English pudding, the qualities of which Dinah had enlightened me with my first Christmas in Cornwall ... and in real life, I would produce hopelessly soggy dough and overdone meringues, probably.

"Of course, the judges are tough as old boots, and the way they argue over a sponge puts cats to shame," said Gemma, scornfully. "Butter wouldn't melt in Miss Hardy's mouth, and as for that French chef, he makes a face while chewing English pastry like it's a stack of old laundry."

I tried not to giggle, since I could picture the face she meant. "Still, that's a little harsh, I think," I answered. "Pierre was really nice to the contestant whose Leaning Tower of Pistachio Sponge collapsed into a big heap. He said it tasted delicious, even if it leaned just a *little* too much." And he hadn't sounded the slightest bit sardonic when he said it.

Pierre Dupine and Harriet Hardy were the two judges for the baking contests in England's southern counties. In every episode, they had been tough critics when it came to flaky pastry and stiff meringue, but especially Harriet Hardy, whose book of English cookery had been on every British cook's kitchen shelf for more than twenty years. I marveled that a woman who made a living crafting biscuit and cake recipes could be as slender as a twig — yet as firm and unbending as a fireplace log when it came to her standards of excellence. As for Pierre, he only seemed laid-back and charming in interviews; the moment he stood in front of a contestant's creation, you could practically hear their bones quaking as the eminent chef sampled it.

A contest winner from Dorset squeaked a narrow victory over other competitors with a perfect cherry chip cake. This one would be just like the other episodes hosted between English counties — a mad, three-event dash by the bakers to complete each task to time and standards as the judges awarded them points, ending with an elaborate recipe that would determine which baker had won.

"What have we here? Savory poppyseed biscuits? That wouldn't be for my cravings, would it, Dinah?" Lady Amanda had joined us, descending upon the platter of freshly-baked treats with relish.

"Help yourself. The ones for the luncheon are already tucked away in the tin," said Dinah, who poured her cake batter into a buttered and floured pan. Needing no prompting, Lady Amanda took three.

"Little Cynthia has such an appetite these days," said Lady Amanda, nibbling the edge of one. Beneath her soft silk caftan-style shirt, the slight outline of a 'baby bump' was now visible. "She won't let me keep anything down, but she insists on being fed regularly, all the same."

"Cynthia? Is that the name you've chosen, if it's a girl?" I asked.

"I'm giving it favor," said Lady Amanda. "I like it better than Violet — that was yesterday's choice. Anyway, it rather feels like Cynthia today. I can sense it in my bones, so I underlined it in the book. Alongside half a dozen others, I'm afraid. Oh, Julianne, I simply can't decide!"

"You have five whole months left," I said. "You've only been thinking about it for a few weeks."

"Yes, I know. Three weeks ago 'Natasha' struck me as a rather intriguing option, so you can see we've made some progress since then." She popped the last bite of the second biscuit into her mouth.

"I've always been partial to Lily," said Gemma. "Lovely name, really. Or Pearl. Then a bloke would always call her 'his Pearl' like in the Hollywood *Pride and Prejudice.*"

"I've never heard a 'pearl' or a 'lily' drop from the lips of the blokes around here," said Dinah. "Blokes around here stick with 'the missus' and 'old girl,' and think those romantic phrases you have in mind are rubbish." She resifted the confectioner's sugar in her bowl, as if she couldn't quite reach the texture she wanted. I was beginning to think this particular cake must be a new recipe for her.

"It isn't rubbish, it's just romance," said Gemma.

"I didn't say it *was* rubbish, only that it's the opinion of others," said Dinah. Her usual sharpness towards giggling conversations in the kitchen had mellowed ever since Pippa left — Pippa, who had been the dreamiest of the two young women of Cliffs House's staff.

As if reading my mind, Gemma sighed. "At times like this, I miss Pip," she said. "Think how disappointed she'll be that the baking contest's coming here now that she's in Hampshire. She told me she didn't even watch the northern counties' contest on the telly because she was busy working those nights."

"At least she got to see Highclere Castle," I pointed out. Pippa had sent me a dozen photos of her posing excitedly on the grounds — Gavin had very sweetly arranged the outing on a day when they could have tea there, leaving Pippa in seventh heaven.

"It's such a beautiful spot," said Lady Amanda. "I quite enjoyed *Downton Abbey*. What was the name of the Dowager again? Violet, wasn't it?" She tapped her finger against her lower lip, thoughtfully. Forget Cynthia: I knew its competition would be receiving a double underline in the baby names book tonight.

"Do you think they'll let us sample the leftovers after the contest?" Gemma asked. "I mean, we'll be helping set up and clear away and all — not that any of them can hold a candle to Dinah's recipes, even Leeman himself." At this, Dinah's kitchen utensil let out a furious rattle, ending with a crash between pot, pan, and stirring spoon on the floor.

"Blast!" She seized a dish rag and began mopping it up. "Gemma, mind the chocolate on the stove, please." Gemma sprang to the double boiler as I ran to help Dinah.

"Is everything okay?" I asked.

Dinah paused. Her eyes sneaked a quick look in the direction of Lady Amanda, who was in quest of a clean spoon for the chocolate. "Not quite," she whispered back. "May I — have a word with you?"

It was nervousness in her voice: the first I had ever heard in the usually-unruffled calm of Cliffs House's cook. "Sure," I said. Nonchalantly, I withdrew to the pantry, where Dinah followed shortly.

She lifted an extra box of confectioner's sugar from the shelf, then turned to face me.

"I entered the contest," she whispered. "And they accepted me."

My eyes widened. "Really?" I said. "Dinah that's gre—"

"I can't believe it, even after a week," she continued, hastily. "I'm going to be on the program — a woman who's never so much as stirred in the direction of the spotlight before! Whatever shall I do?"

"What do you mean?" I asked, puzzled. "You're going to be on the show, of course. What else?"

"I haven't a clue which recipes or what flavors I'll choose, to begin with — and I can't help thinking what it means for this place. It means a week of this place shifting with only Gemma in the kitchen, and a temporary cook, since I'll need time to prepare and practice ... they make those contestants work night and day before the grand finale."

"You'll do whatever you have to do to get by," I said. "We'll all be so proud of you. No one will be surprised when you announce it, because everyone thinks you're the best, Dinah. Your marmalade and your saffron biscuits are perfection."

"Pish posh," Dinah scoffed. "It isn't that I don't have confidence in my own skill. But this is television, my girl. And besides, I never dreamed I'd be chosen. I don't go about fantasizing about life, you know." Her voice softened a little. "Once, after I graduated from Paris, I thought about opening a little shop of my own someday — I never really thought about being top chef in a Michelin star restaurant, like the others dreamed. But I sent that application on a lark...I thought I'd just go on being content like always with a few compliments for a tea spread or a proper cake."

"It's lucky they chose you," I said. "You'll have a great time. You might even win, Dinah."

"Against a pack of cutthroat competitors and two sharks for judges?" she said, with a short laugh. "Leeman's not the only professional in that lot besides myself. There'll be proper pastry chefs and confectioners among them, and more than one who's been trained in Paris as well."

"Paris isn't everything," I said, thinking of Pierre's begrudging compliment for a contestant's flaky sweet rolls inspired by mince pies. "I think you being yourself will be more than enough to rival the rest of the group, regardless of your training."

"I'm just glad I've told someone at last," said Dinah. "It's been preying on me for weeks now. I've made daft mistakes in my cooking because of it ... but now I suppose I'll have to go through with it all." She pressed her hand to her cheek — one which was unusually flushed for Dinah.

I squeezed her arm. "Go for it," I said. "I think Lady Amanda will be thrilled. Even if the rest of us are eating pickle sandwiches and shop biscuits for the rest of the week."

***

On Monday morning, the first delivery trucks arrived with The Grand Baking Extravaganza's official equipment and crew. There was a crowd waiting at the village sign, cheering excitedly as the lorries motored by en route to Cliffs House.

Flour, sugar, icing sugar, rising agents, treacle — all non-perishable goods had been delivered in advance. For the first event, we had arranged for them to set up in the manor house's ballroom, where, thankfully, Wendy Alistair's concert had created plenty of electrical outlets we could use for baking ovens and fridges, once the village electrician made some modifications and extensions. Now, the piano, chairs, and sofa were gone, replaced by matching rental tables covered with neat white cloths — row after row of work spaces for the contestants to lay out their supplies and ingredients. No cooking implements were provided, since each contestant was expected to supply everything they needed for their recipes, from mixing bowls to piping tools.

The only decoration was the program's official logo, featuring the title and a slice of sponge with a fork stuck in it. Two crewmen suspended it from the ceiling in the form of a two-sided hanging sign.

With the lorries of tables and baking ovens, arrived a rental car conveying the two judges. The first to emerge was Harriet Hardy, slim, imposing, and elegant in a rose-colored suit, not a stray curl escaping from her tightly-pinned, sleek hairstyle. Then Pierre Dupine, a swarthy Frenchman who might have looked at home on a pirate ship if not for his tailored suit — the graying hairs in his dark mane and crinkles around his eyes were a sign he was obviously well past middle age, and in another life would be a retired swashbuckler by now.

"There they are," whispered Gemma, as we peeked from behind the lace curtains of the manor's front parlor. "Goodness, Harriet Hardy looks more frightening in the flesh than on the telly, doesn't she?"

"She's imposing," I said, inwardly wincing for Dinah's sake. Dinah, who had taken a week's holiday from Cliffs House starting yesterday, to avoid any accidental conflict of interest as the estate's cook, wasn't here to join us for this sneak peek. "But I think Pierre's the one to watch out for. Eight times out of ten, the lowest marks come from him, no matter what he says about the contestant's bake."

The two judges lingered in the garden, surrounded by Matt and Pollock's most recent effort — an ornamental herb garden featuring the southern counties' plants in particular. I saw Miss Hardy pinch a leaf between her fingers and sniff it, then speak to Pierre.

"Think they're making small talk?" I asked. "Soaking up the sun?" Pierre had complained about the rainy days in England more than once, so maybe the slightly more Mediterranean climate of Cornwall would soften him.

"More likely they're bickering about something," said Gemma.

"Already? They haven't even tasted a soggy sponge." Lady Amanda was behind us, peering through the curtains, too. "Although I could eat a whole one myself at this moment, no matter how underdone its middle." She rested her hand on her baby bump. "Little Violet is famished."

"Violet?" I echoed. "You're back to choosing that one, are you?" I imagined the baby book's predictably crossed-out names and erased lines of negate, but managed not to smile.

"For the moment," said Lady Amanda.

"And if it's a boy?" asked Gemma.

"Anything but Adolf Hitler is a possibility," answered Lady Amanda. "I suppose I must now go greet them as the lady of the house. Wish me luck." She withdrew again, leaving us to our covert observation.

Gemma clutched the curtain. "There are the contestants," she said, excitedly. "Do you see Dinah?"

"Not yet," I answered, feeling my stomach muscles clench a little, as if it was me marching up the pathway with a box of kitchen supplies instead.

They were mostly strangers to me, even the other Cornish contestants and Leeman from the Devon border village. Men and women with armfuls of electric mixers, whisks, wooden spoons, and nesting bowls, filing past the judges and Lady Amanda — and there was Dinah near the end of the line of a dozen or so, a bright yellow stand mixer peering over her box. I was pretty sure her expression of grim determination was pure nerves from steely Dinah.

"Let's go," whispered Gemma.

The contestants were assembled in the ballroom when the two judges, Lady Amanda, and the two of us, joined them. The judges posted themselves at the head of the room.

"Welcome, all, to The Grand Baking Extravaganza," said Harriet, in the precise tone I recognized from the show. "This little gathering will be a review of the contest's rules and schedule, as well as an explanation regarding the filmed portion of the event, so you won't feel quite so lost when the camera crew is present."

Dinah's words about appearing on telly came back to me as I listened, facing the nervous-looking contestants who were doing the same thing. Sheets of paper were being passed out to them by one of the production associates during the judge's speech.

"There will be three major events, with forty-eight hours between each one to allow for practice and preparation. Your score will be tabulated after each judging, and combined with your previous score. As you know, the final event being worth fifty percent of the total points in the contest."

"That's a lot of pressure," muttered Gemma. "No wonder someone always goes a bit wobbly."

"Filming will take place only during the events themselves, of course, so you needn't worry about anyone interfering with your practice. However, this room, and any other sites prepared for the competition, will be off-limits to contestants during the hours between events. Which means you will exit this room as soon as we have concluded our remarks, and will not be allowed to return until tomorrow."

This protected recipes and supplies from sabotage, I supposed. Not that anyone in this crowd looked desperate or devious enough to cheat.

"The rules for the contest are clear and simple. No fraternizing with the judges from this moment until the end of the competition, except at open gatherings where all are present — and even then, no private conservations between any judge and contestant," continued Harriet. "No contestant may give gifts of any kind, or additional baked goods, to the judges. No recipe step for any event completed during the forty-eight hour practice interval may be included in the final presentation. And, last — but not least — of all, no contestant may in any way influence, intimidate, or circumvent another contestant's recipe."

Harriet glanced at Pierre Dupine — evidently it was his turn to speak. "I hope you will all try very hard, and enjoy your time as part of this contest," he said, in his familiar dusky French accent. "I wish all of you good fortune."

The assistant handing out the papers handed me one as well. It was a basic outline of the events, not the detailed dossier which Dinah and the other competitors had been given with their acceptance notification. The days and times for three events were listed: a morning bake, a mid-morning one, and an afternoon bake for the finale. The first was a tea dainties' bakeoff, the second, a grand biscuit challenge. The finale — a centerpiece sponge with the theme of love and passion.

I imagined Dinah tackling this first one. Would she be tearing through her recipe collection one more time, in search of Cornish-themed biscuits or savory treats? Every other contestant was wearing the same expression of shaky composure as they read the list of challenges, a few exchanging nervous whispers.

"Thank you all for coming," said Harriet, so Pierre's speech was at an end. "We will see you all tomorrow morning for the first challenge."

The contestants filed out of the room, leaving behind tables occupied by cooking utensils and stacks of colored mixing bowls. Then Lady Amanda and I locked the main doors to the ballroom.

***

"The tea challenge should be easy for Dinah," I said. "She's a master of dreaming up little cakes and biscuits and savories — just think of any event we've hosted, and there's an example of Dinah's genius. I think she has a good chance to impress the judges."

"It's far more challenging when you have to face your toughest critics before an audience of competitors," chuckled Matt. "This first one will be the hardest. And it may make or break her chances, psychologically."

"They didn't mention the surprise today," I said. "Do you think there will be one?"

Sometimes, the judges instituted a 'surprise' challenge in addition to the usual three — it meant bonus points, in essence, if the contestants did well, but a major setback if they didn't.

"I hope not. It cost one of the northern counties' contenders their chance of winning," said Matt, grimly. I remembered the 'oozy pudding incident', and shuddered a little for its poor baker's sake.

"Enough worrying about surprises, then," I said, feeling Matt kiss my earlobe as he wrapped his arms around my waist from behind. "Are you ready to teach me a few things?" I teased. "You promised, remember?"

"Only if you're sure you want to go through with this decision," he answered, sighing against my cheek.

"I think it's high time, don't you?" I said, turning to look into his eyes as I leaned into his embrace. "Besides, I thought it would be nice to surprise your family when they come." Matt's 'family' was his sister Michelle and her new fiancé Liam, currently stationed in Asia. "Can you think of anything better?"

"All right, you win," he said. "Open the recipe book to page twenty-two."

My cooking skills were pretty poor when I first came to Cornwall, and even with lessons from Dinah, my talents were still minimal. The baking challenge had made me reassess my woeful limitations and resolve to do better — at least as well as Matt, who was far more comfortable using a decorative sponge mold than I was.

"First step is to sift the flour," said Matt, who handed me one of our kitchen aprons, a very frilly one printed with cherries. "Then we measure our wet ingredients in a separate bowl..."

I succeeded in making a mess with the flour, my kitchen trademark, and had a narrow escape from adding the wrong seasonings to our recipe, Matt rescuing the container from my hand just in time.

"Exact measurements, love," he said, as I trickled molasses — or 'treacle,' as Matt called it — from the cupboard jar into a measuring cup.

"You don't measure things exactly," I pointed out, having watched him make the recipe a time or two. "You use dribs and drabs, and pinches of seasoning whenever you mix it up."

"Trust me, in the beginning, it's better to do it precisely," he said. "You'll get the hang of it over time, and then it's less of a necessity." He opened an extract bottle from one of the cupboards, releasing a pleasant aroma into our kitchen. One of Matt's mum's 'secret ingredients' in her treacle pudding, he had told me once before.

"This is really sticky," I said, my fingers tacking themselves to the jar. I licked one of them. "Bit strong, isn't it?" I said, worriedly. I had tasted molasses when I was a kid, and remembered it being less pungent.

"This is extremely strong treacle," said Matt. "I bought it at a roadside stand in North Carolina when I took a weekend excursion along the southern coast. It's the sulfurous flavor you're noticing. 'Blackstrap sorghum molasses,' as they call it in the South. It's an acquired taste, but adds an interesting element in cooking."

I tried not to make a face. "What's next?" I asked.

"Honey," he said. "Just a spoonful or two." He lifted a jar of honeycomb from one of Rosemoor's kitchen corner nooks, near the percolator.

"One of your mom's secret ingredients?" I asked. It wasn't anywhere on the recipe before us. In fact, we'd added several things that weren't mentioned on the pages of Harriet Hardy's *Everyday Recipes of the British Kitchen*.

"It is indeed," said Matt.

"How many times have you made this?" I asked, as I dutifully stirred in the honey. "Since you know it forwards and backwards, I mean."

"Many times," said Matt, with a smile. "I made it more frequently when Michelle was still close to home. It brought to mind memories of childhood Christmases after only the two of us were left. It was a way to keep part of the past with us."

"Does Michelle know the recipe, too?" I asked. I was nervous about surprising Matt's sister with a dessert that she, too, knew like the back of her hand. I crossed my fingers that I wasn't the only one ignorant around here about the secrets behind English puddings.

"Not as well as I do," he said. "I was usually the one who helped my mother — Michelle was too young those first few Christmases. And when my mother worked, and our finances were limited, our Christmases tended to be rather small. Once, when I was nine or so, I found the cookbook in the cupboard and attempted it myself."

"A dangerous task for a little boy, wasn't it?" I asked. I knew Matt had spent a lot of after school hours on his own while his mother worked. A 'latchkey' kid as the phrase says, without a baby-sitter for him and Michelle many an afternoon.

"Imagine the secret horror of a nine year-old boy's mother when she finds out he's been using lots of electrical appliances and a gas oven while she was absent ... and you have an excellent picture of my mother's face when she first arrived home that evening," said Matt. "The finished product was a sticky mess, I fear, served once the lectures and tears were finished that night. Even so, when it was served, my mother pretended it was brilliant when she took a bite."

I pictured a childhood version of Matt helping in the kitchen. Probably standing on a kitchen stool, pouring ingredients into the bowl as his mother stirred. I had only seen a couple of pictures of the patient, hardworking single mother who had done her best to raise Matthew and Michelle, and who hadn't lived to see how well their lives turned out. Matt had her eyes, I noticed. And there was a little of her in the shape of his cheekbones, too.

"Now for the tin," he said. "It's in the top cupboard, behind the bread pans."

The tin was old and battered, elegant-looking except for a dent in one side. It was Matt's mother's, one of the few things from his childhood that was still around, besides a handful of items tucked in shoeboxes. Somehow, he had saved this one, despite relocating his life multiple times on this side of the Pond and the other. I turned the tin over in my hands, examining it with reverent admiration.

"Now, onto the cooking stage," said Matt. He kissed my cheek as he placed our newly-mixed pudding on the counter beside the stove.

The pudding was more Matt's effort than mine, but we ate it as soon as it was decanted from its mold, with a brown sugar toffee sauce on the side that Matt made to sweeten its flavors for my sugar-coated American tongue. He cut two generous slices and put them on the chipped blue and gold china tea plates I retrieved from the top shelf of the kitchen cabinet.

After his first bite of pudding, an odd look crossed Matt's face.
"How much treacle did you add, Julianne?"
"Just the amount it said in the recipe," I said. "I topped off the measurement of the cup you gave me." I held up the measuring cup, which was sitting in the heap of dishes to be washed.
"That's not the measuring cup I gave you. I handed you two — one for the sugar, one for the treacle. Didn't you see the measuring cup I set in front of the book?"
"What measurement?"
Matt opened the cookbook again and pointed to the recipe, where the correct amounts were printed, partly obscured by a crusty bit of flour I had spilled earlier. I read it, feeling my cheeks flush at the substantial difference between the recipe's amount and the cup I had erroneously chosen. I had switched the measurements for the sugar and the treacle.
"Oops," I said, cringing. "Sorry."
"At least your sauce will come in handy," he chuckled, spooning a generous helping over his pudding before he took a second bite. "Maybe next time, we'll try sticky toffee pudding instead."

***

The first day of The Grand Baking Extravaganza dawned with bright summer sunshine, the lush trees and jeweled greens of the garden herbs stirring in the coast's faint breeze off my beloved cliffs. The drapes were open in the ornate ballroom, where the program's camera crew setup had been old hat for all of us, thanks to Wendy Alistair's concert.
All of the contestants were at their marks, all wearing matching aprons printed with the program's logo. Most of them were muttering recipes under their breath, or gripping a whisk or a spatula as if primed to go when the judges gave the word.
Each of them had been given the basic ingredients, but had to supply the rest of what they needed. Their recipe was meant to be unique — their own special twist, not something unaltered out of a standard cookbook (like Harriet Hardy's *British Cookery*, for instance). And, of course, it must be a dainty selection perfect for serving at tea.
From behind the set, I watched Dinah wait with hands folded for the

official start. I crossed my fingers behind my back, and glanced towards Lord William, who had sneaked in also, and was watching with a serious look of anticipation. Lord William had a streak of baker's sympathy, too, I remembered — Lady Amanda spoke fondly of his lemon poppyseed bread which he sometimes made for their tea.

"Each contestant at their place, please. When the bell sounds, you may begin," said Harriet Hardy. As a member of the production crew sounded a single chime, all the bakers sprang into action.

"What did she choose?" Lord William whispered to me.

"I have no idea," I whispered back.

I hadn't seen Dinah since the day before the Extravaganza arrived at Cliffs House — only Geoff Weatherby had, and that was because he had dropped off Dinah's special spice blend which she had forgotten and left at the manor's kitchen. He had reported somewhat reluctantly to Gemma that Dinah's cottage kitchen seemed 'a bit of a mess' at the time. I got the impression that she hadn't been in the most cheery of moods, either.

"Keep those fingers crossed," said Lord William.

I watched as Leeman, the former star baker of Ceffylgwyn's village fete, stirred fresh raspberry juice and sugar together in a double boiler pot. It was certainly the main ingredient for his once-beloved jeweled raspberry tarts, which Gemma had spoken of reverentially.

The bespectacled, goateed figure looked perfectly confident about his chances, as he rolled out a pastry tart with a little French rolling pin without handles. On the other hand, the young woman at the neighboring table had already covered her apron and her hair with generous daubs of flour.

I could definitely sympathize with her.

At her station, Dinah was whisking cream and lemon juice over heat, which I recognized as the base to her lemon curd tarts. They were a delicious recipe, but not one of Dinah's most creative ones, which surprised me. Had she decided against her special orange saffron iced biscuits as too bold? Her basil-thyme scones served with fresh crab meat in rosemary cream as too different? A dozen snacks from the past came to my perplexed mind as I watched her strain the vanilla beans from her custard cream with a tiny sieve. Dinah playing it safe in the face of a cooking challenge — it couldn't be true.

A contestant who looked no more than twelve years old was shaping puff pastry into little frog-shaped cakes, I noticed; meanwhile, a woman in a cotton sari was measuring a yellow-colored spice into a mixing bowl of dry ingredients, with miniature mountains of chopped fruit piled on the cutting board at her elbow.

Dinah was cutting circles of pie crust and pressing them into tart tins. Her hands were shaking less than when she had begun, at least. She seemed sure of herself as she trimmed the edges with her worn-handled kitchen knife. My doubts about her choice of recipe erased themselves when she placed a new saucepan on the stove, and lifted a bowl of oranges onto the table beside it. Anything with Dinah's magic marmalade was sure to impress.

All tea dainties must be finished by noon. There would be a coffee break before judging began, and I knew I still had to finish overseeing the reception room for when the crew and contest participants were finished. I slipped quietly from the ballroom, and made my way to the parlor, where Gemma was laying out stacks of white tea plates and the silverplate coffee service belonging to the manor's service wares.

"Purchased biccies," she said, making a slight face as she laid out the pre-packaged shortbread rounds on a glass platter. "I loved 'em as a kid, but they're not as good as something from a proper kitchen."

"We'll have to make do," I said. "These iced buns from Charlotte's shop will be worth sampling, at least." I had arranged for three dozen filled snack buns to be baked and delivered from the village fish and chips shop — its owner Charlotte made the best pasties in all Ceffylgwyn, and one taste of her homemade dessert buns at a Christmas party convinced me she was the right choice for entertaining the Baking Extravaganza crowd.

The buns were iced in pink, white, and yellow — the baking contest's official colors. Gemma and I hastened to bring in the muffins and crocks of preserves; without saying anything we knew that we were both hurrying to see the finish of the first bake.

"Done," I said, breathlessly. "All that's left is to serve the coffee and bring in two pots of tea."

"Lady A will be pleased enough, although it would be better if we weren't short a cook and a hand in laying out service," said Gemma, stirring her gingery bangs from her eyes with a short puff of breath.

A suitable full-time replacement for Pippa still hadn't been found, and no part-time schoolgirls were available today, it seemed. "I'll have Kitty come down to clear away," I promised. Gemma and I scurried from the sitting room, thankful no one but a production assistant saw us hurrying towards the ballroom doors left open a crack.

"They're garnishing," whispered Gemma, peering through it.

Then it was almost over. I felt a twinge of anxiousness. I could only see the shoulder of Dinah's blue blouse through the crack, then her fingers sprinkling something from a little dish. Gemma and I withdrew before the doors would open and release the contestants for their break.

Dinah was shaking like a leaf. "I've never been so nervous in all my days," she said, accepting a cup of tea from me as the rest of the contestants and judges helped themselves to a treat. "I've never been in greater need of a cuppa, either." She took a long sip from it.

"I'm sure you've done great," I said, reassuringly.

"It's only a little bite of curd tart, I told myself! I've made a wedding cake for artistic royalty, and made scones for that posh footballer and his model wife," she continued. "But it didn't help none. I only hope I remembered the proper ingredients." She took a bite from one of the shop biscuits, and wrinkled her nose a little.

"I know," I said. "Gemma bought them last minute. She was afraid we might run short." I was beginning to wonder if these were last holiday's biscuit tins only newly-discovered in the back of the shop.

"See if Charlotte can do you some savory biscuits for tomorrow," she said. "Or some of her nice cold roast sandwiches on rolls that the American tourists like so much." She brushed the crumbs from her hands. "I feel quite bad that I'm not allowed to help out in between the challenges. If I could just make a bit of something —"

"We don't want any accusations of cheating," I reminded her. I scanned the room, watching the contestants with their cups of coffee. "Who's your biggest challenge?" I asked.

"Leeman's quite good," said Dinah, quietly. "But the girl in the flower print — name of Emily — she's sharp and precise. If her flavors are as steady as her hands, the rest of us are doomed to fall short."

"We'll see," I said. "They haven't tasted anything yet." I glanced towards the two judges, Harriet Hardy's nose wrinkling as she discreetly disposed of one of the shop biscuits, and Pierre Dupine utterly charming a wide-eyed Gemma as she paused in the midst of refreshing the teapot.

In the ballroom, platters of finished tea dainties awaited the judges. Plate after plate of perfect miniature cakes, scones, and biscuits, garnished with dried fruits or fresh herbs. Harriet Hardy and Pierre Dupine, each armed with a fork, began their verdicts.

The little raspberry tart gleamed like ruby glass in the sunlight as Pierre cut through its surface. Leeman managed not to break into perspiration during the interminable silence that followed as the French judge closed his eyes and chewed his bite.

"Piquant," he said, at last. "Very rich. How you say ... effervescent on the tongue, even." As the judge opened his eyes, Leeman beamed for the benefit of the camera behind the judges.

Harriet Hardy tasted it now. "Too much gelatin, perhaps," she said. "It's very pretty...but it's a bit *chewy*, don't you agree?"

Pierre made a face that, technically, didn't constitute agreement or disagreement in my book. Leeman looked a trifle less confident.

"But I agree that the flavor is, nevertheless, very lovely," said Harriet, afterwards.

"A fine dessert," declared Pierre, at last.

The frog puff pastries from a boy named Gil were somewhat the worse for wear after baking, with overly-browned edges and not enough minty cream inside. And the savory lamb finger sandwiches by Imera in the blue sari produced a debate between Harriet and Pierre regarding too much turmeric. They tasted cranberry biscuits, lemon-lime spritz shortbreads, and glass candy walnut tarts — and, in line with Dinah's shrewd judgment, found flower print-clad Emily's white chocolate ganache and coconut spirals 'delightful' and 'heavenly.'

Dinah's lemon curd tarts were topped with a layer of her signature marmalade, and a tiny sprinkle of candied citrus peel. She was doing her best not to wring the lap of her apron as Harriet Hardy's fork sliced through the pastry crust.

"A very zesty lemon," she said. "The tartness of the marmalade balances it, however."

"It is the *spice* that one notices, not the bitterness," contradicted

Pierre. "It is perhaps too strong, the citrus and the cream, if not for that tiny bit of heat. We must credit a little cinnamon, perhaps."

"Yes, perhaps, but one cannot have both sweet, and the spices are irrelevant without the true citrus neutralizing the sugared cream," said Harriet. "It's the tartness that carries this off. It's well done for that reason alone." She moved on to the next contestant. I could see Dinah breathe a deep sigh of relief as soon as the judges and cameraman were gone.

After the last tasting, the judges withdrew to a separate table to compare notes before releasing each contestant's score. In first place, Emily Pierce. In second place, Leeman Lawson. And in third place, Dinah Barrington.

"I guess Jenny Bryce is disappointed," said Gemma, who was beaming as she applauded — but only after the ballroom door was safely closed again. "Her magic whisk had only landed her in tenth place."

"I think it was the soggy pastry crust that was responsible," I said.

Dinah had survived round one of the competition. If Matt's estimation of human psychology was correct, she stood an excellent chance in round two.

***

Lady Amanda had arranged for the judges to have tea with the lord and lady of the manor — the principal staff was invited, excluding Dinah. As soon as the contest judging was at an end, Gemma and I donned aprons in the kitchen and helped Lady Amanda prepare cucumber sandwiches, buttered bread, mini crab-and-cream scones, and iced petits fours with raspberry filling.

"Thank heavens Dinah had some of these tucked away in the freezer," said Lady Amanda, as she split open the herb-flecked scones. "Gemma, mind the soft spot on that cucumber," she cautioned, as she brushed aside crumbs from the serving platter using the hem of her apron — one printed with a cartoon baby wearing a chef's hat and the words 'future bun baker in the oven.' A joking little gift from Dinah, perhaps.

"Did I get the cream dressing right for the crab?" I asked. "Quick, someone taste it —" I held a spoonful towards Lady Amanda, who waved it away.

"Not now," she said. "Little yet-to-be-named has changed their mind about food. I might send back my lunch if I take a bite."

Gemma stuck the spoon into her mouth. "A little more dill," she said. "And I think Dinah garnishes with rosemary. Do we have any fresh?"

"A little," I said, hastening to add the lumps of flaky white crab to the salad's sauce. "If those cakes are fully thawed, there's some raspberry jam ready to pipe in the pastry bag by the icing."

"Brilliant, Julianne," said Lady Amanda. "My attempts to fill piping bags are always too messy." With energy, she began filling the extra little yellow sponge cakes Dinah had saved after a recent charity luncheon.

Harriet Hardy only ate a bite of her bread and butter, I noticed, and one tiny little cucumber sandwich, while Pierre Dupine ate nothing but two cucumber sandwiches. Sampling a dozen tea treats in advance of the hour itself leaves you without much of an appetite, I suppose. The rest of us tucked in with energy, however, as Lady Amanda poured tea for our guests.

"I hope your stay at Cliffs House has been comfortable thus far," said Lord William. "We can't say how terribly pleased we are to have you. The whole village is thrilled, in case you've missed the rather obvious crowd of observers along the drive."

"We are quite used to crowds," said Pierre. "I fear the program's vans draw them wherever they go. Yours seems a very charming village, though."

"If you can tell us," I said, "what is it about Cornwall — and Ceffylgwyn itself — that impressed the producers to choose us?" I sneaked another crab scone from the platter as I asked this question.

"I believe it was the charming photographs in your proposal. A rather zealous young man presented a sort of scenic slideshow to us, emphasizing the 'magic' of this atmosphere for the program," said Harriet Hardy, who stirred a lump of sugar into her tea.

"I believe that would be the American event promoter," said Geoff, who managed not to smile at this accurate description of Nathan. "He's rather enthusiastic about his work, it seems."

To my right, Kitty snorted at this remark, but said nothing as she picked apart her tea sandwich.

"Your beautiful coast is the true reason," said Pierre. "But it helped, of course, that there is a rather popular program that is here ... you must know what I speak of ..."

"*Poldark*," said all of the women at the table — including Harriet Hardy, I noticed. Her cheeks colored faintly, her expression composing itself behind her teacup, taking another dainty sip. Her intimidating, perfect posture was on display with this gesture — she looked exactly like the picture on the back of her cookbook's jacket, I realized, even twenty-something years after it was taken.

"It is this, yes," said Pierre. "And your village itself is unique. Perhaps not its cuisine — unless I will have the privilege to dine upon something other than the very oily dish I sampled from one of our assistants. It makes the paper wrapped around it very soggy."

I wished that the production assistant had chosen Charlotte's pasties instead of old-fashioned fish and chips. "I suppose English 'fast food' is very different from France's version," I said. "As an American who moved here, I know how different cuisine can seem from country to country."

"True. I remember my first taste of a proper American McDonald's," said Lady Amanda, with a laugh.

"American cuisine is fast," said Pierre. "We have a joke in my city — Americans like the oil, and the English like the boil. Except when it comes to their fish and potatoes, it would seem."

"I think England has produced some of the finest chefs in the world," said Harriet Hardy. "France has always believed itself to possess a monopoly in the world of cuisine, but it's hardly true now."

"That is because the English always believe their good breeding makes them the best," said Pierre. "But in France, we know simply we are the best. It is a simple bite of food which proves it, without words."

"I'm afraid we have the same argument often," said Harriet to the rest of us, apologetically. "We've stumbled into its boundaries once again it would seem. I'm sure you all share my perspective on this, leaving poor Pierre quite in the minority."

"I like French food," piped up Gemma. "Not snails, but, you know, cream puffs."

"Ah, the *patisserie*," said Pierre, with enthusiasm. "That is where we are undisputed masters, surely. The pastry I taste in your country —

forgive me — is heavy and very soft. Sometimes I put my fork into a tart and *voila*, a wet blanket where there should be crispness, lightness, flakiness —"

"I believe what you are tasting, Mr. Dupine, is merely prejudice against British bakers in general," said Harriet, in a steely tone. "It's nonsense — I've tasted the same pastry crusts you have and most of them are equal to any Paris patisserie I have visited —"

" — and even in Paris, there is *patisserie* invaded by English cooking," said Pierre, scornfully.

It was just like the arguments they had during the northern competition's episodes of The Grand Baking Extravaganza. I was amazed — it was surreal that it was happening in Lord William and Lady Amanda's private parlor, with her mum's best tea service on the table and an awkward audience of estate employees.

"More tea, anyone?" said Lady Amanda.

***

Dinah's cottage was a small one tucked in a street mostly converted into flats and lease properties — a small, remodeled, painted one that seemed to have retreated beneath the shade of a nearby tree and some very thick shrubbery. I made my way up its stone pathway, taking care not to jam the heel of my Prada shoes in the cracks between, and rang Dinah's bell.

Day two of the competition was tomorrow — the grand biscuit challenge. I had seen the dossier for the challenge, which required contestants to build a 'gingerbread scene' with at least four separate elements involved. No ordinary gingerbread house would do, apparently; I knew that past competitors had built amazing biscuit creations, including Santa's workshop made from chocolate shortbread, and a Swiss ski lodge from savory rye and white cheddar biscuits.

No one came, so I rang it again. Just when I had given in to the assumption that Dinah had gone to the market, the door opened. On the other side, a slightly disheveled Dinah in a frosting-splattered apron greeted me.

"Quite sorry," she said. "I'm afraid I had just dozed off. Come in, Julianne." I stepped inside and found the 'slight mess' of Dinah's kitchen had found its way into her sitting room. Scissored-through cardboard boxes were piled on an armchair, while sheet after sheet of large paper draped itself across a little study table, where I was fairly certain a geometry compass was driven through them rather savagely, pinning them to the table. A fine dusting of icing sugar on the table, the floor, and a nearby needlepoint throw pillow completed the look.

"Cuppa?" Dinah asked. Despite looking and sounding tired, she managed a note of cheeriness beneath it. "My teapot is here somewhere." She stepped through to the kitchen and rummaged beneath a pile of tea towels and empty flour sacks.

"I just wanted to stop by and see how things are going," I said. "I don't want to disturb you while you're working — I know you're probably really busy practicing —" I noticed the sheets of paper had blueprint sketches on them for Dinah's gingerbread creation. It looked like a castle, possibly.

"I've been working since yesterday afternoon," she answered, with a weary chuckle. "Practically from the moment judging ended on the first, if you can believe that." She had located her tea pot, its cozy's yarn bobble sticking out from beneath a pile of dirty pots and pans. Brushing off some flour, she removed its lid and turned on the cold water tap in the sink.

"Third place, though," I said. "That's amazing, Dinah."

"Rubbish. It was too simple," she said. "It was written all over their faces. I was being far too safe by choosing a curd tart. You saw Leeman's creations — looked like a proper patisserie window, they did. And as for that girl Emily —" she poured water from the kettle into the newly-tidied teapot, " — well, all I can say is, I'm lucky to still be in this thing at all. I'll have to work twice as hard at the biscuit competition if I want a chance."

"I'm sure whatever you're designing is brilliant," I said. "On par with any masterpiece you've created in the manor's kitchen. And you've got a whole day to figure it out, and practically a whole day to complete it in the competition."

Dinah was still frozen at the counter, her hand on the teapot. "I've a bit of a problem with that," she said, at last. Her voice sounded funny.

"What is it?" I asked, concerned. Maybe Dinah's gingerbread design was at a creative roadblock already.

"Have you read the rules for the bake?" she asked.

"Not exactly. I know it's ginger biscuits and construction," I said. "Is there a complication? Some trick behind the assignment?" I imagined that Pierre and Harriet were more than capable of coming up with an extra 'twist' that would cause contestants to scramble to the finish.

"Sort of. They told us beforehand, and I thought my sister and a friend of hers was coming from Leeds. I used to always make a proper gingerbread with her at Christmas....it's a group bake, you see," she said, looking at me. "I'm supposed to have helpers, and assign things for them to do. Part of testing a baker's ability to delegate and unify, I suppose."

Which Dinah could do blindfolded with one hand tied behind her back, I knew; but the judges of The Grand Baking Extravaganza didn't. "What happened to your sister?" I asked.

"Not coming. Her little grandson has the flu, and her daughter and son in law both work," said Dinah. "There goes my crew — felled by germs, for there's no one else to look after the lad. I'll have to tell the judges that I can do it on my own, and see if they'll bend the rules."

"No, you won't," I said. "Dinah, we'll be your crew."

"I couldn't ask it," she said.

"You don't have to ask," I said. "It's already done. You honestly can't think any one of us would leave you stranded in a situation like this?"

"Lady Amanda's already having to make do without a cook while the place is crawling in visitors needing refreshments," Dinah argued. "And there's loads of summer visitors besides, which means there's already a dozen maintenance tasks for everyone."

"And none of that will matter if it waits a day," I said. "All you have to do is assign us our part. And since you've done that dozens of times in the past, what could be better?" I brushed some cinnamon from the nearest chair and sat down.

"It's a great deal to ask," said Dinah, reluctantly.

"You didn't ask, remember?" I said. "Now, show me your designs." I reached for the sketchpad behind the tower of spices.

Gemma volunteered instantly, of course. "Not help Dinah win?" she said. "That *would* be a load of rubbish, wouldn't it? 'Course, I'm rubbish at baking," she admitted. "I burn biscuits at home all the time. But I can always pipe, of course." She swept the carrots she was chopping into the soup pot — soup was on the menu pretty much every day without Dinah here to bake savories for the Extravaganza's crew.

"And so can I," I said. "And I'll brave the baking part — just don't ask me to mix up the ingredients." I still remembered my bland-tasting treacle pudding from last week. "Kitty, you know how to bake, don't you?" Her previous job had been at Charlotte Jones's shop, where I was sure she must've spent as much time turning out Cornish pasties as she did frying fish and chips.

"A bit," said Kitty. "Charlotte taught me to make the pastry. It wasn't my strong suit, really."

"But you'll do it?"

"'Course I will," said Kitty, in her usual scornful tone. "I'm not heartless. "

"It will be good enough, I'm sure," said Lady Amanda. "All hands on deck for this one, including me — I'm sure there's no conflict of interest, is there?"

"Actually, there probably is," I said. "We need someone else, just so the producers can't say that the estate was favoring one of their own, for instance."

"Geoff. He makes vol-au-vents for the New Year's party," said Gemma.

"I don't think Geoff would agree to appear on a television program, even for Dinah's sake," I said. "Besides, he's helping Lord William with the new field fences — and Lord William, of course, is yet another conflict of interest, so we can't ask him, either."

"Oh, heavens, we will be on the telly, won't we?" Gemma flushed several shades of pink and red. "I can't be on a program — I haven't had me nails done in weeks!"

"With a bit of luck, nobody at home'll notice," said Kitty, dryly. Unlike Pippa, Gemma took the high road and ignored Kitty's remark. I could see her flushed cheeks, however, as she confiscated Kitty's newly-chopped potatoes and dumped them into the soup with a trifle more force than necessary. Even after two months, Kitty and Gemma hadn't become friends in the manner of the original Cliffs House duo.

"What about him?" said Lady Amanda. She was looking through the window, where a man was standing in our garden. *Matthew*, I thought, who was a master of treacle pudding and decent meat pies at home. Only it wasn't him — it was a figure in a suit, talking on a mobile phone.

"Him?" said Kitty.

Lady Amanda opened the window. "A word, Mr. Menton," she said. He turned towards her, then turned off his phone call and approached.

"Lady Amanda?" he said. "What can I do for you?"

"You can don an apron tomorrow morning and help out Dinah in the contest," she said, smiling brightly.

"Um ... what?" he said. His smile became a puzzled one.

"Please, Nathan," I said. "All you have to do is take a few simple directions from Dinah — just cut some cookies out of some dough, probably. She needs some volunteers for her team if she wants to stay in it."

"You do have an afternoon to spare, don't you?" said Lady Amanda.

Nathan looked as cornered as a mouse in a live trap. I could tell he was desperate to think of an excuse to get out of saying 'yes' ... but even with his awkward body language signals, he wasn't quite escaping this one. After all, it had been his idea to bring the baking contest here in the first place — and to leave part of Cliffs House in a lurch after all his talk of fondness would be nearly impossible.

"We're all chipping in," said Gemma. "Even Kitty, for all her prickly ways." She shot an arch glance in Kitty's direction, where Kitty was pretending suddenly to be very hard at work chopping up leeks. I could see the event promoter was wavering.

"Please, Nathan," I said.

***

Challenge number two took place in Cliffs House's grand dining hall — an impressive room that generally hosted luncheons for conferences, not baking challenges. But now, with the massive mahogany table and damask chairs removed, it played host to the signature rows of white-clad tables, colorful stand mixers, and mounds and rolls of gingerbread dough.

The contestants had teams of friends and family with them — no more than four were allowed to a baker. Dinah had exactly four: me, Gemma,

Kitty, and Nathan.

Dinah's blueprints unfurled across the table like a massive treasure map. "This is it," she said. "I call it, 'the Grand Cornish Castle.' It's based on a print in a book I had as a little girl, actually," she added, with a slight blush. "I always loved it. This one's made up of a lot of pieces — but there's a whole afternoon, so it won't be impossible."

We were all gathered around, wearing logo-printed aprons provided by the program, staring at a sketch of a towering, multi-tiered gingerbread castle with jagged towers that looked as imposing as the snow queen's fortress. A large dragon with biscuit wings inserted on his back was partway wrapped around it, and a row of horseback knights filed from its open drawbridge.

It was massive, impressive ... and maybe a tiny bit ambitious for a crew of relatively inexperienced bakers? I felt a tiny wish dawn inside of me that Dinah's sister would suddenly show up with her magic gingerbread skills.

"It'll be simple enough," said Dinah, reassuringly. "I've got the recipe here for the dough, and all the spices and dry goods are measured out in these bags. I'll need someone to mix and to bake, to make the construction icing, and some to help assemble the smaller pieces. I'm going to cut the pieces out myself, and put the main pieces together." As she spoke, she removed a series of cardboard templates from her bag, a lot of complicated pieces that reminded me of a jigsaw — the only ones I remotely recognized on their own was a dragon's head and a miniature horse.

"I'll bake," I said, hastily. I was more adept at not burning stuff, in my estimation. And construction gingerbread was meant to be crisp, right? "Gemma can mix," I added, since I knew her dread of burned baked goods.

"If she can make the construction frosting, that would be lovely," said Dinah. "You always make good icing, love," she said to Gemma.

"I can roll out dough," said Kitty, who was pinning her dark curls up as she spoke. "I've got a strong arm, Charlotte always said."

Now Nathan snorted. "Really?" he said, raising one eyebrow.

"What's that supposed to mean?" said Kitty.

"That I'm looking at a skinny arm in that sleeve —"

"I'll need you two on the assembly line," interrupted Dinah. Her drill sergeant self in the kitchen was back now, taking charge in a way that had been missing these past few weeks at Cliffs House. "There's the horse and the knights, and the little stands that hold them up.

"Assemble things?" said Nathan. "You mean stuff that will actually be on display?"

"Well, I don't mean to hide it under the table, no," said Dinah. "It'll be simple. Mix a bit of frosting and put them together. Gemma will be doing the decorative piping on those, and I'll be doing the castle, and the head of the dragon."

"Attention, everyone," said Pierre Dupine. The room fell silent, suddenly. The camera crew was in place, making us all terribly self-conscious as the little red power lights became noticeable, and the judges took their places for opening the challenge. I wondered if the stubborn little frizzy curl I hadn't been able to tame this morning was sticking up on the crown of my head, but I couldn't bring myself to find out. Beside me, Gemma pasted on her best close-lipped magazine smile. Even Kitty made a self-conscious swipe towards her makeshift hair knot, as if to check it. I couldn't help but notice that she was wearing a touch of lipstick today.

"We have seen your blueprints and your templates," Pierre said. "We have confirmed your designs and your assistants. Now you will have until five o' clock to bring your creations into fruition. We wish you luck."

The bell sounded for the challenge's beginning. Gemma turned on one of the mixers and began creaming butter and sugar. Around us, the room was alive with the hum of electric motors and the scent of cinnamon and cloves as all of the teams sprang into action.

***

Dear Diary,

There I go with that corny introduction again. You're not real, you're just a diary, so I have to stop addressing you like you're a person.

I had a dream last night that I was being attacked by gingerbread men. I think it was inspired by Dinah's sketches of her imposing gingerbread castle, which looks like something that gingerbread Game of Thrones characters would probably live in. Dinah is in the top five, so we're hoping to help her advance. Of course, I don't know anything about baking, but Gemma's been Dinah's assistant forever — and Kitty knows a thing or two, not that she's willing to admit it. I think she's forgotten how well I know Charlotte Jones.

Then again, I think Kitty's always afraid that everybody knows about her past.

— Julianne

***

Kitty:

"Any clue what you're doing?" I asked Nathan.

"Of course," he said. "Relax. I've baked before."

"Frozen dinner trays?"

"No," he answered, sarcastically. "I used to help my grandma make gingerbread cookies." He paused. "Well, I used to help cut them out and put sprinkles on them, anyway. So practically baking, right?"

He cracked a smile for his joke. I didn't, but only because I was too busy trying to get the edges just right as we cut little horses out of the sticky dough. When it got a bit warm, it tended to tear, so I was having to chill little rounds of it in between cutting. After my second horse tore in half, I wadded the rolled dough into a ball and swapped it once more.

"Let me." Nathan rolled up his shirtsleeves and reached for the rolling pin. "We'll save your strong arm for after I'm worn out."

"Right."

"You can talk to me, you know," he said. "I don't bite. I know *you* do, but I'm willing to put up with that."

The teeniest edge of a smile now. I couldn't help it, really. "I don't bite," I said. "I just don't have much patience with prats. There's always plenty of them about. I guess I tend to think of everyone that way. Not exactly fair, I know."

He didn't say anything now. But the dough was more or less a thick oval waiting for cutting at this point, so maybe silence was better.

"I can see baking as a nice hobby," he said, laying a knight on the baking sheet. "You know, maybe learn how to knead bread. Roll out pasta. I love fettuccine, tortellini."

"Those aren't baked pastas."

"Did I say 'bake'? I meant 'cook.' Boiling stuff, baking stuff. It's all good." He laid another knight beside the first.

"Further apart," I pointed out.

"Why?"

"So they don't grow together in the oven," I said. "They'll spread. Even after chilling."

"Right," he said. He moved it an inch to the side, and it tore in half across its middle. I bit back a smile and kept cutting horses as Nathan's cheek twitched with irritation. He wadded his biscuit into a ball and started again.

"So, do you bake? Boil? Cook in any form?" he asked.

I shrugged. "No one bakes in my house," I said. "Mum's a bit of a processed foods nut. I'm never home long enough to care whether there's flour or sugar in the cupboards."

"Somebody told me you worked in the pasty shop in the village, though," he said.

"Why did they tell you that?" A tiny bit of suspicion in my voice — can't help it, honestly, since my ears are usually burning from village gossip about Kitty Alderson's checkered past.

"Um...uh...it came up in conversation," he said. "We were talking, and something was said about your old job. Where you worked before you worked here."

"Oh."

"Nothing bad, I swear," he said. "Julianne was talking about how your potential was getting lost behind a fish fryer until you found your calling as an event planner in training."

"More like she found it for me," I said, half-muttering. I paused in cutting. "That is ... Julianne gave me a shot. Not many in this village would do the same. I figure you can guess the reasons why."

He laughed a little. "I'm not as connected to the village grapevine as you think I am." He cut another cookie. "Does 'grapevine' have the same meaning over here?"

I glanced towards Julianne, who was busy trimming the rough edges of Dinah's gingerbread castle. I had hoped that Dinah would assign me to work with her — or work with Gemma, even — rather than stick me in this situation.

Nathan broke the silence. "I'm trying to end the tension," he said.

"What tension?"

"Very funny," he answered. "I'm just trying to be friendly. Nice. I thought maybe since we work together sometimes, we could have a civil conversation."

"About the cooking skills we don't have, eh?"

He sighed with frustration. "You know, you don't have to be such a —"

"Relax. I'm kidding." I broke into a grin — pretty rare for me — and gave him a look. "Talking's fine. I don't dislike you. I don't even know you, so how could I?"

"You are a very weird girl," he said. But in a way that sounded like my mate's brother when he talked to his sis — not the way he talked to her annoying friends. There's a difference.

"And you're cutting your knight's arm off."

"Oh. Hm. I'll just kind of smush it back on him. There."

That would never hold, but I didn't tell him.

After cutting, we helped mix more dough, then more icing, as the biscuits chilled again. Two hours had already passed, and it was time for the midday break before the second half of the challenge. And with four times the crowd in the sitting room, that was a long line and a quick cuppa.

"Where's Dinah?" said Gemma, who had snagged one of Charlotte's buns from the trays that Lady Amanda was hastening to refresh.

"Still working on the castle," said Julianne. "It's still threatening to topple on one side."

"What about the dragon?" said Gemma. She lowered her voice. "It's a bit complicated, isn't it? How will she ever get it to stand upright?"

I had seen Dinah's drawings, and it looked tough. But I'd also seen the other competitors — one of them building a gingerbread replica of Whitehall, even. Dinah had looked quite rattled for a second when she saw it.

Ten minutes after break, Julianne baked the biscuits me and Nathan had cut. Rows of little horses and knights, fresh from the oven, were cooling in front of oscillating fans — some were a bit burnt, but not badly. I mixed decorative icing for piping as Gemma mixed construction icing for Dinah's towering castle — Julianne was holding up one of those tricky pointed towers as Dinah tried to cement it in place with the hardening sugar paste.

The little knights and horses were merely piped outlines with a bit of fancy work where the armor should be. Dinah showed me how, and put one together for me and Nathan as Gemma piled the cooled gingerbread cookies beside us.

"This should be simple." Nathan lifted a bag of construction icing and snipped its tip. A little big, but it would do, so I didn't point out that he'd be shooting great gobs of frosting on his target.

"It takes a lot of icing to hold these together," he said, as he glued a knight to the horse along the little space between the knight's legs, then glued the horse to its stand. "He looks like he's wading through the snow."

"Just keep gluing," I said. Dinah would probably fix that part later. Besides, it was closing upon two o' clock, and we only had a quarter of our army glued together properly.

"I'm gluing," he said. "Only they're falling apart." One soldier slid off his horse and lay sideways in the clotted icing, like a Norman conqueror fallen in the snow — just like a picture I remembered in an old history book of my gran's.

"Hold him together," I said. "I'll put a bit more icing around its feet."

"I think the horse's feet snapped off," said Nathan. "It'll be shorter than the rest."

"It's a pony, then." Something was wrong with this icing, obviously. Gemma must have mixed up the wet ingredients when compounding it.

"Darn. I killed another one." Nathan's soldier had snapped in half at the knees. He looked a bit depressed — Nathan and the soldier — as the biscuit pieces fell amongst the globs of icing. I snorted back a laugh. It really oughtn't be funny that everything was going wrong.

"I'm mixing up new icing," I said, dumping ingredients in the bowl as I spoke. "This stuff will never hold. Pipe some design on those last soldiers while I'm working."

"Hold on. Whoa. I'm not a decorator," he said. "I don't pretend to have any knowledge about glitter glue or scrapbooking, so I'm not the person to ask to dress up toy knights with frosting."

"It's just a few lines and squiggly bits," I said. "And you've got to do it, because we're running out of time, and there's still the dragon to finish."

The dragon, thus far, was nothing but a three-sided biscuit frame with lots of scaly things piped on it. Dinah was trying to attach its tail, which didn't want to go on it, but simply fell over on the newly-piped moat door instead.

Nathan looked doubtfully at the piping bag I handed him, as if it contained a snake instead of frosting. With a grimace, he put a bit on the coat of the nearest knight.

He wasn't bad at it, really. He drew nice little lines that looked almost like proper chain mail. Even a little sword belt and sheath outline on one, instead of the little curly things and rivets we'd been painting on the rest.

Bite your tongue, Kitty. If I said a word, he'd probably muck up the rest of the lot due to stupid masculine pride or something, and we needed every good bit coming our way. One table away, the little gingerbread carousel now had multicolored biscuit animals circling its turning post. Leeman Lawson's legendary signature design, as all Ceffylgwyn knew.

"What's this piece for?" Nathan said, lifting an odd-shaped long gingerbread biscuit from the pile. "This one spread way, way out of control. I think it must be two or three cookies in one."

The 'cookie' sagged a bit, then snapped in half. Nathan looked startled. I couldn't help the laugh that escaped me.

"It's an extra piece," said Nathan. "I'm sure. We'll just toss it or something."

"It's not ours ... oh, blast it, it's the *dragon's*," I said, dropping my voice to a hush. I heard a gasp from Gemma just then — but it was for a castle tower that attempted a nosedive.

"Hold it up, quick now!" said Dinah, who leaped to its rescue. None of them noticed the two of us and the broken bits in Nathan's hands.

"What part?" he said to me. "This doesn't look like a dragon in any way, shape, or form."

"I dunno. It's the neck, or a bit of a leg or something, but that's what it is," I said. "Dinah's not even begun the part of it that's supposed to be upright."

"No problem. Nope," said Nathan. "We'll just glue it back together." He flipped the pieces over, and I put some glue along the seam.

"It's oozing out the front."

"She'll cover that part with decoration," he said. "Put a lot on there."

"She'll kill us, you know. The dragon's the important part of all this."

"It'll be fine," said Nathan. "Just let it dry a little." He grabbed the fan and held it close to the frosting.

The glue might have held the pieces together — but it also fastened them to the parchment below. I heard a ripping sound as we tried to peel it away a minute later, and then a *snap* as another piece of the biscuit came free.

We were huddled too close for my comfort, pressed even closer when he reached for the frosting bag again. I could feel Nathan brushing up against me by accident, and noticed there was a decent bit of muscle evident beneath his rolled sleeve — I admitted to myself that he was probably better at rolling gingerbread. The dining room felt terribly hot, suddenly, from all the ovens crisping the gingerbread. I edged away from Nathan a little.

"Darn," said Nathan, who was trying to peel the bits of paper off now. "Quick, get some more icing —"

"What is that?" said Dinah. "What are you two — oh, for heaven's sake! Put that down," she said to Nathan. Her eyes were wide as saucers at the sight of our handiwork on the dragon's missing part.

"I'm sure it can be fixed," he began.

"It's in three pieces!" she said. She closed her eyes. "Never mind it — we'll salvage what we can. Hand me a knife," she said to me. "We'll shorten his neck and see what else can be done." She sliced away the jagged edges, reshaping the pieces.

The dragon ended up with gills extending from its face, and a neck that now hugged around the castle rather than towered above it. It was Dinah's piping and a bit of extra shaping on the leftover pieces that saved it. Plus, the nice curly tail had managed not to break.

"Soldiers in a line," panted Dinah. "Two by two out of the moat.

Quick now," she said, glancing over her shoulder at the clock: a quarter to five. She swept away the bits of icing left around the castle.

It looked a treat, especially the massive dragon. But it didn't stand a chance against the working carousel, we all knew, as we watched the little colored animals turn to the sound of a music box tune. And maybe not against the toy box or the gingerbread lighthouse that Jenny Bryce was sitting smugly behind.

"It's practically cheating," muttered Gemma under her breath. "Leeman used to build that same carousel every year for his shop window. He used a set of shop biscuit cutters, too."

I saw icing on the bridge of her nose, and wondered if she knew the camera was on us right now. At the same time, I felt something brush against my hair — Nathan's fingers were responsible.

"Just a little frosting," he said. "Thought I'd take care of it for you." He hadn't bothered to clean the icing sugar from his own person yet, I was tempted to point out to him.

Dinah's dragon was good enough for fourth, even beating the pirate ship made by the boy whose frogs had turned into burnt little lumps last round. Fourth was good enough, judging from her relief when the judges announced it. The rest of us had a proper cheer when it was announced, and got crushed into the fold of a group hug by Julianne.

***

Julianne:

"A little more to the left," I told Kitty. "There. That's got it."

Now that the grand biscuit faceoff was over, we were rearranging the dining room's tables to take up less space without teams to occupy them. I had assumed we'd simply have them moved until the day of the final challenge — but that wasn't what the producers had in mind.

"Gemma was a little hard on Leeman Lawson's carousel," I said, as we straightened the tablecloths. "I don't think it's necessarily cheating since it's really his own design."

"It's only because Leeman was a bit of a snob in the village," said Kitty. "He rubbed in the fact that his recipes were the best, and always said he'd take his secrets to the grave. But his carousel was always a proper job. When I was a kid, he used to put it in the bakery window every spring. I wasn't even as tall as me mum's knees, so she'd lift me up to see it."

A nice memory, I thought. Leeman might have held up his nose a little too high for Ceffylgwyn, but it hadn't prevented his skills from making others happy — and he wasn't in the grave yet, so maybe there was still time for him to share his secrets. Not that winning The Grand Baking Extravaganza would encourage him to do it, I imagined.

"Need a hand?" Nathan, who had appeared unnoticed, seized the other end of a table that Kitty, with a grunt, had begun moving aside.

"I've got it," said Kitty, who was grasping both corners. Her stubborn tone was back, even though its conviction was lacking a little.

"Which way?" said Nathan. "Towards the windows, right?" He lifted one end and carried it as Kitty and I carried the other.

"Thank you," I said. "And to what do we owe the honor of your visit? I thought you'd avoid us a little after the dragon mishap." Nathan actually blushed for a moment, then recovered himself.

"Nothing," he said, as he helped shove the table into place. "I'm just here to check in with the production crew before they get started today. They promised some commercial footage would be ready for the tourism board to review. If people don't see proof that Cornwall is the latest home of the Baking Extravaganza, then we can't sell fans on visiting here, right?"

Kitty and I exchanged glances. "What's the production crew doing today?" I asked.

"You didn't hear yet? They summoned all the contestants to be here in two hours. The crew will be here any minute." He checked his watch. "Something about whenever there's an extra day between the second and third challenges, there's always a pop quiz bake, or something."

I knew it. "Any idea what they have in store?" I asked.

He grinned. "It wouldn't be a surprise then, would it?" he said. "Speaking of surprises, do you know anything about the Minack Theatre?"

"Of course," I said. "Anybody's who's lived in Cornwall for more than a few weeks knows about the amphitheatre on the sea."

The Minack Theatre possessed a view breathtaking enough to rival my beloved view which gave Cliffs House its name, as impossible as this confession seems. I had been there once before with Matt, and had been dazzled by the soft horizon at nightfall, and the ancient grandeur its modern stonework conveyed. It created a harmony between history and nature that seemed alive during that concert, with me and Matt under the stars and facing the sea, with imaginations capable of transforming those stones into a castle's ruins, or a second Stonehenge.

"Well, my next paying gig — pardon the distinction — is some tourism promotion work for one of their upcoming events. Anyway, they gave me a couple of tickets to something they're having tomorrow night, and I thought maybe I'd let you have them, if you and your husband are interested."

"We'd love them," I said. "But I really can't. I'm still helping fill Dinah's shoes around here until the end of the week. Besides, you should go. It's worth seeing, trust me."

"It's not that I'm not a theatre lover," he said. "It's just that I thought maybe somebody else would enjoy it more than a guy sitting alone on some stone bleachers." He looked at Kitty. "Unless maybe ... you'd like to see the show?"

Two spots of pink had invaded Kitty's cheeks during this conversation — a quick flash of color I'd seen appear more than once whenever people talked about theatre and performance art.

"If you're not busy, then think about it. I could pick you up tomorrow afternoon," he said. "I've got a little meeting with the manager, then it's basically showtime. Very good seats, I've been told."

"I've got things covered here," I supplied. Which wasn't even remotely true, of course — but that was beside the point.

A long pause of debate lapsed. "I guess," said Kitty, at its end. "I've never been there, so seeing it might be worth the ride."

"Great," said Nathan. "I'll see you then. I'll text you about the when and where."

I was careful not to say anything as Kitty and I went back to moving tables. Somehow, I had a feeling this would be the wrong moment to make any sort of remark about this decision. And something in Kitty's face and body language made me fairly certain she was doing her best to be totally indifferent about having said 'yes,' even though she would never admit it.

Then again, I was pretty sure Nathan's nonchalance about her accepting the ticket was fake, too. But who was I to make that claim? If I were, then I would have known that the doors to the dining room were about to open and admit twelve very nervous contestants.

"Most of you are quite aware of the nature of our surprise events." Harriet Hardy was the sole judge present for the introductory part of this challenge, as was customary for the surprise bake. "You will open the envelopes in front of you, and will have one hour to complete a recipe — from memory — which fits the requirement inside."

Twelve white envelopes had been laid on each of the tables. Inside would be a card printed with a single phrase — but with a difficult surprise twist. Not just 'Victoria sponge,' but 'Victoria and Albert sponge,' for instance; or 'crown and cake.' It was up to the contestants to make something of it, with the blindly-chosen ingredients they had brought to the challenge.

The cameras were rolling, so I couldn't get close enough to see what the card inside said. Instead, I saw a flurry of cards dropped on the counter as bakers dove for their baskets of supplies.

Bowls beneath mixing beaters, clouds of flour, cartons of eggs. I saw Dinah rummaging through her basket, the color draining from her face as she paused. I felt my blood chill a little at the possible reasons for this.

The challenge was a soufflé. Not just any soufflé, but a fruit-themed one. The card simply read 'pink fruit' for its description of the dish. Bakers made a mad dash to cobble creations out of extracts instead of fresh fruit, or make sauces with dried fruits and food dye. Some of the creations which emerged from the ovens looked more like bulbous, hideous science experiments than dishes fit for human consumption.

This is why the 'pop quiz' bake, as Nathan called it, is a dreaded Baking Extravaganza event.

First up was Emily's. It was studded with tiny little flecks of dried fruit, and had a strawberry sauce to spoon over its top, which Pierre and Harriet both claimed didn't taste too artificial.

Second, the boy whose frogs and pirate gingerbread ship had been noteworthy for different reasons. His was a perfectly puffed soufflé dyed a very pale shade of pink — with a 'surprise' citrus flavor that pleased the judges.

Next, Dinah's.

Even before Harriet's fork sank into its top, I could see something had gone wrong. The top was dipped below the rim of the soufflé dish. The whole dessert seemed to list to one side, and was far too pale for one of Dinah's usual soufflés. Even the clear red-pink syrup served beside it wouldn't fix that.

"It has fallen," said Pierre, with a *tsk* of sympathy.

"I think it's never risen," said Harriet, suspiciously. "I think it's missing an ingredient or two. Look at that pale texture," she said, splitting it open further. "And the sauce is the only shade of pink and the only fruit flavor we're getting with this one."

"Yes, but the card simply says *'fruit and pink.'* It does not say how much. And the edge, look at the edge — it has risen a little, no? It has sunken. That is the mark of an improper oven temperature."

"Surely you don't think there's a proper rising agent in this? And that sauce —"

"Ah, but it is that overripe fruit taste that you English cooks love, is it not?"

Dinah came in ninth place. The only soufflés which fared worse were the neon pink one, the explosive one that was oozing from its baking dish, and the undercooked one that was practically soup inside. Poor Leeman Lawson came in eighth, while the magic of Jenny Bryce's new whisk finally paid off with a first place finish.

***

After the surprise challenge, Dinah barricaded herself in her cottage for the rest of the day. She didn't answer the door, and didn't answer her mobile when any of us called to make sure she wasn't giving up. Dinah couldn't and *wouldn't,* we knew ... but what we didn't know was how she was planning to face the final challenge.

"Made a proper mess of it, I did," she muttered, as she had packed up her remaining ingredients. "There were too few eggs. Harriet Hardy wasn't wrong about that — and I'd nothing of fruit in my basket except a bottle of cherry extract and a bit of cordial, wouldn't you know? I couldn't have done much worse if I had brought a poke with a pig's head in it."

"Don't be so hard on yourself," I soothed. "You've been in the top five before, and you can do it again. Besides, at least Pierre thought your flavors were nice."

"Like scrambled eggs with jam, I'll wager," said Dinah. She had scraped the soufflé into the garbage with considerable vigor. "I'll not have any of that again. What a mess, what an utter disaster."

No reassuring words would end her self-scolding. And now even Geoff and Gemma hadn't a clue what Dinah was doing to win back her old confidence.

"I'm not coming out again until I know I can make myself proud in the final," she had told them. "That's all I can do. And I'm going to work as hard as is necessary to do it." And with that, she had ended contact with the outside world for the time being.

I sought out Gemma for further updates, but she was busy helping clean the breakfast parlor. There was nobody in the kitchen except for Pierre Dupine, who was in the midst of making bread.

Various mixing bowls were on the table, along with a canister of flour, a bottle of oil, and a cutting board sprinkled with fresh herbs. The French chef's sleeves were rolled above his elbows, his arms and hands coated in flour as he kneaded a large wad of dough on the table's surface. There was even flour flecked here and there in the weathered ridges of his face.

"Sorry," I said. "I didn't realize someone was using the kitchen." I turned to go, but I heard him speak.

"Stay, stay," he said. "It is fine. It is bread, not a private affair." He smiled. "I bake when I wish to clear my head — and my palate — between judging. Come, do whatever you wished. It will not be an intrusion."

"I was going to make a cup of tea," I said. "Want one?"

His smile changed subtly — one of humor, I thought, from the spark in his eyes. "You English and your tea," he said. "I have had to learn to acquire a taste for having it served at many unusual times of day."

"I'm not English," I reminded him.

"Ah, but you are," he said. "In the heart." He tapped one flour-stained finger against his chest, but his eye was on my ring finger. "Or am I wrong about your *mariage*?"

I blushed. "You're correct," I said. "I'm married to the estate's former gardener, actually." I turned the heat on beneath the kettle, and took two everyday teacups from the nearby shelf.

"Love...patriotism...food. They all have the same root. But which is stronger?" he asked. "Some would say love. It can make a person leave the other two behind. You live in England, no? You drink tea instead of your beloved coffee, and give up your doughnuts for biscuits."

I had lifted down a tin I had kept hidden behind a box of rice, one which held several cherry pistachio snaps that Dinah had frozen after a ladies' luncheon. "I do miss doughnuts," I admitted. "And I miss America. But I love Matt...and I think we'll always find a way to compromise, and share each others' worlds." As we talked, I posed the biscuits neatly on the plate, the way Gemma did at tea.

"As for myself," said Pierre, who twisted his dough into a beautifully complex shape with one hand, "I think about love when I cook. But I think there are passions stronger than love. And when there are — there is no easy compromise, perhaps. Then what does one do?"

"I don't know," I said. "I guess I've never thought about it." I placed the plate on the table. "Have you?"

I remembered that neither of the Baking Extravaganza's judges was married. It was surprising, given that they were both talented, famous, and fairly attractive — a baker as handsome as Pierre, up to his elbows in delicious, aromatic dough, would surely have caused more than one female French chef to swoon.

"Often," he answered. "Bread makes me very philosophical, you would say. One could solve the world's problems, perhaps, if all its leaders would only bake bread." The spark in his eye became a twinkle with these words. In one quick motion, he popped the beautiful globe of dough in his hands into a bowl. Carefully, he covered the top with a little cling film, then with a cotton cloth.

"As my mother did, long ago," he said. "Only without the *plastique* underneath."

I poured the kettle into the waiting teapot, then poured a cup of tea and handed it to him. "You must really love cooking," I said. "So do you love judging other people's dishes, too? Especially English ones?"

He laughed. "I must do something to get out of my restaurant now and then," he said. "An old friend asked me if I would do this. I obliged. It is a good adventure. And even when the food is not the same ... the passion is. You understand?"

"I think so," I said. I took a biscuit from the plate, then nudged it closer to Pierre. I dunked my own in my teacup before taking a bite. Pierre reached for one and snapped a piece out of it. He inspected it between his fingers, his expression the same serious one from the television program, before he took a bite.

I waited a long time as he tasted it. At last, Pierre spoke.

"Rich...delicate...and not too sweet," he said. "This baker should be proud of their biscuit. Its simplicity is deceptive. I would give it a place in a patisserie showcase."

"Would you?" I said. "Would you say its baker is ... let's say ... worthy of top marks in The Grand Baking Extravaganza?"

"Worthy of winning, you ask?" The knowing twinkle in Pierre's eyes grew brighter. "I would agree that it is so."

"Have another, then." I took a sip of my tea.

Matt was in the newly-planted herb garden, trimming the bug-damaged stems and leaves when I found him. His figure was outlined in the fierce light before sunset, with the coastal wind ruffling his dark hair as he lifted his gaze and smiled at my approach. Studying his features, the ruddy, swarthy touch of the sun, I imagined that Pierre Dupine's face was similar to what Matt's would be in twenty years, with creases along his brow and a touch of white in his dark hair ... but I stopped myself before this fantasy had Matt and I as pensioners kneading bread together in a tiny French village boulangerie.

"Are you only just now finished?" he asked, pocketing his plant shears. "I thought they cleared away the dining room crowd long ago."

"I was doing some covert research," I said, nestling against him as I laid my head on his shoulder.

"Then shall we be homeward bound?" he said. "We could try out a new dish, a bit of a challenge for your budding skills. Pierre Dupine has a recipe for two-bird roast, which I found online this morning. There's a quail and a chicken in our fridge ... and a bit of liver paste that would mould nicely with some veg for the innermost stuffing."

Eerie coincidence? I found myself giggling at the thought. "No, thanks," I said. "It's too soon after the treacle pudding incident. I think I'd like to postpone my cooking resolution temporarily in favor of scrambled eggs."

"Then let us go toast some bread instead." His arm wrapped itself around my shoulders as we took the long way to the manor's driveway by way of the cliffs path.

I wondered if Matt would bake a loaf of bread tonight if I asked him. Just curious.

***

Dinah's campaign of silence continued along with her effort to restore her confidence in her talents. From outside her cottage, the three of us — Geoff, Gemma, and me — stood beneath Geoff's umbrella on a drizzly morning and watched Dinah through her kitchen's window glass.

She took no notice of us as she thumbed through various notebooks and recipe cards, pounding something with a pestle, tasting it with a shake of her head, then turning to slice something paper-thin at her cutting board, tossing it into a little pot on the stove.

"It's like a chemist's shop in there," said Gemma, as Dinah scrutinized her latest ingredient's portion, leveling off the top of the spoon with a surgeon's precision.

"It puts me more in mind of alchemy," said Geoff. "The olden days of skills part wizardry, part science," he added, in response to Gemma's confused expression.

"That could be the very definition of the culinary arts themselves, couldn't it?" I said, with a smile for this joke. "It takes a little of both magic and science to make a perfect dish."

"You mean like Harry Potter or something," said Gemma.

There was something about Dinah's intense concentration that put me in mind of the Sorcerer's Apprentice, I had to admit. She was furiously grinding some spice into a red powder in one of the many bowls crowded haphazardly between the table's contents, dipping in a quick finger to taste the quality before scribbling a note on a sheet of paper.

When she raised her head, we waved, quickly. Disappointingly, she didn't see us, already turning rapidly to whatever was bubbling on the stove.

In the pocket of my rain coat, my mobile rang. I pulled it out, and saw Lady Amanda's number onscreen. "Hello?" I said.

"Julianne, where are you?" she said.

"I'm just running a quick errand," I said, trying to think of a reasonable story that didn't involve three desperate friends standing outside another's house.

"Hurry back, please. She's taking over the kitchen ... dinner plans ... not a clue where ..."

"Lady Amanda? You're breaking up," I said. I checked the mobile's signal, seeing the cursed symbol for weak coverage. "What did you say?"

"...she wants everyone there tonight, too." This was the last intelligible line from Lady Amanda before we were disconnected.

"I have to go," I said to Gemma and Geoff. "I think there's a crisis in the manor's kitchen." I had given Kitty most of the day off to ensure that she wouldn't find an excuse to miss seeing the performance at the Minack, so there was no one at the manor right now to help.

"I'll drive you there," said Geoff. "Let's be off, shall we?" Beneath the umbrella's shelter we three moved reluctantly down the walking path from Dinah's house to his car.

The kitchen wasn't in chaos, but it was definitely abuzz with activity when Gemma and I entered. Total strangers in restaurant smocks were unpacking boxes of groceries, pots and pans, and crates of wine on Dinah's scrubbed work table and the various counters. In the midst of this stood the ever-sophisticated Harriet Hardy in a dark designer dress and un-sensible patent leather heels by Valentino, directing her staff where to go.

"Hi," I said. "Is all this for the show?" There couldn't be another 'pop quiz' for the bakers, right? They were all in the midst of practicing for the final challenge — and besides, I didn't recognize any of these people as members of The Grand Baking Extravaganza's production crew.

Harriet turned away from one of her assistants, to whom she had been speaking in French until now. "Of course not," she said. "This is the staff from my restaurant, Ms. Rose. As per my tradition, we are cooking dinner for the contestants, our hosts, and their friends. No, Rupert — put the chard by the sink, if you please."

So that's what Lady Amanda must have meant by 'she wants everyone there.' "Is there anything I can do?" I asked. "I can cook. Sort of." This last part I felt obliged to add, even though Dinah considered me a decent hand in the kitchen.

"I see," said Harriet Hardy. "It would be lovely to have additional help, if you have time." She snapped her fingers, and an assistant rushed up with an apron. "There is a great deal to be done, and there is no one assigned to the chopping station as of yet."

Assigned? "Sure," I said. "Wherever you need me —" But the assistant had already laid out chopping boards and knives, and what looked like a boatload of vegetables. I saw Gemma donning an apron as well, giving me a look somewhere between excitement and bewilderment for all this.

Harriet Hardy herself never donned an apron or a smock, yet managed never to splash anything onto her silk dress as she patrolled the kitchen, inspecting the prep for every dish, and tasting everything in each pot with the same skeptical expression she wore when tasting contestant's bakes. In between, she consulted some very yellowed recipe cards and a threadbare French cookbook that I realized must be from her personal recipe collection.

Two soups, three vegetable dishes, two meat dishes with sauce, and a dessert served with custard. Sounds pretty simple, doesn't it? So why did it feel like we were cooking for an army as we scrubbed, peeled, chopped, and boiled everything from carrots and onions to spinach and chard? No sooner did I finish with a vegetable, then one of Harriet's assistants whisked it away to one of the many pots boiling or simmering on Dinah's stove, where Harriet stalked ceaselessly, checking the temperature and consistency of every dish in between whisking and stirring her own ingredients.

"Two pinches," said Harriet, to the assistant who held a bowl of spices the chef had grated herself, a small mountain of nutmeg as she whisked a pot of cream.

"Two? Doesn't this recipe usually call for one?" he said.

"Two," she repeated, in a crisp tone that suggested that Harriet's staff would find it easier not to argue her, and probably seldom did. He obeyed this time, then went to fetch another ingredient, during which time, Harriet reached for the dish and added a third pinch to her sauce before tasting it. A satisfied expression appeared on her face, and she gave the whisk a firm tap against the pan's side.

The open recipe book was turned to a Provencal gratin dish involving green leafy vegetables and a sauce of some kind. I saw several notes had been made in pencil to the side of the recipe. As quickly as my eye landed on the page, Harriet closed the book's covers — but not before I saw the last page held its author's picture, a very familiar weathered profile beneath a mane of dark hair.

I caught the chef's eye, and saw an unusual twinkle in it. But Harriet said nothing, merely lifting my board of newly-chopped onions and scraping them into the dish of prepared greens with one deft stroke, as her assistant began pouring the sauce over them and added fresh-grated Parmesan.

"It smells like a proper Sunday dinner in here," said Gemma, as she laid aside a series of peeled, parboiled onions. "There's enough veg on the stove to feed us all for a week."

"Maybe Harriet meant 'feast' instead of 'dinner'," I suggested, as I watched the female chef began lifting the skin of three plucked chickens away from the meat, a dish of some sort of greens-and-ricotta stuffing at her elbow.

"I can't believe she hasn't splashed that gown even once," said Gemma. Whose apron was like mine — covered in green stains from spinach and leeks after an hour's rinsing and chopping.

Even Lady Amanda found her way downstairs and helped mix the stuffing for the onions as Harriet finished trimming a very large fish with an herb bouquet before popping it in the fridge. By the time the oven was at baking temperature, Lady Amanda made a pot of tea and mixed coffee for everyone present, not that Harriet and her crew availed themselves of a break — apparently, that would be detrimental to the preparation of the delicate onion dish being treated like pages of the Voynich manuscript, which was the last of the dishes being readied for the fridge.

"I smell a proper custard, and baking apples," said Lady Amanda. "It's making little Harold positively ravenous." She took a bite out of a biscuit from my dwindling 'secret stash' of Dinah's, the ones used to impress Pierre.

"Is that the boy's name you've chosen?" I asked.

"I certainly hope so," said Lady Amanda. "On a dreadful note, William wants to name the baby for his great-great-great grandfather Edward if it's a boy. You've seen his portrait in the gallery upstairs, haven't you?"

I recalled a picture of a rather sour-looking gentleman in spectacles who looked as if he'd just consumed a disagreeable dinner — or was wearing too tight a pair of breeches, possibly. "Edward's not a bad name," I said, trying to sound supportive. "Even if its original bearer is a little ... grim."

"Exactly. Imagine naming the baby for such a grumpy old bore," said Lady Amanda. "I can't abide it, frankly. I can't believe he's suggesting it." She took a sip from her teacup, then patted her stomach. "Never fear, little Violet. I shan't let your papa have his way in the end."

"What happened to Harold?" said Gemma, dunking her biscuit in her tea.

"I feel quite sure it's a Violet in there," said Lady Amanda. "Woman's intuition." She glanced at the clock. "Goodness me, we must get a wiggle on if we're dressing for dinner." She untied her apron and tossed it aside. "They'll be putting the chicken on soon."

"Dress?" said Gemma.

"It *is* a feast worthy of kitchen royalty," Lady Amanda pointed out.

Fortunately, 'dress' meant neither white nor black tie in this case, but more of a continental evening casual. Pierre Dupine was in his usual suit, while Lord William wore something a little more stylish, which I knew he usually reserved for weekends in London. Lady Amanda's flowing blue summer smock hid much of Violet — or Harold — from sight; it was from the same shop where she persuaded me to buy the summer dress I was wearing, a light black dress with sheer sleeves.

Dinner was served in the temporary pavilion built behind the manor for the final event. Tomorrow, it would be filled with cooking stations, but tonight the tables had been put together to form one long banquet, surrounded by rented chairs. The white-clothed surface didn't hold decorative cakes and puddings, but the manor's second-best china.

All of the contestants were there, including Dinah, who seemed perfectly calm despite what we'd seen through the windows earlier. She wore a pink summer lawn dress that seemed light and filmy — it was one of the rare times I saw her out of the kitchen smock and in something posh.

"You look beautiful," I said to her, as soon as I broke from Matt's arm's embrace and the conversation we'd been having with Geoff and Lord William. "How are you feeling?" I thought back to this morning with slight uneasiness.

"I'm perfectly fine," she said — not with a touch of forced bravery, I hoped. "I couldn't miss dining at Harriet Hardy's table due to a little cake, could I? It's a real treat to be asked to dine on something she's cooked, and there's no mistake about it."

"Are you — close to a design?" I asked, half-afraid to know if all those notes and concoctions had come to nothing today. We'd hardly stuck around long enough to see the outcome of all Dinah's labors, not that I wanted to tell her we'd all been standing outside, dying to know, but afraid of disturbing her.

"Oh, let's not talk about it," said Dinah. "Not tonight. You'll see tomorrow morning. I'll be back to my notes as soon as this dinner's concluded." And the look of determination from before was back in place, proving Dinah wasn't satisfied with this day's efforts.

One by one, Harriet and her kitchen staff presented the courses. We ate garlic soup with lightly-toasted croutons, or a creamy broth with pureed broccoli lending it a pale green color, and a salad of simple greens. Then came the fish served with lemon wedges; it was delicious despite the fact it still had eyes and seemed to gaze mournfully at me when the platter was passed my way. And that compliment comes from a woman who does *not* eat dishes that stare at her, I promise.

"This flounder is delicious," said Matt. "My compliments to the chef and her kitchen."

"Here, here," said Lord William, lifting his glass. "You've outdone yourself, Ms. Hardy. One assumes you must be missing your restaurant very badly to concoct a feast like this in a mere afternoon."

"It was quite simple, I assure you," said Harriet, who was pouring a new bottle of wine for her dinner guests. "When I grow weary of dining from other people's kitchens, I find myself compelled to bring to life a quiet dinner of well-prepared dishes. Perhaps you are right. It is because I miss my quiet bistro — or prefer something more satisfying to the palate than fish and chips or a hotel salad."

"Then you have accomplished it," said Pierre, who raised his glass to her also. "It is not quite true French cooking, but it is very charming." As one of the kitchen staff served him the spinach and parmesan grating, he took a small forkful and tasted it.

"Ah," he said. "*Piquant*. It is truly savory." He took another bite. "This has the hand of a French cook in its preparations. The nutmeg — it is perfection."

"Is it?" I said.

"Yes. The English cooks — they limit such a spice when they make the sauce, never more than two pinches. It must have at least two to bring out the hidden nature of the sauce, as any French chef knows. *Exactement.*"

"Two pinches. Really," said Harriet, taking a sip from her glass of wine. "I've always found three to be more suitable." I was sure she was hiding a smile behind her glass just after these words.

The stuffed chicken was delicious, and as for the kitchen's baked apples with custard, words failed even Pierre Dupine for the English twist on a Mediterranean favorite. I was almost too full after having sampled so many delicious things, so I discreetly let Matt polish off the last of my baked apple.

We walked home afterwards, leaving the eager contestants to claim the judges' conversation on the eve of the last challenge. I couldn't help but think about Dinah — and probably everybody competing against her — staying up late to try one last icing technique, or experiment with one last flavor.

"Where are your thoughts?" Matt asked. His arm was around my shoulders, steering me along the familiar cliffs path in the moonlight. The lingering smell of summer rain was lost in the sea's breeze, the only evidence being the gleaming droplets the clear sky illuminated on the rose hedges.

"Food," I answered.

"Food? We just ate a six course dinner," he said.

"I didn't finish my baked apple," I reminded him. "Compared to you, I'm practically starving."

"I see," he said, his arms sliding around my waist as he turned to face me in the pathway. "So what can we do to quell those hunger pangs?"

"We'll think of something," I said, playing with a button on his shirt as I lifted my eyes to his own. "I'm sure there's a recipe that can cure it."

"Page sixteen should be the right one," said Matt. "I think there's some cinnamon in this cupboard." Back in our cottage, he opened the cabinet above our fridge, searching behind a tin of tea and a bag of jasmine rice. I tied an apron over my dress, tossing Matt's suit coat onto the sofa in the next room. For good measure, I kicked off my stiletto heels, too.

I ground dried cloves with a mortar and pestle as Matt sifted flour into a bowl. I carefully spooned allspice and ginger from their respective spice jars, and packed brown sugar into a measuring cup.

"I hope this tastes better than construction gingerbread," I said. "I had a bite of some in the competition, and it was a little crunchy for my taste."

"This is softer," said Matt. "A little more like the American 'cookie' than a crisp biscuit. You'll see. It's quite delicious, I promise." He opened a tin of bicarbonate of soda, and pushed the jar of treacle across the table to me, where I was cubing butter.

"Uh-uh," I said. "No way. No more molasses measuring by me. That part is all yours."

"If you want." He kissed the top of my head as he joined me, lifting the measuring cup from beside my bowl. "You pour, I'll watch. That way it's still you who's accomplishing it."

"That's more like it. Thank you."

We mixed, rolled the dough into balls, and chilled it as we hunted for biscuit cutters, and succeeded in coming up only with a bird-shaped one someone had given me as a gift and a scone cutter. Together, we rolled the dough out while it was still somewhat cold and stiff, where Matt's muscles contributed more than my own. It became a smooth, shiny brown disk, with a few grainy bits of clove here and there like bits of black sand — proof my grinding skills needed a little work.

"I should've bought that adorable biscuit cutter I saw in the London shop a few weeks ago," I said. "It was shaped like a tiny little cottage. It made me think of Rosemoor."

"Next time," said Matt. "What were you looking for in a culinary shop, incidentally?"

"A biscuit cutter shaped like a stork with a bundle," I said. "I was going to get a second little gift for Lady Amanda."

"Another one?"

"You know me. I like giving gifts." My cheek brushed against his as we drew the rolling pin towards us in its steady rhythm. "I thought about getting her a baby book instead. Maybe *The Mousehole Cat* — there were copies of it in a shop window back in December."

"A clever title for its American readers to pronounce," he said. "Not so much for Cornish ones, in some respects, is it?"

"Stop reminding me, okay?" I blushed red for the memory of Matt's teasing, even after all this time. "I know, I was a naive American, an easy target for one of your silly jokes."

His finger lifted a lock of my hair and gently tucked it in place behind my ear again. "I enjoyed teasing you then," he said. "But not because I wanted to mock you. I wanted your attention and had no other way to get it that didn't seem so terribly ... polite. Too formal. You'd relegate me to the status of friend and fellow employee far too quickly like that."

"Maybe," I said. "I don't think you realize how hard it was for me *not* to notice you back then."

I glanced into his eyes, which was both easy and challenging with us in our cheek-to-cheek position. I wondered if he really had no idea how much power a look from his eyes had over me — then and now.

"Then feel free to tell me all about it," he said, softly, a wicked gleam in his eye.

"And forget about our biscuits?" I said. "Not on your life." I smudged a little sticky bit of ginger dough across Matt's cheek, hearing him laugh in protest.

The biscuits were crisp around the edges, but softer in the middle once they cooled from baking. We snapped a beveled-edged circle in half and each tasted it. "Mmm," I said. "Perfect. It tastes like my mom's gingerbread cookies at home."

"It reminds me a little of some from my own childhood," said Matt. "I think Michelle would like this recipe. Not that you need to impress her,

Julianne. I hope you realize that."

"I know," I said. I brushed some crumbs from my apron. "But I want her to feel at home when she's here with us. And I want to feel more at home as part of your family, and not as much like an outsider."

"You're not." He leaned forward and kissed my cheek. "This was what we wanted. A collision of cultures, a relationship between two very different people whose pasts will become one future. You needn't think I expect you to change, because it's simply not true."

"It's not about changing," I said. "It's not about forgetting what I've known, but about embracing something new. It's important to me to find my own place in this life we're sharing. I'm just looking for a new way to be part of your traditions."

"And maybe we'll be making new ones," suggested Matt. "Ones that include your recipes, your favorite things, too."

"New traditions. That sounds nice," I said. "Like the beginning of something meant to last for a lifetime. Maybe even pass down to someone else." I lifted my eyes to Matt's with these words. "You know. Someday."

"Save *The Mousehole Cat* for when that day comes," he answered, softly. "It's a bit of our own story."

Our cups of tea were empty, so we toasted to this with two bird biscuits instead. A little crazy, but not more so than two people baking biscuits in the wee small hours while talking about building a lifetime of possibilities together.

"Speaking of the future, did you hear the latest dilemma over Lady Amanda's baby names?" I asked.

***

I let Kitty have the day off today. I was afraid if I didn't, she might bury herself in the planning process for an upcoming event, and avoid going out this evening. She's still pretending she doesn't care about going, but she can't fool me. I saw the look on her face when Nathan mentioned having an extra ticket.

I just wish I knew whether that look was for the theatre or for him. Call me crazy ... well, call me curious instead. I think the only cure for it will be too busy myself in studying recipes for Scottish shortbread, because I've DEFINITELY decided against building a gingerbread house this Christmas. And as for Christmas cake — well, I'm afraid I'll dream tonight that Dinah's topples over right in front of Harriet and Pierre. How's that for dreadful psychic premonitions? — Julianne

***

Kitty:

I hadn't wanted to take a day's holiday, but Julianne all but forced me to do it. She hid most of our work in one of the locked filing cupboards, and I knew that she'd see the marks if I picked it open, so I left it shut up. She's a bit mental sometimes, I've decided; but there was nothing for me to do except tidy up our office and sneak home around three o' clock.

Nathan's text mentioned half past as the hour for us meeting to drive to Porthcurno, so he hadn't been making a joke about arriving early. Funny that I'd never been to that theatre, really. I had lived in Land's End, which was only a short bus ride to Minack's place on the map. But I'd had other drama on my mind in those days than seeing plays in my free hours.

As usual, the telly was blasting some program at full volume when I let myself inside the house by way of the kitchen. I slipped past the doorway, spotting Mum busy clipping something from a magazine as an advertisement on Channel 4 boasted about some brand of pasties.

I kicked off my shoes and tossed my jacket onto the sewing table. Opening the closet, I unzipped the garment bag I kept near the back. In it, a 'posh frock' that I had bought once, and never had a notion of wearing. A bright pink pattern of silk with splashes of wine-colored flowers on it, like a watercolor someone had spilled water over to blur the picture. Quite snug in its curves, with a wide neckline and sleeves that dropped almost off the shoulders. There was a flimsy scarf to match it.

I took a deep breath. My last chance to turn back was here. Reaching over, I pulled the dress from the closet and began squeezing myself into it. I put my hair up quickly and pinned it, then dug through a little box on the table, where I kept an old pair of fake diamond earrings that had been Mum's ages ago.

I slipped on my shoes again and grabbed my pocketbook. Time to creep away before Mum knew I was home. I made it halfway to the door before she popped out of the front room and ran straight into me.

"Katherine, for land's sake!" she said, clamping one hand over her chest. "You scared me witless, creeping about like that — what are you doing?"

"I'm just leaving —"

" — and what on earth are you wearing?" She took note of my appearance with a look of dismay.

"It's a dress, Mum," I answered sarcastically. "I thought that much would be fairly obvious."

"Where did you get it?" she asked. "And whatever possessed you? It makes you look a bit tarty, love. Go pop into your room and change straightaway. What if Nigel saw you wearing that?"

"I don't have time, Mum, I've got to go," I said, impatiently. "Nigel's not even here, besides."

"Where are you off to in such a rush?" she asked, sounding suspicious. "I don't like secrets, Katherine. If you know what's good for you, you'll keep away from that crowd in Truro —"

The sound of a loud snicker from the kitchen interrupted our conversation. "Well, well, isn't that a bit of a show?" said a third voice. "Is that a posh frock or your mum's old curtains done up, KitKat?" My cousin Saul had come in through the second door, unannounced, as usual. "Makes you look like that painted doll you had as a kid, the one Teddy and I buried in the garden."

"You're a right comedian, that's what you are." I rolled my eyes and pushed past him to the door.

"Don't be peeved, I'm only having a bit of fun," he said. "Come back, Kitty. I need a favor — just a few quid —"

"I don't have any," I said.

"You can't ride your motorbike in that getup," Mum argued. "Kitty, come back here!"

"I'm riding with a friend," I said. "Tatty-bye."

At the end of the lane, a decent piece from home, I waited for Nathan to meet me — there was no possibility I would let him collect me from Mum's house. I saw the little car whose lock I picked slowing down as its driver spotted me.

Nathan emerged from the driver seat when it stopped, and the look on his face made me blush despite my best try. "Hi," he managed, after a moment. "I .. um ... wasn't sure I had the right place ..."

"Sorry I'm late." I opened the passenger door and climbed inside. "Thanks for the ride."

"No problem." He'd recovered himself, at any rate. "Is this your house?" he asked, glancing at the nearest cottage — one a bit better off than Mum's, with the garden properly tended in front.

"No," I said. "Let's go." I motioned for him to go on — there was a distinct chance that Saul might be by at any second and see us. I didn't want questions about who the 'posh boy' was who gave me a lift.

"Right." He shifted into gear and began driving again. He glanced over at me. "That's ... quite a dress," he said. "It's pretty, I mean. You look nice." The skin of his face had turned a bit pink. I could see it from his profile, even. "Not that you don't usually look nice. This is just different for you."

"Not exactly my usual style, I know. Try not to laugh, all right?" I said, wryly. "Let's not make a fuss about it." I felt self-conscious as I adjusted the skirt a bit. Sitting down, it was even more snug against my knees.

"I'll try not to," Nathan said. "Promise." He was still kidding, but in a nice way. Nicer than when we were building the biscuit knights, even. I felt a bit less weird about it when he sneaked glances a couple more times — I didn't think it was because the dress looked a mess, although this made me feel weird in a different way.

"What play is it?" I asked. "The show we're seeing."

"*The Tempest*," he said. "Are you a Shakespeare fan, by chance?"

"Only seen it once. When I was at school," I said. It had only been a drama club play of sorts, and I hadn't been a student of good standing who was allowed to participate. That wasn't a tale I wanted to share here and now, however.

It wasn't the most uncomfortable car trip I've ever been part of. It was a bit quiet at the start, but it gradually became less so, when we had both grown tired of silence. It was safe enough to talk about the baking contest, and the summer diary of Cliffs House's events. And it was a stroke of fortune that Nathan had never driven these roads before, and needed my knowledge of the roads from Land's End and Penzance to find his way there.

Minack Theatre was nothing more than a postcard in the Land's End shop where I worked, a pile of stone above the sea, one that looked a bit like some old Greek ruins. But Julianne would say that everything changes when you see it in person, and it was the same for me when I took the stone steps that wound down to the amphitheatre's seats.

I'd never had a funny moment where I felt breathless, but I did for just a second, looking at the blue water flecked with white foam, like a big piece of silk rippling over a tabletop the size of the world. There were little strips of green between all the stone levels of the theatre, and sprays of something blooming with little pink flowers cropped up along the path below, leading to the stage and background of false ruins.

"Are you okay?" said Nathan. He looked a little bit concerned that I was so motionless all of a sudden on the topmost step.

"Me? I'm fine," I said. I followed him down, where the people he was supposed to meet were waiting in the front row. He started to put his hand on my arm when I caught up with him, but hesitated at the last second. I managed not to break into a little smile, imagining he'd make some remark about my 'bite' being worse than my bark, probably. But the theatre had taken the mood for joking out of Nathan, too, maybe.

"The theatre of the gods," he said, softly. We were at the bottom now, looking up at the rows of seats carved from stone, which looked fitting enough for Greek gods to occupy.

"Pick one," said Nathan. "I'm just going to talk to them for a little while about some concert stuff." He motioned towards the two men waiting at the stage's edge. "You can come if you want, or just hang out here."

"Which seats are we supposed to be in?"

"Any of them," he said. "Pick one of the good ones, if you want — the ones carved for the gods and not the back benches. Just save one for me." He crossed to the stage, where the two men waiting were now shaking hands with him.

So I picked a place in the second row, and sat watching the sky change to a pinkish shade as the day drew to a close. Some tourists were taking photos of the sea and the stage until it was almost time for the play to begin, when the big lights came on to illuminate the stage as the sun disappeared.

The show was a local theatre company onstage — there wasn't much in the way of props or backdrops, but that was the point of playing the Minack, where the sea and the stone ruins like an old Mediterranean fortress were the real backdrop. At nighttime, the sea was a velvety darkness that washed against the far shore, where a little white light burned across the way.

"I hope you understand Shakespeare better than I do, because I'm totally lost," Nathan whispered to me. Even the cooler temperatures of Cornwall versus the hot summers across the Pond didn't stop him from taking off his suit coat and tucking it over the seat. He didn't move his arm afterwards; I felt it brush against my shoulder as he leaned in to whisper, "Who is the guy on the left supposed to be?"

"Sshh," I said. "You're ruining my concentration." I leaned forward, pretending to be totally engrossed in the play. Not that it wasn't a good local performance — but it was mostly because I didn't want to get quite so close all of a sudden. But he didn't move his arm from the niche between our seats, except to stretch it out along the top. I tried not to roll my eyes as I settled back in my place.

"You're stealing part of my seat," I whispered. "The back bit's mine, too."

"This? This is the neutral zone," he said. "It's outside the seat's technical boundaries." A smile twitched at the corner of his mouth, briefly. "Besides, I'm getting cramped sitting the other way. And aren't you too busy watching the play to notice?"

"Touché," I muttered.

When we rose at the end for the standing ovation, he tucked his suit coat around my shoulders; I felt its silk lining sliding around me before I was aware what he was doing.

"It's a little cool," he said, speaking louder since the audience was cheering.

"Thanks," I said. It was a little too warm for it, really, but I felt suddenly that I didn't want to be rude to him.

He wasn't in a hurry to go after the cast's bows were finished —

besides, we were trapped in place until the rest of the audience had filed up the stone steps to the carvings and natural boulders looking down at us from on high. Nathan sat down on the back of the first row's seat, using its 'neutral zone' as a resting spot as we gazed at the now-empty stage and let time pass.

"Won't they kick us out?" I asked. I had seated myself next to him, since we seemed to be waiting for something. "Your friends with the theatre, whoever they are."

"No. They said I could stay as long as I wanted," said Nathan. "So long as we can find our way out of here in the dark." As he spoke, the stage lights disappeared. There was just moonlight, but it was bright enough since the rain clouds weren't hiding it. It made the sea look different, and the chairs of stone and the leaves and flowers in the garden beds above. Like a great big spotlight that made everything seem bright, but not cold.

"So," he said. "Did you like it? This place. Tonight."

"Of course I did," I scoffed. "It was different for me. Sort of like...something magic." Rubbishy words, really. My cheeks turned pink, and I was glad he couldn't see them. "At least a bit like it."

"They said it was beautiful here," he said, resting his hands on either side of the seat's flat back as he gazed at the carved cliff around us. "You know how it is, though. Just words until they become reality."

"Whose words are those? Your mates in Truro?" I asked, teasing him. "Ceffylgwyn's posh set that absconded from the village?"

A sound between a grunt and a groan came from Nathan's throat. "What's with you and them?" he asked. "Would you just tell me what you have against them? Or what they have against you?"

"They didn't tell you to stay away from me, then," I said, airily. "Guess you need better mates."

"Why would they tell me that?" He looked me firmly in the eye at this point. "Come on, Kitty. Tell me the truth."

I let his coat slip from my shoulders, to the back of the seat beside mine. "I was a bit wild in my past," I said. "You must've heard the stories." I didn't stay locked with his gaze for this remark.

"Oh. Those. You mean about you stealing the motorbike," he said. "And spray-painting the primary's walls —"

"That wasn't me," I said, quickly. "Some of the lot I followed about, maybe, but I didn't do those things." I might've stated this with a little more force than necessary, but I was still prickly after all these years whenever my name was connected to village vandalism. Gossip had grouped me in with the louts who had been cruel and destructive just for boredom's sake, which was the worst part of it all.

"I never said you did." Nathan leaned back a little. "I'm not an idiot. I don't believe everything I'm told. Well, the motorbike I believed," he clarified. "Especially after you picked my car lock with all the prowess of Catwoman."

"I'm not proud of it, you know," I answered. "A skill like that."

"Like heck you're not."

I bit my lip to stop the sudden twitch of a smile from becoming real. He was partly right. It was a mixed bag, showing off with something I wished I hadn't learned, with the 'showing off' being the part I liked about it sometimes, wrong as it was.

"So why did you leave the village?" said Nathan. "You think most people run away because they're looking for something bigger, or more exciting. Did you decide excitement wasn't all it was cracked up to be?"

"You've obviously never seen Land's End, or that wouldn't be the thought popping into your head," I said. "That's where I ran off to." I paused, feeling a bit of the sea breeze ruffle my dress scarf and my hair—I could feel the pins holding my style in place were starting to slip. "I guess I wanted to get away after my gran passed. She was the only part of my life back then that held me there."

"What was she like?" he asked.

"Gran was fantastic," I said. "She made flowers look like works of art, like something out of a painting, whenever she put them together. She could bake the best oggies of anyone, even Charlotte Jones — and she made stories out of patchwork." Bits of those quilts in my room made me think of her whenever I laid aside my things at the end of the day. Maybe that's why I was still living there.

"But you came back," said Nathan.

I snorted. "To look after Mum," I said. "But she didn't need me around to fuss at her until she crept off the sofa now and then, or so she said." I studied my fingers with their nails clipped short, as if it was interesting

I'd left them unpainted. "She still thinks of me as trouble waiting to happen. And maybe she's right. I picked your lock the other night without a second's thought, didn't I?"

"Maybe she would see it as a good sign," said Nathan. "You're using your powers for good now, and not evil." That made me laugh — me with powers, and not two pins that had once let me crack into any room in the primary school after hours.

Nathan's gaze moved to the water again. "You know, leaving home wasn't easy for me," he said. "I came here in the first place because I thought this was a career opportunity I couldn't pass up, not if I wanted something bigger in the future. But now ..." he hesitated, "...now I'm not sure what I wanted, really. Bigger's not always better. When I quit the tour, I guess I was just trying to find myself outside of ladders and goals."

"You sort of live for your job," I said. "Least that's what everyone says about you."

"Yeah. That's the problem for me." He drew a deep breath. "Maybe I should be a more enthusiastic theatregoer," he said, after a minute or two. "Shakespeare's not exactly my thing, really. But I guess it's yours," he added, looking at me. "Julianne said you liked the theatre. You know, plays, musicals."

"When?" I challenged. "Not when we were in her office, and you offered me the ticket."

Now his face was shaded a little darker in the moonlight. "It was just a random remark," he said, his voice going a bit awkward all of a sudden.

"Yeah. Must've been," I said.

"Anyway, since you liked theatre, I thought you'd like this."

"If people didn't know better, they would say this was a date," I said. "You and me on the town for a night — me in a posh frock like this one."

"They would, wouldn't they?" said Nathan. "I mean, it looks exactly like it. Even the two of us just sitting here, talking."

"Especially that part," I said. "Everyone knows we can't talk to each other." We both laughed. Nathan's grew quiet first.

He cleared his throat. "You know, there's a chance I was working up my courage to ask you somewhere," he said. "And maybe this event sort of presented itself as an opportunity."

"To ask me out."

"Your words, not mine," he said.

"So you were asking me out tonight," I clarified. "That's what this was all about."

"Like I said, Shakespeare's not my thing," he answered. I imagined that his face was probably redder than ever, but he was still looking me in the eye. "So, I confess. I asked you out tonight on a kind of pseudo date."

"Why?" I asked.

"Maybe because I find you sort of ... fascinating."

"Me? Fascinating?" I echoed, raising one eyebrow.

"Don't make me say it again," he answered. His face must be blushing harder by the minute. "It's not exactly the right word, but you know what I mean. I think about you — I mean, I can't stop thinking about you on some level." He sounded helpless. "There's something about you that defies explanation for me. In a good way, not a bad one," he added, quickly.

It suddenly seemed really funny when he said it aloud. As if I hadn't been truly aware of it the whole evening, which was the reason I was wearing this dress that my Mum found so mortifying. I was laughing at him because it was the only thing that would keep me from melting into a puddle of messy confusion over the revelation that someone was actually thinking about me on a semi-constant basis.

"What?" he said, as if he knew what I was thinking about somehow.

"I'm just thinking — you, me. Out on a proper date," I said. "Everybody knows what you think about me. And me with a posh bloke — the kind of toff whose opinion of me I didn't need you to confirm."

"It's not that funny to me," he said, in a sort of amused-but-perplexed voice. "I don't see anything weird about the idea, really."

"I think the rest of your mates would have some serious questions about that," I said. He took my smile for mockery — which was what I wanted him to take it for, as if I couldn't stop teasing him.

"Will you stop using them as an excuse to keep me away?" said Nathan. "What do you think of me? Seriously, not as some British cliché of a white collar businessman, or whatever. Give me a straight answer, Kitty."

Quite serious, that voice, even with his smile. All the humor was disappearing from his face, but it wasn't angry or disappointed, the look confronting me. Maybe his earnestness was getting to me, because I felt the color rush to my cheeks again.

I was wishing things were different right now. That somewhere inside, I didn't still feel like I didn't belong in this posh frock, in this moonlit place, and especially not with him. I wished I didn't find myself liking him so much. Because this moment wanted to be the beginning of something as amazing as this place had felt tonight, and that didn't seem possible.

"What do you want me to say?" I was still being coy, but I didn't feel like it. I didn't know what I was feeling anymore.

Nathan leaned towards me. I felt his lips against mine, kissing me; I kissed him back. It was a little one at first, but growing more serious by the second. From pleasant to good, then like waves of hot sparks that make you feel quick and breathless.

At first, I didn't want it to stop, then I knew it had to. It had to stop before it was too late to turn back from something that just couldn't be true.

I put my hand on his chest and gave him a gentle push to end it, drawing away from him. "It's late," I said. "They don't want us hanging about here forever." I slid down from the back of the seat and away from Nathan, because I needed distance — a good bit of it to clear my head, which felt hot and muddled, not that I could tell him so.

"What's the matter?" said Nathan, who hopped up from his seat now. "What's wrong?"

"Nothing," I lied. "I just have to go, that's all."

His face fell slightly. "Fine," he said, after a moment. "We'll go home." He slipped on his coat again.

"You needn't drive me," I said. "I'm staying with a mate here. I forgot to tell you before that I'm popping around to their place for tonight. We're meeting up with friends later ... doing some stuff."

"Okay. I'll give you a ride to their place," he said.

"I can walk." I was going up the stairs with these words. "Thanks, anyway." I wasn't riding the miles back to Ceffylgwyn by his side, in darkness and silence after what just happened. Things had all shifted with that kiss. It was us both being crazy in the moonlight, giving in to some silly impulse.

"Kitty, what's the rush?" he said. He sounded exasperated. "At least let me drive you there."

"I'm good. I can take care of myself," I answered.

"Is this because I kissed you?" he said. "Was it that bad?"

"G'night," I said. "I'll see you around." I made it to the top of Minack's stone steps before Nathan even set foot on the first one.

It was a lie. I didn't have a mate in Porthcurno, and my only one left in Land's End didn't answer her mobile when I rang it. Obviously, I couldn't call Mum and explain that I had stranded myself here. So I rang Saul instead.

"H'lo." He sounded grumpy, as you would expect at one in the morning. I'd rung him twice before he even bothered to answer. I pictured him sacked out on the sofa, probably under a pile of old clothes and empty takeaway wrappers.

"It's me — Kitty," I said.

"The waitress at Tilly's A-Go-Go Club, what asked for me number last Saturday?"

"Hilarious." I rolled my eyes. "I need a favor. I need a ride home from Porthcurno."

"Porthcurno? At this time o' night? Are you mental?"

"It's important," I said. "Look, I'll give you twenty quid if you'll just come and fetch me." It was all I had in my handbag when I looked.

"Thirty quid," he grunted. "That's what I owe Louie." Louie was probably a bookie — Saul was always losing his wages over a bet or two gone squiffy with some local shark, especially now that the racetrack at St Austell was open again. "I'll come for thirty and not a pound less."

"Fine," I sighed. I told him where to find me, and then waited. The bench I was sitting on was hard, not more so than the theatre's seat, but it felt like it. I think my brain wasn't doing a decent job of escaping what happened tonight. Trying to transport me back, maybe, as I sat alone. But what good was that, since I obviously wanted to get away from there in the first place?

I put my head in my hands. It throbbed a bit — the funny feeling from kissing him hadn't gone away completely. It made me a bit dizzy; I was shaking a bit, even though I wasn't cold. But something inside me felt frigid and sick ... that was a new feeling, one that had come over me after

I made my escape.

You can't regret it, I told myself. *What was going to come of it, in the end? When he went back to America, and you drifted to another village? Nothing, that's what. It always comes to nothing.*

I spent the night curled up in an out of the way alcove, wrapped up in my dress scarf. Not the roughest night's sleep I've had, but close to it. Two hours after I had called, Saul still hadn't arrived. I rang his mobile again, and it went to his voicemail. Blasted lazybones — he'd probably fallen asleep again after we spoke.

At five in the morning, I heard the sound of a familiar motor in the distance. There was my motorbike speeding towards the village crossing — Saul was riding it, the spare helmet clipped to the back of the bike. He screeched to a stop, then lifted my helmet from his head.

"You look like something the cat dragged to the kitchen door," he said.

"Where's your car?" I said, with dismay. "What's Mum about, letting you take my bike?"

"Dad's borrowed mine. Gone up to Newquay for a bit of business," he said. "Think you can ride in those togs?" Another smirk for my dress. I felt stupid once again for choosing to wear it last night.

"Don't be daft," I answered. I put on the spare helmet, then climbed on the back of the bike. "Just take me to Cliffs House."

"Cliffs House?" he echoed.

"I'll be late for my job if you don't," I said. "It's the final day of the contest. Now let's be going, if you don't mind." I clung on tight as he revved my little engine unnecessarily to take off again, my scarf trailing behind in the breeze as we turned towards the village's road. I buried my face against the back of Saul's jacket, smelling the odor of smoke and stale beer, and tried not to think about Nathan's last words before I left him.

***

Julianne:

The tables were in place, the appliances arranged. From the pavilion's open sides, you could see the restless surface of the sea, the summer fields of Cliffs House, and the back gardens and stately manor itself. All that was missing were the twelve contestants for the final baking challenge.

"I'm nervous," I said to Gemma, as we watched from the windows as the crew set up. 'They'll start arriving any minute now."

"There's two hours until it begins," said Gemma. "Think she's still practicing?"

"By now she must know what she's doing by heart. They all will." I thought of Leeman's carousel gingerbread construct, which had been practiced dozens upon dozens of times even before the contest began — he would have thought of something fantastic after years of decorative baking.

"Jenny Bryce's bloke's been bragging that hers is spectacular," said Gemma. "Says no one who eats it is satisfied with one piece. Been dropping hints about it all over social media."

"We'll see," I said. Personally, I was more worried about Emily's cake, whatever it might be. And what about that serious boy, who had managed to redeem himself after the burned pastry frogs? A come-from-behind move was distinctly possible — and it was distinctly possible that it wouldn't be Dinah's.

I bit my thumbnail distractedly as I watched the two judges stroll towards the pavilion from the garden. I turned and retreated to my office, to avoid any more suspense. Dinah probably wouldn't be arriving for at least another half hour.

Kitty at her desk — dressed in her old clothes, I noticed, a worn pair of denims, and sneakers that had seen better days. This was an unusual rebellion against Cliffs House's posh status. "How was the theatre?" I asked.

"Okay." She was deeply absorbed in double-checking an event's attendance list. I smelled an evasion.

"Just okay?" I said. "That surprises me. The theatre's so beautiful. And I know how you love plays. Was it a poor production?" It was basically Cornwall's version of Shakespeare in the Park, so I couldn't imagine that was true.

Kitty sighed. "I don't know. It just ... was okay. All right?" Her tone was snappish. She stapled together an event scheduled with more force than was necessary.

I saw a spare garment bag crumpled out of sight behind the office's big antique floor globe. A bit of bright pink fabric stuck out at the bottom, where it was partly unzipped. Underneath it, by Kitty's old knapsack she kept lying around here, a pair of sleek little high-heeled shoes.

I sat down at my desk. "Did Nathan like the play?" I asked, quietly.

A few seconds ticked by. Kitty knew that I knew something was wrong, and was evidently trying to figure out how to get off this train of conversation. "I've been thinking about taking up a language," she said, finally. "You know, learn something useful for the job. What do you think about French?"

"Kitty," I began.

"There are loads of books on it. After the baking contest, we'll probably have guests from restaurants in Paris and Marseilles. I thought it might be a proper way to welcome them ..."

"Katherine Alderson." My tone had become very firm. Just then, there was a knock on the frame of my open office door.

"Julianne, the event promoter's here, if you want a word with him," said Gemma. "I think the spectators are starting to arrive, too." Crowds always gathered for the final event of The Grand Baking Extravaganza, local fans and curious visitors alike.

"I'll be right there," I said, gathering up my digital planner. I noticed Kitty's face had washed itself a whiter shade of pale, exposing all her freckles. She rose from her desk and escaped the room as if it were on fire.

I followed. Halfway down the path to the cliffs, I caught up with her. "Tell me the truth, Kitty," I said. "What happened last night?"

"Nothing." She crossed her arms and stared out to sea. A very bad feint of indifference, in my opinion. "We saw a play, that was it. Maybe things got a bit stupid for a moment, but it'll sort itself out. Always does."

"So that's why you're wearing a hoodie to work that looks ready for the dustbin?"

Kitty's expression was blank. "Go on," she said. "I'm fine. You have stuff to do."

"He likes you, doesn't he?" I said.

She didn't answer.

I sighed. "Kitty, if you want to shut people out of your life forever, then fine. Do it. It's your life, and no one can live it for you. But I thought after all that happened, you believed in second chances. And I think — maybe — underneath that prickly surface is someone who desperately doesn't want to be alone."

Kitty's crossed arms seemed less like defiance than protection at this angle; I knew she was listening to me, even if she didn't answer. And I knew that whatever happened last night, she was afraid of it the same way she had been afraid deep down to take a chance on Cliffs House's job at first.

"Shutting people out has a price," I said, softly. "Being complicated and contrary just for habit's sake will only get you hurt. Don't do this to yourself, Kitty. Give yourself a second chance with Nathan."

"What makes you think I want one?" she asked. Her voice stumbled a little bit, even though she tried to sound defiant. She blinked hard, even though the sun wasn't all that bright in the garden.

"Because even though you're wearing those clothes, *you are wearing lipstick*," I said, close to Kitty's ear. "And I really don't think that's for The Grand Baking Extravaganza's benefit."

I turned and went back up the pathway without Kitty. She needed time to think, I suspected, and I had several things to do, as she pointed out. Especially if I wanted to catch Dinah before her big moment in the baking pavilion.

***

Dear Diary,

Darn — I did it again, didn't I? Anyway, my premonition came true. Last night, Dinah's cake collapsed into a big, oozy mess, right in front of the two judges. To begin with, it looked like a tower of underdone puddings, which was probably the reason why ... and then I stepped up to the table and poured Matt's toffee and brown sugar syrup all over it, like that would help. Not really sure what that part was about, but there you have it. Now, let's hope it's not a cosmic warning about the future.

— Julianne

***

Kitty:

It wasn't long after Julianne left me, that I heard footsteps on the pathway. A man's — I can tell by the shoes. I don't turn around, because I know it's going to be him.

He hesitates behind me on the pathway, so he's not coming closer. I tuck my hands deeper in my hoodie's pockets. "It's sort of ... awkward ... for me to talk to you," I said.

"I could say the same," he said. A sound that might be a laugh, only bitter. "Call me crazy for trying it again, I guess."

"It's not the same." I turned to look at him, my tone becoming a bit fiercer than I wanted. "You don't understand how hard it is for me. And it's not about what happened last night —"

"What, then?" he asked. He sounded frustrated. "Is it just me? If it's something about me, just say it — get it over with." He braced himself, trying to be brave enough not to duck this blow, or fall back when it came. "We're both grownups. I can take it."

"It's not you," I said. A band tightens in my stomach, and I know it's fear. "I'm that way with everyone. It's not just my past that makes me do it. But I have one that I don't like ... and you've come someplace where no one knows yours."

It was quiet.

"I'm not close to anybody. No one since my gran, anyway. But I told you things I never tell anyone, and I don't know why." Right now, I can't believe I'm saying this to anybody, much less him. "I was never any good at connections with people. No ties, no nothing, not in a long time. There was never anybody who had a hold over me. So ... I'm not sure there can be."

"I don't have to be a stranger, if you don't want me to be," said

Nathan. "Unless the other night was just a mistake for you. Unless the looks between us, this ... thing that was happening ... it's just my imagination. To you, anyway." He stressed that last point.

"Don't be daft." I blinked to erase the burning tears under my eyes before I looked at him. I didn't mean to look as long as I did. His expression made me feel funny enough that I was glad I was sitting down on one of the pathway's big cliff boulders. My hands felt weak, even.

He wasn't leaving. "So what does that mean for us?" he said.

***

Julianne:

The theme of the final challenge was 'passion.' The bake had to be a cake or a series of mini cakes, either one — but it had to express the concept of romantic desire in some way, shape, or form.

Dinah arrived next to last to the pavilion with her box of supplies, and a single page design sketch rolled up tightly. She greeted us with a smile, which, while tired, was more relaxed than the last one she offered us at Harriet Hardy's dinner.

"I'm proud of myself for making it this far," she said, "and I know I've done my best with what I'm doing today, even if it doesn't come out quite right. I'm only glad I've stayed the course. And the best part's been all of you supporting me — I couldn't have done it without all of you, and I'm ever so grateful."

"Oh, Dinah," said Gemma, giving her a hug. "You'll do wonderful today."

"Chin up," said Geoff. "The day's not over. You've as good a chance of winning as anybody, and better than several of them. Look how close you've come to winning first place in all the previous bakes."

"I know," said Dinah. "But it's best to be prepared, either way it goes. Now, wish me luck, because I'm off for one last time." She gave us all a final glance before she entered the pavilion.

"Fingers crossed," I said, and hoped that the fallen pudding cake was truly a fiction of my imagination last night.

Jenny Bryce was unpacking her mixing bowls, while Leeman was studying a very complicated-looking diagram with patterns attached to it. I saw Emily dusting off a set of deep, nested metal pans that promised to yield a towering cake in the near future. I sucked in my breath, and retreated to the garden momentarily, pretending to be busy inspecting the roses in bloom to hide a little flutter of doubt for Dinah's chances.

At noon, the cameras were ready, and Harriet and Pierre addressed the contestants one last time.

"Today, you will present your final bake — one worth fifty percent of your total points in this contest," said Harriet. "The theme is passion, and the dessert you present to us must reflect that theme in an unmistakable manner."

"We wish to see it — to taste it," said Pierre. "It must convince us that your passion for food, for life, for love, can be expressed physically by your skill. You will have four hours when the bell rings."

"We wish you all the best," said Harriet. And with that, the bell rang for the final challenge.

"I can't watch," said Gemma, from outside the pavilion. "I think I'm going a bit dizzy." Inside, mixers whirred to life as small clouds of flour rose from sacks poured into sifters, and pots clattered into place on the heated eyes of stoves.

"Four hours isn't long," I said, even though right now it felt like it would last forever. In the distance, I could see fans of the program watching hopefully, trying to glimpse the ongoing action. "Let's go have a cup of tea."

We had one in Lady Amanda's office, three of us sitting anxiously and watching the clock. Little Violet — or Harold — was lively today, so Lady Amanda couldn't bring herself to touch the last of Dinah's biscuits, the only thing left in the kitchen that wasn't from a shop tin.

"I should have had William make some shortbread," she said. "He's quite good at that sort of thing. I'm a bundle of nerves these days, between the baby and all this excitement." She pressed a hand to her stomach, where a moment before a tiny foot had made a decided movement beneath her blouse.

"Do you think it's in the oven now, at least?" Gemma propped her chin on her hands and gazed mournfully at a sculpture on Lady Amanda's desk, one that sort of resembled a cupcake at the right angle.

"They'll be halfway through with making decorations by now," I said. The clock's hands were both on the two. "The real test will be assembly, if Dinah's making a layer cake."

In the pavilion, cakes were cooling, while contestants were now whipping up icing and putting the finishing touches on cake toppers and other embellishments. Emily was making bowlfuls of white icing and had already filled two piping bags, Lord William reported to us, while Leeman had cakes of three different colors cooling on his racks.

"And Dinah?" asked Lady Amanda, eagerly.

"She was painting some sort of flower," said Lord William. "That's really all I could see of it, I'm afraid. She's quite near the back."

"And her cakes?" I said.

"Round, I think. I think there was a bit of chocolate involved, but I couldn't be certain. A biscuit, too, if you please, my love." He accepted a cup of tea from Lady Amanda. "I will say that I glimpsed a bit of Jenny Bryce's work ... and it appears to be quite flat."

"Flat?" we echoed. An exchange of glances proved we were all equally puzzled, both by his description and the possibilities it presented.

"On purpose, I presume. Rather unusual choice for a show-stopping presentation."

Jenny's was indeed flat — that is to say, more like loaves than Victoria sponges, although she was deftly cutting them on the diagonal using a large bread knife. I circled as far to Dinah's side as I could without being in danger of the camera's lens, but all I could see was a glimpse of Leeman swirling white frosting streaked with pink over three unusually-shaped sponges layered together. Dinah stepped to one side, holding a tray of something — but my view was blocked by another contestant hastening from the freezer to their work station, carrying some sort of meringue creation made to look like a giant rose.

At four o' clock, the event was over. Each presentation was concealed by a folding white screen made to look like a big present with a bow on top, ready to be pulled away as the contestant revealed his or her creation to the judges. Harriet and Pierre entered the pavilion, each armed with the program's trademark 'tasting fork' to sample the goods.

First up, the meringue rose — pretty impressive at first glance, except for the fact that the meringue's piping didn't look very petal-like up close, and wasn't quite swirly enough to be a flowered hat, either. Next, a 'volcano of love' made from chocolate that pumped a strawberry lava glaze down its sides and into a little chocolate-made paradise — that was the effort of the boy who made the frog pastries and the pirate ship of gingerbread. Pierre and Harriet had a heated debate over whether a volcano merely represented destructive powers or 'flowing passion,' as its creator claimed — Harriet, the detractor, won. Still, it was the more impressive of the two, I felt.

An Eiffel Tower, a cake iced like a valentine card, a couple of wedding cakes, and even miniature cakes that looked like roses and engagement ring boxes followed. And that was before Leeman unveiled his sweetheart cake. Three layers of heart-shaped sponge, each layer a different shade of red or pink, and topped with three sparkly-sugared marzipan roses.

"An excellent sponge," said Harriet. "And the flavor is very satisfactory. Cherry?"

"And vanilla," said Leeman, proudly. Pierre said nothing, his fork flattening a bite of the cake as if testing its spring.

Next up, Jenny's. The cake loaves had been pieced together to form a daisy shape, iced bright pink and decorated with candied cherry bits. It was a 'love cake,' she informed the judges: a special family recipe that was guaranteed addictive. "And it brings everybody love who tastes it, legend says," she claimed.

Already, Harriet didn't look thrilled by the sight of it. "Such a ... *uniform* pink," she said, at last. "Perhaps it needs just a bit more of something to give it definition. Don't you agree?" She looked at Pierre.

Pierre chipped off one of the candied cherries, a curl of contempt briefly evident in his lower lip at the same time. "What is this, this candied fruit you English prefer?" he said. "This kind is so sticky — it is so heavy. It has the — the texture of a piece of leather, no? The fruitcake of the *supermarche* is so ... I cannot eat it." His fork clattered against the plate as he dropped it in apparent protest.

"The cake itself is quite nice," said Harriet. "Do taste it, Pierre."

But the same candied cherries were chopped up inside the sponge, and the French chef declined on the grounds of a sensitive palate. Despite all the social media boastings from before, I felt extremely sorry for Jenny at this moment, who looked crestfallen as the two judges argued heatedly about the virtues and drawbacks of candied fruit.

Their argument came to an end when Emily's cake was unveiled. A three-tier wedding cake like the ones before, its surface was smooth, perfect fondant over vanilla cream, a scrollwork of frosting creating a collar-like design around each towering layer. Miniature blood red roses surrounded the topmost edges, while a pair of marzipan turtle doves nuzzled each other at the very top.

Emily sliced the bottom layer. A perfect yellow sponge was inside, with a tiny pink flower-shaped center cut from strawberry cake embedded in it. Harriet proclaimed the sugar work to be the finest she had witnessed in the whole competition. She declared the cake itself 'heavenly' upon tasting it — and even Pierre was charmed by the perfect — and non-burned — second cake embedded in the main sponge.

"An almost perfect creation," he said. "You have my compliments. *C'est* a cake magnificent."

Dinah was last of all. She didn't look nervous as she unfolded the white screen hiding her final sponge. I crossed my fingers one last time as I teetered nervously on my heels just outside the pavilion, behind the production crew filming the event; I felt Gemma seize hold of my arm, anxiously, as Dinah's creation came into view.

Three layers of sponge iced in ivory white, each tier separated by cake posts almost lost to sight behind blossoms and miniature fruits. Not real ones, but ones crafted from marzipan, fondant, and chocolate, looking so real I almost didn't believe she had made them.

Red and pink roses with chocolate petals, passion fruits with a blush of red on their pale green skins, brilliant hibiscus blossoms in shades of wine and crimson, white chocolate throats and marzipan stamens flecked with velvety, tinted cocoa powder like red pollen. At the very top, a split pomegranate — its rosy flesh and scarlet seeds of chocolate and seedless raspberry jam as artistically deceptive as the rest of the ornaments. It was surrounded by red fairy roses, passion flowers with soft fringe petals made from colored chocolate in dusky red, and a large Stargazer lily fashioned from painted fondant.

"Well," said Harriet, after a moment of gazing silently at the cake. "That's quite impressive." She paced from one view to the next, examining it. "I really don't know where to begin."

"We begin by cutting it," said Pierre. "What is this cake, madame?"

"Chocolate," said Dinah. A slight tremor made her voice sound slightly different, but otherwise she was calm. "It's red velvet cake and devil's food in alternating layers. Spiced with a little cayenne to add some depth to it. The filling between is preserves made from pomegranate and passion fruit."

"Pomegranate and passion fruit *both*?" he said. "With the red pepper? It is too much." He shook his head.

"I've been very careful," said Dinah, stoutly. "The flavors are balanced, so that the pepper brings a bit of heat and savory to the chocolate, and the fruits bring a bit of sweetness to it."

Inside, the cake dark chocolate layers contrasted with the deep scarlet ones, a smoky shade of red. Harriet's fork pierced it, lifting a bite to her lips. "And the frosting?" she enquired.

"White chocolate. With a bit of spice to temper the sweetness."

Harriet had her first bite. Beside her, with a sigh, Pierre cut away a miniature square with his fork and did the same. My stomach tied itself in knots as I watched. Dinah didn't close her eyes, but I could see her hands clench her apron as she waited.

Pierre was the first to speak. "I was not wrong," he said, at last. "It is too much. But in the way that passion itself — the very heart of it — may burn with too much also." He cut away a second forkful, and I felt the breath of the pavilion's occupants leave their lungs in collective shock. Was Pierre Dupine taking a *second* mouthful of something?

"It is almost like a perfume made with chocolate," said Harriet. "It is very aromatic. Very rich — but not too sweet. You have managed to balance the elements so that the chocolate's bitterness is rich, and outlasts the sweetness of your fruits."

"A wine of chocolate, perhaps," said Pierre. "It has a bouquet of its own. Congratulations, madame. It is a *piece des merveilleuse.*"

A little cry escaped Dinah's throat. She took a deep, shuddering breath. "Thank you," she said.

Pierre and Harriet exchanged glances. "We must now retire and make our decision," he said. They laid their forks beside the plate of Dinah's cake.

It would be close. Really close. But after those words about the 'chocolate perfume' of Dinah's passion cake, I knew that there were only three possibilities in the judges' minds. When the multi-flavored sponges of Leeman's three hearts valentine cake came in third, there were only two possibilities left — Emily and Dinah.

"In second place, with a total of eighty-eight points ..." said Harriet, "... is Emily Pierce."

Emily looked pleased and disappointed all at once — Dinah looked as if she was about to faint, even before Harriet finished speaking the all-important words.

"And in first place, with ninety-one points, is Dinah Barrington."

***

"I was never so afraid of anything as I was those words," said Dinah, with her hand pressed against her chest. "Heavens, I thought my heart might leap out of my chest before I heard the final scores read."

"I can't believe you won!" said Gemma, who was squeezing Dinah's other hand in a congratulatory death grip. "I mean, I can — but I can't — you know what I mean!"

"Goodness, you'll turn my finger bones into bits of glass candy if you're not careful," said Dinah, extricating herself from Gemma's unconscious hold. "I'll need that hand come tomorrow, you know." And with that, Dinah was back to her old self.

"A toast," said Pierre, opening a small glass liquor bottle. "It is sherry from Jerez de la Frontera — to celebrate your gain. I have opened a bottle with every winner, so it is a privilege I will share with you and your friends now also." He filled a row of delicate glasses which shared the dining room's table with the contestants' entries, Dinah's triumphant passion cake as its centerpiece.

"No French wine?" said Harriet, accepting her glass, and raising one eyebrow. "I thought you would disdain toasting love and passion with anything so removed from your homeland as a Spanish liquor, Pierre."

"Love makes us all do strange things," he said. "To passion. To *amore*. And to the many flavors in which it comes."

He clinked his own glass against Harriet's, and they both raised the drink to their lips — in that moment, I witnessed a gleam in their exchanged glances that made me think there was a possibility of something more between them than the program's onscreen rivalry of tastes and nationalities.

Maybe there was something to Jenny Bryce's famous family recipe after all.

"To Dinah," said Geoff, now raising his own glass in a toast. "Who today proved herself what most of us already knew her to be."

"Go on with you now," she answered, with a scoff. "It was a narrow squeak. If Emily Pierce had only added a bit of citrus to her sponge, I'd be a happy second place contestant right now."

"So what comes next?" I asked. "Now that you're the winner of The Grand Baking Extravaganza?" And, for that matter, the substantial prize awarded to each of its victors, something that hadn't occurred to me until now.

Here was Dinah's chance for an old dream — not necessarily that of being Cliffs House's longest-serving chef. I knew that everybody was thinking the same thing, now that the realization sank into us all that Dinah was the winner.

"Well," said Dinah. "I don't know. It's a decent heap of quid, I suppose. Enough to do a great many things." She gazed at her glass of sherry, pretending to study its color. "I did think before about having a little bakery someday...not that I want to be disloyal to Cliffs House. You've been quite splendid to me, really," she said to Lady Amanda and Lord William, who were standing among us.

"And will be whether you go or stay," said Lady Amanda, putting her arm around Dinah's shoulders. "We're simply proud of you. That won't change in the future, whether you're the cook in Cliffs House's kitchen, or a proud businesswoman. Although," she added, "we will miss your marmalade and your saffron biscuits terribly."

"Quite terribly," added Lord William, with a smile. "But we still wouldn't stop you, if you decide you would be happier elsewhere."

"Enough talking about people leaving," said Gemma, looking unhappy. "It's bad enough that Pip's gone without Dinah going, too." She took a sip from her glass. "I wish everything would stay the way it is for a little while."

"Even your being single?" I teased. "No proposal from Andy, or anyone else?"

Gemma looked slightly taken aback, then blushed. "Well, almost everything," she clarified. "A few changes wouldn't do any harm."

"I can't believe we're not allowed to tell anybody what's happened," said Lady Amanda, disappointedly. "I would so love to call my parents — and a few friends — and tell them how delightful this has been. Our lips are sealed for five whole weeks."

"I know," I said. "Isn't it awful?" As soon as Lady Amanda had rejoined Dinah, I knew I would make a discreet move to tell the one person from whom I could never keep secrets....and not the pages of my newly-adopted journal, before you ask. My finger was already itching to press Matt's number on my mobile and tell him the amazing news.

"I believe that a tasting of the cake is in order for the rest of us," said Lord William. "This is a celebration, isn't it?"

"Permit me the honor, if you will," said Pierre, who began cutting the sampled layer of the passion cake into narrow slices. "We must save some for tonight's farewell party, of course — but it will do no harm for Ms. Barrington's friends to share its secret in advance."

As Pierre was speaking, Kitty and Nathan joined the fringes of the celebratory circle, standing apart from each other as the samples of Dinah's cake circulated. A moment later, however, Kitty's fingers stole across to lightly brush against the palm of Nathan's hand. His eyes met hers instantly; in that look they shared was a very different secret from the one behind the desserts being served today.

Unless, of course, love really is the secret ingredient, and not just in the air.

A Castle in Cornwall

By

Laura Briggs

I stood at the crescendo of the walkway, where the two biggest stones become a wall to the eye — a short one that only blocks you from taking two or three climbing steps down the plummet before it becomes sheer, yet jagged stone to the bottom. From here, the sea's restlessness is an ever-changing picture, one that I, Julianne Rose, never grow tired of watching, no matter how many times I come here.

No place is more special in all of Cornwall than this one, not to me. Here, I met the love of my life, who mistook me for a tourist the same instant I trampled his endangered native plant. Here, I would tell him I loved him only a few short months later, before we were temporarily parted. Best of all, it is the place where he asked me to marry him after we weathered various storms in our relationship.

I first laid eyes on the fierce and rugged beauty of the county's shore in this place, and it changed my life forever. Now, as I take a deep breath of sea air, and hear the wind and waves collide with the stones forming these heights, I ask myself how I could ever leave it behind.

But that, sadly, is exactly what I have to do.

***

Three Months Earlier

I hadn't the slightest intention of entertaining thoughts of going home. My life in Cornwall was — well — perfect. As the event planner for Cliffs House manor, I had the career I'd always dreamed of, right? Better than my old life in Seattle, where I'd been the bottom dweller on Design a Dream's staff. And the ring on my finger symbolized a relationship more amazing than any from my romantic past, too.

But it only takes a phone call from a friend to change things. And when that phone call is from your best friend, it's difficult to say 'no,' even if it means a major disruption in your own plans — which is exactly what happened to me. Aimee, my best friend in all the world, was having surgery and had no one else who could run her business during her recovery time. Months of lost revenue meant she'd have to close her shop unless someone could take over for her, someone she trusted and who knew the vision she'd been trying to create with her work ... and that's where I come in. Me, who helped her choose everything from wall color to business plan over five years ago when Aimee first dreamed of doing it.

"It would only be for a few months," I said, wrapping my arms around my legs, resting my cheek against my knees. A good huddling position when I was in need of some self-comfort. "She thinks she'll be back on her feet by next March, once her physical therapy is complete. But ... it'll be months. Definitely sure about that part." I bit my lip after these words.

"It's your decision, my love," said Matt. "But as strongly as you feel about it, I can't see you choosing any differently. We will make it work. I promise." From his place on the floor, where he had been drawing a garden layout, he leaned back against the sofa, his hand brushing against my bare foot.

"It's not me I'm worried about," I said. "It's you. What will you do in Seattle?"

Matt was going with me, of course. When I first explained the situation, I had tried to talk him into staying behind in Cornwall, but he declined. This time wasn't the same as our first separation, when we had barely been dating for three months with no commitments between us, as Matt pointed out to me. Even then, we had both been miserable while apart, proving long-distance relationships weren't our cup of tea.

Matt laughed. "Don't worry about me," he said. "Haven't I told you before? I'll find something to keep myself occupied. There is a natural world in Washington as well as Cornwall, and, I have no doubt, plenty of opportunities for employment in either plant science or propagation."

I pictured Matt in wading boots, collecting botanical specimens from along Washington's rocky coasts. This wasn't exactly on par with Matt's Ivy League career from before in the U.S. It was true that Matt changed careers frequently — from classrooms to digging in the dirt in historical gardens, for instance — but I hated to tear him away from opportunities like his most recent one: designing a special landscape tribute to botanical artist Constance Strong's work, in honor of her gallery show opening in Marseilles.

America was a long ways from France. And I wouldn't have a lot of free time for travel while learning the business ropes before Aimee's surgery.

I sighed. "I just don't want things to change," I said. "I love our life. I love this place. And I feel like we're losing everything somehow, just by crossing the Pond ... even if it's only temporarily."

"That's normal," said Matt, softly. "Anyone feels that way when facing a decision like this one. But we can't change the fact that life changes, Juli. And we change with it. I'm afraid it's true. I've loved this place all my life, yet I still left it for a time after university ... and even after coming back, as you well know. Had circumstances been slightly different, I might never have come back at all."

I was indignant, thinking he meant had he gone to New York with Petal, the former model whom Matt had once loved in America — then I realized he was probably talking about the career he gave up after their breakup, his teaching position and the historical gardens in Massachusetts. Even so, I didn't soften towards his suggestion that a few random choices meant he wouldn't have been on the cliffs path the day I took my first walk in Cornwall.

"Well, I'm not changing," I said, stubbornly. "There was nothing wrong with my life in Seattle, and nothing wrong with Washington ... it just wasn't what I truly wanted. It didn't make me happy the way this life does. You weren't there, for starters."

"But I will be now," he pointed out. "Happily combing the beaches of Seattle, and helping you stock boutique shelves when needed. Won't that make a difference?"

"It'll make it more fun," I conceded. "Compared to life at Design a Dream, anyway." Where my former boss had been all too eager to lay credit to any pathetic little bit of an idea she gave me the chance to share for any event we planned.

"You don't think you could change your mind about that life?" Matt raised one eyebrow. "You'll be home again, Julianne. The land of Starbucks and Coca-Cola, of Thanksgiving dinners and fall foliage like a fireworks display in nature —"

"You're thinking of New England," I said. "In Seattle, it rains nearly as much as England." I was exaggerating a tiny bit, maybe, but I stuck with my point. "In that respect, you'll feel as at home as you do in London, I suppose." I was desperately maintaining my pout. Trying very hard not to concede that Matt's argument was logical, and not entirely without possibility, no matter how much I wanted otherwise.

"Don't you think there's a chance you might someday want to return to Molehill?" He referred to my true hometown, the one I had left behind for Seattle in the first place.

"Not if I can retire to Mousehole first," I answered. To Matt, they both seemed equally small, but vastly different, I supposed. And even if I did miss landmarks from my past — my childhood home, my elementary school, the park where I used to play — would I ever miss them enough to live there again, the way Matt had come back to Ceffylgwyn?

"Still," he edged closer, now encompassing one of my hands with his own, "it's only fair that we give life on your side of the Pond a decent chance after the time we've given my home. I've never had a chance to see your former place in the world, since I was on the other side of the country."

Matt hadn't visited Washington during either our engagement or the first months of our marriage — my parents had flown to England twice, and Aimee had come once, but we'd never had the opportunity before to visit my old haunts in Seattle. The bookstore where I used to curl up with a cup of coffee ... the site of the very first wedding I had helped coordinate, be it in a very minor role ... the places where Aimee and Nate and I hung out, or even the spots where I had gone on an occasional date (not counting my rather fruitless relationship with Dwight, of course).

"I could show you around a little," I said, as Matt rose from our threadbare carpet of cabbage roses. "After all, it's only fair, as you said."

"We'll be there for Christmas," he said. "You can show me your family's traditions firsthand."

My family would probably insist upon joining us, I knew — we'd all cram into a small space and maybe forego my mom's usual pre-purchased ham dinner for something a little more special.

"Those traditions involve baking lots of cookies," I said, foregoing the word 'biscuit' since we were talking about America anyway. "And decorating the tree weeks early with really awful handmade ornaments and all the really beautiful ones we love ... and driving around the neighborhoods to see all the houses decorated. Maybe walking past a few — hand in hand, of course. And everyone's windows are lit up, and you see glimpses of parties, smiling guests and hear holiday music when the door opens ... and you dream about the evening your own home is full of friends and as alive as the one you've just admired."

I couldn't help the fact that my voice softened for these words; the picture in my head was an old one, but one I loved, even as deeply as I loved this cottage, and the view of the restless waters of this coast.

Matt's arms slid around my shoulders from behind; I rested my head against his shoulder.

"I guess maybe it's worth seeing for one Christmas," I said. "I wouldn't want you to be deprived of some of our many American holiday traditions. And I shouldn't abandon Aimee to frozen turkey dinners for Thanksgiving." I smiled, even though Matt couldn't see it with his face buried against my hair.

It meant a year without a tree in our cozy corner in Rosemoor Cottage, of course. But we would bring along Matt's beloved childhood reindeer ornament, and hang it next to the souvenir snow globe I had treasured as a child. We would welcome his sister Michelle and her new husband in whatever place we called our own, if they wanted to come; and top our tree with her childhood handmade angel one last time before it returned to its rightful owner. We could learn to live without Dinah's fantastic puddings and a proper Cornish 'cream tea' for a few months while we contented ourselves with Seattle's amazing coffees and biscotti.

"We can come back," Matt whispered close to my ear, as if sensing my thoughts. "And we can give the life wherever we are a chance in the meantime, making the most of it. As long as I'm with you, I'll be content ... and you've already said the most important part for you is being with me."

"True," I whispered back. I closed my eyes, too, picturing the future we would have on the opposite side of the Pond. One that would create new memories, be captured in new photographs, and commemorated in all the 'bits and bobs' that would fill shelves, tables — and moving boxes — for the rest of our life together.

But it won't be the same as this life. And no matter how good it is, I know that I want to come back, because this is home for me.

***

"Happy birthday," said Nathan.

On Kitty's desk, he placed a white box tied with a glittery pink ribbon, an eager smile on his face as he waited, hands tucked in his pockets. Kitty eyed the gift as she lifted it, as if it might contain live insects, or maybe an unwelcome charge card bill instead of a present from someone who was obviously infatuated with her.

"How'd you know it was my birthday?" she asked. Her fingers tugged the ribbon loose.

"Dinah squealed," he said. "Come on, open it up." He sat down on the edge of her desk, looking as eager as if he was the one with a present to open.

He looked completely smitten with her at this moment. Frankly, it was almost adorable, which must be making it tough for Kitty to keep up her usual air of indifference towards him ... one which was rapidly revealing itself as a feint to anybody close to her these days.

She lifted the lid and from inside, lifted an intricate-looking Eiffel tower made completely of chocolate. The label on the box from a Paris *confeterie*, undoubtedly.

"Thanks," she said. Two pink spots invaded her cheeks at this point. "It's pretty." The tone with which she uttered those understated words was proof that she was secretly pleased. After all, Kitty's French was more than a little intelligible now after several weeks with books and online pronunciation guides, as our new cook Michael from Nice had admitted; this was no doubt the reason why Nathan had chosen this present.

"I, um, thought you might like it," said Nathan, who was blushing now, too. "There's more to the present than just the chocolate — the rest just didn't arrive in time."

"You don't have to get me anything," she said, although she was still turning the little tower ornament, taking in its ornate detail. It had a ribbon at the top, as if it was an ornament and not an edible — and highly meltable — object. "I mean, it's not obligatory, since we — since I didn't say anything about it, or whatever. Besides, Paris chocolate's not exactly cheap."

"So?" said Nathan. "Like I said, I wanted to get you something. And I wanted to stop by and see you today." Suddenly, he was very busy studying the carpet, and then the framed print of the Duke of Wellington on the opposite wall. "I thought maybe if you weren't busy tonight ... I'd take you somewhere. Since it's your birthday and all."

"Oh." Kitty's blush was a little different now, and rapidly turned pale. "Thanks. But ... I've got a thing already. With the players."

It was Nathan's turn to look disappointed. "Right," he said. "The community theatre. I forgot that was coming up." He studied a random paperweight on Kitty's desk. "So ... is this time something important?"

"It's auditions," said Kitty. "I'm thinking about trying for a part this time."

She looked embarrassed, although she shouldn't — Kitty was a surprisingly good fit for Ceffylgwyn's amateur players. It had taken her weeks to work up the courage to attend one of their meetings, where the sullen looks that cover up her shyness had finally melted away in the theatre's diverse and sometimes eclectic society.

Then again, maybe that shyness was now about something different, since both she and Nathan seemed to be suffering from it. Their glances were brief, their body language that of two people who are trying desperately to *not* give in and let stronger feelings take charge.

"That's — that's great." Nathan still looked slightly disappointed, but undaunted. "Maybe later, then," he said. "I mean, I know that rehearsals always mean you don't have as much spare time, but I ..."

He hadn't seen me sitting at the table by the door, sending a few emails to a London bakery about an upcoming wedding's cake prices. Not until I rose and approached Kitty's desk with a list of vendors did he realize that I was in the office, too, leaping up as if the desk's corner was covered in hot coals.

"Hi," he said — too brightly to be a comfortable or genuine greeting, since it was obviously covering up his guilt. "Um, I just thought I'd stop by and catch up with things here — you know, discuss the upcoming wine competition —" He stuffed his hands in his pockets, since he had no idea what to do with them up to this moment.

"Save it, Nathan," I said, with a grin. "I know about you two. You don't have to pretend." I gave them each a knowing look before I departed. The blushes of both Kitty and the event promoter were dead giveaways that things had progressed since what happened between them this past summer.

Everyone knew it was true. The fact that they had been seen together several times that fall and winter only confirmed it — not that either of them actually used the word *relationship*, of course, as if their dating was a covert operation. Uncertainty, undeclared feelings — was all too familiar from my own past, and I wondered how long until the two of them admitted the truth to each other about how serious they were.

I knew I could probably twist Kitty into admitting details on its seriousness later. But now, I had something more important, and more personal, to do. I followed the sound of voices, and a repeated soft *thud* not in the direction of Lady Amanda's office, but to the long hall upstairs that served as a portrait gallery for Lord William's long line of ancestors who occupied Cliffs House before him.

Despite the dour-looking expression of great-great-and-so-on-grandfather Edward, little Edwin picked this spot as his favorite place for playing fetch. Of course, his mum did most of the fetching for him, since five-month-old Edwin could only sit up — but as Lord William, inventor of this particular baby game, had pointed out, it might be the arm of a future cricket champion which hurled that red ball an impressive distance of three feet.

His name was a last minute choice in a compromise between his parents, since the baby name dilemma had stretched on until the mystery was revealed with his birth. The rest of him definitely favored his mother, all except his newly-growing hair, which was Lord William's bristly brown thatch instead of Lady Amanda's ginger color.

"Who's a little bowler? Yes, he is!" Lady Amanda's baby talk voice produced giggles from the future heir of Cliffs House, who was seated on a blanket knitted by his grandmother, wearing a pair of ducky overalls that Gemma herself had picked out as a gift, and a pair of tiny red boots. He clapped his small hands, which were momentarily not occupied with either his favorite red ball or with mussing up his hair.

From the gleam in Edwin's eye as he watched my approach, I knew it wouldn't be many more months before he gained mastery of his tiny feet; it would be his destiny to walk early and lead his mother into many panicked scenarios involving disassembled bouquets and upset biscuit trays.

"Lady Amanda," I said. "Can I have a word with you?"

"Of course," she said. "Would you mind terribly retrieving that ball from behind the podium for Lady Mulgrove's bust? Honestly, it's the second time this morning the silly thing has rolled there."

She was seated cross-legged for the moment, a binder from her huge shoulder tote bag now open on her lap to a list of local boat charters — despite being wife, mother, and lady of the manor, Lady Amanda's tireless efforts at small business growth and public relations in the village took a back seat to nothing, not even Nathan Menton's efforts to put us on the map.

"What is it, Julianne?" she asked. "If it's about the wine competition, I have a complete inventory list on my desk — the master of ceremonies emailed me by mistake." She pretended to make the red ball disappear — on Edwin's face, a momentary look of astonishment as his toy disappeared up the sleeve of Lady Amanda's flowing blouse. "Where did it go?" she asked him, making her eyes as wide as his own.

"Actually, it's something more serious," I said. "Sort of a problem." I sat down beside her.

"Do tell," she said. The red ball reappeared, and all was right in Edwin's world for the moment.

"My friend Aimee in Seattle has an emergency and needs my help," I said. "Specifically, she needs me to run her business for a few months while she recovers from a medical procedure. She doesn't have any parents or siblings to do it for her, and there's no one else she can trust." I swallowed. "And I told her that I would do it."

A moment of silence. Lady Amanda looked surprised. "I see," she said, at last.

"I don't want to quit," I said. My face had begun to burn hot; my hands tingled horribly, the circulation gone from my fingers in my anxiousness. "But I understand that you can't possibly hold this job for me while I'm gone. I mean, we're not talking about a normal holiday, are we?" I laughed, although it felt very fake to do so. "So what I'm saying is ... I understand if you have to replace me."

"Replace you?" said Lady Amanda.

"You need an event planner, a coordinator," I said. "Now more than ever, since you've got little Edwin on top of your own business to run.

And I know that you're probably not ready to trust Kitty to do it."

Kitty had come a long ways in a short time, but even I didn't know if she was ready for the pressure of handling Cliffs House on her own. The chaos, the difficult clients who were sometimes picky about their hors d'oeuvres, or angry about a last-minute change — would Kitty revert back to her old self, the opinionated hothead who thought nothing of challenging or insulting her antagonist?

As if sensing this was a serious moment for his mother, Edwin handed me his red ball, his tiny face suddenly solemn. I accepted it, turning it over in my hands as I spoke, as if it were a Magic 8 Ball that would predict the outcome of all this.

"I was going to hand you a formal resignation in a few weeks, but I wanted to talk to you first, so it doesn't come out of the blue," I continued. "I thought I would help you choose a successor, if you needed help doing it."

"I don't see why you should resign for good," said Lady Amanda. "Not if you're planning to return."

"But for months?" I said. "What will you do?" I pictured her hiring a nanny for Edwin, letting her own business affairs fall slack to tie up loose ends for the public side of manor life. It was hardly fair.

"We'll do what you suggested," she said. "We'll give Kitty a chance. After all, she's proven herself quite competent the last six months or so. She deserves a chance ... and, anyway, we'd probably be leaning on her skills until we found someone to replace you, wouldn't we? And it's not as if you're asking us for a paid extended holiday, are you?"

"No," I admitted. "But it's too much to ask, having you hold the position for me." *And if I don't come back,* I could add, even though it didn't seem possible in my mind. But if I didn't, then Cliffs House's affairs could, well, go 'over the cliff' as they say ... unless Kitty proved herself worthy enough to take my place on a permanent basis.

"Nonsense," said Lady Amanda. "It's my decision, you know, more than William's, even. And I wouldn't choose someone to take your place unless your decision to stay in America was absolute. Besides which, I must admit that I've grown rather fond of Kitty these past few months — she's really quite good with Edwin, you know. He positively adores her."

I thought of Kitty's protests that she was terrible with kids, and hid my smile. "If you want to give her a trial period, I would support you," I said. "We both know she's gifted at this work, whether she admits it or not."

"I had been thinking she might handle the wine competition on her own," said Lady Amanda, whose tone was decidedly thoughtful with this reply. "It would be a good test, really, now that I consider it from all angles. If she can handle that crowd, then we'll know she's practically ready."

"Ag gug goo!" proclaimed Edwin. I handed him the red ball and watched as his throw landed it a disappointing two feet away from his own.

The *'had been thinking'* of Lady Amanda's speech caught my ear. "Really?" I said. "You wanted Kitty to be in charge of the event?"

Don't get me wrong — it wasn't professional pride that made me ask, but genuine surprise. This particular competition involved a rather posh and serious subset in the wine community — a group we had dealt with before, who were now hosting a few English winemakers and a few small French vineyards for a blind tasting. The sort of clients who made Lady Amanda nervous, due to the list of pet peeves and preferences that accompanied their booking.

"She wouldn't want to budge from the manor this summer, anyway," continued Lady Amanda. "Not with the players staging a new production, of course. She and Michael get on swimmingly, so the menu for the brunch and the hors d'oeuvres would be simple for the two of them."

"Of course," I said. "But what do you mean by 'budge'?" Was Kitty planning to go somewhere, and I had been clueless about it?

"Yes, well...I had rather a favor in mind from you." Lady Amanda hesitated. "I suppose I've been putting off asking for it — but since you've confided in me, and you're not leaving immediately, I believe that I'll take advantage of your skills while they are still at my disposal. You *are* here for the summer, I trust?"

"Of course," I said. "And I'm happy to help with anything." Nevertheless, I felt puzzled. There wasn't another major event on Cliffs House's calendar for the summer — unless there was one I didn't know about —

"I don't suppose you've had any experience with royal weddings, have you?" said Lady Amanda.

My eyes widened. "What?" I said.
"Ga-ga woo!" declared Edwin, clapping.

***

Azure Castle, home to the Honorable Samuel and Marjorie Ridgeford, stood at the top of a hill in the village of Aval Towan, or 'sand apple,' as it means in Cornish, named for a once-famous orchard which stood close to the sea. The tongue-in-cheek nickname of the castle locally was 'Towan Castle,' Lady Amanda explained — even with only a smattering of Cornish at my disposal, I was quick to get the point, since 'towan' means 'sand.'

"Marjorie's ever so grateful for this," said Lady Amanda. "You can't imagine, really. She was almost in tears after Helen rang her and positively *begged* to use the place for the wedding. 'Bullied' would be the proper word for it. Helen's one of those women who always has her way, whether it's by the pressure of tears or words. And ever since the scandal with her husband, she's had a positive fear of the press, her London house practically a cloister since he left."

Helen was Lady Helen Lewison — and somehow closely related to William's cousin Marjorie, it seemed, although Lady Amanda had yet to explain how close. Enough so that she couldn't refuse to let her family's home be used for a family wedding, it seemed.

"Honestly, I don't know how her daughter endured it, short of being at school most of the time — then again, I don't know how Marjorie let herself be persuaded to leave her flat behind for weeks, merely so Helen and the others can avoid a few photographers."

Lady Amanda was at the wheel of her car as we drove to Aval Towan, passing road signs for Land's End and other villages along the Cornish Riviera's coast. I was in the seat beside her, while Gemma and Pippa were squeezed into the rear seat beside a snoozing baby Edwin. Yes, our very own Pippa, who wouldn't miss an opportunity to be part of a royal wedding — even if the royalty involved was as distantly removed from the crown as these two lovers.

"Isn't he a prince, though?" piped up Gemma. "That means he's probably really famous in his country — the entertainment reporters will be mobbing the family for all sorts of juicy details."

"Imagine marrying a prince," sighed Pippa. "It's so romantic. Like the movie where the girl finds out she's a princess, but was living like an ordinary nerd in some American city. Remember the one?" she looked at Gemma. "With Anne Hathaway?"

"He's in the line of succession," answered Lady Amanda, "but very distantly in line for actually inheriting a Scandinavian throne, I assure you. I believe several uncles and their descendants would have to die first." Her lips cracked a rather wicked smile as she caught my eye. "Josephine won't be crowned anytime soon."

"Josephine?" echoed Pippa, dismayed. "What sort of name is that for a princess-to-be?" She wrinkled her nose with distaste, although I couldn't see anything wrong with it.

“But well suited to an empress, I suppose?” Lady Amanda winked at me. "Magnus's choice," she explained to Pippa, referring to Helen's former husband. "It was popular in whatever part of Canada his shipping line was headquartered once — the island where *Anne of Green Gables* was written, I think."

"Josephine Barry," I said. "The unlikely 'kindred spirit' to Anne."

"Who?" said Pippa. "I've never heard of her. Was she some sort of psychic?" But the only reply was a sleepy gurgle from Edwin, who was beginning to wake up for his lunch.

"How much farther?" I asked Lady Amanda.

"A little longer. Aval Towan is above Penzance on the coast. Not quite part of the Cornish Riviera per say ... the village faces the sea to the west," she said. "I'll show you on the map — where is it?"

"Here's one for the Newquay township," I said. "There's one for the inland roads —" I sifted through the glove compartment's assorted objects, finding mostly extra brochures from the businesses Lady Amanda represented, a bottle of hand cream, and a spare pacifier.

"Is the prince at the castle already?" ventured Gemma.

"Everyone's at the castle," said Lady Amanda, abandoning our search for the map after several sample brochures landed on the car floor. "Even Josephine's grandmother, the antiquated Lady Astoria, who has deigned to leave Paris just to bestow her blessing on the girl ... or stop the wedding, whichever decision her sharp mind entertains upon arriving.

And Kristofer's branch of the royal family is there, of course..."

I heard Gemma issue a contented sigh. "There's not a chance there's a few royal brothers, I suppose?" she asked.

"Afraid not. At twenty-two, Kristofer is the oldest and only child of Prince Gustaf," said Lady Amanda. "I'm afraid any younger siblings that might unexpectedly be added to his family would be more eligible as playmates for Edwin than suitors for either of you."

"She didn't say that the royal cousins wouldn't be there," pointed out Pippa. Edwin gave a louder burble of concern.

"I agree, lambikin," said Lady Amanda to him, in a soothing voice. "I believe it's time to luncheon, dear ladies," she said. "Then on to Azure Castle." She turned at the sign indicating Penzance, the nearest sizeable village to the apparently quiet-and-rustic Aval Towan. Our future destination sounded a little like Ceffylgwyn — only perhaps even sleepier, as hard as that would be to imagine, as it wrapped itself around its resident castle on the hill.

Above that sleepy village of whitewash and granite was indeed a hill that looked like a gently-sloping mound, heavily blanketed in timber, with towers of stone rising above the tree tops like sentinels watching over the world below. It was not the gentle slope it appeared, when Lady Amanda's car rumbled up the winding, mile-long wooded lane that curved suddenly to reveal the courtyards, gravel car park, and gardens that formed the grounds of Azure Castle.

"Here we are," she said. I drew a deep breath, unprepared for this first encounter with a true Cornish castle, its appearance as far removed from Cliffs House's stately grandeur as an ancient Norman cathedral is from Windsor Palace — two distinctly breathtaking sites which share the common grounds only of being historical buildings.

Like sand, Azure's newer towers seemed pale and tawny, almost white in the bright sunlight above its wooded glens. Turrets and fortress walkways abounded in its square portions and the serpentine curve of its original structure, especially on the oldest part which now faced us — a darker granite which did seem almost blue in the shadows, as if the trick of the sea's colors on a stormy day had been imparted to it. The whole construct was married together like puzzle's sections harmoniously joined at the corners, with impressive windows surveying us from three floors.

Its sleeping self seemed to awaken as the sun broke from behind its clouds once more, bathing the high walls and the bright shades of flowers in the massive carved urns placed along its facade. It could be a Mediterranean palace overlooking the sea — if only the sea was visible as more than a pigeon's view from the back gardens, as I would later learn. It could be the home where Sleeping Beauty lay for a hundred years, so peaceful and beautiful it stood in the garden's clearing.

"Wow," I said, softly. Nobody heard me, since they were busy taking notice of a second arrival, a rental car parking a short distance away, which was the only thing which drew my attention from the castle before us. From the driver's seat, Dinah emerged.

"Dinah!" Pippa's scream was echoed by the rest of us — as a group, we launched ourselves at Cliffs House's former cook, who almost dropped the box of pots and pans in her arms as a result.

"Heavens!" she said. "You would think it's been thirty years instead of a couple of months! Pippa, mind that decanter, child, it's fragile!"

Among the many favors that Marjorie had called on Lady Amanda to fulfill was the search for an exemplary baker whose prestigious bakery wouldn't try to cash in on the chance to make a royal wedding cake, as cousin Helen evidently feared. And there was nobody as talented or discreet as Dinah Barrington, winner of the southern counties' Grand Baking Extravaganza and owner of the newly-opened Sponge & Scone bakery — whose cakes had formerly graced the receptions of celebrities ranging from footballers to artists.

"It's been longer than that for me," said Pippa, giving Dinah a pouting look. "Aren't you the least bit glad to see me?" Pip had only been at Cliffs House once since her marriage to Gavin a year ago. The former kitchen assistant, along with Gemma, had always been wont to drive Dinah crazy with gossip about celebrities and speculations on the romantic status of Ceffylgwyn's natives ... although I always suspected Dinah enjoyed their company more than she admitted.

"Of course I am." Dinah's customary scolding, but softened, as usual. "And not the least bit surprised you're here, given the grand occasion." She shifted her box of supplies into a more comfortable position. "I only hope that my sponge doesn't fall flat — this filling is rather tricky, and in practice the whole thing is wont to lean."

"It will be brilliant," said Gemma. "You've never had it fail when it's a necessity to pull it off."

"Just like in the baking extravaganza," said Pippa. "Only your souffle was a bit wonky, come to think of it. And when Pierre pointed out —"

"Enough of this chitchat," said Dinah, before Pippa could detail the exacting sting of judge Pierre Dupine's critique. "Where is the kitchen?" she inquired of the caretaker, who was helping unload our luggage.

"Right this way," said Lady Amanda. In his carrier, Edwin began fussing, his pacifier having lost itself in the blankets, so Gemma lifted him up.

"How's my little fewwow?" she asked him, in exaggerated baby speak, as he beamed up at her, tears vanishing — Edwin was definitely aware of his power over the rest of Cliffs House, and knew how to use it. It resulted in him being fed tiny animal-shaped biscuits dipped in milk from Gemma and me, and getting loads of 'horsey rides' from Geoff whenever he came to tea.

"Here, you're not holding him right," said Pippa. "He needs better support. I'll show you." Pippa now worked at a child care center, where she probably spent hours holding babies and toddlers; but this was mostly an excuse to cuddle Edwin, I suspected, who found her pixie haircut fascinating. The six of us made our way inside, where Marjorie was waiting to meet us.

"I'm so glad you're here," she said, pouring a cup of tea from a brown china teapot. "I've been positively frantic for the past few weeks — Samuel's still in London, will be until the end of the trial, and meanwhile, everybody's popping up, from a Danish ambassador to the dowager herself." She sat down in one of the kitchen chairs. "I told Helen 'the house isn't ready — it hasn't been open since Reginald died, not even for tours by appointment!' But she was so dreadfully insistent ... going on about how Josephine was positively hounded by the press after Magnus left, and there were whispers that Kristofer's family dislikes family drama ... that I broke down ere the end of her pleadings."

She poured tea for all us in turn, as Dinah bustled around in the background, unpacking her personal utensils. "And what a dreadful mess I've made of things," she continued. "I was never lady of the manor, as you know. After all, when Reginald was alive, his second wife — the one from Greece, remember? — she did the smile and wave bit for the tourists, and at the Christmas Eve open house for the village, while I was busy worrying about Downing Street and Whitehall's matters."

Marjorie had a position in government finance, I had learned, while her husband was part of the judiciary. "And now that she's gone, I've no one to turn to but you. Well ... and Aunt Darlene, I suppose. But she's a bit potty these days, isn't she?" She took a sip from her mug.

"Practically senile," said Lady Amanda. "Never fear, though. I've had loads of experience in your shoes — keeper of the castle, that is. And I've brought my very best to answer your needs."

"Thank heavens," said Marjorie, blowing a wisp of bangs from her forehead. "They've placed almost everything about the reception and the decor in my hands. Of course, that gimlet of a wedding coordinator is slithering about, but she's only here to pass judgment, it seems. Helen's so dreadfully nervous that someone will find out about the wedding that she won't let practically anyone of note provide so much as a tulip!"

"You won't hear a peep from *me*," said Dinah, who was sampling biscuits — shop ones — with a look that suggested they were better quality than the ones that Gemma typically favored at home.

"Nor any of us," I said. "We promise that no word of weddings or royal ties will cross any of our lips, here or at home."

"Helen will be relieved," said Marjorie. Whose voice took on a slight edge when uttering this name.

"Why's she so afraid of the papers?" asked Gemma. "It's not like Prince Harry's getting married."

"Or someone else famous, even," added Pippa, who snagged a biscuit from the plate as Dinah passed it within her reach. "That is, I know the groom's practically a prince — and she's from some branch of the Queen's family tree — but even so, it's not the event of the year when there's loads of celebrity gossip and scandal happening every day. Footballers getting married, actors caught cheating. M.P. candidates upsetting the national polls — selling national secrets, even."

"Ah, well, scandal's the problem," said Marjorie, with a sigh. "Helen's husband left her, you know. Magnus Oppenheimer — the shipping tycoon here and abroad. Five years ago, he absconded with his masseuse — off to Malta on his yacht with nary a word of warning. He left Helen in tears. The whole thing made for a horrible story in the papers, and poor Josephine was scarcely fifteen when it all descended on her."

Marjorie poured a cup of tea for Dinah, who joined us now. "Poor child couldn't stir from her own home without nasty questions about her father plaguing her," Marjorie continued. "She ended up in boarding school in Switzerland to get away from it all. Helen was a bit of a disaster then."

"Is that how she met the prince?" asked Gemma, whose mind undoubtedly leaped ahead to romantic meetings on a ski slope, the prince and his princess-to-be sharing a sleigh robe for a moonlight ride in a reindeer-drawn sled.

"I suppose it was," said Marjorie. "In truth, I think this proposal was rather ... arranged." She hesitated. "His parents were very eager to have him nicely settled — they're a bit strict, quite afraid of their only son choosing a wild child, probably. A lovely, educated girl from a noble family, albeit a foreign one, probably seemed like an excellent stopping point in love, in their eyes."

"And her mother?" I said.

"Agreed right along with them. No doubt because she's afraid that Josephine will make a less-than-sensible choice herself. Magnus wasn't always a tycoon, you know. And he had a reputation — a small one — when they met." She set aside her teacup.

"It can't be a loveless match," said Lady Amanda, scoffing. "The parents can hardly be forcing these two into a union unless there's *something* there."

"Oh, they seem fond enough of each other — Kristofer especially — but this whole courtship has been rather rushed towards the ceremony. Stiff old upper crust forcing youth into its proper roles." Marjorie smiled. "You'll have a chance to see for yourself these next few weeks."

Dinah was showing everyone the sketches for the cake, two drawings encased in plastic sleeves, along with a photograph of a trial version. I carried my teacup to the tray on the sideboard, gazing at the formal garden which resembled a neat square of bright emerald between stone walls, with hedges like leafy marbles on twiggesh trunks.

"That's the bride," said Marjorie. Referring to a girl in the garden, occupying the middle of the square. Posed like a dancer, or maybe playing statue, she seemed so perfectly still and graceful.

"Ballet, or something from its modern school," said Marjorie, as if reading my mind. "She was a student as a girl — once, when she was quite small, I brought her to see an interpretative Eastern European dance company at the Royal Albert Hall. One of the rare holidays I wasn't fretting over an M.P.'s upcoming vote."

Now, as the girl struck a different pose, I could see the resemblance to some little ballerinas in a jewelry box from my childhood. Josephine had the proper build — slender, a 'slip of a girl' as prim little old ladies would say, in her fitted leggings and leather riding boots, a soft summer top with sleeves flowing around her arms like a dancer's light costume. Her brown waterfall of hair was obscuring the sight of a pair of earbuds, I suspected.

"She looks so young," I said. "She looks sixteen or seventeen, not old enough for marriage."

"She's nineteen," said Marjorie. She was carrying all the tea things to the counter now. "And very bright — she finished her studies early by spending every waking hour with books and classes. Art history and literature. She's only recently been free of scholarly duties, and wished to travel for a bit before settling on a future — I suspect that's why Helen pushed for the wedding, really."

"I see," I answered, feeling sad at the thought of Josephine's possibly-dashed dreams. "What about after they're married?"

They would live in Kristofer's country, I suspected; but surely Josephine wouldn't be the antiquated 'lady of the castle,' sitting around planning formal teas ... or whatever passed for them in Scandinavia. Kristofer wasn't a future king — and this was the twenty-first century, anyway.

"She wants to start an arts program or literacy foundation for children, I think." Marjorie's brow furrowed, as if she couldn't quite remember. "It's practically the only thing she talks about, while Helen and the rest talk above her about couture gowns and the nuptial theme for the formal hall."

"And Kristofer?" I felt a bit nosy asking, but I supposed we would all be meeting Marjorie's royal relations in a matter of hours anyway. It was better to know now than ask them dull questions later.

"Something in government or finance, I think. He's only a few weeks away from accepting a position. He's a charming boy — a bit shy on the surface, but quite personable and kind. Josephine spoke so fondly of him ... well, until their families began meddling." Marjorie's tone was a bit darker at this point. Underlying family tensions, I perceived.

"Go and introduce yourself, if you like," continued Marjorie. "She has to be summoned inside shortly anyway — a meeting with the aforementioned dictatorial coordinator begins in a quarter of an hour. Practically high tea around here." She rolled her eyes. "Just mind the security agents of Helen's, if they're about. They're quite touchy about strangers."

Security agents? "Sure," I said. I opened the outside door, finding a slate pathway outside it, branching in three directions at its crossways. I chose the one leading to the formal garden.

Josephine was inclined almost earthwards, one leg extended behind her, arms stretched in a graceful upside-down 'V'. I paused until she noticed me, then smiled.

She smiled back: a charming, small one that I expected from a newly-minted adult assuming a role in society. She rose, and removed the earbuds; I caught the faint strains of classical music. "Hello," she said.

"Hi. I'm Julianne Rose," I said. "I'm here with your cousin's wife, Amanda. I'm her event planner at Cliffs House, and she's asked me to help out with your wedding's plans."

"You're an American," said Josephine. "From what state?"

"Washington," I said. "Have you ever been there?" Maybe Josephine and I could talk about travel — I had no idea what one discussed with a possible future princess. Were normal subjects acceptable? Should I say something polite about the royal family, or remark on the beauty of castles or crowns?

"Never. I've never been outside of Europe," she answered. "Mummy doesn't like air travel. It gives her a headache. And until recently I was quite busy with my studies, even for holidays. My father has, though." Her tone was short for this remark.

Magnus wouldn't be at his daughter's wedding; Mrs. Lewison had been insistent, not that he had complained or protested at being banished. He had written off his wife and daughter entirely after running away with his masseuse, it seemed.

I switched the topic back to something more cheerful, since we had inadvertently stumbled into sensitive territory for her. "This is such a beautiful place," I remarked. "I think it's a perfect choice for a wedding."

"It was Mummy's." A slight inward pinch of the lips, then Josephine smiled again. "I've always been curious," she said. "Is America really anything like it is on the telly?"

"I'll tell you anything you want to know," I said. "At least until we reach the drawing room where your wedding coordinator awaits."

Josephine's smile dimmed. "Of course," she said. "Duty calls." She turned off her music player and followed me towards the castle's entrance. To my relief, not a single bodyguard materialized from behind the manicured hedges as I began explaining life in Seattle.

***

While Josephine freshened up, I found my way to the drawing room, hoping for a quick introduction to Marjorie's 'gimlet,' the wedding coordinator. The tiny staff Marjorie had hired for the wedding was busy elsewhere, along with the caretaker, so the first two doors I opened upon my guess turned out to be some sort of nearly-empty armory and a vast hall that must surely be the site of the wedding ceremony, with the simple majesty of an ancient throne room, and tall windows filling the whole space with light.

Third try lucky: I found myself in a room with a beautiful modern suite of furniture, a handsome carved fireplace, and bookshelves occupied by leather-bound editions and curious antique knickknacks. Given Marjorie's home in London, I suspected these were mementoes of the house's former owners, Reginald and his wife — including the piano near the windows, where a young man was now playing a song.

Kristofer, I surmised. Not just because of his wheat-blond hair or blue eyes which would immediately suggest northern Europe to most people, but because there was no conceivable reason for anyone else this young or attractive to be waiting for a dull meeting in a drawing room.

"Sorry," I said. "Didn't mean to interrupt. I was looking for the wedding coordinator."

"She will be here in a moment," he said. "Come in, please." The music had ceased when I opened the door, but what I heard before then sounded classical — an echo of the song from Josephine's music player.

"Don't stop playing," I said. "It sounded really beautiful."

"I must stop anyway, when everyone else comes," he pointed out. He rose and extended his hand. "Kristofer Rijink," he said. He spoke English extremely well, although I could detect his accent easily when he spoke at length.

"Julianne Rose," I said. "I'm here to help plan your wedding."

He laughed. "I didn't think there was room left for anyone to help," he said. "The coordinator, my mother, and Lady Lewison — they seem to have done a very remarkable job in very little time. They have made a wedding appear out of thin air." He smiled for his joke, but I wasn't sure it was a completely humorous smile.

The door opened and the rest of the company appeared: a very cool, elegant, and slightly plump woman who was introduced as Anneka — Kristofer's mother; a strong moustached, weathered General Gustaf — Kristofer's father, the prince; and a well-tailored middle-aged man with the family nose and a disarming smile, named Anders — a relative, I presume, although he was introduced as a diplomat.

Helen Lewison was exactly as I imagined her: tired, sad, and extremely dignified. With her fair skin and light ginger hair she looked more like a relative of Lady A's than William's — but with a formal bearing, even in casual situations, that seemed as old-fashioned as her formal — and expensive — afternoon dress.

She tended to interrupt the coordinator every third or fourth sentence to contribute some exacting detail — while Anneka said nothing, only telegraphed her opinions with her eyes to either Gustaf or the diplomat. Countering details or suggesting changes was apparently the job of Anders, whose disarming smile had the power to momentarily stupify both Mrs. Lewison and the coordinator.

The coordinator. Marjorie's brief words hadn't painted a picture of someone this ... *commanding*. I felt I should stand up straighter as I lingered on the outskirts of this party — or maybe offer a salute instead. Daria Krensky was as stark as her own black-and-white glossy business card. A sleek black helmet for hair, a dress so perfectly black and fitted it must have been sewn onto her body this morning. A long and grueling train trip and cab ride from London to here, yet she looked as business-like and unruffled as if she'd taken a leisurely fifteen minute stroll here.

"I have taken great pains to ensure the privacy and security of this wedding," said Ms. Krensky, as she drew off her black gloves. "Private photographer, private dress fitting, private magistrate for the ceremony — all with such 'hush hush' in the arrangement that no member of the press will be aware until the affair's conclusion." She accepted a cup of tea, and for the first time, I thought I detected a glimmer of human relief in her face. But it might have been the light reflecting off her eyeballs instead.

"Of course, your dear friend has discreetly arranged the rest," she said to Helen. "The food and the flowers — small details — but preserving the utmost secrecy. I look forward to seeing the menu and the flower arrangements in the coming week."

Marjorie looked as if she was suffering a sudden attack, judging from the sudden widening of her eyes. I wondered what detail she had forgotten, and winced inwardly.

"Dearest Marjorie," said Helen, with a sad smile. "My cousin, as you will recall," she clarified to Ms. Krensky, who apparently forgot 'small details' like this one from time to time. "There is no one so capable and efficient as Marjorie. Or so fond of Josephine when she was a little girl." I noticed that Mrs. Lewison had evidently not considered the possibility that her cousin's business talents were not honed for decorating a castle for a wedding.

During all this conversation, Josephine had sat by, saying next to nothing.

She arrived at the drawing room last of all, wearing a powder blue dress that complimented her skin tone and her chestnut hair. The moment she entered, I detected a new light kindled in Kristofer's eyes. He automatically chose the loveseat, the logical choice for Josephine also, glancing away from his fiancee only when Anders addressed him momentarily.

Josephine smiled when he spoke to her — but shyly, with her gaze sometimes averted. It was several minutes before she warmed up enough that they were chatting quietly and laughing together like a real couple — but by then, 'Commandant Krensky' — as Marjorie referred to her — had called her meeting to order.

"Might I ask who the other young lady present is?" said Anders. He had been studying me from the corner of his eye during Ms. Krensky's narrative.

"Julianne Rose," I piped up. "I'm an event planner. I'm assisting Mrs. Ridgeford with the reception and flowers."

A collective murmur of acknowledgement and polite greetings followed. Daria Krensky surveyed me with a steely gaze that I suspect found me lacking in sophisticated qualities. Until now, she hadn't given me a second glance — but that was before she knew I was the latest lackey at Azure Castle.

"Let's talk cake," said Ms. Krensky, snapping open a leather-bound cell phone case, a stylus in hand. "Would Marjorie care to enlighten us on the chosen baker?"

I was glad when the grueling interview on Dinah's skills was concluded, and the portfolio of her magnificent creations and her sketches were tucked aside again. Now the conversation drifted towards more casual subjects — as casual as it got with this group, that is. For Mrs. Lewison, it was the subject of the Proms; for Anneka and Gustaf, the proud subject of their handsome son's achievements.

"Of course, he is rewarded for his difficult studies," said Gustaf, whose casual gruffness sported its own version of a beaming countenance. "He was the first choice in his field — no one else was so qualified. He finished early, you see," he added to me, the only person here who probably hadn't heard this story before. "He even had a — an internship — during the holidays, when other boys would be having their fun or at home with their families."

Kristofer blushed. I tried to come to his rescue.

"That must have been really hard," I said. "Having no free time like that — you're obviously really dedicated, because half the people I know would burn out." Did 'burn out' have the same meaning in a Scandinavian culture? I pondered this too late.

"I have free time now," he said. "I do things I enjoy, although I must leave for Copenhagen in a few days. Until then ..."

"It's Josephine who doesn't have a minute to spare, it would seem," said Anneka, softly, whose sudden remark was a surprise to more than me. "She is so busy with the wedding she has not time for Kristofer, even."

An accusation, I thought. Josephine's cheeks reddened, but her expression remained the same.

"I do not mind." Kristofer's smile was unfazed. "Her work is important, and the wedding must take much time to plan as well. And I have a great many things to keep me occupied. I practice my music — I was saying before — and there is so much to see in this castle. It has a very interesting history. I knew nothing about Cornwall before I came here. These are Josephine's ancestors who lived here, yes?"

I detected disappointment in his voice, although he was trying to hide it. I liked him even better for it, truthfully.

"There are a great many responsibilities for a bride," said Helen, at this point. "And Josephine has always been a rather busy young woman." She smoothed her skirt, which didn't have a single wrinkle in it to smooth out, but her hand obviously needed an outlet for her sudden agitation.

I found the first statement odd, since Josephine — odder still — had made scarcely any contribution to the conversation about her wedding cake or her photographer. Perhaps there was some sort of legal formalities involving Josephine before her wedding day ... or maybe she was working on her foundation's plans instead?

But tea was concluded now, evidenced by the fact that Ms. Krensky had closed her cell phone's little cover and tucked it in her Gucci handbag. I couldn't help but notice her shoes were the very latest in the Paris fashion windows — putting my pair from last year to shame. As my old boss Nancy would see it, that was the mark of the industry's top professional: the kind of person who has a staff of sensibly-shod minions to do her bidding. And it goes without saying that one of those minions would be me.

"If you have time, Mrs. Ross —" she began.

"'Rose'," I corrected.

"I see." She didn't make a note of this. "I would like to speak to you and the rest of Mrs. Ridgeford's temporary staff about a few little points regarding the reception —"

"I'm sure they would love to discuss them," I said, brightly, although I hadn't a clue what sort of plans Marjorie had — or hadn't — made regarding the castle's decor or the reception's food. "I suppose we could all meet over an early dinner?"

"Dinner? Impossible. I never eat before five o' clock, unless it's a formal occasion," she answered. "Unlike some people, I haven't the time for 'quick bites' or 'early suppers' in casual settings."

Over her shoulder, I saw Kristofer and Josephine talking again, momentarily free from their relatives — until Anders laid claim on the groom. And while her mother was busy in conversation with Kristofer's mother, Josephine slipped from the room.

***

Kitty:

"Let's prepare ourselves, darlings!" said Millicent, clapping her hands together. "Gather your thoughts!"

She's a bit theatrical, Millicent. Not just for wearing that fortune teller's turban, but in everything else. In Ceffylgwyn, where most people want to keep their heads down and whisper secrets, Millicent tells everyone anything they want to know — what comes of being a bit of a scandal in her younger days, most villagers point out. Not that you'd know it now, with her running a tea room for tourists along the new bypass to Penzance, and managing to blend in now and again despite her bright scarves and blouses.

As it's ten minutes before auditions, I feel my stomach clenching a bit, and wish I'd had a bite when Michael offered to make me an omelette in the kitchen earlier today. I doff my old apron — one I'd been wearing to tidy things in Gemma's stead — and take a deep breath or two.

"Everyone has a copy?" said Gerard, holding up a script from his box. There's random bits of everything in that box, playbooks and loose leaf scripts from Shakespeare to *Streetcar* — they'll let you read anything in the Society for Amateur Players, if you've not brought something of your own.

There was about twelve of them before me: mostly the pension lot between here and Truro, at least those with dreams of the stage, or loneliness for showing off talents with a brush or a bassoon. Besides them was Rosie, known locally as 'that crazy cat lady,' who was one of the principals, Martin, the local curate, and Lorrie, who taught at the primary now, and who I remembered as a girl a year advanced of me.

We're not the only younger members of this set — Gemma's boyfriend Andy joined, the first of a few youth in the village who had a secret yearning towards what might be the only romantic escape in Ceffylgwyn, even if it's an imaginary one.

"What are you reading?" Rose asked me. The whiff of cats clung to her clothes from the pet shelter, although she was trying to spruce herself a bit with deodorizing spray and a flowered shawl.

I shrugged. "Something from Shakespeare," I said. Hadn't a clue what I would choose, although I'd rehearsed a few bits lately — feeling a bit awkward in the process, thinking that any moment someone from Cliffs House would pop into the empty dining room and catch me.

"Read the scene from *The Taming of the Shrew*," she said. "You're quite good at that one —" here, she lowered her voice, "— and rumors abound that the play Millicent's chosen is Shakespeare, maybe *The Tempest.* Just a word to the wise."

The Tempest. A shiver made a path down my spine for these words. That was a play I had seen last summer at the Minack. Coincidence only, but I thought I might blush. "I've only read the part a few times at best," I said.

"So? We only live once — have a bit of moxie," she said. "I'm reading from one of those murder mystery scripts in the box. A hen night I was part of last year hosted one of those mystery nights."

"A hen night, eh?" I echoed, one eyebrow flickering upwards.

"I might be past forty, but I'm not in the grave," she retorted. "Me schoolchum who finally met the man of her dreams named me chief bridesmaid. How do I look?" She had been adjusting a large floppy-brimmed hat on her head this whole time, one from a costume box by the stage, next to the mirror.

"Smashing," I said.

"Good." She struck a dramatic pose. "Remember — read out! This is your chance, love."

I sucked in a deep breath. I hadn't tried out for a part before — last time, I'd stood in the background as one of the Queen of Heart's Knaves.

Mostly, I painted scenery and helped eighty-something year-olds Nellie and Nora sew costumes — the 'sequin biddies' as the society affectionately titled them. Their seamstress costumes were generally outlandish ensembles made from all the bits and bobs leftover from past productions.

The society's usual players and stagehands were scattered through the auditorium — the makeshift one, that is, populated by lots of old theatre seats loosely bolted down, and mismatched padded folding chairs that had seen better days a decade ago.

The whole theatre's a bit that way. A high stone house that was some sort of tavern, once, until an eccentric got hold of the idea of having a theatrical society — that's how Millie puts it. In reality, it was her and Gerard's idea; he built the stage, she sewed curtains, and they built a few walls in front to make a receiving area at the front entrance. The big painted sign for the 'Cliffs Edge Playhouse' is rather dramatic and outlandish — just like Millie, who spent hours painting the big man in the moon and the Harlequins in red and gold, with letters like a circus playbill's. Years in an artist colony, she claimed.

Most of the regulars let the first night's audition go to newcomers and outsiders who popped in, so I knew most everyone here. Even though I'd never really performed, I hadn't come last night because I was in conference at Cliffs House until late. That's why I wasn't celebrating my birthday ... not that anybody here knew that. Short of Mum and Julianne — who had evidently told all of Cliffs House — the only other person was Nathan.

He would've taken me to dinner. My cheeks went a bit pink for this idea. I knew he would've chosen some posh place in Truro. Not the sort of place we usually sneaked off to visit — sneaking was the word for it, too, since I still hadn't told Mum that an American bloke was courting me. Thus far, gossip about me and a boy never included Nathan's name ... or the fact it was the same boy each time, for instance. That was the part that would have her attention in a minute. It had mine, to be sure ... not that I let him know it. And maybe that was wrong of me.

"There's a proper crowd here tonight, no mistake. And I thought all the newbies would've come last night." Lorrie plopped down on the seat next to mine. "Look at you, you've snapped up Shakespeare," she said, pretending to be scornful towards the book in my hands. "I haven't rehearsed a thing — two boys at the school plugged up the toilet and I spent all afternoon —"

"Attention, everyone," Gerard had set aside his box and made his way to center stage, moving with the stiffness of old age. "Time we get started. Millie, come along." The stage manager and official prop master and jack of all trades moved aside for the society's current director and president.

"Evening, dears," said Millie. "So glad you could come. And welcome to night two of auditions. As you know, we've a meeting tonight to settle the details for the Passion play at Cliffs House's stage — our dear Kitty is here to bore us all with details about permits and so on." Cheers and whistles followed this, and I found myself blushing a little bit. "But before we get started on the rather tedious side of theatre, this *is* the second night of casting auditions for our upcoming production. So if you've scripts at the ready, we'll begin." She accepted a clipboard from Martin, which had been passed 'round the room.

"First up — Andy."

He bounded up the rickety side steps. "Um ... I'll be reading a monologue from a Noel Coward scene," he said, thumbing through his script. He took a deep breath, then plunged into his lines.

"Help me run my lines," whispered Lorrie. "Hurry — I'm right after Blake." I turned the pages quickly through a copy of *Love's Labor Lost* — so Lorrie had heard the rumors of Shakespeare, too.

"Line four," I whispered. Lorrie's inflection was pretty good for a scene involving a case of nerves — of course, it helped to have the added drama of Blake onstage, whose auditions were always a bit unpredictable.

"Next up, Lorrie."

We both climbed onstage, since her scene required two people for its dialogue. I had done this a couple of times before. If I could do this, maybe I could survive a speaking role. Not something big to begin with, but a small one.

Next was Martin, then Sy, then me. I opened my copy of Shakespeare, and took a deep breath.

"Evening, all ... I'll be reading as Katharina from *The Taming of the*

Shrew," I said. "Which most of you would say is a good fit for me." A bit of laughter from the crowd. I wet my lips, and pushed my nerves deep inside. I paced a few steps with anxiousness, pausing with a fierce expression as I stomped one foot.

"What — did he marry me to famish me? Beggars that have come unto my father's door — upon entreaty have a present alms. If not ... elsewhere they meet with charity. But I, who never knew how to entreat, nor never *needed* that I should entreat, am starved for meat. Giddy for lack of sleep, with oaths kept waking, and with brawling, fed."

I paced some more, restlessly, during these lines, then paused. "And that what spites me more than all these wants ... he does it under the name of 'perfect love.'" I made a scornful sound in my throat after these words. "As who should say — if I should sleep or eat — 'twere a deadly sickness, or, else, present death." I waved my hand at an invisible servant. "I prithee, go and get me some repast," I said, with pleading and exasperation. "I care not what, so it be wholesome food."

I pretended to collapse at this point in a dead faint. I heard applause, and I opened my eyes, hearing the laughter of the rest of the company. I scrambled up and collected my book to exit the stage.

"Next — Loreena," announced Millie.

"Nicely done," whispered Martin, as I seated myself in the front row again.

"I practiced a bit," I said, brushing it off. Although I'd fainted twice on the floor at home to be sure I could do it onstage without wincing or flinching.

Onstage, one of the newcomers read a passage with Blake from an old *EastEnders* script, while old Callum did a number from *The Music Man*, because he auditioned for every production as if it were a musical, mostly for laughs from the rest of the company.

"Next — Nathan."

Nathan. I hadn't heard that name before. I glanced around, looking for the face of a newcomer, and saw him climbing the steps, a book in hand, looking somewhat sheepish.

My Nathan.

Well ... not really ... but you know what I mean. My face caught fire, and I heard some whispers around me — no doubt about this latest stranger, maybe recognizing him from around the village. Nathan cleared his throat.

"Um ... I'm new here ... I'll be reading —" he checked the script in his hand, " — from, uh, *Alice in Wonderland.*" He fumbled it open a few pages into the script, then cleared his throat. Twice. He scanned the lines a few times in the awkward silence that followed, before his lips finally moved.

No one could hear anything except a faint mumble. Millie spoke up. "Louder, darling," she said. "Enunciate from the stage for us all to hear."

It was a stiff read. Louder didn't help, except to prove that Nathan had never done this before, although he pushed on earnestly. Stumble, stammer, pick up at the next word and plod woodenly forward with haste — but haste was probably for the best. Especially since he was reading the scene's four parts as one.

What possessed him to do this? It felt like a dream where you run into people in impossible places — a dead celebrity at your wedding, for instance — and you know all the while it can't be real. Nathan didn't care for theatre; I knew he only went to plays because I did. He said he had avoided plays and pageants in his youth like the influenza —

Nathan stumbled to the last line of his dialogue, then closed the book. There were a few hesitant claps in the company, the society wanting to show encouragement for anyone fool enough to try out ... but it would be hard to applaud something as painful as what Nathan had just endured, except as bravery's reward.

He climbed down a trifle more quickly than he climbed up, and dropped into the seat beside me. "Hi," he said. Some of his embarrassment was fading away now.

"What are you doing here?" That whisper sounded a bit upset — but it was only surprise, I swear to you.

He shrugged his shoulders. "I thought I'd try out," he said. "See what it's all about." He glanced around. "There's a lot more people here than I imagined...here watching, I mean."

I felt Lorrie's stare boring through the back of our seats. She leaned over, keeping her voice hushed as the last actress for the evening recited. "You look familiar," she said to Nathan, her gaze scrutinizing him. "Friend of Kitty's?"

"You met him at the pub," I said. That was the place where most everyone who'd ever met Nathan would remember him, except for Cliffs House, possibly. "He comes with me sometimes."

"A Yank, without a doubt by that accent," she said. "Are you living in the village?"

"Truro," he whispered back. "I'm an event promoter. Kitty and I —"

For a moment, I thought he was going to say 'are boyfriend and girlfriend,' or 'a couple,' but he finished with "—work together at the manor house on major events in the village."

"That's where I've seen you," she whispered, excitedly. "It was The Grand Baking —"

"... and Nora concludes our auditions for the evening," announced Millie. These words snatched everybody's attention. "We'll take a quick breather, then we'll meet to discuss plans for this summer's Passion play. Gerard has the script, I believe —"

"We only want to know what this next production is," piped up Sy, as everybody laughed.

"In good time," promised Millie, mysteriously.

"*I* want to know the name of your friend," said Rosie, elbowing against me as soon as we began to mingle. "Isn't he that bloke you brought to quiz night with Juli and Matt? Your mystery friend? I had no idea he had ... er ... theatrical leanings."

"Um, they're new," I said. Now that everyone was moving about, I spied a chance to talk to Nathan without too many listeners, near the prop box. To ask, for instance, why he hadn't mentioned coming here tonight earlier, if he'd been planning to do this all along.

"That was the longest three minutes of my life," said Nathan. "I felt like I was in the dentist's chair at home — how you stand up there like it's nothing is beyond me. You were great up there, by the way."

"Thanks. But I thought you didn't like theatre," I said. He was putting his script back in the box. "I mean, you never mentioned coming here. You said that you thought theatre people were a bit weird."

"Yeah. But this is your thing, right?" He shrugged his shoulders. "I thought maybe I'd give it a try. I didn't know we were supposed to bring something, so I just grabbed the first thing in the box. Turned out it was the last play you were in."

His gaze wandered momentarily towards the old scenery still onstage from that production, a plywood house with Alice's arm stuck out of its window, and the backdrop of the rose garden with half-painted red and white rose trees.

"Yeah ... I just ... guess I was surprised." I didn't know what I was feeling. It was a bit awkward ... but it was a bit nice, too. Him being here, trying to support me. Even if his reading *was* rubbish.

"I'll probably do better the next time. I didn't exactly have time to practice this week. Shows, huh?"

"I would've helped you, if you wanted," I said. "I would've read lines with you, if you'd only said something."

"Then it wouldn't have been a surprise," he said. "Hey, look — we're spending your birthday together after all." He stuffed his hands in his pockets. "Besides, I don't expect to get a part — not a speaking one, anyway." He grinned, briefly, and I thought he was relieved by this. "I thought I'd just hang out. Paint some scenery, watch you practice. Spend time with you in between."

"I'm not in the cast," I said. "Not yet, anyway. I'm probably too new for them to pick." I thought maybe it looked like we were having an argument to anybody watching, so I tried to lighten the mood a little. I wasn't angry, anyway. It was thoughtful of him, the sort of thing every girl wants from a bloke. I just hadn't expected it here and now.

"I'm pretty sure you will be," he said.

I blushed three shades deeper than before, although I tried not to. That look in his eyes had an effect on me. Months of trying to figure it out, and I still do nothing except give in when it happens.

"So when will they tell us who gets the part?" he asked. "Not that I'm in it, obviously."

"Monday," I said. "That's the next meeting. That's when they'll announce what play we're doing."

Nathan hanging around here, getting to know my friends outside Cliffs House's crowd — it was sure to reach my Mum's ears soon. Uncle Phil and his lot would make jokes about the two of us that would emphasize Nathan's foreigner status and posh job ... knowing my luck, they'd make the same jokes to his face, once some sort of meeting was forced between us all. He wouldn't be 'some bloke I'm seeing' anymore.

"This'll be fun," he said. "I'll hang around and drive you home after the meeting. I'll be at the pub when you're ready." He pulled on his coat and gave me another smile.

He looked a lot more comfortable, now that he wasn't holding a script. A bit boyish and earnest, really. I almost gave him a kiss on the cheek then and there, but realized someone was bound to be watching us now. I sneaked a quick glance to make sure there wasn't, before I stole against him and laid my lips against his face.

"See you later," I said. I knew he wouldn't be gone twenty seconds before someone asked me about him.

"Who *is* that dishy newcomer?" asked Nellie. Across the auditorium, Andy caught my eye and gave me a knowing look, since he knew full well why Nathan was hanging about Cliffs House. If it wasn't before, my relationship with Nathan was now going to be very official to the society, and the rest of the village soon after.

And what was wrong with that?

Nothing. Only it kept hopping into my thoughts all the next day as I finished the menu with Michael, and packed for my weekend in Aval Towan. Nathan's gesture wasn't the sort I could forget easily, especially since I couldn't put into words that I was flattered and pleased *and* exasperated by it — the summary of everything between me and Nathan, in reality.

Me and Nathan — what would it mean if those two words were coupled as an *us*?

***

Julianne:

I was looking forward to Saturday morning. Not just because it was the first day we would begin serious discussion of the grand hall for the ceremony, but because the one person I missed the most during this extended vacation was coming here. Matthew had promised he would arrive before lunch, and I could hardly wait.

"Yes, but is he trustworthy?" Helen had pursed her lips.

"The soul of discretion," soothed Lady Amanda. "Besides, you have to trust someone with the wedding's flowers. And who better than someone I've relied on so many times?"

It was the photos, ironically, of the bouquet for Petal Price-Parker (*ne* Borroway) that convinced her that Cliffs House's floral staff would suit her needs. In addition to Matt, I summoned Kitty to help us create sketches that would impress the bride's family — and, I hoped, the bride herself, who seemed mostly interested in classical music on the iPod, thus far.

The moment he stepped through the door, I wrapped my arms around Matt, burying my face against his collar. "I've missed you," I said, not caring that my voice was muffled.

"It's scarcely been a day," he said, chuckling. "You do realize I wasn't even at Rosemoor yesterday?"

"That's not the point," I said, drawing back to look at him. "Anyway, I desperately need you to help make this wedding a success ... and promise your lips are sealed in the presence of tabloid journalists."

"Of course," he said. "I have a few samples in here —" he held up the basket in his hand, "—that I think will impress Josephine and her mother with regards to the floral selection. Kitty will have to be the voice on arranging them, of course."

Kitty had entered behind him, wearing her best business clothes and heels, looking the part far more than Matthew in his casual attire. As soon as Matthew had gone through to the kitchen, we were joined by Gemma with Edwin in his stroller.

At the sight of Kitty, Edwin began gurgling, extending his hands towards her as if he could reach her from meters away. Kitty's smile broke in its full splendor.

"Upsies?" she asked him. This was her name for Edwin's game with his favorite person — Kitty would lift him overhead, then back down and up again a few times. Shrieks of joy always resulted, and in seconds, Edwin was chortling with laughter as Kitty lifted him once again.

"You there!" A commanding, yet frail, female voice addressed me from an open doorway. "You — wedding planner — are we going to be lolling about all day? I haven't much time left, you know, and I don't want to spend it standing around while Helen powders her nose once again."

The dowager — the legendary Lady Astoria — had deigned to be present for Josephine's dress's arrival. Despite her ninety years of age, she walked with a cane more for the sake of dignity and providing annoyance to others than any real need of it. She had escaped from the private sitting room where I had strongly hinted for her to wait, while Marjorie struggled with a conference call regarding Whitehall business.

"The garment fitters haven't arrived yet," I answered. "Josephine will be down soon, however, so why don't you go back to the parlor and wait for her?"

"Dreadfully dull room," muttered Lady Astoria. "Not a speck of imagination in it. Reggie's wife took all the decent prints and curios after he died. Might as well be a chiropodist's office." She noticed Kitty now, who was giving Edwin a quick spin for good measure before restoring him to his stroller.

"Who's that girl?" She pointed with her cane.

"That's my assistant, Kitty Alderson," I said.

"I like her," she said. "Energy and youth. She's more interesting than half the lot Marjorie's dragged in for this thing. You there," she said to Kitty. "Come here for a moment."

"Kitty, this is Lady Astoria," I said. "She's Josephine's grandmother. She just arrived from Paris for the wedding preparations."

"You're a sharp-looking young woman," said Lady Astoria. "Speak any languages besides the Queen's English?"

"Bit of Cornish I've picked up," said Kitty. "Bit of French. I've been learning, at any rate."

"Not the Queen's English," said Lady Astoria, upon hearing Kitty's accent. "But that's quite all right. Never liked all that mincing talk — came to a point that the staff was more proper than the lord of the manor on that count." She scrutinized Kitty from crown to foot, as if reading her like a label. "French, you say," she continued. "Any good at your job?"

"She's excellent at her job," I answered, giving Kitty a smile.

"Hmph. How'd you like to leave her and work for me, girl?" asked Lady Astoria. "My last assistant walked out. Old crank without a sense of amusement or energy anyway — always tucking hot water bottles into my bed, or telling me to climb the stairs more slowly. I need someone with a bit of youth and fire."

"I'm not exactly looking for a position," said Kitty. "Don't you think it's a bit hasty to offer a job to someone you've only just met?"

Lady Astoria quirked one eyebrow. "Blunt, aren't we?" she said. "At my age, time is of the essence, Ms. Alderson. I know my mind well enough. Can you run errands? Answer telephone calls? Get rid of annoying relations or acquaintances who stop by? As for looking after my things and my wardrobe, you'd learn quickly enough. Better to learn by mistake than learn and make them anyway, I say."

"Never heard that one before," said Kitty.

"Think about my offer." Lady Astoria pointed her cane at Kitty, then swung it in my direction. "Now, if I can be forgiven for attempting to poach your staff, will you be so kind as to send in whatever dreadful help Marjorie employs with a cup of tea? My throat is parched from boredom."

"Absolutely," I said. Gemma hastened away to fulfill this request, giving Edwin a swift ride in the direction of the kitchen, much to his satisfaction — Edwin hates slow perambulators.

Kitty glanced at me. "Is she always that bold?" she asked, as soon as the dowager disappeared.

"Lady Astoria knows her own mind — as she no doubt informed you," said Marjorie, who emerged from a room that served as her office; I made a mental note to remember it and not to wander in there in search of the breakfast nook tomorrow.

"Probably what happened to her last assistant," said Kitty. "They knew theirs as well."

"You might give it thought," said Marjorie, glancing from her to me. "I know she's a dreadful old bat at times, but she's quite active socially in Paris. Her apartment's a fantastic posh suite of rooms, practically a time capsule full of antiques and furnishings that Coco Chanel would have coveted. And the company she keeps ... mark my words, it wouldn't hurt your career's future to rub shoulders with *them*."

"Thanks, but I'm quite content with not-so-posh society," said Kitty.

"Even so, I'm sure that Julianne wouldn't stand in your way if you changed your mind," said Marjorie. Gemma, who had returned with a tea tray for the dowager, was now at my elbow.

"The fitters are here," she announced. Marjorie's cheerful expression vanished with these words.

"Oh, blast!" she declared. "And Helen is still moping somewhere in the gardens — Julianne, run and fetch Josephine, will you? Kitty, be so kind as to show them into the sitting room —"

Upstairs, I knocked on a door that turned out to be a large linen and storage closet, then circled back to the suite that Gemma and I shared before finding my way to the wedding parties' chambers. The arched door to Josephine's room was partly open, so I gave it a hesitant push.

"Josephine?" I said. "Are you here? Your dress has arrived, and your grandmother's really eager to see you in it ..." I stepped inside, seeing a neatly-made four-poster bed with an embroidered coverlet, and a dressing table occupied by a couple of binders and books, a computer tablet and keyboard, and a coil of earbud wires belonging to the bride-to-be's iPod.

A few books on the bedside table — poetry — and a few DVDs, romantic titles like *Bride and Prejudice, Ever After, Letters to Juliet.* A tiny box which must have once held Josephine's engagement ring, but was now occupied, oddly enough, by a plastic gold one with a fake diamond rhinestone.

Josephine must have gone for a walk. I stepped away, then the ruffle of paper in the breeze caught my eye. On the other side of her computer, a piece of paper — a note — was pinned beneath the keyboard.

There. Relieved, I reached for it, only to realize my mistake. It wasn't a note written by Josephine to anybody here. Oddly-printed letters ... elaborately printed fonts ... spelled out words. *'I know it's your birthday. Here is something to remind you that one is thinking of you today.'* And another: *'I wish you the best for your final exam. You are far too brilliant to fail, so never fear of it.' 'Your goal is so inspiring. I think of how many children's lives you will change and I am amazed by you.'*

There were more of them, along with small toys, a few hair ornaments, and some dried roses. Besides these, there were black and white photographs of a young man in a hooded sweatshirt, walking along a boardwalk somewhere, and paying for an ice cream cone. His face was obscured, but the photos had been taken in quick succession. I touched one, and the business card for a private detective peeked out from beneath it.

"Are you looking for something?"

The sound of Josephine's voice made me leap, half with guilt and half with surprise. "Sorry," I said. "I came to tell you your dress is here — I thought you'd left a note on the desk ... with the work for your foundation." Obviously that's what the binders and books — business ones — pertained to; but the rest of this stuff clearly didn't belong.

"Of course," said Josephine. She smiled, but it wasn't just reserve I noticed in it — it was uneasiness. "I'll just fetch my cardigan and be downstairs momentarily. Please tell my grandmother it will only be a moment."

"Sure," I said. "Whenever you're ready." I knew that wasn't the opinion of Ms. Krensky on the issue, but I felt guilty for having glimpsed something which was private and none of my business. Something that Josephine was now tucking away in a small jewelry box as I exited her room.

"Where is she?" demanded Lady Astoria. "That child is scarcely twenty — she should have more energy than I, rather than creeping about upstairs like an old woman looking for her shawl." She adjusted her own shawl, a Paris silk one, around the shoulders of her houndstooth walking suit. "She's perfectly aware that Wilson is supposed to drive me up the coast to dine with Balmy Brightweather today."

Balmy Brightweather? I tried not to laugh — he sounded like a made-up character from a British comedy. "She'll be down in a moment," I promised. The two fitters, for whom 'silence is golden' appeared to be a lifelong vow, were busy unpacking their sewing utensils, as Ms. Krensky impatiently tapped one foot.

True to her word, Josephine came down a moment later, and smiled politely to the impatient Ms. Krensky as the wedding coordinator unpacked the giant garment box delivered from London. Inside, a stunning dress of white satin in an elegant, modern style, with an asymmetrical neckline that descended from a single sleeve.

"Oh," said Helen, with a small cry of happiness. "Why, darling, it's beautiful." She glanced towards her daughter, whose smile was ... well ... the same as before. "I had so hoped to help you choose it ... if only I hadn't been so dreadfully ill that week ... but you've done so well on your own."

"I'll try it on for you to admire," said Josephine. She stepped behind the folding changing screen provided by the London garment alterations team; the sound of rustling fabric followed.

"It's by Gotan," said Ms. Krensky, proudly. "Josephine certainly has excellent taste. Rumor has it he'll be the toast of Milan in fewer than two years. When I saw her selection, I will admit that I was stunned beyond words."

"Come on, Josie," said the dowager. "We haven't all day."

When the screen was folded back, Josephine looked like a photograph ripped from a high-end fashion shoot. The dress had a long train which trailed past the elevated stool the fitters had provided, the bodice and skirts fitted to her slim curves without being confining. She looked beautiful and elegant, as the reaction of her mother, the coordinator, and even the silent fitters proved.

"That's quite a stunner," said the dowager. She lifted one eyebrow — a mark of approval in this case, I gathered. "Well done, dear girl."

"Turn towards the mirror, dearest," said Helen. Josephine did, and the reflection it offered in the bright sun and shadows of this room revealed a very young girl who looked uncomfortable and unhappy in some manner.

Josephine's lips formed a very small smile. "It's quite perfect," she said. Then looked away quickly. "I suppose we must hurry with these alterations. I have a conference call with my solicitor about the foundation's grant." The fitters tucked and pinned in the appropriate places before she stepped behind the screen again.

"I'm glad this was quick enough," said Marjorie, who was watching over my shoulder. "Despite thick walls, you can hear every one of the dowager's words in my office, and *I* have a conference call with my secretary and someone from the Ministry of Finance in half an hour."

"It certainly was." Too quick, I thought. Someone like Josephine should have looked happier to be wearing her dream wedding dress, not as if she was trying on a school uniform. Something was very wrong.

"Maybe it's just wedding nerves," suggested Matt, in our phone conversation later that night. Already back at Rosemoor, his visit to the castle had been far too short—with far too little time spent with the two of us together. This conversation was already longer than most of the ones we had managed to share in between the flurry of wedding details that morning.

"If it were nerves, I don't think she would manage to be so calm on the outside," I said. "I think she's holding back something bigger. Maybe she doesn't love Kristofer. He's certainly in love with her, but that's not always a two-way street."

"True," said Matt. "But if she doesn't really love him, she's rather waiting until the last moment to run away from her engagement."

I pictured Josephine going through with a loveless marriage. There are worse things in the world, I suppose, but for a lot of people, that would be the beginning of a miserable future and a disastrous split. And the photos on her desk ... who was that person? A former boyfriend? Kristofer? And why were the photos all taken by means of stealth?

"How is life other than wedding preparations?" Matt asked. "Have you seen much of the surrounding village? It's practically a historical landmark in itself, it's so well-preserved in its origins — the old tavern is more than seven hundred years old."

"I'm afraid I don't escape very often," I said. "I'm afraid the security guards will tackle me." I was still learning to make my way around the castle as it was, having discovered a chapel with an altar and cross, a library, and a sitting room done in an alarmingly pink shade of coral, all while searching for both a modern bathroom and Ms. Krensky's temporary office.

"Security guards?"

"Mrs. Lewison has a morbid fear of the press," I said. "Oh, Matt, honestly, it's a tiny bit like being trapped in an English comedy novel. They're like caricatures more than characters — Lady Astoria with her fearsome walking stick, and Mrs. Lewison with her nervous headaches. Even the groom's family might as well be Scandinavian stereotypes. They're even all blond."

I heard him chuckle heartily. "It sounds dramatic. Somehow, I can't imagine you're not enjoying it a wee bit, at least. Not you, who love a challenge, the odder the better."

I sighed. "I miss you," I said. "I miss our cottage. Don't get me wrong; Azure Castle is beautiful, and the view from the back gardens is breathtaking —"

"I rather think I could have spent days sitting there," said Matt. "I envy you."

"Well, don't," I said. "I'd trade it to be home at Rosemoor, and have the view of the cliffs at the manor house." Whether I liked it or not, the number of days I had left in Cornwall was dwindling, and I wanted to spend most of them with the place and people I had come to love.

"Speaking of home, I started packing this evening," said Matt. "Charlotte scrounged some boxes for us from behind her shop. I haven't gotten far ... just the prints in the living room, and a few books."

My throat tightened, oddly enough. "Wow," I said. "I hadn't even thought about it yet." All of our things, our mementoes from this life, couldn't be left in place on Rosemoor's shelves or in its cupboards. It wasn't our cottage anymore, once we vacated — even Matt's beloved plants couldn't be left behind.

"Charlotte's offered for us to store a few things in her shop's loft, if we'd like. We'll be shipping some of it, of course, but it might be a good option for your desk, and my gardening tools and pots."

Not the rest of the furniture, of course. It belonged to Rosemoor Cottage. And whose home would that be when we were gone? I couldn't bear to think about it yet.

"Did you know that some of the village is organizing a farewell party for us? Charlotte told me when I collected the boxes."

"That's sweet," I said. "And if it didn't make me want to cry, I'd probably be thrilled."

"I miss you," he said.

"I miss you, too. But I already said that, didn't I?"

You can find a way to keep the cottage. There's still time, I told myself. *You're going to come home to it again.*

***

Kitty:

On Monday, Millie kept her word, and had the cast list ready for the meeting. As usual, she made a dramatic fuss over telling us the play and the players.

"In less than three weeks, we will dazzle the community with ... *A Midsummer Night's Dream*," she announced from center stage.

A chorus of groans from some for this rather overdone chestnut of community players, with cheers from those who love Shakespeare in any season. I calculated my chances of ending up as a handmaiden for the Amazonian queen, when Nathan joined me in the neighboring seat.

"Did you get a part?" he asked. Copies of the cast list were being passed out now; my hands held one, but my eyes were having trouble finding my name. Nerves, I suppose.

"Lucky you," said Lorrie, who popped into our conversation from the row behind us. "You landed Hermia — first time out of the gate, too."

"Hermia?" said Nathan. "Who's —?"

"She's the girl in the love triangle," said Lorrie. "And I — I am poor, sad Helena, who wants so desperately to be loved by Hermia's unwanted fiance Demetrius. Just my luck to play the unwanted woman."

"Looks like I'm close to the bottom," said Nathan, studying the list. His eye was scanning the rest of the cast. "Who's playing your fiance?"

"Martin," I said. "And Lysander is —" I looked at the name, but that couldn't be right. Lyle Groves? 'Twasn't possible, was it?

But it was him, walking into the theatre just now. Ripped jeans, work boots, leather waistcoat, t-shirt — the same overly-long, straight hair cut just above his shoulders, and jaw in need of a good shave. Lyle Groves in the flesh, who had already seen the cast list, and now spotted me.

"KitKat!" he said. And before I could say anything, he picked me up and swung me into his arms like a doll. "How's tricks since I've been gone?"

"Are you daft?" I wriggled free of his embrace so my feet touched the floor again. "Is that a way to greet someone you've not spoken to in three years?"

Nathan's face was one of shock at this moment — not pleasant at all. He twitched once as though to do something about Lyle holding onto me; I think it was a good bit of effort on his part to make his countenance normal again when Lyle let go of me.

"It's been an age, hasn't it? You haven't changed a bit. Got a proper job, I hear, no more peddling fish 'round the village."

"Yeah," I said. "I didn't know you'd come back, though. Got tired of wandering around in a caravan? Or did it leave you stranded on the side of the road?" His leaving — that was the important part three years ago, when he'd tossed everything he owned into his brother's old camping van and taken off.

"Got on with a mate in construction," he said. "Pouring concrete and what not. Doin' a bit of work over Falmouth way for the summer. Ginny talked me into joining this lot. Long time since the old drama crowd at school. Gawd, but Mr. Tremworth was a rotten old ghoul, wasn't he?"

That careless smile — it hadn't changed a bit, either. But the part of me that had been angry enough to kick his teeth out had faded over time, so I didn't feel a twinge of longing to give him the long-overdue farewell blow from before.

"So ... you two know each other?" Nathan glanced from him to me. "Old friends from school?"

"'After' is more like," said Lyle, sliding his fingers into his denim's pockets. "Kat and I used to get up to all sorts of things in the village, though, before we hooked up in Land's End. Remember that party down by the coastal scenic park? Ginny got nabbed by the fuzz, o' course, when they crashed in. That's what she gets for having too many and taking her top off."

I squirmed a bit. This wasn't the sort of story from my past that I wanted Nathan hearing — the days when I was part of a rowdier crowd, who drank a bit too much, got a bit careless when drunk, and did things in any frame of mind that were simply vandalism, or messing about with property of Ceffylgwyn's uptight residents. The Kat Alderson who was guilty of hanging about on their fringes at first; then, among other ambitious errors, of believing that a jerk like Lyle Groves really fancied her.

"Sounds like quite a party," said Nathan. "So you're into community theatre, too?"

"Aw, did a bit of playing at it when I was at school," said Lyle. "Got the knack for it, not that I ever use it. But like I said, one of me mates said they'd be short of players 'round here, and since I'm sticking around until the job's done over Falmouth way, I thought I'd pitch in."

"Nathan," I said to Lyle, by way of introduction. "My ... good mate from work." I didn't know how else to put it, really. Nathan extended his hand and shook Lyle's.

"I'm an event promoter in Truro," he said.

"Got stuck across the Pond?" said Lyle. "They got planes that fly both ways, mate, in case you didn't know." A cocky smile with this joke; Lyle loved needling people. I didn't like to think about the fact that I once laughed when he did it.

"Cornwall grew on me," said Nathan, who didn't seem to mind the joke. "I was working from London, but I decided to take my chances here for awhile. Guess I was persuaded by some of its charms." He almost sneaked a glance at me — not quite, but enough that Lyle didn't miss it.

"You two?"

Until we stood up a few moments ago, Nathan had been playing with the curls at the hollow of my neck. Probably not the most discreet maneuver on his part, if we were still a bit of a secret.

"Come off it, Lyle," I said. "Don't be poking about in other people's business for a change, aye?"

"So this is the new Lysander," said Rosie, sidling up to join us. "I remember you better for heaving a rock through me car's window at the park. Cost me a fair quid — and put you under the constable's nose for a bit, it seems."

Lyle did have the decency to look embarrassed. "I've grown up a bit since then," he said. "Maybe I'll make a decent Lysander now." His wink for this line was quick, and for both me and Rosie. Did he always have to behave like such a flirt around women? There was a time I overlooked that, too.

"What part do you have?" Nathan asked Rosie.

"Titania the Fairy Queen," she said. "Only way I'll ever be queen of a man's castle, it seems." Her grin was saucy. "At least it's a proper part with a bit of sex appeal — last time, I ended up the old handmaid in *Romeo and Juliet*. No balcony scene for me — not even as Margaret in *Much Ado*."

"Balconies are overrated," I muttered. "Who wants some bloke yelling at them from the garden below?" All this talk of love stories was making me a bit uncomfortable.

"Who are you playing?" Lyle asked Nathan. Who checked the cast list one more time.

"Um ... Starveling," he said. "A tailor. Somebody with next to no lines, I'm pretty sure." He noticed Lyle's place on the list. "Wow. You're

... practically second billing, aren't you?"

"Like I said, I've done this before," said Lyle. "Only I'll be onstage snogging you this time, love." His words were for me, but the grin and wink that came with them were a show for the general public now. "Where's our Demetrius slipped off to hide?"

"Martin had an emergency," piped up Lorrie. "Gerard's reading for him tonight as a favor."

"I could ..." Nathan began, but Millie was calling us to order for the first reading. I caught Nathan's sleeve and held him back as the others gathered around the stage.

"Don't be jealous of him," I said, glancing in Lyle's direction. "It wasn't anything." Lame and awkward, these words, and not saying at all what I needed him to know. Not properly, anyway.

"I'm not," he said. "Relax. It's theatre, right?" He gave me a smile.

"All right, everyone!" said Millie. "Let's begin our read through so we're not here all night..."

***

Julianne:

"I wondered where you were," said Pippa. "Weren't you hungry? Gem's eaten practically all of Dinah's muffins —"

"That isn't true!" protested Gemma. "I only took one extra to make a mush porridge for Edwin. He likes it soaked in sugared milk."

"Heavens, don't feed him anymore of it," said Lady Amanda. "He's quite the solid little chap as it is — it'll be like carrying about a bandbox of bricks soon." In reply, Edwin giggled, then flung a handful of his creamed carrots and yams onto the baby tray.

"I didn't mean to be late," I said, slipping into my chair. "I got lost again. I took a wrong turn looking for the room where Ms. Krensky left our sketches of the formal hall. I ended up in a gallery instead, and it took me forever to find my way back."

The gallery had been full of tapestries that looked so old and frail I wondered if they were the preliminary trials of William the Conquerer's wife before the Bayeux's panels. A right turn at the end had taken me to a series of mostly-empty rooms, one of which had a glimpse of Azure's narrow sea view. In the end, I found my way back to the corridor where the guests rooms lay ... but not to Ms. Krensky's would-be office.

"It's really a simple house to navigate," said Marjorie, buttering what had undoubtedly been the last of Dinah's muffins. "I can't imagine how you've become so lost. First floor is the grand hall and the main chambers, second floor is bedrooms and the old servant's wing, third floor is the private family quarters —"

"I have the map you gave each of us," I said. "I just forgot it." I had left it — unfortunately — somewhere in the midst of my notes for Ms. Krensky. Since there were no muffins left, I took a slice of toast instead, and consoled myself with a jar of Dinah's special marmalade. One bite reminded me how much I had missed it.

Today we were putting the formal hall's carpet and chairs into place, and moving in several massive stone flower urns that would hold the wedding's bouquets. The arrangement was regal, formal, and conveyed a hallowed elegance. It also seemed a touch cold right now, but given the odd behavior of the wedding party, maybe that wasn't completely out of character.

I hadn't told anybody about Josephine's odd mementoes, of course; and nobody was talking about the fact that Mrs. Lewison and Ms. Krensky were the dominant opinions behind everything we were doing. Instead, I tried to focus on putting the urns in just the right spots — Kitty's floral arrangements called for generous sprays of baby's breath and stunning white lilies with mottled throats, with a bouquet of lilies, both large and small blossoms, for the bride.

Josephine had seemed pleased with them. But it was a detached sort of pleased that really bothered me. If she wanted something else for the wedding, she needed to tell us. If she wanted to change things in secret, we would be her co-conspirators in undermining Ms. Krensky's regime of perfection, for instance.

"Our commandant will insist on seeing the table's layout today," said Marjorie. "The presiding minister, a magistrate, and a society hostess whom she 'just *dotes* on' will be at tea to discuss the seating arrangement and the ceremony." Our seating chart currently had dubious gaps, where Helen simply couldn't decide whom to seat where. "I won't be here, since

I have an errand to run on Samuel's behalf. What a pity." She smiled with this joke. "But I'll be back as quick as possible, in case she has questions you can't possibly answer."

I was in the hall, retrieving a folding ladder that the caretaker had kindly located for me, when I saw a figure walking across the courtyard. A young woman in a pair of skinny denim jeans and a stylish long blouse, a looped scarf around her neck and a pair of sunglasses. Josephine, carrying a shoulder bag, was making her way towards a car turning around in the courtyard.

Josephine was leaving. And that was completely *not* all right in her mother's book, since the whole point of being here was to hide until the wedding — and the furtive glances she gave the house before climbing inside the car proved that this was a secret outing. With less than two hours before Ms. Krensky's mandatory tea time, I wondered what Josephine could possibly be thinking.

Was she running away?

I couldn't throw open the window and call her back — the car was already pulling away. Marjorie was gone already, along with the only transportation I knew of — except —

On impulse, I opened the door to the morning room. Despite her abundant energy, Lady Astoria was asleep in her chair, an open book on couture designs in her hands. I nudged her shoulder, gently.

"Wha—Wilkins, what is the meaning —?" she began, then realized who I was. "What on earth do you want?" she asked. "Speak up, girl!"

"Can I borrow your car?" I said. "Please. I have to ... to run an important wedding errand in the village." What the village could possibly supply, I hoped she wouldn't ask.

"What the dickens? The car? Oh ... very well, I suppose. Ask Hidgens to give you the keys." She turned the page in her book, peering at a very stylish midnight-black gown in a shop window.

It would be better for Hidgens to drive me, but I knew that meant someone else would observe Josephine's escape. I found the chauffer in the kitchen, having a cuppa, and he obligingly handed over the key to the Bentley parked outside.

Behind its wheel, I took a deep breath, reminding myself it wasn't that hard. Matt had given me lots of pointers, hadn't he? And I hadn't scratched his car in the handful of shaky trips I'd made between home and Truro. I turned the key in the ignition, and shifted into gear, trying not to drive too fast down the steep lanes of Azure Castle's private road.

If I could catch up, maybe I could get the driver's attention. But I hadn't any right to stop Josephine, unlike her mother's security team — just as I wasn't responsible if they discovered her missing come tea time. So what on earth did I think I was doing?

The hired car was only now driving away to my right when I reached the bottom, and there was plenty of space between us. Josephine didn't recognize her aunt's hired vehicle, it seemed. We passed a road marker — Penzance was ahead. At least now it was clear that Josephine's errand wasn't in Aval Towan.

Traffic was a bit trickier in Penzance, and I found myself growing nervous. But the hired car pulled over near the Pavilion — and Josephine emerged.

By the time I managed to climb out of the car, she had disappeared. I hurried inside the first door, finding myself in the midst of a carnival.

Family Activity Centre! proclaimed the nearest sign, with others directing visitors to food, video games, and other family-friendly entertainment. An abundance of large stuffed tigers and My Little Pony greeted me from prize booths — I realized that the miniature sparkly figurines in one of the display cases were identical to the one I had seen on Josephine's desk.

A crowd of guests were busy at the fruit machines and the mechanical claw. I scanned the crowd for any sign of Josephine. I spotted a girl with long hair and darted in that direction, cut off by a group of children running excitedly from the bowling alley.

Like me, Josephine was moving swiftly through the room. Looking for someone, I imagined — probably whoever gave her the sparkly pony, and wrote the notes to her. My heart sank as I pictured what this meant for poor Kristofer.

"May I go, Mum? May I?" A child clutched his mother's arm and pointed towards the enticing lights and music of the video game zone. By the time they were past me, I caught only a glimpse of Josephine disappearing outside through the opposite door.

"Wait! Josephine!" I yelled. If she heard me, she didn't turn around. I exited the entertainment venue, and spotted Josephine in the midst of a crowd enticed by some sort of street performance near the car park. In the distance, a boy in a hooded sweatshirt was watching the show as he talked on a mobile, his other arm holding a slim package. And it was towards him that Josephine's steps were carrying her rapidly.

I took off running. A few people moved aside for me, and I heard someone scold me for pushing my way past them. The band's music drowned out any chances Josephine had of hearing me, and I had no idea what I would do if she did. What could I do to stop her? Should I? Ahead, I could see Josephine's target was emerging on the other side of the crowd now, in the car park, his quick stride moving faster than Josephine's as the crowd of onlookers hampered her steps.

The boy in the sweatshirt had climbed into a van. It was pulling away by the time Josephine reached its parking space. She stopped and watched as it drove away. I could see disappointment etched on her face. Breathless, I caught up to her, watching as she turned away to gaze at the disappearing van.

"Josephine." I tried to catch my breath after this word. She whirled around.

"What are you doing here?" Her tone was accusatory — and very startled.

"I followed you." I drew a deeper breath, trying to slow my pounding pulse. "I'm sorry. It's just ... you can't do this. Not to Kristofer, not to your mother. If this wedding is a problem ... you have to talk about it."

I had no idea what I was talking about — except for the fact that I was very sure that this secret meeting with this young man wasn't something meant to help Josephine's engagement. The pieces in my mind were trying to form a picture, and it was fast becoming one of Josephine loving another person than Kristofer.

"I don't know what you mean. I just wanted some fresh air." She gazed off towards the desert-like trees and shrubbery which grew alongside the Pavilion's Victorianesque arched entrance. "I've been trapped in that castle for more than a week now. It's unbearable how much everyone worries about someone finding out we're there."

"I think you came here for something besides fresh air," I answered. "I saw the guy you were following, Josephine. You came here to meet him."

I paused, seeing the bride to be blush slightly, although she tried to hide it. "You can tell me the truth. Really. I promise."

All the color drained from Josephine's face. "I was so foolish," she muttered, at last. "What an idiot I've been. I knew someone would find out. Please," she said, looking at me. "Don't tell my mother. Don't tell anyone about this."

"I'm not going to," I answered. "I'm not trying to expose you, I just want you to face whatever's wrong before it's too late. Consider the truth about your feelings for Kristofer. He doesn't seem like somebody who deserves to get hurt, if there's someone else in your life."

One word from Josephine, and I could go back to Azure Castle and pack my bags. There wouldn't be a need for my skills here any longer, and it would be Mrs. Lewison's and the royal family's turn to find the truth about Josephine's cold feet. And as for the groom-to-be, his heart would be broken in two. It wasn't fair, but if Josephine was seeing someone secretly, nothing about this engagement would be fair or happy.

"He doesn't deserve it, no." She had turned away from me, hugging herself. "It isn't what you think ... it isn't like that. It had nothing to do with Kristofer, really ... not directly." She looked at me. "Promise you won't tell anyone, and I'll explain everything. Only don't tell them I left the castle."

"I promise," I said. "I mean, you're an adult who should be able to go wherever you want. But considering the event you've let your mother and Ms. Krensky create, it's awfully hard to justify leaving them alone with their guests at tea without so much as a note."

"I know." She sighed. "But I wasn't planning to be gone for very long. I only wanted —"

"Everything all right?" A man whom I'd never seen before jogged up to us after climbing out of one of the cars. "Bit of a problem, Josephine?"

"No, nothing at all, Stefan," she said. "Thank you. Everything's quite fine."

"All right," he answered. "I'll be going, then." He got into the car and started the engine. I wondered if he was one of the security guards Marjorie warned me about, although his name was familiar. Then I remembered: the same name had been printed on the card of the private detective.

"You can let your hired car go, if you want," I said. "I'll drive you back to the castle. It'll be less conspicuous that way, since no one will notice your aunt's car."

"Thanks," she said. She followed me towards the Pavilion again.

We weren't late for tea, of course, but Ms. Krensky had apparently been hunting for the bride-to-be for the past hour. "There are so many things to discuss," she said, taking Josephine by the arm the moment she found her in the garden. "We haven't even *begun* to determine the number of dignitaries who might be present —"

"If you'll excuse me, I haven't had a bite to eat all day," said Josephine, extracting herself from the wedding coordinator's grip. "I would like to attend to my personal matters before the guests arrive." Such a polite, posh tone — and a smile that I wouldn't quite like to have directed at myself, I decided.

Ms. Krensky froze. "Of course," she said. Politely, although her voice carried daggers now. "It is your wedding, after all."

"Thank you." Josephine marched into the kitchen. I followed, seeing her take a strawberry tart from a platter of them fresh-baked by Dinah. Who had expressed a need to clear her head by cooking before she began sculpting the molds for her wedding cake decorations.

"Care to see the progress on your wedding cake?" Dinah asked her, lifting her eyes from the form of a bird carved in soft wood, the shape for the mold. "I've had a thought or two regarding the top layer —"

"Perhaps later," said Josephine, who had looked interested in joining Dinah until the word 'wedding' was spoken. "I have some things to do."

Dinah glanced at me, but I was helpless to do more than shrug. I had to keep Josephine's secret, so I made myself busy with a cup of tea, to appear as little involved as possible.

In the hall outside, we heard voices raised. Helen and Josephine were now having a discussion about her day's plans. The sound of footsteps taking the stairs swiftly in the distance, undoubtedly the sound of Josephine going upstairs alone to dress for tea.

Mrs. Lewison appeared in the garden a moment later. Through the partly-open kitchen windows, we could hear worried and distressed voices as the matriarch and the wedding coordinator engaged in a quiet but intense conversation.

"What do you suppose all that's about?" said Dinah.

"Wedding nerves?" I suggested, stirring sugar into my tea.

"I think it's a bit more than that," she said. She drew her glasses down and rubbed the bridge of her nose. "It'll be a relief to have the prince come back. It's not fair to have only the poor bride as the object of that scheming planner with her clipboard army."

Kristofer might not be coming back to good news, I thought. And despite her promise to me, I wondered whether she would be willing — and brave enough — to reveal it to her insistent family at all.

***

Kitty:

Rehearsals began Tuesday night for *A Midsummer Night's Dream*. After hours at Cliffs House, I hurried to the theatre, where Gerard had already begun painting forest backdrops with lots of foxgloves and Canterbury bells, and Nora had begun molding a donkey headdress from papermache.

Millie was trying to get the drapery right for the dresses, swathing Rosie in gauze as she protested, "But it's not me who'll be wearing this stuff — I'm in an evening gown and wings!"

Nathan was late. I didn't see him anywhere as I tucked myself into a seat with my script, trying to remember my first cue before we began scenes tonight. I glanced around when the theatre door closed in the distance, but it was only Martin hurrying inside.

Lyle approached. "Like the armor?" he asked. He had decked himself out with an old cardboard shield and sword. "I'm thinkin' maybe Lysander's a bit more of a fighter than lover this time." He made a few jabs in the air, poking me and my script.

"You always were a scrapper," I returned, without looking up from my pages.

"Come on, Kat —" he said.

"Don't call me that," I said, sharply. "I don't like it."

"Why? 'Cause it was my pet name for you? I didn't think you'd care anymore. All water under the bridge, as they say, since you've got a new bloke hanging 'round."

"Just stop using it," I said. "Don't make me ask politely."

He laughed. "You haven't changed, have you?" he said. "What are you doing with that bloke anyway? You hate posh types. And he's one of those toffs who lives on his mobile — probably has an accountant and plans for a little retirement place on the coast." He swayed closer, looking into my eyes as he teased me. "Does he take you to Topshop for your birthday? Or Cartier's?"

Until now I forgot how much I hated the silly faces he made. "Who are you to question what I choose?" I asked. "Runnin' off like that without a word — that's what our relationship came to. Maybe I thought I'd try someone with a bit better manners."

"Oooh — Kat's claws. I remember those well enough." He held up his hands, defensively. "Here comes loverboy now — best make myself scarce." He gave me a wicked smile as he retreated. A moment later, I felt Nathan's hand brush against my back.

"Sorry I'm late," he said. He pulled off his coat and rolled up his sleeves. "Are we doing the whole play tonight?"

"Just a few scenes," I said. "Yours'll probably be one of them." Millie liked to pace through the minor bits in between the principle ones.

"I'm ready," he said. "I've only got a couple of lines, so I guess it's hard not to be." He flipped open his script. "Not exactly a dynamic role, Starveling the tailor. It could be worse, though. I could've been somebody called 'Bottom.'"

"Better than ending up as a fairy," said Lorie, sagely, as she tucked a flower into her hair.

"Mostly kids from the primary play those parts," I said. "Some of Lorrie's class."

"Didn't you know?" said Nora, who was passing by with an armload of gauzy fabric. "No kids this year. They're doubling up the cast, so all the minor players get two parts." She shuffled a series of printouts in her hand, then gave one to Nathan. "Congratulations."

He read it, the look on his face growing perplexed. "*Peaseblossom*?" he said.

The fairies would all be costumed in spangled leotard and glittery wings. I bit my lip, fighting the urge to laugh as Lorrie did the same. It was taking a good bit of Nathan's nerve to hold himself together in this sudden turn of events. Even so, he didn't collect his coat and leave.

Millie was sitting on the edge of the stage. "If I could have my Titania and Oberon take the stage, please," she said. Rose hastened up the steps with her script, her hair wreathed in flowers from the prop box. "And her attendants — Nathan, Andy, Louis, and Mickey."

Nathan made it through both of his lines without stumbling too badly — as Starveling the tailor, since the scene with Titania didn't have any lines. Two of my scenes with Lyle were on Millie's agenda for tonight, and afterwards, we all stayed late to help Gerard paint the scenery.

At lunchtime the next day, I was doing the same thing. It was quiet at Cliffs House since the posh master of ceremonies was finally satisfied that Michael and I would deliver top-tier dainties for their event, so I donned an old pair of jeans and an old apron from my fish and chips days, and added a touch of color to the fairy lights on the forest backdrop.

"Want some help?" I gave a bit of a jump. Nathan had come in without me hearing the door swing shut. He leaned against the frame for Oberon's castle, watching me paint.

Nathan was a better artist than actor — that much I knew from our time together during The Grand Baking Extravaganza. He put earnest effort into helping me paint the colored fairy lights in the forest. That look of concentration was the same one from when we were decorating Dinah's soldier cookies.

"You don't have to be serious about it," I said. "From the last row, they'll hardly see that we painted anything."

"Yeah, but this is a part I can do," he said. "Let me enjoy it, will you?" He grinned, sheepishly.

"It's not about being a brilliant actor," I said. "It's about having a bit of fun, you know. That's why I do it."

"Lyle's pretty good," he said.

"He's all right." He was better than all right, actually. Even as a lad, he'd been good at acting, and in school plays when he wasn't in too much trouble. Most of us who behaved that way wouldn't be considered, but Lyle always had a way of persuading people to give him another chance. It came in handy for persuading constables a time or two as well.

"I thought he was pretty convincing last night," said Nathan.

I wasn't quite sure what he meant by this. "I could help you run lines, if you want," I suggested. "We could practice together sometimes. If you want to come to Cliffs House while I'm working, it'd be easy."

"We should run *your* lines," he said. "As Peaseblossom, I only say two words." He laid aside his brush, careful not to get paint on his suit. He took my hand and drew me to my feet.

"Think you could make me a better actor?" he said. "Good enough to move up in the cast ... let's say, as Snug?"

I almost laughed at that. "All you need's a bit of practice," I said. "That's all it is. Learning to put what you feel into a few words."

"In that case, maybe I want to set my sights further than the town laborers," he said. "Something more dashing. Maybe your friend Lyle can give me pointers."

"That cad?" I scoffed. "I wouldn't ask the likes of him for help crossing a zebra stripe."

"I'll put more enthusiasm into my performance, then," said Nathan. With that, he embraced me, and dipped me low suddenly. I let out a little shriek, even though he caught me perfectly.

"What's his line when he asks you to run away? Something about 'the course of true love never did run smooth — but was to different ...something, something."

"'Too high to be enthralled to low,'" I said. "It's not Lysander then, it's Hermia."

"Right. So he says 'or if there was ... sympathy in choice, war, death, or sickness seized it, making it momentary as a sound.'"

That was pretty good, actually, even if it was a bit wrong. He'd been reading the play and not just his lines. But they were better because it wasn't Lysander saying them, but Nathan himself. I liked that bit best.

"Think I deserve the part?" he asked, softly.

"You haven't sold me, really," I answered, wrinkling my nose.

We'd looked at each other too long. He'd been holding me in this position too long for something not to happen. He leaned closer, and brushed his lips against mine. His heart was beating fast, and I could feel it with my hand pressed close to his chest. Mine was beating fast, too.

There had been kisses in the past. One last summer at the Minack, one last Christmas beneath a cluster of mistletoe, a few small, stealthy ones here and there that don't count in my opinion, as plenty as they were. But the trouble with being a secret from everybody, even yourselves, is the limited contact it creates. Secrets or no, Nathan was about to kiss me, really and truly, for a third time.

Suddenly, he drew back. "Breath mint," he said. Apologetically, as he tilted me upright again. "Sorry. I didn't realize —"

"I had a sandwich for lunch, not fish and chips," I snapped. "At least it wasn't garlic —"

"Not for you, me," he said. "I had an onion roll at lunch ..."

"I didn't say anything about it, did I?" I answered, crossing my arms. I was disappointed, angry — and confused that I let such a little thing feel so much more important to me. So what if that was it?

"No, but it shouldn't be like that," he said. "Even in a spontaneous kiss, it shouldn't mean your first thought should be of rancid food —"

"Can't say my thoughts were going there," I retorted. Nathan stopped digging through his pocket and looked at me — a long, searching sort of look that made the heat rush to my cheeks again.

"Well," I said, as we stood there, the distance between us feeling not so far now. "They weren't. Not while there was something else distracting me." My smile was a different one. A bit weak-kneed, the whole sensation, as we looked at each other.

He had given up his search for the mints for good. I wanted to apologize for scolding him, because all I had wanted was to kiss him. The two of us were returning to that moment ... but that was before a thud was audible behind the curtains.

"G'day, lady and gentleman of Greece," said Gerard, emerging from backstage with a handsaw and a carpenter's apron full of nails. "Oh, wait — you're not a gentleman," he said to Nathan, with a chuckle. "You're the tailor, aren't you?"

"Right," said Nathan, with a sigh. "That's me."

***

Julianne:

Ms. Krensky approved of our efforts in the grand hall, and finally gave her consent to Lady Amanda's table arrangement after the conference at tea regarding the who's who of the guest list. With days ticking away steadily until the ceremony, there was no sign that Josephine had expressed any hesitation over going through with her wedding.

"I'm as nervous as a gnat at the thought of presenting it," said Dinah, who was busy sealing six layer cakes in airtight wax sheets. "I know it's only a trial, but I haven't a clue what flavors to choose if they find vanilla too bland ... or want something a bit fancier than gold leaf on the outside."

"What's fancier than gold leaf?" asked Gemma.

"Lots of things," said Dinah. "Chocolate collars are all the rage these days, and the piping on those is quite elegant. And there's the fad for jewel colors to consider."

Pippa was eating crumbs out of one of the cake tins. "I think it's perfect," she said. "I like the chocolate birds — the whole thing looks rich enough with all the bits and bobs you've added."

"They're not 'bits and bobs,'" retorted Dinah. "They're extremely delicate ornaments crafted by hand — and for heaven's sake, mind yourself with those tins! They could still be hot, you know."

This cake was for a 'tasting tea' as Dinah referred to it, when the bride and groom would approve her creation as wholeheartedly as Ms. Krensky. Since I thought the chance of refusal was slim — barring disaster — I didn't feel the same butterflies as Dinah over its presentation.

Mine returned while I was in my room, emailing Kitty about the flowers' delivery time. I heard a knock on my door, which was partly open. "Come in," I said. Instead of Lady Amanda or Gemma, I found it was Josephine who answered.

"Might I talk to you?" she asked.

I remembered her promise from before, in the car park at the Pavilion. "Of course." I closed the lid of my computer. "What do you want to discuss?" It wouldn't be cake flavors or flower colors, I knew. This was about Josephine's secret, whatever it was.

"I want to thank you for keeping my secret a few days ago," she said. "I'm sure you've already guessed why I'm here."

"Truthfully, kind of," I said.

"I have to talk to someone, I suppose ... and I suppose it might as well be you, since you've found out already," she continued. "And I feel I owe you an explanation. I don't want you thinking that afternoon was something it wasn't."

"I don't have any clue why you were really there," I said. "I can't tell your mother anything too terrible, if that's what you're afraid of." I sat up and tucked my legs beneath me as Josephine sat down in the chair closest to my window. She gazed at the garden outside.

"The boy in the car park. I don't know his name," she said. "I've never met him. I don't know anything about him at all. He's a complete stranger to me."

I hadn't expected this. "So why were you following him?" I asked.

She hesitated. "I met Kristofer when I was fifteen," she said. "I was on holiday at a skiing lodge." I imagined Gemma's thrill if she found out this tidbit of the bride's past. "His school was close to my own, so we saw each other sometimes. We texted and emailed each other. He was sweet." She smiled. "He told me even then he intended to marry me. He gave me a silly little ring he won at a holiday fete, and said it was so I would know he was in earnest. Then when I went to Oxford, he came, too."

"Were you two close?" I asked.

"Very." She lifted her gaze to mine. "Don't think I didn't love Kristofer — don't love him, I mean," she corrected. "We were extremely close, and spent every moment we could manage together ... at least until someone found out about us." She sighed again.

"By 'someone,' I'm guessing you mean the press," I said. "Or your families."

"A little of both," she said. "It was our families first. Spies on social media are everywhere, so it was only a matter of time before they knew. Mummy was upset at first, I had to persuade her I knew what I was doing — but she got over it quickly enough after Kristofer's proposal was public. Then we were together publicly, with all sorts of chaperones and lots of people asking questions about our future, and how soon we would be married. I guess you could say all the magic ... all the thrill of being in love ... was lost in the formalities of duty."

"Kristofer didn't give you those gifts, did he?" I asked, softly. "The ones on your table."

Josephine didn't meet my gaze. "A few months ago, I got the first note," she said. "From an anonymous stranger who just wanted to wish me a happy birthday. After that ... there were a few small gifts, a few more short letters. Nothing, really. Harmless...kind...I should have tossed them into the dustbin, but I couldn't."

She rose and parted the curtains, looking out at the garden's flower urns spilling over with vinca and red ivy. "I wanted to know who he was. That's why I hired a private detective. I'd used a tracing app to find out the location of his messages — somewhere in Copenhagen, so I knew it was someone possibly from my past. Stefan was the one who took those photos. He had traced the mobile signal to a park."

"But no name?" I said. "No face, no address — not even from the cell phone trace?" I knew that spying software was pretty impressive these days, and simple to use...not that most people I knew bothered to hide their location, but shouted it out to everyone on social media.

"The mobile was a disposable one. The detective lost his trace shortly afterwards. Then, a few days ago, I received another message. He doesn't text very often, and the user location is usually encrypted — but, just this once, it showed a location, at the Pavilion in Penzance. I called Stefan, of course, but I wanted to go myself. I wanted to see him...just to see what he was like. Just to know if — if the reason he sent me those gifts and notes was something I needed to know."

"A secret romance," I said. That wasn't so hard to believe, given the books and DVDs I had seen in Josephine's room — ones full of second chances for love, and improbable matches.

"You see why I can't possibly have my mother know about this," she continued. "It's harmless, it's nothing. But she would see it as an utter disaster. She would think I'm planning to run away without a second thought on the matter. She would think it's foolish to even wonder about him."

"Is it?" I asked. "I mean, you chased this guy through a car park. That's not a normal way to meet someone who might just be a friend." I met Josephine's eyes firmly for this question. There was no possibility that she didn't know this, too.

Her cheeks burned. "I don't know," she said. Her gaze dropped lower. "I don't know what I feel. I know that I care about Kristofer. I do," she said. "But I feel as if this person knows me — knows things about me that no one else really does. The words in some of the notes, the little gifts that fit the things I love or find funny ... there's only a handful of people in my life who knows those things. And to have a stranger know them, too seems like too much. If this is a friend I've lost somehow, I need to know. And if —"

She didn't finish, but she didn't have to. A small part of Josephine was wondering if she had missed a second, very different, chance for romance. One without royal ties and a demanding wedding's plans.

"You said this wasn't about Kristofer," I said. "It's kind of hard for it not to be. Since you're basically two weeks away from marrying him."

"But if our life is to be like these past weeks — full of people controlling us, coordinating our every move, scrutinizing our every decision — I'm not sure that I want it." She sighed. "I've had that already with Mummy, even before my father was gone. And I want to be free, to travel and to work on the foundation." She looked at me again. "Imagine if the people you love are only happy while they're controlling you. Wouldn't you run away from that? Even if you loved someone who couldn't?"

Kristofer couldn't run away, of course. That was probably unacceptable for someone in a family like his, even if they were a dozen places removed from the throne. But a mysterious boy who traveled across Europe and sent flowers in secret to his crush, was probably exactly the kind of boy who possessed that freedom. In Josephine's place, the future she wanted might not fit with Kristofer's world. The version of it she was seeing up close these days, anyway.

"So what are you going to do?" I asked.

She shook her head. "What could I possibly do?" she asked. "Except continue as things are. It will grow easier in time, I suppose. I can always hope it will improve somehow." The other option would be worse, I thought — the one in which she and Kristofer found their future together impossible.

"There's one thing you need to do, though," I said. "And that's decide now whether to stay or go."

"Now?" she said. "How can I?"

"If you can't make the life you want as Kristofer's wife, you can't leave later, not after your wedding," I said. "Not without making things worse. And if you're going to stay ... harboring a secret crush will only hurt both of you in the end."

"Don't you see how difficult it is for me to do any of those things?" she said. "It isn't that I don't want to decide what's right, but the choice isn't simple. What would you have me do?"

"I think a girl like you can figure out a way," I said. "You've already managed to hire a private eye who either keeps his mouth shut or doesn't know who you really are. You're creating a foundation to help children. That's pretty impressive for someone so young, who's been battling family issues the whole time." I couldn't help thinking her secret admirer was particularly right about her gifts.

"It's much easier to create a charity for books and music than tell someone I care about that their life seems terribly stifling to me."

"You've managed to hold your own life together despite your parents' lives falling apart," I pointed out. "That couldn't have been easy. So don't let two pushy families determine what you do with it now."

Josephine was quiet.

"Just ask yourself if you love Kristofer enough to fight to have him in your life — and fight to make that life what you want it to be," I said. "Or if you think it would be easier to let him go and make that life on your own. It would be easier to figure it out now than later, Josephine. And a lot less painful for both of you."

It wouldn't be easy. This wasn't advice I wanted to give anyone, but with her standing in my room, and me the only one who knew her secret, I had to do it.

"Then I would have to choose," Josephine sighed again. "And either way, I'll have to tell him the truth about how I feel now."

"It's pretty heavy to deal with," I said. "But you owe it you. And to him."

A long silence followed. "What if I don't decide?" said Josephine, at last. "Will you still keep my secret?"

"Of course," I said. I felt disappointed; Josephine was giving up already, it seemed. "I'll always keep my promise," I added. "After all, it's your decision what happens, not mine. If you do this, you're doing it for you. Not because you feel threatened that someone else will bring it crashing down."

"Thanks," she said again. She rose. "Thanks for listening." But that was all she said before leaving me alone again.

***

I stretched out on the garden's grassy lawn after a long day of helping Ms. Krensky sort the guest's replies and debate the merits of the seaview garden for the wedding portrait. Lying here, surrounded by urns of flowers which seemed suspended above me like the hanging gardens' floral clouds, I watched the daylight slip away, and listened to the sound of the sea far below. It reminded me of home — the home I had found, not the one I was returning to. I was still reconciling myself to this last part, one which involved my leaving.

At home, Matt was no doubt sorting through his things, sorting our possessions into boxes that we would both examine and debate before taping closed. A few weeks from now, Rosemoor would stand empty — would our landlady Mathilda lease it again? To some horribly careless person who persuaded her to put the worn-out old armchair by the dustbins on the curb, and cover the walls in some horrible modern paper?

I shuddered. Best not to think about it. Think about pleasant things instead — like coming back to find our cottage waiting for us, and the seedlings of Matt's beloved plants in bloom in spite of his absence. Not of goodbye parties, but welcome home ones —

My mobile rang. My heart leaped, imagining Matt's number would be on the screen, and that our thoughts were connected across the distance — but it was my mother's instead. She couldn't be more thrilled about our coming to America, even if it was as temporary as I made it sound.

I sighed. It wasn't the call I had hoped for, but it was a voice I loved, so I would have to answer it. Maybe a conversation about the life I left behind would help reconcile me to it more quickly.

***

Kitty:

"Now ... fair Hippolyta our nu — nuptial hour draws on pace. Four happy days bring in another moon. But — oh, methinks how slow this old one wanes. She lingers my desires like a stepmo—dame or a dowager..."

Randy had a puncture in Truro and was late for rehearsal, which meant we needed a stand-in, so Millicent appointed Nathan to read his lines. 'Read' being a bit of a stretch, maybe. Pauses abound.

"... I wooed thee with my sword and won thy love, doing thee injuries —" Nathan paused and re-read that line silently, as if not sure it was correct. "But I will wed thee in another key, with pomp. And triumph and with revelling."

He gave it a bit of enthusiasm in places, but it was still creaky. I heard a faint snort of laughter from Lyle and wanted to poke him hard in his stomach with my elbow. Only he wasn't the only one who was having to hold back a laugh this time — and besides, I knew that Lorrie wouldn't like me injuring her onstage paramour, whom she found rather dishy in real life, too.

"Happy be Theseus, our renowned duke!" Peter, also a new addition to the company, launched into Egeus's speech. Unlike Nathan, he overdramatized his lines, making a weird contrast.

"He's not exactly improving, is he?" said Rosie, observing Nathan helping Gerard with the shabby old rust-colored curtains of velvet. "Still a bit wooden when he delivers — have you worked with him, love?"

"A little. But he's not exactly possessed of a lot of time," I said. Even with me and Nathan not da—I mean, not hanging out after hours, regular rehearsals and lots of petty work-related bits and bobs took up the extra time. I was helping with the flowers for Lady Amanda's friend's hush-hush wedding, and Nathan had spent a night or two in London after some meetings.

Right now, he was watching as Lyle and Martin rehearsed their lines in the scene with Puck, a fun, lighthearted scene they were both enjoying. They were both joking around a bit in between. Lyle had been a regular at the cast's table in the pub these past few nights, and had charmed the lot of them in no time in his usual way.

"He has a decent Shakespearean elocution," observed Gerard of Lyle. He was collecting props as Nathan leaned against the stage, watching them, too. "I wish he would speak a bit quicker, though, and pick up the pace of this scene."

"I wish he were six feet under his own concrete," said Nathan. With a bit more venom than he was wont to use. Gerard looked slightly startled.

"Kidding — kidding," said Nathan. His smile wasn't altogether real, though. I knew his smile well enough to be sure of it.

So he was jealous of Lyle. Couldn't he see I wasn't daft enough to be interested in a conceited git like him? When I was stranded in Land's End, knocking around between the shopping village and the kid's park, handing stuffed animals to tourists and counting coins, it was one thing. But not after I was finished being lonely on my own in that place, or being bitter at Mum and the village for all my mistakes.

"You don't fancy Lyle anymore, do you?" Lorrie asked, suddenly. She'd read my mind, and I started a bit in return.

"No," I said. "If you do, you should know, though — he's a bit of a cad. Not just the way he was at school, either."

"I know that part," said Lorrie. "I didn't expect him to have grown up entirely from the boy who smashed windows and vandalized village walls. But it's not as if I've got another option handy for nights at the pub, now is it?"

"You'll have to fight Rosie for him," I said.

"Rosie? She sees through the likes of him from a league's distance," said Lorrie, with a laugh. "I don't even know why I asked you about this, since you have a bloke already. Suppose it's just out of friendly courtesy."

My bloke. They were all referring to Nathan that way. And I didn't correct them, the way I had in the past.

"What's this I hear about you moving to Paris?" Andy leaned over the seat's back to join me and Lorrie in the third row. "Cushy job with a countess, I heard."

"From who?" I demanded.

"Gemma. Who else?" he said. "It's going around that you'll be living the high life in a posh apartment — wheeling the old lady to society galas for champagne and caviar."

I forgot that Gemma was standing by when Lady Astoria was talking me into a job as her assistant. "Don't be spreading that around," I said, lowering my voice. "It's not something that one wants getting 'round — besides, I wasn't exactly charmed by Lady Astoria. When she says she knows her own mind, it's more like a declaration of war than a fair warning."

Lorrie stifled a laugh. "You paint her as a battleship," she said. "I've been picturing some prunes and prisms old dame in a wig and the Queen Mother's dress."

"Why on earth *is* she staying at that castle?" said Andy. "Gemma says it's for some sort of family meeting."

"That's the truth," I said. We'd all been sworn to secrecy, so that was all he'd hear from any of us until after the wedding was announced in the society magazines. I made myself busy with my script, hoping he wouldn't ask any more questions. Across the way, Nathan looked more depressed by the moment, as Lyle and Martin began their lines with Lorrie.

I wanted to tell him he could quit, if he wanted to. I wouldn't cast it up to him later, either. But I realized I would hate for him to go now. The way things had been, this was the only time we saw each other; and while that didn't exactly bode well for us, it was all we had right now.

***

Julianne:

It was good to be home. I dropped my overnight bag on the sofa at Rosemoor, momentarily deleting my mental to-do list: change of clothes, dress for wedding, pick up flowers, remind Lady Amanda to wash Edwin's favorite blanket. Kicking off my shoes, I plopped down in the battered armchair and released a long sigh.

"Glad to be home, I gather?" Matthew kissed the top of my head. I lifted my gaze and smiled.

"Yes, yes, and yes," I said. "Even if it's only for a few days, I'll take it."

"The 'commandant' Krensky released her inmates, I gather?" He raised one eyebrow.

"We'll be back in ample time to set up the hall and the garden," I answered. "Besides, Lady Amanda was growing positively distracted by the coordinator's nagging little hints ... and the rather frosty royal in-laws are back."

"That's a good thing, isn't it?" he said. "It means Kristofer and Josephine are reunited."

"Mmhmm," I said. I had no idea how that reunion was playing out, really — since Kristofer's return, he had been swept away by his diplomat uncle and his military prince father to various conferences by phone or business meetings. While Josephine and her mother had slipped away in secret for a few days, because Mrs. Lewison had a necessary appointment in London.

"I've got something to cheer you," said Matt. "Four lovely pasties, ready to heat and eat."

"Sounds delicious," I said. "Gourmet cuisine."

"Your mail is on the table in the kitchen, if you want to read it," he said. "Next to the tickets to the play."

"Opening night?"

"Of course," he said. "We don't want everyone spoiling the end for us, do we?" He gave me a wink as I collected my heels and carried them to our closet. I couldn't help but notice that most of Matt's books were gone from the shelves already. So were the paintings Constance had given us, the one of the cliffs and the one for our wedding, a miniature version of her famous 'Lilies of Marseilles.' I missed them already — their empty places on the wall looked lonely.

I picked up my floral materials from Cliffs House the next morning, along with a checklist of blossoms. In the kitchen, Michael was removing a delicious-looking cake in a decorative tin, its odor as tantalizing as Dinah's toothsome morsels.

"Cuppa?" he asked, as I entered. A barked request that sounded more like a begrudging inquiry than a genuine offer, but I had faith he meant it nicely.

"Cake?" I asked, with a hopeful glance at the tin.

"Not on your life. It has plans already." He closed the oven door, then poured a cup of tea from the pot waiting by the stove. I accepted it.

"Event promoter's in your office," said Michael. "Said to let you know that when you arrived."

Nathan was indeed waiting in my office, to discuss the possibility of

Cliffs House hosting a British automotive executive's upcoming conference.

"We have an opening, certainly," I said. "Nothing's booked in the coming month at Cliffs House." I was thinking it should really be Kitty at this meeting, not me, since I would be gone by then. "Talk to Kitty and Lady Amanda about it next week."

"Kitty's busy right now," said Nathan. "Extra time for the play." His tone sounded funny when he said this. I bit my tongue — trouble between them?

"How did you come across this idea?" I asked. "We're not the usual choice for an event like this."

"Oh, I ran into some guy in London. He wanted something new for his event, I gave him a card." Nathan didn't have his usual enthusiasm when talking about this situation, either.

My phone rang, playing a sentimental love song that was Aimee's favorite. Nathan glanced up from the calendar. "Turn that off, will you?" He sounded annoyed.

I shut off my phone, but I gave him a stern look. "All right," I said. "What's wrong?"

"What do you mean, 'what's wrong'?" he said.

"Don't make me torture you for answers, Nathan," I said. "What's happening? Did you two have a fight?"

"We didn't have a — you can't have a fight if you're not —" he began, then trailed off. "It's ... just the stress of the play. Lot of rehearsals. You know."

"It wouldn't be because her ex is in the cast?" I said. Kitty had told me that her former boyfriend from Land's End had come back to town. He sounded like a cheap Casanova, judging from her description — but maybe he was something more, if Nathan was so edgy.

Nathan didn't say anything. "He calls her Kat," he said, after a moment. "She won't let anybody call her that."

"She hates being called Kat," I said. "It's because of him."

"It's more," said Nathan, muttering. "I keep picturing his nicotine-stained fingers holding her hand — his snaggle-tooth leer directed at some girl in a dark bus shelter, and I feel like throttling the guy. Or maybe throwing up instead." His expression was unmistakably that of jealous frustration.

My heart melted a little. "She's not interested, you know," I said. It was obvious he felt like the lesser guy in this picture. I had heard that Lyle was the rugged, casual bad boy wrapped up like a blue collar dreamboat. In short, a lot of things that Nathan, with all his looks and masculine charm, was not.

"Maybe. But there's other things, too," he said. "I know she won't stay around here forever. I know I probably won't, either. I guess it hit home for the first time the last couple of weeks...maybe we've been wasting time all these months."

I sucked in my breath. What was he saying? "Nathan," I began.

"Forget it," he said, shaking his head. "I gotta go. I just wanted to give you a heads up about the conference, so you can run it by Lord William sometime soon." He rose. "See you around. At the party, if nothing else."

"You don't have to go, do you?" I was trying to stop him, but he didn't take the hint. I heard him leaving the manor a few minutes later.

I wished Kitty was here to explain exactly what he meant, since nothing about it made sense — unless one interpreted it very pessimistically. And I thought it had been a great idea for Nathan to join the local theatre company, too. Had it broken them up somehow, between her ex and his doubts?

I sighed, and closed the manor's calendar.

"My friend in London is taking the roses from the hothouse," said Matt. "He's a lifelong rose gardener, so there's no one I would trust more. The garden will have to fend for itself, though."

"What about the rare plants?" I asked. I lifted my head from his shoulder. I had been using Matt as a back rest as we sat in the garden. It was a bit overgrown in places where Matt hadn't weeded lately. He'd been too busy packing, I suppose.

"I'll arrange for the preservation society to come collect them," he said.

I picked a blade of grass. "I'll have to pack up my office," I said. "There are loads of folders and sketchbooks I need to go through." I wouldn't be needing them in Seattle. But should I take them just in case ...?

"We've plenty of time," said Matt, softly. "Don't rush. We'll have everything settled long before we're ready to leave for Seattle."

I sighed. "Do you think we'll enjoy the party?" I asked. "The one the village is throwing us?"

"How could we not?" he asked. "Dinah is making a sticky toffee pudding." He snuggled me closer, as I wrapped my arms around his own.

***

Dinah needn't worry about her cake — the moment I saw the finished example, I was sure that any bride and groom would love it. Three exquisite layers of cake with marbled strawberry filling, decorated on the outside with flawless frosting piped in an elegant lacy pattern of flowers and leafy stems around the base of each layer. Miniature white chocolate doves in flight decorated each side, with a carefully-molded pair at the top, surrounded by delicate little frosting flowers.

Even Anneka and Gustaf looked impressed when it was unveiled in the sitting room. I saw Ms. Krensky's eyebrow elevate itself just a fraction of an inch, which I took to be a sign that Dinah exceeded her expectations.

"The sponge is vanilla," said Dinah, "but I've done it with chocolate, and also with white chocolate. The piping's a bit of a tribute to the bride's passion for children's books — inspired by silhouettes in an antique book of children's poetry."

"It's quite good," said Helen, pulling apart her slice's layers with her fork.

"I think the vanilla is a suitable flavor," said Anneka. "What do you think, Josephine?"

"It's perfectly lovely," said Josephine, who smiled politely.

No one asked Kristofer's opinion. That's because he wasn't at this tea, although he was supposed to be. I checked the time on my phone multiple times as I stood just outside the meeting's circle, but each minute ticking past didn't bring the arrival of the royal groom.

"... of course, the wedding sponge will be fresh and not frozen prior to assembly — and if the bride wants something other than gold on the leaves, we can make it look a bit more natural, with soft pinks and greens, for instance."

I had been wondering when I came back to Azure Castle if the bride to be would still be in residence. I saw nothing of Josephine that afternoon; by evening, I had been helping Dinah assemble the cake, the two of us discussing opening night at *A Midsummer Night's Dream* in the village. I had promised Marjorie I would check one last time on the delivery of the garden floral arches for the reception, and stepped into her office while Dinah finished her piping.

Josephine was in the hall when I emerged. "Hi," she said.

"Josephine — can I do something for you?" I was feeling startled, not having expected anyone to be there.

"No," she said. "Only ... I wanted to tell you that I've given what you said some thought. And I've realized that leaving Kristofer isn't something I could ever do. No matter what else I decide."

"I see." I felt relieved, but also a little surprised. "If that's what will make you happy, then I'm glad you're sure of it."

"I love him," she said. "I know I would miss him terribly if I didn't stay. Unless he came with me." She smiled for this joke. "Even to get away from this wretched wedding, I couldn't hurt him. Dreaming my past held some sort of carefree romance ... it wasn't quite the solution I thought it would be. Just a silly notion that distracted me when I should be capable of telling Mummy that my life is my own."

"Maybe you don't have to run away to solve your problems," I answered. I touched her shoulder, sympathetically. "If you talk to Kristofer, he'll understand you're feeling pressured by everyone. Maybe even you mother will understand ... especially if it's a choice between losing her daughter's big day or letting her have some space for making life choices." I pointed this out with a smile for my own joke.

"I hope so," she said. Although Josephine didn't look as if she believed this part was possible, at least. "But if I'm staying, I do have to face these things bravely. Especially if I don't want to be trampled by everyone else's feelings."

"You can do it," I said. "I think anyone as bright and clever as you has what it takes." The pressure of keeping secret Josephine's impulsive sneak-out episode was lessening just a little bit for me, now that she was determined to solve things herself. It looked like everything would be fine after all.

Except, of course, for the fact that the groom was late to their cake tasting.

"Kristofer will be so disappointed," said Anneka, laying aside her half-eaten slice after a few bites. "I wonder what is delaying him?"

"He's always punctual," said Gustaf. "Have you spoken to him today?" He looked at Anders.

"This morning. He said he had some personal business to attend to before he would arrive," said the diplomat. "I assumed it was only a few trivial details he spoke of, and nothing very difficult."

"I hope everything is all right." Helen looked worried; I wondered if she was picturing an auto accident or a jilting at the altar at this moment. On Josephine's forehead, an expression of worry formed, as if these same thoughts were in her head. But that last one was surely impossible, given Kristofer's obvious affection.

"I suppose we're quite finished here," Ms. Krensky said. A crisp tone of voice, since the wedding coordinator was obviously peeved not to have both her clients present. She snapped shut her little cell phone case, stowing the digital diary in her suit's pocket. "Kristofer appears to be unavoidably detained. Thank you, Ms. Barrington, for your time. I'm sure this cake will be perfectly acceptable."

Dinah and I exchanged glances, this time for the snippy words of the wedding coordinator.

As the wedding coordinator had dismissed us, Dinah and I left the sitting room, along with Mrs. Lewison, who complained of a headache. The castle's door opened just as Josephine emerged to go upstairs, and Kristofer entered the main hall.

"Josie," he said. She turned around at the sound of his voice. "I am so sorry I'm late." He held out his hand for her as she approached.

"It's all right," she said. "There's still cake if you would like to try some," she began, gesturing towards the sitting room. To my surprise, Kristofer, carefully and quietly, closed the door before the rest of the room's occupants would notice them in the hall.

"I have something better than cake," he said. "Something I have wanted to give you for a long time." He glanced around, eyes resting on me for a moment in his search. I realized he was trying to have a moment alone with her. I took a step away from them, towards the passage to the grand hall.

Josephine was opening an envelope as I turned away. I heard paper rustling, a short silence, then a little cry of surprise.

"What — what is this?" she said. She sounded astonished.

"For your foundation," he said. "An office for you and your volunteers. I know you haven't had time to find one yet. It was harder to find the right one than I thought — I had hoped that the building's lease would be in your name earlier, but the papers were not ready until today. It is my wedding gift to you: a place where you can begin to make your dream a reality."

"Thank you." Josephine's breathless voice said it all. "Thank you so much." Whatever else she said after this, I was too far away to hear, but I let myself glance back for just a second, to see her arms thrown around Kristofer's neck as he swept her into a close embrace.

***

Kitty:

"Has anyone seen my head?" demanded Bottom. Andy was in costume except for Bottom's donkey's head of paper mache. Behind him, Nellie was hustling to fit a yarn-festooned lion's head over Mickey's.

Dress rehearsal's never a smooth sail for the players. I had already lost two lines by accident in my first scene, and was feeling a bit upset. Even Lyle had stammered once or twice, and so had Rosie, who'd read like a pro all week — but the worst bit thus far was the scenery malfunction with the forest backdrop sagging on its ropes.

Nathan was sitting on a closed trunk in the darkness backstage. He was still trying to remember his cues, and breaking out in a bit of a sweat over it. He had a Mother Hubbard dress pulled over his workman's clothes, as Starveling the tailor is Thisby's mother in the woods play, but the mob cap he was supposed to wear with it was beside him.

"Here." I crouched down and helped him finish buttoning up the dress and fitting on the cap. He shoved his script aside, and gave me a grin.

"I thought at least as the tailor, I'd be dressed as a guy," he joked, wryly.

"You look good," I said.

"That's a lie."

"All right. You look rubbish. Didn't you prefer me lying?"

He leaned over and kissed my cheek. "I like you either way," he said. This wasn't a joke, like the rest of the moment, and I knew it by his voice. My hand brushed his and lingered against it, our fingers touching, then intertwining like an embrace.

"Where's my head?" hissed Andy, close to us.

"Heavens, you haven't found it yet?" Nora whispered. In her black stagehand clothes, she looked like a nearly-invisible wisp of a woman. "It's two scenes from now — quick, everyone look for Bottom's head!"

It went off rough, the rehearsal, but I'd seen worse around here — 'tech night' for *Alice in Wonderland* had ended up dropping the White Rabbit's house on said character and Bill the Lizard. Nathan's nerves didn't totally get the better of him, and we didn't drop any scenery on anybody before the night was over.

"Everybody study, study, *study* your cues faithfully!" said Millicent, at the close. "We've only a little time left before we unleash this beast on the village, as you know, and we don't want it to have the horror of Bottom's ... er ... 'other self,' shall we say."

This produced a lot of snickers among the cast.

I'd never felt so tired as I did pulling on my proper clothes at the end of the night. Many times, I'd been out and about at this hour in the past, but it had been awhile, and it was never for anything as exhausting as staging a theatrical production. I stifled a yawn as I waited in the tiny little foyer of the playhouse, leaning against the wall decorated with old playbills and posters until Nathan appeared.

He pulled off his coat. "Come on," he said. "It's starting to rain." He held it above our heads as we emerged. Summer droplets pattered against the fabric, a gentle rain on the stones outside the old building.

"I won't catch cold," I said.

"Yeah, but you probably weren't planning to take a shower tonight, were you?" he said. "It's a long walk home from here, and you don't have your bike."

"I have my legs," I retorted. Even tired, I still felt a bit playful. "Besides, you have to go home and go to bed, too."

"I'm not tired," he answered.

"Sure you're not," I said, with a knowing smirk. "Walk me as far as the stone wall at the cross streets, then we'll say goodnight."

On the way, we talked about the play's rehearsals, and laughed about a few of the cross purpose incidents — like when the old velvet curtains somehow got wrapped around Theseus' castle and rattled it with the force of an earthquake, just like the fake gravestones in the old movie *Plan 9 from Outer Space* rock in every wind or breeze. We talked a little about the play itself, too, although Nathan avoided any remark which might lead to discussing my character's onstage fiancé.

We paused at the crossway to say goodnight, both still standing under Nathan's coat. We kissed, a light, quick one, not a proper one like the one on the stage would've been. This was the usual kiss we stole when nobody was watching — even nobody but ourselves. But it was followed by another, then still another, because it's hard to stop with just one.

I touched his face, cradling it lightly between my fingertips; I felt his lips brush against the bridge of my nose, then my forehead, a feathery touch that was almost a kiss itself. He drew back afterwards, to look me in the eyes.

"Are you busy this Sunday?" he asked. "After the play's over, I mean."

"Kind of," I said. "I have to do the flowers for the wedding, remember? Julianne's taking them back with her to the castle."

"Oh. Right. I forgot about the wedding," he said. "I guess lately I've forgotten most everything but this play. Even my own work's kind of taken a dive."

"We could hang out Monday night," I said. "Do you want to see a movie in Truro, maybe?" The only decent thing playing was some sort of comedy — my cousin Silas hated it, which was a recommendation in my book.

An awkward smile crossed Nathan's lips. "Um, actually," he said, "I was thinking maybe we could have dinner ... at your place, maybe."

A short laugh from me. "My place?" I echoed. "I don't have a place, Nathan. Me mum's around all the time. There's no way she'd be out on a Monday evening."

"She doesn't have to be," he said. "We could have dinner anyway, you, me, and your family."

"Are you *mental*?" I demanded.

"What? Don't you think I should meet them sooner rather than later? She's probably heard about me by now. It'd be a good time to break the ice."

"It's never a good time to break the ice," I said. "My mum's daft. I told you that before — she doesn't like anyone I date. As for the rest of my lot, they'll talk about how you're a toff, and too posh for the likes of me, and I'll be fighting them in two minutes' time, and they'll laugh about how teasy I am."

It was humiliating. I didn't want to be humiliated in front of Nathan, or have my relatives laughing at him and making fun of him. Even if it seemed like good sport to them, it wasn't. Not to me. Probably not to him, either, although he didn't fully know it.

Until now, I'd managed not to let myself think about it, or worry about it too much, because this moment wasn't supposed to come.

"So?" said Nathan. "So they laugh at me. I think I can handle it."

"I can't," I muttered.

"Kitty, come on. I think it's time to give this secrecy thing up. We might as well tell people what we are ... it's not like saying the words will make it any different, will it?"

"You told your folks about me, I suppose?" I said. I locked an eye on Nathan, seeing his blush come and go as quick as paper in a flame. "That's what I thought. You've never mentioned me, have you?"

"I'm on the other side of the ocean," protested Nathan. "If they had thought I was dating someone seriously over here, they'd be demanding all kinds of details. I thought we'd take a step forward, *then* I'd tell them."

"And we're taking that step with my lot, are we?" I said. "So you don't have to be part of an uncomfortable Skype call in front of your family, or whatever —"

"I'll tell them, I swear," said Nathan. "I was only thinking yours were closer."

"We're not having dinner at Mum's," I told him. "That much I can promise you. I'm not showing up with some bloke whom I've been dating secretly for months, and let her pick you apart." Mum seemed harmless enough at first, but that was before she really found ways to poke her claws under your skin.

"Maybe that's fine with you," he said. "But it's not for me. I don't want to go on like this, Kitty."

We were both quiet, arguing inside instead of with each other. Both probably considering how many uncomfortable things we would face by saying those words. Either breaking up or telling everybody what they already knew, but we didn't: that we were deeper into this relationship then we'd ever been before. At least it was true for me.

"What, then?" I asked him. "Are we breaking up? Unofficially, of course?" I crossed my arms.

"You don't have to be so sarcastic," he said. "You haven't explained how we can keep seeing each other without becoming part of each others' lives. We're not frozen in time, Kitty."

"It's not like no one knows," I said. "Julianne does. Most of Cliffs House, really." I looked at him. "Who've you told?"

"A few people I know in Truro ... I told them I spent evenings with my girlfriend."

Girlfriend — not a word he'd ever said in front of me before. I twisted the button on my coat, trying to think clearly, with my head too crowded with feelings. "Then we're both just as guilty," I said.

"I don't want to be guilty anymore," he said. "That's the difference between us. I want things to change. They can't stay like this, Kitty. I can't stay like this."

"You're not coming to my house for dinner," I said. "If you want me to tell everyone, then fine. I'll tell them, but we're not doing that so quickly."

"Maybe I'll show up anyway," he said. "Are you going to close the door in my face?"

"Is it impossible for you to be sensible?" I said. "I'm trying to protect you!"

"Then stop it," he snapped. "I don't want it, I don't need it, and I've already told you why."

"I guess we've got nothing else to say on that subject, have we?" I answered. Snobbily.

I stepped out from underneath his coat and into the rain, ignoring his protests, and continued on in the direction of Mum's cottage by myself. I could feel his frustrated scowl aimed at my back, even with a blanket of light rain and the darkness between us. But it couldn't possibly match my own, which was growing darker with every step I took, and the thought of what he was asking.

Nathan was being ridiculous about this. A meal with my family, 'round Mum's table — it would send him screaming from her house before dessert was served. He should be thanking me that I wasn't pushing my mental family on him, the way someone else would, not demanding that I introduce him for an evening of mutual misery.

Nothing serious had been said between us yet. It's not as if we were getting married or something. Only I knew he was in the right to ask to be a proper part of my life; and there was only one way to stop it from happening. That's why my face was still hot with anger and unhappiness, and by the time I reached the front door, all trace of our goodnight kiss was forgotten.

***

Opening night. The white shingle with *A Midsummer Night's Dream,* painted in red letters, now hung below the playhouse's official sign. Gerard had decked the windows with posters, but they were all dark rectangles come evening, when villagers were trickling inside the tiny foyer. Backstage, Gerard looked handsome and dignified in his rented posh suit coat, which he wore for every opening night.

I had a case of the nerves, given that I've never been onstage as anything more than a background player. Andy had peeped between the curtains. "It's a full house!" he hissed, with a grin.

I took a deep breath. It came out again like a balloon releasing dribs and drabs of air because I was shaking a bit. The stage was lit up, the scenery was in place for act one, and Nellie in black stagehand garb was putting some last-minute tucks in Rosie's fairy queen costume.

"See you onstage, love o' my life." Lyle drew me against him in a mock embrace. I pushed free.

"Get off," I said. "We're not onstage yet, are we?"

"Kat still has her claws bared, does she?" He made a showy theatrical bow. "Forgive me for friendliness. Break a leg out there, aye?" He passed his arm around Rosie's waist now. "*Here's* the love of my life, then."

"Go on with you," she said, with a protesting laugh. She pulled away from him, trying to fix her gauzy dress — and ignoring a decided smack from behind her as Lyle moved on.

"Cheeky devil!" said Rosie, indignantly. "What a coxcomb thou art, wastrel!" She called after him. Her indignation dissolved into a snort of laughter once he was out of earshot.

"Oh, you dodged a bullet with that one, pet," she said to me. "He's vain enough these past few days, strutting 'round like he's the only rooster in a henhouse. Not that it bothers me at my age." A flirtatious smile appeared on her lips. Rosie maybe young for her years, but loves to play up the fact she's not a lass anymore.

"Never needed to dodge," I answered, finishing tucking my hair up in a knot. "He was never going to pull the trigger." For all his sweet-talking ways, I had known deep inside that Lyle wasn't serious about me. Even when I had wanted to believe otherwise, I had known it: right up to the afternoon he drove away from Land's End and left me behind him, mentally and physically.

"They're pretty," said Rosie. She wasn't looking at my hairpin ornaments, but at the flowers in front of my mirror, a cluster of spotted lilies and two-toned stem roses in a vase, delivered this evening from Marian Jones's floral shop.

I blushed. "Just a bit of well wishing from somebody," I said, shoving the card underneath my powder case.

"Don't be coy with me," said Rosie. "I know who sent them, and it wasn't your mum."

Mum wasn't coming tonight — matinees were good enough for her, she said, and besides which, I was only going to get into trouble running 'round with this lot. Her usual words on the subject, anyway.

"He's a good one, your lad. Thoughtful of him to send you some opening night." She glanced at some of the other dressing tables. "Yours are the only ones 'round here, except for the ones for Millie at show's close."

It was true that none of the other players had more than a rose or two in a bud vase. I tried to do something with the curls at the base of my neck, but my fingers weren't operating properly. "He probably ordered some a few weeks ago," I said. "Thought it was traditional." He certainly didn't order them after the fight we had walking home, I reckoned. We'd said little enough to each other today as a result.

"Fifteen minutes to curtain!" reported Nora, who was carrying her costume draped over one arm, doing double duty as one of the crew and the cast. "Your director will have a word with you momentarily, and Gerard will be along after he's seen to the lights."

It had been lovely of him to send flowers. It was exactly the sort of thing Nathan was good at doing — and the sort of thing that would earn some snide laughs from my oaf cousins, too. All about my posh boy who wasted money on wilting flowers, and wouldn't let me walk home in a little rain shower, like I'd melt into a puddle of sugar.

He said he didn't care if they made a joke of him. But I didn't want to picture his face when he knew that half of what was said about him was spoken in a mean jest — or with pity for him as an ignorant outsider. My stomach clenched fiercely for this thought, which didn't help my nerves one bit.

I snapped one of the roses off short, and tucked it into my knot of hair. I slipped a pin to hold it in place, and tried not to think about how I'd used one of these pins to impress Nathan by breaking into his car. That past was starting to feel like the past... but what was in the future before me, besides this moment onstage with the players? With strangers across the Pond wanting to meet me —

I shut my eyes, seeing only the flash of orange and yellow from the rose in my mirror for a brief second. Then I opened them and went to join the rest of the cast waiting in the darkness for the curtains to open, and the scene onstage to begin.

"Lucky Loreena," whispered Rosie. "She's in a toga and Roman sandals out there. I'm squeezed tightly enough in this corset to crack nuts with my ribcage." The Amazonian queen hefted her cardboard shield and spear into a more amenable position as she whispered something to Sy.

Lyle and Martin were waiting just ahead of me, in costumes that looked a bit like something between a soldier and a gladiator. Behind me, the peasant boys in their loose, ragged work costumes. Including Nathan, who was probably an utter bundle of nerves, too.

If I wasn't still so peeved, and he wasn't so far away right now, I'd give him a kiss for luck — but only because he looked like he needed one.

Millie's voice was muffled on the other side of the old rust-colored drapes. A squeaky sound came from the gears as Gerard hoisted them open. The house lights were low, and the audience was applauding for the first characters onstage, Theseus and Hippolyta.

I didn't feel quite so ill by the time it was my turn onstage. I was too quiet at first, and my voice shook a bit, but I got past it after a few lines. The knots in my stomach were gone pretty soon, and only came back for Nathan's first scene — but even he managed to get his few lines out without a hitch.

Without a hitch. That's description enough of opening night itself. By the time Puck spoke the closing lines, we were all a bit sweaty, tired, and ecstatic as we took our bows. The lights were up, and I could see lots of familiar faces in the crowd, including the staff from Cliffs House, and Lady A and Lord William besides. As always, Gerard emerged with a bouquet of flowers for Millie — showy enough roses, but not as pretty as mine, really.

"Here's to a smashing opening night!" Gerard lifted his pint. "To the cast who made it possible ... and the lovely director herself!"

Millie waved her hand. "It was all Shakespeare," she said. "Well ... perhaps with a teensy *bit* of me involved, of course."

"Then to the bard," said Martin, raising his glass now. We echoed his toast as a group — all of us from the play, mostly still in costume at the Fisherman's Rest as the society's tradition dictated for opening night's post-performance drinks. A headache for Nellie and Nora, who would have to clean all these costumes tomorrow, and repair damages — like the crushed Mad Hatter's top hat last time, which someone stood on in a dare.

Even with the thrill of being onstage, I didn't do more than sip my pint, and not just because I was a bit prudish these days for the sake of my job. Nathan had given me a congratulatory hug after the show, and I'd kissed his cheek and told him jokingly that his fairy wings looked daft — but none of it had felt quite the same as it usually did.

We were still on the outs, I suppose. It wasn't a pleasant feeling at all, possibly worse than stage fright. I had thought feeling sick while standing in the dark couldn't be topped until now.

Lorrie, her hair festooned with fake flowers, looking fresher than my wilted rose, managed to nudge her way across the room to join me. "How did you like your first real taste of stage life?" she asked me.

"I've never been so scared," I said. "And I've never had quite so much fun, either."

"My first was *King Lear*, two years ago," she said. "Opposite Martin onstage for it. He and Lyle are rather enjoying being dressed up like Russell Crowe, I see." They were mock dueling with the cardboard swords from the play, giving the poor shields a bit more beating than they were designed for.

"He's not that much fun, really," she said, reflectively, after taking a sip of her drink. "Lyle."

"He asked you out, did he?"

"Sort of." she said. "More like I persuaded him to have a pint here one evening. Bit of a bore, isn't he? Thinks he's a gift to womankind, pays you a bit of a compliment ... then turns around and pays it to the girl behind you."

"That's a pretty apt sketch of his character," I said.

"You know, I gave him a little gift for good luck," Lorrie continued. "Just a trinket, really. He didn't get me so much as a stem rose for opening night." She laughed. Even if she wasn't serious about him, I knew it stung a bit, being ignored. "He's quite the Casanova, isn't he?"

"He'll grow up someday," I said. "I mean, I grew up, so he's bound to, right?"

Now Lyle's arm was wrapped around Loreena's s waist — he had a sharp eye for spotting a woman weak for his looks, even if only a little bit so. Even Loreena's common sense melted just a fraction for his flirtation under the influence of a pint and all the post-production enthusiasm.

"Nathan's rather brave in his humiliation, don't you think?" said Lorrie. She was watching the other side of the room now, where the cast members in their fairy costumes — minus the fairy wings, but not the glittery head garlands — were doing their best to disguise their costumes beneath various coats or jackets as they sipped their pints.

"It was rotten luck," I said. "Him ending up with those parts, I mean."

"Not many men like that would've put up with it for their first time among the players," said Lorrie. "You should be proud of him."

I knew as well as she did why he put up with it, of course. He could have walked away if he had wanted to, but he never would have gone. And I was proud of him — dreadfully so, even though I couldn't find the words.

He caught my glance, a small, albeit sadder version of a smile on his lips. I felt myself blush quickly, a bit of color in my cheeks under that gaze as I offered him a faint smile in return.

"Surprised he toughs any of this place out," grunted Sy to Lorrie, as he squeezed himself through the pub's crowd to claim the only empty chair beside her. "Probably getting tired of hanging about in some country village. The lad was saying he's had a job offer up London way — some sort of firm browbeating him about a fresh image, or whatever those posh types need when they're in financial straits."

"What lad?" I said.

"Andy. What's been chasing 'round with the old Ben's daughter. Says what's-his-name over there had turned it down twice. Seemed a bit teasy all day to me, so's won't be surprised if he doesn't regret doing it. That's how all those type are — act in haste, repent at leisure."

I reckoned he was regretting it now. Turning it down to stay in Truro, and giving me that daft speech about meeting my Mum and telling his parents — those two things weren't a coincidence. He wouldn't make that mistake a third time, not after what we'd said.

It kept hopping into my thoughts the next day. A drizzly day that boded no good for anybody's mood, since the whole world looked grey through the manor's windows. Even discussing pate-stuffed mushrooms and garlic hummus with toasted brioche, Michael's latest and last creations for the wine competition's menu, didn't take my mind off it.

"Why so glum?" he asked. He snapped his fingers when I ignored him. "Hey, look at me," he commanded. "Don't look at the floor. Eyes are half the conversation."

I gave him a look that would wither anybody else but the Cliffs House chef. "Who? Me?" I retorted, sweetly. "It's the weather, like everybody else," I said.

I hadn't been writing down ideas on the menu sheet — just drawing little stick people on a stage. One of them was Nathan, obviously; it was holding a mobile phone.

"It's not the weather. I know when it is. You know how?" he said. "I get a pain in my right hand — the one I broke years ago. When it's *that* kind of gloom, it affects people's feelings. A wind from the north stripping life out of humanity. This is just a summer shower."

He spoke brusquely, somewhere between a bark and a grumble. Michael's skin was chapped from steamed pots and heat waves from his oven, so he looked as if he'd been laboring over a bonfire all day. That weathered look, the voice, and his rough features, made him seem fierce and aggressive in the kitchen, a general armed with a chopping knife. Pork chops cowered before him. Cakes don't dare emerge underbaked.

Thus far, he hasn't exactly grown on everyone, given his fearsome looks, but he and I get on well enough. Gemma's afraid of him — then again, maybe that's why I like him.

"Maybe mine are affected anyway. You know, if people don't have proper light, they fall into a state of depression. Decrease in Vitamin D does it."

He shoved a skillet onto the stove's eye, and *thumped* a plate in front of me. "Crepes," he said. "Eat up."

"I'm not hungry," I said.

"Who in their right mind seriously isn't hungry for crepes?" he demanded.

"Me," I lied. It was hard, since Michael's crepes are extremely delicious, and sometimes he gives me a French lesson while I'm eating them. But today, I simply hadn't the stomach for them.

"Then you've got a big problem."

I was silent.

"Katherine." It's not fair of him to use my full name. The one only my mum uses, and usually when she's peeved at me, and it instantly rouses me for battle and stubborn replies. "Don't lie to me. Spill it."

"I don't want to." I poked at the edge of the crepes' plate.

"It's about love, then." He dug a fork into its contents and began eating them — I repressed a noise of protest in my throat. It's not like I could choke them down anyway.

"I'm not in love," I said, pretending to scoff. But Michael's scornful reaction drowned mine out.

"You are the worst liar," he said. "What's more, it's pathetic. How long have I been here? How long have I known you? The answer — 'too long.' Now tell me what's happened. I'm getting tired of browbeating you over it."

"I hurt Nathan's feelings." I studied the floor, but it was for my own protection, because I didn't trust my self composure now. "I told him I didn't want him to meet my family. I was trying to be nice ... but he was having some sort of desperate crisis about us. Some firm in London wants to hire him, and he should probably take it. I mean ... we might not have a future together. He knows it, surely."

"He's serious." Michael grunted. "You?"

I bit my lip too hard, and it hurt. The words were squeezed in my throat, not wanting to come out. I'd been waiting for our relationship to be doomed or disastrous for a long time, and now that it had happened, I didn't know what to do. Everything ended at that point in my imagination — no solution, no fight, no period of healing. I'd never imagined past it, because I'd been hoping it would somehow never happen.

Michael's hand on my arm felt a bit like steel wool, given how rough his palm is. He gave it a gentle squeeze and shake. The fact that he didn't say anything at all made me feel better.

***

Julianne:

The farewell party was held at the Fisherman's Rest — not in the back room, where the anchors and mounted fish were once supposed to preside over Pippa's wedding reception, but in the pub's main room, where a noisy crowd was gathered, more than half of whom I suspected didn't know me or Matt at all, but were lured here by the promise of Dinah and Michael's cooking, and St Austell ale.

"I can't believe *you're* leaving, too," said Pippa to me. "First me, then Dinah ... who's next? Gemma? It's awful, really."

"We're not moving away for good," I said. "We're coming back as soon as my friend is well."

"That's what everyone says," said Pippa, mournfully. "Gilbert Tolbien said it six years ago and where is he now? Still in Edinburgh, I tell you, though he's promised to come back a dozen times yet."

"Oh, for heaven's sake, he's a heart specialist," said Dinah. "What possible reason could he have for coming here to work in a clinic? Be reasonable — it would hardly be fair to his career, now would it?"

"Jenny Bryce hasn't come back, either," Gemma pointed out. "'Course, that could be because she put on airs after The Grand Baking Extravaganza, too. Thought she'd make a proper baker in some place with posh tourists."

"Well, *we* are coming back," I repeated, firmly. I realized my hold on Matt's arm had tightened, and released my grip again. "This is just a temporary departure."

"It had better be," said Lady Amanda, who joined us with a brimming glass in her hand. "Even if Kitty is brilliant, she won't have your *panache*. I will rather miss that when it comes to Cliffs House's events."

"You won't be missing it for long," I promised. Or, rather, hoped. Lately I had begun to feel more dismal about these prospects. Was it true, what everyone said about not being able to go home again? Only for me it wasn't my old home, but my new one that would be the victim of this logic. Me starting over as an event planner in Seattle, Matt settling in at some laboratory or college. It seemed more real now than before, when the wedding, and our summer deadline, seemed far away.

"I selected the band myself, you know," said Lord William, proudly. "I thought perhaps you'd like something traditional. A friend of mine saw them at a festival and said they were quite good."

The music was loud and lively, a mixture of Celtic and Cornish folk tunes played with pipes a fiddle, and a stringed instrument that to me resembled a lute shrunk in the wash. I had taken a turn on the dance floor for one of the 'called' dances, but even Matt's skill wasn't enough to keep me from stepping off on the wrong foot occasionally, and making a breathless and humorous collision with a neighbor. Now we retreated to our place near the bar again, greeting the endless number of guests who *did* know us, from Marian and Charlotte to the forgetful Harvey Willow and his son David, the local nurserymen, and even Ted Russert, the farmer whose barn I once borrowed for an unforgettable reception. The first event I had planned with Kitty, actually.

Kitty was leaning against the wall in one of the darker corners of the pub, looking moody and reserved. I had tried to talk to her several times this evening, but her answers were short, and her body language was that of a person trying to discourage all conversation. I thought her restless gaze was looking for someone — surely Nathan was supposed to be here sometime tonight.

"And I've made you a proper pudding to say farewell," continued Dinah, who had been talking without me noticing it.

"Sticky toffee, I hope?" said Matthew. "That's my favorite. And you did promise," he reminded her. He caught my eye and winked at me. I smiled back, knowing he was only teasing her.

"That promise was the only thing which saved me from making a plum pudding," Dinah answered. "No one in the States can make a real English pudding the way a Cornish chef can. You'll be missing it come Christmas."

I would, actually, as strange as that seemed. "Maybe you can mail us one," I said, jokingly.

"There's a kind thought," said Lady Amanda. "We should all send you a lovely Christmas box. With lots of things you can't possibly find in America — that won't perish in the mail, of course. And you could send us some from Seattle. I rather fancy those gooey chocolate-covered puffs now and then — what are they called?" She frowned, trying to recall.

"I *can't* believe you're really leaving," began Pippa again, mournfully.

"Not again," I groaned. Lady Amanda squeezed my arm with a wry smile. Just then, we were joined by another party at the bar.

"I see we be having a bit of a cry," observed Old Ned, who joined us at the bar. "Now, now, it's natural enough. Womenfolk are given to tears when there's a parting. Thank ye, 'tis a kindness of ye, my boy," he said, as Matt placed a pint before him. "I remember once, when Ollie Samuels was going away ...."

At the table reserved for me and Matt, I sat with a plate of Charlotte's oggies, listening to the music and watching as Gemma and Andy made their way through a lively step dance, along with several other village youths and a few older residents, who were the best at it of all. I remembered the first time I had been part of a Troyl, one that was held in an old stone barn. It had been my first time to stumble my way through a called dance — I didn't dare attempt to learn any step dancing techniques — and my first time to see Matt in a kilt ... which had definitely lived up to Gemma and Pippa's promises on that score.

If I never came back, would this be enough? All the experiences, all the memories ... could I be happy somewhere else if I had to be, with this little bit of time here alive inside me? And in the pages of my journal ... well, you can imagine that a lot of them are blank after the first month or so of faithful attempts to document my life here.

Matt sat down beside me. "There's a surprise yet to come," he said. "Charlotte and Julie Finley are doing something a bit special for us tonight, it seems."

"Are they?" I said. "That's sweet of them." I realized I must sound a little absentminded with this answer. Matt glanced towards the dancers.

"Another turn?" he asked me.

"Let's wait until my ankle rests a little more," I said. "I think I twisted it just a little when I tried *not* to step on Pippa's foot earlier."

He smiled. "You're not really such a terrible dancer," he said. "You needn't exaggerate it. A few little missteps are common for everyone the first few times they try."

"Maybe if you'd worn your kilt, it would be easier to persuade me," I answered. Matt laughed heartily in response.

"Did I tell you," he said, after a moment of recovery, "that I found a position for when we come back."

Come back? For a moment, I wasn't quite sure I heard him. "What?" I said.

"When we come back from Seattle," he said. "A friend of mine has a consulting position opening next year for a garden near Falmouth. It involves the application of some research I did several years ago, which is why he thinks I would be the natural choice."

I felt my heart skip a beat. Matt was thinking about our return. He was imagining the two of us here again — not just someday, but someday soon.

"Really?" I said. "You don't think it's too soon to be sure?"

"Unless something changes, no," he said. "I see no reason not to assume I'll be here when it's open. And if something happens to change our minds in America, I'll decline the position. Simple enough, isn't it?"

It was. My heart suddenly felt lighter, although I couldn't explain exactly why. It just made me feel better to know that Matt and I were on the same page, and that despite all the fears I had for leaving my job and saying goodbye to my charmed life here, that his hopes were the same as mine.

"You're right," I said, sliding my arm around his, and drawing him closer. "It's perfectly simple. I don't know why I worry as much as I do." I rested my head on his shoulder.

"What's your favorite thing to do in Seattle?" he asked me, softly.

"I don't know," I said. Come to think of it, I didn't. "Why do you ask?"

"I just thought I should find out," he said. "So I can imagine how good — or bad — I'll be when I try it."

"Mmm...in that case, it's playing paintball. Zombie apocalypse style."

"Very funny," he answered. "If it's drinking coffee, don't be ashamed to say it."

"Har, har," I said. "I did more than that. I bowled, and went to movies and plays, and went to friends' houses for game nights ..."

"That's better," he chuckled.

The magic of Charlotte's pasties and Matt's words were beginning to fill me with contentment. It was good to be home, good that the wedding at the castle was almost over. And it would be good to have one last chance to be home alone with Matt in our cottage before our lives began anew.

I noticed Kitty was still waiting alone on the other side of the room, and I wondered where Nathan was tonight.

***

Kitty:

I wished there was a chance Nathan wasn't coming tonight, although I knew it couldn't be, not unless he'd had a puncture somewhere between here and Truro. But the way he'd rushed off as soon as this afternoon's performance was finished was as if he had pressing business elsewhere. Probably reviewing his employment options in light of stupidly deciding to stay around Ceffylgwyn.

I wanted to see him. And I wanted to avoid him, too. I didn't know which one was stronger, really, as I managed to avoid having anything more than a half pint and a bite of Michael's Christmas cake when it was circulated through the room.

"... and they'll be having loads of fun in America, and won't come back here, probably," Pippa was saying to someone. "Imagine living in a proper city — with skyscrapers and modern buildings, even."

Might as well be London, I thought. Or any metropolitan spot in the world, for that matter. Maybe I should've taken the dowager's advice, and set my sights on something bigger. What would I do with Julianne gone anyway, the only reason I had the job in the first place? They'd probably be ready to toss me out once she was gone. The new planner would want their own assistant to come along.

I sipped my glass, feeling a bit unhappy. I scanned the room, and saw Nathan watching me from near the doorway.

He must have just come in. He was talking to somebody, but he didn't look very interested in the conversation. I knew I didn't look any more interested in mine when Talisha pulled me into a conversation on the best indie comedy films we've seen.

I thought I'd lost track of him, until I turned back to the bar and found him in front of me. Awkward. No avoiding it, though — not without going around him and being rude in front of everyone.

"We need to talk," he said.

"About what?" I asked.

He scowled. "Look," he said. "I'm sorry, all right? If I hurt your feelings, I'm sorry. But I thought ... I feel like I have a right ..." He stopped speaking, because the nearest party guest looked as if they were listening to us.

He took me by the shoulders and steered me out of foot traffic in the pub. We stood in a private nook in the shadows behind the bar, where no one else was talking. "I wasn't thinking that you had different feelings from me," he said. "If that's what made you angry, you can stop feeling that way."

"It wasn't about our feelings, it was about whether you were doing something daft," I said. I wished he hadn't picked here and now to talk about this. "Haste and repentance — those go hand in hand, you know."

"What? Because I said I think it's stupid not to be more open about us?" he said. "Those are my feelings, and forgive me if I think the only reason you would oppose them would be for a very obvious one."

I felt the blood leave my face. "That I don't care for you?" I retorted, incredulously. "Don't be mental." It made me angry, because he couldn't possibly believe it. It wasn't a good tactic if he wanted me to admit I was wrong before, about us being open.

"Is it crazy to suggest, since you're the one holding us back?" he said, raising his voice, then remembering to lower it again.

"I'm not just protecting you, I'm protecting both of us," I argued. "Two people being honest can be messy — even if they have saintly families and spotless lives. And neither of us do."

"Do we always have to argue?" he asked.

"You're the one starting it," I hissed. "Why else would you say that I don't care about you?"

Nathan moved aside, so we could see each other beneath one of the lights, without drawing too much attention from anybody else. His hands were still on my shoulders, as if trying to keep me from looking away. Not without reason, because I was having a hard time resisting the unhappiness in his eyes.

"You could just tell me the truth," he said. "Couldn't you tell me, Kitty? If there's a reason ... if I'm crazy, and expect too much out of this."

His voice was soft and pleading. It took the heart out of me to answer by asking what of his own truths on that score, given his chance for London. I could only think of the depth of what was between us, and how it felt as if it had a life of its own.

His hands framed my face and he kissed me. Hard, the way he had been intending to that day in the theatre, before he worried about mints and other things — like whether I'd fancied Lyle more than him, probably. And I kissed him back, holding the collar of his shirt to pull him closer.

We broke from it. I met his eyes, and looked into the blue of them with a feeling that hurt and felt wonderful at the same time. I was brave enough and mixed up enough to say words I'd been thinking about before he showed up. And they were the wrong ones.

"I think you should go to London if you want to. I won't make you stay here. I won't ask you."

Nathan's face changed in a second's time. I wasn't sure if he'd seen a ghost, or couldn't believe my words. As if he'd expect anything else of me, given how crazy we were at this moment. Given the fact that I couldn't imagine him staying here forever anymore than I imagined us thwarting the odds.

"So that's how you really feel." He looked crushed. "I guess it would be easier if we both go our separate ways, wouldn't it?" he added, bitterly. "No one turns back, no one left behind."

He sounded crazy to me. "What do you want me to say?" I asked. "It's not that I don't —" I almost said 'love you,' and only stopped myself in time, "— it's not that I don't care about you. That's why I'm saying it. I'm being fair to you."

If he told me what he wanted to hear, I knew it wasn't too late for me to say it. If they were the words on the tip of my tongue even now, I would kiss him again to prove it, and we'd figure the rest of it out later. It wouldn't be words of goodbye he was waiting for, because he didn't come to this farewell party to tell me he was leaving me behind.

"What if I want —" he began. "I can't. Not like this." He released a frustrated sigh. "This place drives me nuts sometimes. I can't think of what to say, how to make you understand —"

He would've kept speaking, but there was a commotion as Charlotte and Julie appeared from the pub's back room, bearing with them a huge Stargazy pie to Julianne and Matt's table.

"There won't be a proper one of these in the States, love," said Charlotte, as the other guests whistled and cheered for this variation on the Tom Bawcock's Eve traditional dish. No doubt, they had used Julie's own special recipe, the one she had perfected in her time living near Mousehole, where the festival is held every December.

"Heavens, that *is* a treat!"

"Looks like a proper fisherman's pie, that does."

At the sight of the fish heads protruding from the crust's edges, eyes staring at us in passing, Nathan's own eyes grew wide, his train of words and thoughts coming to a full stop. In this moment, with all the pressure I was feeling, I didn't care about the party or the fish pie or anything else, except getting out of there and being alone.

"I'm going," I said. "Goodnight." And for the third — or maybe fourth — time since Nathan Menton had known me, he called in vain for me to stop as I maneuvered the crowded pub to freedom.

***

"Make certain the flowers have plenty of water and preservative — wait, Gemma, those are for the chief bridesmaid, we need to keep them separate from the centerpieces."

"The photographer is arriving early, apparently, to take some photos of the bride in the garden," said Marjorie, as she slipped her mobile into her cardigan pocket. "Do tell Ms. Krensky that the caretaker has promised to remove his garden cart before that morning, so she won't be quite so rude about it as she was before."

"I probably won't see her for another day," I said. "She had some pressing errands in London, so she'll probably call Mrs. Lewison before she calls anyone else."

"Maybe Josephine will," said Pippa. "She's in the garden, so you could tell her." Until now, she had been busy teasing Edwin with a stray flower, one which he had been trying most desperately to reach from his stroller.

Josephine was standing just outside the hall's windows, and when I looked at her, she motioned quickly for me to come outside. I glanced at the rest of the staff, but they were busy tucking the flowers into the darkening closet, and didn't notice.

Not again. "I'll be back in just a moment," I said. I stepped past the buckets of fresh-cut flowers and made my towards an outside door.

Josephine looked slightly pale. "I have a favor to ask of you," she said.

A favor? I racked my brain for what kind of errand this might be. "If I can help, I will," I said.

"I want to put the silly crush I had completely behind me," she said. "I won't accept any more gifts or notes from my admirer ... but I need someone to tell him that."

"Why?"

"Isn't it obvious? So Kristofer will understand that it's completely over. I can't keep receiving gifts and notes, or he's sure to know about it ... and it would hardly seem one-sided if he learned the rest of the story. I can't begin to imagine how I would explain it."

"Can't you just throw them away?" I suggested. "You could always text him and tell him the truth, couldn't you? Then change your mobile number or something." I was searching for any answer that didn't involve me somehow, because I knew where this was going.

"He never responds to my texts," she said. "And besides, I want him to really understand that it's final. That's something that a blocked number or a few characters on a screen can't do."

"You don't know where he is, though," I pointed out.

"But today I do," she replied." She toyed with the sleeve of her shirt. "You remember Stefan? The detective? I called to dismiss him, and that's when he told me he traced down the van we saw driving away. It's parked at an inn not terribly far from here." She met my glance now.

I definitely had a bad feeling I knew where this was going.

"He gave me the address — the name of the driver renting it is the name of a stranger as far as I can recall. But I want to return the gifts and have him understand I can't accept anything else now. No gifts, no contact of any sort in the future."

In her hand was a paper sack, and a small envelope. I imagined one contained the little gifts and mementoes from before, and the other contained a note that told her secret admirer that she was happily in love and wasn't interested in his attention.

"I want to be sure this becomes part of my past," she said. "I need to take charge of my own life. I'm going to be completely honest with Kristofer from now on, and be open about what I want and need. No more secret dreams or plans. It's what you suggested I do in the first place, really."

I suppose it was my advice, sort of. "I see," I said, faltering. "If you're sure that returning them is necessary ..." *Send the text. Send these things by post, if nothing else. What am I supposed to say to him?*

"There's no one else I can trust," she said. "Mummy would never understand, as you can imagine. Anyone else would ask questions, and I would have to make up an excuse for it. But you already found out, so you're the only person I can ask."

The only person who knew her secret. True enough — and it was my fault I knew it, too.

With a deep breath, I accepted the sack and letter. "Okay," I said. "I guess I'll ... I'll do my best to see that he gets them back."

"Thank you," she said, breathing a sigh of relief. "I'm so grateful. I imagined how difficult it would be to get someone else to do it — even Marjorie."

I knew I should have stayed sensibly behind when I saw Josephine slip away that day. Following her had made me an accomplice in this odd little scenario in the first place, so I had no one to blame but me, right? This was what I told myself inwardly, even though I knew I had done it because I liked both Josephine and Marjorie, and wanted the best for their family for their upcoming big day.

Relax, Julianne. I told myself that if getting rid of a few plastic toys made Josephine feel more honest in her relationship, that it was worth a little extra trouble. After all, Kristofer seemed like someone worthy of the romantic, selfless gesture this represented in Josephine's eyes.

The address was for an inn close to Penzance — a nice one that was more like a private resort, with a small beach, several old-fashioned cottages, and very dignified walls and a gate. After I climbed out of Marjorie's car, one shakily parked at the gates, I had to give my name before I was allowed through to the private cottages where the van's current driver was staying.

Down a tumbled little stone stairway, to three cottages facing the distant beach, and a converted stable, all wrapped in the arms of a shady grove of native trees. The van in question was parked outside the stable-turned-garage, where a town car with tinted windows was also parked, alongside a vintage motorbike painted a very electric blue.

I knocked on the first cottage, the one registered to the van's driver. There was no answer after two tries, so I knocked on the one next door, hoping maybe his neighbors were aware of his current location. After two knocks, the door opened. On the other side was Kristofer.

"Julianne?" he said. "This is a surprise." He looked puzzled. "Is something the matter at the castle?"

I was startled. "Hi," I said. "Um ... I was actually looking for whoever's staying at the cottage next door." I pointed towards it. "The person who drives the rented van parked over there."

"That would be my driver," he said. "And the other members of our staff."

For a moment, I was speechless again, until I realized the truth. For in Kristofer's cottage, I saw a grey hooded sweatshirt draped across a chair, and a bouquet of flowers like the dried ones in Josephine's collection in a vase on the table.

I held out the sack. "I think these are yours," I said. "And I think maybe I'd like an explanation."

***

"It wasn't meant to be a secret," said Kristofer. "Not entirely. That is, I sent the first few things anonymously ... I thought she might guess it was me. We had been spending so much time apart, and I missed our moments together. I thought it would be the beginning of a special surprise."

He had opened the sack of knickknacks, and the envelope from Josephine, which explained much of the how and why of this situation, I imagined. His face was grave as he read it, but with the faintest trace of a gentle smile. He wasn't angry, and he wasn't laughing at Josephine's earnest gesture; he seemed touched by it, and I liked him a lot more for that reason.

"Then you were going to tell her?" I asked. "When? How?"

"An afternoon in Penzance," he said. "I was going to text her to meet me — to slip away somehow and come there. I had flowers —" he pointed towards the now-wilting bouquet on the table, " — and I was going to give them to her with a note printed like the others. I thought it would be romantic."

It was cute, actually. And definitely surprising — although he had no idea how much trouble it had caused. "So why did you leave that day?" I said.

"I was called away for a business emergency before I could text, so I thought I would just wait —" He paused. "How did you know that?" he asked.

"I followed Josephine. Who followed *you* there, trying to find out who you were," I said. "She was determined to know. She couldn't understand how a stranger could sense so much about who she was and what she loved. I don't think it occurred to her that it could even be you. And when she truly thought about you in the midst of it ... that's when she felt so guilty for ever being curious to find out the truth."

"It's my fault," he said. "Only ... I knew she was a romantic. These formal meetings, these teas and wedding planners ... it isn't how we came to fall in love each other. I wanted to return to those times. I thought we could be spontaneous again, if it were only the two of us exploring Penzance."

He sighed. "The person I must be isn't always what I wish to be. I wish for more freedom sometimes, more carefree moments. I want her to see that. Perhaps she would understand me better."

I touched his arm, seeing how wistful and disappointed he looked. After all, with his plans deflated, there was nothing left but Ms. Krensky's endless teas and wedding plans.

"She really does love you, you know," I said. "Plenty of other people would have kept fantasizing about some perfect mystery admirer. Or just tossed all this in the trash and tried to forget it happened when they changed their mind about it. But Josephine wanted to be sure that her life with you was completely honest. To me, you seem like someone who deserves that. And she seems like someone who deserves you."

"She deserves someone who can make her happy," he answered. "I was trying to do it. Although very stupidly, it would seem."

Maybe a *bit* stupidly. But he was earnest and endearing, and surprisingly romantically mature underneath this rather awkwardly-executed gesture on his part. Not many guys would have bothered to think outside a bouquet of flowers, I knew.

It was a shame that it had to end like this. Josephine both embarrassed and awkwardly surprised, the whole thing collapsing into a very silly misunderstanding.

We were both quiet for a few minutes. Kristofer's fingers reached for the little sparkly pink pony, the one that looked just like the carnival toys at the Pavilion. He probably planned to win another one for her that afternoon, or maybe a big stuffed animal — or lose a few games to a girl who was probably as good or better than he was at them. Wander around hand in hand in the sunshine, find someplace to eat and talk where it would just be the two of them....

Kristofer lifted his gaze and met mine. "Might I ask a favor of you?" he said, after hesitating.

I was sure he was thinking the same thing I was.

"Name it," I answered.

Formal tea with the dowager and Ms. Krensky was on for today, since the countdown to the wedding could now be marked by hours instead of days, if one preferred. The commanding wedding coordinator had just arrived ahead of the royal family, removing a pair of gloves and consulting the screen of her cell phone.

"Where have you been?" she said, noticing my breathless condition as I hurried inside from a consultation with the caretaker Wilton. "I haven't been able to reach Mrs. Ridgeford all morning — she spends a dreadful amount of time on her phone, it seems."

Yes, well, when one has a hand in running the government, I suppose they have more to do than wait on inconvenient family and friends, I wanted to snap back. Instead, I smiled nicely. "I was just taking care of a few last-minute details," I said. "Sorry, but I have something important waiting for me." I hurried up the stairs before she could ask me too many questions, taking a quick peek to make sure none of Mrs. Lewison's security guards were lurking about.

Josephine was emerging from her room, wearing a lavender sundress that was a suitable choice for tea, and a pair of leather ankle boots. I grabbed her arm before she reached the stairs.

She gave a gasp and a start. "Julianne," she said. She clutched my hand. "Did you give them back?" she whispered. "Was he upset? Did he agree not to send anymore?" She was trying hard not to seem too curious, especially while ensuring that communication was at an end between her and her secret contact.

"He knows how you feel," I said. "But — there's one more thing you have to do to put it in the past." From the look on her face, I could see she was uncomfortable with this. "If you love Kristofer, then do it," I said. "Trust me."

"All right." As I drew her to the opposite room's windows, I saw a look of determination on her face for ending this matter, then of perplexity for what we were doing. At least until I opened the curtains and revealed the ladder propped against the window. And her royal fiance standing at the foot of it, wearing a grey hooded sweatshirt, a motorbike parked behind him.

She opened the window. He waved at her. "I need you to tell me to my face that you do not want to hear from me again," he said. "Or you will never get this back." He held up the small, sparkly pony.

Josephine's eyes were wide. "How — why —" She looked at me quickly, then at Kristofer, then back again, before her mind made the connection.

"You were right," I said. "Your secret admirer, really did know you impossibly well."

"Do you forgive me, Josephine?" he called up to her.

"Why didn't you sign your notes?" she demanded. Less angry than embarrassed, I imagined. "Kris, I thought you were a complete stranger — and I was engaged to you! Why on earth did you do any of this?"

"All I ever wanted to do was run away with you," he answered. "That's why. If you are willing to do it, then come down and forget our families and their silly fears and teatimes. If you do not mind that life can be impulsive, that is."

On Josephine's face, a look of surprise for this answer. I could tell the breath had been sucked from her lungs, leaving her without means of replying to this speech from her fiance. Suddenly, she laughed. It was a happy, carefree sound that I'd never heard from her lips before. "Gladly," she answered.

She didn't have to give it a second thought, but swung herself onto the ladder, and began climbing swiftly down it. Kristofer reached for her hand when she was near the ground. On the motorbike, there were two helmets waiting.

I waited until they were safely on it before I closed the window; the last thing I heard was Josephine's laughter as they drove away. By now, I suspected the sound of voices and the motorbike's engine had attracted plenty of notice.

Downstairs, I met Mrs. Lewison preparing to come up. "Is Josephine upstairs?" she said. "I heard voices — where is she?"

"She's not in her room —" I began, but Helen now noticed a flash of light on the window, reflected by the motorbike's mirror as it circled around to the long castle drive. "Josephine!" she cried. She threw open the window. "Josephine — come back here!"

I knew it was too late; but that didn't prepare me for the military grip of Ms. Krensky on my shoulder. "What is going on?" she demanded. "Why is my client shouting?"

"She's trying to persuade Josephine to come back for a very dull tea," I answered, politely.

"What? What did — is she gone?" She rushed to the window, then turned back to me, accusingly, as if sensing I had a part in whatever calamity had just befallen her latest coordinator-client meeting. "*Where* is the happy couple?" she asked. One hand on her hip, an intimidating fashion pose as she waited for the answer.

"Don't worry," I said. "They'll be back in time for the wedding." At the last second, I added, mischievously, "Probably."

***

Ms. Kensky needn't have worried. Josephine and Kristofer returned long before the wedding — even if it was hours after her teatime meeting ended. They both looked worlds happier for having escaped the confines of their watchful relatives and security teams, and since no tabloid stories broke the next morning about the royal couple exploring Penzance, Mrs. Lewison could rest assured they hadn't been recognized.

On the morning of the wedding, I was awake extra early. When it was barely daylight, I helped Pippa and Gemma finish putting the grand hall in perfect order, down to sweeping away the last stray flower petal from the bouquets in the urns. Marjorie and her staff needed our help finishing the reception area in the garden also. There was no forecast for rain today, though a weather pattern building offshore was bound to bring a cool shower in another day or two. By then, however, the newly-married couple would be off on their honeymoon, preparing to start a new life together in a Scandinavian city.

I sipped a cup of tea as the sun rose. A brief moment to myself, long enough to watch the dawn light illuminate the harbor, the dark shapes of boats moving on glittering waters. I had seen a glorious sunset in this same spot yesterday — that was the only advantage of Azure Castle's little glimpse of the sea over my favorite cliffs, whose southerly face didn't exactly showcase a rising or setting ball of fire. But who needs a direct view of the sun anyway? Not me, although I intended to enjoy this one morning's glimpse — indirectly, that is — to the fullest.

"Have we finished with the garden arches?" asked Marjorie. She hurried up to me, adjusting her flowered dress and hat at the same time. "I'm in rather a rush — Samuel will be here at any moment, and I hardly want to still be fretting about wedding decor when he arrives."

"Relax. We have everything in place," I said. "You go greet him and let the rest of us worry about Ms. Krensky's last-minute orders. That's why Lady Amanda brought us, after all."

"You're such a dear. Thanks," she said. I could see she breathed a deep sigh of relief as she hurried along the garden path to the gate.

By the time guests had begun to arrive in earnest — and security was blocking any members of the press from accessing the castle road — Josephine had donned her dress and her veil. She looked lovely, and far less nervous than the young woman who had attended Ms. Krensky's business-driven tea parties.

She caught a brief glimpse of me on her way downstairs to the chamber beside the great hall, where I oversaw the delivery of the bride's bouquet from the floral closet. She gave me a conspiratorial smile and lifted her hand to wave her thanks. Tucked in it, I noticed a folded slip of paper, and a tiny pink object: her 'secret admirer's' treasure. For luck, I thought, as I smiled back.

The photographer took their portraits in the garden after the solemn wedding ceremony in the grand hall. With the sea in the background, Josephine and Kristofer posed with eager smiles, and Anneka managed one a tiny bit warmer than her polite-and-proper version. Even Gustaf looked happy today, more like a prince than a stern general; and Helen, after tears in the ceremony, looked far more relaxed than usual by the time Dinah's masterpiece cake was cut.

"Hasn't it been romantic?" Pippa sighed. "Me own was nice enough, of course. But there's something about *royalty* that just seems a bit exciting. Imagine if she really ends up a queen in some rich European castle ... with a jeweled crown ..."

"You heard Lady Amanda," said Gemma, scoffing. "He's twentieth in line, or something like that."

"But you never know," said Pippa. "What if someone abdicates?"

I tried not to laugh, but it was terribly hard. Especially when I caught Lady Amanda's eye.

"Helen looks well," said Lady Amanda. "I think she's rather relieved to have Josephine happy. That's what she really needed all along, if she hadn't been too silly to notice."

She shifted Edwin to a more comfortable position in his baby bunting carrier. She had stayed away until the reception, since Edwin tended to fuss in solemn halls, and tended to howl when babysat by anybody who didn't belong at Cliffs House. In his 'posh baby suit' he looked quite smart today — although Lady Amanda had managed to tame his hair in the beginning, it had returned to its natural disarray, thanks to his tiny fingers.

"Ga wa," he said to me. "Adj-ji-woo." He pointed quite vigorously in the direction of Dinah's cake. Lady Amanda declined to notice, however — and gave the rest of us sharp looks to do the same.

Mrs. Lewison's smile did look happy as she stood with Josephine and Kristofer, talking to the dowager. It wasn't the champagne melting away her nerves, I told myself, even with Lady Astoria being her usual self. Her cane narrowly missed a tray of champagne flutes in the hands of one of Ms. Krensky's staff as she gestured towards the hedges — I was beginning to wonder if the dowager really was doing it on purpose.

"Doesn't Josephine look like a model, though?" said Gemma. "More so than that awful Petal Price-Parker. I never thought she was a proper choice for Donald, anyway." She referred to the football star whose wedding had been my first one to plan — and whose bride had been Matt's first great heartache in his youth. Because of that, I had my own reasons for not thinking Petal Borroway was one of the runway's most beautiful faces, although I did my best to avoid saying it.

"I think Josephine's less interested in clothes than in books," I pointed out. "You know, Kristofer found her an office where she can set up her charitable program of literacy and arts for underprivileged children."

"Isn't that lovely?" breathed Gemma.

"So romantic," said Pippa. "Like I said, it's practically a fairytale."

She sighed again.

Josephine and Kristofer didn't ride away on his electric blue motorcycle, but in a sleek luxury car that was taking them to a private flight. Whether their final destination would remain the planned one or become something spontaneous after they landed ... well, that was their adventure to keep secret, not one for the rest of us to know. But remembering the carefree look on Josephine's face, and the smile on Kristofer's, as they drove away together the afternoon of their 'escape,' I hoped they had something special and spontaneous ahead of them now.

Ms. Krensky seemed satisfied despite all her final orders and the sniff of uncertainty regarding one of the urns of flowers. Throughout the reception, she had been an imposing figure with a cool smile, one that wasn't shaken by even the most intimidating, important guests on the roster — people whose parties she had probably planned, I imagined. She did manage to get a portrait of herself with the bride, Helen, and Anneka. There was probably a whole wall of them in a secret room in her office, a 'who's who' of European society.

Now Ms. Krensky had marched away with her team, whose uniforms did remind me a little of soldiers. Helen Lewison had left for London, Anneka and Gustaf returned to their private cottage, and there were no more security guards hiding behind tapestries, or in rooms that I accidentally bungled into while searching for others. We helped clear away the cake and appetizers, the empty champagne glasses and the flowers, until the garden and hall of Azure Castle was its simple, beautiful self once more.

I stood admiring it for a moment. Matt had loved its clean lines, the green square between limestone walls that seemed like a gemstone in a frame, even though his heart generally belonged to the sprawling cottage gardens that were beautifully-planned chaos to my eye. In his place, I took one last stroll through the grounds, gazing up at the stately castle which waited so patiently above the sea for visitors to find their way up the long and winding wooded path.

Marjorie told me that she and Samuel were planning to spend part of the autumn here, and open the castle to public tours a few days a week. It sounded lovely, but Matt and I wouldn't be here, of course. Our return visit would have to wait a little longer.

"Home again," sighed Lady Amanda, setting the baby bag on the kitchen floor at Cliffs House. "I'm quite glad to say that aloud." She sat down in one of the kitchen chairs, setting Edwin in a high chair first.

"Pour me a cuppa, Gemma," said Pippa. "I'm done in." She propped her chin on her fists. "I told Gavin I won't be home for at least another day. I'm too worn out from this job to take the train home."

"That's what comes of looking after babies all day," said Gemma, loftily. "You're losing all those muscles from cleaning the manor's high windows."

"You're just jealous," sniffed Pippa. "Though I do miss it a bit."

Michael had fixed us tea as soon as we returned, and we took it downstairs rather than haul the tray to Lady Amanda's parlor. Lord William joined us, having been lonely for company — and for his wife and son especially — these past couple of weeks. And when Geoff entered, Pippa and Dinah went positively wild, although it had only been a few days since the farewell party.

"I feel quite popular," said Geoff, as they hugged him. "I haven't been so eagerly greeted in all my past. Not even by my own mother, I daresay."

"Well, I didn't have time for a proper greeting at the party," said Dinah, by way of excuse. "And it's only right, given how long we toiled together in the past, you and I." She made herself busy pouring cups of tea in Gemma's stead — though I noticed she had hugged Lord William just as hard when he arrived at the kitchen beforehand.

"You missed me, didn't you?" Pippa said to Geoff, after she was done embracing him.

"Of course I did," he said. "It hasn't been the same without you, I assure you."

"Go on with you now," said Dinah to her. "Haven't you had quite enough of asking everyone how deeply they've mourned your absence?"

"I only want to know," said Pippa. "What's wrong with that? We know they missed *you* well enough. Not that I'm meaning to offend, Mr. — er —" she said to Michael, who was leaning against the counter near the stove as Dinah attacked his mixing bowls, spatula, and flour and sugar canisters with renewed vigor.

"Michael," supplied Kitty, who was helping Edwin count the plastic keys on his toy ring as Lord William held him. "No last name. He doesn't like it."

Pippa took one look at Michael's rather fierce exterior — including the tattoo exposed beneath his white shirt's short sleeve — and said no more.

"It's like old times, isn't it?" said Dinah, as she placed a platter of fresh-baked biscuits on the table for us, her special marmalade ones. Michael sneaked one and took a bite, he and Dinah exchanging glances — approval was in his eyes, so I was satisfied.

"Indeed it is," said Lord William. "It's quite good to have everyone back. It's been far too empty around here, I assure you — and been quite different this past year as it is." He took two of Dinah's biscuits; I knew that Lord William hadn't quite resigned himself to Michael's recipes yet.

"We're not all here, though," pointed out Pippa. "Ross isn't here."

"Who?" Michael spoke for the first time, sounding puzzled. I hid my smile for this old joke.

"She means Matt," I said. "I could call him, I suppose." He was probably at Rosemoor, potting his beloved plants for transport elsewhere — unless he was already driving them to his horticulturist friend for safekeeping.

"Oh, do," said Lady Amanda. "We'll all have dinner, perhaps. There must be something about useful in making a bit of stew — or a shepherd's pie." Michael grunted his agreement, as he took a second biscuit for his tea.

"Where is Edwin's toy lorry?" Lady Amanda asked, while rummaging through the baby bag for extra nappies.

"It's in the playhouse," said Lord William. "I had a few of his things up there to see if there was room for playing." He looked a bit sheepish with this confession, since more than one of us had seen Lord William enjoying crashing the toy lorry and the fire truck together as much as his infant son did.

"Fetch it, will you Kitty?" asked Lady Amanda. "And Julianne, do call Matthew and see if he'll come by."

I pressed the button on my mobile phone, waiting for Matt's answer. I knew he wouldn't want to miss this reunion, after so many memorable times in this kitchen with Cliffs House's staff. The first time we worked side by side was here ... the second time Matt ever teased me was in this very room ... and right now it was filled with the people who were part of those moments, and as bright and cozy as always.

***

Kitty:

The playhouse wasn't one of those plastic snap-together kits, but part of the set for Theseus's castle from the theatre. It was too big for Gerard to store, and he didn't have the heart to tear it apart, so Lord William had adopted part of the false front for a little play platform for Edwin — one with plenty of safety rails to hold him on the main platform, of course.

It was a bit pointless for a child of Edwin's age, but Lord William was thinking ahead — and couldn't build too many things that an infant could play with, either.

It was beginning to sprinkle a bit as I crossed the garden and climbed the little steps to retrieve the truck, which lay scattered beside a few plastic outdoor toys. I heard a voice call my name, so I rose and looked out the castle window, the one painted with the false balcony and flower box as before. There was Nathan, standing in the garden on the other side.

"What?" I said. I wasn't sure I wanted to talk to him. Since leaving the goodbye party, I hadn't seen him again, and it had meant we didn't have to go on with that awful conversation from before. One full of lots of unpleasant things about love and leaving.

"I don't want to go to London," he said. It was raining in earnest now, pattering a little against his jacket, and against the roof of the playhouse.

"Good for you," I answered. My heart skipped a beat, though, and I didn't feel as casual as I sounded.

"I don't want to go back to the U.S. and have the big career. I want to be with you, and if that means going to Paris, I'll go. I'll go anywhere with you, because I love you."

His tone was determined, almost fierce. "Well?" he said. "What do you say to that? I love you, Kitty. I said it. I want to marry you, even. That's how much I feel for you."

"I love you," I said. I didn't stop to think about it. It came out on its own, no stopping it.

I had never said those words to anyone. The earth might be shaking down to its core at this moment. Sending big showers of lava up, and cracking open the earth because something this impossible actually happened.

Nathan stepped closer. "Then let me come with you," he said. "Because if you don't, I'll follow you there. I'll follow you anywhere, Kitty. I swear it."

It might have left me a bit speechless, except I didn't have a clue what he was talking about.

"I'm not going to Paris," I said, bluntly.

Nathan blinked. "You're not?" he said.

"No. Who told you that?"

"It was going around the village. It was a huge career opportunity, they said."

"The dowager?" I said. "I never even thought of it. It was a proper posh offer, I suppose, but I wasn't interested, not even for Paris."

"Oh." Nathan looked slightly sheepish. It had taken the wind from his sails, I suppose, given there was no place to follow me. And if I wasn't shaking a bit, I might have laughed at this situation.

"I was going to take you to Paris," he said. "Before I thought you were going there for good. Two tickets ... that was the other part of your gift." He blinked hard in the rain. "The idea feels a little dumb now."

"It's not," I said. I'd never had anyone take me anywhere, much less some place that exciting. He must have been thinking about how hard I'd been studying the language; or maybe just thinking it was romantic.

We both stood there in the rain for a second. Nathan was the first to say something. "Look, will you come down from that balcony?" he demanded. "I'm tired of standing down here, yelling at you."

"Learned how to ask proper, did you?" I retorted. But I was smiling.

I reached the bottom of the steps and ducked outside the doorway, into the open air and rain. Nathan's arms were around me, holding me tight. I wrapped mine around his neck and pressed my lips against his own, rumpling his wet hair.

"I'll let you meet my mum," I whispered to him. "I'll let you meet all that lot, even if they're awful —"

"I don't care," he whispered back. His voice was still fierce, even quiet. "We don't have to live with them, Kitty. Or with my family, either. We can go anywhere we want — do anything we want — and it doesn't matter what anybody else thinks. "

He kissed me back. Sweeping me off my feet — literally — and into his arms, which were strong enough for a toff in a suit who ran his life from a mobile.

It was raining buckets now, but we were still kissing. I pressed my cheek against his for a breather as I held tight to him, and thought about the breathless, headlong rush our lives were about to enter, the chaos with his folks and mine. Then I saw the rest of Cliffs House watching us from the kitchen windows. Eight faces were locked on us standing like fools in the garden.

"I think we're being a bit too open now," I said, close to his ear. "Maybe we should stop for awhile."

"What? Why?" he said. But he realized what I was looking at over his shoulder. He turned around, and I could feel the jolt of surprise go through him for our audience, since he hadn't put me down yet.

Dinah opened the window. "Come out of the rain, you two, before you catch your deaths!"

I heard Nathan's voice a minute later, close to my ear. "You're right," Nathan answered me. "Let's go in." He lowered me down again. We took each others' hands as we walked together towards the kitchen door.

***

Julianne:

The sea was a gentler blanket today, turning its edges back in white foam, tucking itself against the crevices of stone far below along the rocky beach. I was at its edge, or as near as anybody could be, thanks to the carefully- arranged boulders at the top. From there, the sea air could reach me, along with the restless sound of its waves.

I tucked my hands in the pockets of my green pea jacket, and remembered the first time I saw this view. Me in this same coat, my hair 'tinged with fire' in the sunlight, as Matt put it, as I approached the sea off the beaten path — and met Matthew for the first time.

Maybe not the most romantic meeting on the planet, I knew, but it would always seem so to me. Just like this place would always be the most romantic spot on the planet in my eyes, too.

The last of our things had been packed up, or sent to Seattle, leaving Rosemoor's rooms bare except for the furniture. I was going to miss the old armchair shedding its stuffing and in need of new upholstery, and the threadbare rug and old sofa. Our glass door cupboards were empty of our mismatched collection of dishes, and the old iron bedstead supported only a mattress, without the beautiful quilt that someone had given us as a wedding present.

I had walked through those rooms one more time. The only time I had seen them empty before was when I rented the cottage myself...but that seemed an age ago, along with the briefly-painful episode in Matt's life connected to it. I closed my eyes, twisting the rings on my left hand, knowing there was a time when I narrowly missed the chance to wear them.

I felt Matt's arm around my shoulders now. "Are you ready?" he asked. "Everything else is in the car." Geoff's, not Matt's. Matt had sold his, rather than have it stored for months.

"I guess so." My hand slid around his own, wrapping his fingers in mine. We both stood there in silence, gazing at the moving waters. I closed my eyes and took one last deep breath. It would have to be enough to hold me for a few months, while I pursued a temporary life in my old home city. Where Matt and I would make new friends, share new experiences, and retrace the paths that had brought me to this moment almost two years ago.

"Let's go," I whispered to Matt. Squeezing my hand, he withdrew his arm and led me up the pathway again, towards Cliffs House's garden. I glanced back one last time as I reached the crest of the garden walkway.

Goodbye for now, I thought. *But I'll be back soon. That's a promise.*

For Sneak Peeks, Fun Facts, Book Club Q&A and more, visit the A WEDDING IN CORNWALL official series webpage at:

https://weddingincornwall.blogspot.com/

~and~

Follow the author on social media for the latest updates on the series:

Twitter

@PaperDollWrites

Facebook

https://www.facebook.com/authorlaurabriggs/

Blog

https://paperdollwrites.blogspot.com/

Special Excerpt from A ROMANCE IN CORNWALL

I was searching for a good spot for a butterfly paperweight, a gift from Aimee, when my office door opened and Gemma's head popped inside. "Have you heard the rumors yet?" she asked.

One thing which hadn't changed — at least not that I could see — was Gemma's love for news, gossip, and all things rumored in Ceffylgwyn.

"Not of an event?" I made the idea sound terrible, even though it was how I made my living as an event planner. But the thought of a celebrity wedding or another celebrated baking show was the last thing I really wanted at the moment. With Nathan in Paris, I thought maybe the manor could enjoy a brief lull in spectacular or surprising events, at least until I felt more like my old self.

"No, nothing like that," said Gemma. "I'm talking about the celebrity sighting. Andy's mum's best friend's sister does for the Pendragon from time to time, you know, when she's not cleaning houses over in Truro; and she said she saw the names on the hotel register the other day and recognized one right away — a *famous writer*, no less. And you'll never guess who."

"Who?" I said. The Pendragon was a hotel not far from Falmouth, and it was known for now and then attracting a few special guests en route to Penzance. Since Gemma's celebrity-crazy days had dwindled in Pippa's absence, I imagined it must be someone extremely recognizable.

"Rowena St. James? The romance novelist?" said Gemma. "You've heard of her, surely. Even my mum's read all her books, and she usually only reads a good spy novel now and then."

"Rowena St. James?" I said. "The author of *The Lightkeeper's Heart*?" I had a copy of her first and most famous book on a shelf at home, tucked next to Matt's *Treatise on the Flora and Fauna of Southern England.* Romance and gardens go hand in hand, in my opinion.

"That's her. And rumor says she's *taking a room at the Dummonia,*" whispered Gemma, excitedly. "Anyway, that's what *she* heard from Charlotte Jones's sister what delivers dairy goods there on Thursdays, when she told her about the register. Mind you, we're not supposed to spread it around, since it's not certain. And the guest book's supposed to be private, too. We wouldn't want to get anyone into trouble."

I tried not to smile, knowing that Gemma was not only breaking this rule without a second's thought, but so was everyone else in the village, too. "Of course," I said. "I won't tell anyone."

"Think we'll see her about while she's here?" asked Gemma. "Think she'll visit Cliffs House to see the gardens? I've always wanted to meet someone famous — Donald Price-Parker and Wendy Alistair don't count, really." Gemma mused over this fantasy. "I wonder if she'd tell me whatever became of Alaric and Georgia in *Love's Winding Path.*"

"Most likely she plans to keep traveling and stay in Penzance for awhile," I said. "Ceffylgwyn's probably not exactly the location she has in mind for her next novel." I read somewhere once that inspiration for her first book had struck her during a holiday in Penzance, so she was probably revisiting whatever site planted inspiration for her greatest literary achievement. I made a mental note to tell Aimee about this in our next conversation — that book was her favorite of all time.

"I wish it were," said Gemma. "Then maybe we'd have a bit of romantic magic around here and not just boys nattering away about rugby and beer. But she wouldn't write about a dull little village when she writes about lonely, wind-swept plains, or islands adrift in the foamy sea. That's a lot more romantic."

How about windswept cliffs? I wanted to reply, but knew that Gemma was quoting the author's description of book settings. "You don't think Ceffylgwyn could be the scene of a fictional romance?" I laughed.

"Maybe. If Rowena St. James made it into someplace exciting or irresistible," said Gemma. With that, she was off to tell the same news to Lady Amanda, probably.

I hung Constance's painting above the mantel in my office. It was the perfect spot for the portrait of my favorite place on earth — which was more romantic than even Rowena's lonely lighthouse, in my opinion. But I'm not a writer, as my long-abandoned personal journal proved, so maybe I'm wrong.

Maybe journaling was the answer to my feeling a little lost upon coming back. I wondered just where it had ended up when we moved.

Coming to major eBook retailers in August of 2017!

Printed in Great Britain
by Amazon

74943676R00302